A SLIGHT LAPSE

A
SLIGHT
LAPSE

Robert Chibka

W. W. NORTON & COMPANY

New York   London

The author is grateful for support provided by Yaddo, Phillips Exeter Academy, and Boston College. Among human beings who have helped, he wishes especially to thank Marjorie DeVault and Barry Wade.

Published simultaneously in Canada by Penguin Books Canada Ltd., 2801 John Street, Markham, Ontario L3R 1B4.
Printed in the United States of America.

The text of this book is composed in Walbaum, with display type set in Walbaum. Composition and manufacturing by Maple Vail Book Manufacturing Group.
Book design by Charlotte Staub.

First Edition

Library of Congress Cataloging-in-Publication Data

Chibka, Robert.
  A slight lapse / by Robert Chibka.—1st ed.
    p.   cm.
    I. Title.
PS3553.H4737S55   1990
813'.54—dc20   89–3263

ISBN 0-393-02774-0

W. W. Norton & Company, Inc.
500 Fifth Avenue, New York, N. Y. 10110
W. W. Norton & Company Ltd.
37 Great Russell Street, London WC1B 3NU

1 2 3 4 5 6 7 8 9 0

For my parents

A SLIGHT LAPSE

First

My indecisive mother tried to abort me, but too late, and I danced out from under the knife in a splash of amniotic fluid, with something of rue but little of reproach. An operative foetus, I was anomalous in the explacental world. I was, if not cute, at least pathetic. My mother took an immediate liking, putting aside her abortive sentiments of a moment earlier. Constitutionally mercurial, I forgave the lapse, but required complete care: not yet uncurled, I was weak, I was not strong. My idea was, everything would have been perfect if she hadn't, first, decided, and failed, to do me in before I got out, and last, lost the will to have done with me once I was excised and could look her, through diaphanous lids, in the eye. This forgiveness was a toddler's cross. What had she to do with excusing a seven-month habitation *and* an untimely vacancy?

I toddled little, actually. My mother and her hatchetman, with uncharacteristic resolve, thought the better of snipping off nurture when they saw my helpless nature. So until it withered and my mouth opened, my umbilicus afforded me about ten feet running room, measured from almost waist high on my mama's person. I

clung mostly, a tenacious watch on a fob, for the first nonincu-
bated month, then started liking crawling up and down her reset-
tling topography. I was not unhardy for a foetal extraction, and
soon mastered the art of clutching, then, set gently on the carpet,
of rolling to and fro on a flexible protospine between her dainty,
as I later learned, feet.

Mother lounged a lot in those days. Bifurcated garments were
out of the question; and dresses, she later told me, produced an
eerie feeling, masking the cord's source. Robes, then, were the
rule. Oedipal usurpation came early in our household: my father
agreed to retire in the nursery, for fear of a traumatic midsleep
crushing; he was, I understand, a flamboyantly fluid sleeper, rolling like dice through the night. Mama slept like a landscape. I
myself was restive, but incapable of crushing anyone.

For a short time, I both suckled and umbilicated, enjoying
simultaneously active and passive nourishment. When the cord
finally atrophied, it did so from the middle out, leaving my mama
and me with five feet each of vestigial cable. My navel was a necessary afterthought, and as such neither inny nor outy; rather, a
more complicated configuration.

If, as I have come to believe, we start aging when we hit the air,
I had a head start on my exact contemporaries. By nine months
after conception, I had more than recapitulated phylogeny; it followed that by the time my mother and I cast off from one another,
my features were of a more articulated character than one comes
to expect of milk-fed month-old-baby bodies. My x-rays (I was of
course a medical curiosity) were less translucent than is normal
for those rounded cartilaginous creatures.

It was not easy, pumping my own blood, breathing my own air,
running that subtle pulmonary exchange. Mercifully, the transition was a gradual one, timed by the sclerosis of my umbilical
artery like a fuse. Nevertheless, digestion has always troubled me,
and to this day I swallow unusual quantities of milk to float food-
stuffs like barges down my irritable alimentary canal.

You begin to see the tension, do you not? A prematurely weathered exterior, a delayed development of internal systems. Out early,
cut off late; like getting to a stop way ahead of time for a bus that's
behind schedule. It's those minutes waiting for public transport
that interest me, those months exposed to the elements with an
untested, nay barely primate, heart; that tug-of-war between my
mother and me. That time, I feel sure, accounts for everything.

During those years when little boys want to be sailors and cowboys and firemen and spies, I wanted to be a bank clerk. I followed none of the regular progressions, pirate to shortstop to astronaut; I wanted to be a bank clerk.

I used to think banks were just fun. All those deposit and withdrawal slips, a little black book to be stamped, coming in with the burden of assets and leaving it safe in someone else's hands, or coming in penniless and leaving with concrete negotiable evidence of trustworthiness and respectability. What could be better?

Being the agent, I thought, of such pleasing reciprocity could be better. Of course you could have an account as well, approaching colleagues on your coffee break to procure your own economic gratification. It was the best, I thought, of both worlds. And such working conditions: contemporary art on the walls, your own cage and nameplate, air-conditioned comfort.

I changed my mind about banks when my parents lost their money. Father put all our eggs in a single unsound basket and hopped on a speculative bandwagon headed for bankruptcy court. They used to buy me Monopoly games, the only toys I craved: I'd take out the money, stuff boards, markers, and cards in a closet, and play Bankclerk. When I tired of the amount I had, I'd request a new game, and get it. But once I asked Papa for a new Monopoly game, and was answered curtly.

'Larry, what are you playing, Bankclerk or High Finance?'

'Bankclerk, Papa, but banks always have new money. All I have is old money.' I enjoyed crispness, I disliked wrinkles.

'Well, Laurence, your mother and I are trying to play Solvent People, and we'd be very happy with used money, but we haven't any.'

'That's no problem, Papa. Go to the bank.' I was amazed that he hadn't thought of this himself.

'Larry, go play with your money. The bank won't give us any.'

'Why not? That's their job.'

So my father explained banks to me, and I was without an ideal profession. I crumpled my bills, discarded boards and houses and hotels, guilty by association, and resolved never to have enough money so it mattered.

'It has been observed, and not without reason, that the color of headhair being but an inconsistent indicator of the color of pubic hair, yet the color of beardhair can in all cases be taken as a true emblem thereof. Can it be considered equitable that one half of the population shall thus walk about displaying on its blushing cheeks the hue of its shame, while the other half ambles protected from the certain surmise of strangers; that one should exhibit, the other conceal? Surely not; nor can clothing be disparaged, its insulating qualities being widely appreciated. Thus has fallen to one half the populace a dilemmic lot: to parade sure sign of private matters, or to dissemble, to scrape and discard the banners of ignominy. So man has learned to shave.'

I believed in this theory at the time of my life when it became an issue. I shaved enthusiastically, always happy to alter or eliminate parts of my body. The joy of shaving did not match that of nail-biting (finger and toe), lip-chewing, or scab-picking, only because I could not bring myself to ingest hair. I preferred recycling, hated throwing parts away.

Have no fear, I never recycled from inside, having no urge to hoard my supply of phlegm or waste. But things that grow outside, nails and skin, things that grow outside and regenerate, my greatest pleasure was putting that protein back in circulation, making by-products into fuel. Hair, though, I could never swallow. I saved it like marbles, like Monopoly dollars, box- and bagfuls on the closet floor.

Returning to the theory, which I still believed: thinking to transcend the ordinary race of men in masking my discredit, I proceeded from vehicle to tenor and shaved my pubic hair, mixing it indiscriminately on the closet floor with hair that was formerly facial.

'She was good manners running sideways. She was breathlessness under a hat. Pretending to circularity, she compassed off equal radii. Her life was a pie, like a government dollar, sliced here and there but impounded beyond allocation.'

That was how I saw her. She was my first love: Irene. She made me feel, in her presence, like a puddle of knives.

It occurs to me like memory, but I may be inventing, that I met Irene on a bus. If so, it was a bus to the hospital during the year my mother was dying. It's strange: my father died one night, and I a child, and my mother died for a year, and I an adult, and I have as little clear memory of the one as the other. All I seem to recall are the bus rides, and mostly, the books I read to and from the hospital. My mother had a diabetic eye problem, and I would read her novels by perusing on the bus and summarizing during our visits. Most of our visits, it seems, were spent paraphrasing novels.

My mother died in the middle of *Moby-Dick*, she never heard the end of it. Foresightful in her old age, perhaps she guessed at the final confrontation. I had met Irene by then; she was summarizing *Madame Bovary* for her father in the same hospital. A major question that year was whether to finish *Moby-Dick*. A minor question was whether to finish the chapter 'Of the Less Erroneous Pictures of Whales.' Irene never had this second problem; her father died at the end of a chapter. My impulse was to finish my chapter, then quit; and to be honest, to finish it before buzzing for the nurse. My thought was, Mother would have wanted it that way. My decision (to finish the book) was a bone of contention when, after finally getting together, Irene and I finally broke up. But I precede myself.

I was a twenty-six-year-old orphan with a provocative navel and no pubic hair. Irene was to me an exciting woman: the first. What had I, a budding heterosexual, to lose? I continued visiting every evening, I continued reading on the bus, I didn't tell Irene my mama had passed on. She found out when, one night on the bus after visiting hours, she sat beside me as always, leaned against me (the first time), and shed tears on several successive pages of *Moby-Dick*. 'Laurence,' she finally said, 'read as fast as you can. Skip unimportant passages. You're almost finished. What's important to them now is closure. My father died tonight, nearly three-fourths of the way through *Madame Bovary*. Thank God it was the end of a chapter. I only hope you can finish *Moby-Dick* for your mother. And if you do, summarize short stories. It will be better for both of you.' With fervor, Irene advised me thus.

I explained that my mother had passed away two weeks earlier, but that I was almost finished with the book. Astonished and reproachful, 'Oh Laurence,' she said, 'how could you!'

'If one is reading a book for a family member and the family member dies in the midst of the less erroneous pictures of whales, one is duty-bound, by respect for a beloved (moreover, elderly; moreover, unsighted; moreover, deceased) family member, to place a permanent and functional bookmark in the midst of the less erroneous pictures of whales, nor to read further in that or any other copy of said book.'

This is a fairly concise capitulation of Irene's theory concerning termination of life functions in middles of novels. It was one small part of her theories concerning behaving like a human being, to which she held especially fast in times of stress. A week later, though, the crisis past, Irene found me not so reprehensible as to merit rejection of a politely offered dinner invitation. Two orphans, we caught our customary bus and ate in the hospital cafeteria, thinking to exorcise grief over the least exorbitant chicken croquettes in town.

I explained sitting *shivah*, my week-long gesture to the aunts and uncles who excused my areligiosity by persisting in thinking of me as the somewhat less than sentient yoyo-like extremity of my mother's anatomy they had finally grown used to when the twisted and diminished cord divvied labor between our separate organs. I explained the stores of coffee cakes and cold cuts jamming my refrigerator. Irene, a lapsed Unitarian, was dumbfounded.

'Why?' she asked. 'Why not let you and your mother rest?'

'An expression of respect, like wearing weeds,' I said. 'A guarantee of a week, at least, of remembrance.'

'I never could have stood it,' said Irene. 'I've all I can do to compose myself in private. Entertaining guests,' she shuddered.

'It's not exactly entertaining,' I said, wondering what it was if not that. 'People have strange ways of enduring grief,' I theorized tentatively. 'I'm through with *Moby-Dick*, and feel much better.'

'Oh Laurence, let's not talk about finishing novels,' said Irene with tears in her eyes. But it was that night, I imagine, that she returned to Flaubert for comfort. In any case, she was all but finished by the night after next, when I showed up at her apartment bearing a sour-cream coffee cake.

'Now I fell like I'm sitting whatsacallit,' said Irene.

'No, just helping with the leftovers,' I said, thinking to put her at ease.

'Oh Laurence,' she cried, setting my coffee cake on the counter and hugging me. 'Sometimes it's so hard to behave like a human being.'

My father had wanted me: before I was conceived, I mean. The method they used was prophylactic and spermicide: foam-rubber, my father called it. These devices were for my mother's sake; my father wanted me. He found a way to replace Mama's foam with shaving cream and pinpricked holes in his condoms. I was conceived by paternal subterfuge, birthed by maternal same: she snuck out one afternoon while he was at work, thinking to miscarry me away. This after a good four months of argumentation at which I was present but in no position to represent myself.

'Birth defects are the incarnation of unwantedness. A woman delivered of a baby she never wanted is delivered of a baby with a problem. Infantile handicaps are parental projections.'

This was my mother's theory of unwanted pregnancies and imperfect offspring. Given her belief in this somewhat metaphysical theory, abortion was euthanasiatic. All my friendly, gentle kicking hadn't convinced her; but one look at my complete, if underdeveloped, corporeal inventory, my pleasing bilateral symmetry, endeared me to her in a way seven months of breaking bread together and shared morning sickness had not.

My father, who returned from a hard day at the office to find me napping, dangling in the open, was shocked: he had been expecting someone older, more aesthetically conventional, someone he could take into the other room and dandle, away from my mother. He was disturbed not to know, even, if I was the son he had contrived to conceive or the daughter he had dreaded (curled as I was, it was impossible to discern; for the first month or so, I was Laurence/Loretta).

Then my father didn't want me, but my mama did. Until I reached the age of somersaults and tossing things back and forth in the yard, I never knew the joy of biparental desirability. But the age of somersaults succeeds the age of resentment: I was by then my mama's little friend, and he was the man who slept in the room he had prepared for me.

'Nine months it takes a mother to learn to love a child enough to live with it for, say, twenty years. With luck, a marriage should last longer. Why should the acclimation period be any shorter?'

Irene, of course, on pregnancy and courtship. I responded, of equivalent course, by drawing a practical parallel between my infantile prematurity and the premaritalization I had now proposed.

I still wish I knew whether she experienced ambivalence during this time or felt secure in her analogy. At the time she appeared disinclined to budge, but appearances can mislead. Now, older, possibly wiser, I could easily explain to her, to anyone, what was wrong with her theory.

In case you're wondering, yes, I was precocious. PTA open-house evaluations (reported by Mama on her return: the only times she smelled like smoke) abandoned early on the usual 'working up to his ability' in favor of 'surprisingly mature,' 'wise beyond his years.' Tops in capability was taken for granted, like the rhythm section of a band; the melodic line was more like 'extraordinary emotional stability' or 'behavior toward classmates saintlike,' with occasional embellishments of 'uncommonly imaginative' or 'always trying to see things in his own way: a joy to teach.'

I won prizes in my least favorite subjects. Expense-paid trips to hear nose-cone designers at MIT, countertenors at Carnegie Hall. Two weeks on a tanker for 'The American Merchant Marine: Key to Defense and Trade.' Saxophone solos in City Hall, math fairs, French contests, All-State debating, more likely to succeed than more popular class members.

If you were devising an SAT, you might put it thus: weathered exterior : late-blooming organs : : youthful accomplishments : emotional underdevelopment. Then you could hide it among plausible alternatives, and everyone would have to choose. Something about repeated commitment made these tests comforting. I had a serious aversion to 'None of the above,' though it was sometimes unavoidable.

Back when test-taking gave a structure to things, I always took fresh No. 2 in hand with a bit of embarrassment tainting my otherwise serene confidence. Through no fault of my own, I knew I'd do much better than other members of my cohort. True / false or multiple-choice just made the injustice more evident; with them, I didn't even have to work for my unearned superiority. My favorites were the questions that ended, 'Why or why not?' Example: 'Did you discuss these problems with your parents? Were they receptive? Why or why not?'

One adjective that ought not to modify adolescent human beings is 'wizened.' Nevertheless, this adjective modified me. I was sickly, I was wan, I was wizened: my body refused to display nourishment. I ate with panache, but couldn't inflate myself.

Thus it was that on a summer afternoon in the year 19— I ran home crying to my mother. Mother looked harried; she wasn't feeling well. She'd sliced a finger cleaving leftover chicken for a dish called mock American chop suey. She was staunchly stanching blood with a paper towel wrapped tightly round the digit; but blood seeped around the pressure point, collecting in her palm, a tiny reservoir.

I hugged my mama, frail arms clasping her waist-high, my face pressed to her pelvic girdle. If my mother was a finger, my head was a stone set in the ring of my arms.

I have always loved the garments known as 'housedresses.' At times like these, there is nothing more comforting to clutch than the homely, thin, clean cotton print of a mother's housedress.

My mama tried to scoop my wizened semi-adolescent face up from its blind involvement with her midsection. My tears diluted motherly blood.

My mother's blood: the only blood I ever could suck from a wound as unself-consciously as my own, the only blood sweet enough. I swallowed the small puddle and kept on sucking through the paper, but would not lift my face. We stood thus engaged for several moments.

My mother said, 'Whatsamatter, Lala?'

I mumbled inarticulately where I stood, as if she had ears in her belly, "Maymemimamemoo.'

My mother, who had no ears in her belly, repeated the question. I raised my head slightly and tried to elocute, but still gurgled in the salt-sweet solution: 'Vaythedimuzenroo.'

'Who, Lonnie? Who said it wasn't true?'

The kids said it wasn't true. The kids. They said it wasn't true.

I was now fairly articulate, though a little smudged. What had happened was fairly simple. We had been playing Red Rover.

The game of Red Rover is played with two opposing defensive lines, hands across the lawn presenting a strong front on either side. One team shouts, 'Red Rover, Red Rover, we call ———— over' (trochaic nicknames fitting best into the metrical scheme). The called-over kid charges the opposing line at what he presumes to be its weakest point. If he breaks through, he returns to his proud teammates with a hostage, a new member. If he fails to break through, he becomes a member of the team that rebuffs him. It is a game of fast-shifting loyalties.

Most kids enjoyed being called over, but for me it was a continual source of anxiety. People were forever calling Larry over, not for his prosodic suitability, but because they knew he was too weak to break through their line. The trouble was, they then had Larry on their side, and anybody could break through *his* wizened little grip. I was a frustration to more serious Red Rover players. Despite my vast fund of experience at being called over, others' skills were always more advanced. Those whose team I was not on appreciated me, but I was never not on a team for very long.

So that after a long and hard-fought game of Red Rover that had me slightly dizzy with shuttlecocking that summer day, I faced a committee of pubescent athletes convened to reproach me with lack of stolidity. I pleaded extenuating compactness. They said if I wanted to play, I'd have to eat more.

I told them I couldn't: it wasn't my fault I was small. I was born at seven, pendant for three, months.

My peers were incredulous. Exhilarated with the declaration, I expanded on my potent secret within the limits of my understanding. I exposed my ace in the hole: a compound navel. The kids were not convinced.

That's when the kids, heady with fresh hormones and budding little muscles and novice knowledge of things procreative—rid at last of their baby fat—said it was impossible, said it wasn't true, called me a conventional weakling and furthermore an unpersuasive liar.

My mother, consternated, tore off fresh, absorbent towels for both of us. The kitchen was becoming less damp in general; but we were both troubled, as families can sometimes be, together.

'Am I a liar, Mommy? Am I?'

'Oh Lonnie, oh Lala, no, you are not a liar. You were born at seven, pendant for three, months.'

'Life is like a lecture series. There is no excuse for sitting, out of politeness or feelings of inferiority, till the end of a lecture one cares nothing about or hasn't the background for. To expend any part of life in wondering, Is it permitted to get up and slip out quietly, is a shameful waste; very much waste deadens the spirit. Of all states of mind, boredom is most fatal. One must sit on an outside aisle, near the red EXIT signs that hang in public places, to minimize embarrassment in case one desires to leave early.'

This is the best I can do with Irene's theory of flagging interest in middles of activities. It is the best theory I know of boredom, but in practice presents certain problems. She could, I am sure, expound it more convincingly than I. It is not unrelated to her theory of pregnancy and courtship, which I found unacceptably inflexible:

'Believe me, I was born ahead of time. My mother's seven-month abortion proved to be a scarless cesarean. I was attached for three months. I still have digestive trouble: red meat, green peppers, purple cabbage, I can't eat them.'

Irene thought I was fabricating. She was bemused, but skeptical.

'Why would I lie about a thing like this?' I asked.

'I don't know, Laurence. You've never lied to me before.'

'I've never lied to you at all,' I said to Irene. 'In over seven months, I've never lied to you.'

'Oh Laurence,' she said, 'if only I could know for sure.'

'Irene,' I said, 'many people do it. It's part of being evolved past fish and trees, of behaving like a human being.'

Irene resented my invoking her pet vocabulary against her. She sent me home to a TV dinner. Forty-eight hours later, though, the crisis past, Irene thought me not so reprehensible as to merit rejection of a politely offered dinner invitation. Linguine with clam sauce, toothsome in the extreme, and a dessert beyond compare: Irene.

If I could describe the loss of virginity, I would do my best, I promise, to eliminate bathos, however true to experience it might have been. Without being vicious or vindictive, the sooner myths get undercut the better.

At the age of throwing things back and forth in the yard, I joined my father for a year or two of variably enthusiastic acrobatics. One of our more frequent routines involved an acquaintance with the principles of linear dynamics and simple machines. The question was one I found in a useful volume entitled *Puzzles and Posers for Fathers and Sons*. The book was a gift from my mother, in commemoration of my dozenth birthday (measured from two months after birth to simplify school matters).

'Imagine a pulley with a rope. On the two ends of the rope, clutching, a monkey and a sailor, of identical weight, thus:

The monkey, unwilling to perpetuate this tableau, starts to climb the rope. As he climbs, nimbly, nearer the pulley, does the rope move?'

The question is not so simple as it seems. My father pointed out that stress on a pulley is exerted in a horizontal direction (so that the problem is one of torque): the weights remaining equal, the rope will remain inert. My thought was, the monkey is expending force, in climbing, on the rope itself, like a sailor hauling in an anchor: the rope will move down on the monkey's side. My father believed that the monkey, climbing, would exert less force on the pulley than when hanging as dead weight: the rope will move, if at all, down on the sailor's side. We agreed to assume the pulley was frictionless. And so on.

My mother declined to venture an opinion. She thought it was nice that we found things to talk about.

But my father died before we could agree. They were trying to excise his prostate when he started bleeding. I persist in believing the monkey could move the rope, though I think that in terms of physics, my father was right.

My earliest memory is of a white frame house without shutters, a late-summer lawn that had given up hope, a sandbox, taller playmates with toy trucks, caterpillars, payloaders. Whence this universal male fascination, I wondered, with commercial vehicles? Don't get me wrong, I found dolls equally vapid.

It was getting dark. Grass was turning greener on both sides of the fence. Lampposts which had been most interesting as things to think about climbing became light sources to throw pebbles at. We had all wandered separate ways into the shadows, knowing a clump of small ones is easier for mothers to locate.

Mrs. McNamara, always the first to fret, was calling her brood. 'John, Gregory, Peter, Constance, Anne!' One by one she checked them in. Within minutes, she was calling, 'Gregory, Peter,' only; then, hoping to appease inscrutable kid-petulance, 'Greg, Pete.'

My mother never called till it was dark in earnest. She was either slower in getting dinner or more skilled in keeping it warm. For whatever reason, she didn't take her cue from the streetlights like Mrs. McNamara, rather usually waited till the sun was all gone, till childhood skin was tingling with evening chill and stars could be clearly discerned.

I saw a star. I wondered if my mother saw it. If so, why wasn't she calling me?

This star was very bright, and I thought wishes made on it would have a good chance. I recited 'Star light, star bright' to reserve my place, then paused to ponder an appropriate hope.

A bicycle: I suspected my parents had one in mind for my birthday (figured from two months after birth to simplify school matters) anyway.

A lot of money: I had no desire for a lot of (most likely wrinkled) money.

No broken bones: it seemed silly to wish against something that might not happen in any case. I needed a wish with positive, noticeable results, so I could know if and when it came true.

To be a handsome prince: too corny.

For everybody to like me: did I really want everyone to like me, even Connie McNamara?

World peace: I had seen that ploy used to good effect with department-store Santas, but I had never lived through a war, and thought it might be interesting.

Personal happiness: too vague.

I didn't need any help with my grades.

Other stars were out by now, but I knew the first was first, there was no hurry. Mine was a beautiful bright star, not to be wasted on an everyday wish. But I couldn't spend so long deciding that I'd come home to cold food, or worse, parental glares.

I wanted to hear my mother calling. Was she hurt? Had she forgotten me? I thought of wishing my mother would call, but that seemed a waste of a perfectly wonderful star. I'd regret falling into a trap.

A long life, a peaceful life, a good marriage, my parents still healthy when I'm eighty-five? The decision was beyond me. I could wish for wisdom. Complete success in all endeavors.

I was getting hungry. Small armhairs were standing on end. Muscles. Lack of insomnia. Marbles prowess, digestive prowess. Permission to run the electric mower. Normality. Distinctiveness. The existence of God.

I could run home, ask for advice; no, once there I would never be allowed to leave. It was well after dark.

A trick. I could wish this star would be back tomorrow, same time same place. I could sleep on it. The hoax would be seen through, I would be betrayed.

I was the only kid left out under the sky. Finally, fear found me. I heard my mother calling. Relieved, my concentration broken, I closed my eyes tight as I ran and perspired and wished: 'Breaded swordfish for dinner.' A favorite, immediately verifiable, not such a bad wish.

Mother looked harried; she wasn't feeling well. She'd sliced a finger cleaving leftover turkey for a dish called mock Texas hash.

Irene and I had been up most all of the night arranging cold cuts on plates and divesting bread of crust. In the morning we shaved together. I started with my upper lip, she with her left ankle.

'Laurence, don't you wish your folks could have been here?' she asked as I was patting dry my cheeks.

In general, I, at the sink, finished my face about the time Irene, in the tub, finished her legs. Then I would move to the tub for my pubis, while Irene took advantage of the mirror above the sink for her underarms.

In the suds floating Irene's yellowish sheddings like a loan, I thought this morning of *Moby-Dick*, of wading in a headful of the choicest spermaceti, and was content that my parents could not attend. I fantasized reasons they might devise why Irene and I should never be joined in lawful matrimony, patrimony, fratrimony: I was glad they were forever holding their peace. But I would have liked to phone them after the ceremony.

Irene's maiden aunt came for the wedding. A narrow Unitarian with a speedy metabolism, she was absorbed into the vortex of uncles and aunts on my side milling about the buffet. While they broadly praised the liverwurst, she ingested primly a deceptive quantity of pumpernickel. When my relatives dispersed, she bobbed up like a cork in water to help finish the cold cuts and move in with us forever.

She sat upright in a corner kitchen chair all the days, evenly timing cups of tea, one an hour, and reading thin mysteries. After sex, I chronically desired a snack with milk, while Irene lounged as if modelling for imaginary Renaissance sculptors. My maiden aunt-in-law, seated in her corner like a vacuum in a closet, inhibited my postcoital appetite. Over meals, conversation was channelled to conform to her preference for generality. More voluptuous newlywed discussions took place in the bathroom while shaving. When we traded tub for sink, the talk invariably took a more personal turn.

We didn't know at the wedding that Irene was expecting. We assumed all brides felt sick that morning. Throughout our nine-month courtship, digestion had been a concern; Irene was imaginative with soothing menus for my touchy insides. Now, with Irene queasy in the early hours, we could devise engaging theories concerning our mutual tendency to nausea.

I lowered myself into the lukewarm tub, soaping my belly with soft terry. Irene was stretching her left arm up and earnestly assessing stubble. Soaking in body temperature, I received the idea with aplomb.

'Irene, do you think you might be pregnant?'

'Yes,' said my wife, and lifted the razor to her moist underarm.

Love being the commonest proof that parallel lines do meet at infinity, Irene and I had not expected a prompt intersection. The immediate fruits of our lovemaking were a conviction on her part that her physique was worthy of marble and a desire on mine to raid the refrigerator. A more concrete production had not been our intent.

When not enjoying the relaxation of shaving, we both viewed the prospect with anxiety. Irene thought it a judgment on us for indulging in the act nearly two months prior to the legitimating ceremony. She blamed me for persuasion, and said this proved I was born at the usual time, in the usual way. I insisted on my good faith and argued that blame should rest solely on the passion that had precluded contraception.

'It might have been that very first time,' said Irene, 'after the linguine with clam sauce. If only we had overeaten.'

'I doubt our desire would have been quelled by another helping,' I said, though the sauce was good. 'Besides, it could have been the second time, with Beethoven on the radio.' The *allegro furioso* had disturbed the accuracy of our *interruptus*.

Irene persisted in believing our moderation with pasta—I, symphonic inspiration—had been our undoing. 'Either way,' I surmised, to dissipate tension, 'clam sauce or Beethoven, the kid will have good taste.'

'No,' said she, suddenly stern, 'no taste at all. I plan to have an abortion.'

Shall I discuss the vehemence with which I protested? I pictured a recessive line of shrinking foeti, bound each to each with diminishing cords, till from a thread hung a pea-sized blastula. 'Never!' I erupted. 'No child of ours will suffer eviction. We started this pregnancy, and we'll finish it.'

'Exactly,' said Irene, with composure.

'No,' I affirmed.

'Yes,' she denied. 'This embryo is not a novel, not some piece of writing that must go on after patience is exhausted.'

'Don't change the subject,' I said. 'It was healthy, finishing Flaubert. And even sonnets have beginnings, middles, ends.'

'This baby is not Flaubert, and this baby is not a sonnet,' was Irene's concluding couplet; and having left no room for argument, she joined her maiden aunt in a cup of tea.

Irene the conceptual minimalist had no mama; rather, a mother. My outer limit of ten feet, give or take inches, was about as close as Irene's mother got. What sort of cord one could devise to maintain such distance is beyond me. A reinforced cable, I suppose, conjuring images of caterpillar and payloader, working men; scaffolds, hods, cranes, and barrows. Still, Irene and Aunt Amelia were very close after the wedding.

She was not the sort of invalid who'd appreciate a summary of Flaubert; her interest in literary theory was next to nonexistent. She preferred to offer advice, in the comfort of her deathbed like a throne or tenured chair.

Amelia favored abortion, though she thought it unfortunately messy. 'You see what comes,' she told Irene, 'of mixed marriages.'

'All marriages are mixed,' I replied for my wife. 'You see rather what comes of carelessness.'

After surviving politely to the end of my thought, but not condescending to bicker, Irene's Aunt Amelia died.

Did Irene credit me with the death of her maiden aunt? It's a good bet. Would she countenance further discussion regarding the fate of our unborn firstborn? Not on your life.

For the first eight weeks or so, they can use straight suction to gather up whatever is in there. Imagine the sensation, like iron to a magnet, calamity in the uterus, womb-tornado; a low-pressure center, eye of the storm, withdrawal, primal grapple, not release. I remembered maternal tugs on my infantile lead, like a bit and brace, painful to us both. Irene thought this best, eagerly willed it: what could she think of our marriage?

She cherished her privacy, was euphoric with the promised expulsion of occupying forces. *Te deum*, she hummed that morning.

Inside Irene was clean as a whistle: nothing to show for our trouble. I had come to dissuade, and out of concern. The doctor pulled me aside to explain one likelihood.

'It's called false (or in less enlightened periods, hysterical) pregnancy. Not very rare, but it usually proceeds from wishful thinking. We almost never see them here, but in this case I consider it a good likelihood.' ('Here' being a clinic whose house specialty was dilation and curettage.)

Good likelihood, enlightened, hysterical? Granted, I'm no doctor. 'How,' I nevertheless thought I had a right to ask, 'does this happen? How do you *do* something like that?'

'Simply put, by means of a small cannula inserted into the.'

Cannula shmannula. 'No, I mean, how does it happen that you execute an abortion without first determining beyond the shadow of a reasonable doubt whether a person is with foetus? Aren't there tests?'

'Indeed there are, extremely reliable ones. We performed what we call endometrial aspiration, a common pre-emptive procedure known in some quarters and depending upon circumstances as menstrual regulation or extraction or uterine evacuation. Completely effective and quite without danger of harm to the mother— or woman, as the case may be. Under the circumstances, we thought it best to accede to the wishes of the patient.'

'Her name is Irene. What circumstances?'

'She was quite insistent, Mr.'

'Paprika.'

'Paprika?'

'Paprika. She insisted on what?'

'On both: forgoing the test and undergoing the procedure.'

'You thought that best? Even if she wasn't pregnant? Even if she was?'

'Under the circumstances, yes.'

'You have no idea what the circumstances are. You don't have the slightest clue as to the circumstances. The circumstances are totally beyond your ken.'

'The situation called for a judgment. We didn't, under the circumstances, think.'

'Under the circumstances, under the circumstances!' I had the feeling I'd been here before: pre-emptive, aspiration, regulation, extraction, evacuation. We could not labor under such illusions. Undo the circle dances: 'The point is, her cupboard was bare! The point is, what are you, some kind of quack?'

'That was highly uncalled for, but I shall let it pass, simply reminding you, Mr. Paprika, that I spoke of likelihoods, not certainties, and informing you that given the circumstances, your wife may feel a certain ambivalence for a time, she may be somewhat traumatized. I mean emotionally, of course.'

She was not. Guess who was. This dry run had given me pause. Though Irene was prepared to resume conjugation almost without interruption (she was well, the doctor said, adjusted), I withheld my favors, having learned that to make one was to condemn it, and early, when it hadn't my seven-month agility. I slept on the sofa, leaving Irene to languish in frustrated diagonal luxury.

You think she was not a good lover? Modest, inhibited, guilt-ridden, frigid, repressed? On the contrary, Irene was full mistress of erotic abandon, of touching, verve, the spice of life. It was no fun on the couch, knowing Irene was there, waiting, willing, ready to bar no holds. The exquisitely cuisinary aroma of our mutual clothingless shaves was almost more than a man could . . .

She was Helen, Salome, Cleo, Cytherea, Diana, Iseult . . .

Divorce was out of the question . . .

What's out of the question is sometimes thought to be the answer. Irene found my embryonic empathy absurd, my abstention from sex disconcerting, and increasingly, my husbandry in general less than satisfying. Why, Irene?

Irene would answer by giving you a recommendation, as if what you wanted were a reference for your next job:

NAME: Laurence Paprika.

AGE: 27½.

BACKGROUND: Frail, underdeveloped childhood; naïve adolescence; cathartic but self-conscious young manhood.

CHARACTER ANALYSIS: Laurence is a very, perhaps overly, conscientious young man, baffled by being, who finds comfort in reason. To explain his shortcomings, he has devised entertaining theories; *e.g.*, that he was the product of an abortive abortion, to elude responsibility for the perception (an acute one) that he is at once older and younger than those around him, regardless of chronology. As he entered adulthood, Laurence found olderness more threatening, just as youngerness had been in childhood. Though he is capable of capitalizing on his geminicism, his more characteristic tropism tends toward that hemisphere which embodies his insecurity, which he can then intellectualize, rationalize, and theorize into oblivion. Thus, his adult consciousness is one of almost classical order and control; while his behavior is riddled with a childishness at best latent, at worst pervasive. Imminent maturity has driven him to refuge in the most provoking infantilism. He is at once progressive and regressive. What wordplay is to language, Laurence is to himself and those around him.

PROSPECTS: Women are likely to find Laurence exhilarating, delightful, in the infancy of a relationship, for a year or, in extreme cases, two; thereafter, he must become a mental and emotional burden. Employment should involve limited compulsiveness: Laurence would make an excellent bank clerk.

Thus Irene, daughter of all virgins, sister of all coquettes, mother of all courtesans, might diagnose me, as a chronic but not fatal malfunction. Nor, given her theory of boredom, would she sit very long still wed to an unpleasant situation, without even fleshly union to keep her warm. Shortly after aborting nothing, less than a fortnight after burying her maiden aunt, a scant month after the wedding, two months and some spare change after consummation, not a year after our first bus ride, we were without a doubt on the decline.

Shaving was irritating. Our smooth timing thrown off, one would finish before the other. Irene stood dripping like a towel, waiting for the sink, or I watched her attend to details of her lower extremities, repeatedly shaving against the grain to get closer. Nicks and scrapes were common when voices were raised; the floor was littered with squares of tissue dotted with single drops of blood, like the aftermath of a homemade Rorschach test. Irene accused me of hogging the styptic pencil. I, aiming to appease, bought her one of her own. We argued over which was whose.

If this was shaving, our personal ritual of intimacy, imagine dining, imagine doing the laundry.

'When all else has failed, and despite the perils of imperfect contraception, climb back into bed.'

My personal theory of last-ditch efforts and what finally can save a marriage. Did it work? About as well as most such expedients do.

I wore two condoms, one over the other, to thwart the most zealous of homunculi. Irene didn't mind, and to me it felt cozy, like bundling up for a cold winter day. We pumped Irene full of foam, like insulating a house. And the élan was there: male superior, male supine, front to back, back to front, upright, crosswise, equestrian, *more ferarum*. Foreplay, tongueplay, lipplay, lapplay, overplay, underplay: of course we could do it all. Oral, genital, anal, alluvial, olfactory, marsupial; contrapuntal, dipuntal, monopuntal, polypuntal perverse. If anything, there was too much thrill in it, too much relief to be taken as part of something else and all right. Too much joy in undressing to believe the bodies were real, too luminous an afterglow to pretend we knew what to do next. The subtle animal pleasures were too much with us. The feeling was of a trap, but a soft trap, equipped with a safety; no trap at all, then: a warning. I beat a sad retreat to the couch.

Love, first or other, is like reading the best book in the world. Aching with the impeccability of each sentence, but craving the shape of the thing as well; wanting the eternal fragment, but peeking round every corner for resolution.

This is nobody's theory; this is fact. Irene, more curious than I, was making our story short, just as I was trying to settle into a comfortable rhythm for the nonce, seeking terms in which to couch an extended family romance.

That she could leave would never have occurred, at least to me. I had to substantiate our loose ends to prove we deserved the longer form.

Since Irene wouldn't see me, I had to move. I couldn't just sit wifeless and not wait, not count the hours. Where, indeed! The City, barrel of fear, trigger of possible release. New York, first home of parents, underground spring, vessel of everything altogether. I would find, and Irene would return when I had found, evidence: an antique placenta, a phone number, an old man with a dull knife, rehearsing technique and wondering what went wrong a quarter of a century and more ago. I would search for a trace, a clue, a sign from the City teeming with signs: a quack. I would bring Irene an offering, a record, a receipt, a coathanger, something to show and tell Irene.

One

So Laurence withdrew what money he had from the fridge—
long a distruster of savings institutions and, of gastric
necessity, an eschewer of flesh, he stored his life savings in
the meat keeper—and taking only what he could carry—skeleton
crew of clothing, ditty of toiletries, worn *Moby-Dick*, can opener,
mottled tenor in a fake-alligator case, shoebox of his own placid,
inert, loosely compacted hair—hopped a bus for the Port Authority, without an idea in the world of what he was up to.

From the outside, he looked like this: cheeks not sunken but
submerged; hair not long but too large, as if it had spread, crowding the brow, leaving the ears no place to go; navy-blue eyes on
the edge of their seats, fidgeting as if they needed to leave the
room; veins and arteries everywhere present but nowhere apparent, despite a dearth of flesh; skin pilatory and nearly opaque; feet
in proportion with the frame; socks that allowed for the inference
of ankles, trousers that allowed for no inference at all; short sleeves
with all due respect; and an open four-pocket vest, with a back of
brownish satin (perhaps he neglected to mention this custom of
never going out without a vest), dangling front panels like ready

wings. Lower lip smaller than upper, less suited to the nose, marked
by thick-walled nostrils, little or no septum, and only an adequate
bridge; teeth nimble; shave clean to the eartops; lashes long and
lithe, his best feature perhaps.

Had you undressed him, you would have seen a slight man, not
without buttocks, hair here and there like pen-and-ink crosshatch,
freckles like pilgrims with a long way to go, joints like rivets, unexceptional scrotum and a penis approaching normal. Flay him, and
you'd find modest organs; gauge him, and you'd find blood under
pressure, determined as salmon; drain him, and you'd find that,
like the rest of us, he was more than mostly liquid; his lungs were
clean, and breathed awfully well; his heart was game, and pumped
like a free-lancer on deadline; battalions of enzymes and hormones were marshalled and mustered; his bowels were unprepossessing.

But if you had been the rather less than more observant driver
of that routine express, you'd have noticed not a word of this as
you riddled his ticket and asked him to watch his step (you wouldn't
have seen, from the light bones and heavy joints, that he walked
really quite steadily); you'd have likely bothered to regard only his
rather more than less remarkable hands.

You never had the pleasure of his palms' acquaintance. The
knuckles looked kind, eager to please. The nails were to hands
what a broken nose is to a face, truncating fingers that, in themselves and afforded goodly manicure, might have been the pride
of a more seemly anatomy. His fingers—could you have guessed
as much?—were all but bleeding: occupational hazard of their
daylong involvement with teeth athletic, almost gymnastic. As he
approached with symmetrical satchels, the hands pumped gently
at his sides, aiding the rhythm of encumbered locomotion. But
when he handed you his ticket, the hands, as if spring-loaded,
applied immediately to the mouth. In the few seconds it took you
to check his destination, punch his pass, hand it over, he effected
the precise excision of two identical cantles from two equally blunt
digits, left and right. This operation, you might have noted, was
timed to conclude with the completion of your minor chore, so
that the left hand, that less recently emerged from the mouth,
reached, salivaless, for the ticket you offered, as if the two of you'd
been rehearsing synchrony all week.

He boarded the bus with hands under wraps and claimed the
seat of his dreams: first row right, with a green picture-window on

what was to come and no one beside. But before you had kicked the luggage latches fast, made the door exhale to a close, dropped your hat on the handle, aligned your rear end for cross-country comfort, and pulled sleekly into traffic, a large man with a cantilevered brow and two elbows found Laurence's lack of sprawl inviting and confined our young man to the width, if that, of our young man's body.

Laurence, shifting his own rear end on spongy springs, had been anticipating, not to say planning, a somewhat metaphysical, not to say romantic, ride, what with the clarion call of memory, the view seen and the image reflected, seen through the window and reflected through the inside from out the other side, trees on trees moving slightly out of phase in and through the heavy green glass of a heavy metal bus speeding over the river and through the woods before his half-closed eyes—that sort of a ride. Elbows hadn't entered in; but now they were there, he resolved to make the most.

The large man spoke: 'Name's Hank, but you can call me Big Jim; most do; who doesn't is a piss-livered faggot.' He paused. 'Been on a bus before, son?'

'Never a cross-country one, Big Jim; these ride higher off the ground.'

'All well and good, son, but what's your name?'

Laurence pronounced Laurence.

'Well, it's a name I guess,' said Jim. 'Lo-rence,' he mused.

'You make it sound like a landlord's nightmare,' summoned Laurence cheerily.

'That's all well and good, son, but it's a name like another. What's your Nicholas-name then, son; that is, outside of buses and strangers, what do you get yourself called?'

'Larry, I guess.'

Big Jim just looked. His eyes were green, but so were the bus's windows, through more than two of which daylight now reflected off him onto Laurence.

'It's a name like another,' put in Laurence.

'Could be better, could be worse,' said Jim. 'Tell you the tale of my given name, time I called my father out on the subject. I say, Listen here, you did wrong to provide me with such a handle, that I can stomach but couldn't like in a million; should have unloaded "Henry" to the highest bidder. He says, Sorry you feel that way, son; my feeling was, it suited you down to the ground. Henry, yes, still couldn't improve on it. I say, No, and you're not to call me it again. He says, What, then? I say, Big Jim, short for Large James. He lets out a gasp, you can see he's grappling with something. Ill-conceived, O ill-conceived, says he. Never saw such emotion in a man, never got such a rise out of him, never found out why, never called me Hank again, never called me anything. It's a wise son that knows what his name's about.'

'God,' said Laurence, 'that's enigmatic.'

'Well and good, but you and me have something in common: names that could be better and could be worse. Plenty of company in that. Mind if I use your knees?'

You should be aware that Big Jim had now produced a poker deck, minus jokers, from his hip pocket.

'In what sense?' asked Laurence.

'Aces. Any luck, I'll have you piled in no time, up to the kings. I win, mostly.'

Laurence wasn't sure.

'Solitaire,' said Big Jim. 'I'm a buff, calms me on buses. If you'd just as soon not, well and good, I know some folks are fussy about their knees. Busful of pairs, no shortage.'

'Quite all right,' said Laurence, planting his feet square on the floor of the bus.

'All right then, sport, let's hit the deck, as I'm prone to saying.' From this point on, Big Jim sustained a patter meet for the son of an auctioneer.

'Stack 'em, split 'em, shuffle 'em up, bridge 'em, sift 'em, straighten 'em up. One shuffle's all a deck ever needs, if it's a good one, provided you didn't win last game. Okay. Seven two three four five six seven. Ten two three four five six. Eight two three four five. King two three four. Seven two three. Four two. Nine. Seven ten eight king seven four nine. Looking good. Seven on the eight, ace on the knees. Deuce. Nine on the ten, five. One two red queen on the black king. Six on the seven, red five on the black six. Seven. One two four. One two nine. One two deuce. One two black trey on the red four. King without a spot. Deuce on the trey, deuce on the knees. Six, red six on the black seven. King and queen to the spot. Ace on the knees. Deuce on the ace of dia-monds. Jack. Red ten on the black jack. Six. One two ten. One two red jack on the black queen. King. One two three four five six seven, no spot for a king. One two queen. Turn 'em over. One two jack. One two five. Red five on the black six, black four on the five. Red four. One two black ten on the jack, red nine on the ten. Eight seven six five on the nine. Five on the red six. Seven. Six five four on the red seven. Spot for a king. Nothing for a nine. King in the spot, nothing for a nine. One two black ten. One two black eight. One queen on the black king. Lordy, another queen. Jack ten nine on the red queen. Deuce. Deuce without an ace on the black trey. Four trey deuce on the black five. Black four on the red five. Trey of diamonds on the knees, baby we need some eights. Six goes on the black seven. Ace on the knees. Trey on the black four. Turn 'em over. One two jack. One two deuce on the ace of clubs, trey under a two. Nine. One two queen. One two king in the spot. Ace of hearts on the knees. Deuce on the ace, black trey on the deuce. Red four on the trey, four, five of clubs on the knees. Five of diamonds on the knees. Filling up the knees. Black six on the knees, red six on the knees. Trey of hearts on the knees. Seven on the six. Nowhere to go. One queen on the black king. Eight of clubs on the knees, back to the ten. Turn 'em over. One two red jack. One two nine. One two ten. Deuce six eight trey, nine in the hand, four under the seven six. Mother, we lost again.

'Ever play solitaire, son? Let you use the deck, but your thighs arc too small, have to play backwards, probably miss your combinations. These here are seven-pile thighs; fit every card in the deck on these thighs, excepting the ace stacks. That's where you come in handy. Four-pile thighs. Neat.

'This time we get 'em. Stack 'em, split 'em, shuffle 'em up, bridge 'em, sift 'em, straighten 'em up. Don't need but a single good shuffle, provided you lost last time.'

Laurence, between games, momentarily relaxed straining ligaments.

'Steady, son.'

'Right,' said Laurence, tightening four-pile thighs.

'Okay. Eight two three four five six seven. Eight two three four five six. Six two three four five. Deuce two three four. Nine two three. Five two. Queen. Eight eight six deuce nine five queen. Eight on the black nine. One two trey. One two queen. One two trey. One two seven on the red eight. Deuce. One two ten. One two queen. One two queen. One two five on the black six, black four on the five. Five. Turn 'em over. One two trey. One two queen. One two trey. One two nine. One two black six. One two red jack on the black queen. Queen. One two five. Turn 'em over. One two trey. One two queen. One two trey on the black four, red four on the five. Black deuce on the trey. Six on the black seven, five four on the six. Trey, king. King in the spot, queen, jack on the king.

Nine, king. Jack on the deck. One two nine. One two six. One two jack. One five. Turn 'em over. One two trey on the red four. Five. One two queen on the black king, red seven on the eight. Black six five four trey deuce on the seven. Nine. Seven on the deck. One two deuce on the black trey. Ace of hearts on the knees, deuce, trey of hearts on the knees. Jack on the deck. One two red ten. One two queen. One two five. Turn 'em over.'

'Black eight on the red nine,' said Laurence.

'Oops, black eight seven six five four trey deuce on the red nine. Thanks, son. Ace of clubs on the knees. King queen over to the spot. Ace of spades on the knees, deuce, trey of spades on the knees. Red four, black four. Four of spades on the knees. Ace of diamonds on the knees. Seven. Trey of clubs to the four of diamonds, four of hearts, five of spades on the knees. Turn 'em over now, I guess?'

'Turn 'em,' said Laurence.

'One two seven. One two red ten. One two black jack. One two queen. Five of diamonds. Mother, we lost again.

'Son, you're a jinx. 'Scuse me while I find another pair of knees.' Before you could say 'red five on the black six,' Big Jim had shuffled off.

When Laurence found his knees relieved of their supporting role, he sat motionless for a few moments, as if waiting for another gambler to provide his femurs with a renewed sense of purpose. Femurs aside, he then set to thinking; Big Jim had jogged his mind. The original idea of a softly meditative ride undermined, the young man was deliberately ruminative now, like a child's tongue wagging sympathetically with a crayon; though Laurence's was caged, it massaged his incisors palliatively. His hips stopped holding their breath and eventually relaxed into Big Jim's absence.

Laurence's thought was now engaged with possibilities of postponement—flat tire, electrical storm, nauseous child, something to drive the Greyhound safely off the highway for a time. He wished to disembark prior to destination, and to hell with the refund of prorated untravelled miles. Laurence wanted no part of New York today. His wanderlust stopped at the City limits. The arrangements he hadn't made displeased him. Where would he stay, what work would he have? An absence of theory vitiated expectation. He would presently be overrun with fact. Fact did not sit especially well with Laurence.

A voice said, 'Excuse me.'

Laurence was prepared to excuse most anything, but all that was required was to affirm that he had no neighbor. A woman who had been seated next to a pair of knees of fortuitous aspect, displaced by the willing offer of the knees and her own gracious abdication, had found the only vacant seat on the bus was that rendered so by Big Jim's luck at cards.

This was a woman who did not remind Laurence of his mother. Quite understandably, since she had little in common with his erstwhile mama beyond the standard female apparatus. She was thin, as Laurence's mother was not in particular; she was fair, as Laurence's mother was not at all; her voice was low, if not stealthy. Something there was, though, that made Laurence feel she could have been someone's mother: a Mongoloid, a hemophiliac, someone who required of a mother much. Or a block mother she could have been, to whose first aid sundry neighborhood children appealed in the absence of blood relation.

It occurred to Laurence that something was displaced. This woman who did not remind him of his mother was not so old that she should have. She was the age of his mother in the days of Red Rover and mock hash, housedresses and reassurance. The most powerful lack of resemblance was between Laurence's mother dying, he an adult, and this woman asking for a seat: a woman of an age he might have mistakenly followed into the ladies' room in the days of insouciant youth. And this woman the age of his childhood mother was not now much older than he. He recalled Irene's extraction, his presumptive ability to fertilize. Of Laurence's generation this motherly woman was.

Laurence, baffled, pondered age. His happy conclusion was that he had reached one where it wasn't of prime importance. Twenty-seven, thirty-three, twenty-four, forty-eight; Laurence felt himself a man of—as the French say, meaning the opposite—a certain age. Big Jim, early forties, had used his knees like another's; this woman, vaguely trentagenarian, had excused herself to sit beside him; and neither had said, O what a beautiful baby, Does your mother let you travel alone then, Where do you go to school, I have a son your age. He was sitting on an equal footing. Very well, then: he would start.

'Big Jim—the man with the cards—thought my knees hexed. I hope you're not the gambling type.' Laurence felt he could smile and say this; so he did.

'I have all the knees I can make use of,' said the woman. 'I'm not in the market.'

'Fine then.' Laurence was glad to find someone not in the market; he was not, at the moment, in the market himself. The old man with the dull knife was far from his mind; he merely had to make his way in the City.

'Do you spy a discrepancy?' she asked after a decent interval.

Sixteen men could not have spied a discrepancy. Her nose, breasts, posture, inflection? She was pale, but Laurence preferred not to mention.

'My hair,' she said. 'It's dyed. It should be white.'

Laurence wondered how old this motherly woman of his generation was. 'Why should it be white? It's nice the way it is.'

'True,' she said; 'but my eyes. They're pinkish.'

Laurence considered conjunctivitis. Her whites were white as meringue; her irises, though, were pinky-blue.

'Can't you see my pallor?'

'Since you mention it,' said Laurence, 'you *are* all but translucent.'

'Translucent isn't the word; I'm an albino.'

Hard put to respond, Laurence bethought: albinism held for him the vague, benign fascination of the previously unconsidered. He'd never seen a human one: a porcupine one, once, with whitish quills like gullfeather stems and the inevitable pinkish eyes. In its cage, it had seemed a playpen image of himself: hapless youth damped by no prospect of robustion. Pigment problem: lack of something or other, pectin no, carrotin no, tannin negrin no no, lack of something that makes skin safe, furless mammal open to infrared. Are they a race? No. Mutants, sports, random; dwarfs are like that, or midgets, what's the difference, dolphin, porpoise, crocogator, allidile. If fittest survive, what's the point of making some who aren't the fittest? Placeholders, filler, evolutionary ciphers, packing material for the parcel of more viable organisms? I'm that, too. Not the same; I'm that because of what Mother did, tried. Would I have been otherwise ruddy? Father was medium height, weight. You tend to think albinos don't have much blood, or it's buried too deep, but really it's the skin. Her arteries are shallow, blue rivulets in the temples like marble: Roquefort. It's the skin that filters it, but I thought pink came from capillaries, why are some people's blue? Wait a minute, blue is coming back, veins, without oxygen? What do cells want with oxygen? Or is it all blue inside, turns red when it hits the air? You'd think you'd remember these things. She's not the only conundrum around here. Let's say everyone gets one peculiarity to start with, like a stake,

Monopoly dollars, try to build it up, buy Boardwalk with a flashy
personality? Albinos have a head start, highly visible trait. Red
and blue, primary colors; what's yellow? Urine, but you keep that
to yourself. The blood's always running, continuous showing; but
it's not the blood, it's the skin, am I right? I wonder how rare?

'There are only three thousand of us in the City,' the lady
announced.

Three thousand of anything—dollars, earthquakes, lemons,
albinos—seemed to Laurence plenty.

'Is that not much?'

'It's a handful, a pittance. We're a minority's minority.'

Were they then organized, meet the third Tuesday, get dis-
counts on hair color and dark glasses? For twenty bucks a year,
could you become a supporting member, honorary albino?

'There's a bar on Park Avenue South a lot of us frequent. Do
you know the City?'

'I'm about to.'

Visits to grandparents in the Bronx long before Father died.
Racket, clatter, more people than you knew what to do with. Father
hated to drive in the City. Don't run, don't jump, there are people
living below, china menagerie, don't touch, breakable, everything's breakable. Grandpa had a heart attack, right in this bed,
convulsions—what's a convulsion, never mind—lucky Grandma
knew to rub his wrists, woke up and rubbed his wrists like her life
depended on it. His did: why should that be? Empire State, Radio
City, Madison Square: no, I don't know the City. The lady's waiting. A lady in waiting.

'I haven't been since I was ten. Now I'm going to live there.'

'You won't recognize the old place.'

'I wouldn't have done so then.'

'You'll be staying with family, then?'

'My grandmother's gone. Grandpa cut off touch after my father
died. He didn't appreciate my mother. I have aunts and uncles in
various boroughs I'd just as soon avoid.'

'Is your grandfather living?' she asked gently.

Right in this bed, convulsions—what's a convulsion, never mind—
rub his wrists, attack, grab, pump seized up like an engine. Is my
grandfather living?

'I don't know,' said Laurence. He rapidly tucked the question
away as perhaps of crucial importance; but conversation was proceeding.

'What do you do?' was next, and she reminded him, but not of his mother.

What Laurence did was something of an open question. He had never been a bank clerk. He had taken drawing courses, but was no artist. Had delivered letters, but was no mailman. Swept, but was no janitor; watched, but was no watchman; driven, but was certainly no cabbie. His profession, in short, was something indeterminate.

Laurence wanted not to tell this lady in waiting from the City he didn't profess; it would be the wrong note, exposing his own misgivings. He thought of his tenor, lacquer spotty, pads matted: an instrument suited for jazz. 'I'm a musician,' he improvised.

'In what sense?'

'Sax,' said Laurence.

What could *she* do? What *couldn't* she do? Airline pilot, lifeguard, decathlon, suntan commercials. Was she frail? No reason to think so: it's just the skin.

The lady was a cellist, and told him as much.

'We could make ludicrous music together,' she said.

You have no idea how, thought Laurence, considering his saxophonic expertise like a closed empty box between them on the bus's vinyl seat.

'If you have in fact no place to stay, I have a chamber in the Village where we could make such music.'

Though she played with words, her meaning was clear. Laurence worried, though, that something might be expected of him in a musical vein. It must be admitted, also, he thought of Irene. In fine, Laurence was gently torn between the warmth of remembered Irene—the damsel, after all, was she not, of his quest—and the projected summer chill of the City. As the lady had offered, apparently, a rhetorical proposition, Laurence took the liberty of sidestepping.

'The Village?' he posed.

'Greenwich,' she said, and Laurence knew he had blown his cover. Could he claim, then, to be a baroque, a marching-band, a mood-music or *bar mitzvah* saxophonist? She seemed willing to let him step aside once more.

'Where in the Village?' asked Laurence, trying to save the question from sounding prurient.

'I've a loft near where Tenth meets Fourth.'

'Avenue and Street, or Street and Avenue?'

'Street and Street.'

Laurence had an arithmetical interest, but was afraid to ask. What could cause such a pleat in the City? There was silence for a moment, during which Laurence pondered the fate of six missing blocks: red four on a black ten, somebody in city planning had been cheating.

Before Laurence could pin the culprit down, the bus stopped for coffee. He had it, iced, and the pale lady's companionship, avoiding as he did so the menacing glance of Large James. But just before reclaiming seats, the gambling man brushed by and warned the lady: 'Watch out for the kid, ma'am: bad knees.'

Assimilating whatever undertone, she examined Laurence's lower extremities for signs of—what, malignity, rickets?—but Laurence's trousers suffered no inference. He was confirmed in his baggy predilections.

'How are your knees?' the lady articulated when they were once again seated.

A predicated quandary: how to characterize one's patellae?

'They'll do,' said Laurence.

'In a pinch?' she pursued.

'In or out of one,' Laurence now said confidently, though he had never before considered his joints *per se*.

Intrigued, the lady quizzed our hero's anatomy. How were his shoulders, how his eyes, how were his pinky fingers? The postpartum foetus and the albino cellist talked at length about his parts. Laurence was a man of many parts, and the game made the ride pass quickly.

Anatomy led—as it so often does—to birth. Somewhere in Westchester and late afternoon, the story of Laurence's escape and dependent infancy was told. There was, as always, a moment of suspense as he watched for signs of dissent. The lady showed more interest than belief, more belief than disbelief.

'Omphallically,' she said, 'you must be something.'

Laurence felt a kinship of difference: he was taken with this pinkish-blue-eyed lady.

Be it known, then, that by the sultry time you reached your furnished rooms on the West Side or flat in Brooklyn or waiting wife in Hoboken or other Jersey clime, Laurence and Gretchen were lolling in Greenwich, near where Fourth meets Tenth, in a loft furnished largely in early baroque—sheet music everywhere, viola da gamba propped against a wall—a makeshift navel observatory.

As he had done not countless, but a number of times, Laurence was gripping the downtown edge of whatever shirt he wore, preparing to disclose his unique belly button and confirm the fact of his complicated incunabulation.

Two

Never had Laurence had, for his navel, a more generous
audience than Gretchen. She cheered: 'It's gnomic,
gnostic, labyrinthine!' Spurred by his nodal whorl, she
demanded encore. She hooked her cellist's fingers below his belt
and made as if to tug his trousers off.

Laurence had expected a more Brahmsian tempo, *adagio con
moto* before the *vivace*. He tried to inject a *scherzo*, but Gretchen
was all for the *presto obbligato*. Exigent as metronome, she would
not be put off. '*Allegro,* yes,' thought Laurence, '*ma non troppo.*'

With Irene, undressing had always been a sublimated shave:
measured removal, caressing the complexion between strokes as
if to locate signs of something overlooked, still covering the naked.
Gretchen conducted herself differently: she wanted the cutaneous
and sub-, bare bones *sforzando*. Laurence heard vehicles and
altercations below: he was in the City, he'd have to adapt; but what
had happened to the *moderato?* He thought of his clean-shaven
pubis.

'Hold on,' said Laurence, 'let me undress *you.*' He always preferred exposing before being exposed. Here was Laurence, show-

ing a New York cellist the way to remove clothing. Off, you lendings! she had cried, but Laurence had kept his shirt on. Deliberate, he began.

Gretchen was wearing: garnets in her ears, garnets round her neck, garnets round a wrist; on the other, a timepiece of coppery gold; two tortoiseshell combs inlaid in her thin brown hair; pumps, two; a cotton shift gathered and darted; ephemeral bra with a single clasp in front, between; a half-slip of satin, the color of maize; a brief that fluttered like a moth when Laurence let it go. He removed these items as languorously as he could without seeming unenthusiastic: examining, nuzzling, tracing outlines and reporting back. He wanted a process of some anticipatory majesty, a beauty not merely inferred.

What he found was this: ears like leaves; skin like a mushroom patted dry and ready for salad; good bones; chin with a sexy underside, baby-blue circulation shining through; breasts unbridled and drifting on breathwaves, anaureolic, unpigmented nipples; contoured elbows; shampoo the only scent; pelvis prominent, abdomen placid; mons like moss- or lichen-covered humus, bleached peat; joints like paper clips, toes that could burrow: an unlikely, well-proportioned organism, shimmering before dinner like staff paper without notation: stippled and deckled on closer inspection, embossed with demure subliminal pores; onionskin, vellum, a stationer's dream. Her rising blood made a texture that suggested etching. She made Laurence want, for the first time in years, to engrave.

The City was punch-drunk with heat collected since morning, but Gretchen was dewless, undewed.

He praised her surface, and she grabbed for his leggings again. Intently iridescent, she required. She was igneous, opalesque, deepsea; still fully dressed, Laurence tumesced. He felt contingent, six-legged, evanescent.

Gretchen was quick and precise, using all her limbs to extricate his. Finally, they were bodies in air. Crowd seated, baton raised, a silence, the concert began.

Laurence and Gretchen made love like playing a duet, twelve-toned, harmonic, full of stops and entrances. Trilling and arpeggiating, chorically vibrant and leafily attenuated, suspending and resolving, in unison and counterpoint, they elaborated chords both vertically and horizontally, thirds and sevenths and ninths, increasingly jazzy and syncopated runs and changes. Double plucking, triple tonguing, they were almost a quartet. First he was tacit while she played riffs and licks, then she kept the beat while he improvised a progression. Always she returned to his navel for direction: her maestro, her oracle. They achieved intromission to mutual acclaim. His downbeat, her upbeat, *da capo, dal segno,* they repeated and developed, then took the coda to the finishing cadence. 'I die, I spend,' she sang. Then Laurence emissed and they rolled off the bed and flattened Bach. They tumbled past Monteverdi and Corelli and came to rest, panting, in a heap of Scarlatti. Handel, Haydn, Mozart, Purcell floated in with the tide. Enisled, they lay amid alto clefs and hummed a tune of tandem sleep.

Laurence awoke with his head at home on bleached peat, forceptual legs embracing his neck, ankles crossed on his stomach. He was more than comfortable. His hands capped the knees on his chest and squoze; Gretchen wiggled toes in greeting, rocked his head in her pelvic cradle.

It was just after midnight in the City, and Laurence and Gretchen were ravished, darkly latticed by the blinds.

Intermission: Laurence considered his placid manhood. It seemed content enough. Revision was called for. Irene he loved, but sex had become impossible. Gretchen he hardly knew, but sex was majestic, magisterial, fun. With Gretchen Laurence had little in common. Apprenticed to the trade of all jacks: position on a queen of a different suit. Strangely, Irene and Gretchen felt almost the same; differences were trivial, unromantic: the set of a hip, a tongue's preference, pitch of a vocal cord, estimated time of arrival. Monogamy beat a shocked retreat, stranding random ideas of order in its wake. Puzzles and posers were framed in Laurence that could stump a son and father both.

'You're not half so fragile as you look,' he said to Gretchen's toes.

'Most people aren't. You're fairly sturdy yourself.'

Gretchen did a sit-up and draped her breasts over Laurence's head: odd earmuffs. He was surprised to find that he felt intact, neither wretched nor abashed nor the least bit ravenous. Gretchen, though, was a hungry albino. She lithely wriggled out from under and cantered to the kitchen. Laurence, lying alone, wondered where were the Renaissance sculptors.

In a minute, Gretchen returned, bearing a blue-willow plate heaped with liver, rare, and a tumbler of skim milk whose milk-glass tint reminded Laurence of Gretchen's own lymphatic glow.

'You're going to eat that?'

'Chew it up, swallow it down. The taste of life; God, what texture! Want a bite?'

'Thanks, no. Are you anemic?'

'Hardly; I eat a pound and a half of this a day.'

While Gretchen chewed her magenta delicacy, the naked pair talked. She glowed like mother-of-pearl with a bluish cast. The combination of reddish, whitish, and bluish made Laurence think of birth.

'In case you're worried,' said Gretchen, 'I can't have children.' Laurence imagined the dimly lustrous distension of a Gretchen with child. 'Which is funny, 'cause my name's Barron, only spelled different.'

'Why not?' he asked, if it wasn't too personal.

'Nothing personal about physiology,' said Gretchen. 'Hormone imbalance; makes me like sex more and worry about it less.' She gnawed at the rich corpuscular organ. Her hands were stained with watercolor juices.

Gretchen, it seemed, was a voluntary postcoital talker; contact made her voluble. She chewed her liver and shot the breeze, while Laurence took it all in, considering sautéed onions in their absence.

'You get on a bus in Providence, you just don't expect this sort of a find. Look at us, a comical pair, I'm so pale and you're so.'

'Wizened?'

'Wizened? All right, wizened. The pale young lady and the wizened young man; we sound like a nursery rhyme. You're an only child, I'll bet.'

'Yes,' said Laurence, 'and a mistake at that.'

'We're all mistakes in our various ways. All my brothers and sisters are healthy and ruddy and businesslike. My parents figured someone was trying to tell them something, so they made me a cellist. They reserved me a chair in the Providence Symphony, but I got tired of Tchaikovsky and Rachmaninoff.

> *'So the pale young lady, she came to the City,*
> *And the wizened young man did too,*
> *And he thought she was very, very pretty,*
> *And she stuck to him like glue.'*

'She did?'

'That remains to be seen. You know, you beat the band in bed.'

Laurence was a conscientious lover, and had always wanted to hear that he beat the band. Now that he had been told as much, he was worried about adhesion, but comforted by the literal fact of Gretchen's sweatless skin. He thought it would be easier to peel oneself away from a lover who didn't perspire.

'I'm no expert,' said Laurence.

'When I was twenty-three, I dated a medical student. OB/GYN guy; what you might want to call an expert. He's the one who told me I can't have children. I found all sorts of things in his textbooks, but always in Latin, and I had to ask what the names meant. He knew the names, but he wouldn't indulge in any. Imagine such a wealth of knowledge going to waste. We could have called out fancy signals—*Manipulatio ad tertium molto con brio; Emissio vice versa sostenuto*—but all he wanted was the stroke, stroke, stroke of the coxswain. Made me feel like a dinghy. He should have been a missionary, wouldn't even play on his own terms. I left him *a capella*. So much for experts. Then when I first came to the City, I made it with an illiterate trombone player, didn't know an orifice from a hole in the wall, but ohmygod, his *glissando*, his *cadenza! Rubato prestidigitato*. Last year, there was a shrink, sixty-two, sixty-three years old, and he said, "I never thought I'd get involved with a kid like you, but damned if I haven't learned a thing or two. Where in hell did you grow up?" I told him Providence, and he packed up and moved to Rhode Island two weeks later, started a whole new practice. How's that for reaction formation? I thought you weren't hungry.'

Laurence was startled by direct address; in his concentration, he had been picking at his toenails with his blunt-honed fingers and absent-mindedly ingesting the trimmings. It was a practice he generally kept to himself, but Gretchen's unself-consciously devouring liver before him had short-circuited inhibition. Now, attention called, he didn't know whether he felt embarrassed or proud.

'I run out of fingers,' Laurence explained.

'You do such a neat job. Don't you wish you could reach them with your teeth?' Gretchen asked fetchingly.

'Ah, the supple pleasures of youth,' he reminisced.

She strolled her toes in front of his face. 'Would you like to try a bite of mine?'

Laurence had never worked on nails or cuticles not attached to himself. The not untitillating idea had been suggested once before, by his mother, as a step toward quitting. 'I'll let you bite mine,' she had said, offering her hands, 'if you'll leave off biting your own.' The archetypal proposition of a mother's love, conducing to a childish guilt, though never calculated to. Laurence had turned his mother's fingers down. Now he was faced with ten pale, chewy little toes, inOedipal, freely offered, without ulterior motive to be seen.

Every biter knows there's nothing more covetable than the untasted splitless half-mooned nail of an alien hand, untouched by human teeth. One deriving from the less dextrous foot would be, to some, even more enticing: more stocky, so more of a challenge; less often in view, so with less disfigurative danger, even if one hadn't Laurence's microtomizing dental virtuosity. To trim with oral loving care another's virgin metatarsals. And Gretchen's toenails were elegant, finely striated, custom-fitted, seasoned to taste. Though scarcely sybaritic, Laurence was blessed with human frailty. How could he refuse?

Gretchen lay on her back, right ankle tucked under left knee, left heel on a pillow, propped. She splayed her toes to air interstices, then relaxed her every muscle. Head to one side, eyes shut in trust or anticipation, her toes lay dormant. Laurence shivered.

'You're sure?' he managed to ask.

'My toes are in your hands.' Indeed they were, docile as newborn, tractable, serene.

Laurence felt privately calm, professional, expert as a faceter of gems musing on his exquisite task. Gently, he pedicured Gretchen.

A Bach cantata of 'This Little Piggy Went to Market,' at once substantial and spiritual, ethereal and elaborate, proliferant with notes like so many nerve endings, would have been the only fitting accompaniment for such an operation:

> *Dieses kleine Schweinchen ging zum Marktplatz,*
> *Dieses kleine Schweinchen,*
> *Dieses kleine Schweinchen,*
> *Ging zum, ging zum, ging zum*
> *Marktplatz.*
>
> *Dieses kleine Schweinchen,*
> *Dieses kleine, dieses kleine,*
> *Dieses, dieses, kleine, kleine*
> *Schweinchen blieb' heim,*
> *Blieb' heim, blieb' heim,*
> *Dieses blieb' heim.*
>
> *Dieses, dieses, dieses, dieses,*
> *Kleine, kleine, kleine, kleine,*
> *Schwein, Schwein, Schwein, Schwein,*

Chen, chen, chen, chen,
Dieses Schwein, dieses Schwein,
Kleine chen, kleine chen,
Fraß wiener, Schweinchen,
Fraß wiener, Schweinchen,
Fraß wiener, wiener, wiener, wiener
Schnitzel,
Fraß wiener Schnitzel.

Dieses kleine Schweinchen hat' kein,
Hat' kein, hat' kein, hat' kein, hat' kein,
Dieses kleine Schweinchen hat' kein.

Und dieses kleine Schweinchen schrie
Dieses kleine Schweinchen schrie
Und, und, und, und,
Schrie, schrie, schrie,
Und dieses kleine Schweinchen schrie
Wie wie wie wie wie wie wie wie
Wie wie wie wie wie wie wie wie,
Schrie wie wie wie den ganzen Weg,
Schrie wie wie wie den ganzen Weg,
Schrie wie wie wie wie wie wie wie
Wie wie wie wie wie wie wie wie
Wie wie wie den ganzen Weg
Heim,
Den ganzen Weg, den ganzen Weg,
Schrie wie wie wie den ganzen Weg,
Schrie wie wie wie den ganzen Weg,
Und dieses schrie wie wie wie wie
Den ganzen wie wie wie wie wie,
Dieses kleine wie wie Weg heim,
Den ganzen Weg heim.

Gretchen didn't wriggle, squiggle, waggle, or squirm, but lay loosely deliquescent *den ganzen Weg heim,* while Laurence nipped and tucked, incised and caninized her shuddering, tingling piggies. This little, that little, five in all.

Laurence took a developmental approach, starting with the bite-sized hors-d'oeuvre of a pinky and working gradually toward the harder, more horny excrescences of the larger toes. As he whittled at Gretchen's extremities with scalpel-like teeth, her whole life flashed before his eyes. The delivering doctor explaining the exigencies of raising such a one to parents who only wanted to know how and why this colorless child had been awarded to them, of all the expectant couples in Providence, in Rhode Island, on the Eastern Seaboard . . . the lifelong avoidance of sun as if it were a deadly raygun aimed at your fragile pupils and potentially puffy skin; bundling up for heat as if it were cold (and the adaptive value of not perspiring when you must cover as much in summer as in winter) . . . the lectures to your fifth-grade class on the nature of your anomaly; your own epidermis a surefire hit at show-and-tell . . . the troubled looks of cosmetic-counter personnel as you approach . . . the annoying persistence of bunny-rabbit allusions . . . the trip to the zoo, where you saw people huddled three-deep to ogle the albino porcupine, while the regular porcupine languished nearby without an audience; and wondering, which was the freak, popular oddity, or neglected normality? But most of all, Laurence heard and heard again as he clipped and carved these five left toes, the questions, endless questions, that could drive one who really wanted you to know to falsify hair color. Questions as if it were her fault, his fault, they were as they were.

But whose fault was it? he wondered. If you don't hold people to account for their characteristics, for what do you hold them to account? If the body's peculiarities are the mother's fault and the mind's the father's and behavior's society's and the soul's history's, can one be more or less likable, more or less forgivable than any other? One must, Laurence concluded: some will let you bite their nails, and others won't even let you bite your own. Did the first little piggy go to market out of anxiety, a wish to overcome agoraphobia, or a need for groceries? Did the second stay home out of deep-seated guilt, or because he had a well-stocked pantry? Did the fourth ever express a desire for roast beef, or was he content with feed corn? And if the fifth was really a whiner, did it make him any less distasteful to know that he had once had reason to whine?

Taking between his teeth responsibility for Gretchen's continuing podiatric outgrowth, Laurence wondered, how can you ever assign responsibility? How ever make choices without knowing all the facts? And what might constitute a valid reason for anything? And wasn't every move a drastic move, drasticity a matter wholly of degree, the shuffle Big Jim's whole ballgame, the opening at chess as crucial as check and mate? He recalled arguments with pubescent athletes over his own origins, with Irene over those of a nonexistent embryo: Beethoven or clam sauce, clam sauce or Beethoven, what's the difference if there's no way of knowing for sure?

Gretchen's foot twitched with nervy enervation. Laurence's mouth had all it could fathom of feeling. Head to toe, it was an open question whether either could stand the excruciating intensity of the opposite foot. Cheek to sole, they took a communal breather. Laurence and Gretchen slept together.

Biters don't generally pay the attention to nails that trimmers do. They know the calcareous growths are far from their best feature. There was no special time of week or day Laurence set aside to attend to fingertips. He was to his nails like the parent with custody, who has the kids all week, not the one who takes them to the circus and spoils them on weekends. His typical concern was not how did they look, but what were the chances of infection. He had had an infected thumb once, the size and color of a small lime. Outpatient surgery had been the only answer. But the lancing hadn't soured him on nails, only made him more precise: he stuck thereafter more closely to the nails themselves, leaving the abundance of surrounding tissue to take more or less care of itself.

Undertaking Gretchen's piggies, then, was the most concentrated observation of nails he'd ever made, like staring into another's eyes for the first time, when all you can do with your own is blink. More than a physical, it was a metaphysical experience. While Bach played in and around his head, Laurence could have taken notes for a dissertation: 'Tooth and Nail: The Ontology of the Other.'

A heady day for Laurence: his trip to the City (though he'd as yet seen none of the City), the second woman of his life in bed (he imagined a bogglingly logarithmic progression: twenty-six years had produced one partner; twenty-seven, two; what would the sum be at thirty?), and now an unacknowledged lifelong craving satisfied: five remarkable nails at his disposal. One might think he had trouble sleeping; but he had not. One might think, if he slept, he'd be swarmed by significant dreams:

Irene is restless, so I go to the kitchen to fetch a drink of water. When I return to bed, I find not Irene, but a translucent cello, and the water changes in the glass to calf's blood.
Or:
I am transformed into a playing card, appropriated to a game of solitaire in which I am being used to cheat. I try to protest, but find I cannot open my two-dimensional mouth.
Or:
I am in bed with Grandpa Theo when he has a heart attack. Thinking quickly, I try to rub his wrists, but find myself instead biting his nails, and he dies. I wonder if there's any point in finishing the manicure.

But no; he enjoyed a repose prenatally, almost preternaturally sound. Neither he nor Gretchen stirred for a full eight hours. When he finally woke, he did so in his favorite way, with slow delight and a gauzy vengeance.

Suppose you don't like a particular aspect of your tennis game; your lob, for example. There are two choices open to you: avoid lobbing, or lob and lob until you like your lob and love lobbing. If you take the latter course—and it is meet that you should—you may find, after many a lob, that you enjoy your lob best of all your shots. You lob inordinately, lob in fact more than anyone else you know of.

So it was with Laurence and waking up. The end of sleep each day jolted his system like birth trauma, and gave him a panicky sense that he would never sleep again. His choices were clear: avoid waking up, or wake up a lot. Laurence chose the latter course, and was capable, from years of practice, of waking up for hours on end, without being fully awake, without getting out of bed.

Waking up had become, in fact, the highlight of his typical day. Softness, comfort, warmth were never greater than during the indulgent, gradual extrication of his mind from the unconscious, his body from the horizontal, state. The deliberate, exigent sensuality of sex could scarcely compare with the diurnal ecstasy of this communion with the sheets. That he should wake cuddled under cotton comforters, a muffled, undifferentiated mass, and only slowly rediscover the unnerving specifics of form, meet again his long-lost elbows, renew the acquaintance of his lower extremities, only then hear from internal organs, hungry or cramped or otherwise unpleased with the new day; that he should have the time for this disturbing process to be conducted in slow motion; that he should be prepared for the shock, as early election returns prepare a candidate destined to lose; this Laurence considered a gift, a daily grace vouchsafed him.

For a good nursery rhyme, Gretchen should have been an early riser, splasher of face with icy water, runner around the block or sunrise calisthene. In fact, no such Jack Spratt symmetry obtained between this pair, both of whom characteristically nursed their dreams like drinks till the shocking ice of wakefulness had melted and thoroughly diluted the heady draught of sleep, till brainwaves played a stable counterpoint of alpha and beta. The halfway point was what both liked best: not quite responsible as one is for waking thoughts, but implicated as one can never be in dreams *per se.* Transition, when the eyes could be open or closed—are

you dreaming your own room, or seeing someone else's?—when
thought is too slow to be consecutive or awareness is too sleepy
to see how fast thought is, conscious of being unconscious, or yet
unconscious of being already conscious: the extended birth of
sentience.

Irene, a splasher, had worried an hour or so away each morning
while Laurence indulged his luxurious, liminal, almost metem-
psychotic revery. He had always been alone under daylit covers,
his most private of times. Now, with Gretchen beside him humoring her tandem twilit self, Laurence felt as if someone were joining him in side-by-side vice. He felt onanistic, exposed, unwantedly
self-conscious, and what was more, guilty for sucking his dug of a
dream to the dregs.

When Laurence identified, with surprise at its pleasurability,
what he was feeling as guilt, he caught himself thinking, 'Irene,'
and was associationist enough to conclude that his unease had to
do with his wife. Not, surely, that he was betraying her by waking
in Gretchen's bed; rather, perhaps, that he was in danger of
entangling alliances—'And she stuck to him like glue' was echo-
ing—that he should have alerted Gretchen to how things stood.
Well, how, he wondered, did things stand? Who the devil knew;
but should he have mentioned Irene, marriage, shaving, Amelia,
false pregnancy, life-as-a-lecture-series?

Half-awake Laurence, then and there, renounced such scruples, the religioid notion that every first date is an oblique trial
marriage, that one is obliged to warn the world before undressing:
I may not be totally rational, I have a mole on my left nether cheek,
I sometimes snore, I never believed in Santa. No! thought Laurence; and with the force of this conviction he woke more nearly
up. I'm not required to confess all, as if my life were a turnpike,
and autobiography the quarter I'm to toss in a basket every twenty-
five miles. For the privilege of her hollow, she gets my protru-
sion—for her toes, my teeth—not exclusive rights to my life story.
I'm in the City, not in court; under compulsion to get by, not to
tell the whole and nothing but. In fact, thought Laurence as he
completed the bumpy ride to wakefulness, in fact, in fact, in fact,
I'm not under any oath at all; in fact, in fantasy—I needn't have
told her anything, needn't have explained my navel—*infantasia*—
I could be mum or lie—yes, lie, why not? (the thought had never
seriously occurred to Laurence!)—on any subject.

Alert now but lying still, Laurence tried to recall every tidbit of biography he had already offered, preparing to subject his further disclosures to the test of not truth or completeness, but consistency or felicitous composition. He lay concocting stories of his life to give Gretchen when and if the question arose, and chuckled out loud at his fabrications, chuckled private little squirrel- or chipmunk-chuckles at the fantastic acorns he could contrive to stuff the pouchy cheeks of his life in the City.

Gretchen, at this involuntary guttural proof that Laurence was awake, and as if she had been waiting for merely that assurance that she wouldn't be leaving her brand-new lover to wake alone, leapt from the mattress and headed for the shower. Alone, Laurence found himself—like the first realization that he could ignore a stop sign at midnight with no one around, or break wind in private and enjoy it—chuckling still at his newfound resource of invention, as if it were a set of wings, or a set of genitalia he'd never thought much of till puberty. He was a happy confectioner with a fresh cake to frost, chuckling and chuckling as Gretchen stood in the shower on toes he knew better than his own. The gushing shower sounds pleased him, the competence and serendipity of his arrival in the City pleased him, the loft, the sheets, the physical setting pleased him. Gladsomely he lay, awaiting Gretchen's damp return.

Gretchen arose with a passion to clean. She cleaned herself and then she cleaned her loft. She stacked her sheet music by composer and decade, and within these categories, in alphabetical order by key. She dusted her viola da gamba, carefully tracing scroll and *f*-holes, and resined all her bows. She washed her dishes and mopped the kitchen floor. She whistled while she worked. She angled her refrigerator out from the wall and scoured at the private interface where floor and baseboard met. She unplugged the appliance and piled victuals, smorgasbord-style, all over the counter; then set off to polish her floor-to-ceiling loft windows while the fridge defrosted. Sunlight activated slats of dust through the panes; and Gretchen, in a cleaning frenzy, swiped determinedly at the splayed shafts like a mind grasping facts, gladly catching and releasing handfuls of motes.

Laurence, assembling a semblance of breakfast from the counter, felt enhanced by a tinge of illegitimacy, as if he were strolling through a supermarket, plucking one of each item from the shelf: a piggy gone to market with no intention of paying. He was startled by Gretchen's Nietzschean will to tidy. It made him wonder if there had been anything wrong, for her, anything messy or polluting, about their night together.

'Why so cleanly?' he asked, trying to sound casual and unFreudian.

'Happens every time I take a lover,' said Gretchen. 'Freudian, I suppose.'

What Laurence found surprising was her undaunted, unworried, unromantic, undemanding stride, in which everything, it seemed, could be taken as a matter of ongoing fact. Surprising, charming; admirable, almost: cause to chuckle.

And chuckle Laurence did—with a stamina he hadn't known since early Irene—through a shower long and hot in the already steamy stall. He emerged to find billows of visible vapor, some content to billow, some more given to condensing on Gretchen's mirror. He considered wiping it clear to comb his hair, but then with his recent resolve to become whoever he pleased, whoever pleased him, in fact, in fantasy, left the bathroom dripping and unkempt.

'You lied to me,' said Gretchen when she heard him coming.

Laurence referred the accusation, as was his wont, to the story of his birth. 'I never,' he said.

'You at least once,' said Gretchen, who was, he could now see, rummaging through his saxophone case.

'What are you doing with my sax?'

'You run out of fingers; I run out of things to clean. I thought of doing you the favor of giving it a once-over. It needs a lot more than that. This thing looks like it hasn't been touched in years: a piece of junk.'

'Hey, watch how you talk about my ax.'

'This is no ax; it's a crudded thing that's dying of neglect. There's not even wax for the keys. You lied when you told me you were a musician.'

'I didn't.'

'Had any gigs lately?'

Now her rhetorical questions were losing their charm. 'I play sax,' he said.

'Play it, then.'

'I'm not going to perform for you.'

'You are if you don't want me to think you lied. I don't like being lied to, Laurence. I didn't bring you here to lie to me.'

'I am not a liar, and I didn't lie to you. I play the saxophone.'

'Play, then.'

'What would you like, *Symphonie Fantastique*, "The Teddy Bears' Picnic"?'

'Suit yourself; but play, or admit you lied.'

What if he did? What if he admitted he lied?

'I did not lie.'

'I don't see why people think they have to lie,' said Gretchen, aggression giving way to upset.

'I didn't think I had to; I mean I didn't have to; I didn't; I don't; I'm not a liar.'

There was coldness in her voice now. 'I'm sorry, then, Laurence; I've done you an injustice. But I do so love the sound of a saxophone. Won't you please condescend to vouchsafe me just a single small melody?'

'Some other time.'

'Then I'll play for you. I guess I can manage a few scales.' She grabbed a gristly reed from the case and began sucking. Laurence paced.

He paced himself back into the bathroom, no longer misty, where he shakily combed his hair and began to dress. He always felt less vulnerable when dressed; he'd often thought if he had to be shot or run over or incinerated alive, he'd feel better about going clothed. In the bathroom, steamless now but humid, he heard tentative notes from his unmistakable sax—the sticky keys, the flatulent low D, the leaky tone like stale cotton candy, like a drunken or smoke-filled saxophone; a lousy imitation-boozy blues singer, pretending to age never reached: fake degeneracy, phony pain. Pathetic and ludicrous, Gretchen's shoddy scales clawed at his ears like a mob assaulting the royal carriage. He ironically applauded, tried to shout 'One more time' as bitterly as he could; but instead, and without meaning to in the slightest, he cried. Thank you very much, he thought. Just what I needed, he thought. God damn, he thought. Bitch, he thought. From somewhere—he couldn't have told you where—he remembered some words in a language not his own. *Cania*, he thought. *Donnaccia alla breve; putana poco più mosso.* Hilarious with the thought of cursing Gretchen in the tongue of her profession; and though he was crying, laughing too, as he dissolved in a rain of imperfect bilingual malediction.

It was years since Laurence had felt the petulant tyranny of moods, the uncontrolled amusement-park ups and downs; but now, the raging helplessness, and the horrible spiteful acquiescence an overtired mind gives to their smug sway. *Acquiescat in pacem*—an epitaph for a mind that's relinquished its reins to capricious and vicious moods. 'You're fairly sturdy yourself,' she had said to him not twelve hours since; and his surprise at crumbling wasn't half so great as his surprise at so hatefully and childishly holding against all logic to his first and only lie, at inviting Gretchen to play the notes that gratuitously proved what neither doubted. It was he who had forced her to hit him at the moment of greatest vulnerability— in sports there are penalties for that: roughing the passer, roughing the kicker—he who had set her on an end run around his feeble, unpracticed defense, to scamper the length of the field, the bright field of falsified possibility he had only just then seen open before him. He resented his own stubborn pride, and he resented her accidental ruthlessness; and two separate parts of him resolved at once never to hold it against her, and never to forgive her.

So that that night, in the midst of a lovemaking reprise that made their morning recriminations and Gretchen's ugly solo seem less like something that had happened than something they had feared might happen; in the afterglow of restoring Gretchen's right foot to near symmetry with her left, Laurence's feelings were mixed when she said, in a tone of demure seductivity: 'I too have a favorite perversion.'

He was startled to hear her refer to their so recent ecstasy in this manner. Were toenails his favorite perversion? Did she wish to nibble some part of him? Was he obliged to let her?

He tried to sound open-minded. 'Yes?'

'*Mictio in os.*'

Latin. An act of esoterica sexualis her medical student had refused to perform. She had a store of vocabulary in a dormant language, saved for a rainy day and a willing partner. He pretended not to have an inkling.

'Micturate in osculum,' she glossed.

'Whose?'

'Mine.'

Better yours than mine, he thought; but to her he said: 'In your *mouth?*'

Her expression brightened. She sat up straight. 'Where else then?'

Silence. 'No?'

He had hesitated, not because he couldn't say no, but because, never having considered *mictio in os*, he didn't know what he wanted to say. He was thinking. 'Wait,' he said.

'Yes? *Tant mieux.*'

'Wait,' he said. Suddenly, slightly abashed, he knew. It was not the act that daunted him; it was Irene and her maddening behaving-like-a-human-being. Oh, she held her sway over him. It was not the sort of thing he'd do in spite. If he did it, it would be—he amazed himself by thinking this—from love. And if from love—he saddened himself by thinking this—it would be with Irene and only Irene.

'No,' he said.

'No? *Tant pis.*' Gretchen headed for the kitchen and liver. Laurence regarded his sax, dull metal, and felt he was himself dull metal; animal no, vegetable no, mineral yes, a tarnished clipper: he felt enormous, *largo*, and too old to be playing games.

Three

$\sim$

Experience—self-satisfied stepmother of knowledge, bullying big sister to inexperience, self-proclaimed expert on this and that, court-appointed guardian of us all—teaches that loneliness and remorse afflict indiscriminately, without regard to gender. No spreader of greatcoats over puddles, experience; nor was Irene supremely happy without her Laurence.

Thus one summer night, as Gretchen Barron, a woman profoundly aware of her vaginal lubricity, transferred half a mouthful or so of saliva into the palm of her hand and then sculpted and frosted it on and around the glans of Laurence Paprika (a gesture whose homely charm was not lost on him), Irene was dialing in Providence the number which had served her and her husband and her Aunt Amelia throughout most of their married life, only to learn from a recording with an annoying echo that the number was no longer in service.

Her image of Laurence hadn't allowed for his leaving town. She had called with reconciliation on her mind, ready if need be to announce that she would bear him a child, would do a full nine-month term of penance for her impetuous false alarm; that she thought him, far from a chronic malfunction, both necessary and sufficient; that two months of symmetrical solitude could bring them back to recognition of their mutually orphaned needs. Irene was all but ready to beg, ready to yield to Laurence's theories and promise to love, honor, obey, and even to believe.

As she cradled the receiver, her thoughts went something like this:

A human being is conceived on the evening of the first snow-fall—mid-November—grows toes, say, in February, eyes, say, in April, a stomach, say, in May, though none of these goes to work in earnest until the tail end of July, when the infant emerges—a month premature and a bit undersized—and is incubated—fed, perhaps, with an eyedropper—till, say, early September, when, like all good children, it sets off to make its fortune.

It—she, say—is told to eat right, exercise, and learn a thing or two, so she will be happy, healthy, generally viable in years to come. She does well in first grade to give herself a good opportunity in second grade; in second, in third; in third, in fourth; in fourth, in fifth; in high school, in college; in college, in career; in career, in life; in life, in what—posterity, afterlife, death? And she begins to wonder, in junior high school which is good preparation for high school, or on a date which is good preparation for marriage: When does it start, the real thing, life—post-rehearsal, pre–cast-party, the performance—when does it start, the *Ding an sich*, how will she know, what will the signs be that the clock has started ticking away her life, that incubation is over? When is the pump primed, where is the big time? Childhood—which experts tell us didn't exist two centuries ago, and which seems to be growing steadily, encroaching on adulthood, so that soon we will be children till the last minute—when does it end? When she loses her virginity? When she's in debt? When she lands a steady job? When she misgives her parents? When she sets up housekeeping? When she fears for her life? But all these things have happened, and she stills feels preparatory.

And it occurs to her—say, me, Irene—that childhood ends when I have a child; that it must, or lines would be backed up behind schedule, pastries plopping undecorated off slapstick assembly lines; and that that, among several other things, is what children are for: to make adults of parents, to put the cherry atop the layer cake of childhood and clear the moving belt for its next passenger. Like houseplants: water, drain, water, drain, parent, child, parent, child.

Irene thought then of her own parents, of how, especially now that they were gone, they seemed nothing more than grown-up children playing House. She thought of any couple, any marriage; and they all had that air about them: children playing House. Boys will be boys, girls will be girls, and couples will be couples; and if you're going to play House, you may as well play it, patter of tiny feet and all.

To Irene, a lapsed but not extinct Unitarian, it seemed almost religious, this voice of vocative maternity. There used to be tenses, moods for that: *I would have a child! O that I were a mother!* Despite anachronism, Would that I were a mother, she thought; now, this minute, or allowing for the red tape and paperwork of gestation, nine months hence. Already, though, she felt enlarged by contrast to the tiny toes, reinforced in comparison with the tender skin, invulnerable to diaper rash, articulate in the extreme. 'O where is my husband?' she cried.

Laurence awoke, as was virtually his wont by now, amidst frets and staffs, in a room filled with clefs but not with Gretchen. Only vaguely did he recall an earlier abortive waking: Gretchen's diurnal Bach cantata, her characteristic stereophonic *Reveille,* and the swishing shower sounds and the door's closing click that had put him firmly back to sleep. He ran his lonesome tongue over each of his fingernails in turn, absently checking prospects for the day. Only after showering and shaving extensively did he wander into the kitchenette in search of juice. Magneted onto the refrigerator, at eye level, a note from his hostess, explaining *in absentia* her absence: 'Out to buy a new G-string. Back soon.'

Laurence was growing used to a chronic confusion about whether Gretchen was referring to music or sex; now feeling horny himself, he thought to take advantage of her absence by practicing a few scales. When Gretchen returned not many minutes later, he was assiduously sucking on his reed. She sat to restring her cello while he lubricated his keys and did his best to fluff the melancholy pads of his down-and-out sax.

'Laurence,' she said, stretching a spanking new filament over her bridge, 'there's one less rabbit in the world today.'

She was clearly shaken, and Laurence, still not fully awake, marvelled at the extent of her sympathy for a fellow pink-eyed creature. What sort of accident had she witnessed on the streets of the City?

'One less rabbit?'

'I seem to have taken in a boarder.'

For a moment Laurence thought she meant himself. Then the images clicked, and he was fully awake. 'But you can't have children.'

'Not only can't; don't want to. I'm already the proud and busy mama of a viola da gamba and two violoncelli.' One of which, having restrung with the nonchalant loving care of a diapering mother, she patted on the behind and set against the wall.

'But your medical student.'

'Chris Crickenberger, M.D. Either he flunked Endocrinology, or he was handing me a line. Or maybe hormone balances can change that much over three years. I never thought to audition my metabolism again.'

'You could be wrong?'

'I was supposed to be a blood bank ten days ago. Instead I've become an incubator.'

Laurence recalled Irene's gratuitous abortion: *But when she got there, the cupboard was bare . . .* 'Are you sure, are you absolutely sure?'

'Laurence, a rabbit has given its life!'

He recalled his image of both Gretchen and himself as evolutionary placeholders—'packing material for the parcel of more viable organisms'—and his question: 'If only the fittest survive, why make some who are not fittest?' Recollection provided no answer, only an additional question. What of the offspring of two ciphers? How could their child be anything but pale and wizened? He envisioned a brief, macrocephalic, nursery-rhyme life, with all the limbs and outward flourishes, none of the staples, of humanity; a child with cellophane for skin, exposing scarcely any organs to speak of, an overgrown protozoan. An overgrown protozoan, yes, thought Laurence; but then a Darwinian extrapolation presented itself in bearded tones that seemed too sage to be his own. 'What are we all but overgrown protozoa?' He transposed the query into his own voice. It sounded no less wise; moreover, gave rise to corollaries. Then there's no particular reason why any of us should or should not have been born.

Suddenly, Laurence thought he understood that natural selection is an inductive science. Evolution has to work, like a high-school coach, with what it's got. It can't invent bonus babies to groom for the majors, but must wait to see who comes out for the team. And if a given year is not a particularly good one for fielding a genetic team, if it's a building year after losing a number of seniors through graduation, then maybe even the product of a Laurence and a Gretchen could make the first string.

Laurence's outlook, in a single movement, like a kaleidoscope or geologic fault or uncomfortable sleeper, shifted, rearranged, and resettled itself. I don't owe it to the embryo, he thought, or to any-one else, to see that it gets born. It's just a choice, my small free-will contribution to the phylogenetic potluck, nothing in the way of moral obligation for or against. With this thought, the pressure relieved, Laurence decided to make it his business to see that this child *would* be born. Why? He remembered his Yiddish grandpa's answer to every 'why': '*Noor vee doos.* Just like this.' And he thought it a signal of growing up, something in common with Grandpa Theo, that he could accept this answer.

'Just because': the prerogatory response permitted the very young and the very old. Ask a six-year-old why: 'Just because.' 'Oh. Okay.' Ask a sixty-year-old why: 'Just because.' 'Oh. Okay.' But ask a sixteen-year-old why: 'Just because.' 'I'm sorry, Larry, that's not a sufficient reason.' But Laurence now saw every 'Just because' as a glorious, and what was more the only, reason. First, final, mate-rial, and efficient cause; the unmotivated motivator, unpremedi-tated precipitator: *Noor vee doos.*

He was committed, as one could only be for no particular rea-son. But what of Gretchen?

She sighed a sigh she had been saving up. 'Laurence, you and I, we have no business being parents.'

Gretchen's insidious intent was incubating in Laurence's mind, growing little teeth and claws, familiar, unmistakable.

'No!' he shouted, much too loud, with pent-up anger at his mother, at Irene, at the imaginary old man with his recurrent dull knife.

'It's just a little bunch of cells, Laurence.'

'Cells dividing and differentiating, goal-oriented cells, genes with a full itinerary. What are you, what am I, what was Bach but a bunch of particularly genial cells?'

'Oh, life, liberty, pursuit: foetal rights. Mothers have rights, too, especially inadvertent mothers misled by opportunistic medical students.'

'What about fathers? What about fathers' rights?'

'Fathers aren't mothers. I'm not about to raise a child.'

Gretchen raised, instead, her voice, and a discussion of major proportions ensued. For Laurence, a reprise, a reprieve, new lease on the argument he'd lost to Irene. After several months to review mistakes and revise his case, he was prepared to be rational and persuasive. But as they heated, he doubted how persuasive his 'Just because' could prove; and he couldn't rid his mind of the unreasonable imagery of incineration.

She wants to be an incinerator, he thought.

'A baby isn't trash!' he claimed.

How he had arrived at this line of thinking was not exactly clear to Gretchen, but she was willing to engage him on whatever terms. 'A baby born to you and me might well be better off as trash,' she said, thinking perhaps of cellophane for skin.

'Gretchen, if you want to annihilate something, don't for gods' sake add to that the insult of saying you're annihilating it for its own good. They could have said that about you. They *did* say it about me, and I'll be damned if I say it about any poor little blastula.'

Laurence realized that his 'Just because,' though privately reason enough, hadn't an embryonic chance of swaying Gretchen, and that his argument, as if instinctively, was composing itself not of free will, but of moral and pragmatic red herrings he would himself have rejected. Conventional sentiment, dumb and useless, was fuelling a stance that had its roots in the power of mere impulse. He felt the gears of his argument slipping, and in desperation made an offer whose impulsiveness more nearly resembled its motivation than any debater's Q.E.D. could have done.

'I'll be the mother,' he said.

'There are limits to sympathetic labor.'

'After it's born, I mean. You be the mother till delivery, and I swear to you I'll be the mother from the minute you're out of the hospital. Bear with me for nine months and you'll never give another minute of your life to me or the child if you don't want to.'

'You want a child that much?'

'I don't want a child at all! But I've got one, helplessly dividing in there.'

'You expect me to do that for you?'

'I'm begging you to. I'll do anything you want. I'll *mictio* in your houseplants, in your cello, in your ear.'

'Rear?' she shuddered.

'Ear,' he clarified.

'Nine months, huh?'

'Less by now.'

Silence from Gretchen. 'Yes?' he asked.

'Wait,' she said.

Inwardly, Gretchen smiled. She had often thought she'd like to be pregnant, she'd like to give birth, she'd like to have that singular nine-month experience under her belt, if not for the burdensome aftereffect of a child. She was thinking this might be a rare opportunity, a criminal act with no threat of prosecution, a sanctioned trespass.

'I guess it wouldn't get breast-fed,' she said.

'Not unless my hormones are as unpredictable as yours.'

Laurence could see she was coming, quite unexpectedly, around.

'I'd want the kid named after the person responsible,' she said.

Not an unreasonable condition: Larry Junior, thought Laurence. Loretta the Second. Lonnie the Younger. Lala *fils*.

'*Tant mieux*,' he said. 'Laurence if it's a boy, Loretta if it's a girl.'

'Absolutely not. I said the person responsible: Christian.'

'Christian?'

'After Chris Crickenberger, Quack. Christian if it's a boy, Christian if it's a girl.'

'Gretchen, be reasonable.'

'Take care, Laurence. If I'm reasonable, this little clump will be no more than a gleam in its father's eye by tomorrow noon.'

Laurence remembered how treacherous was his footing, and retreated. He would, he had said, do anything. But Christian Paprika?

'And you find out where that bastard of a Chris Crickenberger, M.D., is practicing, and we go wherever that is and have him deliver his namesake.'

'Gretchen.'

'Take it or leave it.'

Take it or leave it. Love it or leave it. To be or not to be. Was this the upshot of all his free will?

'Deal,' said Laurence. 'Shake on it?'

'Unless you want a formal contract with my belly notarized.'

'Gretchen, you're a jewel.'

'Laurence, you're a fool.'

'I'll buy that; and furthermore, I have a confession. You were right: I'm a lousy saxophone player. I used to be not bad, but that was quite a while ago.' *And besides, the wench is dead* popped comically into Laurence's head.

'I never doubted it for a minute. How are you going to support this kid?'

'I don't know.'

Gretchen chucked him under the chin. 'Such a good provider,' she said, smiling.

'Yeah,' he said, trying not to.

Directory Assistance listed no Paprika in Providence. Irene concluded, not that Laurence had dispensed with phone service, but, correctly, that he had flown the coop. Where was another question: the Alps, the Aleutians, the Indies, the Hamptons? For just a moment the long-distance whereabouts of her errant husband seemed an insoluble riddle, a crossword definition outside her vocabulary. But then she outflanked her own ignorance, thinking what she did know of Laurence; she knew he'd have given himself a reason for leaving, in the form of a destination. He'd be off consulting, looking for allies, hunting out collaboration. Researching, documenting. Family, possibly; New York, then.

Irene was amazed at how unmistakably letters combined to form words, astonished at how easily the cars of her train of thought were coupled and caboosed and confidently chugging toward Grand Central. How simple to eliminate every global locale but one! A single municipality in which to locate a single husband she'd recognize on sight, even in a crowd. And it wasn't as if she hadn't some clues, sundry intersecting Paprikas in various metropolitan white pages, maybe even a mercantile Paprika or two in the yellows—'Uncle Izzy's Carwash,' 'Aunt Elaine's *Salon de Beauté.*'

Irene winced at the detective work ahead of her. She conjured painful imaginary phone calls to Laurence's relatives, clannish unlikable folk she'd met only once, at the wedding, and whose names and faces she'd had a hard time keeping straight to thank for the color-coordinated cookware they'd conspired to provide, daffodil-yellow stainless darkening to a rusty brown toward the nonstick edges: Autumn Harvest.

'Sounds more like a rest home or cemetery than a color for frying pans,' she had said, disgruntled with the shiny uniformity of their spic, span, and spanking new kitchen.

Laurence, seriously weighing a toaster, had apologized: 'They mean well, even though my mother's side of the family has always been sort of separate.'

Irene stopped short: 'my mother's side.' These weren't Paprikas at all. Aunts Tootie, Snookie, Fluffy were Laurence's mama's married sisters; Uncles Benny, Ellie, Julie were by marriage, and as far as Irene was concerned, of indeterminate surname. These were not clues, then, but distracting needles in the urban haystack. Had there not been a single Paprika sprinkled about the wedding buffet? She wished she had paid more attention to introductions, less to her preoccupying bogus morning sickness.

Who, then, occupied the father's side? As far as Irene knew or could guess, only the grandfather with the bad heart, who had never acknowledged their announcement, and who, for all she could imagine, might be deceased or disapproving or otherwise unpromising as a means of pinpointing Laurence. New York might be, after all, a gigantic crossword puzzle of unfamiliar thoroughfares, diagramless, and Irene with no idea of where to start.

Gretchen, no welsher, did her best as a mother-to-be, not smoking, not drinking, taking good care, and eating what she imagined would one day be the baby's favorite dishes, though that imputed list did not coincide with her own. For herself, she insisted only on her daily dose of rare liver. Iron she always personally craved; and though exempt for the nonce from her portion of the world's menstrual duties, she was determined to thwart whatever chromosomes might be conspiring in secret to make Laurence's baby pale like herself. Once committed to bearing, she feared subversion. She invented a patron saint of pigmentation, prayed for an infant of ruddy opacity.

Though her coloring was orchidlike, Gretchen was no shrinking hothouse plant. Resolved throughout her pregnancy to postpone confinement, she played cello at least as often as before in public, and more at home. Her feeling was, the gestating offspring of pregnant musicians are entitled by heredity to a foretaste of good taste, a rhythmic, harmonic, vibrating rehearsal hall of a womb. Strings in general, she thought, and a cello in particular, could produce a virtuous lullabic tone when played as she knew how; and she played for her embryo mainly ruminative liturgical motets now, with breathless dedication, hugging the curved wooden body of the instrument between her knees as if it were a lover, almost as tall and fully as wide as herself. She rested the polished belly firmly against her own, planted its umbrella tip steadfastly before her, and played for the diversion of her private audience a command performance.

Eavesdropping from the nearby bed, Laurence felt lyrical, domestic, blessed. Gretchen completed a heavenly cadence and lay beside him.

'You know why I think I let you talk me into this?' She implicated her abdomen.

Laurence didn't. Her surrender had come with a sudden impish mysterious ease he couldn't attribute to his command of rhetoric, and to explain which even Gretchen's habitually acceptant stride seemed insufficient.

Her question, though syntaxed like a challenge, was delivered in a tone of comradeship, both-in-this-togetherness. 'No,' he rejoined in kind, 'I don't know why you think you let me talk you into that.' He too poked playfully, but respectfully, at the general region of her womb, and fancied it fuller, riper, more like the taut precision curve of a cello belly than it had been. He was touched by her upcoming distension, wished in a peculiar way it could be his, but knew there were limits to sympathetic labor.

'Chris Crickenberger, M.D.,' she said, and with that brief utterance—two words, two initials, barely an utterance at all, a lowest common denominator—did away with the serene and magical mood her music had induced.

What oddities of cause and effect were at work in Gretchen? A young man with no knife at all, administering endless pelvics somewhere in Rhode Island. By what impossibly remote control had *he* rescued the burgeoning clump *in utero?*

Chris Crickenberger: the vapid beetlish alliteration of the physician's name nettled Laurence. That charlatan, mandrake, metabolic misreader: what was he doing in their story? What right had he to even a cameo role in the biography of a namesake he had ruled out? Laurence felt his alien presence like an unhealed abrasion you forget till you come in contact with something, anything: all roads, for Gretchen, seemed to lead back to him, 'the person responsible,' the medical man irresponsible. Couldn't he let them be? Couldn't he stake out a recurrent claim on some other uterus?

It occurred to Laurence that such a man might have similar first dibs on dozens of fallopian tubes, might have lulled countless women into a false sense of sterility, might have babies twice removed from legitimacy scattered about the industrial Northeast like air-dropped pamphlets. Vaginas and cervices were his business, but he left his lasting and sinister mark in the female neocortex, brain cells across the land embittered by his wayward speculum, betrayed by his insincere, manipulating disposable rubber gloves. The man was a menace.

It must be admitted, though, since it was just now being insisted by Gretchen, that he *was* 'the person responsible' for her accession to Laurence's impassioned but shaky argument. According to Gretchen, and who should know better, only he, somehow, had made ongoing pregnancy bearable. Laurence had to resent him for the existence of that embryo, but had also only him to thank for its deliverance.

O how Laurence hated to be bracketed, even inadvertently, with the mountebank! To be in cahoots, he thought helplessly, with an incompetent or conniving intern, a disgrace to his stethoscope, betrayer of Hippocrates. Fertilization, concluded Laurence without a hint of comedy, makes strange bedfellows.

But Gretchen, his present bedfellow, was embarking on an exposition.

'Chris was in Gynecology at Brown Medical School; I was still living at home, playing with the Providence Symphony. He had a season ticket, and a fascination with my body which at the time I thought was more than merely professional.

'I don't know why doctors become doctors. Some say money; others insist altruism. I suspect, more often than not, it's an interest in bodies. Not lascivious, I mean, but somehow prurient. Chris, at least, wanted to be privy to others' secrets.

'Once I asked him what muscles look like. He flexed, but I explained I meant under the skin. So he showed me.

'If some guys want to impress you, they show you their cars. Others show you their etchings or their generosity or their diplomas or their waterbeds.'

'Or their navels,' put in Laurence.

'Or their navels. Well, Chris Crickenberger showed me his cadaver.'

'His what?'

'His body. His dead body.'

'You saw a corpse?'

'Several, actually. Yes.'

Laurence had never thought of such training in anatomy as other than a medieval or Renaissance, surely pre-Enlightenment, practice, bygone with cupping and bleeding. That apprentice physicians still dissected cadavers as part of their education was news to him. His interest, moreover, was piqued. What more piquant, after all, than bodies? Actually seeing them seemed taboo. Sheets, blankets, hospital johnnies, eyelids, police officers' coats: something, at any rate, always seemed, and properly so, to cover them. He'd never imagined naked death.

He imagined it now: a sight to make eyes sore, smarting with indecent exposure and morbid curiosity. He himself, it occurred, was displaying an interest not lascivious, but somehow prurient—and not so excusably vested as a doctor's—in the graphic after-image of the doctor's art. Of anyone's art, he thought: the universal upshot, dust to dust, organs to organs, tissue to tissue.

Fascinated, Laurence settled in as if, popcorn in hand, waiting for a show to start. Gretchen was his reflecting screen; after animated shorts, coming attractions, no minor, unaccompanied by parent or guardian, he awaited an X-rated feature, feeling, in fact, a slight pornographic tingle. Foetally huddled, lit only with inferential streetlight, he listened to Gretchen as a child to a ghostly tale, fully prepared for the extraction by fear of his living daylights.

It was midafternoon, said Gretchen, but the med-school morgue was dark and airless, unwindowed, secret as a catacomb at the end of the hall. It felt like midnight in a parking garage, cool, damp, concrete. There were aisles of four-wheeled stretchers like an auto showroom. The fixtures were fluorescent, blue-white office light, and buzzed with a stupid insistence. For a second she thought it was her own head that was buzzing, and feared some idiotic feminine vertigo; but the thought of being unconscious in that place was more frightening than being conscious. On every gurney was a shiny green vinyl heap that zippered down the front like a garment bag, like something you carry suits through airports in.

Laurence was surprised at the prepared, literary quality of Gretchen's depiction; he felt distanced, spectatory, and remembered the days of saxophone solos, the adrenaline calm just before going onstage.

Every student has a partner, said Gretchen, and the two of them share a cadaver for the semester. Chris told her there are more than enough bodies for each to have his own, but the problem is space. He said there's a surplus, a waiting line; half the people who will their bodies to science get turned down or put on hold. It's expensive; they have to be preserved and stored till the start of a new school term.

Laurence imagined warehouses, giant meat lockers, flophouse freezers for indigent corpses waiting to be of use. That even in death, people should be at the mercy of curriculum and the semester system was disturbing. But he was far from being scared out of his wits. He was—it astonished him to think so—merely interested.

'Interesting'—the language's word of faintest praise, adjective of least resistance. How was the movie? Interesting. What do you think of food additives? Interesting. The Holy Roman Empire? Interesting. What was it like to look Death in the eyeball? Interesting. Interest, not death, was the bulldozing leveller, homogenizer, eraser of distinctions. 'Interesting,' Laurence realized, was how one characterized life's least interesting experiences, barely a cut above 'boring.' Yet interest, in all its blandeur, was what he felt. Maybe, he thought, when she describes the actual *corpus delicti*, the look, smell, feel of mortal viscera, maybe then I'll itch with something more than interest.

She kept thinking it would get worse, said Gretchen, scarier, eerier, otherworldlier; but entering the room, with the lumpy silhouettes, before he turned on the lights, was the nearest thing to fear. The *idea* made her queasy; but once he unzipped the vinyl bags, it was just dead things, undeniably there, and loss of affect. No petrification or putrefaction, no nausea, no supernatural awe or demonic sublime. She was just . . . interested. Could he understand that?

Laurence nodded. It all seemed so very familiar, but he couldn't fathom why it should. Why he should be equipped with a doctor's detachment, an undertaker's solemnity masking, really, neutral unperturbed indifference, humoring mortality but uninvolved. Why should he be encumbered with a businesslike cool? Death was not his profession.

There was no particular smell, said Gretchen. It could have been any place of business after hours, an insurance office maybe, with the stretchers all around like desks; and she thought, Some custodian comes in here and sweeps up every day, like a school auditorium or post office or bakery, and his job is just another job, cleaning up a room full of things that don't concern him. That was how it seemed: a room full of things that didn't concern her.

Chris unzipped an old man who'd died of lungs. He warned her that the lungs wouldn't look normal. The part that's diseased, he said, doesn't take the preservative as well; it stays a kind of jelly, while the rest is made lifelike but leathery, like a definitive suntan. The lungs were messy, but the rest was like porcelain; even wrinkles were intact: smooth, clean wrinkles. The face was sunken, but looked alive, or just dead; it looked like a face. It had lips and eyelashes and a little stubble.

Like a grandfather, Laurence thought. Grandfathers always have a little stubble.

But what got to her was the hair. The hair, said Gretchen, was perfect. It was hair. She wanted to congratulate somebody. Maybe because living hair is dead protein; it looked exactly like living hair. Each one came out of its follicle (the pores were a little enlarged) and went its merry way, like any hair in the world, curving around its fellows like wood grain, like migratory birds, like hair. She could see so clearly every single hair on his balding head, the surprise was like getting a new pair of glasses and seeing everything the way you were meant to in the first place. They were all there, ageless hairs, a perfect sculpture of hair. It was beautiful.

Yes, thought Laurence. But why should he know what she meant? Why should her account not rattle him in the slightest?

The bodies were half-&-half, harlequin clowns, split down the middle. One arm, one leg, one side of the neck, fifty percent of everything bisymmetrical was dissected, and the other half intact. The skin was bedclothes, slit to be folded back and expose the innards, muscles and arteries and nerves with Latin tags strung onto them, seeming appropriate as prices on groceries. Chris would peel back a flap, like lifting the hood of a car, and there were the works, all labelled and anatomized, not slimy but not dried out either, the perfect consistency, like something edible and baked to a turn.

Then Chris showed her his—he'd been working up to her, she was the most impressive of the lot and he knew it. He and his partner had nicknamed her Marcia, after Beethoven's *Marcia Funebre.* She was a young woman, but fully grown, maybe in her thirties. She had been very beautiful. Whatever she died of didn't affect her looks: her breasts were almost full, only a little deflated, with nipples and aureolas, the real thing. (Chris made a leering jest about bickering with his partner over who got to do the thorax, but Gretchen wasn't entertained. She found something offensive about the locker-room humor, and something not at all solemn but not at all funny about Marcia's beauty embalmed.) He lifted them back, dough from a breadboard, and showed ribs and organs, everything tucked neatly in its place, a hope chest. She was like some kind of gorgeous fruit, attractive. That was the part that heartened Gretchen even as it took her breath away: she was sexy!

Her pubic hair, for instance, was specifically enticing, as if she'd
shampooed it just before she died. You could see she'd been one
of those women who exude eroticism and make everyone around
them feel sexy too. Gretchen wondered if that had made her happy.
She was sorry not to have known her; she would have liked to soak
some of that up. It was the only time she had ever felt that way
about another woman. She wished Marcia would wake up for just
a minute so she could reassure her that even in death she was
beautiful. She wanted to tell her she was beautiful. She told Chris
instead.

'She's beautiful.'

'She was,' he corrected.

'No,' she insisted, 'she is. She's lovely, she's gorgeous, she's very
sexy.'

'Lord, Barron,' he said, 'don't go kinky on me here. I'm not
about to climb up on one of these gurneys and make love to a half-
dissected corpse, and I don't want to make love to you either, here,
not here. Christ, I didn't bring you here to turn you on.'

But of course he had, in a way. He wanted to scare the hell out
of her and then take her home and screw the hell out of her. And
his plan, though he wouldn't admit it, was working better than he
had hoped. He took her there to be titillated with some unspoken
connection, and once she was titillated, he refused to recognize
the connection himself. She wasn't thinking about necrophilia any
more than he, but she was seeing the connection. He couldn't see
that Marcia was sexy. After months of enjoying himself rummaging around in her interior, nicknaming her, joking at her expense,
he claimed it was all for course credit.

Gretchen was heated, as if espousing a cause.

She didn't think Chris would admit the connection between sex
and birth, either; he told her she couldn't have children; he took
whatever stimulus and response he could get, but he wouldn't face
the cause and effect of conception.

'And I think that's why I let you talk me into this, to spite his
bloody clinical hypocrisy, that could treat bodies like textbooks
and take Marcia as a case history.'

Gretchen caught Laurence's eyes with her own, which were teary
but coldly, directly challenging.

'Can you see it? Can you understand that she was sexy?'

Laurence understood that he was now being cast as antidote to
the physician's bad medicine, and something larger, burden-

some—redeemer possibly of an entire gender. He nodded, carefully, but his mind was elsewhere. Jolted and tearful, he had remembered why it all seemed so familiar.

He *had* seen death, not naked but as good as, in the midst of the less erroneous pictures of whales: his moribund mama, with her skinny skin and hairy hair, looking too like his mama to be anything but. If a mother could be, had been, motherly in death, a flat definition of motherhood under sheets, then of course the *femme fatale* could be beautiful, even magnetic, and the greedy greedy, the obnoxious obnoxious, the generous generous, the hypocrite hypocritical. Death made x x, y y, and z z. Death, in fact, it seemed to him now, was the point at which people were most themselves; and if something preserved them at that moment, for better or worse, they'd be themselves forever.

He recalled what Gretchen had said: the *idea* that frightens. If death was the becoming most oneself, that made sense: familiarity breeds acceptance. Doctors dying, morticians dying, don't panic; in fact, dying, nobody panics, except at the means of execution. Hit by a truck, you panic; bumped off by a thug, you panic; but dying on your own, of heart, lungs, liver, sugar, your body and its built-in fallibility, you exhibit a courage and acceptance that's the norm, not the exception. If you have the strength and your wits about you, you probably make jokes to relax those around you, watching, who are afraid. You yourself are too busy negotiating with and encouraging yourself, dying and trying not to, to waste time on fear. An aphorism presented itself: 'Death is Nature's way of relieving us of the fear of death.'

Laurence was far afield in his revery, while Gretchen still reflected on sexy Marcia. He wanted a reconvergence, a merger, wanted to give her something in return for her rueful portrait of the morgue, tit for tat, morbid but heartening tale for morbid but heartening tale. He told her the story of his mother's disappearance:

After Father's demise, Mama feared for her visibility. With increasing frequency he would find her, preoccupied, waxing edgy, gaping quizzically at an arm or a mirror. He soon learned just the calming tone in which to appease her fear: 'I can see you, Mama, I see you.' Then she felt better, her brow unfurrowed to its usual smooth and motherly self. But he wondered, if he, external assurance, hadn't been there, what would have happened? Convinced that she was disappearing, what would she have done?

Gretchen, visibly lounging, hadn't a clue.

Even in the hospital, dying—especially in the hospital, dying—
when she herself could no longer see at all, she needed to be told.
The encroaching opacity of her world only intensified her sense of
personal transparency. Describing the fantastical garb of seagoing
men, their tribulations, customs, vocabularies, or the silver spray
of flukes—even in his valedictory portrayal of the less erroneous
pictures of whales—he saw his mama's mind's eye was roving,
searching as frantically as seamen did for flukes, pressing lids shut
as a binocular spyglass in which to image herself. In vain. It was
up to him to interrupt Melville, lean closer and squeeze the hand
that was taped down to steady the IV, stroke the twitching forehead, and croon in his tone of comforting: 'I can see you, Mama,
I see you.' But who was there after nine p.m.? Each day he had
twenty hours of accumulated disbelief to dispel in four short visiting hours.

By the end, there was nothing he could tell her, no final perfect
summing, no calculitic integration of the minute tropisms of off-
springhood, no balm to offer but 'I can see you, Mama, I see you,'
his last words to her. And hers to him: 'Who are you to see me,
when I can't see myself? What right? What point? I am dying,
Larry, dying.'

O his allusive mama! As if he were a groundling, needing to be
told in words; as if he couldn't see for himself orphancy imminent.

His mama, in death, though, alluded to nothing but herself; she
became more opaque, more a substantial, studiable, incontrovertible presence: a fact. He wanted to wake her and say, 'Look, Mama,
how far from invisible you are. Look how beside the point were
your fears. Not disappearance, but stolid inanimate appearance,
was the threat. Observe how the light bounces off you. Look at
you there, like a blueprint of impermeability.'

Then, his mama gone, he did not follow her example and doubt
his own reflectivity; he was seeing Irene, Irene was seeing him.
Nor had he since found disappearance a real or present danger.
The crystallization of incipient bone, the tentative gelling of flesh,
usually hidden, top-secret, in the womb those last two months, he
had himself observed himself achieve. He knew what it was to be
translucent, and what opaque.

Gretchen, with a pretty clear idea herself, shifted quizzically from
one elbow to another.

His father's father, Grandpa Theo, hadn't made matters easier
when Papa died. He behaved not as if Mama had disappeared,

sending out search parties, but as if she had simply dissolved in air, sublimated, vaporized, resolved to a dew, as if both she and his baffled grandson existed no more. Obverse of fearful Mama, he positively preferred to drop from sight.

'When will Grandpa Theo visit?' Laurence asked.

'Lonnie, I don't believe he will.'

Why not then? Was he deceased along with Daddy? Had the death of his one and only begotten son attacked his heart, known to be weak, with sympathetic infarction?

Laurence imagined Theo—stubbled, grouchy—intemperate at his son's untimely undoing, throwing a myocardial tantrum, his ticker holding its bloody breath till he got what he wanted—the resurrection of the son—failing which, he turned a loathsome blue and died. It seemed a so much more juvenile reaction than Laurence's own.

'Tell me, Mama, is Grandpa Theo dead?'

'No, Lonnie, just hostile.'

Mama and Laurence: an innocuous, touching, lovable pair. He could scarcely fathom hostility.

Theo was his favorite relation, parents aside. He would gladly have sacrificed all the multi-boroughed couples and their progeny, the incommensurate cousins, players of Johnny-on-the-pony and hurlers of slushballs, to retain Grandpa Theo. Couldn't they have been dropped a line, given a buzz or a jingle from time to time? No, said his mother, Theo had never liked the match; and Papa gone, he had nothing to say to them. The match? He sounded to Laurence like City Hall, civil, ceremonial, reducing marriage to blood types. Of what, specifically, had he disapproved? Though Laurence was his mama's one bastion and mainstay, she declined to answer. She knew, she said, but divulge she would not.

So the question Gretchen had innocently raised on the bus was a not inconsequential one?

Yes, he had to agree, not by a long shot.

He remembered, possessed at fourteen of a novel idea, asking his mama, 'Mama, do you *have* to love *all* your relatives?' It had just then occurred that perhaps you did not. The concept was invigorating and not a little scary. 'Of course not, Larry.' Of course not? His Mama's calm response seemed to decree a whole new ballgame. Heady with unsurmised freedom, he announced on the spot, 'Okay, then I love only you and Daddy'—though Daddy was dead—'and Grandpa Theo.' He cringed as soon as he spoke, expecting lightning like a well-thrown slushball to strike him down; but was struck only by his mother's smiling reinforcement: 'You can hardly be blamed for that, Larry.'

Like a Tenderfoot lost in the woods, Laurence, trying to find the original trail, had only hiked further afield. He was, he knew, all but irrevocably removed from the issue of Marcia's appeal. But he decided, not to attempt to circle back, but to forge ahead (since Gretchen appeared rapt) and find, if not their base camp, then some new and suitable site where they could bed mentally down together for the long sylvan night of discussion's end.

Gretchen, typically, had other ideas. Circling back was in fact what she had most in mind. She hadn't, as it fell out, been trudging scoutingly along behind Laurence through his woodsy talk, but had stopped and stooped to examine a bit of moss he'd unconsciously picked up and dropped a ways back. 'I was seeing Irene, Irene was seeing me': logical enough as a reason for believing in one's visibility, but who was Irene?

'Who is Irene?' she asked when he stopped for breath.

'Irene?'

'Irene. You said you were seeing Irene, who was seeing you. Who is Irene?'

Laurence felt, as he had felt before with Gretchen, a quandary of disclosure. How are your knees? What do you do? Who is Irene? Since fertilization, Gretchen's queries had grown decreasingly rhetorical; and Laurence could see she wanted, for this one, not just any, but the true response.

Why was he so utterly loath to tell her? Recovered now from the initial exhilaration of fictive autobiography, he had, in general, no objection to telling Gretchen who *he* was; but who Irene was was another, and for some reason a more unnerving, question. Was it his still technically intact marriage he preferred not to discover? Was it the precedent of having once given in to apparent abortion he wanted to hide? Was it the admission that he, Laurence Paprika, was the sort of person who married? Or was it simply an instinctive desire to keep separate the parts of his life, to prevent their adding up to a whole for any interpreter but himself? For whatever amalgam of reasons and nonreasons, Irene was the part of himself, given a single fig leaf, he would cover. Now that his leaf had blown away in the careless breeze of unpremeditated talk, would he deign to patch together a more clearly defensive screen?

Gretchen was once again a lady in waiting, and Laurence's very

hesitation put his cards on the table: that Irene was someone significant had been admitted, else why give a second thought to
saying? Damn, thought Laurence, damn not my impulsive disclosure, but my passive, stupid need to pretend. Damn all bushes that
need to be beaten around, damn all inscrutably tender spots, all
supersensitive nerve endings, all unreasonably private parts.

'Irene,' said Laurence, 'is my wife.'

But Gretchen did not then, as he had feared, recriminate or
proclaim reprehensible cover-up. She did not have recourse to
broken Commandments or accusations of betrayal. She did not
demand Laurence stand and deliver explanation, why she should
carry a child more properly assigned a different vessel. She did
not evince hurt at being kept in the dark, or jealousy at playing
second fiddle, or even justifiable curiosity. Instead, touched by
honest exposure, she responded with genuine mercy, and huddling closer to the body beside her, said, 'If it's all the same to you,
let's call it a night.'

Another thing Laurence liked about Gretchen was that, like
himself, she was almost always willing and able to give sleep its
sound and restorative due.

Four

Blue-green, green-blue, red-orange, orange-red, brown, black, above all magenta—these were the tones eight-year-old Irene favored. Before yellow-green and carnation pink even reached the paper-peeling stage, her black and magenta were pathetic stubs with no paper left to protect fingers from slippery, waxy deposits. The rich certainty of darker shades appealed to Irene's youthful sensibility; what was more, their thick opacity didn't let the telltale lines show through, lines at staying within which Irene's skill was not of the best. She was always pleading with one parent or another for a new box of crayons.

Her mother: 'A whole new box? But Aunt Amelia just gave you one for your birthday, not three weeks ago.'

'I know, Mommy, but my magenta's almost gone, and I can't color without magenta. My black rolled under the bed, and I can't even find it, it's so small.' She sometimes used black more than she would have liked to ideally, in an attempt to forestall the inevitably premature depletion of her magenta.

'Irene, there are other colors,' was the solution of her mother, ten feet distant at the sink. Indeed there were, sixty-four in all, with a built-in sharpener. 'You never even touch your flesh. Really, those faces you color magenta are unseemly, grotesque. No one has magenta skin.'

'No one has skin the color of my flesh crayon either.' Irene had discovered this truth by doodling on her forearms. 'I can't draw without black and magenta, Mommy,' she cried, teary with the injustice of it all; but she knew her case was lost, and she'd have to wait till evening to appeal to her more malleable father.

Her father: 'You're going through those colors awfully fast, aren't you, sweetheart?'

'Mostly black and magenta, Daddy. It hurts my fingers to color when they get so small.'

That precisely the colors she was most partial to should be painful to use struck Irene as cruel and unusual, like developing allergies to favorite foods just because one ate too much of them. She considered herself a martyr to love.

Her father, who might have had something of the same self-image, and in any case couldn't stand to see his daughter weep, generally advanced her the price of a new set of colors. Thanks to his sentimentality, Irene had a closet floored in a parquet of virtually unused pastels, the by-products of box after fresh box acquired for love of magenta.

It is useful, in general, to note formal resemblances, parallels, echoes, but rash to jump to conclusions; for unlike Laurence with his hair and hotels, compulsively closeted and never used, Irene eventually pressed into service her vast hoard of colors, thanks to Donna Forenza.

The job of sitting babies is not a secure or lifelong profession. Its pay scale makes it something girls do in high school; and no girl, in the overall scheme of things, is in high school very long. Being a baby sat, therefore, is a position calling for adaptability, since the turnover in those doing the sitting is so great; always a new trainee to be broken in. And if you are a lucky enough baby to be sat by one you come to care for, you are by the same token an unfortunate baby, and bound for disappointment. Detachment from the mother aside, this may be the child's first experience of what will become increasingly a fact of life as age brings other, intersected lives to a close. For sitters and babies are not, by definition, peers; and few sitters develop as strong a devotion to their weekly charges as vice versa. So it was with Irene and Donna Forenza.

Donna was seventeen when Irene was eight, a mere nine years her senior but at that ideal distance that sometimes obtains between eight and seventeen. Irene remembered Donna as fair of face and thin of hip, accommodating but with a slight professional aloofness that served only to span the gap of half a generation and intensify the eight-year-old's positive identification.

Donna Forenza liked Irene and was not above some casual comradely coloring with the girl. Donna, proud of her own artistic sense, taught little Irene that coloring with a gentle, circular motion optimized odds of staying within prescribed outlines. Irene's image of Donna was colored in just such circlets, and in the thoughtful pastels whose ungrating compatibility she taught Irene was more pleasing than the impulsive and lurid combinations an eight-year-old fist more instinctively grabbed. Under Donna's chromatic tutelage, Irene willingly did what her mother's firm denials had never induced her to do: she brought her pent-up colors out of the closet, and in so doing learned the immense joys of melon, thistle, sea green, cornflower, periwinkle, grey, and many another lovely addition to her hitherto severely limited spectrum of play. Her bedtime prayers embraced, in the final position of special reverence, the hallowed name of her weekly sitter:

> *'Now I lay me down to sleep,*
> *I pray the Lord my soul to keep;*
> *If I should die before I wake,*
> *I pray the Lord my soul to take.*

'Amen. God bless Daddy and Mommy and Grandpa and Grandma and Aunt Amelia and Uncle Herbert and Cousin Sue . . . and the milkman and the mailman and Miss McCarthy and all my classmates . . . and God bless Donna Forenza.'

Donna Forenza, who taught her, too, the firmer control paradoxically afforded by light fingertip grips than by the power-hungry overhand fist, so inappropriate to gentle circlets. Less pressure, more finesse: an incipient aesthetic was, all in all, what Donna offered; a virginal sense of something approaching personal decorum. The formula of behaving-like-a-human-being Irene had from her mother; but whatever concrete appreciation of the axiom she achieved, whatever subtlety of tone she was capable of investing it with, must be credited to Donna Forenza.

Donna Forenza, whose Crayola technique embodied for Irene the essence of her mother's constant admonitions to behave and so forth, stood in Irene's world as the model, for all intents and purposes, of supremely human being, worthy above all others of emulation. If Donna's handwriting tilted backwards, like playing cards braking at Alice's command, then Irene's pengirlship would exhibit the same cautious posture, letters like bathers testing temperature with toes before plunging, despite all teacherly exhortations that letters should be aggressive and forward-reaching. If Donna's eyebrows were plucked to stylized gullwing shapes, then Irene's would receive the same conspicuous attention. If Donna, seventeen and Catholic, took an interest in boys but frowned on premarital sex, then Irene, eight and Unitarian, tried hard to comply, though boys represented at her age a singularly boring set of characteristics, and though she'd have to wait a number of years to conceive of, let alone frown upon, anything premarital.

It is difficult to overstate the influence Donna had on Irene, to whom she offered an example, in the flesh, of what was, from her mother, a demanding theoretical proposition. What was part of Donna and could be part of Irene was embraced as essential; what was not part of Donna was rejected as inappropriate; what was part of Donna and could not yet be part of Irene was longed for and meanwhile, with varying degrees of gracefulness, fervently imitated. Eight is not an age of discrimination: Irene wanted no less than to *be* Donna Forenza.

But Donna, seventeen and Catholic, soon turned eighteen and collegiate, and was replaced in the living room, if not in Irene's heart, by young Lucy Fern, who colored in jagged zigzags; knowing which, Irene concluded she knew all she needed to know regarding her substitute sitter.

Like Dante, Irene possessed a remarkable memory for women seen early in life; and like Dante, displayed a tenacious loyalty to her first ideal. Though Donna was, as far as sitting went, removed from Irene's world, the girl colored that much more furiously (and that much more genteelly) in honor of her memory. Throughout adolescence, Donna of the pastel coils was Irene's implicit guide; when faced with choice, she asked herself, What would Donna do? Irene's theory of flagging interest in middles of activities was an extrapolation of Donna's reactions to certain Friday-evening television shows. Irene's theory of pregnancy and courtship was an *ex post facto* distillation of hints dropped in her presence at eight and stored for later use. Even Irene's theory of termination of life functions in middles of novels was a blossoming of seeds planted by Donna Forenza: one summer evening Donna had squashed a bug with the fan magazine she was perusing, and refused to read further in that or any other copy of said magazine. Indeed, Irene's entire elaborate arsenal of theories concerning behaving-like-a-human-being was a monument erected to the joint memory of her mother, who craved theory, and Donna Forenza, who behaved like a human being.

Studying his subway map—as he would for several months, sure sign of recent arrival—Laurence would have liked to disclaim, to anyone in the rattling vicinity: 'Though I consult my map in full view of you all, I'm no tourist. They left before I knew what was what, but I live here now, a repatriate, an immigrant. You understand immigration, you New Yorkers: the magnet's pull away from origins to the City. For me, *to* origins, to the City, one and the same. You with your Statue of Liberty, United Nations, and all, you understand. I'm not asking for special dispensation, mind you, just to be flung into the melting pot with the others, not resting atop like a spice sprinkled but unmixed. You're familiar with the expression "melting pot," aren't you?'

Laurence saw, dimly, faces on all sides, leather jackets, hand-knit sweaters, raincoats, shirt sleeves, wraparound skirts, shorts, sandals, boots; as if no meteorological consensus could be reached. Faces possibly bored, not quietly amazed as he still was to be standing underground as a matter of course, if anything mildly annoyed to be not yet back on the surface, wavering slightly in the wake of passing trains, like weeds inopportunely taken root too near a highway. Thinking this loitering inside the earth neither wonderful nor loathsome, but something to be merely waited impassively out, laundry spinning in a machine, no thought that the event might be worthy of prolongation or curtailment, nothing but a blankness so contrived and studied as to be not even aloof, but truly blank. So many so close to so many others with no more acknowledgment than if they'd had no senses. All was rote for those around him: avoidance of one another's glance so consummate, he wanted to shake them up, make them register something, human sameness, human difference, fear, pride, anything but this blankness like the fluorescent hum of the med-school morgue, that can't be bothered even to be ominous. The faces covered a good deal of the chromatic spectrum, but none of the emotional.

The subway station was, then, a melting pot with the heat turned off; not mingling but juxtaposition prevailed. A train approached, sounding off like glass marbles in an aluminum vessel, random noise overdone. Soon he and those around him would be glass marbles in an aluminum vessel, clinking and scraping to no end but acoustic excess. The subway system, whose colorful stylized chart Laurence held in his hands, seemed a municipal monument to the harder, more desolate forms of philosophy: an elaborate, graphic argument for predestination, a concrete Calvinist Q.E.D.

The movement of certain others, who had no doubt this was their train, reminded Laurence of his own uncertainty. His excellent map skills were called into play, and provided him in the nick of time with a conviction that he should board the train. He did so, drawing from those already seated the stares that characteristically greet a late arrival.

Inside the car people were different. Motion, seating, closer quarters, combined to relax them. With the excuse now that regarding one another was scarcely avoidable, some showed curiosity, cupidity, concupiscence, a gamut of appetites. Under pretense of scanning the car for hints of possible danger, passengers exchanged a thorough looking-over. The moving box was composing itself into a collective personality, which none of its components wished to be the last to discern.

Clothing was loosened; brows were mopped; tired calves were kneaded, stiff necks and stinging eyes massaged, newspapers unfolded, shopping bags rummaged in, legs crossed—at the ankle, at the knee, at the thigh—all to the tickety-tackety rhythm—'Catarrh, catarrh, catarrh, catarrh'—of the swaying car.

To Laurence, the change was startling. People, assembled with no more in common than a need to get from here to there and the wherewithal to purchase a token, seemed to vibrate, as the subway vibrated, together, in phase, a chamber orchestra of tuning forks set humming by an unseen conductor.

Laurence would have liked to position himself near the front, with a view of what was to come: lights, green, yellow, red, white, and a surreal vibrant blue, tracks and cables and tunnels and tiles; but he knew, among natives, only youngsters ogled details of the trip, the mechanical articulation of conveyance, and his imagined platform speech had pretended to nontourist status. Besides, he had a conflicting desire, no less strong, to observe his temporary neighbors. A nicely dressed young woman down the aisle was reading Dickens; that was nice. It was a sort of identifying badge, what one read on the subway; Laurence put his map away. Others perused best-sellers and the sports pages, horoscopes, fingernails, lovers, makeup, palms; they seemed engaged in an act of communal divination, looking up from time to time as if to confirm results.

These lookings up and lookings down, though certainly not coy, were nevertheless flirtatious: roving eyes in an intimate, promiscuous setting. Despite frequent stops and changing clientele, a consistent sense, almost an odor, of burgeoning humanity accrued. As he had, on the platform, been aware of clothing, now he perceived bodies riding loosely within: endo-, ecto-, mesomorphs, each with its personal provision of variably jiggling flesh. A yeasty intimation of cells dividing every which way enveloped him. The subway was lush and luscious, fertile, fecund, feral, and though far from orgiastic, in its own rank way, loving. The termite queen, palpitating with the upstart lives inside. Yet it was not amniotic, and like Gretchen in the morgue, Laurence felt now a sudden, unlooked-for revelation: the subway was sexy. Twenty or thirty offerings to Eros overlapped for a moment, sharing space. Laurence revelled.

The subway clanked and careened and careered like some madly companionable itinerant *Bierstube*; its passengers, like alumni mobilized *en masse* by irrationally binding old school ties, jolted in cartoonlike unison. Laurence almost felt his undelivered platform appeal answered. Had not, in a sense, this chance cross section of Manhattan unthinkingly embraced him? Was he not suspended colloidally along with them, an alien spice no longer, jostled, just as they, to the syncopated bumps and steely grinding turns of the percussive car? Remembering Gretchen's textbook improvisations, Laurence felt like calling out fancy signals himself. What was it the Germans did, drinking, swaying, singing, elbow-linked?—*'schunkeln.'* *E schunkelnibus unum*, he thought. *Syncopatico sub terra firma.* How often, in the City, he found use for his paltry random store of foreign diction!

Yet something in the ride reminded Laurence of the less felicitous aspects of smatterings: those unnerving moments of darkness. Every half minute or two, the lights went out: completely out, in a way they never did above ground. Laurence hadn't the slightest idea why: metal wheels squealed over some switch or other on the tracks, and the lights went dead out, out like a light, intensifying the sounds of the benighted train. Unnerving, not for what happened to the car—for Laurence, taking his cue from natives, could see this periodic darkness was routine and unalarming and put no crimp in their impassive collective swaying style—but for what happened to his thoughts. When the lights went out, Laurence's mind stopped, suspended like breath held. Lighted-subway thoughts were not succeeded by darkened-subway thoughts; only 'Catarrh, catarrh, catarrh, catarrh' filled the blank. Vehicular blankness produced an inky mental void, disjunction, caesura, as if his brain, along with the lights, were briefly short-circuited. When the lights and the schunkelling, impervious companions reappeared, his thoughts picked up precisely where they'd left off, even in mid-sentence. But why should even this be so unnerving? You're reading, the lights go out, and before you have time to think, 'The lights are out, what shall I do?' the lighting is reinstated: should you not simply go on reading? Why should such a minor outage seem a major disturbance?

Before Laurence had much time to ponder issues of cerebral discontinuity and the psychology of transportation, the train pulled to a histrionic halt amid the bright white tiles of the Seventy-Ninth-Street station: his stop. Though he knew it was silly, he wished the others would make it their stop as well, and tumble out of the car with him. They seemed a nice enough group: couldn't an impromptu outing be arranged?

No. No outing. Laurence recalled that subways are deterministic in nature, ferrying each and every soul to its particular underworld stop. But sentimental, he turned from the platform, disconcerting traffic, wistfully waved, and said aloud, 'So long,' to oblivious northbound travellers as the doors bumped shut before him.

He made his way through and up the labyrinth of crossovers, stairs, and turnstiles to the street, where, like one emerging from a matinee, he was mentally and retinally startled to find that the outside world was bright and busy, and hadn't, in its tall airiness, seen the same show as he, nor cared to. The reflective brilliance that obtains, on brilliant days, in cityscapes surrounded and galvanized him; soon he was happily one fish in the streaming school, headed hither, headed thither; everyone, it seemed, was headed, except a small, casually intent group on the opposite corner, randomly munching street-vended edibles, and its lyrical focus: a stocky young man with a baby face—'just a kid,' elements of the crowd variously noted—playing Brandenburg concerti on richly wooded homemade vibes in front of a jeweller's window.

Beyond insulating shocks of apple-red hair, the boy was smiling cherubically, appreciated and appreciating, beatifically blessing the flock with his solo arrangements. Mallets, three per hand splayed at mock-floral triadic intervals, flashed with the remarkable ability to reproduce orchestral harmonies. More remarkable still to the crowd was his continuous regard of them; never glancing down at his wooden keyboard, he smiled forever outward, at *them*, and yet his mallets neither faltered nor misstruck.

The boy's unself-conscious artistry reminded Laurence of Gretchen, whom he now imagined seated at her cello on a city sidewalk, playing for the diversion of whoever had time to pause: a haphazard multitude, graced with an average of—what, five minutes?—of incidental Bach. Laurence wondered, though, whether even Gretchen could match this youngster's natural and unlikely charm. An apparent country boy, rosy, corn-fed, winsome, he might have been seated on the porch of a general store playing folksy mouth-harp or banjo tunes for fellow yokels; but behind the primitive's charisma was a sophisticate's styling. Street-corner vibes resounding Bach: more than a nice touch, elegant.

Laurence fingered his baggy pockets, among tokens found a quarter, itself a token of his gratitude for an unlooked-for midday concert. He sought a receptacle, tin can or other repository set on the sidewalk for passing recompense. None was there. No professional, this boy hadn't provided for commercial reimbursement. He wasn't—Laurence again remembered Gretchen—in the market. Gratis diversion was what he offered, having apparently no use or no desire for Laurence's two bits. All right, then: Laurence would pay him back the only way he could, by lingering, forming part of the human advertisement for the boy's free interlude. O generous boy! he thought. Innocent nonulterior entertainer! You have made my day. Gratuitous melodiousness had replaced in Laurence any gloomy sense of world-as-subway-system, predetermined, group-dynamic, goal-oriented, ultilitary network of hapless to's and fro's.

Then a florid jeweller emerged with an apoplectic clatter, genuinely annoyed and livid at the spectacle obscuring his display window. How was he supposed to make a buck? Did the kid think that diamonds and rubies and sapphires and six-point marquis settings and more karats than you could shake a stick at were out there sunning, for their health? He bet his life they weren't; they were there at the jeweller's behest, and for his profit, there to attract paying customers, not to be shaded and overshadowed by free-loading softheaded music lovers with nothing better to do.

Jeweller—merchant—*Merchant*—Shylock—Jew—jeweller: a pernicious circle of associations appalled Laurence. Would the populace submit to be pushed around by such backward, unre-generate, dyspeptic, typecast values? Now, thought Laurence, a fine test case for the citizenry's mettle! Surely a grass-roots move-ment will reinstate priorities—pleasure before business—and shame mercantilism into retreat.

But there were no grass roots in this concrete. Aimlessly, the crowd dispersed; and even the performer, good-humored but resigned, as if long acquainted with rude commercial injunctions to play his music elsewhere if at all, efficiently dismantled his instrument and moved on.

Disrupted, Laurence rejoined the particulate flow, now become, to his eyes, once again raw traffic, unknown things to do, unnamed places to go, aggressive, jockeying, territorial. Oppressed by anon-ymous inertia and prodding, he was relieved to exit at the massive steps of the Museum of Natural History, his original destination achieved through all these innocent ups and disillusioned downs.

His pilgrimage this day was to pay homage to a mockup of *Tyrannosaurus rex*, its osteoporotic gaps filled in with plaster of paris, at the feet of which his parents had first laid eyes (but as far as he knew, nothing else) upon one another. Laurence, the prod-uct of his mother's early middle age, felt far removed from the Great Depression, which had been, nevertheless, a crucial defin-ing and orienting fact of his parents' young adulthood. They were not the sort of progenitors who would encumber a son with object lessons or even anecdotes of their own harder or more adventure-some times; but a skeleton crew of tales had been handed down, and had attained all the more for their small numbers and isola-tion the mythic weight of parents' preparental lives.

There was, first of all, the arrival at Ellis Island; for they passed on nothing of their parents' lives in the Old Country: history began, for Laurence, on Ellis Island. The canvas baggage, burlap sacks, cloth coats, swaddling clothes ensconcing his own infant father: the entire story seemed to Laurence wrapped, mummified, in lay-ers of cloth, a narrative tapestry of a textile arrival in the promised land. And the hunger and the colic and the quarantines and the overworked immigration sub-subs struggling with alien diphthongs until they gave it up and took to putting down, as surname, whatever English word most resembled, to their untrained ears, the identifying phonemes babbled by polyglottal relocating hordes. Customs-office fatigue had resulted, for Laurence's paternal forebears, in the ludicrous monicker Paprika, overactive phonetic fancy's approximation of Priapka or Periopescu or Porpoiaschchko or something along those lines (since history began at Ellis Island, Laurence had trouble recalling).

There was Laurence's maternal grandpa, unmet by him, a cabdriver so conscientious he would dream through the night of taxiing fares through the City, his right foot urgently depressing his dormant wife as if she were an accelerator, saying, though sound asleep himself, 'Where to, lady, where to?' until she woke and told him, 'Far Rockaway,' hoping to get some rest; but soon enough he would dream himself back to the Bronx, rev up his snoozing loving wife and ask again, 'Where to, lady, where to?'

There was the strange machine by which, while Theo and Molly were settling for distasteful parts of beasts, they could squeeze all the blood from a precious little square of sirloin, leaving a paper-thin, paper-dry sheet of beef fiber and a baby whose corpuscles were thriving on beef tea.

There were incidental tales of Teutonic matrons, extrapolating English from the three or four languages they did know, politely informing butchers, 'I will become a nice plump chicken,' and other mislingual pleasantries of the sort; but these were marginalia, vague matting for the absent portrait of Laurence's own background.

There were also more recent, more epic tales, of uncles in World War II, tales he was never told, conspicuous in the nontelling, horrible enough to be unsuitable for children and maybe even for the men whose stories they rightly were. Laurence sensed that not just the war stories but all of life before the move to Providence was suppressed, out of painfulness or wishfulness or defensiveness or protectiveness, out anyway of some -ness that left unquestioned, centrally located voids in his own natural history.

Perhaps these pervasive and glaring ellipses could account for his uncanny feeling that dark moments on the subway were more than mere dark moments on the subway. New York was for Laurence a metropolis of gaps, manholes, more rent than fabric, possibly irretrievable original loss. As he had come in search of an old man with a dull knife, he remained in search of all old men with dull knives, all myths of origin swallowed up by the City in time like a black hole in space.

Hence, the magical, nuclear force of a simple, unremarkable fact: in the days of the Great Depression, when jobs were few and generally unattainable, bright young people spent afternoons at concerts, in libraries, in museums, not the least of which was that monumentally dedicated to Natural History, where this day Laurence had ventured to stand on the spot where his mother and his father, bright young people unemployed, had met, in front of *Tyrannosaurus rex*. It was virtually all he knew of his parents' courtship, *Tyrannosaurus rex* and romantic expeditions to the Automat, where a couple in love could recklessly squander twenty cents apiece on lunch. The Automats had gone the way of all private enterprise, but the immutable Museum and its mammoth immovable tribute to defunct giants remained, and Laurence was grateful that the incident in question had graced so unephemeral a spot. Would his parents' spirits linger among articulated casts of prehistoric bone? No, Laurence was far from that much of a romantic. Nonetheless, despite rationalism and areligiosity, he felt a soulful tingle, an adrenaline tickle, in the elevator lifting him to the Hall of Dinosaurs.

Unlike Gretchen in the med-school morgue or Alice in Wonderland or Dorothy in Oz or even Gulliver in Brobdingnag, none of whom was particularly awestruck or incapacitated by the fantastic or grotesque, Laurence in the Hall of Dinosaurs was all eyes and could scarcely catch his breath, so rarefied was the atmosphere of extinct presence. Overwhelmed by the stolid, substantial age of the exhibits themselves, let alone what they represented, vertiginous, purgative, he almost, anachronistically, swooned.

He was standing with eyes shut before *Brontosaurus*, light-headed, transitory, when a girl half his height, yanking on his vest, demanded, 'Mister, how big is this one?' Laurence looked down at the girl, up at the skeleton, down at the plaque, read: 'Sixty feet, thirty tons.' Sixty feet big? Thirty tons big? Puny figures. Seventy million years big? As big as rock? He crouched to kid level: 'See those bones? See that stature?' She nodded: of course she saw. 'That's how big,' said Laurence.

'Geez,' said the girl, genuinely impressed.

'Yeah,' said Laurence, 'geez.'

'I know,' said the urchin, 'but, Mister, how many feet, how many tons?'

'A million feet,' said Laurence. 'A billion trillion tons.' He
pointed: 'That big.'

She puzzled a moment, inhaled deeply, then skipped off toward
a doorway overhung by a gigantic aquatic jaw, singsonging:

> *'A hundred million thousand feet,*
> *A million billion hundred thousand*
> *Dillion gillion tons.'*

Laurence moved reverently to the smaller *Tyrannosaurus*, its ribs
staking out in his eyes a floating cross-ventilated temple, a shrine
to Hymen. 'Largest terrestrial carnivore in Earth history,' he read.
Though not in general overly impressed by superlative forms, 'Geez,'
said Laurence. For a long while he stood and stared, trying to
imagine his parents' first words to one another on this very spot.
Was his father suave? Was his mother coy? But he could call forth
no other first words in such a setting than some such quasi-sac-
rilegious vulgarism as 'Geez.' They must have stood side by side
in silence, save the odd 'Geez' emitted inadvertently from astonished throats. 'Astonished'—turned amazed and amazingly to stone,
like the bygone dinosaurs themselves: had the startling fact of
extinction expressionistically petrified its victims, preserving the
affect of the event, transferable to mothers and fathers and transfixed unforeseeable sons? Laurence trembled before the recon-
struction. 'Largest terrestrial carnivore in Earth history': what did
it *mean?*

A couple in mock-marine attire and a casual embrace bantered
jovially as they passed, impressing one another tremendously. 'Hey,
paleontology, there's a racket for you. Find a bone, intuit a couple
million years of evolution. Nice work if you can get it,' said the
man.

'Never have so few extrapolated so much from so little,' said the
woman, strolling under the mandible with its six-inch teeth.

Spellbroken, Laurence thought. Was the magic he felt conventional, shamanistic? Was he the dupe of sleight-of-hand, carnival
conjuring? What was he all but worshipping here? Mere human
fancy, sloppy sentiment?

The dinosaur business was, after all, almost totally a world of
fantasy, conjecture, confection and confabulation. From a few bones
or a couple of teeth, man-sized men fabricated entire life-styles
for dino-sized saurians. Oh, there were misconstructions, some
even famous, crania placed on tails instead of necks, limbs mis-

articulated laterally, plains-dwellers mistaken for marsh-brows-
ers. And oh, there were disputes, petty professional squabbling as
well as serious theoretical disagreement, hot blood, cold blood,
warm blood, cool blood. A hit-or-miss vocation, resurrection;
imaginative riddling of Sphinxy organic stone, a guessing game.
Thirty tons? What if this brontosaur chronically overate? Carnivore? What if this stegosaur more favored vegetables? Laurence
himself, technically omnivorous, couldn't stomach red meat, green
peppers, purple cabbage.

If his parents were articulated here in osteoimaginative postures, could he recreate the Great Depression from worry lines
etched on skulls? Could he, from the structure of his mama's pelvic girdle, derive a proof of his own traumatic birth? Would
Gretchen's eye sockets imply myopia to an expert, or her teeth
proclaim love of liver? From involutions intaglioed on Irene's
braincase, could research in the year of some people's Lord seventy million infer behaving-like-a-human-being? Laurence suspected not.

Why then this monstrous powerful affect, this excellent hoaxy
susceptibility (for it would be months before Laurence could munch
on chicken without thinking these bony, dinosaur thoughts)? What,
he wanted to know, were these diggers up to?

Up to fiction, up to myth, than which truth is reputedly stranger.

Midnight in Providence: Irene pondering sitters—their unique
function, midway between hat-check girl and National Guard—
and wishing, if truth be known, that one could be assigned to her.
Babies have sitters, and the elderly have companions, but what of
us in the vast plural middle, she thought, who keeps us company
of a Friday evening? We fend for ourselves, I guess: we're the ones
who leave the very young and the very old well cared for and pursue our interests outside the home.

Irene had one interest now; his name was Laurence, and she
knew not how to pursue him. To be sure, she had plans—vague
and intimidating plans of scouring the City—but in the meantime,
she longed for a sitter. She'd long ago lost track of old friends: her
father's protracted death, her marriage and setting up housekeeping and catering to Aunt Amelia and the preoccupying dissolution
of life with Laurence, all had conspired to make her feel she had
neither time nor need for friendships. Friends, after all, were such

a responsibility, such a juggling act of time and energy, almost like having a child. But Irene wished now she had one or the other, someone to make demands, someone to blame for something, someone to resent.

One of her wishes, at least, was coming true: Laurence, the only person in all her life still in touch (she felt this, though she didn't know where to reach him), was beginning to provide an outlet for resentment. There were limits to the remorse she could feel for the emptiness of her life, and soon enough she was ready to turn frustration outward: where else but toward Laurence? How could he just leave? How could he not have known she would want him back? And wasn't it marriage to him that had largely precluded establishment of other ties? Irene resented the exclusiveness of their brief love, its greedy consumption of her life at a time when she could have been storing up friends like nuts for the solitary winter to come. What had been the point of funnelling all her desires into Laurence, if he was gone so soon? What right had he to monopolize her attention? Life with Laurence now appeared to her a waste, and what was more, a waste of her perhaps most crucial year, when, a newly established orphan, she ought to have been erecting structures against loneliness, shoring fragments against ruin. Never mind that that was precisely what it had seemed at the time she was doing—what more classic bulwark against loneliness than marriage?—she would have done better, it now appeared, to take up a hobby, join a club, adopt a charity, develop a skill, memorize phone numbers aside from her own, practice techniques of meeting men, meeting women, anything but sitting and wishing for a sitter.

Behaving-like-a-human-being was supposed to leave you well fortified with human beings who appreciated your behaving like one, and who'd be willing to sit for you of a Friday evening. But behaving like an adult human being apparently meant taking care of yourself, or following accepted channels of locating comfort. What did that mean, of a Friday evening? Irene guessed it meant her local bar.

Irene had been inside a bar once in her moderately youthful life to make a phone call, and once to get change for a laundromat next door. Her parents had ignored fermentation in all its forms; she too found the urge to abandon sobriety foreign. She now appreciated that liquor might have little or nothing to do with patronizing bars. Thinking herself needlessly innocent, she resented her parents' sober limitations.

Resentment was coming, in general, easier to Irene these days.

She dressed, but not to kill, since she wanted it clear she wasn't looking to be picked up. People in bars, she assumed, were looking for lovers; she wanted a sitter; maybe they could effect a compromise, and become just good friends. The very novelty of the idea might appeal to others who, like herself, didn't know exactly what they were doing there.

Irene walked by three bars before she found one that sounded, from the sidewalk, friendly and not overloud. There was music, to be sure, emanating from her choice, but music soft and rhythmic that struck her almost as a lullaby, conducive to quiet, comforting talk, not the embarrassment of having to ask virtual strangers to repeat themselves. Irene walked in.

The failure of anyone to react to her entrance both relieved and a little hurt Irene. No one took her wrap; no one sold her a drink; no one showed her to a table; no one looked her up and down, leering. She considered going out and coming in again, with a bit more flair, but then surmised that perhaps no one was *supposed* to sit up and take notice. Already she was learning things.

Her confidence dissipated as she realized that others ignored her not from politeness or reluctance to disconcert her with requests, but because they all of them, to a human being, knew what they were doing there: had their drinks, had their friends, had palpably no need of her. Though none still looked her way, she grew self-conscious, standing as she was in the middle of an aisle without the slightest idea of where to sit. The protocol of such places was beyond Irene. She imagined all these people were 'regulars' and would, if they noticed her at all, resent her intrusion. Desiring therefore a less conspicuous posture, she sat herself at the bar, unsure whether it was good or bad that the stools on either side were vacant.

The bartender seemed as unaware of her presence as everyone else, so that Irene was uninterrupted, thinking, God damn, God damn my inexperience, which she assumed was visible to all around.

A large and woozy man, whose flab naughtily protruded from interstices of clothing, sat down beside her. He listed insinuatingly in her direction, aimed a pectoral at her face, and addressed her as anything but naïve.

'They say it's better in the dark,' he said, 'but I like to see what I'm getting myself into. You?'

Verging on tears, but too startled to release them, Irene cursed her sheltered past, which hadn't taught her to deal with this sort of interrogation. Should she ignore him, at the risk of having an angry drunk on her hands, or act worldly, at the risk of inciting him with spunk? The honest answer—the one she would have given Laurence—occurred to her—'I'm not particular, I like it both ways'—but she was horrified at the thought of encouraging the man's lewd drift. 'What would Donna do?' was her refuge, and she swivelled and surveyed the room as if expecting to see Donna herself.

Irene was not, of course, literally expecting anything of the sort; it came as no mild shock when her searching gaze encountered none other. Across the bar, through the smoke, alone at a blue-lit corner table, swirling a drink in the manner of one who thinks swirling makes a drink more potent, like a vision: Donna Forenza, answer to Irene's improvised and hopeless prayers. Not just any sitter, mind you, but Donna Forenza! Feeling grateful and generous, she turned back to the man beside her and said as she slipped off her stool, 'You raise an interesting point. I'll think it over and maybe get back to you later in the month.' To her surprise, he seemed content and only wobbled placidly on his stool as she headed for friendship—haven—at the far end of the bar.

Proximity disclosed nothing gentle about the circlets ringing Donna's eyes, receding from recent tears. Her coloring under messed-up makeup was pastel, but laced with capillary red, bloodlines exposed through an eroding complexion. A woman clearly divorced, worn and discarded, was how she struck Irene, who wondered if her own separation could be so easily inferred from face, posture, eyebrows—Donna's, unplucked for days, straggled irregularly, like a recently seeded lawn, about her eye sockets and the bridge of her nose.

'Donna,' said Irene, gingerly, the way one addresses a patient during visiting hours, abashed at disturbing but expecting forgiveness will follow recognition of a friendly face. 'Donna?'

Donna moved her eyes, not her head. She'd been such a constant mental companion and guide, Irene never thought just shy of a score of years would have made recognition unlikely. Donna shook her head and returned to deliberately nursing her drink.

'Donna, it's Irene Embler.'

The seated woman seemed reduced to essential movements, jealously guarding her energies with only the briefest of shorthand gestures. She shook her head without, this time, raising her eyes. A simple negative: Irene Embler rang no bell.

'You sat for me eighteen years ago. You taught me to color. Your last year in high school. Back then. You taught me to color. I'm Irene.'

Irene was running short of clues. 'I was eight,' she said. 'Irene.'

'Leave me alone, can't you?'

Irene despaired for the eighteen years lost between them, eighteen years she'd wished to see Donna again, now wasted on some cruel joke, a double or identical twin. 'Aren't you Donna Forenza?'

'No.' The head shook with unshakable certainty, but the brows bristled, busy as an ant colony.

Mistaken identity? Wish fulfillment? Psychotic episode? Irene sat down out of pure bafflement.

Donna drank as if to sober herself. 'I was. Yes. I'm sorry. I'm married now. Donna Groat. Now, who are you again?'

'Irene. I was a lot littler then. You taught me to color. You were the favorite sitter I ever had.'

'Oh. Hello, Irene.' She straightened. Irene waited. Introductions dispensed with, she didn't know where to start. She felt infantile, inarticulate, her precious memory clearly useless to this melancholy woman.

'I taught you to color? Irene, have you got a man?'

'Yes.' I assume so, at least, thought Irene.

'Is anything drastically wrong with him?'

Frightened, Irene thought. 'No.'

'Then what the devil are you doing here? Shall I teach you something else?' Donna took a final gulp and put her drink down. 'Listen, Irene Embler, if you can walk all right, I advise you to walk out of here and find him. If you'd rather not, I'll ask you to walk to the bar and get us both a drink, and then I'll tell you a story you'd probably rather not hear.'

Irene took Donna's glass to the bar and asked for two of whatever had been in it. She returned with two double bourbons, neat.

Donna Groat was a mezzo-soprano of some notoriety in the greater Providence area. Had Irene read the Arts & Personalities section of local news, she'd have known that Donna Groat, in the midst of a promising career as well as a Verdi aria, had broken down onstage and refused to be removed, but insisted on sobbing through to the end of the scene, to the considerable discomfort of the assembled opera lovers of greater Providence.

Irene now perceived the failure of her 'What would Donna do?'

in even the most pedestrian vocational sense. Opera, Irene had
never stomached; it seemed a needless torturing at once of the
vocal cords and eardrums, and further, so unconvincingly artificed. She'd never have guessed that what Donna would do was
sing opera. Still less could she have intuited the rest of what Donna
would do.

Donna was one who had lost religion in reaction to a family
crisis; an oddly conventional reason to lose religion, thought Irene,
who could imagine several better. Unworthy of Donna, thought
Irene, whose notion of her was to suffer a string of revisions, losses
and reinstatements, in the ensuing twenty-four hours.

Victor Groat, crop duster and free-lance master of his own twin-
engine Cessna, who in younger days had buzzed highways and
shopping malls and state-park beaches just for fun, flew an inch
too near an acre of peas, heedlessly sunning themselves on the
surface of the unyielding earth in a season of near-drought. His
wings cracked and flamed, leaving him, inverse Icarus, back-bro-
ken and badly burnt about the legs, mercifully anaesthetized but
unmercifully paralyzed from the waist down. More daredevil than
hero, more showoff than martyr, Victor Groat was not then thankful for small favors—ongoing life, viable mind and upper torso—
but resentful over large mishaps. Petulantly unforgiving toward
the wings, the peas, his own faulty judgment, he withdrew from
Donna's kindly ministrations and refused her cold comfort, till
their primary form of conjugal recreation was the lavish drowning
of mutual sorrows over casino and related games of chance. Many
a ten had been precariously built, tipsily taken in, between the
two.

Donna Groat, née Forenza, whose mind tended toward the sim-
pler oppositions, could no longer worship a God, by and large
benevolent, who in some perverse and capricious retraction of
benevolence could inflict or allow to be inflicted not only suffering
in the abstract, but suffering so concrete and grotesque on her
reckless, hapless husband as well as her own fairly circumspect
and unexceptionable self. She had of course been aware of fire,
famine, and slaughter abroad in the world; but self-pity and apos-
tasy, like charity, begin at home. The Gods of both Testaments
now seemed equally malicious and sophomoric practical jokers.
Unfamiliar with various theological resolutions of the Problem of
Evil, Donna suspended on the spot all ritual and sacred thoughts;
and innocent at thirty-four, felt such suspension as a drastic, sys-

temic shock, like a childhood disease contracted too late in life to be innocuous. The shock was only partially absorbed by drink, and hardly at all by a canasta winning percentage just a hair over sixty-two.

Chronic anxiety, as is well known, lowers resistance to chronic infection. An irksome band of renegade yeast drove disconsolate Donna to the gynecologist, who cured the infection and then addressed himself to the anxiety. Aware of her recent domestic disruption and Victor's indisposition, he offered himself as understudy to her incapacitated spouse. Triumph over yeast invested Donna with renewed desire for a man, lost on her disabled and embittered husband. Not unbitter herself, and feeling she surely deserved something for all her troubles, she entertained thoughts of the doctor who had treated her so well; then, pleased with the thoughts, progressed to entertaining the doctor himself, and being entertained by him in turn.

This physician, expert at his craft, took advantage of Donna's shipshape pudenda, painless thanks to him but possessed of a different sort of itch, and of her marital status, which promised to preclude unexpected demands or continuing entanglements. He was not averse to sleeping with patients—had, in fact, a convertible sofa in his office—so long as they were, in the larger and long-range sense, unavailable. He took them one at a time, and generally a short time at that. Most women soon enough harbored guilt and returned to the unadulterated state, not much the worse for wear, within a month or two, more often than not switching doctors once they'd had their fun. But Donna had a husband for thumper and crazy eights, none for conjugating; and the doctor saw with some dismay no declension in her interest, her almost need. Declining was his usual mode, though, and nothing in Donna made him feel like abandoning it; so that when Donna was ready to feel at home, her doctor was all for moving on. He grew to resent her office visits; other patients were waiting, a booming practice.

Adultery, like atheism, hence also like a childhood disease, affected Donna Groat rather more strongly than it might have had she indulged earlier or more than just this once. She clung to the specialist's treatment of her cervix as something special, more than just another set of cell formations and smears; this treatment which, along with her music and her alcoholic games of more chance than skill, formed the single bright, comforting, orienting constellation in the otherwise dark and tribulatory night sky of her life. In her grew, tumorlike, a transference to make a strict Freudian blush with patient-envy.

In short, Donna Groat fell in love with her gynecologist. She still loved Victor, too, but this was different. Victor was for imbibing, reminiscing, mothering, and double solitaire. More dynamic modes of loving she redirected, as an irrigation system revises the landscape, toward Dr. Crickenberger.

Even before her husband's minute altimeter miscalculation, Donna had a weakness for bourbon, neat; a weakness, more precisely, for bourbon itself, neat being simply the most efficient way of getting at it. Victor's accident only reinforced her dipsic bent. As she knew of no specific Scriptural or liturgical injunction against bourbon, neat, a dram had never conflicted strenuously with the Romish scruples of a successful mezzo-soprano and wife of a dauntless crop duster; still less, then, did additional jiggers contradict whatever scruples remained for a faithless, notoriously troubled contralto (hardship had lowered her range) and custodian of a boozy, complaining invalid. Since Victor's crash, inebriation was largely responsible for maintaining the marriage intact; and given Chris's increasing aloofness, it naturally became as well the primary means of maintaining Donna intact.

Irene's head was reeling with Donna's autobiography and a couple of sips of unwonted bourbon. Her uninitiated metabolism adamantly rejected the alien and discombobulating molecules; only rapt attention had kept her doubly astonished body from luxurious complaint and reverse peristalsis. But now Donna's glass was empty, and she implored Irene to make it full again. Eager to comfort the former sitter, Irene stood to navigate her wobbly way to the bar, but veered instead impetuously and wisely toward Ladies, where her stomach emptied of its own accord and with an absurdly meticulous, indecorously prissy thoroughness.

Retching impatiently over the unfamiliar drain, Irene tried to mold Donna's life into a tolerable syllogism—Victor's accident + loss of faith = affair with the promiscuous Dr. Crickenberger—whose logic seemed at once self-evident, insanely trite, and impossibly contrived. How could Donna submit to such blatantly literalistic cause-and-effect, wondered Irene, who was just then herself submitting to the ineluctable overblown histrionics of an insulted and injured GI tract. She cleaned her face lightly, rinsed her mouth, caught a disturbingly pallid reflection in the mirror, grabbed for the door; but for all her urgency to rejoin Donna, Irene was distracted by a sequence of graffiti pencilled and penned on the door:

GOD LOVES YOU —A Christian
I DON'T LOVE GOD —A Pagan
GOD LOVES YOU ANYWAY —A Christian
GOD CAN GO FUCK HIMSELF —A Rationalist
GOD CAN DO ANYTHING, DON'T YOU WISH YOU COULD —A Christian
GOD LOVES MEN, NOT WOMEN; WE MUST LOVE ONE ANOTHER —A Feminist
SCREW MEN —A Sister
I DO —Ginger
SCREW YOU —A Woman
WOULDN'T YOU LIKE TO? DON'T TRY IT —A Real Woman
IF YOU ARE OPEN TO GOD'S LOVE, YOU FIND IT EVERYWHERE —A Christian

Suspended in momentary fascination with this colloquy, Irene tried to attach personalities and lives to each assertion, response, rejoinder: fragmentary glimpses of histories that had led, like Donna's, through what unknown trails and trials to these instantaneous postures. Then stymied by this interpolative impossibility, she shook her head to clear it, headed for the bar, ridiculously distant, with Donna's glass, hefty, bottom-weighted, still firmly clutched in her unfirm hand and tears rimming her eyes, whether from drink or Donna or regurgitation or confusion over disputes documented on the door was more than she knew. On the bar she leaned lightly, tentative, testing the acid-pitted metallic aftertaste on her teeth, in time for last call, and somehow balanced the final brimming, luscious, copper-highlighted glass of the evening back to Donna, who drank as if there were more where it came from and resumed her melancholy narrative.

Though her troubles had grown of late consistently less Victor-troubles and more Chris-troubles, Donna still drank generally at home with her husband, though hiding from him the private sorrows their mutual toasts aided her in facing. But this night, the night she encountered Irene, Irene whom she didn't remember, Irene who remembered her, she felt she couldn't go home to Victor. That would be too hard, on him, on her. She had settled in this anonymous saloon after wandering aimlessly, stricken, away from a disastrous appointment, well after office hours, with Dr. Crickenberger, an interview which had established at last as fact suspicions she couldn't in all good conscience drink away in the presence of Victor Groat.

As if loss, for all intents and conjugal purposes, of husband and loss of God and loss of specialist weren't enough, Donna had this night confirmed by this selfsame specialist that these losses were balanced by a single small gain, more upsetting to her than any loss. Suspicion of this gain, striking her irrelevantly and imprudently in mid-aria, had precipitated Donna Groat's scandalous collapse; this horrible gain, merely inferred onstage as an outside possibility, was the straw that had caused a professional to lose control in concert. The inkling that had visited Donna at an inopportune moment in Verdi, Irene now had with the vivid intuition of virgin inebriation.

'Donna, are you pregnant?'

Donna downed her final bourbon and nodded and wept.

Irene's thoughts began a centrifugal spin, weaving up and down as they spun like carousel ponies. Then they stopped spinning, and finding in her hand the brass ring of an answer, she proposed a single word to solve Donna's immediate life.

'Abortion,' she said.

Donna only cried louder and longer and more helplessly, sobbing so uncontrollably that she reminded Irene viscerally of her own recent submission to importunate paroxysm. A barmaid, swabbing sloppy tables with a sloppy rag in the vicinity, stared unwillingly at the spectacle. Irene pushed the better part of her own double bourbon in Donna's direction. Donna drank, then laughed, ruefully, reproachfully.

'I can't. I won't. I'm Catholic.'

'Not anymore,' said Irene.

'Again,' said Donna.

To a sensibility programmed early in life, this pregnancy suited too neatly the symbology of punishment fitting the crime not to kindle remorse and born-again, full-blown Catholic conscience, frozen but not obliterated by family calamity. The cardinal sin of lust had led to the mortal sin of adultery had led to gravidity, the wages in this case of compound sin. The wages did their job, making sin recognizable as such, thawing conscience and causing confession, repentance, self-hatred, and a resolve forever to forswear the ways of sin. And the modern, efficient way to abjure and negate her original sins—termination, pinkslip with severance pay, detached attachment of sins' wages—was only a way to compound sin with sin with cowardly, irredeemable sin; for abortion was officially as damnable as lust or adultery, and Donna Groat, back in the fold (albeit a bit too late), would never again commit herself knowingly to sin.

'Just this once? Just this sin to purge you of previous sin, and after that no more?'

'That,' said Donna, 'is the way of the Devil. Chris was right, that just once more leads always to just once more. You see me now, drunk as a sailor; and I came in for just one drink, to steady my hand and settle my mind. A clean break, with the Devil, with Chris, with drink, is the only way.'

'Then have the child and raise it with love. Surely that can't be a sin.'

'O Irene,' she said, burbling and sniffling, 'Victor and I haven't been together, that way, since his accident. He'd know, and his knowledge would torture him, and the poor poor man has had enough torture to last a lifetime. All I want is to go back to Victor and care for him and make his cross a little easier to bear. But if I return with another man's child, I'll only add to his misery. And if I don't return, he'll think it's because he's crippled, and I'll only add to his despair. Poor Victor, poor Victor. What can I do?'

God had Donna in a bind, a stranglehold from which it seemed only death could release her. But that bet was covered, too, by a canon set gainst self-slaughter. Good Christian that she once again was, she would gladly have endured pain if only she could keep from inflicting it; but it seemed she could no more save Victor from pain than herself.

What in the world had become of Donna's seemly penchant for pastels and the delicate beauty of gentle circlets, now her life was palled and immobilized in ugly swaths of bile and oxblood, unsubtle interior hues no impressionist sunlight could reach? What advice or solace could Irene the former baby conceivably provide one so encumbered and overcast? What pastoral response could Irene the lapsed Unitarian offer to such confession? And if no advice, then what? Sanctuary, at least?

Irene offered the best she could, a place to sleep off the oppressive combination of fact and alcohol. The devastated *diva* accepted, and a cab took the two despairingly drunken women the handful of blocks to home, where Irene put her erstwhile sitter gently to bed and remained herself incontrovertibly awake and violently, fruitlessly ill.

Laurence fled the Museum in an inscrutable rush, not stopping as he'd planned for a postcard remembrance of *Tyrannosaurus,* pushing instead with angular expedience out the door and down the steps, vest aflutter, like one who thinks he may be ill any minute. He had some thinking to do, away from the engaging, intoxicating aura of age so strong that animal, vegetable, mineral are confounded and indistinguishable.

The street was clouding up in appeasement of the sky's gathering heat. He decelerated without noticing it for a couple of humid blocks, wondering what in the world it was that he wanted, what sort of thundershower could clear his mind as it seemed one was about to clear the City's air.

An old man dressed wildly, gesturing wildly, a broad, fluid man with several days' growth of beard, distracted Laurence from a block away and grew larger as he approached till Laurence could discern rheumy eyes and spacious nose and hairs growing incongruously on the outer rims of ample ears. Now Laurence could tell he was lecturing, preaching actually, on the fairly busy corner. He was bobbing and weaving next to a waste can, under alternate-side parking, No Left Turn, and electric Walk and Wait signs, where a loose knot of people stood nodding and smiling at one another in full view of the object of their amusement.

'I tell you, brothers, the Jewish people are a nervous people. They're nervous in their talk, they're nervous in their walk, they're nervous in their business dealings and in their home life, and why? Because they know they missed out, they took a wrong turn on a one-way street, they can't find their way, they're lost, they're in the dark. They're waiting. The train is out of the station, brothers, the horse is out of the barn, do you hear what I say, they're nervous because they missed the boat. They rule the world, but they missed the boat and they don't know peace, and they don't even know what they think they're waiting for.'

An elderly man, frail, birdlike, who made an attempt to dress well, whose eyes were yellow, whose hands were wringing one another, who had a droplet of drying blood on the tip of his beak— had the large fluid man punched the frail birdlike man?—paced back and forth at a distance of ten feet as if caged, blinking and shaking his head and repeating over and over in a mynah's voice to anyone who would listen, 'I *gnome,* he's Joosh him*self,* I gnome already a long time, *he's* Joosh.'

The broad man, shaped like a chicken croquette and possessed of remarkable eyebrows echoed in the hairs flying like banners from the edges of his ears, spoke to anyone, no one, everyone, improvising, changing his tune every minute or two, moving from stance to stance like a mail-order catalogue, making all within earshot, Jew and gentile alike, nervous, while the frail man repeated the same one note: *'He's* Joosh, *he's* Joosh.'

'Did you know why their God pulled them out of Eden, did you know? For eating a fruit? Fools! Their God couldn't stand for them to be like Him. Same deal at Babel—"lest they become now like us"—did you know that? They wanted to make a name for themselves, lest they be scattered. But they're scattered, and the Lord knows they made a name for themselves, and what is it? A nervous name for a nervous people.'

'I gnome from a long time, *he's* Joosh,' said the thin man, pacing, darting his yellow eyes from the sidelines like a coach or parent. He *sounds* Jewish, thought Laurence, but so does half of New York.

'They don't even know their God is colored. The Book says His hair is woolly—woolly! Do you know what race has the woolly hair? You and I, my friend, are under the thumb of a nervous people that worship a colored God that couldn't stand the competition. He confounded their speech so they could never be like Him, but I'm speaking to you now. My speech is clear and you can hear if you aren't too nervous over the price of potatoes to hear what is not confounded. You were meant to be gods, but He demands a blood sacrifice, and if you find a dime in the gutter you give praise, but you lose everything you own and still you give praise. It's a nervous people, I tell you, a nervous people praying to a colored God.'

'Don't listen tomb, *he's* Joosh, the Jew bestid.'

'Did you know there's a man Ishmael that was cast out with every hand against him and never did a blessed thing but have a kid brother? Did you know there's another man Ishmael that they called a hero, that invited other men into his own house and killed them just like that, and they called this man a hero?'

He's Jewish, thought Laurence, like I'm Jewish, without knowing it. He calls them nervous because he's nervous, nervous about being Jewish, Jewish about being nervous. Is the old man his father? He knows him already a long time. I'd like to know, what brings a man to such a pass, what makes a man such a spectacle? Why should this man be shouting and the kid with the vibes shut up?

He preaches at will, while the City goes about its business for miles on each side and the lighted signs above his head switch from Wait to Walk and back again to Wait. How can a man live like that?

How, Laurence started to wonder, could anyone live in this City that won't leave you alone? It's all traffic. I come to fill in a finite number of specific gaps, and after this short time I already have a lifetime of irrelevant information to sift. How can a person live in a place that won't answer a simple question? Why does a place answer a question with a question? How do I get to the subway?

Laurence had a festive-looking diagram to answer this question. He consulted it and headed for Gretchen, shaken by his foray and looking, no doubt, as blank as any other straphanger that afternoon.

Gretchen, who fancied she had felt something kick, though it might have been a burp of her own, was mercifully in a serene and patient mood when drained Laurence returned. She was humming a song related to the food that was simmering on the stove, and she was swaying gently in hopes that someone would appreciate the free ride. For one her size, she gave Laurence a surprisingly inclusive hug and kept on swaying and humming to calm him and anyone else who might be listening in.

It seemed to him that to explain what had happened, or more precisely, to explain its effect on him, he would have to start long before the subway ride. It seemed to him that to explain, he would have to tell Gretchen everything there was to tell.

And now, alone in the small city night with a digestion closed for repairs and the worrisome erratic rhythm of restless shifting sounds and the disarming arrhythmia of restive shiftless silences, Irene indulged a lushly fearsome review of the life sleeping fitfully under her narrow roof and light conforter, the life Irene had undressed and put to bed as it once undressed and put her to bed, and which now requested no more than to spend itself in unwished tending of another, undressing and putting to bed and taking from bed and dressing and reaching things down from cupboards and dusting what trinkets or mementoes remained from half a life spent flying as near things below as seemed wise and distracting a mind too much given, perhaps, to recalculating a single minute and momentous error and assuring that mind that half a body of living willful flesh and half of dead weight were sufficient for another half a life of moving at an even, steady wheelchair level and pace through a world of varied and unreachable heights, of diminished variety and unvarying diminishment.

Irene was this night keeping for the first time a vigil over another life, tending the night-blooming plant of another's fragility, leery of seeming overwatchful but feeling, for once, the whelming burden and uneasy absurdity of an organism open to all shocks and ills—nightmare, microbe, failing heart—that flesh and mind are heir to, breathing in her space and therefore somehow by her leave and so, potentially at least, upon her conscience.

She thought of Donna's marriage and her own, how much more expressly Donna's embodied what every marriage meant or could be made to mean: another one, or more than one, whom if he needed feeding you would feed with more than half a mind to taste and nutrition both, planning balances as you wouldn't for yourself; whom if he needed bathing you would bathe with more attentive care to soft and tender spots where moisture gathers and can chafe than you give to your own; whom if he needed breathing you would breathe for, giving your life over to resuscitation, becoming an unfailing, full-time iron lung. Would she have done that for Laurence, or he for her? For even the most thoroughly childless union held implicit the seed of a parent-child relation, through accident or disease or breakdown or simple age. Could she without resentment or homicidal inkling spend each day and every night in just such responsible fretting and full accountable logging of each and every breath or breathless pause as she now felt for Donna? Had Donna herself once lavished, for her three cents a minute and all the soda she cared to drink, such rich and fastidious attention upon Irene's own continued functioning? What *did* Donna do, after an eight-year-old's bedtime in the days of sitting and being sat?

How simple for a husband to take a tumble from his chosen hobby-horse and become once more a child, helpless, demanding! And how hard for a wife to watch him and watch over him, an inn guest somehow roped into doing the gardening and keeping up not only her own maid-bereft room but all the extensive grounds of the declining estate. And what ever made her think of herself as a guest, her life as a vacation? Merely signing in with the desk clerk and being handed a room key in no way ensures a safe and happy visit. And calling room service for an overpriced bottle and bucket of ice is no guarantee that bottle and bucket will be sent, or if sent, will successfully drown waterproof, waterlogged sorrows. Who ever promised one would not end up sitting for someone else's child at a meager rate of pay and without even refrigerator privileges?

Yet Irene was grateful, despite it all, to have Donna back, and more than grateful for the chance to take reciprocal care. She half suspected her lugubrious fancies had chemical origin in the bowels of a system spooked by its first encounter with a popular poison. And along with the fears and fancies, at the same contradictory moment, she felt competent and almost cozy in her tallying. All she had to do at the moment was make sure Donna exhaled for every inhale and inhaled for every exhale, and for this she had a much greater return than Donna's old dollar-eighty an hour. She had gone out looking for something like a sitter and come back with one; she had gone out wanting someone to care for and come back caring for someone. She wanted Laurence, but in an odd way Donna would do for now.

Victor. Should she wake Donna and remind her of responsibilities of such magnitude? But Donna slept more peacefully now, and Irene felt her own primary responsibility was to protect that slumber. Surely the dauntless flyer could manage on his own till Donna was sober.

Sitters: Donna so apposite, Lucy Fern so opposite. Had Donna stayed, Irene might have waited years before prematurely proclaiming adulthood; but her dislike of Lucy was so intense, if vague, that she whined childishly to her parents that she was old enough to go without. Irene felt her illogic—Lucy was not specifiably deficient—but if she couldn't be sat by Donna, she preferred not to be sat at all.

One crucial night nothing had happened. The Emblers at long last yielded to the briefs Irene endlessly presented in favor of being released under her own recognizance. They were only to be gone for half an evening—two hours perhaps—but they took precautions, writing out, going over, and posting on the refrigerator a slew of local phone numbers. They would only be in one location, but there were contingency plans; if that phone didn't work, if it was busy, if they were in transit, there had to be numbers and backup numbers—failsafe redundancy—at every stage of the operation. There was a thorough review of victuals, electrical safety, whether to answer door or phone, which lights should be on, whether food was permitted on the living-room rug; all the things Irene knew and had known for years were iterated for her first few hours alone. And Irene didn't mind, taking every admonition with a new and precious solemnity. Like a flight crew gearing up for a dangerous sortie behind enemy lines, the Emblers checked and cross-checked lists and strategies. Then the door clicked shut, and Irene immediately wished her mother hadn't been wearing that chinchilla coat, whose tight pearly-grey curls Irene found soothing against her cheek in times of anxiety. She knew her parents were standing on the far side of the door, waiting to hear that she had properly double-locked it from the inside. She almost couldn't bring herself to lock them out, but pride turned both locks, and she stood with her ear against the door and her mouth open and her tongue against its roof, filled with remorse and self-pity, incredulous that her parents had taken her at her word and left her alone in a house after dark.

Irene spent fifteen minutes trying to isolate something illicit, some license she could never have taken before, private drawer or secret cupboard or adult volume she could take this opportunity to discover and peruse and put back exactly as it had been with no evidence of tinkering. But she had no sooner located a half-crumpled tube of something inscrutably gynecological and read what she could of the tube's label without the slightest glimmer of enhanced understanding than she imagined she heard the car pulling into the driveway, and visions of stern parents tiptoeing upstairs to find her *in flagrante delicto,* footstool in place, top drawer wide open, mysterious tube in hand, made her wipe everything she had touched with the edge of her blouse and lug the stool back to the kitchen and seat herself demurely in full innocent view in the living room, with the television on but the volume way down, with all the lights on the ground floor blazing and her hands carefully covering the hem of the blouse that had wiped off the evidence of her mystified quest for grown-up things that belied her protests that she was herself grown-up.

So it started almost immediately. Seated primly in front of the flickering bluish screen that she couldn't make herself pay attention to, she imagined everything that could possibly go wrong. She started with minor plumbing leaks, spills on the rug, blown fuses, power outages, flashlights with corroded batteries, candles tipping over, conflagration, phone lines dead, doors sticking, trapped like a rat in a flaming split-level. Soon she refined her fancies to include

intruders, possibly escaped from mental institutions or correc-
tional facilities, with knives or guns, machetes, howitzers, hordes
of wild men splintering the double-locked door for ingress, gagging her so she couldn't warn her returning parents, forcing her
to watch as her mother and father were cut down gangster-style,
a perforated line of bloodspots opening diagonally across the chinchilla, her father's teeth plucked out one by one with no anaesthetic, her mother's eyeglasses painted over with nail polish, what
atrocities would these demented strangers stop at?

Worse, what if ten o'clock rolled around and Irene, still parentless, tuned in the grown-up news and saw films—no, worse, live
on location, minicam shaking with the reality of it all—of her own
dear parents being excruciatingly extricated from the tangled
wreckage of a head-on collision, and she had to watch as the paramedics searched frantically for vital signs?

Worse yet, what if eleven or midnight rolled around and Irene,
still parentless, had to imagine the worst? Imagining what it would
be to imagine the worst, she had to wonder what the worst might
be. And though the little hand was still nearly as close to the eight
as to the nine, Irene was already in that eleven or midnight frenzy,
wondering at well before quarter to nine whether it would be
excessively worrisome to call one of those numerous numbers at
just after ten, or the hospitals at quarter to eleven, or the state
troopers at quarter past. Worrying when to start worrying.

So that by the time her parents redomesticated themselves, a
little before ten (they too had been slightly worried), and found
Irene safe and sound with hands in lap and transfixed, they presumed, by television, she had done them in in every conceivable
way, no holds barred, no gore spared, had gotten their estate
through probate with half a dozen different results ranging from
hidden treasure to total indigence, each of which, however, afforded
her a trip around the world, as poor beggar girl or lost heiress to
the throne of Bohemia, all in the name and guise of genuine fear.
Such a flutter of mixed emotions welled up in her on seeing once
again her own unexceptional parents with their usual ten-o'clock
demands involving toothbrush, hairbrush, laying oneself down to
sleep and praying the Lord one's soul to keep. Irene was, on the
one hand, so thrilled they hadn't died or absconded with her
inheritance that she almost jumped up and gave her distant mother
a hug; on the other, so dispirited at the contrast of her lushest fears
with her plain old unmelodramatic mother and father that she
stared at them with something approaching disdain. As she resigned

herself to the humbling procedure of brushing and brushing and praying and sleeping, she already knew that the dominant residue of her first dark hours alone would not be relief that they were alive and well but disappointment that nothing had happened. And even before the humiliation of being bossed around by those she'd disposed of in so many spectacular ways, she knew that her dearest desire, since nothing had happened in fact, was not to let on that anything had in fancy. She convinced herself that what she really wanted to hug was the chinchilla, which she had after all inherited half a dozen times in the last half hour. She refused to speak till she had regained her composure.

'Back already?' she finally said.

Her mother, ten feet distant at the closet where she was ferreting her fur away, and her father, loosening his tie with one hand as he double-locked the door with the other, exchanged a look of mutual accusation—how silly each other had been to worry.

'Everything all right?' asked her father.

'Of course. What could go wrong?'

'Then brush your teeth and hair,' said her mother, 'and say your prayers and in bed by ten,' which was bedtime when nothing had happened.

She hit the streets at the usual time, but the stimulation of her earlier thoughts and the mortification of her parents' return kept her from sleeping for several hours. She felt, even then, that something had gone terribly wrong; her fantasies proved she felt helpless and scared, but she had only demonstrated to her parents that she didn't need them or a sitter either. Pride would keep her from confessing; and later, when she understood the hostility displayed in her hour and a half of terror, she would be glad it had done so. She had behaved like a human being, though she had never before wanted so much to spite her mother. And to be sent to bed at ten! She almost wished something *had* happened: not the worst, to be sure, but something. How could being alone for the evening be so thoroughly uneventful?

Well over a year since being orphaned in fact, Irene knew the answer to that question now, but she was sure she had no desire for anything to happen to Donna, or to Victor while Donna was in her care. And her knowledge of what *had* happened to Donna made her flush at her youthful desire for drama. Did drama have to be tragedy?

Irene thought of her delusive pregnancy, of her silly self and her possibly silly husband and her silly visions of combing the City for clues. Would a farce or comedy of manners afford satisfaction? Couldn't Donna's tragedy, by a slight twist of attitude, become one? Couldn't her own story, by a complementary twist, evoke as much terror and pity as Donna's? Wasn't there a third alternative? Why should the categories of the stage apply at all? For Donna, perhaps, it was fitting that life should be stagy and larger than life. But seeing what Donna had done in eighteen years, what eighteen years had done to Donna, Irene was left without a model, even in theory.

When Laurence was finished telling Gretchen what he thought she needed to know, she knew what Laurence knew about dinosaurs and dull knives and uncles in World War II and monkeys and sailors on pulleys. She knew more than she had bargained for when she asked, 'Who is Irene?' She knew, as truthfully and fully as he could say, why he was in the City at all and what had been stirred on the subway and sidewalks of this heated and overcharged day.

There was something she didn't know, something she thought had a bearing. She asked a question she had asked him before, unsuspecting, on a bus from Providence.

'Is your grandfather living?'

Good heavens, the undeniably crucial things happening all this while in the great wide world! Races starving, loyalties shifting, currencies collapsing, superpowers intervening, cures being sought, ozone dropping, entire continents underdeveloping and overdeveloping like kids with a thyroid condition. You may wonder, on the day Laurence arrived in New York, what did commuters on the Long Island Railroad read in the morning papers? On the night he pedicured Gretchen, what did Hawaiians see on the evening news? What was Bolivia thinking, whom were Italians electing, whose civil liberties were abridged, did the Cubs go into extra innings, were there hot spots and shortages, did someone make a statement, were babies tossed in desperation from third-floor windows caught, were young men *bar mitzvah*'d, did young women fight back when attacked, was welfare curtailed, did someone drive drunk, did the Jaycees meet? You may wonder less ambitiously, who, for heaven's sake, was President? Were we at war? What year of anyone's Lord was this?

What you are asking is, Laurence, are the limits of your life so narrow? A mother, a father, a wife, a lover? Do you overlap? Don't you intersect? If England dies, are you not the less for it? For whom tolls your bell? Are you more than a clanging cymbal? What you are asking is, why *this* story?

The question is out of order. Ask instead why Greeks live in Greece, why hydrogen is the lightest element, whether different causes have different effects, can goodness be taught, why are bees magnetized, who invented food, why was Buddha fat and Jesus thin, which was Muhammad, what is the opposite of spaghetti. Inquire into the volume of mountains, the shape of air, the power of addiction; demand to know why your cat was run over, whether leaves are really green or only appear so, what advances will be made after your demise. A miss is as good as a mile, and beside the point may as well be light-years off.

But has it occurred to you, while washing dishes or stuck in traffic or licking a stamp or swimming the Channel, to wonder whether Gretchen Barron, promising young Providence cellist, and Donna Forenza, promising young Providence mezzo-soprano, ever made one another's acquaintance? They were, after all, approximately of an age, and very proximately of a profession. The musical circles of Providence, after all, are not so extensive as to provide very many symphonic ensembles to back up choric extravaganzas. Have you thought that the Providence Symphony perhaps accompanied Donna's not unstellar debut, and further accompanied her rising, then falling career? Have you supposed that Donna, a known admirer in early adulthood of gentle circlets, was drawn to the complexion of a rather strikingly pastel cellist when the two collaborated on a production of *Die Walküre* or *Messe in H moll* or *Prometheus: The Poem of Fire* or *Peter and the Wolf?* That Gretchen, whose taste ran to the baroque and pre-baroque, may have forgiven a fetching mezzo the turgid excesses of Verdi and Rossini? That the two may have lunched together, dined together, swum together at the Y, thus showered, dressed, undressed, soaped their privates, together? That with the single exception of her boyfriend Victor, Gretchen may have been the human being Donna felt closest to? That the former's move to New York may have dismayed, disheartened, even thrown for a loop, sensitive Donna? That, in short, these two women, one known to Irene, the other to Laurence, may have shared more than an unscrupulous gynecologist? That, for all you know, one may, in private consultation in the Y's drying room, have referred the other to the M.D.? You know how

Gretchen met Crickenberger, for she's told Laurence in your hearing; but Donna, troubled with yeast, may she not have turned to her longtime friend and swimmate, and may Gretchen, with as yet no reason to resent, detest, or execrate the man, not have heartily recommended her personal physician? Have you any reason to believe otherwise? Can you doubt it?

Would it surprise you to learn that, so far, all your conjectures are true, and that when Laurence met Gretchen on the bus she was returning from a visit to her old friend Donna, who had been having a difficult time of late?

In that case, has it occurred to you that, while highly unlikely, it is by no means impossible that by sheer coincidence Gretchen might be telling Laurence about her Catholic, operatic, alcoholic friend Donna at the exact moment when Donna might be telling Irene about her albinic, cellic, hepatophilic friend Gretchen? That Laurence might respond, by means of some more or less plausible transition, with more information about his theoretical, hysterically impregnated, and now deserted wife, while at one and the same moment Irene, in some parallel, equally unlikely but equally plausible discursive turn, might be telling Donna about her premature, unpredictable, dangling missing person of a husband? Might Gretchen remark on the strange new lover in a letter to Providence? Might Donna mention the former charge who put her up for the night in a note to New York? Might the missives cross in the mail? Might Irene, in this way, learn of the disconcerting whereabouts of her lawfully wedded man, or Laurence, in this way, learn of the reconcerting second thoughts of his lawfully wedded wife? These things are not inconceivable. Do you expect the four of them to converge in some grand farcical roundelay of an encounter, with Big Jim as the master of ceremonies and Dr. Crickenberger (who we now discover is Big Jim's bastard son?) as the catalyst and the little girl from the Hall of Dinosaurs (who we now discover is Crickenberger's bastard daughter?) as the innocent source of reconciliation and dénouement?

Would it bother you to learn that these further conjectures couldn't be further from the truth, that Donna never mentioned Irene to Gretchen, nor Gretchen Laurence to Donna? There is no blood relation whatever between Big Jim, Chris Crickenberger, and the little girl (let us call her Emily).

As for the opposite of spaghetti, I'm doing the best I can.

Five

~~~~

Theo's Ties is six hundred square feet of busy floor space on Fordham in the Bronx, fifteen by forty with racks and shelves obtruding obliquely so the walkable floor is shaped like a four-in-hand tie. At approximately the spot where a tack or diamond stud might pierce such an item, a cut-glass cooler regales Theo's clientele with a seemingly endless supply of bubbly Vichy. Mineral water, Theo is known to say, soothes the nerves, makes people happy, so they're more willing to buy ties. What he actually says is this: 'Minirill fought air, suits din knives, mex pippil gled, entice day foot pie chess fit abet air fill ink fin Tayo.' The bubbler, like the Windsor-knotted floor and the hand-painted one-of-a-kind neckwear draping racks like a ticker-tape parade down Broadway for some historic occasion, is a New York tradition and landmark, as is the sign that boldly proclaims Theo's location on the street. Fire-engine red on battleship grey around the doorway, the word 'TIES' appears in every language Theo knows someone who knows. Esoteric strangers have come from as far as Cherry Hill just to add an entry to Theo's single-minded glossary. The most English-speaking of English-speakers, the most thorough monolinguist in the borough, would know at a glance that each of those cryptic slapdash morphemes must mean 'TIES.' Six-and-thirty urgent polyglottal messages, so obsessive, so clear, one wouldn't need the English word to translate by. Waggish Theo has recognized as much: the English does not appear. Dutch, Croatian, Nepalese, Iroquois, Aramaic, Greek (modern), Greek (classical); but over the lintel, not English but Esperanto reigns, the universal tongue over all the rest—'KRAVATOJ'—so Theo's storefront looks like an inverted family tree of Indo-European neckwear.

Theo lives upstairs. Not an erudite man but a reader, a self-taught shirttail immigrant who learned to make ties from remnants during the Great Depression so he and his son could look sharp applying for jobs that didn't exist. Soon Theo, unemployed in only the financial sense, was hand-sewing, hand-painting, hand-pressing ties faster than he or his son or their friends could apply for jobs. There were many like Theo in those hard years who, desperate for something to believe, believed a cravat might procure them an income, that America was a land of well-groomed opportunity. It was for them, the immigrants out of work, that Theo started making ties then, and to them he started selling them for next to nothing; often, like an employment agency, for a commission if the client landed a job while wearing one of Theo's ties. By the time hard times eased, Theo could scarcely stroll in any part of the Bronx without his tie-height eyes noticing necks sporting samples of his handiwork. As the Depression cheered up and more men were seen in Theo's inimitable ties, more men were also known to be finding work. Some logical or magical connection being assumed, Theo became known not only as a master haberdasher, but as something of a wizard.

'Expent, fie dun jew?' friends would ask. 'Ah *shneider* saw chess yes elf, eye coot sip row due sink hets, gluffs, ah payer pents, *eppis* ah nice vesteleh. Fought coot be bet?'

Theo saw nothing bad in that, but was committed to neckwear, and hand-painted neckwear to boot. 'Fought expent, fen affray fawn knit snake tice? Fen New Yaw kiss foot tint buy no mower tice, den foot beady tie em tech spent. De hole foiled poot sawn ah tie fife dace inner vick, in affray bawdy stents awn lion farah hent-pentit tie, dawnly gahmint day coot pie chess dots pentit fitter crefty hent. Mine fa dare cess to me indy old ace: "Fawn tink, bit fell." In dot's dot.'

Stageleft of his carefully knotted personal tie, looking like a pack

of cigarettes in his shirt pocket—but why would a man carry cigarettes who walked always to and fro in a pungent self-generated
cloud of thick blue-white smoke, choice latakia billowing from his
ever-present meerschaum?—was a battery-powered electric device
that told Theo's heart when to beat. At the appropriate interval,
provided his batteries were replenished on schedule, the white
plastic box sent an impulse through a hair-thin copper wire that
trailed under Theo's tie, through a buttonhole, and straight on
into his chest, where a permanently implanted electrode informed
his central muscle, day and night, every minute sixty times, give
or take a few: 'Beat . . . now, beat . . . now, beat . . .' Systole, dias-
tole, and by the bye, life, were sustained on schedule and, in theory, forever by this primitive, monotonous reminder. Like Theo
himself on his father's advice, it did just one thing, but well.

Theo had been one of the earliest subjects when the pacemaker
pulsed its unlikely way off the drawing board and into experimental production. Had his heart forgotten when to beat two months
earlier or research and development come up with the white plastic box two months later, Theo would be dead without regrets,
ignorant of the artificial stimulus about to be placed on the market. To the dumb-luck timing of a dicey technology that seemed
at the time miraculous, Theo knew, he owed his life. And though,
in the twenty years or so since he played guinea pig so fortuitously,
remarkable advances had been made in the art of reminding hearts
when to beat, Theo clung to the primary advance, the one that
had saved his life when it needed saving. He showed no interest
whatsoever in newer models smaller than a single cigarette, in
microchips embedded within the chest itself, in transplant, in open-
heart surgery, or in any other device or technique that could now
do away with the cumbersome pocket-sized circuit that had once
seemed compact and that for twenty years had never once failed
to say, 'Beat . . . now, beat . . . now, beat . . .'
  'Fen doos fawn fill giff op, den foot be tie em to tinker bout sum
odor tink. Tilden, fa now, in sew lung my hot ticks, eye coo tint be
mower kin tent.' And this was Theo's way, generally, with consumer goods. Since the unfortunate death of his beloved wife and
lifelong friend, Molly Nečz Papyrushchka, Theo had added nothing to the appurtenances of his life and had replaced precious little: light bulbs, perishables, sewing-machine needles as called for,
but not the machine itself, a sixty-year-old treadle affair that had
been the means of his livelihood even in the Old Country, and

that had sat placidly by when he discovered the New Country offered no such specialty as sewing fancywork ornamentation on the leather uppers of the boots of the upper classes, and that had still been patiently waiting when he devised a new specialty, and that was, since Molly's death, his dearest and most constant companion, with the crucial exception of the white plastic box which ensured not only his ongoing life, but also that his pajamas, no less than his shirts, all bore pockets on the left side of the chest.

The implements in Theo's kitchen, original equipment from half a century ago, were caked and blackened outside, worn and washed smooth and shiny inside; one frying pan in particular, his favorite, had a bottom warped and battered with tens of thousands of meals and resembling a relief map of Poland. Theo's belts were a fraction of their original thickness. Theo's best-loved coffee mug was porcelain webbed with a thousand cracks and stained with fifty thousand doses of rich, oily black brew. But most extraordinary were Theo's pipes, fragile meerschaums darkened till they could be taken for conventional briars, kept impossibly intact over decades of heating and cooling, filling and emptying, combustion and condensation. One Theo had still from the Old Country, its bowl delicately carved to a bust of Heine, but so smoothly eroded from a lifetime of handling it more resembled a newborn infant's features. How many bitter smoldering dottles had been gently knocked out of this pipe into Theo's calloused palm is beyond knowing; but the pipe itself, empty, smelled more pungent than most pipes filled and lit.

Theo's cilia were permanently weathered and charred; Theo's tongue, though long ago cured and tanned, still stung every morning and evening, and could perceive only the strongest coffee, the strongest tobacco, the most strongly seasoned foods; Theo's canines, skewed with clamping against gravity the weight of pipes, were as brown as his tongue; Theo's breath was dense and painful, more like a noxious gelatin sucked through a sieve than a wholesome admixture of life-giving gases; Theo's doctors had warned him before the days of the white plastic box to give up tobacco or die before his time. But the doctors enjoined him also, for his pressure, not to worry; and Theo didn't. The low-lying cloud of stagnant smoke in which his head resided while awake was synonymous for Theo with the absence of worry. The bit between his teeth was solace, and so although the cardiologist still punctuated every visit with the traditional injunctions, not to worry, not to smoke, Theo now left his office drawing on a fresh-lit bowl of latakia, saying, 'Duct air, ewer unintelligent men. Eyeful tally oo fawn tink eye foot tint foury: eye foot tint foury inny mower dot eye shoot die yunk.'

A pipe is many things to many people. Some will tell you it's phallic, vaginal, mammarial, or affords some other variant of psychosexually fixated oral or manual gratification; others will insist it's a political signature, announcing aristocratic, bourgeois, or proletarian standing or sympathies; still others will call it affectation or prop, habit or obsession, seductive, disgusting, arrogant, insecure, private, public, tainted, safe. To Theo it was none, or all, of these: it was no less than a language, 'ah complit lank fetch.' Most anything anyone else could say in any native or acquired tongue, any attitude or tone, argument or implication, compliment or insult, creed or image, thesis or antithesis, Theo could express through some combination of eyebrows, meerschaum, hands, and a mouthful of smoke. His inhale was eloquent; his exhale, ineffable; all the sundry stage business in between, with palm, lips, teeth, and tongue, bowl, shank, stem, and bit, matches, tampers, reamers, and pokers, composed a semantic system so various and communicative that Theo scarcely needed to speak. And when smoke could say his piece, he saw no need to waste empty breath; with the result that Theo was a man of relatively few spoken words, but of many opinions decisively expressed. Each meerschaum was a lexicon, each puff a gaseous morpheme; and Theo, not to put too fine a point on it, was the consummate poet of combustion.

Theo's voluminous pipetalk was familiar to anyone who had ever, in want of a tie or merely curious, made the trek to his notorious though unadvertised corner of Fordham, and even to any who'd strolled innocently by and remarked in passing the cloudy white overflow billowing above the sidewalk from inside the shop, editorial surplus cut out from Theo's first draught and sent wandering through the streets in search of a likely interpreter, or hanging stagnant in the windless air about the wordy doorway like a vocabulary, ready to be of use. But Theo's cloudy articulation was surely best known, among the living, to the two-and-twenty members of Paideia, a monthly discussion group held on his own four-in-hand premises.

On the second Thursday of any given month, the cooler was drained of Vichy and half filled with two gallons of the choicest

shnapps; and from eight o'clock till the shnapps or the topic was
exhausted, whichever came second, Theo's Ties was transformed
into a private forum—members and rarely invited guests only—by
the addition of firmly slatted wooden folding chairs, lining the
shop in a long, thin ellipse. At the foci, on one hand, the cooler,
gleaming with russet liquor; and on the other, a small, dark table
of ruby-stained walnut on which were set, at eight, two dozen jel-
lyjar glasses, fewer as the shnapps and the evening wore out and
on, and three Dutch porcelain humidors of latakia, on the house.

The chairs, some with added cushions provided by members
who required them, were sat and shifted and eagerly leaned forward in for these few hours a month by twenty-two gentlemen,
full-grown though the mean height was four foot eleven: elderly
gentlemen, shrinking in only the literal sense, in every other sense
holding boldly forth with thoughts as varied as their aspects: slicked
and dapper or frail and wispy, in suits whose lapels were wide or
narrow, whose breasts were single or double, shirts whose collars
were buttoned, tabbed, or pinned, frayed or impeccably, staunchly
new or starched. For Paideia knew no boundaries of income or
social standing, knew rather only long-established bonds, the
homemade tradition of four-and-twenty immigrants given to the
life of the mind and the civil, energetic monthly exchange of views
on issues topical or timeless, in comments trivial or telling, but all
equally, unequivocally attended to.

The sole sartorial commonplace, embracing every neck like a
bad communal pun on the group's solidarity, was the Paideia
Society tie, reverently hand-painted by Theo, each and every one:
though various in width depending on wearer's preference, fash-
ionable or no—some ordering a new Paideia tie each autumn in
keeping with restless modes, others sporting still their original
Paideia ties from forty years since, imperceptibly touched up by
Theo's crafty hand—they all displayed on a field of rich maroon
silk flecked with threads of a lighter red the Paideia Society insig-
nia in a substantial but decorous charcoal grey: an open book to
connote an open mind, a sword broken clean in half to symbolize
the mighty pen, the owl of Minerva above the book, and below the
sword, vanquished, the narrow and hideous dragon Error, culled
from a fortuitous first reading of Spenser by a charter member
exercising his adopted tongue.

But Paideia included no member who wasn't charter, save the
four 'Youngsters' (ranging in age from fifty to sixty-five) who had
proudly assumed their fathers' chairs on the decease of those

respective gentlemen, and the single 'Pup,' a man of thirty-five who had taken the chair of his father, who had taken his father's chair in turn: the first and thus far only third-generation Paideian, whose views were nevertheless greeted with the selfsame thoroughgoing, deliberate, and upright respect as any other member's.

This mutual respect, which amounted almost to monastic veneration and was the one and only cardinal written rule of Paideia—'Each member heard, no viewpoint ridiculed'—might not have been apparent to an outsider, since members were heard and ridicule withheld above a continuo of comings and goings, to the cooler and back to refill a glass, to the humidor and back to refill a pipe; of standings and sittings, to rest or relieve a spine that had stiffened or foot that had nodded off; of affirmative grunts and disputational puffs; of the bubblings and churnings of two-and-twenty sipping, smoking, evaluating, dissenting, variously assertive, concerned, flatulent, eructative, or borborygmous aging gents. But for all the rustle and continuous shuffle of refills and excrescences, influx and efflux and politely ignored effluvial commentary, shiftings from weary cheek to cheek and rhetorically preparatory realignment of plates and trusses or mindful clearing of phlegmy throats or purging of formidable smoke-clogged emunctories into overworked, wrinkled, tobacco-stained handkerchiefs; for all the random, busy noise unavoidable in such a gathering, a second, unwritten rule reigned over Paideia—'No whispering.' When a Paideian had the floor, the floor was, verbally, his alone; and any member would sooner expire on the spot—indeed, one member had—than interrupt a colleague's say with any apt or irrelevant, oratorical or offhand, trivial or urgent two cents of his own.

The floor rotated, regular as subway stops and with amazing equanimity on the part of all concerned; for each Paideian knew that on each round of every topic or subtopic or even point of information, the floor would rotate to his chair and he would be granted as long as he needed or wanted, to say what was his to say. The only chairs onto which the floor did not devolve were the two untenanted chairs, one at either end, left vacant years ago by the untimely demise of two unhappily childless members; childless, at least, as far as Paideia was concerned, for these men's sons had not cared to join, nor, since that preference was established, had been referred to as extant by any voice in any gathering of the members of the Paideia Society.

At the regularly scheduled meeting following the death of a

member, the sad truth was silently announced to all by the draping of his folding chair with a single modest streamer of black
crepe next to his Paideia tie. The vote was invariably unanimous
to offer the tie and the vacant seat to his firstborn son. The offer
was made as soon as humanly possible, by a committee of two
Paideians who knew they would find the son at the house where
shivah was being sat for the deceased. The offer, moreover, was
made once only; for there was no place in Paideia for halfhearted
offspring of charter members: better a perpetually vacant chair
than a new generation of Paideians who might, when they attained
a majority, turn Paideia into a drinking or partying fraternity. Better the eventual extinction of the Society altogether than a single
member who hadn't been waiting, patiently and with awe, his whole
adult life for the moment when fresh grief would be mitigated by
the solemn pride of assuming his primogenitally rightful spot in
Paideia. 'Better naked bread than rancid *shmalts'* was a motto
accepted without question, to a man, among Paideians.

Theo's extreme reaction to his one and only son's death is perhaps understandable in light of Paideia's strict structure of descent
and order of ascendancy. The son of a dead Paideian father was
assuaged by assumption of his chair; but the Paideian father of a
dead son had no such salve for his wound, into which instead was
rubbed the salt of knowing that his chair would be vacant in per-
petuity, moved to the far end of the ellipse so that those who were
still alive and hard-of-hearing might be more closely grouped. There
was absolutely no provision in Paideia for a chair to descend to
the distaff, let alone the in-law distaff. There was, moreover, not
even the hint of a Paideia Women's Auxiliary; though some of the
remaining wives enjoyed the pleasure of one another's acquaintance, this was quite apart from any Societal doings. Paideian wives
were ideally, and by another unwritten rule, relegated to the role
of sustaining aging mates, keeping track of cholesterol, nursing
stiff limbs, even rubbing wrists (as Molly had) like mad when a
Paideian heart attacked; keeping husbands alive and functional
was their function, as far as Paideia was concerned. Theo's own
Molly had done a splendid job as long as she herself survived, had
kept Theo in fact so well fed and intact that the intertia of his
Molly-coddled vitality had continued, with a little assist from the
white plastic box, to sustain him, breathing and digesting blithely
on and exchanging fifteen additional years of views beyond her
own demise. She was the very model of the Paideian helpmeet.

Small wonder, then, that Theo, with Molly as his standard of comparison, mustered not much respect or patience for a wife who'd allowed her husband, and furthermore his son, to expire at an early and unforeseen age. Never mind that the prostate was diseased and that, in the attempt to remove it, a prominent specialist had severed a bleeder or two; never mind that there was nothing, in all good conscience, his daughter-in-law could have done; never mind that she had her own reasons for wishing, at least as fervently as Theo possibly could, her husband would survive; never mind that, traditionally, grief at a well-loved husband's loss is recognized as commensurate to that of a bereaved parent: most bereaved parents haven't Theo's urgent good reason for mourning the loss of a son, and most wives, however loving, haven't a chair in Paideia to keep husbands alive for, a chair now consigned to eternal limbo, toward which murky destination, for all Theo cared in his amplified grief, the chair could transport his daughter-in-law and little Laurence, his only blood survivor.

Theo had never known for sure that his son would have entered Paideia on his death. Devotion to the Society was not something to be preached or inculcated: it appeared in a son at the crucial moment or it did not; there would have been no wheedling or coaxing. And while his son lived, Theo had reason to doubt his son's acceptance of the legacy; had he not, after all, disdaining his rightful place as cravateer by Theo's side, upped and emigrated to, of all places, Rhode Island? Theo had no reason to believe a change of heart might bring him back to Fordham and Paideia. But once his son was dead and gone, such doubts quickly vanished from Theo's mind: of course his son would never have moved, if not for that woman—'dot voomin'—that woman who couldn't keep a spouse alive till the time came for him to see straight, return, take over Theo's Ties, and host the monthly meeting from the folding chair at the endpoint of the short axis of the ellipse. Of course, had she succeeded in her proper wifely function of dying before her mate, he *would* have returned, a prodigal son, that Theo might have slain the fatted bolt of watered silk and proudly sewn and painted the legacy that would then lie waiting in the safest keeping for his own departure: his son's Paideia tie. Of course, then, if not for that woman, Theo might have died content in the knowledge that his business, and his status as host of Paideia, would live on through his son and his son's son after him: Laurence, who would, as his grandfather had done before him, revert to his proper name, Papyrushchka, and devote himself to the exemplary haberdashing of New York necks and the gracious filling of Paideia's monthly pipes and glasses with only the finest latakia and imported shnapps.

Toward Laurence, last seen by him as a bright but weakling ten-year-old, Theo felt a soulful tug, sentiments mellowed as they never could or would toward his disgraced mother. But to seek out Laurence any way but through his mother seemed impossible; and to reestablish contact after such abrupt truncation and so many intervening years ran counter to Theo's pride as well as his common sense. And saddest and most definitive in determining Theo's failure to attempt to locate the grandson he yearned more strongly with each passing year to locate, a sticky Paideian problem: there was, in all Paideiana, no precedent for offering a member's chair to any but the firstborn son—a hard, a fast, an unbreached tradition—and Theo knew, as host, he would put fellow Paideians in a statutory bind by requesting special dispensation; a rule for the nonce and his personal satisfaction might seem crassly like reimbursement for the gallons and pounds of liquor and tobacco. Moreover, Theo had even less reason to think that Laurence would show the necessarily thoroughgoing interest, nay devotion, to Paideia than to think his lost son would have recanted and returned. Nor could he ask for a special ruling on the case without knowing Laurence would show such devotion. Nor could he contact Laurence without offering him such a dispensation in return for asking the boy—how old *would* he be now?—to forsake his worthless mother and his chosen career, which, whatever it may be, was most likely not hand-painting ties.

Some time ago—was it months now or over a year?—a smallish envelope the color of squirrels' tails in winter had arrived. When Theo saw the Providence postmark, his rage at the wife who had allowed her husband to perish welled up, and he discarded the letter without opening it. With some remorse, he later realized that it might have come from the son and not the mother; and he came, in gradual stages, as close as reaching down from the shelf in the public library the Providence phone book, feeling the time had come to contact the son, worthless mother or no; but he replaced the floppy book unopened, stymied by spleen at the thought of calling the detestable woman. Had he gone a step further, he would have found a Paprika, Laurence, separated finally from the mother from whom he had dangled, so separate that even the phone company listed him on his own. Had he gone yet a step further, he'd have found, as Irene once found, that the only Paprika in Providence was disconnected.

Laurence and Gretchen: two late risers in blowsy juxtaposition. Long before any other part could get a rise out of him, Laurence's bladder pressed in its repletion lightly against his prostate, with the result that first his most sensitive part and then all of him rose and sleepwalked to the bathroom for relief. Such an excursion put Laurence in small danger of waking irrevocably up, and he looked vaguely forward to resuming the extension of sleep he granted himself. Balancing like a bowling pin wondering whether to drop, he stood waiting for things to calm down sufficiently for water to be made, when suddenly he heard from the other room a jarring knock at Gretchen's door—three strenuous metallic raps. He jumped and immediately dismissed thoughts of the Gestapo, which were instantly succeeded by other thoughts: an ancient lover, shrink back from Providence to avenge a bum steer, intern to expand vocabulary, trombonist to slide back into her life? And would she think to cover anything before answering? They were in the City, after all; it could be anybody. One blessing at least from the startle: his member withered, then disgorged a lemony arc. He did not flush, but listened, heard two bolts, then a chain, undone, and the massive metal portal opened like a castle gate.

Awake and alert as something small that lives in woods: where was he? Could there be someone now in Gretchen's loft who shouldn't hear his flush? If worse came to worst and the knocker was hostile, better to keep himself secret; if there was to be a fight, surprise would be his only advantage. Paranoia, that. Should he emerge nonchalantly, despite nudity and ignorance of whom the exposure would regale, scandalize, or incite? Should he, cowering on tiny cold tiles amid porcelain fixtures and frosted glass, wait word from Gretchen? He felt like an adulterer in an old joke—'What are you doing here?' 'Everybody has to be somewhere'—realized that of course he *was* an adulterer, but knew it would not be Irene's knock he had heard. An absurd situation: trapped like a rat in your lover's privy, *sans* apparel, *sans* inkling of whom you were hiding from, or whether. Amazing, really, how small a change in circumstances could make you feel again eight years old, sitting on the stairs out of sight and listening in on adult conversation, fearful and illicit. And of course the question to which Laurence was all too susceptible: *was* he illicit, was he contraband? If he'd found refuge, why should he still feel like a refugee? Though somewhat alien, he was not significantly illegal. For heaven's sake, this woman was carrying his child!

He manfully flushed and donned, with some confusion as to the proper usage of silk strips apparently intended for closure, Gretchen's brightly ideographic kimono that hung on the door. He took a deep breath and strode as purposefully and naturally as he could out, to the great amusement of Gretchen, who had just dismissed her caller and climbed back into bed, where they had less trouble undoing the silken strips than Laurence had had doing them up. When they finished, she explained how she had tried to decline but her friend had insisted and she had finally agreed.

So that evening Gretchen Barron, reluctant possessor of a condition that reminded her not a little of the general periodical misery of premenstrual blues, mitigated only slightly by a twinge of pride at full-blown fertile and fertilized femaleness, took Laurence Paprika, empahetic nonparticipant in female troubles, to a party—self-conscious debauche vaguely in spite of Ramadan, which was just about then placing its annual curb on various dispensable human appetites throughout the East, the sequel to an infamous soirée earlier in the year that had flown in the face of Lent—at the uptown apartment of one of her more successfully musical friends: doorman ('Gretchen Barron and friend for 5-C'), view of the river, very classy; bouillabaisse with actual fins and heads afloat, cold sesame noodles with matchstick cukes, various colorful and pungent dips, talk of a roasted lamb to come, though where one roasted a lamb in such a dwelling was beyond Laurence, open bar in a crowded other room, smoke of several sorts and white powders making the rounds like confectioner's sugar, rolling surf of chat and laughs and party voices that treated every topic as startling audible from the other room, where Gretchen Barron and friend for 5-C now headed.

Once again, he found the traffic distressing as he balanced tentative soup and gingerly noodles in two disposable vessels in one hand, mineral water and lime wedge in the other, and tried to understand how to keep these items intact in the crowd, let alone ingest them. He found that he could only with difficulty refrain from hanging on Gretchen's arm, an accessory like the massive pocketbook slung over her other shoulder; if not for the tipsy edibles, he would have literally gripped her. As it was, he followed her about like a police tail, eyes nervously searching her out when the crowd intervened.

They were almost all musicians: those who weren't declared as much by hanging on the arms of those who were. Laurence tried to gauge, by highly developed forearms or embouchures, who played what, since their persiflage afforded little in the way of clues: these music-makers were damned if they were going to talk shop; instead, the talk was, mostly, of Literature.

'But these neonaturalists are all alike. Sure, I want to fuck my mother as much as the next guy, but at least I have the decency to keep it to myself.'

'It's based on a principle of entropy, stunning really, perhaps as far as formal experimentation has yet taken us. The pages get larger until the midpoint—computed by number of characters, including spaces!—and then they get smaller. The paper reacts to human perspiration by disintegrating, I suspect to make the point that no two people can ever read the same book. It's the death of reread-ing; just the *idea*, really, is worth the price.'

'It's just another off-color chunk of what Dostoyevski hath wrought, as far as I can see, cut off by the sphincter of literary history and incessantly plopped in the laps of reluctant readers, who inherit the unappetizing task of cleaning up. They should publish this stuff in airtight boxes, with a little shovel stapled out-side as a warning.'

'But can you really *read* Dostoyevski? With pleasure, I mean?'

Some of the talk, though, was of Art.

Yes, the symbology of Van Goghian colors was so significant, Laurence had to agree; a mistake, since he was then treated to the inside story that, for Van Gogh, yellow represented the loving sun; red, the passion of blood; blue, the serene or threatening sea (or, by reflective implication, the serene or threatening sky); green, organic nature; brown, decay and the cloacal earth; black, night and, by analogy, death. Had he ever noticed that Van Gogh never employed white? Never? Never ever. No, he hadn't noticed, but professed to be enlightened, nodding in phase with his edifier.

A man who played synthesizer interposed: the thing was, it was all wavelengths. Sooner or later, it all boiled down to wavelengths. Colors weren't colors any more than notes were notes. It was all just wavelengths. Even this talk they were having right now: wave-lengths!

A percussionist on a toot: 'Ever wonder what Cézanne did with the leftovers? Man, that dude must of gone through enough apples to keep the whole damn AMA away. At least those old Dutch dudes had a more balanced diet. Christ, apples up the wazoo!'

Laurence scanned for Gretchen, but had lost sight of her back in the midst of the Van Gogh nods, and presumed she'd returned to the bouillabaisse room. On the way, he encountered a knot of males in animated disagreement. A glutenous reed man, who looked like bread dough on its second rising and whose tweedy clothes had an air of crockery about them, was proclaiming, not surprisingly, that his semen smelled for all the world like active yeast. 'No really,' he insisted, like the recipient of a vision, 'like yeast!' A concert pianist begged to differ: his smelled like Clorox bleach, no more no less. A tall black bassist with the calm voice of a seasoned bedside manner claimed his was odorless, colorless, tasteless, and anyone whose wasn't should have himself checked for social diseases.

Gretchen wasn't in the kitchen, and Laurence quickly gobbled noodles, sipped soup, and set off with only his drink to locate her. Back in the larger room, two twelve-tonians were exuberantly developing the idea that ontology recapitulates philology. A high countertenor was declaiming on the inverse relation of the names Lipschitz and Butkus. Laurence was accosted by a discussion of Film.

'Daringly uncontrived . . . movingly contingent . . . flatly three-dimensional . . . wrenchingly ambiguous . . . mordantly filmic.'

Mordantly filmic? Where was Gretchen? She found him, and he looked to see whether she shared or sensed his discomfort. She did and could. 'I had to get away from the other end of the room. The synthesizer fellow, the one with the wavelengths? He used to play trombone. He's the one I told you about. After Crickenberger. Switched to Moog. I'd rather not talk to him.'

Laurence felt a not totally pleasureless chill. The trombone man he'd conjured up in Gretchen's bathroom this morning, here in this room tonight. As he and Irene had surrendered virginity to one another, he'd of course never been in a position to spot a former lover of hers. Seeing this one of Gretchen's made him feel a piquant mixture of competitive, surly, proud, and disappointed. He wanted to stare, but Gretchen, serious about slipping away, was leading him into a bedroom, where they joined a conversation already in progress, involving an older man of striking aspect and a younger woman with dainty, jagged teeth. This conversation was quiet, an oasis, it seemed to Laurence, of sanity. These people talked about music, and he was shocked at what a solace that was to him. Even more shocked by the manner in which Gretchen introduced him.

'Laurence plays saxophone,' she said, and the old man's brows shot up in what may have been disapproval. With a telling look that seemed to appease him, 'Tastefully,' she added.

What a relief polite and vacuous small talk seemed after impolite and vacuous discussion of the arts. The *tête-à-tête* on which they'd intruded had apparently not been saxophonic, and the subject was changed to accommodate newcomers: weather, crosstown buses, parking regulations, dog droppings—oh, blessedly pretensionless topics! It occurred to Laurence that just by looking, these two could tell he didn't profess musicality, could divine, as he had tried to, a party's instrumentality. Yet they were being friendly enough, not the way you'd treat a supposed impostor, and indeed after half an hour or so—during which Laurence thought, in fact, very little about buses or droppings and a good deal about saxophones, synthesizers, and Gretchen, who having deposited him securely in less egregious company had once again wandered off— the older man stopped the chitchat short with an unexpected proposition.

'Young man, I should like to lunch with you. Tomorrow, if convenient.'

'Surely,' said Laurence, annoyed with himself for chameleoning into his interlocutor's diction.

A place and a time were proposed and accepted, and the old man seemed then finished with Laurence, just when the latter, thinking to find here, if anywhere, a sympathetic audience for the kid with the homemade vibes, had been about to launch anecdotally into the details.

'Young man, if as I seem to gather you are some way attached to the charming Miss Barron, I suggest that you bundle her off, and away with the both of you, for she verges at this moment on behavior not at all charming, and as I have had the misfortune to witness her previously under similar circumstances, I assure you she will highly value your quitting the premises with herself in tow.'

The man had an accent not quite British, having clearly learned his English in books. He pointed a very long finger, graceful in a way no other part of his anatomy was, over Laurence's shoulder toward the other room, where Gretchen, transformed, was rubbing more than elbows with the Moog-musician she'd professed half an hour ago to wish to avoid. She looked clumsy, rasping, vampish, erratic, distinctly unGretchenlike.

'What in the world?' asked Laurence aloud, though he thought he was addressing himself.

'I assure you, young man, there are half a dozen, at least, substances in circulation at this gathering capable of producing such alterations in aspect and behavior. I assure you, also, that we have scarcely a moment to lose, unless you wish an untoward scene.'

The bookish idiom and not quite placeable accent that had previously enticed Laurence now irritated, as did the 'young man' and the cocksure condescension of the man. But even if he was right, Laurence hardly knew what to do. Was Gretchen making moves for the trombonist that was, or unable to repulse his moves for her? Had he, Laurence, in any case proprietary rights over Gretchen? Had he a duty to protect her from herself? Could he sweep her away in a leading-man gesture? Did she want him to, as the enticing and irritating old man suggested? On what authority could a false musician intervene in an encounter, however distasteful to witness, between two old friends? Her own good? Gretchen didn't look at all like Gretchen; she was flushed—a startling change—and woozy, and Laurence had just about determined to do something—but what?—when the old man, apparently as irritable as irritating, addressed him again.

'Sir, you are hesitating.'

Sir? Only functionaries, part of whose job it was, had called him that before. The old man clutched him with lengthy fingers and all but dragged him toward Gretchen with a flustered exhale of exasperation at the younger generation. As they two-stepped across the floor, he hissed through his teeth, 'For God's sake, man, get her out of here!' But Laurence stood a foot from her, still stymied before her normal complexion and abnormal deportment.

The prompter assumed an unbidden and unconferred proxy from paralyzed Laurence. Ignoring the quondam trombonist entirely, he urgently confronted unnaturally colorful Gretchen.

'My dear, you are doing what you don't wish to do, and have no doubt been saying what you have no intention of saying. Gretchen, you are really beyond the pale. Why don't you just go home now with your nice young man. Here, I've brought him to you.'

He handed her over to Laurence, who supported her uncertainly while her self-appointed protector tucked, dusted, and plumped her like a throw pillow that had fallen off a couch onto a maculate floor. The Moog man rolled his eyes, heaved a heavy breath, and looked to Gretchen to declare her intention.

She felt weighty and rubbery in Laurence's arms. She bent over backwards and looked up at him. He thought perhaps he should try to smile, but feared his expression evinced horror instead. Gretchen started sobbing with a choking helplessness that frightened him and made him think the old man knew whereof he spoke.

'Oh Laurence,' she gurgled pathetically, 'can't you get me the hell away from here?'

Authorized now from her own lips, he hesitated no longer, but shooting a look both accusatory and apologetic at the younger, a look both grateful and apologetic at the older man, he hustled her out and down, past the doorman with his years of experience at behaving as if nothing whatsoever were taking place. He splurged on a cab without thinking twice. The ride was longish and thoroughly silent. Gretchen fell quickly into sleep, a tot after a tantrum, while Laurence pondered propriety and proprietariness and appropriation and appropriateness and the young woman he was caring for tonight and the old man he might be lunching with tomorrow.

He had to wake her when they reached home; a woman's worth of dead weight was more, he feared, than he could lug, and he had a horror of dropping her. He dreaded, too, waking her—what new Gretchen in what tone of contempt or recrimination would he be face to face with?—but saw no alternative.

Her recriminations were self-directed and almost casual-sounding. Her tongue was thick with tears and sleep and—Laurence now knew the old man had been right—whatever drug she had used. He made coffee while she drawled remorse and rue and self-reproach. As she sobered, less gradually than she would from alcohol, quickly enough in fact to refuse coffee on the grounds of pregnancy, her reproach shifted to the former trombonist, for taking advantage of the weakened state of a woman, disoriented by the drug, who wanted to be taken advantage of, then to Laurence himself: 'Obvious that I wanted to; in which case, the thing for you to do was to get me the devil out of there and take advantage of me yourself. Thank God Gerry was there.'

Laurence had a few things to say in defense of the failure of his position to make anything obvious, and a few things to ask regarding Gretchen's delicate condition and Gerry and substance abuse and advantage-taking. But Gretchen, now lucid, was also drained, and he remembered her having once refrained from grilling him at an inopportune moment. He gently undressed and put to sleep Gretchen and himself.

Gretchen woke fuzzy but needy. She rolled him over and took advantage of the same bladder that had pressed against the same prostate the previous morning. In the process, Laurence awoke and enjoyed, bouncing her back against the old mattress till she bottomed out like a jalopy in need of shocks. When they were both happy, he wondered whether to say and ask his few things when they were both happy. She decided first, and wondered aloud what had passed between him and Gerry at the party.

'He asked me to lunch!' yelped Laurence, checking the time. He had about ten minutes to get out of the house.

'He wants you to mow for him,' said Gretchen casually as he jumped out of bed.

'Mow? How do you know? What do you mean? Who is he?'

'Mowing is always the job he offers youngsters he's taken with.'

'Taken with?' stretching socks up calves.

'Likes. Wants to support. While they get their musical feet on the ground.'

'Feet? Ohmygod, will he ask me to play for him?' buckling a belt.

'Unlikely. He'll probably be content with overpaying you for mowing his estate.'

'Estate?' flapping into a vest inside out.

'Don't you know who he is?'

'No. Mow? Feet? Estate? Who?' removing the vest.

'You really don't know?'

'Clearly not, Gretchen,' reversing the vest, annoyed once again with her rhetorical questions.

'Listen, Laurence, you're about to be requested to trim the flora of Geripold Dempler.'

Vest in place, heading for the bathroom: 'Geriwhat who? Who *is* he, Gretchen?'

'When's lunch?'

'Any minute.'

'It's a long story. I'll tell you when you get back.'

'Great. Beautiful. Wonderful. Lovely. I've got to go. I hope you'll tell me a few other things when I get back, too. Terrific. Good.'

'Bye.'

If not so rushed, Laurence would have been lumbered with
doubts. There was a good chance the man wouldn't show up; he
had, after all, witnessed with growing dismay Laurence's helpless
inaction the night before. He had had to take Laurence by the arm
and hand Gretchen over to him. If 'taken with' Laurence when he
proposed lunch, he certainly wasn't fifteen minutes later. On the
subway Laurence was still late but not rushed, sitting still in the
screaming box and thinking: Mow? Musical feet? (Laurence's
weren't even wet, had desiccated years ago.) Estate? (As far as he
knew, there were no estates in Manhattan.) Was this all a ruse?
Was he a butt?

Laurence was still a novice enough urbanite—would he ever
transcend the status?—to feel somewhat disjointed by entering
midtown establishments that didn't feel like midtown, cut off by
walls from street noise and huddling masses. And as if he weren't
disjointed enough this day, the restaurant where he was to meet
the man was in what is called the heart of midtown; but he'd never
have guessed its cardiac locale from the inside.

Four garish South Seaish totemish poles, rough-hewn and acry-
licked, cornered the space; perhaps it had been Polynesian before
going Japanese. For East Coasters, the associations were fuzzily
close enough: it sufficed that the decor was exotic, and the poles
remained, heedlessly sustaining the roof under new management.
Waiting was done in pastel chiffon kimonos, so that the staff, no
doubt attractive enough under all that drapery, resembled a band
of jumbo shrimp chips.

All the other patrons were suited and coated, and the black-tied
host looked askance at Laurence, merely vested; but he was
expected, and ushered to Dempler, where he started to sputter.

'Last night . . . you were absolutely . . . Gretchen . . . if I had
. . .'

'I should much prefer to dispense with any consideration of yes-
terevening, young man.'

'Laurence,' said Laurence.

'Laurence, then. And you may call me Gerry,' though Laurence
had doubts he could bring himself to.

Dempler had a voice . . . if a soft-boiled egg could have a voice,
that would be the voice Dempler had. He ordered something teri-
yaki, and Laurence, avoiding red meat and green peppers, requested

a sushi-sashimi platter. A pastel shrimp chip brought damp white washcloths, slightly above body temperature, and Dempler swabbed not only hands but forehead, neck, and postauricular flesh; shivers of hair on the cloth bespoke recent tonsure.

'My boy,' said Dempler in his half-runny underdone voice over soyish broth with a single brothlogged leaf sunk clear to the bottom, 'I was given to understand that you are a musician. Be so kind as to remind me of what species.'

'Sax,' said Laurence, adding politely, 'ophone.'

Dempler cleared his throat of some albumenic effluvia. He literally said, 'Ahem,' as if it were an utterance of some semantic import. Under the circumstances, in fact, it was. 'Saxophone is somewhat irregular. And you are, currently, shall I say, at loose ends?'

To say the least, thought Laurence, nodding.

'You transpose, of course?'

'Yes,' said Laurence slowly, 'slowly.'

'European or American system?'

Laurence hadn't known more than one existed. He guessed American.

'That, my boy . . . forgive me, Laurence . . . is a shame.'

Solid food arrived, Dempler's on thick white restaurant ware abraded around the edges like an emery board, Laurence's on a pedestalled oblong. Chopsticks in paper sheaths, needing to be separated like wishbones, splintering when they were, and tiny porcelain trays cast in bamboo-shoot shapes, containing tiny amounts of sauces, curly pink sheets of pickled something, dangerous green mustard. Laurence stared at deceptive fish, squid, eel, tuliped, rolled, pinked, escalloped, topiaried, espaliered. Vividly tinted polymerish flesh inlaid in contrasting cross-sectioned fish, rice, seaweed, like jewelry, candy, glass beads, a miniature rock garden of slippery tissues arranged in the enamelly découpage of multiplex *maki*.

Dempler fished a chubby, ancient tortoiseshell fountain pen and a pocket-sized pad of staff paper from inside his jacket and sketched a dozen clefs, many identical but placed variously on the lines. Every Good Boy Deserves Fun, thought Laurence.

'The *soi-disant* American system of tranposition relies on clumsy, distracting rote memory of intervals. In keeping with the American passion for illiteracy, it employs a minimum of clef structures. Whereas the European system, which is transposition properly so called, wisely requires that its practitioner become fluent in the twelve clefs that collectively exhaust the possibilities of suboctavic displacement. Do I make myself clear?'

He did by the end of lunch, and Laurence was not unimpressed with the idea of fluency in a dozen distinct musical languages; it made him think of the United Nations. As Dempler polished off his disquisition and his lunch, he modulated to the key Gretchen had predicted.

'Twelve Clefs, by the way, is the name of my estate. In Riverdale, Laurence, which is part of the Bronx. Well, then, can you mow a lawn?'

A final bite of fish masquerading as something else slid smooth against Laurence's esophagus, splitting the difference, as each bite had, between pleasure and revulsion. A bit prematurely—he'd not quite succeeded in swallowing—'Yes,' said Laurence, then coughed convulsively and had a moment of panic, envisioning Heimlich maneuvers.

Dempler, less *unheimlich* himself now, mentioned a sum of money, three days of the week, an address, a time of day, appropriate footwear, and, his business transacted, was ready to take his leave as abruptly as he had the night before. The bill was paid. Hands shook. Dempler's, in Laurence's, was smooth and moist as sashimi.

History—the whole sociopolitical ball of wax—had always seemed just around the corner: the corner formed by the intersection of Irene's life with everyone else's. The World War—clearly, for every life that had seen it, the central fact, after which all else, even Vietnam they insisted, must be anticlimax—was no fact at all for Irene, who had come on the scene just as the political, moral, and psychological dust was settling. And, in a word, she resented it. The War created such a gap between her and her parents' generation; it was what she had missed and would never understand. War and Depression made her life pale by comparison, and as pubescent athletes did to Laurence, made her small and inauthentic. These events, conspicuous in their absence, made her inconspicuous in her presence.

The enthusiasm with which Irene participated at an early age in practice air raids—the repeated conviction that the Russians were smart enough to drop something right after the rehearsal, when everyone would think it a false alarm or equipment mal-function—she now understood as an odd form of wishful think-ing: the perverse yearning that her life might contain something as catastrophic, as purely big, as the lives directly adjoining hers.

Sobering like a thought, Irene again examined in minutest detail Donna's face, so vulnerable in sleep, every muscle flaccid, its depths as unguarded as a shallow puddle when a cloud passes in front of the sun. Even the pathetic, translucent mask the face had borne in its cups was dropped, and Donna was as exposed as a bowl of consommé.

Irene half-held a belief throughout childhood that everything—the world, the people who peopled it, the schools that taught it, the products it consumed, the effluvia it gave off—everything out-side of herself constituted an elaborate game, a ritual drama staged for her diversion. Her parents were actors hired to play parents. Her classmates were midgets hired to play classmates. Rocks were rocks hired to play rocks. The world was a hoax; its purpose, to fool her into thinking it other than hoax.

Her life, then, was a test. To expose the hoax would be to pass the test. But her life consisted precisely of being fooled. If the hoax were exposed, the jig would be up, and her life—her turn to be toyed with—would be up as well. Thus her suspicions must be communicated to no one. She opened doors with trepidation, for fear of catching actors out of character, thus committing inadver-tent suicide. The triumph of her mind would be the utter defeat of her and the end of life as she knew it. The actors were of course all consummate, but if she through no fault of her own or theirs caught them out, happened upon them lounging in green-room disarray, she would really only be hurting herself, as the actresses hired to play teachers used to say to the actors hired to play cheat-ing students.

Would she then become herself an actress, devoted to the illu-sionment of some other novice mortal? What fate awaited those perspicacious enough to denude the world of artifice? Irene didn't know, nor particularly wish to. But if indeed that fate meant tak-ing the boards and pulling the ontological wool over someone else's eyes, her life as it now hung suspended in a tenuous balance between knowing and acknowledging what she knew would be good practice for what was to come; for it consisted precisely of acting, of disingenuously playing the ingenue and not letting on that the entire cosmic illusion was to her, perhaps, transparent.

'Perhaps,' because she could never be certain, without throwing in the towel of her suspicions and more likely than not thereby giving up the ghost, that the ruse through which she claimed to see was more than a self-induced delusion—of grandeur, persecution, or whatever. And the subtle dilemma on whose razor edge her childhood was thus pendant had probably as much as anything else to do with her chronic difficulty in deciding what exactly it meant to behave like a human being, which with help from her mother—or the actress who played her mother?—she was at pains to decide.

Irene, in short, was an anxious child, never sure whether she knew what she knew, merely suspected what she suspected, or merer still, fancied what she fancied. That corner history was just around became a busy junction where perpendicular apperceptions whizzed so fast that to attempt a crossing was to invite a fatal collision.

This mildly pathological expression of youthful egocentrism Irene now understood as a reaction to her perceived egoperipheralism. The illusion that all the world was a stage she saw as a defensive response to the fact of having missed the first two acts. Seeing Donna so unmasked, Irene had a rueful smirk for her own former masks and trappings. Surely adult Donna had more cause to suspect extravagant staging and melodrama plotting than child Irene had ever had. And what had adult Irene gained, after all, by vocally doubting her husband's hardly less plausible aetiology?

Now picture Laurence guided by a dour underling to, and abandoned in the midst of, a small complex of sheds and outbuildings. Picture Laurence on the broad estate of the magnanimous squire Gretchen has in the meantime identified as a virtually mythic musical mogul: 'Pianist, then composer, then conductor,' she thumbnailed him, 'and tops at each!' Picture Laurence fitted out with a riding mower for large expanses, a pushing mower or two for tightly planted corridors, an edger for edges, a hedger for hedges, gas cans, oil cans, funnels, spouts, pruners, clippers, spreaders, sprinklers, hoses, nozzles, rakes, grass bags, weed tweezers, aerators, visors, gloves, and a complete line of assorted chemical encouragers and discouragers of respectively domestic and alien botanical development; Laurence, looking for all the world like a semiglossy ad for Grogreen Lawn and Garden Centres

(Riverdale, Ossining, Mattituck); Laurence, feeling all in all like a one-man army mobilized for a major offensive, or the proprietor of some kinky boutique specializing in horticultural polymorphisms hitherto unimagined; Laurence, in conclusion, surveying private landscape in all directions and pondering, with humble solemnity, with almost reverence, where to start.

The idea of so very much lawn had never occurred. Amidst clicking chopsticks and shuffling shrimp chips, Dempler had asked, 'Can you mow a lawn?' Laurence had mown a few—microscopic compared to this—in adolescence, so dared say he could. And in fact, he *could*—who couldn't?—but this job more resembled greenskeeping a links. Indeed, he would soon learn that six holes of pitch-and-putt accounted—what with greens and fairways, six of one, half a dozen of the other, rough but not too immodestly rough, tees to be cropped to civilized tee length, bunkers to be raked to unruffled bunker smoothness, doglegs to be sculpted as shapely as a poodle's—for a full third of his three-day work week at Twelve Clefs.

Laurence stared, a translucent eyeball, at a park of municipal proportions. What could anyone disinclined to touch football do with so expansive a backyard? The sheer multiplicity of blades was dizzying: landscape spun, Laurence teetered oh! far more precariously than he had in Gretchen's bathroom, a bowling pin once again, grazed and unsure whether to fall for a strike or leave a tough spare. He had for a moment a rotary-sprinkler's-eye view of the Horticultural Sublime. Regaining his balance then, he dropped everything and made for the mansion to tender his premature and overwhelmed resignation.

Beyond a welter of timelessly well-appointed chambers, in an alcove designated for private dining on an intimate scale, Laurence finally located his patron at demure midmorning tea with a woman whom, had he followed Dempler's career in glossy magazines, he would surely have recognized as Astrida Äussterschucher. Instead, she appeared to him, as Dempler himself unusually had, a stranger, and a queer-looking one at that. Picture Laurence, then, faced with a couple of queer-looking strangers and, knowing by now who one of them, at least, was, taking a closer look.

Dempler's appearance was no less remarkable than was meet. A high forehead marked off with five more or less parallel creases, like a paragraph marked for editorial excision or a staff hung out as professional shingle, announcing a source of music. The jaw fitted out with so many jowls and chins so equitably arranged that it resembled nothing so much as a distant hillside terraced for cultivation; a well-pruned moustache adorned a narrow, convex upper lip like an ornamental hedge atop the hillside furrowed for planting. A neck emerged superfluously from a collar like a cap from a mushroom stem. Ears were small and delicately whorled, contrasting with the neck's lavish, floral softness. The nose was too small, and the eyes, and mouth, as if all these features had been extracted from some more modest head and grafted into and onto this more billowy silhouette. The complexion pinker than a baby's, possibly as irritable, then dull beige in shifting light. What hair there was, ignored in proper genius fashion. Arms and legs softly stunted, the former ending in digits whose extraordinary extension was tempered only by a slight pudginess and whose genteel delicacy, which might have saved the entire figure from ludicrousness, was diluted by a somewhat liquid hint of the palsy. A trunk whose rotundity, too firmly ripe to qualify as flab, might have done, in waistcoat and tails, as a model for 'Phiz' completed a person that could have emerged, with much less fuss, from the fluent and perspicuous pen of 'Boz.' It was a body that seemed to squirm in its tight-fitting garments, a face set in motion from time to time by random tics, especially about the eyes, so that one might wonder how meaningly or with regard to what one was being winked at. What with squirms and tics, Dempler gave the impression of a man either discomfited in the extreme or with secrets to tell: a man it would be equally easy, were he not renowned, to dismiss as alienating or ingratiating.

Laurence was amazed at how much he saw in the man, now no longer merely the self-appointed guardian of Gretchen or mysterious lunchmate. How could he not have seen the man was a genius? Was the woman one, too? She looked odd enough: hair, of a quantity that defied estimation, done up behind in an impossibly poised bob that seemed, like a small sloop under full sail in a headwind, ever striving to tumble forward, but in far greater danger of toppling aft; maquillage, prodigious, with enough cosmetics to initiate a small finishing school into the decorative arts of womanhood caking and positively hiding her face, affording only a blatantly general hint as to the exact locale of human features; habiliments, as jealous as the makeup, protecting from view any semblance of a nature-born form, substituting an anachronistic illustrator's conception of the feminine, bulged and stuffed, prodded and corseted into the sort of caricature that might be thought necessary onstage to suggest, to the distant reaches of a third balcony, a physique. She was literally a great deal larger than life: overpainted, overclothed, a figure from a costume ball in a century of more mandatory plumping. Working counter to the idea of bejewelled and gracious surplus, however, was a certain effect of anatomical insufficiency that Laurence realized emanated from her left arm. This extremity, though only an inch or two shorter than its opposite number, dangled as a small girl's legs might from an adult-sized piano bench. Somewhere between hand and shoulder, an ellipsis of limb covered but not disguised by the black embroidered glove altered to mimic the more conventional proportions of the other, not quite symmetrical, arm. Though she clearly possessed a left hand and arm of an almost everyday sort, she struck Laurence as a disconcerting monoplegic. So struck, he momentarily forgot his own near-swoon and his reason for interrupting this private repast *à deux*.

The staff on Dempler's forehead contracted, his right eye did something like winking, and he made introductions. 'Madame Äussterschucher, Laurence; Laurence, Madame Äussterschucher. Laurence is here to do the mowing,' he said, implying a clear dichotomy between that task and what Laurence was doing at the moment. Madame dipped her chin an inch and raised it again.

'Madame,' said Laurence, dipping more than his chin. 'Sir,' he said, turning to Dempler.

'Gerry.'

'Yes. I came to tell you that, I'm sorry to interrupt your . . . morning, but that, well, your grounds are very extensive.'

'We,' nodding at Madame, 'are aware of that, Laurence.'

'And that I'm not at all sure.' He hated himself for mimicking a different class of person.

'There are very few things in life of which one may be sure. One does one's best.' This opinion the genius pronounced with an understandable air of impatience at the most recent addition to his entourage, but a certain more mysterious undertone made Laurence wonder what he had yet to learn about Dempler's checkered career. Whatever it was, he decided he'd have to learn it from Gretchen.

'I can't,' said Laurence, adding against his will, 'I'm afraid.'

'Of course you can, and under the circumstances it would be absurd not to. I offer you a most generous stipend simply to do to the grass what for some years Madame Äussterschucher did to my thoughts and me.' The allusion was lost on Laurence, who dropped his eyes as if to seek a footnote among the floorboards. Instead of a reference, he received a reprimand of sorts. 'Do get on with it, or you will force the entire staff to delay their luncheon. You are expected at half past one, showered. I detest cunctation.'

Quite mystified as to what his employer detested (besides, as he now pretty firmly suspected, himself), Laurence retraced his steps and found, of course, that he could mow a lawn, even one that seemed as big as all outdoors.

'That,' said Donna, 'forgive me, Irene, is absurd.'

A heck of a thing to say to the person who brought you home and let you use her toothbrush and tucked you in and made sure each and every one of your breaths was present and accounted for through most of a long night; who patiently permitted you to wake up of your own accord and then had grapefruit juice and coffee ready but waited to ask you before deciding on pancakes or eggs or muffins; who then—while making from scratch the finest pancakes she knew how, separate whites beaten to froth with back-to-back forks, throwing in at no added charge unsweetened coconut, poppy seeds, splash of real vanilla extract, pinch of cardamom, and warming the maple syrup and serving the yogurt from china instead of the plastic tub it came in—told you a story maybe not so melodramatic but fully as pertinent to those involved as the one you told her last night in the bar.

'Well, it might be absurd, Donna, but it's not funny.' This in response to a barely suppressed fit of giggles.

'I'm sorry, Irene, he he, he said he, he he, was just dangling, just hang ang ang anging there from his mud mud mother? He he he, he must be out of his my my my mind.'

Irene started crying, and Donna stopped laughing.

'I'm sorry, Irene, I don't really think it's funny, sometimes I just start to laugh lately. Or cry. I don't think it's funny. Those pancakes smell like heaven. Don't pout. I said I was sorry.'

'Well, it's just hard. I didn't believe it either, and he went away, and now I think I was stupid to make an issue of it. I mean, who cares? Except him. He went *away* over it, Donna. Here, the syrup's warm and there's yogurt and jam and butter. I could make more coffee.'

'I could use another cup. Well, when he comes back, you could just humor him. It wouldn't hurt to—'

'Oh Donna, I don't know if he *is* coming back. I don't know where he is or anything. I think he might be in New York, because that's where—'

'You've got to find him, Irene. Find him and tell him you're sorry you doubted him. It's just his pride that—'

'How can you find a person that just—'

'You can. You can call the—'

'Police? How do you think that would make him feel? That I sent the cops after him. Besides, how would they—'

'Bureau of Missing Persons? Here, I'll drip the coffee, you eat your pancakes, they're getting cold, just eat, we'll figure it out, a person can't just—'

'I'll get the coffee, but how *can* we figure it out? It's not like making a decision. Wouldn't you think he'd write? A change-of-address card, even. You know what I'd like to do?'

'Eat your pancakes, I'll get the coffee.'

'You know what I'd like to do?'

'Eat your pancakes, here, the coffee's dripping. The pancakes are really delicious, Irene. I'm sorry I laughed.'

'You know what I'd like?'

'I know it's not funny, but—'

'I'd like to color.'

'Here's the coffee. Color what?'

'Color. You know, color. With crayons. We could color together, like when you were my sitter. Remember? You used to love to color, you even did it with a little kid like me. After you left, I had a sitter named Lucy. I didn't like her. Donna, do you know, I think I had a crush on you or something.'

'Irene, this is really horrible, but you know, I don't remember.'

'I wanted to do everything just like you, you know? Eyebrows and everything. You were my idea of a human being.'

'A human being?'

'A real human being. And later when my parents died, I would think, What would Donna do, what would Donna do?'

'What would Donna do?'

'You. What would *you* do. I thought you'd always know the right thing to do.'

'Ha ha, that's rich, that's a good one all right.' On the instant, full-sized tears went slaloming down her cheeks. Her ravaged, harried, weathered, pitted, aged and aging cheeks.

'Maybe coloring wouldn't help, huh?'

'No ho ho ho,' Donna was weeping, 'coloring wouldn't help at aw haw haul.'

'Laurence had a grandfather. In the Bronx. I think he might have gone to him. They were out of touch since before I knew him. He never answered the wedding invitation. He might be dead. I could call him or something.'

'I think you should. Coloring wouldn't help. I'd better get back to Victor.'

'I dread it,' meaning the phonecall.

'Oh, I'll be okay,' meaning Victor.

'Donna, I'm sorry.'

'For what?'

'You know, everything.'

'It's not your fault.'

'I know. I'm not guilty, I'm sorry.'

'You and me both, kid. We're both sorry. A sorry pair.'

'But I'm glad I found you.'

'Yeah, me too. Listen, thanks for everything. I'm sorry I told you to get lost last night, I thought I wanted to be alone.'

'You don't.'

'I know.'

'Me neither.'

'I know.'

'You know, I thought I was pregnant once, but it was hyst . . . it was wrong. I mean, it seemed to turn out that I wasn't.'

'Irene, he's an M.D.! Let's not talk about it. I've got to get back to Victor.'

'Yeah, I'm sorry, I didn't mean to—'

'I've got to go, Irene. Look, here's my number. I've got yours.'

'Yeah, okay, you know, I'm sorry.'

'I know.'

'You know.'

'I know.'

At quarter past one, Laurence finished hosing the mower's housing down and started doing the same for himself, having

trimmed, if not a full sixth, no less than an eighth of Twelve Clefs.
The entire staff thus gathered with minimal cunctation for a meal
about which one more firmly rooted than he might have been
tempted to write home. The affable staff greeted him pleasantly
enough (just the merest hint of reserve for the latest in a longish
line of transient and disappearing mowers); but it was the meal
that merited note. Hearty but not too hefty, a genuine credit to all
four major food groups, it pleased not only the palate but less
accessible organs as well. Unused as he was to strenuous physical
accomplishment, Laurence savored nutrients like a new invention, welcoming their timely arrival in a way members of the more
sedentary classes rarely can. This reaction set him apart from most
of the staff, whose work, though taxing, took place indoors, and
whose muscles, though not exempt, were far more accustomed to
taxation.

More accustomed, also, to the manifold skills of the talented
household cook, who had nothing if not range. For Maestro and
Madame, she prepared only the most refined gourmet fare, of whose
surplus appetizers Laurence would sometimes encounter appetiz-
ing bits and pieces at half past one. For staff lunches, though, she
chiefly fixed unpretentious and wholesome foods, enhanced from
time to time by a tasty trick or two from the more demanding
dishes she whipped up for those who detested plain food as much
as anything else. Taken by both betters and peers for granted, thus
doubly undersung, she understood better than most the optimum
balance of downhome and upscale, of simplicity and sauce, of meat-
and-potato and *fines herbes*, gut and garnish, fundament and frill.

There's a glass plate reminiscent of ninth-grade biology, and it
seems no matter which way you insert the plastic it's either upside
down or backwards. You wonder what 'fiche' means, is there a
macrofiche, a jumbo fiche, a family-size fiche, or only a micro-
fiche? You can see there's printing on them, but it's *so* small, eight
million stories in the naked city reduced to illegibility, and it's the
damnedest job getting it into the machine right. *Je m'en fiche de
cette fiche*, you think, smugness at recalling high-school French
displacing annoyance with microtechnology. Finally, you get
'PAPAYA-PAPUZINSKI Area Code 212' under the lens, focusing, cuss-
ing, and then you have to learn the dyslexic art of moving the lever
right to left to move the image left to right: *Je m'en foue de cette*

fiche. Papillon, Pappy, Papst, too far, back up, Paprikas, imprtr. Imprimatur? Importer: of course, Paprikas, spices, teas, things like that. The grandpa you seek is imported, imported Paprika, unlisted. Wait: not Manhattan. Back to the fichefile, Bronx, 'PAPERGRAPH-ICS-PARDEE Area Code 212.' *Diable. Peste.* The names that are words stand out to your scanning eyes: Parchment, Paramount, Paragon, Paradise, Papsmear Associates ('See our display ad, Yellow Pages'). No Paprika in the Bronx, imported or domestic. Dead? Unlisted? Too old-fashioned to use a phone? *Bougre. Foutre.* Stalled, sitting here staring into this peepshow box, trying to find Paprika in the Bronx. *Merde.*

Never a homely aging ingenue so stumped by this intractable problem: how to find a husband. Irene can't even find an in-law. The wedding: Aunts Tootie, Snookie, Fluffy, Uncles Benny, Ellie, Julie: 'my mother's side.' But the grandfather with the bad heart never acknowledged the announcement; but to announce they must have had an address; but the list was so long ago discarded. But. But. *But:* the groom wore a *tie,* and the tie bore a *label,* and the label credited a *maker,* and the maker was . . . Grandpa!

Out of the library, walking down Empire, bus at the corner, home again, home again, jiggedy jig. Laurence wore his one and only tie to the wedding, stiff maroon *peau de soie,* hand-painted with a boy in Western gear and an Appaloosa pony: 'Old family ties are the strongest,' he joked as he knotted the silky thing about his collar. 'Grandpa's not here, but his handiwork is. Irene, could you give me a hand here? I never wear these things. I can't get the ends to come out even.' And she gave it a try while he stared at her hair as if it were something you could be in love with, and she had to keep chucking him under the chin to keep it up, and the skinny end had a label sewn onto it, and the label was embroidered in that wonderful way labels are with the name—and the address, the address?—of the grandfather's business.

Into the closet, locate the tie, boy, pony, skinny end, on the back, that gorgeous machine embroidery:

THEO'S TIES
Fordham Rd.
Bronx, New York

Theo's Ties, Fordham Rd., Bronx, New York! Three thrilling amphimacs Irene chants as she waits for the bus. Off at Empire, walk to the library, yellow pages, fishing through fiches: Ties?

Neckwear? Haberdashers? Men's Clothing & Furnishings—Whol
& Mfrs? Men's Clothing & Furnishings—Retail? Ah. Theo's Ties
2386A Fdhm . . . . 552-8273.

Five five two eight two seven three. Area code two one two. One
two one two five five two eight two seven three. The miracle of the
fiches. Let your fingers do the walking.

Bring.
Bring.
Bring.
'Hollow?'
'Hello, is this?' Who? Grandpa? Grandpa-in-law? Mr. Paprika?
Euphoria over the miracle of the fiches had propelled Irene right
to one two one two five five two eight two seven three without
planning how one might present herself under the circumstances.
Hello, Sir, this is the granddaughter you never had? Now don't
get excited in any way, I know you have a bad heart, but I just
thought I'd tell you your grandson hasn't been heard from in a
month and a half? (Come to think, though, you haven't been heard
from in a good deal longer yourself?) Is this the actor hired to play
Laurence's grandfather? This is the actress hired to play his wife?
'Hollow? Hollow? Hiss doos hoo?'
'Is this Theo's Ties?'
'Off causes Tayo's Tice. Fought else you foot get fin callink Tayo's
Tice?'
'Mr. Theo?'
'Tayo spicks fit chew. Naught ah lodge feck tree. Cents you half
colt, dough, ewer fontink to say sumtink.'
'Yes. Mr. Theo. You don't know me.'
'Doos hiss naught ray air indy bee's knees.'
'Yes. But. I'm sorry, your last name is Paprika?'
'Tice hiss lest nem findy bee's knees, Papyrushchka findy men.'
'Mr. Pappyrush—sh—'
'Coal me Tayo.'
'Thank you. Theo,' the tears welling up, 'my name is Irene. I'm
looking for Laurence.'
'Lawrinse hess ah lest nem?'
'Pappy—, Paprika. Laurence Paprika. Your grandson, Theo. I'm
sorry to call you like this. I thought you might know where he is.
Theo. I'm his wife. Irene.'

'Liddel Lawrinse hess ah vie if dot shill lukes fa him?'

'Mr. . . . Theo, I'm sorry, but I don't know where he is, I'm calling from Providence, and I found your number in the phone book.'

'Lung distints?'

'Yes, Rhode Island. I didn't know where else to turn.'

'Red Eyelid? Ewer mare rid fit migrained sin?'

'With Laurence, yes. But he's left and . . . Oh Theo . . .'

'Dun vip, Eyerin fin Red Eyelid. *Loiter koomen tsoorick.* Pippil calm beck.'

'I thought he might have gone to find *you.*'

'Dot fa beck ah pie sin paheps foot naught calm. Eyerin fin Red Eyelid, eye emma knolled men, eye em loose ink my iceheight, in you mecca knolled men *fardraight.*'

'I'm sorry.' I'm *always* sorry; why am I always *sorry?* 'I'm worried about Laurence.' Is that true: I'm worried about Laurence? I'm worried about myself. What is *fardraight?* What am I making an old man?

'*Maydeleh,* yonk leddy, you spick Joosh, you spick Yiddish?'

'No. I'm s—'

'Dun be sawry. No fawn coot spick affray tink.'

A kind old man, an appealing old man, and I'm making him *fardraight.* What is *fardraight?* 'What is *fardraight?*'

'*Farmisht. Fartumelt. Farfufket. Fardraight* hiss kinfused.'

Imagine a language with so many words for confusion. I'm making an old man confused. 'I'm confused myself, I'm afraid. I think Laurence is in New York, but I don't know where.'

'Iss ah bicks itty, Misses Lawrinse, ah lodge moon easy pellet tea.'

'Yes, I know. I thought maybe he would have—'

'No, eye em sawry.'

'You shouldn't be sorry, it's not your fault.'

'Eye set sawry, naught gill tea.'

'Yes, me too,' said Irene. And suddenly, again, alone in Red Eyelid, she was vipping.

Now the way Laurence tackled jobs that were bigger than he was, was this. He started by delineating a portion of the task, not insubstantial, but clearly not the measure of his endurance. He would do that, and that done, he felt a certain satisfaction, less for the amount already done than for the knowledge that it had not exhausted him. On the adrenaline of this satisfaction, he would stake out another portion, smaller than the first but far from piddling. That done, he would eagerly define a third portion and push to complete it, though fatigue would now perhaps be setting in. A fourth, a fifth, each smaller than the last, in a way that recalled golden means, chambered nautili, Fibonacci, pinecones, and youthful wonder that parts could have such interesting relations to wholes. By the time his stamina was depleted, then, he had two sources of gratification: first, that he had established a progression that diminished in a regular and extrapolable manner and convinced him as he wound down that all the work in the world that needed doing was getting done; second, looking back from the weariness that now resulted from doing even the slightest portion of the job, he could affect a complacent surprise that he had done so deceptively much, both more than it seemed in retrospect he could have done and more than it had seemed in prospect he could possibly do.

In earlier days, no task had better suited this method than the carrying of a saxophone to school. It had to be with him for daily rehearsals at school and for nightly practice at home, so twice daily he transported the vinyl-over-plywood case with the then well-kempt instrument inside over the fifteeen-furlong course. Even before the wide spread of molded high-impact plastic, a saxophone case, even one replete with rags, extra reeds, lyre, wax, sheet music and a volume or two of études, was not a particularly weighty object in the overall scheme of things; but as elementary gave way to secondary, there were more books that needed to be carried by a Laurence scarcely less wizened. The handles of saxophone cases, moreover, dictate that the burden of such objects rests largely on the metacarpal joints, which over a distance Laurence found could become stiff or even cramped. At such times Laurence switched hands, shifting books, carried in the crook of an arm, to the side whose fingers needed relief, and the saxophone to the still supple opposite hand. But the more frequently he shifted, the more cramped the fingers of both hands unfairly felt. So Laurence would set himself goals—'I won't shift hands till I reach that stop sign two blocks ahead'—but when the sign had been reached, he would append another lamppost or two into the bargain, thus affording himself a sense of general competence, will, and stamina, as well as saving his fingers from excessive stiffness by resisting the misleading temptation to make life easier by shifting more often. This system of inconsequential self-delusion allowed Laurence to arrive at school in the morning, at home in the afternoon, with a sense of self-possession and manly capability.

Mowing now proved a felicitous discipline—the first in many years—to which to apply the method perfected in lugging the sax. His job was already crudely subdivided when he arrived, into three quite equal allotments of a day's groundskeeping each. At first, these portions made for long days, since the terms of employment demanded that Laurence stay on the job till one day's work was done; and more than once he hosed down the bottom of the mower after dark, stepping blindly into puddles of squinchy, fecal, matted, gasoline-scented grass, squeamish and grumbling and wondering why, of all the things one might find to do in New York, this was the thing he did. As days grew shorter, Laurence naturally sought ways of simultaneously doing the work more efficiently and convincing himself it could be done, and his saxiferous methodology proved an invaluable resource. His program now was so much more complex than that of moving a saxophone from one locale to another that he built on the foundation of sensible apportionment a superstructure of personal lore geometrical and terpsichoreographical.

Gretchen was amused and only infrequently disturbed by Laurence's late ponderings over diagrams that looked like haywire Mondrians: graph-paper maps of real estate revised compulsively into ever more pleasing mosaic subdivision. Because the Village loft was not itself particularly subdivided—one large and lofty chamber with only conceptual boundaries, nothing to thwart a determined photon from one end to the other—Laurence would sometimes retire, after bedtime for Gretchen, who was doing her best to keep regular hours for the sake of Laurence's entail, to the bathroom, where he had experienced several of his most significant urban thoughts. There, supine in the dry old clawfoot tub, clipboard erect on his abdomen, he reproduced the Dempler estate in sketchy scale on many a quadrille leaf and parcelled and portioned and assigned to the turf arty bird's-eye views of sequential shearing. He condemned or reprieved thousands of blades at a mechanical-pencil stroke, revising configurations weekly, so that grass never knew at what angle or time of day or from which direction he'd be coming.

One spot, ten feet square at a forgotten corner of the grounds, Laurence always started by blackening in on the map, as if releasing a crossword puzzle from diagramlessness. This spot he reserved, without permission, unmown. A joy of mowing more sensibly sized lawns for Laurence had always been to see, by the contrasting height of surrounding, yet untampered swaths of sward, what he had accomplished. He had waited as long as he could without irritating neighbors, so that when he finally mowed, the unmown was clearly unmown, the mown clearly mown, and the extent of his achievement clearly marked. But all Twelve of Dempler's Clefs were to be gone over weekly, giving Laurence little sense of the necessity, hence of the rationale, for his labor. The ten-foot square, then, served as a measure of the week's work's worth. Like the Bronx Zoo not very far distant, it maintained a bit of the wild in the midst of the tame; and like the zoo, was so neatly circumscribed in its alien setting that it sometimes seemed to Laurence the tame, or at least the placid, in the midst of the wild, or at least the contentious. For although he derived a serene pleasure from mapping in the tub, his hours on the full-size hectares made him struggle, against time, against spineless buzzing creatures, against the implacable tendency of nature to make more nature. And though thrice weekly, returning to his square to check the progress of unchecked greenery, he attempted to convince himself of his utility, he could scarcely help liking that patch the more, the more he learned to dislike the dauntless other grass. Not the grass itself he disliked or disliked tending, but the needless frequency, as he saw it, of his passes over the same helpless weeds, the needless meticulousness, as he saw it, of nipping each blade so often in the bud, the weird fear he thought it bespoke of grass-as-grass, opposed to grass-as-carpet. He hated never giving it even a chance.

Whence this odd empathy with leaves of grass, so different from his attitude toward hair? Especially when mapping Twelve Clefs in the waterless tub, engaging in feats of landscape architecture that really did no more than rearrange a single job into another version of the same but that nevertheless engaged him as thoroughly and repeatably as the game of klondike did Big Jim, especially then, in the posture that held such memories of marriage and depilation, Laurence sensed mysterious connections between mowing and shaving, mysterious chiefly because the parallel was skewed. Didn't he sometimes see Twelve Clefs as a giant anatomy with chins and upper lips and groins to be tended with blades but without styptic pencils? Didn't he mow carefully around ponds as if shaving around a mouth, clip assiduously near fences as if eliminating sideburns, rake gently as if towelling off the estate's tender skin? Yet shaving was something to do as often as one reasonably could to preclude evidence of the substance removed, whereas grass already short took for Laurence the joy out of mowing. He attacked stubble with a purpose and a vengeance that seemed to him uncalled-for in responding to lawn.

To some extent, the pleasure he took in form distracted him from the substance of what he was doing. First day on the job (his plodding, pedestrian back-and-forth thwarted by bushes, trees, annoying plantings of every sort), he discovered retrograde, then curved, sinusoidal, and catenary movement. He avoided when he could the rider's monotony, revelling in the pusher's superior maneuverability. A week later he had a repertoire of ballroom moves: a waltzy boxstep, cha-cha for the overgrowth, sarabande for particular obstacles, two-step for his two-stroke engine, square and circle dances, reels, a tango that didn't take two. Then he educated himself in relations between his movements and the patterns they created; he found that spiralling inward on a rectangle left a pleasing chevron formation that produced the illusion of depth. He understood that this way of proceeding wasted energy in turning twice as often; but moving toward the center of the quadrilateral, he seemed to accelerate by making right angles more frequently, squaring off diminishing oblongs with the end in sight, and he found an inscrutable value in coming at something from four sides at once. An early devotion to flashy arcs—the parabolic, hyperbolic, elliptic conic sections and the compound curves of cycloids that adornamented Dempler's estate with rick-rack, ruffle, party-dress flounces and flourishes—faded, while the mature geodesic potential of the simple polygon consumed Laurence more and more.

The essential and epitomal triangle, world's most stable structure, became all his study. These shapes, alarming in both their infinite variety and their universal commonality to every high-school kid who pays the slightest attention, had a practical advantage: they seemed to disappear more rapidly than other shapes, geometrically, logarithmically, exponentially, hypotenutically! And Laurence suscepted to a sort of mesmerization, a foggy meditation upon the sums of the squares of the other two sides—out of sight of the mansion, out of the smells so pungent of suffering foliage and potent petrochemicals zillions of years in the making, oblivious to: internal combustion and the racket it made, salt precipitating to a grainy film on forehead, bugs abuzz, wind in the willows, quaking aspens, birches to and fro, strange genius-coot tinkling up there in a turret and expecting him for lunch, gravid Gretchen and her fingertips calloused from pressing silver-wrapped gut to the ebony fingerboard, Irene being human somewhere in the distance, Providence, the fact, even, that he had a body whose muscles were doing things, whose mucous membranes were paranoiacally allergic to much of what surrounded them, whose nails, recovering from what he did to them this morning, awaited what he would do to them tonight, whose spine was alive with a system it would not be inaccurate to call nervous. Oblivious to all but the sums of the squares of the other two sides, until something happened.

Laurence never saw the mole alive. The mower made a kind of rasp and sploosh, and the creature was dead instantly, on the spot. It lay with its absurd feature pointed toward the heavens and no expression whatsoever on its face. How could such a face, dominated by this fleshy protuberance, this snout in the shape of a Christmas-tree ornament, have an expression even in the best of times? Ridiculous, thought Laurence; I should be laughing. A joke: How do you *breathe* through that thing? posed the elephant to the naked man. This must be the thing called a star-nosed mole, he thought. To go through life with a thing like that on the end of your face, and then to meet your fate under the rotor of a power mower pushed by a fellow thinking about the sums of the squares of the other two sides!

And Laurence thought—but why is open to question—*Is your grandfather living?* Death was not the connection, exactly. It was something about that nose, that eponymous feature whose explanation did not present itself right off the bat. The birdlike man with the single bead of blood dried there like a ruby. *I gnome, he's Joosh.* The ungenerous jeweller, Marcia Funebre, Mama under a sheet, the monkey, the sailor, the other two sides. His eyes never left the star-nosed mole's star-nose. Why should he, why should I, kill something with a nose like that while cutting the grass of a genius, thinking polygonally, a missing person in New York trying to prove something about how I got here in the first place, and a cellist, a trombonist, Aunt Amelia, Red Rover, shoebox full of my own *hair*, for Christ's sake! But is it even a nose at all? What exactly makes a nose a nose—breathing, smelling, sneezing, picking? There was something in *Moby-Dick* about whether the whale has a face.

I was born here. New York, Providence, New York: round-trip, I was *born* here. In this place of seven millions being human and no one knows how many moles, I gulped searing oxygen and screamed bloody murder and saw the light of day.

'This place' in the municipal sense only. Not the pitch-&-putt, not the baby grands, not Maestro's thin-sliced sesame bread with anchovy, rosemary, drizzle of imported virgin oil, not the single leaf of romaine under heart-of-palm almondine, not sliver of melon, not svelte tumbler of iced English Breakfast garnished with fresh mint, not even, exactly, the humbler staff fare that followed at half past one. Not bouillabaisse, not Greenwich loft, not viola da gamba. None of these. Nevertheless: I was born at seven, pendant for three, months. Born. Here.

Borne. Hear. Father's fight song: *The scarlet and the blue wave over me / Ess tee you why vee ee ess eh en tee.* Mama's sister slapping her for eating a banana on Fifth Avenue, unladylike. The Triangle Shirt Factory Fire. Washington Heights like the prow of the *Half Moon* heading up the Hudson. DiMaggio on a rampage. Bakeries that hired a gentile to stoke their ovens over the Sabbath for neighborhood women to bake their own bread in, cutting into profits for the sake of goodwill. Central Park as a sensible spot for a stroll. La Guardia reading the funny pages over the radio. East Side, West Side, bicycle built for two. None of this was his, but like *Tyrannosaurus rex* it must have some bearing. And that strange club Grandpa Theo was in, with the Hawaiian-sounding name: Pineapple, Mai-Tai, Pie-O-My, Paisano, Pandora, Pehee-nuee-nuee? Paideia. Paideia. And behaving like a human being. *Is your grandfather living?* Is your landfather giving? Is your land, Father, grieving? Is your landgrabber thieving? Is your grandlather fibbing? Is your grandfather leaving? 'No, Lonnie, just hostile.' My tie.

Tay-O, Tay-ay-ay-O, daylight come an me wan go home.

Six

You get on a bus, your mother is dying, you meet a woman, her father is dying, one of you makes linguine and you both get married. You get on another bus, you meet another woman, she's got ten toes and a gamba two and a half centuries old, she takes you to a party, next thing you know you're a gardener and every week for lunch you're eating leftovers of appetizers you thought were only served at wedding receptions. What's the point?

Sometimes it seems you just drift into things; they wash over you. The trajectory of an object on the sea is up and down, up and down: the waves move from Lisbon to Provincetown or vice versa, but the object just sits, a piston in an engine, a grampus in a rocking chair. That's not exactly what I mean.

Watch an insect sometime: constantly in motion, every movement composed of six or eight smaller ones, jointed like crazy, putting on a show like a gymnast who never dismounts, one trick to the next without thinking. As if it's all planned out beforehand and practiced a thousand times; but the insect, presumably, never gets the big picture, never understands why it's sniffing out this or crawling over that or lugging the other between its pincers. That's not it either.

I realized at one point that I'd hardly been outdoors in months except to get from one indoor place to another. Words like 'sunlit,' 'blooming,' 'verdant,' 'backpack,' 'snowblindness,' 'mud'—nature words—weren't even in my working vocabulary. Now along comes this job, and it seems like I *live* outdoors. Three days a week I rub sunscreen all over my face, and I spend three hours in the morning and four in the afternoon walking around in the grass smelling like a coconut. And muscles: it isn't as if I decided a person should develop them. All my life I was wizened. Now along comes this job, and I come home ('home'? Is Gretchen's 'home'?) all healthy-tired with aches and pains and knotty little muscles poking out from under my skin. I'd have dirt under my fingernails, if I had fingernails.

Or take living. Did Gretchen and I decide to cohabit? *Do* we? When Irene and I were married, I used to sing an offhand lyric whose final couplet rhymed 'birds of a single feather' with 'happy to live together.' Then, on another bus, 'I have a chamber where we could make such music,' said Gretchen. Fine. I certainly don't seem to be living in Providence.

Lately I've been falling asleep in the bathtub. I climb in there to play with Twelve Clefs, I catch my eyelids drooping a couple of times, but it seems such an effort to get up out of that tub: old, with clawfeet and sides so high it's like a kid mounting a ten-speed to hoist yourself in or out, so deep inside, before showers is my guess, when they made tubs for serious bathing without splashing on the floor, not for lounging, mapping conductors' estates. Not a comfortable place to lie down in, let alone sleep. Porcelain abraded from decades of scouring powder, like the edges of cups in that Japanese restaurant; if I had fingernails, I could make myself jump out of my skin just by scratching it.

It has occurred to me that someone whose muscles ache from grooming a conductor's estate and who voluntarily spends the night in a scratchy, clammy old bathtub in lower Manhattan may be avoiding something in the other room. If it occurred to Gretchen, she didn't mention it. She's always taking things in that stride of hers, like a majorette without a baton.

Speaking of taking things, speaking of stride: one Wednesday I return from Riverdale, beat, having greenskept the links. Gretchen isn't home. Maybe rehearsal ran late. I have a bite and climb into the tub. Gretchen isn't even home: I could be lying on the bed. But instead I'm in the tub, naked, moist pilonidal indentations getting cold against porcelain. I hardly even pretend to be playing with the maps; in a couple of minutes, I'm asleep. The next morning I dream that the grass rake won't work, its teeth have turned linguinic, covered with sticky grass like a failed pesto, and I awake to a clatter, a racket, a brouhaha. Gretchen is cleaning. Everything.

I remember last time I was so careful to sound unFreudian. The small of my back has stiffened up, and I'm kneading both kidneys: 'Wow, you're really cleaning up a storm.'

'Call me the white tornado.'

That would be funny, except she really is in one of those frenzies, obsessive, straightening up for all she's worth, compulsive, dusting her heart out.

'Gretchen, is there anything you want to tell me?'

'No. Is there something you want to know?'

'Are you cleaning for a reason?'

'I guess so.'

'Glissando?'

'?'

'Trombone? Synthesizer? Wavelengths?'

'Well, Laurence, what do you expect? You've been sleeping in the fucking bathtub for weeks!'

Is it fair to call two weeks 'weeks'? Two is the next number after *one*. That's like saying you've had problems with all the women you've ever slept with, when there are only two. It's misleading, that word 'weeks'; however, I can't deny that two is, technically, plural. I didn't consciously decide to sleep in the tub, though; it was one of those things you drift into. I guess that's irrelevant. The point is, she's right: I have been sleeping in the tub. Rubadubdub, One man in a tub. *Is* that the point? No, the point is, what's a couple of weeks? A person could spend months, years, sleeping in a tub, without another person taking such a step. I myself spent twenty-six years without taking such a step, though, granted, no one was sleeping in tubs. The pale young lady and the wizened young man. 'And he thought she was very, very pretty, / And she stuck to him like glue.' Little Jack Horner, / Sat in a corner, / And frightened Miss Muffet away. *Dieses kleine dieses kleine dieses kleine Schweinchen.* 'Oh Lonnie, oh Lala, no, you are not a liar.'

I'm trying to be sensible about this. One little part of me just wants to cry *wie wie wie den ganzen Weg heim.* That little piggy in the market while this little piggy stayed home. But parts—'a man of many parts'—other parts, larger, older, wonder about rights, wrongs, what right I have to say what's wrong. I dragged her away from him once, but not till she begged me to do it. That was the nice thing about her in the first place: not virginal, vaginal, clitoral, clutter all my thoughts are clutteral, guttural, gutter all my thoughts are gutteral. 'What do you expect?' You got picked up on a Greyhound. What do you want from someone you meet on a bus?

That's one way of thinking about it.

But you're carrying my child!

That's another. Perhaps irrelevant. Immaterial. Objection: badgering the witness. Sustained.

Your honor. Am I really that old-fashioned? Not the point: am I really that hypocritical? Couldn't Irene feel the same about me? Well, no, I didn't buzz around cleaning up in front of her face. At least I had the decency to. Just. Disappear. 'I can see you, Mama, I see you.' I'm not in much of a position to be asserting anything here. Besides, what's a little intromission between old friends? Would he micturate in osculum? Objection: speculative. Sustained.

Your honor. I'm holding you in contempt. Your honor. Counsel is turning these proceedings into a circus. Pro seedings into a cervix. Order in the court. Ardor in the part. All rise. I do sullenly swear. Nothing but the tooth. 'Ohmygod, his *glissando,* his *cadenza! Vibrato prestidigitato.*' Objection: hearsay. Sustained. So. Help me. God.

Boredom is my least favorite emotion: life-as-a-lecture-series. After that, jealousy. A part of me stands aside, finds this interesting; not the adjective of least resistance, truly *interesting.* Little Laurence, Lonnie, Lala, such a grown-up conundrum: how does he feel about an albino cellist having sex with a spacey trombonist, excuse me synthesizerian? How does he feel? Gutteral. Interested. Vested. Civil. Rights. Sleeping in the fucking tub, fucking in the sleeping tub, seeking out the tupping flub, cuffing in the pleasing butt, this is getting out of hand.

I tried on several traditional responses as if they were clothing off a sale rack: How could you do this *to me?* How could you do that *with him?* How would you like it *if I?* Objection: argumentative. Sustained. They didn't fit anyway: closeout on discontinued styles. Clearance.

Irene would never have done this. What is that, past perfect subjunctive? Would never *do* this. Never? Probably has by now. (I know *I* have.) If not, not for reasons I admire in any case: innocence, high fidelity, sound reproduction, dumb ideas. Besides, why should Gretchen be Irene? She shouldn't: the party of the first part nipped a misconception in the bud, wouldn't agree to deliver even when she *wasn't* pregnant; whereas the party of the second part is distending, even as I ponder, just for me.

Precisely. Try to remember which deals are big. It's only sex. Grow up. Mow up. Throw up. Toe up.

How does he feel?

Objection: calls for a conclusion.

'Your triangle is known from high-school geometry and B movies as a marvel of design, unimproved upon since ancient times. Builders ever since Tut have confirmed its status as least collapsible of two-dimensional forms by making it their common first-order component of three-dimensional structures; recent visionary architects compound it in the most amazingly arc-generating ways. The apex of resiliency, one two three turns adding always to a complete about-face: the most enduringly chronic of polygons. But your vertices, acutely exposed as they are, can take quite a pounding as this most hardy of shapes tumbles uncrushably, unflappably about. Equilateral, isosceles, scalene, right, acute, obtuse. Time cannot wither nor custom stale. Sum of the squares of the other two sides. What immortal hand or eye.'

Laurence's theory of triangles. For your trigonometrician, your pilot, astronomer, surveyor, or sailor, triangulation is a fine means of getting bearings; for your lover, it's the perfect way to lose them.

For the longest time, unconscionably long in retrospect, she has believed that he and she are going through a phase (as who is not? But she means the sort parents attribute to offspring: humorable, aberrant, condescendable-to, patiently-to-be-sat-through). She has been, at the worst, waiting for him to give her back her life, as if it were a book he borrowed and is unforgivably writing in, breaking the spine of, dropping in puddles, thoughtlessly misplacing. She doesn't want a new, a critical, edition, complicated with footnotes, marginalia, scholarly apparatus tracing variants both substantive and accidental and disallowing naïvely definitive readings. Nor does she want back a tattered paperback for the inscribed and dedicated hardbound she imagines she lent. She wants simply what she gave: limited first edition.

Now, though, her view has changed. Somewhere along the way, she has lost sight of the limits of endurance. 'Patiently-to-be-sat-through'? Is she not inventor and sole proprietor of the theory of life-as-a-lecture-series? She now believes that grace periods are exhausted, needs the volume back, cannot work with any other. She almost wishes spitefully to impose overdue fines, demand restitution. In any case, fines or no, she will *not* wait like a polite librarian for a delinquent patron; she will make a noise; she will remind him of his debt; she will hire private investigators, collection agencies; she will authorize form letters threatening legal action. Better that than this legal inaction, resentful, resigned, chairbound, paralyzed, Groatesque.

'Iss ah bicks itty, Misses Lawrinse.' Yes, is a major metropolis, but she misses Laurence, and somewhere within its limits, she is convinced, a man is carrying around a biography that belongs to her. And if he *is* in New York, vipping in Red Eyelid will not bring him back.

Bring.
Bring.
Bring.
Bring.
Bring.
'Yeah.'
'Hello.' Victor. 'Is Donna there?'
'Lady, I'm dead from the waist down. Would I be answering the phone if somebody else was in the house?'
'Do you know when she'll be back, or where I can find her?'
'Good question. If you get an answer to it, let me know.'
This bitterness. Imagine living with this man. Make a note: avoid Groatism at all costs.
'Tell her Irene called, okay?'
'Sure, sure. After I tell her a few other things.'
'Victor?'
'Who is this?'
'Victor.'
'Who are you?'
'She loves you, you jerk.'
'Who the hell *are* you?'

'I'm somebody none of whose business it is, but for some reason she loves you a lot, and you're not making it easy. Tell her I called to see how she's doing, and I'm leaving town for a while. Irene. An old friend. You don't know me. Give her a break, Victor, she loves you.'

The first thing he said out loud was, 'Overruled.'

'Overruled, my pretty pale ass! You have no right, Laurence.'

'No, Gretch, I didn't mean you. I was talking to myself.'

'Well, don't go around responding to my sleeping with someone else by saying "Overruled," when you're just talking to yourself. It's misleading and it's insulting, and you have—'

'Gretchen,'

'—no right to—'

'I know, wait, Gretchen, just a minute.'

'—judge.'

'I wasn't judging, I was following a train of thought.'

'Well, don't.'

'I was talking to myself.'

'Well, don't.'

'Okay. I'll talk to you, if—'

'*Talk*, then.'

'—you will, Gretchen, if you will just stop *sweeping*. I can't talk to you when you're sweeping around.'

She dropped her broom, leaving a rabbit-sized bunny in the center of the room, and smiled as airborne motes swirled about her. 'That's funny. That's pwitty funny, Wowence. Sweeping awound.'

'Freudian, I guess. Slipping around.'

Dust settled like a paperweight snowstorm on the chucklish couple, embracing in the cleaning mess for what seemed a long time, during which Gretchen trembled slightly and her giggles turned to sobs. 'Weeping around,' said Laurence, hugging, chortling, while Gretchen, confusingly, blubbered, snivelled.

Laurence subsided while she labored to catch her offbeat breath. Her convex abdomen jostled against him, syncopatible, and he rubbed a soothing counterpoint on her concave lower back. Autonomic, she quaked: *tempestuoso*. Metronomic, he soothed: *dolce, dolce*.

Now what was this? Gretchen, of all people, somehow had lost the beat. Gretchen the Olympic walker, Gretchen the marathoner:

something had broken her stride. Gretchen the viola da gambler, off whose ducky back things were wont to roll, somehow wet and getting wetter, lamenting, alarming, *larmoyante*. Gretchen the unflappable: what could thus flap her?

'I hi didn't hnt hnt think hink it hit hit would hood hood matter her her her,' sob-hobbed Gretchen.

Laurence, assuming the antecedent of 'it hit hit' was 'sex hex hex,' continued to soothe: 'It's okay, Gretchen.' Hen hen. 'I'm not upset.' Het het.

'It's not, Laurhorrencehence, it's not hot okay hey hey.'

What's not okay, hey hey? Am I on the wrong track hack hack? 'Gretchen,' still hugging in the center of the room, 'let's sit down. We'll talk.' Hawk hawk.

They lowered themselves to the mattress on the floor: she supine, staring at ceiling, steadier now on her back, lucid calm after storm; he recumbent on his side, elbow on mattress head on hand a steady little triangle, free hand tracing ovoids now lightly on her belly, now becoming calm, becalming, breakers receding to gentler lapping of shallower breaths.

'Gretchen.'

'Laurence.'

'Baby, what's the matter?'

'Baby's the matter.'

Didn't think it would matter her her her. Baby's the matter?

'Laurence.' Her eyes shut tight.

'Gretchen?' His open wide.

'I want the baby haby he be he be.'

And she's off again. Habeas corpus. Heebious jeebies. Baby as porpoise. Crocogator, allidile. Shaking, quaking. Weeping and wailing. Gnashing of teeth.

'You want the baby?'

Sobering, sniffling, 'Yes. I want the baby.'

Fardraight, farmisht, fartumelt, farfufket Theo. Despite his fourscore, despite his seven, this forefather, long since established on this continent, knows not how to take the news. Laurence, last known as a babe not quite in arms, both married and missing at a stroke. A wife Irene who doesn't speak Yiddish looks for him, calls at the shop a *zayder* who hasn't seen the boy since the middleman, son of the father and father of the son, expired. She sounded nice.

What, then, became of the daughter-in-law he cut off, the mother so closely attached to the son that cutting off one was cutting off the other, the wife who failed in a wife's mission, her bones should only implode?

Now Theo understands that what he held against her even more than the dead son was the unreachable grandson. And he understands that he wants, more than he wants anything else, before he dies to know his grandson, sole-surviving Papyrushchka, crowning twig of the family tree, end of the line, next, last, and all of kin. Why couldn't they fuse? And hopes that the boy, if found, could carry on the line, making ties and Papyrushchkalehs to bear the fortunes of the house toward an uncertain future—even vague hopes of the boy's acceptance by acclamation into Paideia—now preoccupy Theo as he drains and half-fills the bubbler, as he sets out jellyjars and fragrant humidors, as he transfers the white plastic box that keeps him alive to the pocket of a freshly laundered shirt, as he knots Theo's tie around Theo's troubled and stubbled neck, as he sits on the folding wooden chair embracing Theo's ribcage and keening, *daven*ing like an Orthodox at prayer while he waits for fellow seekers after wisdom.

The ruby liquid in the bubbler shimmers before his rheumy eyes, loosing iceheight more rapidly, frighteningly, these last few months. The geography of his shop, his apartment upstairs, his neighborhood, is so familiar that you wouldn't know from the faultless, unfaltering way he negotiates these spaces that he sees them as if through moving liquid, that objects dance about and edges that used to be hard waver, that he lives mostly, in these latter days, by touch. You might not even guess if you saw the ties he has been decorating more and more by rote. You might think his career is recapitulating art history. You might think his style, strictly representational these many years, is becoming impressionist, fauvist, cubist, abstract by willful experimentation. You might think he's on his way toward photographic superrealism, might not suspect he's painting as clearly as he is able, might credit the effects of glaucoma and cataracts to artistic license, might give his creations the benefit of the doubt. And if you gave him a twenty instead of a ten for one of his involuntary abstracts and had to point out to him that he owed you ten in return, and if you heard him say, as he gave you your change, 'Ah knolled men docent pay ah tension,' I hope you'd give him, too, the benefit of the doubt. Because you'd never get him to admit that a foot from his face a twenty and a ten are indistinguishable. Theo has his pride.

All the more extraordinary, then, that off guard and offhand he told Irene, a stranger on the phone, the simple fact he would generally do what he could to hide: 'Eye em loose ink my iceheight.' Waiting for guests, he thinks he understands why. He wants to see his grandson. And illogically, though she called to say she didn't know where his grandson was, he wanted to say to her that he wanted to see his grandson, *see* him before the eyes film over for good. Waiting for guests, the failing eyes that inconsequentially leak tears all day long leak a few for a reason as an old man mourns his mistakes.

Theo is startled from his revery by the bell. Someone awaits without, and he knows it must be Moshe Blender, always the first Paideian to show up but this time uncharacteristically early, more than fifteen minutes, maybe his nephew has somewhere else to be and so drops him off ahead of time. Theo is not pleased: Moshe isn't quite his least favorite Paideian, but close, talking always about his nephew's accomplishments in the field of medical-instrument design. But a person can't be left standing on Fordham Road for fifteen minutes, and Theo, not bothering to dry eyes that drop saline in the best of times, shuffles reluctantly to the door.

Triangles seem to be proliferating here, connecting and combining chronically, tetrahedronically, octahedironically, icosahedonistically: Laurence, Irene, Gretchen; Laurence, Gretchen, Moogman; Laurence, Gretchen, Christian; Donna, Gretchen, Crickenberger; Donna, Crickenberger, Victor; Laurence, Dempler, Theo; Irene, Theo, Laurence. The possibilities seem endless. Thankfully, mercifully, they are not.

So Gretchen wants the baby haby he be he be, wants to rechristen Christian Paprika Christian Barron. Is it just that simple to cut and paste a person's biography? Sure it is, when the person isn't born yet, is still hypothetical, hypodermical. Hypotenutical. What has this desire to do with the Moogman?

Now how does he feel? He is wondering—I am wondering—what one thing has to do with another, what one person's place is in another's life. Will he enter Gretchen's standup routine, one-liner sketches of her exes? How would she put it? 'Met a fellow on a bus, wizened young man with a novel navel. A saxophony, but he beat the band in bed. Convinced me he'd make a good mother, and he did: me. Little Christian's daddy. Last I heard he was mulching in Riverdale.' Could some such breezy dismissal be what would become of him? He, of all people, a thumbnail?

Getting yourself a child is the hardest damned thing. To think of the billion-dollar industries supported by people trying not to, devices hermetically sealed, fallopian knots, applicators, cornstarch, calendars and thermometers, merry-go-round pill dispensers, plastic gizmos, incisions, excisions, decisions, precisions . . . and Laurence can't seem to get one when he *wants* one. Truth to tell, he *never* wanted one; was ever willing, though, having made (or thinking he had made) one, to accept it, a free sample that arrives in the mail, door prize or COD package, bonus or penalty, occupational hazard, fact of life, birds, bees, climate, pores, birthdate, anything you please taken in stride. His stride in some ways as remarkable, really, as this albino's.

But now don't this beat all? The cream of the gest: Laurhorrencehence, who never flinched from paternity, signs a nine-month lease on a cellist's womb, and the landlady, who never sought maternity, decides to occupy the premises herself. What, exactly, are the premises? What, exactly, is at stake here? 'Yes,' she says, 'I want the baby.' And he? Does he? Amniotic sac's a phony? Piggy in the market, piggy at home? Comic operetta: *Orifice and Your Idiocy.*

A lot of people, he imagines, would say, 'Laurence, pull yourself together, get your bearings, see straight. What has happened to Love? Are you in love with Irene? Are you in love with Gretchen? You have a wife, you have a mistress'—surely that's not the right word for Gretchen, the woman carrying his child? her child?—'you've deserted the former'—has he?—'and you're living with the latter'—this, too, in his mind, remains open to question, though demonstrable both *de jure* and *de facto*, and though he can't figure how to label the sense in which it isn't true, he has a sense that in a sense it isn't true.

You'd think he'd have an answer for these people. They or he don't or doesn't understand. What is at stake. The premises. The point. Dip pint, Theo would say.

What we have here is just a tremendous amount of room for misunderstanding. Hadn't they better talk?

'You want the baby.'

'Affirmative.'

'After it's born.'

'Affirmative.'

'To raise it, to bring it up.'

'To have and hold, for richer and poorer, for ruddier and paler. I do.'

'You do. *You* want to be the mother.'

'*I.*'

'Feed, clothe, send it to school.'

'In sickness and in health.'

'If I ask you a question, will you promise not to get upset?'

'Negative.'

'I'll ask it anyway, because I'm confused about something.'

'Good luck.'

'Here it comes.'

'Shoot.'

'What does this have to do with? I don't even know his name.'

'Garson Farfield. But his nickname is Flash.'

'Flash?'

'Right.'

'We're talking about the wavelength guy?'

'Right.'

'Right. Him.'

'What does my wanting to keep the baby have to do with Flash?'

'Right. Now are you upset?'

'No. I don't know.'

'You don't know if you're upset?'

'No. I'm not upset. I don't know what my wanting to keep the baby has to do with the fact that I slept with Flash again last night.'

'But it must have something to do with it.'

'If you say so. But I don't see why, and I don't know what.'

'We're both confused.'

'I don't know. I don't feel confused. I slept with Flash because I wanted to. I want to keep the baby because I want to.'

'*Noor vee doos.*'

'Huh?'

'Just because. Yiddish. My grandfather used to say it.'

'Nervy dose?'

'Close enough.'

'Dozey dotes.'

'Huh?'

'Kiddily divey too, wooden ewe?

'Oh.'

'Now I have two.'

'Have to what?'

'Have two questions.'

'Have to halve two questions?'

'A: Are you upset because I slept with Flash. B: Are you upset because I want the baby.'

'A: I don't know. B: I don't know. I told you I was confused. Are you sure they don't have something to do with each other?'

'I didn't say I was sure. I said I don't know what.'

'Shouldn't we try to figure it out?'

'I don't know. Might be a waste of time.'

'Got nothing better to do. 'Cept sweep.'

'You know, Laurence, sometimes I just love you.'

'Aw.'

'Awe?'

'No. But you know, sometimes, Gretchen, I *am* in awe. Of you.'

'Awe of me. Why not take awe of me?'

'Croon on. You told me we could make ludicrous music. But yes, of you, and of us.'

'Of us? We . . . we . . .'

'Den ganzen Weg heim.'

'Yiddish?'

'German. Never mind.'

'I don't.'

'Could we get back to Flash and the baby?'

'As you wish.'

'Do you think either one is the cause of the other?'

'You mean is Flash the cause of the baby? You and Chris Crickenberger share that honor between you.'

'I don't mean that.'

'What do you mean?'

'I mean, A: Do you want to keep the baby now because you slept with Flash again? And B: Did you sleep with Flash again because you want to keep the baby now?'

'Yipes.'

'Does the close proximity of these two events imply a causal link, or are they perhaps both effects of some as yet indeterminate constitutive factor?'

'Geez.'

'That's what a kid said to me in the Museum of Natural History.' See those bones? See that stature? That's how big.

'It's a versatile expression.'

'But the question, Gretchen.'

'Hey, Laurence. It's a good question, two good questions. You know what, I'm not trying to be evasive or something, but would you mind if, what I really want to do is take a shower. You were in the tub before. You don't mind if I take a shower now, do you?'

'Actually, I think I'd feel better if you did.'

'Want to come along?'

'I think I'd feel better if I didn't.'

'I'll be back in a fl—, I mean in a minute.'

'I'll make coffee.'

'Great.'

With child. Great with child. Concerto for cello and accompaniment. Still life with Laurence. Snapshot with Flash.

Theo knows right away that the woman nervously smoothing her hair in the shimmering streetlight is Mrs. Laurence. How does he know? She is clearly not a customer, since she carries a pullman. She doesn't look Jewish, but this could be said of any number of New Yorkers—more and more, it seems to Theo, in recent years. Never mind; he just knows, and addresses her as such immediately with inflection that indicates she might attempt to deny this proposition, but he wouldn't believe her if she did. She says simply, 'Theo' (as a thirsty person might say 'Water,' he thinks), and the two withdraw through the polysemic fire-engine-red-and-battleship-grey doorway into the shop.

Had you been loitering across the street and watched them recede into the welcoming yellowish light together, the old man's hand gently guiding the young woman by the triceps, you would have sworn that he had been expecting her at precisely this hour and that they knew each other already a long time.

Inside, Irene's gaze is fixed in turn by a stunning array of polychrome silken pseudo-fauvist neckwear draped over peripheral racks, then by the setup in the middle of the room, bubbler amid jellyjars amidst an ellipse of chairs like a shrine to Bacchus or a séance awaiting a medium, then finally despite distractions by the rounded weathered angular innocent altogether unprecedented and fascinating features of Theo, who doesn't laugh or cry but shows on his face a mixture of expectation and dread, fear and hope, almost everything, thinks Irene, but surprise. The eyebrows, dingy beige, superior, full and almost fluted like a lathed newel or nar-whal horn, do not move. Like an Olympian caught in middive by electronic flash. Where, wonders Irene, could a man get such eyebrows but from wisdom, and is glad she has come.

There's not much in Irene's eyebrows to elicit such scrutiny, and Theo is looking instead at her hands, moving with a nervous grace that reminds him—oh he can hardly think it—of Molly. Molly's hands, not in age but when they first met in Poland, Molly's hands in youth, with all of life spread out before them, wars and regimes and eventually, though they didn't know it yet, an entire continent to escape from, the curiosity of an almost new century to enliven them, the blush and flutter of love alone to guide them, all the strength and grace and impatience of Molly's hands to grasp and caress whatever might come, Molly's *hendeleh*, Molly's hands like two independent, separable creatures who, like their owner, loved him and whom, like their owner, he loved. He hasn't thought of Molly's hands in years, in decades, hasn't really remembered them since her death. Laurence married a woman with Molly's hands. Theo can hardly contain himself, Molly's hands on Mrs. Laurence mean so much to him.

So they stand, he on her hands, she on his eyebrows, gazing, rapt, and too, not knowing what to do or say next, each hoping the other will know, until Irene, seeing the tears that incessantly trickle from Theo's eyes and taking them for a sign that he's moved, starts to weep herself, and makes him shed the tears she mistook his for. Then an old man and a young woman weep in concert until they laugh in unison at their own unison. Neither has spoken a word when the bell rings again and Moshe Blender follows it up with his customary knock.

'Mississ,' Theo calls her, without the 'ippi,' 'Eye half ah prop limb. Eye em trilt dot jew half calm, trilt eye coo tint tally oo, bit he ear stotts ah mitt ink, dot jew kent attent. Eye fill bet, bit doos mitt ink hiss naught ah pop lick fawn. Foot jew fate opstayers, in eye fill calm op fen doos mitt ink foot be entit?'

'I'm so sorry, I didn't mean to intrude . . .'

'No no no, Mississ Lawrinse, you dun tint root, bit at doos mitt ink you kent attent. Fill you plisse stay op destayers, in mech yes elf et hum day rent ill eye fill be ebble to calm?'

'Yes, certainly, of course, but I . . .'

'No bots, eye fill calm fen eye ken.'

'Yes, of course.'

After a minor skirmish over the pullman, Theo carries it and shows her op his stayers, a thin case with two landings where flights turn ninety degrees, worn, creaking, bowed in the center to a catenary swoop as if by gravity. He opens the door at the top and directs her into a single room subdivided into various areas merely by virtue of the furnishings: she sees a kitchen corner, a bedroom corner, a reading-room corner, and a tailor's shop, all in a fifteen-foot square. Theo holds her tentatively by both shoulders, leans and places a tentative kiss on her cheek, then turns and leaves her, closing the door. As she hears him creaking down the stairs they just ascended together, she is almost overcome, not by emotion but by Theo's breath, a noxious blend of ancient flesh and recent smoke that makes her momentarily light-headed. She breathes deeply, noticing that the room is nearly as smoky as Theo's kiss, and sinks into the reading-room chair, whose batting emerges in brownish wisps from the arms.

Shuffled abovestairs in huggermugger, left solo and unre-stricted but feeling almost padlocked in, Irene is baffled. Theo didn't look unkind, but what could make a man behave in such a way to his long-lost, or rather first-found, granddaughter-in-law? Some sort of meeting; her imagination goes to work on what sort of group would necessitate such a gesture. Apparently a clandes-tine one, whose activities are not to be looked into by outsiders, and Irene quickly concludes that she is sunk into an armchair over an outlaw confab, a revolutionary cadre perhaps or organized-crime powwow. Her old alone-in-the-house fancy engages. Theo's Ties a front? For what? Drugs, numbers, violent overthrow, white slav-ery even? If the FBI raided at this moment, in what would she be implicated, or from what rescued?

It occurs to her that Grandpa Theo cut off contact because he didn't want young Laurence's life tainted by the family connec-tion to The Family. He wanted to give the boy a fresh start, he was in hock to the Bosses, up to his eyebrows, and his only way of repaying the debt was to . . . to what? To serve them claret in jel-lyjars? Something doesn't quite make sense yet.

Perhaps Theo, an old patriarch, member of an old patriarchal culture (it does not occur to Irene to add, And what culture is not?), has joined some ultra-Orthodox fringe, cabal of warlords, or some occult branch, coven of warlocks. Perhaps what she saw downstairs are the trappings of a satanic, demonic, or chthonic ritual, some splinter conventicle of covenanters who worship the ruby liquid and believe in the folding chairs as the seats of unspeakable spiritual empowerment. What was in those jars, those two giant Dutch urns? Ali Baba and his twenty-two thieves flash across her thoughts, and Popeye's parodic decree: *Open sez me!* Irene imagines ashes, of course, remains of apostate members or victims or spouses, yes, surely, of spouses, some perverse masculate underground dedicated to the elimination of their own race by the selective neutralization of the child-bearing sex. But then the fabric of her vision, her worst-case invention, disintegrates, strained by the incongruities between its evil spinning and the innocuous, even jolly appearance of the two-and-twenty jellyjars. Jellyjars!

The trouble with jellyjars, for Irene's current purposes, is that they lack the ability to appear ominous. Who could press jellyjars into service as bearers of bile? Irene's sinister scenario cannot accommodate jellyjars, more compatible with birthday or block party than with underworld plot or fanatic fringe. And slowly, sense takes over as Irene subliminally surveys the homely, innocent surroundings of the upstairs room into which she has been unceremoniously deposited. A room comprising kitchen, shop, bedroom, den, all clean as a whistle, down to the area about the sink, about the stove, the pristine peppermill (no salt on the table—'His heart,' she thinks), the pipes splayed about the ashtray in a fan pattern, bowls down stems up for proper drainage of unseemly residual fluids; the neatness, the almost primness, the unprepossessing niceness of it all, dashes Irene's semiconscious hopes that she's stumbled into gothic romance or intrigue beyond the naturalistic or the canny.

Only around the old Singer is the pin-neat aspect of the room disturbed, yet the scraps of gaily colored fabric and threads and brushes and paints do not so much disturb as enhance the homely and welcoming atmosphere. Pins with little beads of color on their heads lie about as if they hadn't a function in the world other than to make it a prettier place. How could she think the things she thought: Underworld, coven, violent overthrow, pipeline for helpless women, captive, drugged, ruined? Theo's old Singer is engraved in swirly patterns and ornamented with faded and peeling floral decals, and the shreds and patches that languish all around it in disarray bespeak the pleasant, the comforting, the generous and uselessly gorgeous and almost pure facets of life. Her breathing slows, pulse calms, and spirit swells with appreciation of the unugly spot she has been relegated to. Examining the worn and scrubbed surfaces around the sink and the battered but unbowed pans in the dishdrain and the old grey percolator with its glass-bulb top, Irene is warmed.

But something filters up through the floorboards besides the pungent odor of latakia in flames: a gradually more insistent muffled brouhaha, vague crowd sounds, ambling, fumbling, shambling, rumbling, ruffling, shuffling, shifting, and settling sounds, and voices of various timbres waft Ireneward as if from across some border, garbled, jammed, or encoded, a faraway buzz of almost intelligible activities from the far side of a wide lake on a misty night. Where she sits, between the burned-on kitchen tones and the dingy fade of everything else save the swatches and filaments where all the colors in the room concentrate in one festive and festooned corner, sounds come through like shortwave, full of static and climatic interference.

Were she there, the twenty-two matching ties might rekindle her ominous sense of a secret society of dark intent; but the twenty-two octo- and septuagenarians would jar: she would see a brotherhood of grandpas, reunion of the class of '16. Not there, she can only imagine what manner of convention ripples the smokewaves below her. Abashed at her own curiosity but thinking too she has as much right as any captive to explore, to gather intelligence, Irene kneels and places her ear to the floor between two faded Persians, a Tonto in espadrilles harking for hooves.

Mowing, as it turns out, is good for thinking. Laurence has used his hours in the grass to consider numerous topics, in addition to geometry and the star-nosed mole. He has considered, for instance, what happens to this job in the winter. Does he blow snow, force bulbs, water houseplants? Is he unemployed through the most inhospitable months of the year? Will he still be in the City when those months arrive? Is he any closer to knowing what he came for than when he stepped off the bus? Is Irene still sitting still, a lady in waiting? Does she want him back? Is your grandfather alive? So forth, so on.

Now he thinks of new questions. What are an unwed presumptive father's legal rights concerning his presumptive child? What are an unwed lover's moral obligations concerning his presumptuous lover? Isn't Flash Farfield a silly name? What has he got that I don't have? What have I that he doesn't? Soon Laurence sees these questions as endless swaths of weed, his job to cut them down ruthlessly and without remorse. Legal rights are beside the point. Moral obligations are not the issue. No sillier than Christian, or for that matter, Laurence, Paprika (not to mention Äussterschucher). Who cares? Who cares?

If mowing, indeed, is good for thinking, surely it should lead to focus, focus on the issues that need resolution, issues that prompt behavior. Have you noticed the phrases that emanate all day long, every long day, or at the very least (to remain empirical about it) three days weekly, from Dempler's turret? Six-note, eight-note, three-bar, simple phrases like those a flawed musical memory would take away from a performance of *Lieder*, phrases repeated, altered slightly, repeated, without progression, haunting in their purity, fearsome in their constancy, yet almost merely irritating in their idiot similitude. For all the headway Dempler makes, he may as well be mowing. Forth, back, forth: a phrase, a phrase, a phrase. Like goldfish in a bowl, always making the same, always indifferent and inconsequential, decisions. Has a man of genius come to this? And shall Laurence's mind, once thought not unpromising, come to the same?

Does all Dempler's gentility, his crustless sandwiches and uppercrust sprigs of arcane parsleys, amount to no more than this at last? A sterile, a fruitless bent to iterate, a twice-told, a manifold sameness? Laurence considers types: the frantic need some have (Gretchen? he wonders) to change, the need that not only accepts novelty in stride (Gretchen, he thinks) but requires, craves it, that masks essential sameness in the guise of novelty, making thumbnail sketches of each and every person and day as proof that today, tomorrow, yesterday, differ more than they resemble, as if every person were quite an original and every day an unprecedented dawning. Like me myself, turning mowing into design, imagining myself a worker in monotint, starving artist bequeathed a truckload of viridian. Despite my warps, my woofs, my arcs and chevrons, houndsteeth and florals, wildly successful paisleys and oversubtle plaid failures, my best-foot-forward attempt to transform bucholer into eclogic, to transpose a single lawn, however more-than-lawnlike, into a multitude of keys, all my lawndramatic spins and cycles notwithstanding, the fact remains that Twelve Clefs is one gargantuan lawn, no more, and I mow the same flat acres every livelong week.

And the opposite (Dempler, yes), the less spectacular but equally frantic need to repeat, to wear a groove, to replace each young supposedly musical mower with another, to soothe with those nearly identical phrases not because one can't think up another, but because their very sameness comforts, familiarity that masks the essential difference of each and every person and day, proof that yesterday, today, tomorrow resemble more than differ.

The nails that every morning present again the state suspended between destruction and regeneration, sixteen hours of nibbling undone by eight of regrowth, the patterns of tooth and nail that prove competence and balance and yet refine rather than change. Laurence thinks of meteorology: having a sufficient past gathered to predict future on the basis merely of likenesses, prediction never absolute because based only on patterns of past observation: this is the kind of cloud pattern that, in nine cases out of ten, results in . . . this is the kind of personality that, you can bet your bottom dollar, results in . . . this is the kind of feeling that, the kind of talent that, the kind of relationship that . . . Is this the kind of probability theory that underlies everything we know about ourselves and others? This the kind of educated guess on which we base our own lives as well as those of dinosaurs, this the kind of gamble that makes of all of us oddsmakers, bookies, betting our possibilities against our probabilities?

I take it back about Dempler. Pianist, composer, conductor, Gretchen said; not repetition but modulation ruled. And about Gretchen. Anytime you think you've located the opposite ends of a spectrum, between which all else falls, watch out: you're in imminent danger of concocting a theory, sure sign of brain-rot exacerbated by pride.

V-Victor, V for victory, a glorious, a heroic name, a name for a god. Groat, buckwheat groats, oatmeal, groatmeal, stoat, a name for a pig, for a grain, I don't care a groat, shorthand for the negligible. A large, a magnificent name; a small, a particular name. Little did he know: all his life, he took Victor at its word, thinking, or knowing without thinking, that name was his lot. Lot was a man's name, too, whose wife turned into a pillar of salt. When Victor was a child, Sunday-schooled, he used to wonder how a man's wife could turn into a pillow of salt, what a pillow of salt would be, imagining the stony lick that would make a man's rest gritty. It connected in his mind somehow to beds of nails, sheets of rain, blankets of snow, Job's comforters. Lot and Job: when Victor was small, he could never keep the two straight, righteous men with different stories that both made life seem a veil of tears, crown of thorns, Bible belt, feet of clay, fisty cuffs, hem and haw, gee and haw, hee and haw. When Victor was a mere groat of a boy, the world was an unvanquishable puzzle of phrases whose relations he could not, but ached to, understand. The words built around O's gave him problems: Lot, Job, Sodom. He comprehended, or thought he did, better those built around A's: Cain, Abel, Jacob, Ishmael, even Isaac with the A clipped though doubled. The world of the O-words was more frightening but less scrutable, stories about traps for the unwary that were themselves traps for the unwary, stories that transformed the world into a pop-quiz filled with trick questions. When Victor was a small boy who believed himself destined for victory, he much preferred the Real Stories, the Greatest Stories Ever Told, of loaves and fishes, of blighting olive trees and mushrooming mustard seeds, all suffused with the sweet fertilizing and preservative name of Jesus and the sanctification or condemnation of organic provisions. Eliminating disease and making crops flourish and above all the promise of a pestfree exurban eternity with built-in modern conveniences led Victor onward toward that clean well-lit place or time or not-time suggested but never quite blueprinted in the stories.

Victor learned to fly like the Holy Spirit, joined in marriage with a woman who made a joyful noise unto the season-ticket holders of the Providence Symphony Orchestra. And Victor loved his work, rescuing crops from pestilence, annihilating diseases and blights of all sorts from a vegetable world he vaguely connected with ancient Judea. And Victor loved his wife, her operatic stage presence and bedtime arias and even her backstage bags and puffiness when she emerged from the lavatory morning or night freshly scrubbed, looking as if she'd been crying or allergic or newborn. Victor loved his prima Donna who despite her education in operatic tongues and flawless elocution never, even in quarrels, lorded it over him that he'd not been schooled past ninth grade and had always paid more attention to Sunday than weekday school and had accepted Jesus Christ as his Personal Savior at the age of eleven in a most unroman manner. The elder Groats, hardworking folk who bought the farm young, had lived just long enough to disinherit Victor for marrying a papist; and despite the years of ground maintenance he had to put in to hoard cash for the Cessna he'd expected their estate to pay for, despite intermittent fears over spending eternity with sweet Jesus but not dear Donna by his rapturous side, despite it all he'd never regretted his imprudent match for a moment.

And Victor had time enough on his hands for regrets, Lord knew, since the accident, time between hands of solitaire, casino, canasta, time off his feet, without his legs, or rather, and this he hated most of all, *with* the damn things, those sticks, stones, lumps, bones, dead limbs he had to carry around by the strength of arms, had to pick up like sacks of turnips and place where he wanted them but could never leave behind, infernal counterweights to every impulse; time to regret nearly everything in his stupid hotdogger's halflife, time enough to regret even faith that the good Lord would provide victory to a man who thought his Christian name would ensure it, time enough to damn every angel and preacher he'd ever known or imagined to fiery hell for the lousy stinking eternity they'd always promised him with such smug and beatific grins. Yet Victor had never found the time to regret marrying Donna Forenza, and by damn she deserved a whole man, a man with legs to stand on and to run through fields with, if he had just not felt the need to fly so close to a crop of peas that his crash had eventually flattened and ignited anyway, a savior and keeper turned destroyer and useless half a man.

No natural creature on earth with arms without legs. Limbless, worms and snakes and fish; legs without arms, birds and lizards and every kind of quadruped; but arms without legs, not a blessed creature on this damned green planet. Not a one.

Victor was grateful for few things in his life, but Donna was one, though he knew he should act more like it. Another was that they'd never had a son, a boy whose precious growing limbs would mock his deadwood sculpture of legs, a boy to wonder why he had the only dad in the world who couldn't have a catch in the yard or take a kid camping or teach him to ride a two-wheeler, running behind with a hand on the seat and then, when the kid felt secure and steady, taking the hand away without a word and watching the kid recede in the distance, thinking his dad was still balancing him from behind and then calling out, 'Enough, enough, okay Dad let's stop now, isn't that far enough?' while Dad just stood and smiled a dadlike smile at the kid balancing himself without even knowing it, a dad who could say, 'Son, that's just how my dad taught me, and it's the only way I know to show a kid he can

handle a bike,' and the same with swimming, the pigskin, the
horsehide, even the fatal joystick. And Victor Groat, confined too
long to his own two-wheeler, thanked sweet Jesus that he'd damned
to hell a hundred thousand times for never giving Donna a fertile
womb and him the fruit of that womb.

But such consolations scarcely constitute a meaning for it all,
an excuse or rationale, a salve for the bitter bitter remorse and
hate and despair of one who thought that legs made the man.
There was no balm in Providence for such a one, no saving grace
save Donna; and he knew, though she never gave a hint of it, that
even she must despise, resent, and hate him for the travesty of
legs, the things shaped about right but functionless, the treetrunks
turned to igneous stumps that he dragged from place to place like
a cross up Calvary to mock him with his own name: Victor, King
of the Groats, a man without a father or son or holy spirit, a legless
creeping thing chained to a wonderful woman to drag her down.

No natural creature on earth. Not one.

A man can't live like this, said Victor Groat aloud, as he did
every day of his dismal damned cripple's self-loathing so-called
life.

And now some Irene—he's never heard a word of any Irene—
calls to torment him with the thought that she loves him. 'She
loves you, you jerk.' It's nothing more than what Donna herself
has told him countless times, but almost always after some
prompting, some self-pitying apology that she has to do for him in
so many ways: 'Dammit, Don, you know if there was any way I
could do this for myself, I wouldn't dream of subjecting you . . . '
'Aw, Vic, Vic, Vicky, don't do this to yourself, just don't think about
it, you know I love you, ya big lug.' Big lug indeed, who needed to
be lugged from spot to spot, dragged from bed to john, john to
wheelchair, wheelchair to bed. And Donna, realizing her favorite
epithet was hurtful to him now, starting calling him instead 'ya
big nut,' or catching herself halfway, 'ya big lugnut.' Was that
love? 'Give her a break, Victor, she loves you.' And God knows I
love her. But how the hell am I supposed to show it?

Irene's leaving town for a few days. What's that to Donna? Why
have I never heard of Irene? Who cares that she's leaving town for
a few days? Lots of people—people who can walk—leave town for
a few days. Who is Irene, and what's it to her if Donna loves me
or not?

It doesn't take Victor long to decide, on the basis of nothing at all, that Donna and Irene have been intimate since shortly after the accident. It would explain a lot. It would explain why, every time Donna left the house and Victor expended tremendous, heroic amounts of energy to carry himself to the medicine cabinet and peek inside, Donna's diaphragm was sitting there, inert, placid, smug as an inscrutable grin, to torture her already guilt-wracked husband with his own unmotivated jealousy. He'd imagined that she'd bought a second one, leaving this one always in the cabinet as evidence of innocence; but he'd never been able to find the second one, not in her purse, her dresser, her closet, not any-where. Well, he didn't know a lot about what dykes did, but by God he knew enough to know that they didn't need diaphragms to do it.

What she hears, after her ears acclimate to deciphering the mingled murmurs, are sequential declamations, punctuated with snippets (though she doesn't know this) from Heine and Leibnitz, Chekhov and Kafka, Freud and Einstein, Trotsky, Emma Gold-man, Walt Kelly, Goethe, La Guardia, Nietzsche, Emerson, Push-kin, and the *Bintel Brief.*

The topic this Thursday, proposed by Moshe Blender, is 'What Is Work?' Everyone suspects that Moshe has suggested this topic because he wants one that will lend itself to encomia on his neph-ew's advances in the field of medical-instrument design. For a month now members have been formulating positions, inventing their colleagues' responses and appropriate rejoinders, working out ways to say things on the subject not only true but impressive, not only impressive but true. Some work on microscoping a single thought into prolix oration, others on telescoping a wealth of thoughts into concise proclamation. As always, though, prepared statements and projected directions are sidetracked by statements that startle, directions unforeseen; and despite foundations laid and objections anticipated, a certain brand of spontaneity takes over, unlikely given the ground rules of the rotating floor and their provision that any objection to what was said on one's left must wait through twenty other comments until the floor arrives from one's right. To take notes would be thought gauche, and memo-ries not being what they once were, some Paideians sit patiently through twenty-one remarks only to draw a blank when their turn finally arrives. Nevertheless, the following views, among others, replete with instances, anecdotes, aphorisms, *Reden,* and *mots* of all sorts, emerge and drift through the ceiling toward Irene's left ear:

Work is what makes life worthwhile.

Work is what no one would do unless starvation were the alternative.

Work is what needs to be done.

Work is what someone chooses to do.

Work is what someone will pay for.

Work is what someone takes pride in.

Work is what someone would prefer not to do.

Work is what makes a product come into being (especially a new product, such as forceps of specially treated aseptic space-age polymers).

Work is what destroys the autonomy of the individual in the service of the institutions that oppress little people.

Work is ergs and ergs alone.

Work is whatever someone loves to do.

Work is whatever someone does.

This last viewpoint comes as close as a viewpoint can come in Paideia to being ridiculed. Various members attempt to invent something that someone could do that could not possibly be considered work. Succeeding members find themselves imagining circumstances under which the foregoing examples might be considered work. Getting a tan: but if you were a model who needed one for a commercial; ordering from a menu: but if you were a restaurant critic; *kvetch*ing: but if you were any kind of critic; *kib-bitz*ing: but if you were a consultant; taking a nap: but if it contributed to greater on-the-job efficiency later in the afternoon; daydreaming: but if you were an inventor; the conjugal act: but if you were a . . .

Others object that being able to imagine circumstances under which a phenomenon could be called work does not make that phenomenon by definition work, everywhere and always—must work be activity, must it be effortful, must it be recognized by society as having value?

Along these lines and others, a shopful of retirees (Theo the exception) pursue the work of defining work. All of which leaves Irene quite perplexed.

Much of the meeting is taken up with exchanges so ingrained they have reached the status of the monthly, the generic, the chronic.

Benjamin Flinchmesser, for instance, when declaiming displays a propensity to commence his remarks with the phrase 'In life.' Matthew Pelff invariably opens his next statement with a meditation on the superfluity of such a phrase: 'In lie if? Esso post *fought*, Benchmen? In debt? In deft ally if? Out off lie if? Inny tink fawn coot say hiss "In lie if"; fawn coot hotly tink off ah tink, it hiss naught "In lie if." Deuces ah minninkliss piss redrig.' Month after month, Matthew's own redrig is deployed to neutralize Benjamin's, with no other member taking up either side in the debate. Reseating Matthew at the far end of the ellipse from Benjamin does little good; the former always remembers what the latter says, and takes him to the same monthly task for it. Likewise, Paideians await, along with Moshe Blender's monthly dissertation on the importance of medical-instrument design, Rudolph Furman's considered opinion that, let the topic be what it will, 'Hit sly canny teen kells . . .'

All Paideians, without exception, know that Theo will bring to the topic a laconic wisdom that often takes a linguistic and relativistic turn. In this case, 'Voik,' says Theo in turn, 'hiss avoid, in avoiders allface dissem. Avoiders dot, dot ah pie sin mince fit devoid. You min doos, eye min dot, in feel itch min sumtink, fun diffint fin deodor. Bit avoiders even avoid, enspy toss: naught ah *tink*, bit red air ah *void*. Devoid mince fought de pie sin mince, in devoid fit out de pie sin mince naught ink. Deuces fie ah pie sin most imply voids fit cay air. Rim ember *Arbeit Macht Frei.*'

Home, however painfully, Donna must go. What to tell Victor has overtaken even what to do in her mind as the burning question. Couldn't they just call time, take it again from the top, or if not from the top, from some recognizable spot after the accident? Donna knows she can't wish to contravene facts, but besides facts aren't there attitudes, tones, that could be eliminated, adopted, or done without? Couldn't Victor know she loves him, couldn't she repent and redress? No secrets from this day forward between Donna and her Victor, Vicky and his Don.

With relief, reform, without recrimination, with resolve, Donna will tell all, come clean, start fresh, breathe deep, go straight and narrow, and have at least a fighting chance of making it work. 'It': whatever, the whole thing, make it work. 'In a spirit of reconciliation, I come to you today to propose a new . . .' 'Victor, darling, there's something I want to tell you, and before I do I want you to promise not to . . .' 'Forgive me, Victor, for I have sinned . . .'

Donna doesn't know how she will find the words to say what she needs to say, but with God's help she will find them, and when she has found them she will do whatever Victor requires of her to make things right, make things work, make Victor as nearly happy as Victor can be in this life. With her foetus, she will do whatever Victor sees fit. And by God if it doesn't work it will not be for lack of trying on her part.

Home, with a newfound will and slate-wiping optimism, Donna goes. All she hopes is to find Victor sober. If Victor is sober, she decides, everything will be all right.

Victor is sober as a judge, soberer than a judge, the soberest judge, in fact, that Donna will ever see. Donna is not long in comprehending why, despite her absence, Victor is uninebriated beyond all hopes and recent precedent. Not despite but because of her absence is Victor sober. He long since emptied every bottle in the house, long enough to recover entirely from their effects, and even from the effects of recovering from their effects. So sober is Victor, in fact, that he scares Donna; instead of reviling her, he maintains an ominous, maddening silence.

'Vic, I'm sorry, I'm so sorry, for lots of things, I've got so many things to tell you, I don't know where to start, Vic, listen, I love you, and, but I've been such a wreck, such pain and confusion, I've got to talk to you now, honey.'

Victor's eyes, Victor's mouth, Victor's forehead, even Victor's stubble doesn't move. It's as if they're all as dead as his legs.

'Victor, I can't stand it when you won't talk to me; it's like a death to me; it's worse than a beating, Victor talk to me.'

Victor's nares quiver, and now he's a small vulnerable creature that freezes because it has no defense, but can't stop its heartbeat from betraying life and fear. Donna approaches quietly, carefully, not to frighten the woodland creature, to let it know it won't be attacked, to touch it if possible with kindness, to stem the quivering with gentle lullaby care.

'Don't you,' he bellows, 'touch me,' and suddenly he's large and threatening, untamed, drops of a tearlike salivalike liquid whipping in and out of his nose with his fierce rapid savagely hyperventilating breath.

'Victor, I would have come home if I could, I would have called, you know I would have . . .'

When he speaks, it is with such exaggeration that she thinks he is possessed by an alien presence, a voice whose sarcasm, in all the years of bitterness, she's never heard: 'IIIIrrrrreeee-eeeeennnnne caaaaallllllled,' he oozes, as if these two rolling semantic waves, crashing on the shore of her ears, should wash away all doubt and tell her all she needs to know, as if, knowing now that *Irene called,* she should feel all he feels, curl like a dead leaf, and disintegrate, as if these words are the key to the mysteries of the ages, the Sphinx's reply, the words that announce the end of the world, the apocalyptic told-you-so of life as we know it on earth.

Irene called? A phone message? 'While You Were Out'?

Bewildered, Donna replies without forethought, without managing nuance, in a tone as blank as Victor's eyes were a moment ago: 'What did she say?'

'She told me everything,' lies Victor, grimly triumphant.

Now Donna's blood crystallizes in her veins, and her tissues bristle against the air that surrounds her. 'O God,' she says, not to the deity, not to Victor, not even to herself. 'O God,' she says to no one.

Seeing her face, Victor thinks he knows, finally, what a pillar of salt looks like, and he hatefully feels: vindictive, vicious, vindicated, victorious.

If you don't have a car and you can't afford a cab, the route from Gretchen's loft to Dempler's estate is a straight shot from Fourteenth Street to Two Forty Second Street on the One train, the so-called Broadway Seventh Avenue Local, and then an increasingly affluent walk as the neighborhood changes from the first few blocks of graffiti-covered storefronts and grim-looking tenements under the el past the high-security high-rises nearer the river and finally the gates of the unnaturally kempt and fully fledged and fenced estates of Riverdale. To save a bit of time, you could hop on the Two or Three train, the Seventh Avenue Expresses, to Ninety Sixth, after which Two and Three veer off under the top end of Central Park toward the South Bronx, while you wait for the local (the One you ignored back in the Village) that will trail along under Harlem, under Washington Heights, then up to the elevated tracks for a short time before reaching its terminus in a part of the Bronx more different from where the Two ends up than you'd expect if you judged from the names of the stops: Two Forty First, Two Forty Second.

Laurence prefers the straight shot, partly in honor of the fact (unless it was a fiction) that Gretchen told him: that Broadway, 'the longest street in America' (limited-access highways aside, she must mean, thought Laurence), is itself a straight shot that starts at Battery Park, New York, New York, U.S.A., and ends in Montréal, Québec, Dominion of Canada. Imagine a street with such a span; the very Broadway under which he rumbles and that rumbles along above him, is it in Montréal called *Cheminvaste*? Such perseverance, such crosscultural continuity, dumbfounds Laurence, and to honor it in his own small way he opts for the One. Besides which, when you debarked at Ninety Sixth, wouldn't you be waiting for just the train you thought was too slow at the other end; or are expresses so fast and locals so frequent that a Two or Three overtakes one or more Ones between Fourteenth and Ninety Sixth? How frequent they are is something he's not sure of, since he always takes the first One that comes along.

Soon enough, though through no conscious effort and despite the grasses toward which he burrows in the morning, the cellist toward whom he retraces his stops at the end of the day, and not a few other less definite points of arrival and departure he ponders in between, Laurence knows the stops of the number One by heart: Fourteenth, Eighteenth, Twenty Third, Twenty Eighth, Thirty Fourth, Forty Second, Fiftieth, Fifty Ninth, Sixty Sixth, Seventy Second, Seventy Ninth, Eighty Sixth, Ninety Sixth, One Oh Third, One Tenth, One Sixteenth, One Twenty Fifth, One Thirty Seventh, One Forty Fifth, One Fifty Seventh, One Sixty Eighth, One Eighty First, One Ninety First, Dyckman, Two Oh Seventh, Two Fifteenth, Two Twenty Fifth, Two Thirty First, Two Thirty Eighth, Two Forty Second. And on the way home, Two Forty Second, Two Thirty Eighth, and so forth, of course. The single anomaly— what's wrong with this picture?—Dyckman, fascinates Laurence. Is this street, alone on the One line, too interesting to be numbered? What about it requires a name amid this welter of arithmetical thoroughfares?

'What's the story with this Dickman Street?' he asks Gretchen, who is practicing breathing, getting a head start on third-trimester homework.

'Dickman? You mean Dykeman? In Washington Heights? What about it?'

Washington Heights sounds so honorific, so high, Laurence always likes the name. 'It's Dykeman?'

'Right,' says Gretchen, perhaps a bit annoyed at having to confirm what she has conveyed once so clearly, especially when she's trying to breathe, 'Dykeman. What about it?'

'Well, it doesn't have a number. Is it like One Hundred Tenth Cathedral Parkway, with a name *and* a number?'

'I don't think so. It's just Dyckman. Lots of streets don't have numbers.'

'I know, but it's the only one on the whole One line without one.' So his limited experience has taught him.

'That's not true, south of here none of them have numbers.'

Laurence considers: south of here. He hasn't the foggiest idea what's south of here on the One. 'What's south of here?'

'Oh, Christopher, Houston, Canal, I don't know, Chambers, no Franklin, then Chambers; what's your *point*, Laurence?'

Come to think, he has the foggiest idea: he knows Christopher (which, because it reminds him of Crickenberger, he prefers to call Sheridan Square), and he's heard of Houston and Canal, but they do seem beside the point in the present discussion. Though between breaths Gretchen has posed a reasonable question: what is his point? 'The point,' says Laurence with earnest emphasis, 'the *point* is simply that from Fourteenth to Two Forty Second all the streets have numbers except one, which has a name. Doesn't that strike you as strange?'

'All the stops, not all the streets. And no, it doesn't strike me as strange in the slightest. Not even a little bit.'

'Well, maybe you've been living here so long you don't see what's right in front of your nose' (which is, in fact, the point she, in her gravely measured attempts at gravid breathing, has been taught to focus on). 'I mean, you're going along, One Fifty Seven, One Sixty Eight, One Eighty One, One Ninety One, then suddenly out of nowhere, blammo, Dyckman, then Two Oh Seven and Two Fifteen and . . .'

Gretchen's tightly controlled exhale underscores sarcasm: 'I *know* the stops on the Broadway Local, Laurence,' though actually, as she hasn't ridden it above Seventy Ninth in a long while, this may be a fib, 'but I still don't see what's strange. There's no law that says stops have to be numbered.'

'Exactly,' shoots back Laurence in a checkmate tone. 'Precisely! There's no such law, no such law at all. And *given* that there's no such law, decisions had to be made—where to put stops, what to call them—and from the prevalence of numbered names, you generally get a pretty good idea of where you are on a north-south axis. I mean, it could be One Ninety Eighth, Two Hundredth, whatever it is up there. But there's one street above Fourteenth that has the, the, the courage or something to exercise its perfectly legal right not to be numbered.'

'Oh brother, stop, not street, and God, Laurence, what's strange is you're what's strange, talking about subway stops with the courage of their convictions. What you're saying is *beaux arts*, Laurence.' *Beaux arts* is Gretchen's cute way of saying bizarre; she is constantly classifying events on the streets of Manhattan as *beaux arts*. 'Streets don't name themselves—some guy named Dyckman gave somebody some money for something or something—and they certainly don't have courage or cowardice or rights.'

'Well, logically, of course not,' concedes Laurence. 'But aren't you the least bit curious about this street without a number, this Dyckman?' As he repeats the name now, he pictures the brave little Dutch boy with his heroic finger, now full-grown and holding things together in Washington Heights. The more he thinks about it, the more he wants to visit Dyckman.

'Laurence, I am not. Not a jot, not a tittle, not even a *soupçon*.'

'Never mind, I'm interested enough for two.'

'You're more than interested enough, I'd say, for the whole world.'

'Okay, somebody's got to be. Let it be me. But tell me what you know about this Dyckman.' Laurence is imagining a plaza with a monumental statue of the Dutch man, eyes bulging, neck veins straining, finger inserted in a brick wall, inverse Pyramus saving the municipality from the flood. In fact, wasn't there another Pyramus, wife of Decathlon, who *had* a flood? Or was there? Was Paramus, New Jersey, originally a Pyramus that got, Paprikashically, on its way through Ellis Island, mutilated? Laurence groans at the quantity of things one doesn't know; but Gretchen, having given up finally on breathing, is waxing informative.

'There's not a damned blessed thing in the world to know about Dyckman Street. It's a street like hundreds of others in New York, it's got a subway stop on it, it's mostly Spanish up there now I think, and it's probably got cigar stores and *grocerías* and Spanish graffiti, which looks the same as English graffiti, since you can't read any of it anyway.' Gretchen is certainly irritable today, thinks Laurence, knowing she's usually rather a fan of the City's *beaux arts*, stylized signatures. 'And lots of fairly poor people walk back and forth and spit on the sidewalk and stop to pick up a paper or bawl out motorists or play their number' (Number! thinks Laurence) 'or buy an ice-cube tray or a can of tomato paste or probably up there lots of different kinds of beans. Laurence, here's what, if anything, is interesting about Dyckman Street: on Dyckman Street, there's more kinds of beans in cans than you ever thought existed on the face of the earth. It's *all* beans on Dyckman, white beans, black beans, pink beans, pinto beans, and names you can't imagine, pigeon beans, fava beans, babalooey beans, blidgewidget beans, the street is paved in beans, Dyckman is Bean Street USA. All right? Okay?'

'Beans?'

'Yeah, beans. With names, not numbers.'

'Wow.'

'Wow is right. I hope this kid of yours is less *beaux arts* than his bonkers bozo papa. I can't believe we're having this conversation; you know, when you came in, I was trying to breathe. Besides, doesn't the train go elevated at Dyckman, don't you see what it's like up there?'

'Only from the air, but elevation just supports my point, that there must be something special, worth seeing, up there. What else besides beans?'

'What else besides beans. Oh boy. Nothing. It might be the stop where you'd get off for the Cloisters, or maybe that would be One Ninety First. I'm not sure anymore. Gee, you know about the Cloisters?'

Conversations between the pale young lady and the wizened young man have always, from their first colloquium on the state of his knees, taken these farcical turns. When they were both in the right mood, it felt just fine. When one of them wasn't, it was usually a good bet that the other would be, and then . . . well, Laurence is pleased that Gretchen's dissertation on the Beans of Dyckman has gotten that out of her system, and she's ready to have a serious conversation.

'No, tell me about the Cloisters,' encouraging, happy with the change in her tone, even happier to have a reason (maybe) to get off at Dyckman, thinking (maybe) they'll make the trip together sometime. Cloisters sounds a bit parochial for Laurence's taste, but if it would get them up to Washington Heights and off at Dyckman (maybe), it might be worth it.

The Cloisters, according to Gretchen Barron, either was (or were) a single European monastery brought over in numbered, disassembled, then reassembled chunks, or represented parts of various monasteries gathered piecemeal and combined for the first time on this side of the ocean by either some wealthy industrialist or the City back in the nineteenth or the first half of the twentieth century. Truth to tell, Gretchen doesn't know beans about the Cloisters, except that it's a magical place to visit, free on Tuesdays, and the more she thinks about it the more she thinks that maybe she and Laurence, who have scarcely been out of the house together since the disastrous Upper West Side party, ought to go up there some Tuesday and have a truly lovely time. She also recalls, almost alone among a myriad of *beaux arts* objects, a boxwood rosary bead about the size of a tennis ball, with scenes from the life of Jesus unbelievably carved inside in layers, giving the illusion, which was really no illusion, of depth, perspective, relief.

'Hey,' says Gretchen, 'let's get off at Dyckman sometime soon. How's about Tuesday?'

Donna, of course, was wondering what could possess Irene to spill her friend's personal beans to Victor, whom Irene had never met, had even heard of for the first time only a week or so since. Granted, from Donna's point of view, Irene had known her longer only in theory; but if Irene was to be believed, Donna had been a significant figure in her distant past and recent memory, even a model, filling in the blank of 'What would _____ do?' 'If Irene was to be believed,' indeed! Why had she trusted a virtual stranger with her most intimate and potentially incriminating or at least conjugally explosive secrets? A person says you sat for her, and you spill your guts, for what? Though she couldn't have sworn under oath that she'd actually sat for Irene, she would have bet that Irene was a friend, worthy of trust and desirous to help. Was Donna not the judge of character she thought herself? How could she be so wrong? And if she wasn't wrong, how could Irene have thought that telling Victor 'everything' would help? Donna, who had resolved to tell Victor all, nevertheless could not imagine by what rationale Irene Embler Paprika could have imagined that *her* telling all would be of service to herself, to Victor, to Donna, to anyone on earth.

Victor took Donna's baffled silence as sure confirmation of the truth of his suspicions. If parts of Victor's body were nonfunctional, other parts were more than adequate: his hackles, dander, gorge all rose at this proof that his wife not only was confirmed, avowed, admitted, but had the gall not even to try to deny it. If she did, of course, he knew what to say: 'Don't try to deny it.' But still, since she didn't, he wished she would, because if she didn't try to deny it, he had no idea what to say; but by some preconscious apothegm of contrapositivity, it seemed to Victor that maybe he could figure out an appropriate response.

'Just try to deny it,' he essayed. 'Just try. This explains why your diaphragm hasn't moved from the shelf in a year, how you can get your perverse kicks without paying the price and without any telltale evidence. Yeah, it all comes clear.'

Not for Donna, who, just now, found it all becoming rather less than clear. If a pregnancy wasn't paying the price, and a foetus telltale evidence, of perverse kicks, then Donna wasn't sure what would be. What *had* Irene told Victor? Of course, whatever she told him would later be characterized by him as 'everything,' because it was everything she had told him. Had she *not* told him Donna was pregnant? If not, what would 'everything' consist of? A simple affair with a gynecologist? Yet how would that explain the diaphragm? Irene wouldn't have told him about Crickenberger's diagnosis of infertility without following it up with the story of its disproof, would she? What would be the point of that? To ask Victor exactly what Irene had told him might raise suspicions that there was more to be told. Better to let 'everything' remain undefined for the time being than to start playing cat-and-mouse with Victor in this mood. Yet leaving 'everything' undefined put Donna in a rather strange, a rather inverted position, one that would have made Irene feel as odd as it made Donna: the position of wondering, incessantly and inconclusively, 'What would Irene do?'

'I thought,' said Irene, 'he might have contacted you. That he might be looking for you.'

'Eye fishy foot. If eye new vayer, eyeful be loo kink fa *him*.'

'When his father died, you know, when he lost contact with you, he didn't know why you . . . disappeared, but he thought maybe it was something he had done.'

They were drinking dark coffee despite the hour, the darkest

Irene had ever seen, and Theo was smoking, floating in a blue cloud that made him seem impermeable, not unapproachable but invulnerable, and reminded Irene oddly of Superman, the blue of his hair, though Theo's was greyish brown or brownish grey with age and nicotine.

'Eye luff dot buy.'

He loves that boy. Irene thought she could almost hear Theo's tears sizzle in the hot smoke.

'I know I've been wrong, and believe me if I could undo it all I would, and I'll do anything I can to make it right. I'll do whatever you want, Victor, whatever you think is right.'

'Whatever I *want*, whatever *I* want. What the fucking Jesus aitch Christ do you damn well *think* I would fucking want you to bloody fucking do?'

'I don't know, Victor, I truly don't know. But since I've gotten into this mess trusting myself, I'm going to trust you to get me out of it. Whatever you think is right, I'll do.'

'Damn, bitch, don't play games with me. There's only one thing you fucking *can* do. You just fucking stop it, that's what you fucking do, you fucking *stop* it.'

It was unclear to Donna whether Victor would be referring to the affair, already stopped, the pregnancy, ongoing, or some other aspect of 'everything' that was either slipping her mind or had entered his by accident. Now it occurred to Donna for the first time that maybe Irene had covered for her, had lied, had told Victor some less incriminating story to hide the real one, and . . . and then had to leave town in a hurry, so couldn't convey to Donna the nature of the cover story. This seemed about as likely as any other notion she had of what had passed between Irene and Victor—that is to say, not very.

'Stop what, Victor?'

'Oh, for sweet fucking Mary's holy sake, Donna.' And she had, for the first time in their troubled married life, a sure conviction that if he could reach or outrun her, he would have hit her. For a moment, she was grateful for his handicap; but she immediately deposited that gratitude onto the growing heap of things for which she felt guilt.

Why a vest? Think of a vest: it covers nothing up, holds nothing up, *does*, really, nothing. It is not something you need, not something that protects from wind or rain or indecent-exposure citations. It has a purity rare in garments, rare in almost anything. It makes you think again about garments. Its name, you note, is the generic term: vestment, 'vest' meant clothing. Try to think of another garment whose name means clothing. It represents the entire class of entities of which it partakes. Try to think of one other.

Always the last remnant of an old suit, the vest endures. For this reason you can find it cheap at used-clothing shops, thrift stores, garage sales, yard sales, sellouts of all sorts. What else can you find for a couple of bucks that has lasted so long and stands for so much?

The vest—points hanging down around the loins in front, swaying a bit in the breeze, sides crossing belt-level up to the sateen back cinched about the reins and faded to a fine soft luster, collarless shawl about the neck, sleeveless, easy on and off, replete with gratuitous buttons and pockets—combines extremes: economy and luxury, thrift and superfluity.

Grandpa Theo used to say: Look at him, he meditates whether a flea has a belly button. He said it in Yiddish. Mama would translate. Belly button is 'pipik': a funny word. Highly unlikely that the Yiddish for vest means clothing. It doesn't in most languages. It so happens that in English it does, but that's hardly a firm foundation on which to build. Just because a guy's name is Guy doesn't mean he's less atypical than the next guy.

Theory. 'Teary,' Theo would say. What does it have to do with anything? Why a vest? I like the way it feels. *Noor vee doos.*

'What do you know about Laurence's birth?'
'Hiss bite?'
'Yes, his birth. *How* he was born. Was there anything unusual?' Irene wasn't at all sure she wanted to know the answer to this question, but thought she owed it to Laurence to ask.
'He force bawn in Menhettin, ah smott buy, pie ficked.'
'But the actual birth. Was there anything unusual?' She didn't want to name the disputed fact she sought; she wanted (or did not want) Theo to volunteer the information. She worried about his memory, though; he was quick, he was alert, and seated a foot or two from his eyebrows she still couldn't avoid the idea that he was

even wise, but a man of this age, his recall might not be definitive.

'Deckchill bite? Eye force naught dayer.'

'When did you first see him?'

'De buy force naught fell, ah smott buy bit fickly. Day taught dizzizzizz foot indenture him, in dayer force no fizzit ink entill fun munt edge.'

Fun munt edge! thought Irene. My God: fun munt edge!

'Dear Lord, I ask You to forgive me for thanking You that Victor is incapacitated. Believe me, Lord, I would give anything to have him healthy and whole in mind and body. I just thought he was going to strike me. You understand: it was not a true prayer, the last one, it was more like flinching at something that scares you. I don't mean You, Lord, I know nothing scares *You*. But so many things scare *me*, sometimes I don't know what I think anymore. Forgive me for thanking You. Thank You.'

Seven

⁓

Expectant Gretchen's encounter with the infamous Dr. Crickenberger had long since soured her on the faculty in general; but needing, for the protection of all parties concerned, a guide through the obstetrical course she had to run, she sought one she could trust. For her that meant one who possessed the organs in question, and tabloid ads provided names and numbers of several who met this criterion. Wording of the copy eliminated practitioners of more occult branches ('Tune newborn's bio-aura to planet's electromagnetic harmonies! At Special Delivery, we give you more than a baby, we give you "serenity"!'; 'Give your child a head start on the market—Up-to-date techniques link offspring's Saturn cycle to Dow Jones peaks—Labor Market, Inc., is bullish on your baby!'), as well as those who sounded prissy, reluctant to mention what they were about ('Reliable and efficient—Discretion assured—Major credit cards accepted—Full refund if not satisfied'); but Gretchen still had a handful of M.D.s, a handful of midwives, and a choice to make. After weighing the names, she decided to give Audrey Poole a try.

Laurence couldn't help thinking of 'Audrey' as an adjective, reminiscent of British place-names (Locksley Hall, Cholmondeley Heath, Tunbridge Wells), maybe because when he first heard 'Audrey' he thought of 'tawdry,' the only word that occurred to him that rhymed. He wondered if this was true, and spent a while trying to think of another. Well, 'bawdry'; and if there were two, there might be more. He put his mind to it: laundry no, chowdery no, dawdly no, maudlin no; why did all these words strike him as vaguely British, faintly damning, slightly tawdry? It hardly mattered, of course, since he would soon discover that almost everyone, including patients, called her 'Aud,' clipped as if short for 'audacious.' 'Aud,' too, seemed British, even literary, Briterary, clubby, diminutive of Auddlington or Audmer-Randolph, with perhaps a roman numeral understood. Of course, it also homonymed with 'awed,' but that participle, from what he'd heard, would not aptly modify Dr. Poole.

Gretchen didn't ask Laurence to come along, but seemed touched that he wanted to. He vaguely understood she'd need a coach for birthing exercises, and he (recalling 'I'll be the mother') thought himself the natural candidate.

That was how Laurence learned about Aud, who taught birthing classes to a packed house at the Greenwich Wimmin's Oasis, in what had once been an upstairs parlor. Monday evening, freshly bathed (though he showered at Twelve Clefs, the subway ride always made him feel like a dip when he got home), hair slicker than normal, torso dewy as a fresh-rinsed vegetable, best vest pressed, he felt crisp and slightly complacent as he waited anxiously for Gretchen to take him to the Oasis. She appeared anxious, though, in a different sense, and he wanted to know why.

'I've never seen a man at the clinic, Laurence. I think you might feel out of place.'

'If they don't mind and you don't mind, I don't mind,' chirped Laurence.

'They might. I don't.'

'If you don't, I don't. Why would they?'

'They just aren't used to men on the premises.'

'Well, if you don't want me to come, I won't.'

'I do, but I think they don't.'

'They?'

'Well, Aud in particular.'

That was what Laurence learned about Aud.

'I'm worried they might find it intrusive, or disruptive.'

'By "it," you mean me.'

'Not you. A man.'

'I see.'

'I don't mean that how it sounds.'

'I know.'

'But I think they, I mean Aud, might.'

'Might what?'

'Mean it the way it sounds.'

'I'm lost.'

'Look, I'll go alone this time, but I'll ask about your coming in the future.'

The future sounded formal to Laurence, almost forbidding, but he let that pass. For now, though, it seemed he was all dressed up with nowhere to go.

'Very well then, I'll see you on your return.'

Gretchen caught the Briterary tone, didn't know quite what to make of it, but knew Laurence wasn't happy. 'Look, I'll ask, maybe it's fine, I don't want you to feel bad about this.'

'Then I won't.'

'I hope not,' said Gretchen, as if he shouldn't be too sure.

From the page Victor left the Book open to, Donna was not exactly sure which rule he was accusing her of having broken; it covered such a multitude of sins. Most of these applied exclusively to males: those who uncovered their fathers' nakedness or lay with their daughters-in-law or uncles' wives or with a woman having her sickness, uncovering the nakedness of her fountain. Only a handful applied directly to women: 'If a woman approaches any beast and lies with it, you shall kill the woman and the beast; they shall be put to death, their blood is upon them.' Donna would have surmised their blood would be upon the one who put them to death, but in any case it was unlikely that Irene had told him *that*. 'A man or a woman who is a medium or a wizard shall be put to death; they shall be stoned with stones, their blood shall be upon them.' If they were indeed stoned with stones, this last seemed an incontrovertible likelihood, but Donna could not convince herself that Irene would tell Victor she was a medium or a wizard, or that he would believe her if she did. 'And the daughter of any priest, if she profanes herself by playing the harlot, profanes her father; she shall be burned with fire.' Though Donna had admittedly played something like the harlot, her father was an electrician, not a priest; if he had been, he wouldn't have had a daughter.

Other passages she found difficult to interpret: 'None of them shall defile himself for the dead among his people, except for his nearest of kin, his mother, his father, his son, his daughter, his brother, or his virgin sister (who is near to him because she has had no husband; for her he may defile himself). He shall not defile himself as a husband among his people and so profane himself.' Donna, who associated defiling oneself with incontinence, had trouble picturing how one might do so as a husband among his people, or why in heaven's name he ought to for his virgin sister. Victor did from time to time defile himself, but his sisters were hardly virgins, and Donna could not make applicable sense of the scripture. She puzzled over Leviticus for some time, amazed at its tonal difference from the verses she tended to attend to, amazed too at the inventive wealth of crimes and the general applicability of a single punishment. Though she failed to find her own sin, she was taken aback at how few of those listed were not capital. Is nothing sacred? she thought. Or rather, is everything? She wondered if she hadn't been right after all to thank God for Victor's motor incapacity (though, if he had access to stones, he could certainly throw them, and she shuddered to think that these could be divinely sanctioned tosses).

After lengthy study, Donna realized that a passage she had already read over several times held relevance for her household: 'None of your descendants throughout their generations who has a blemish may approach to offer the bread of his God. For no one who has a blemish shall draw near, a man blind or lame, or one who has a mutilated face or a limb too long, or a man who has an injured foot or an injured hand, or a hunchback, or a dwarf, or a man with a defect in his sight or an itching disease or scabs or crushed testicles.' What could Victor be trying to tell her: a man blind or lame, a limb too long, an injured foot, crushed testicles? Victor, apparently, felt debarred from approaching to offer the bread of his God. Perhaps he wasn't accusing her after all, but excusing himself. From what? From approaching to offer the bread of his God? Had she ever expected him to? There had been some talk, before the marriage, of conversion, but never of ordination, which would have precluded the nuptials.

Bring.
Bring.
Bring.

'Hello?'

'Hello, is this?'

'This is Laurence. Did you want Gretchen?'

'Yes, yes please,' strangely imploring, as if he might be inter-ested in keeping her from Gretchen, as if she'd do anything to convince him to put Gretchen on.

'Gretchen's not home right now.' She's at the Oasis, but who knows if this is somebody she wants to know that. 'Can I take a message?'

'Oh yes please, please. This is Donna. We're old friends, from Providence. If she could call me back. No wait, I don't want her to call me. Do you know when she'll be back?'

'Should be, I don't know, I'd think about an hour maybe. Two, to be sure.'

'Okay, tell her I called, please. Donna from Providence. She'll know. Tell her I'll try back later.'

Bring.
Bring.

'Hello?'

'Is Gretchen there?'

'Is this Donna again? I'm sorry, she's not back, I'm really not sure when it will be, is there a number where she can?'

'I'll call back in an hour or so.'

'Is there some message I could?'

'No. I'll call back.'

'I'm Laurence, by the way.'

'That's fine. I'll call.'

Bring.

The third time, Donna sounded different, or maybe just more so, more scared, possibly more drunk, thought Laurence. He was sorry, was she sure there was nothing he could. No. He was sorry, he thought she'd be home by. Never mind, she'd call.

Donna had no way of knowing which verse Victor expected would leap forth from the page to accuse her in her own eyes: 'If a man lies with a male as with a woman, both of them have committed an abomination; they shall be put to death, their blood is upon them.' And I figure that goes double for women, thought Victor. More believer than exegete, he had failed to notice that the male and the female of the species were often quite strictly differentiated in the Pentateuch; he assumed, and assumed Donna would assume as well, that a man lying with a male as with a woman was and had been since time immemorial the moral equivalent of a woman lying with a female as with a man. Having spent some time searching in vain for an equivalent passage regarding the explicitly lesbic, he took the liberty of assuming equal rights: since he himself found Donna's presumptive behavior an abomination, the passage seemed apt enough. As for putting to death, he was unsure whether that was his own responsibility; he was convinced, however, that if they died their blood would be upon them.

Putting to death had always been one of Victor's strong points. In childhood, he put countless insects, fish, amphibians, and small mammals to death. He crushed them under his heel; he fished them; he speared and squoze and crunched them; he hunted them with slingshot and air rifle, and later in life, with shotgun and .22. Once, without even trying, he hit a dog with his car, and was genuinely surprised by a warm feeling of accomplishment. Less pleasing had been the task of cleaning out the remains of luckless birds from jet engines when he worked in ground maintenance. And though he thought of himself as sustaining and nurturing abundance rather than putting to death, if we think for a moment about what those drums contained, what he sprayed through those nozzles, what blanketed those crops, it may occur to us that, dealing as he did in herbicides, pesticides, insecticides, fungicides, Victor Groat was a man of many cides, annihilating some that others might thrive. Every giving, considered Victor, involves a taking-away, and whosoever giveth must therefore . . .

Putting to death abominable human beings seemed quite another matter, though. In the Air Force, Victor, a bombardier, had in fact put to death not a few human beings, though it was anybody's guess how many of them had committed abominations in the eyes of the Lord. More recently, he had considered, long and often, putting himself to death, in response to frustration rather than abomination; and the notion had become rather more familiar and comforting than alien and shocking. He had never gotten around to selecting a method, even in fantasy, but he knew the choice of means would not be a problem if the time came when it felt like the right thing to do: he had, if nothing else, in the front closet behind the combat boots, tucked away in a ditty, a bottle that contained enough Malathion to do the business of an army of six-legged, and perhaps a platoon of two-legged, abominators.

Victor, in a casual search, had found neither in Leviticus nor anywhere else in Old or New explicit sanctions either for or against self-slaughter; if it was an abomination, though, he suspected he knew what the prescribed punishment would be. This thought threatened to lead to a conundrum of the sort that he usually dismissed as not worth the mental effort, and he declined to watch it ramify.

He knew that the laws of Rhode Island were somewhat more lax on these matters than Leviticus, of which he himself found parts rather harsh; but he reminded himself that Jesus came not to abolish but to fulfill the Law and the Prophets, and that not an iota, not a dot, would pass from the Law until all was accomplished. It was clear to Victor that all had scarcely been accomplished; it was equally clear that Rhode Island was not about to enforce the Law.

Gretchen returned toward eleven, looking drained and exhilarated at the same time. She had had the most marvelous talk with Audrey Poole. A Donna had called, three times, from Providence, sounding anxious or tipsy, maybe both, especially the third time, about a half hour ago. Gretchen picked up the phone.

'She doesn't want you to call. She said she'd call you.'

'That's ridiculous.'

'That's what she said.'

'She just wants to save me the money probably. I'll see what's up. It's okay, I know her husband.'

Bring.

Bring.

Bring.

Bring.

Bring.

Bring.

This many rings meant Victor was home alone, but once she'd got him started toward the phone, she didn't want to hang up.

'Yeah.'

'Hi Victor it's Gretch.'

'Gretchen, you know where the hell Donna is? She with you?'

'I was about to ask you the same, without the expletive. No, I'm
in New York. Isn't she in Providence?'

'Who the hell knows? She's so damned secretive, never tells me
a fucking thing, where she's going, who the hell with, when she'll
be back, fucking nothing.' Victor sounded even more embittered
than usual. 'What did you want with her?'

'Jesus, Victor, what kind of a question is that? I wanted to see
how she's doing.'

'Wanted to see how she's doing' sounded familiar to Victor.
Doing, doing. What's wrong with these women? Why do they all
want to see how his wife's *doing?* What's she been telling them?
What's she been *doing* with them?

'Gretchen, you know somebody who knows Donna, somebody
named Irene, in Providence?'

'No. Well, actually, I do know *of* an Irene in Providence, but
never mind.'

'What the fuck's that mean?'

'God, Victor, what's your problem? It means I heard about
somebody in Providence named Irene, but it doesn't matter, I don't
want to talk about it, Donna doesn't even know her.'

That's a damned lie, thought Victor.

'You okay, Victor?'

'Me? Oh yeah. Beautiful. Fucking peachy.'

'When she gets back, tell her I returned her call, okay?'

Bring.

'Hello?

'Donna, what's the matter? I tried to call you.

'Yeah, at home. Where else?

'Uh huh. Donna, what's the matter with him?

'Well, he sounded pretty weird, Donna. What's wrong with him?

'I don't know, like usual, but more so, really angry. He was pissed
that you were out, I think. Said you're secretive and never tell him
where you're going. He sounded weird, Donna. What's been happening?

'He asked if I know somebody named Irene. I don't think he
believed that I don't.'

Of course Laurence's ears perked at the proper name. Gretchen
thought they might, and now that his attention was caught, turned
as if to ask if there wasn't something he could do in the other

room. The other room, of course, was the bathroom, where there wasn't really anything he needed to do, but where he allowed he could probably find some way to occupy himself. He'd been less interested of late in cartography, but there were other things one could do in a tub, so he gathered up an armful of pillows and something to read and left Gretchen alone with A, T, T, & Donna.

Twice or thrice he clambered out of the pillow-lined clawfoot tub and opened the door to determine whether the conversation was finished. Once long silence convinced him that it was, and he emerged to find Gretchen, phone at ear, deeply engaged in frequent silent nodding. Back in the tub, he continued, without much interest, reading an article concerning the current crisis in post-secondary education, then another on whether tragedy is possible in the modern world.

Gretchen found him uncomfortably scrunched but not quite snoring. She woke him, sorry her call had taken so long: friend Donna was awfully upset and needed to talk. What time was it, Laurence wanted to know. It was late, past one, and tomorrow was Tuesday, promising excursion to Dyckman and incidentally the Cloisters. She'd tell him tomorrow about her talks—with Aud, with Donna. He should just get up and into bed and go back to sleep now. More oblivious than obedient, he did; but Gretchen, troubled, shaken, lay massaging her abdomen and slightly swollen breasts with both hands. Ankle propped against his calf for contact, buttocks squished against his thigh for comfort; Gretchen awake on into the night like a vigilant sentinel sensing danger.

How the hell do they *think* she'd be doing, a woman who's committed abominations, and (or *because?* shuddered Victor) married to dead weight? We're a hell of a pair, a dyke and a stick: no natural creature on the face of the earth with arms and no legs, and none that lies with its own kind as with another, an unnatural pair of beasts. And now Gretchen's in on it too; 'see how she's doing,' my ass. And she clammed up fast on that Irene business, realized who she was talking to, probably thinks she got away with it. And to think that Gretchen's slept over here maybe a dozen times and I never suspected a fucking thing: out there late into the night, 'talking,' 'old friends,' 'girltalk.' Fucking women, shit. Damned lucky we never did have a fucking kid: 'A dyke? You want to know what's a dyke, son? You know the little boy with the finger? Well, a dyke is like that only female, like your fucking mother and her fucking friends, a dyke is a woman with her finger in a dyke, that's what a fucking dyke is, son.'

God damn it, Donna, I loved you. Shit, I'm fucking crying, I still fucking love you, crying like a god damned woman and can't stop. If you just never would have done it. Or even another man, I could understand that, I could live with another man, I'd know how to fight that, and even if I lost you, I'd know you were at least a woman worth fighting for. But this. And you're never around when I need a little help or tenderness or even just a goddam *drink*, for Christ's sake! Is that too much to fucking ask, while you're out doing abominations and all I need is a fucking glass of fucking booze? Drink your damn tears like a woman, pillow of fucking salt.

Wait a minute. Whoa. 'Returned'? Time out. 'Returned her' fucking 'call'? Hold everything. You're out there calling people up on a fucking public phone? You're calling your dykes out on the street? You're out there dropping dimes in a pay phone when you've got this perfectly good phone here at home? Oh, yeah, I'll tell her you returned her goddam call. She's scared to call her dyke friends from the house, but they don't think twice, they call her right up, 'Hi Victor it's Gretch,' like nothing, like fucking *nothing*, like I'm supposed to give her a god damned fucking *message:* 'Coupla lesbos called. They want to know how you're *do*ing. How are you *do*ing, honey? How are you *do*ing? Who've you been *do*ing? What the fuck do you think you're *do*ing?'

Crying, defiling my damn self like a fucking woman.

Despite repeated round-trips to Riverdale, despite memorized stops and the complete obsolescence of his ingenuous previous notion that the subway was in any way sexy, it was, if less than a miracle, still more than a banality to partake of this mode of conveyance. And as if to emphasize that nothing quotidian was happening, the wizened young man rose early this day, not lounging in quilted luxury but sprouting from bed like a piece of nature in time-lapse photography. This Tuesday provided for both the special prospect of unwonted excursion: for Laurence, a journey to the unnumbered and elevated land of Dyckman; for Gretchen, escape from lofty confines to lofty expanses, greeny park surrounding the otherworldly age and isolation of the Cloisters.

Gretchen, though, when Tuesday arrived, was all for slow motion, in a state of near-exhaustion thanks to a fitful night thanks in turn to a call from a disturbed contralto. She chose for her morning cantata the slowest and longest she could find, the one whose *largo* was most *molto;* Laurence found it lugubrious and said as much, but Gretchen insisted on hearing it out over a lingering breakfast. Itching for Dyckman, he begged her to leave the dishes: he'd do them when they got back. Then he sat through enough time for three sinkloads while she made herself ready to leave, assuring him every few minutes it would only take a minute. He was just about to wash them after all when Gretchen emerged from the other room, scrubbed and kempt but still sluggish, the pinky-blue of her eyes surrounded by reddish whites.

On the train her face still looked splotchily bluish. Laurence, concerned, inquired.

'A restive night, restless. My friend Donna's in a bad way.'

'What's the story?'

'A long one.'

'So's the trip to Dyckman.'

'True, but I'm barely awake. Give me a few stops to deploy my brain functions.'

'Sure. The story starts at Fifty Ninth?'

'Make it Seventy Ninth.'

'Sixty Sixth?'

'Seventy Second.'

'You got it.'

'Deal.'

Screeching, squealing, whining, whirring, grinding, thunking subway train. Lead, rhythm, bass: catarrh, catarrh, catarrh.

'You know what, though?'

'What, though?'

'I wish she'd come to New York. I asked her, but she's scared to be away from home another night.'

'Another?'

'She spent one night at this person named Irene's house, and her husband just about threw a fit. By the way, I really appreciate how you've been about the Flash thing.'

He'd just about forgotten the Flash thing: another story. But the story about the woman he didn't know had a part about a woman with a name he knew, and that part interested Laurence particularly: 'I thought I heard the name Irene.'

'Victor wanted to know if I knew one who knew Donna in Providence.'

'Victor's the husband? Not my Irene, I guess.'

'Not likely. This was somebody Donna sat for years ago . . .'

Laurence recalled something about a revered Donna who sat, something about crayons, something about eyebrows, but the name escaped him. 'What's Donna's last name?'

'Groat.'

Groat didn't ring a bell.

'. . . that a couple weeks ago, out of the blue, she ran into again in a bar. After all that time, pure coincidence, Donna didn't even recognize her. But Donna was looped, and went home with Irene. Thought they'd be friends, then blam, out of nowhere, this Irene ups and betrays her.'

'Betrays?'

'Secretly tells some secrets to Victor, who's livid with Donna.'

'I thought you said they were married.'

'No no,' she shouted over the sound of the train, 'liv*id*, live *id*.'

'Oh,' mumbled Laurence, turning the opposite of the now clarified term. Pale and starting to be more or less visibly pregnant, shouting 'livid' atop her lungs, Gretchen attracted some anxious and a few amused stares on the not empty One.

'Imagine being betrayed by someone you took care of when they were little.'

'Sounds like parenthood. What manner of secrets?'

'Jeeps, it's convoluted. This Irene never even met Victor. Why would a person?'

'Search me. Clearly not my Irene, though. She doesn't drink.'

'Donna does more than she should. Victor does hardly anything but. I never understood what Donna saw. He was always a hotdog, and now he just sits on his buns.'

'Beg your pardon?'

'Victor was a pilot: dashing, exposed chesthair, goggles and silk-scarf type, lots of leather, a show-off. Had a horrible crash, which you couldn't help feeling sorry for. But he acts like it's the only thing ever happened to him. Now he's a rueful, reproachful semiplegic. I mean, who are we to judge, but you'd think a person would find a way of living with something that happened, finally find a way of taking it in . . .'

'Stride?'

'Right. Donna's done everything you could ask. She's had a hard life too.'

'How do you know her?'

'She's a singer, did a Strauss thing once with the Symphony.'

'Johann?'

'No, Richard. Used to do laps at the Y.'

Laurence wondered how one could become habituated to dew-laps at the Wye. Wattles at the blue Danube? Not Johann; this couldn't be right. Due lapse at the why. 'The Wye? The why?'

'The *Y*. We swam.'

'Double you see, eh?'

'Roger.'

Considering how difficult it was for Laurence three days weekly to avoid eavesdropping on random irrelevant conversations, he was amazed how difficult it also was to comprehend a well-known woman three feet from his face.

'Gretchen, here's Seventy Second. It's time for the story, but I'm having trouble following. Could you kind of start at the beginning?'

'Willco. Donna and I both have our periods, and we meet in the ladies' during intermission. She's fresh out of feminine hygiene, so I lend her one and we hit it off. The lights start blinking, so we meet after the show. We start swimming together—I used to swim a lot—and we're like best pals. Victor's a jerk about the whole thing, I think he's jealous or something. Member when I met you?'

'Course. On the bus. Did I ever tell you,' gazing down at her now more significant abdomen, 'I thought you were motherly?'

'Motherly? Far from it. I was coming back from Donna's, where . . . well, suffice to say, Victor can really be lunchmeat when he feels like it.'

'Wait, I'm lost.'

'Okay, so we're friends, and she's got a problem, and I refer her to this gynecologist I know.'

'Cricken?'

'Berger, yeah. So like a dope, but who am I to talk, she gets.'

'Involved?'

'Right. You aren't going to believe this.'

'Pregnant?'

'On the nose.'

'That bastard!'

'Victor?'

'No, Crickenberger.'

'Right.'

'You mean it's?'

'Crickenberger's bastard. Like father, like.'

'It's a boy?'

'Nobody knows. She's amnioagnostic.'

'And Victor is?'

'Having a cow.'

'I mean.'

'Impotent?'

'Yeah.'

'To put it mildly. Crickenberger's a bastard, Victor's impotent, and Donna's pregnant.'

'God.'

'He's in the story too. She's Catholic.'

'That's why she's still?'

'Right.'

'And this Irene told?'

'Right.'

'And Victor?'

'Is being absolutely a shit about the whole thing, and Donna doesn't even know for sure *what* Irene told him.'

'What else?'

'Who knows? But he doesn't talk as if he knows. I mean, he talks as if he knows *some*thing, something bad, but he doesn't talk as if he knows what Donna thinks Irene might have told him.'

'Why doesn't she ask him?'

'Laurence, think a minute.'

'Oh. Because if she asks him.'

'He'll ask her.'

'What she thinks.'

'Irene told him.'

'Geez.'

'Right.'

Not quite the Largest terrestrial carnivore in Earth history, but close enough.

Fun munt edge, thought Irene. She could see only two possibilities. One: Laurence, born in the usual manner, at the usual time, was afflicted by some neonatal syndrome that made him microbially vulnerable or otherwise unpresentable for the first munt edge. Two: Laurence, born at seven, pendant (hence equally unpresentable) for three, was introduced to his paternal grandpapa immediately upon receipt of his maternal walking papers, at which time, ten months since conception (effected, as Laurence had claimed all along, by paternal subterfuge?), Grandpa, ignorant of the facts, would credit his grandson with having attained not tree but fun munt edge. Where did he first see the boy, Irene wanted to know.

Proud papa brought the swaddled bantling to visit his grandpa here, in the Bronx. Theo invested the boy at that time with a piece of customized neckwear he'd designed and executed specially and kept on hand an unexpected extra expectant month for the occasion: bib with hand-painted pony happily feeding at hand-painted trough. He'd thoughtfully chosen a baby-blue washable terry and nontoxic lead-free droolproof paint (of a sort developed for heavy marine applications and not easily procured in nursery pastels). Little Laurence looked so adorable in that bib. And loved that bib: some corner or other of it, wrapping a pudgy digit, was almost never out of his mouth for the first year. When they took it away to the laundry, he gurglingly, chokingly wept and sucked his unadorned but equally washable, droolproof, and lead-free thumb. Memory of that so suckable bib brought a lump to Theo's leathery throat.

So sweet, and possibly so proleptic with regard to fingernails, thought Irene, but was more interested in the aetiology than the ethology of infant Laurence. Was there anything Theo could recall, other than being weakly, unusual?

The object of parental and grandparental affection was not so very weakly by the time grandpa met him. Only, for the first month, Theo was told of the child's infirmity. At a mere munt edge, in fact, the boy seemed so (how should Theo say in English?) developed, such a ma chewer *mench* with such a face, and already he could crawl. 'Kit chew imedgin dot, crow link et fun munt edge!'

Irene could, she could imedgin dot. But what she couldn't do just yet, at risk of appearing to this old man obsessed, and though it made her feel like a cross-examiner, was drop neonatal physiology: please, could he think, try to remember, was there anything at all, besides crawling and facial development, different about this baby?

Theo taught and taught. 'Dayer force, bit naught ah sicken afghan tink.'

It *might* be significant. What, what was it?

'Dayer force ah, ah raidniss.'

Inflammation!

Responding to her enthusiasm, Theo too perked up. 'Ya ya, ah nun phlegm asian dot gift dot buy ah tearbill pen, sew bet dot iffen de bip coo tint soot him. Tearbill, oy.'

Where? The pain, the infection, where?

'In hiss, hiss, hiss.' Theo, stumped, didn't know the word in English.

Yes?

'Hiss. Hiss. Hiss.' Groping for the word, forgetting Irene spoke no Yiddish, Theo blurted: *'Pipik!'* He gazed at Irene in momentary triumph, then disappointment, linguistic despair. She didn't know *pipik?*

Flushed with recovered long-term memory trace, eager to be of help, Theo lifted the downtown edge of whatever shirt was holding the box that told his heart to beat and exposed his own, prelinguistic, ace in the hole.

'His belly button?' warbled Irene.

Despite six decades this side of the ocean, this locution was unfamiliar. Nevertheless, willing to take Irene's word for it, Theo nodded and beamed and jabbed himself repeatedly, triumphantly, in the navel with his thumb.

At which Irene burst into tempestuous sobs.

Thinking he'd scandalized a demure *shikse*, Theo apologized and covered up rapidly, redressed though he didn't quite fathom her gentile grievance. But Irene just sobbed and burbled, bit her knuckles, shook her head.

'Oy, oy oy,' crooned Theo, lulling her by, 'dun vip, dun vip, Eyerin fin Red Eyelid, dun vip, no nid to vip.'

Rattling into a station under the northern half of the island, Laurence observed the platform, the changes he'd come to expect. The wan subterranean flower vendors of midtown yielded to stalwart skinny acoustic guitarists up around Columbia, who somehow managed to keep their place despite inevitable rackets on various tracks, summoning courage to warble 'Where Have All the Flowers Gone?' amidst commuter comings and goings, velvet-lined cases open to receive spare change; these in turn gave way to tough guys, hassled women, barely portable stereo rapspeakers, bottom-heavy basslines fading as quickly and despite amplification as irretrievably as gentler waves of folk had done at previous stops. Kids (they're just kids!) hanging out on benches, slouching against posts like they owned the place, menacing maybe. Why would kids hang out underground? What went on above to make the tunnel a more appealing spot to pass the time of day?

'So I asked, almost begged her, to come stay with us.'

Yes, thought Laurence, she should come stay with us, despite stringent space limitations; we could all knit booties, cottage industry, and help each other learn to breathe, always good to have someone to share your interests.

'But she's scared of what Victor might do, and besides.'

I'd be scareder of what he might do if I were *there*. 'Besides?'

'Victor can't really get along on his own. Well, can't, I mean won't, never has been willing to do for himself since the accident.'

'You mean he doesn't?'

'Cook, clean, get up, go out, do much of anything but sit and drink. I'd hate to be his liver.'

Wouldn't want to be any of his organs; sounds like a case of too much spleen, not enough heart. Underdeveloped, overdeveloped: out early, cut off late, there ahead of time for a bus behind schedule, public transportation. A jarring ride today: the subway isn't sexy.

'Men,' mildly expleted Gretchen.

'Men?'

'Maybe not each and every, but the great mass of men.'

'Lead lives of quiet desperation?'

'Not on your life: of noisy self-pity. They think they're so strong. They think they're so . . . manly. They're just a bunch of overgrown babies.'

Overgrown protozoa; Laurence has thought this before, including himself and with no gender attached. And it's not like Gretchen to cast generalized aspersions—how did she get from Victor Groat to Men?—but then the cusp of the trimester must be a touchy time. And what about himself? *He* didn't think he was so manly. Even as a boy, he didn't like caterpillars, payloaders, trucks.

'They? You mean us?'

'For the purposes of this discussion, Laurence, I will consider you an honorary woman.'

'Thank you, I think.' And he did think, did thank, felt grateful for that. At the very uptown stop they were now pulling into, the women, to him, looked sensical and determined, with various household staples, infants, groceries, angled on hips or in crooks of arms, toddlers in hand; it appeared that they, not little boys with impermeable fingers, held things together in Washington Heights, while the boys and men with fingers looked to him neither staunch nor heroic but hopeless, helpless, belligerent, defensive, blameworthy, blaming. Laurence hadn't been an honorary anything since high school's public triumphs, hadn't been presumed unmale since he uncurled and they dropped /Loretta from his name. Now Gretchen unmanned him; though somewhat disarmed, he rather enjoyed the deletion.

Victor had wanted to fly ever since it occurred to him, stunningly, that one might. This occurrence took place during purposeful perusal of his Boy Scout Handbook, specifically a chapter on badges: a mail-order-style catalogue of areas in which young males could excel, wherein each icon of a badge was followed by a brief description of the field and of what a Boy had to do to excel in it and the reader was referred to separate pamphlets devoted to respective badges. Victor needed as many badges as he could come by, because Victor wanted to be an Eagle. He wanted to be an Eagle because, well, what Boy didn't? All through the Cubs, he had no other goal, never rested on laurels or took the slightest pride in attaining Bearhood, Lionhood, even purgatorial Webelosity, because he knew these were no more than necessary stations on the pilgrimage to Scouthood; and Scouthood itself, to Eaglehood.

Victor could tie ('And *un*tie; that's the part most folks don't consider,' he liked to think smugly) more knots by a factor of twenty than he would ever have use for; could tell time, direction, latitude, or anything you please by sun, stars, or whatever the sky afforded, save overcast; could construct a lean-to in nothing flat from whatever materials happened to be on hand; knew what manner of feathers were most apt for a warchief's headdress, could place an arrowhead at sight as to tribe and give you a ballpark estimate as to decade; amassed tons of newsprint and tuns of bottles on various drives through the years; could distinguish simple and compound fractures long before simple and compound fractions, and unlike the latter, knew exactly what to do about the former (never quite grasped the difference between simple and compound sentences: no merit badge in Grammar); had the most extensive collection on the Eastern Seaboard of braided gimp lanyards, more key chains than keys by a long shot; understood habits of indigenous woodland creatures, knew how to nurture most kinds of baby animals and slaughter most kinds of adult ones, could identify more kinds of birds than you could shake a stick at. But the only one he wanted to be was an Eagle. Victor didn't, early on, think symbolically—of soaring, daring, the endangered species of bald-headed patriotism; he just knew that the highest thing a Boy could be was an Eagle, and he wanted to be the highest Boy there was. Being an Eagle was the best preparation possible for whatever might follow (it was simple logic to Victor that the most prepared Boy would grow into the most prepared Man).

Early in the chapter, after Acrobatics and Armaments but before Banks and Savings Institutions and Berry Identification, young Victor came across Aviation. Suffice to say he was uplifted. He had been raised, thus far, to think of the airport, if at all, as the mysterious but not terribly relevant locale through which letters with a few cents extra postage passed. Flying was what letters, to his knowledge, did more than people, and among the latter, what statesmen, celebrities, and perhaps the odd industrialist were privileged to do; at that point, even baseball road trips were largely a chartered-bus affair. Could a Boy, then, aviate? Could a Boy not only fly, but merit a badge for doing so? Could life and Scouting possibly be so magnanimous? If asked, young Victor would have said that of course any Boy could be President; but the very idea that any selfsame Boy could fly took away his breath: by golly, this truly was the Greatest Nation in the World!

To merit his Aviation badge, Victor had to visit a local airport, persuade a local pilot to sponsor him (let the Boy watch, take him up for a joyride, teach him principles, model the role), learn rudiments of aerodynamics, whittle balsa into something that would stay aloft for ten or more stopwatched seconds, and demonstrate in a written exam that he could tell, for instance, Orville from Wilbur and a Zero from a P-39 by their profiles in silhouette, approximately how much air flowed above, and how much below, a standard wing, how a cabin was pressurized, what a windsock was for, what went wrong with the *Hindenburg*, why dark meat differs from light, how to read an altimeter. This last was his undoing when he first took the exam, but the second time he crammed assiduously; and so proud was he of his Aviation badge that years later, when all his other merits were in mothballs, he had Donna seam-rip it off the jam-packed badge sash and sew it onto his flightsuit (no seamster's badge adorned this Eagle's most

Miss America-like accessory), where he displayed it daily on the left shoulder like a vaccination, meritorious mark of antibodies developed early, of immunity.

And Victor *was* an Eagle, veteran of countless Camporees and many a Jamboree and even one Jubilee, adept at survival; forest (deciduous), forest (coniferous), forest (tropical rain), desert (arid), desert (semi-arid), steppes, pampas, veldt, icecap, bayou: no natural terrain on earth could faze him in theory, and none did in fact until the by then puckered despite preshrinking embroidered cotton patch burned to an illegible crisp in an acre of crackling immature peas at the easternmost tine of the North Fork of Long Island. The fate of that patch was what most immediately concerned him when, still dopey, he awoke in a burn ward, floating on jets of air so wounds could heal. Later, the doctors explained that the badge was the least of his losses.

Oh, he was clean, thrifty, loyal, helpful, honest, obedient, brave, true to the law of the pack, and all the rest; he knew there was no other way to attain aquilineage. But what Victor was, more than any scouting thing else, was reverent, reverent with a vengeance, so much so that the minister who was also Troop Leader and who signed the form to certify the Boy's reverence to the Records Division of the Rooster Council at Headquarters couldn't resist appending a personal statement to the effect that Victor Groat, in his humble estimation, was not only the finest and most fundamental Boy he knew (clean, thrifty, *et al.*), but had a gift, a calling, a vocation, was destined for more than mere merit, for the cloth, the pulpit, The Word.

When Victor was seventeen and three quarters, on the very verge of relinquishing Boyhood forever, a buddy was slashed by a wayward shard toward the glassy-eyed tail end of an exhausting bottle drive. Eagle-eyed Victor, prepared, saw an opportunity, seized it, applied pressure to the appropriate point, saw quickly that more drastic measures would be called for, fashioned neckerchief into tourniquet, and got himself written up in the nick of time as National Boy of the Month. There followed a seamy and squalid sequence of suspicions, innuendi, formal investigation, and finally court (Kangaroo! opined the Boy of the Month) where several Scouts testified on their honor and also under oath to the effect that some years earlier, in a gathering of Tenderfeet, they had heard the accused voice a wish that someday, somewhere, somehow, something horrible would happen to someone in his vicinity. They had heard him reckon that Boys of the Month didn't earn the honor, just happened to be in the right place at the right time; the place and time, that is, when a pickup's parking brake lets go, sending the infant (thoughtlessly left alone in the cab while the harried mother acquired provisions to please and refresh the weary bread-winner on his return) careening downhill, when a child too young to read warning signs slips through thin ice into frigid waters, when a wayward shard slashes a buddy's wrist. Fellow erstwhile Ten-derfeet, now more calloused, swore they had heard Victor opine that a *real* hero, a truly deserving Boy of the Month, would actively seek situations, not wait for them to happen, would sally forth with a mission and *find* a life or two to save. The Toughfeet now were convinced, to a Boy, that Victor, about to turn fateful eighteen, had panicked and found a way to save a life by putting it first in jeop-ardy. The most devastating testimony of all was that of the oppor-tune Boy whose wrist had been slashed, whose bleeding had been stanched, whose picture had appeared in all the papers as foil to Victor's, helping him to look helpful by looking helpless in steri-lized gauze himself, and who, it turned out, lost the use of two fingers because Victor, in his zeal to apply the tourniquet tightly enough, had irreversibly damaged nerve tissue. This ambiguous victim or beneficiary Boy, grateful enough at the time, claimed in retrospect that the milk bottle in question had smashed on the table he was working at with, it seemed to him though he couldn't be absolutely sure, more than accidental force (he had a merit badge in Physics, with a special project in Gravitation). He averred, moreover, that though he hadn't actually seen the bottle hurtle toward the table, his considered opinion was that it could only have hurtled from Victor's hand, which a moment earlier he believed had been seen gripping a bottle not unlike the one in question high above his head.

'Not an Eagle in the bunch!' Victor carped when he took the stand in his own defense: 'They begrudge me my good fortune, envy my plaque. Pure green-eyed, disloyal, and unScoutlike jeal-ousy!' The Troop-leading minister, though he expressed himself with more discretion ('Thou shalt not covet,' he admonished, 'thy neighbor's nationwide publicity'), seemed not uninclined to con-strue the Toughfoot tribe's accusations similarly. The investiga-tion thus proved inconclusive—the National Council, though convinced to a former Boy of young Groat's meretricious and pos-sibly actionable opportunism, thinking it incumbent on them-

selves to demonstrate to youth the presumption of innocence
(principal bulwark of democracy) in action, couldn't find airtight
justification for stripping him of his award—and though the Council
was unprepared to pursue his countercharge of libel, neither did
it cause to be printed (what the Toughfeet had demanded) a formal retraction in *Boy's Life*. But the attendant scandal effectively
erased young Groat's chances for Boy of the Year (first prize, a
two-man pup tent and, most likely, a Presidential handshake or
hairtousle: 'Big frigging deal,' thought Victor). And the ordeal, the
humiliation of mounting defense against subaquiline smears, soured
Victor on Scouting in general. 'Besides,' he consoled himself, 'I've
done it all, Eagle, Boy of the Month, where's left to soar?' With
enemies, apparently, on the National Council, better, he thought,
to lose himself in the relatively anonymous enlisted ranks of the
USAF than aspire to notorious and possibly unwelcoming Explor-
ership. Victor, now a Man, knew when he wasn't wanted.

His former Troop Leader stressed the gift, recalled the parable
of the talents, pleaded with him to join the chaplaincy, but Victor
the former Eagle just wanted to fly. He crammed again, but didn't
pass the entrance exam for flight school, which included several
questions about knots, but not of the twiny variety. The closest he
could come, in the Force, to flying was bombing, and he bombed
with chipper resignation because it kept him at least in the air. He
learned something, too, about ground maintenance, which served
him in good stead when he cashiered out and returned, with a lot
of hours but no license, to the World.

The World had forgotten the youthful honors of Eaglehood; and
the moot scandals of same, kept under wraps at the time by the
National Council, were scarcely remembered even by that organ-
ization's changed leadership. But Victor never forgot that he wanted
to fly. His Troop-leading minister, let down by the Boy's refusal
to follow in his clerical footsteps (and perhaps still nagged by doubts
about Victor's life-saving alacrity), had found a fresh protégé and
declined to provide the requested glowing report to the well-known
flight instructor in his congregation; Victor's parents, by now likewise let down by mixed marriage to Donna Forenza, declined in
tandem to bankroll his dreams; and Victor was on his own, back
at Tenderfoot stage: sweeping out fuselages, soaking impellers in
kerosene, saving pennies for a Cessna, once again clean and thrifty,
variably reverent but now more loyal to his favorite mezzo-soprano
than to anyone else, more hungry than helpful, true to the law of
a different pack.

All that, of course, was far behind him now: former Scout, former Eagle, former eleventh-hour Boy of the Month, former flyer, former sprayer of lethal substances from bellies both military and civilian, former devoted husband, former former of highflown dreams for the future. His past receded in asymptotic perspective behind him, but the future stretched, as far as his eye could see, nowhere. Victor, in Victor's eagle eyes, was maker of nothing but former in every way. And Donna, former mezzo, former performer, former homemaker, was now, in those predacious patriot eyes, abominable destroyer of home, man's castle; of family values, community standards; of God's law and man's; of the loyal and true, the scouting and Christian American way. Those yellowing eyes now scanned, from wheelchair height, the flight plan of options, map of marriage, and found no strip for landing, no fallow field or trafficless highway that would do in a heroic pinch, no safe or sound spot to touch down in this emergency. Victor's eyes saw tailspin, impact, fireball, wreckage, cinders, wailing and gnashing of teeth, the search for the little black box.

'But listen, here we go now: time for your favorite street.'

That classic Barron stride; Laurence couldn't match it. He was still considering Men, and in particular the Crickenberger-Groat one-two punch that seemed to have Gretchen's friend Donna down for the count. Not to mention God: by and large dubbed, whether vengeful or merciful, woolish-haired or metaphorically dovelike, Him.

Laurence the honorary woman wasn't ready for cultural adventure. For one thing, he wished to know how permanent the honor was likely to be. Speaking of Men, Gretchen had a question to ask on his behalf the previous night at the Oasis, and he still didn't know the response. He craved to know was he welcome, could he coach: was that what she meant by 'honorary woman'? Preoccupied with Donna, Victor, Christian, Aud, he'd lost track, despite demographic changes that hadn't been lost on him, of the train's destination. He felt unprepared for a street with a name, for beans, let alone for monastic cubicles transported, one at a time or by the boatload, at private or public expense, from an Old World to a New.

But Gretchen wontedly strode, notwithstanding a top-heavy hint of waddle, toward the door; and as she moved the train broke without warning into air and light, elevated steel box now magically lighter than air, suspended on invisible underfoot girders over traffic: not, at this stop, platform, turnstile, tunnel, stairs, then the street, but platform above the street to begin with. So recently, to his mind, *the* street, mysterious unnumbered arena for a kind of showdown, single combat: fantastic Dutch boy meets realist beans. And Laurence, up in midair, theater loge, reviewing stand, honorary superterranean vantage, got himself to think: Let the show, the parade, the games, begin.

The street was all double-knits and silver-spangle signs that the breeze made to sparkle like sun on a lake. The street was all broken-down Buicks and souped-up jalopies and gypsy cabs. The street was all stains from unknown liquids emitted from passing crankcases or throats. The street was open-air displays of unfamiliar vegetable matter: casaba, plantain, bokchoy, taro, leaves and earthy roots of other cultures. Gretchen was right about the cigar stores: Garcia y Vega, Antonio y Cleopatra, Comidas Chinas y Latinas. Chinese and Latin comedies? he wondered, then asked Gretchen, who knew better and suggested they pop into one for lunch.

Into one they thus popped, a nearly empty luncheonette despite the hour, ice-cream and soft-drink posters up behind the counter faded and splotched from decades of sunlight and splatters, hand-lettered daily-special Spanish signs tacked over them palimpsestically here and there. Did Gretchen know Spanish? *Un poquito*, and she thought they could get by. He thought how nice that the Chinas and the Latinas got along so well, in business together, a cooperative cross-cultural venture (Niagara Falls sprang momentarily to mind), until Gretchen explained what she knew of immigration and exploitation patterns that conspired to form the limited partnership and bring into being an unlikely mix-and-match cuisine. The waiter (who also cooked and for all they knew might own) seemed to take special interest in the almost translucent customer; helping her with the menu, he leaned close, attempting, Laurence assumed, to suggest entrées that would put color in those cheeks. His own were sallow, quasi-Asian; a pathetic excuse for a moustache reached out toward them like a houseplant after a distant sun. He rippled on in Spanish like a foreign brook; Gretchen understood a little, Laurence none. '*Parlez inglese?*' he tried, with no discernible effect. '*No comprehendo españole,*' he said with as winning a smile as feasible, proud that he knew enough to admit his ignorance. This at least got the man's attention, but elicited only a swipe at the unruly moustache with thumb and middle fin-

ger and the previously engaged shrug people sometimes give in
the City when asked a question not germane to immediate con-
cerns.

What worried Laurence in particular was how to avoid red meat,
green peppers, purple cabbage on a menu he couldn't read. Milk,
he thought, might be *leche*, so he could probably get himself a
glass of that; he believed that *cerveza* was beer rather than service,
so he wouldn't ask for that. He tried, beyond these simple premises, to improvise a plea: '*No carne ruego, no jalapeño verde*,' but
purple cabbage had him stumped. Gretchen, eager to help, familiar with '*roja*,' '*pimienta*,' '*repollo*,' '*púrpura*,' took over, and the
man, pleased to help *her*, moseyed back of the counter for a tumbler of *leche*, then to the kitchen for heaven knew what. While
they waited and Laurence, trying hard not to think about puer-
peral ripples, manfully sipped his milk, Gretchen reflected and
pronounced.

'That man's a lech.'

Dairy farmer? In Manhattan?

'Hardly. I didn't follow it all, but he was definitely making a
play for me.'

He *was* leaning close, but Laurence had assumed it was a purely
linguistic gesture.

'I think not. The minute he found out you don't speak Spanish,
he started saying such things.'

'Such?'

'*Macho* stuff. That's why it's Spanish. They *need* a word for it.'

Laurence, trying to reconcile *latino* swagger with the waiter's
unswarthy features, recalled the musicians' party, Dempler's advice,
Gretchen's helpless state and final plea: should he get her the hell
out of *here?* Should he sputter sentences beginning with the phrase
'So help me, if he'? 'What should we do?' he asked, as if there
might be any number of alternatives.

'*Nada*, it's cultural, he doesn't mean anything by it, but it pisses
me off to be treated that way.'

'*Hombros*,' shuddered Laurence, testing the solidity of honorary
status.

'*Sí, hombres*,' she smiled back, taking a sip of his milk.

Gretchen had ordered something like kidney stir-fried in spiced
porkfat with unintelligibly wilted greens. It wasn't exactly the liver
she tried to convey, and she found it nonambrosial but toothsome
enough. The collaborative effort to find something agreeable for

Laurence was less successful, but he took lukewarm comfort in a dearth of beans. As he picked and nibbled around the edges of lunch, a wary squirrel, Gretchen told him all about the visit that had made Donna's calls miss her the previous night.

The Greenwich Wimmin's Oasis: a nonprofit clinic in a rehabbed three-story brownstone run collectively by its founding mothers: two M.D.s (one a G.P., the other an OB/GYN), three R.N.s, two N.P.s, a D.D.S., an R.P.H., a J.D., an M.S.W., and a licensed C.P.A. These profusely alphabetical wimmin disapproved of hired help and all took turns at clerical, receptive, and maintenance jobs. The clinic, which ran, in a remarkably efficient, proficient, congenial, self-sufficient, and mellifluous fashion, sixteen hours a day, three hundred sixty-five days a nonleap year, featured a roomy waiting room where wimmin from surrounding neighborhoods could sit, sip, chat, and raise consciousness with or without an appointment. Lovely chamberish music written and performed by wimmin circulated continuously (the J.D. doubled as D.J.); herb tea and protein-oriented snacks, covered by the sliding scale for those who sought care, were available at a nominal fee for those who came just to pass the time. The place smelled more like mandarin orange than rubbing alcohol, and there wasn't a board foot of fake-woodgrain Formica or a square inch of stainless steel in the room.

Gretchen couldn't remember having seen a more welcoming spot. A viola and clarinet duet wafted, hung in the air, volume just right for conversation, and the calico upholstery invited sitting. Nine or ten wimmin, student bodies of the birthing class, had accepted the invitation and lounged in variably bellied postures like a convention of postimpressionist odalisques.

As Gretchen described the scene, Laurence, despite alien spices and tubers that defied categorization, despite or maybe because of frequent recourse to good old milk, found it so comforting that he thought of his mother: her housedresses, her blood, her eyesight. He had not expected to compare this clinic with the hospital his mother had languished in, where he'd read about half of *Moby-Dick*, where he'd shared chicken croquettes and mourning and his first date. He'd expected to compare this clinic with the one he took mistaken Irene to later, where you could smell the suction hoses and sterilized stainless, where doctors in white lab coats talked of routine procedures and of being well-adjusted, where everything possible was done to translate the organic, fluid-filled nature of the business at hand into graduated cc's. He now found himself with some dismay comparing this clinic instead with his refuge against conception, the living room in Providence on whose couch, when things weren't going right with Irene, he cloistered himself, a decision he now thought of for the first time as a medical one.

Women in layers, laces, sateens, woolens, and voiles with an awful lot of gathers but very few darts, pleats, or tucks, embroidered and tatted shawls and scarves held at precarious unforeseen angles by brooches and cameos, sandals over socks, sashes over skirts, kerchiefs over heads, spectacular earrings tugging at belabored lobes: women outfitted from forgotten corners of closets and attics, looking like the slouched aftermath of a parade, and Gretchen, awed, wondering where were the floats.

Into this room, almost immediately on Gretchen's arrival, came a woman of a different cast, though not even vaguely medical-looking: not one whom rubber gloves, surgical masks, or white orthopedic shoes would become. Instead, a darkly black woman, a woman in black, brushed black denim, head, toe, in between, unremittingly black and browns so deep they seemed black at first, save the whites of her eyes, like pinholes in polarized glass that allow you to view an eclipse. She approached with a stride so steady Gretchen had to wonder what manner of footwear she used. She hugged Gretchen as if, instead of planning to, they'd already been through something long and taxing together.

This, of course, was Audrey Poole, whose name and apparent distaste for men was virtually all Laurence knew. But newly honored and degendered, would he still be so distasty? (That blue-green turnip-textured thing next to the gingery probably chicken certainly was.) He gripped his milk like a subway straphanger, as if it would steady him. Knowing so little, suspecting so much, he couldn't help interrupting Gretchen's chronology: 'Well, what did she *say?*'

'About you?'

'Yes, yes, me, me, can I come, can I coach?'

'I told her you're willing to be my coach. I quote her response from memory: " 'Willing?' Willing to be your coach? Oh, isn't it a dear one? Gee, Gretchen, we're all just so thrilled that your Master Paprika is 'willing,' we can't think of words to express our communal pleasure that he's 'willing,' and such a sacrifice too, so large a gesture; convey to him, won't you, that we of the Greenwich Wimmin's Oasis are speechless.'"

Laurence didn't want to make any assumptions. 'That's irony, right?'

'As rain.'

He might have thought they'd take to a man who wanted to be a mother. He didn't exactly expect them to thank their lucky stars, but the rationale of such vitriol directed toward strangers wasn't quite obvious. 'But why?'

'Some of them don't like men, some of them aren't used to men, for some it's the only place they can go to get away from men.'

'Why it's called Oasis.'

'Yup, and frankly, a lot of men deserve it. Think of Victor, think of Crickenberger.'

Once again blamed for the medico's sins, once again hating to be bracketed with the mountebank, 'The lech!' erupted Laurence, louder than he intended.

The waiter, thinking he'd heard the gringo place an order, emerged from the kitchen with a beetled brow for Laurence and a toothy off-center lip-curling and moustache-bristling smirk for Gretchen. And if, at that moment, Laurence had had the slightest clue how to heap Spanish obloquy, how to visit with Spanish opprobrium, he might have been in for a scuffle. Instead, he maintained a rocky silence while Gretchen issued a retraction to clear up the linguistic aftermath of his outburst: *'Dispense Usted, no leche, la cuenta por favor.'* The man dispensed with the milk and dispensed the check; Gretchen dispensed with further explanation and dispensed enough singles to cover the check with eight cents to spare, and parting, shot the phrase *'Guardo el cambio'* over her *hombro* as she hustled her *hombre* out of the establishment.

When Irene's sobbing heaves subsided to shuddering ripples, Theo felt better. He didn't know what, if anything, he had done to help quell them, any more than he knew precisely what he had done to bring them on. He had no way of knowing that not his own personal *pipik per se* but just glossing the word had so upset her; nor could he know that his eyebrows, so unlike Donna Forenza's or even Donna Groat's, had the soothing effect they did on Laurence's wife. But Theo was not one to puzzle out cause and effect unnecessarily. She felt better, or seemed to; he felt better, seeming aside; that was all he knew, and all he needed to know.

It was not all Irene knew, nor all she thought she needed to. A question remained, despite recently uncovered circumstantial evidence of spousal veracity. Take it as given that Laurence was not displayed till fun munt edge. Fine, but if he truly dangled, tenacious watch on a fob, for twelve weeks hitherto, then anyone visiting the mother-to-be during months eight, nine, and/or ten would surely spy something amiss. Oh gosh, this gets complex, thought Irene; she'd be the mother, not mother-to-be, but those visiting couldn't be allowed to perceive her as such until month ten? But regardless of what they called her—here Irene had a shudder of chagrin at wedded bliss's brevity as she realized she didn't know Laurence's mother's given name; he invariably called her simply Mama—disregarding indeed all nomenclatural ambiguities, they'd be *bound* to see that her pregnancy had turned itself inside out, that her premature newborn was taking the air, was by his own theory beginning to age before their indubitably astonished eyes. It would not be something you'd fail to notice. It would not be something you'd forget, even at Theo's age; and much to the old man's dismay, since he'd seen these questions lead to the wracking convulsive dismay of their poser, Irene posed another, to wit:

'Did you see Mrs. Paprika, I mean Laurence's mother, before he was born?'

'Off cause,' said Theo carefully, seeing no potential for tears in this, 'shiff force my dot-en-la.'

'I mean just before, the last two months of her pregnancy.' The first two months of his life?

'De less too munts?'

'Right. They lived in New York then, didn't they?'

'Shoe air.'

'Sure you saw her?'

'No, shoe air day lift in Menhettin, Fest Sight, Hunted Intent.'

'In a tent?' Huddled in a tent? Hunted in a tent? Haunted intently?

'*Fun* Tent, Hunted Intent in Ate Ever New.'

'A Hundred and Tenth and Eighth Avenue?'

'Shoe air.'

'Sure that's where they lived?'

'Shoe air.'

'But did you see her when they lived there?'

'Shoe air.'

'But during the last two months?'

Somehow this question seemed loaded. Theo didn't know why.

Aided thus far by linguistic confusion, he didn't see how he could evade it any longer without deliberate recalcitrance. He had a horrible feeling the answer would open saline floodgates, though he had to admit he hadn't the mistiest idea of what made Irene weep or why. She was staring, studying his forehead as if her life might depend on memorizing his eyebrows. There was nothing for it but to tell her.

'My dot-en-la force naught fell, Eyerin. Force naught fa huh ah smoot bite.'

'Not smooth? You mean.'

'Shiff force naught fell, Eyerin.'

'You didn't see her, did you?'

'My dot-en-la coo tint half fizzits de less too munts.'

Coo tint half fizzits. Naught smoot. Two munts, fun munt, tree munts edge.

The hands that looked like Molly's hands gripped, wrung, trembled as Theo had never seen Molly's tremble. She wept.

Dyckman, Shmyckman, thought Laurence, peeved at being lumped with Men with whom he had in common little. He'd hoped for special dispensation, hoped against hope his maternal instincts would preclude exclusion. Why must a mild Paprika be treated like a belligerent Groat or an unconscionable Crickenberger?

Further, for Cloisters, One Ninety First would have been the right stop. Dyckman entailed a longish walk down fading commercial blocks of Broadway: fruit, liquor, off-track betting, dry cleaning, gasoline, news, tobacco, more gasoline, more liquor, dry cleaning, news, tobacco, fruit, more betting even, then yet again tobacco. These uptown Broadway blocks repeated themselves more frequently than seemed to Laurence profitable, storefronts like chain-smokers, starting as soon as they stopped. Another Comidas Chinas y Latinas made him wonder for a moment whether they'd somehow walked a circle; but this one was flanked by fruit and tobacco, the other by cleaning and news. Regardless, thought Laurence, damn all Comidas Chinas y Latinasses, to hell with all iterative blocks of Broadway, screw all streets seductively unnumbered, bugger all waiters who also did the cooking, fuck all unknown tubers likely to foster heartburn: all x, all y, all z.

He stopped just short of all wimmin, caught himself doing unto others precisely what he resented. Instead, Damn all nothing, he thought, damn all undiscriminating, insinuating, incriminating *alls*. Damn this sentence itself, he concluded, recalling his prize-winning grade-school essay on hating hate. 'Why can one love love without contradiction, when hating hate gets one in such logical hot water?' Something akin to double negatives, he supposed: I don't not want to fail to eliminate less than all but one of these negatives. Don't I want not to be barred from not being not a woman?

'I thought I was an honorary woman,' he pleaded, innocently.

'I'm afraid the Oasis is more literal-minded than yours truly. Sometimes anatomy is destiny.'

'But isn't that kind of discrimination unconstitutional or something?'

'I'm afraid not.'

Laurence himself felt like a frayed knot, ravelled, unravelling, a sleeve of care, unrevelling in the trip he had looked so forward to. Dishevelled, split-levelled and floored by double negations, badly in need of contemplative calm and undisquietude just in time for Fort Tryon Park and the Cloisters, where the absence of liquor, dry cleaning, tobacco, and news—as they now climbed a hill in the sylvan glade, worlds, though only a block or two, away from Dyckman, Broadway, One Ninety First—gave him pause, rapid respite from gravelly, grovelly thoughts; and unlike Twelve Clefs' kempt facade, this hill in a glade in a park on an island was for all he could tell Nature without graph-paper floor plan, motors, rotors, spades, or blades, a spot where even a star-nosed mole might survive.

'This is lovely,' said Laurence, matter-of-fact.

Gretchen, remembering Aud ('We of the Greenwich Wimmin's Oasis are speechless'), Victor ('Me? Oh beautiful. Fucking peachy'), misheard his tone and chided putative irony.

'No, I mean it, this is beautiful, so peaceful, I can't believe we're in Manhattan, I'm simply.'

'Amazed?'

'Awed.'

A sign at the door read, 'Pay what you wish, but you must pay something.' Extravagant multidollared suggestions that followed for adults, for students with ID, for minors or seniors with proof of dearth or abundance of age, made Laurence think again of the prerogatives of very young and very old. He wondered of what the sign reminded him. Christmas gifts, maybe: give what you want, but you must give me something; and if you're up a tree, let me suggest a tennis racket, graphite superflex special strung with nylon-wrapped gut at 78 lbs., and don't forget the zippered airtight vinylized waterproof cover with mod graphic logo. If they meant 'what you wish,' why the 'suggestions'; would they really be satisfied with 'something'? Ground rules and expectations: if one gave less than the suggested adult donation, would heads turn, tongues wag, art lovers of all properly documented ages sneer? What if he gave a penny? Was anyone keeping track? He could always watch what Gretchen did, he guessed.

What Gretchen did was walk through the turnstile without even flinching, without even looking around. Did she expect him, date-like, to pay for her, to spring or plump for suggested donations? He dropped six dollars in the slotted box, not quite so much as suggested for two adults, but not, he hoped, an embarrassment.

'What are you doing?' she asked. 'It's free on Tuesdays.'

Oh.

'Fie vip, fie vip?' crooned Theo, who by now was rocking, keen-ing, *daven*ing in synch with Irene.

'Oh Theo Theo Grandpa Theo, I'm afraid you wouldn't under-stand.' She thought she knew how Laurence felt: 'I'm afraid you wouldn't believe me.'

Theo, in whose ripply lifetime all manner of unbelievabilia had come true—internal combustion to Manhattan Project, quinine to quark, penicillin to penile implant, Versailles to video, pogroms to programmers, Everest to electric toothbrush—craved to be told and promised, if humanly possible, to believe.

'Oh Theo, all my life I've just tried to behave like a human being, and to the most important person, my husband, your grandson, Laurence, I haven't behaved like a human being.'

Theo didn't understand, and knowing what he knew, Theo didn't believe. 'Doos,' he said, 'hiss naught paw sybil.'

'I knew you couldn't understand,' Irene gurgled saltily but not unsweetly.

'Dun vip in dun dispayer, Eyerin. Bit icksplen fie ah hue men pink coot be naught leica hue men pink.'

Irene stopped vipping momentarily to consider: when is a door not a door? When is a ship not a ship? When is a man not a man?

The wisdom of Theo's eyebrows, regarding this riddle as some others, consisted in recognizing linguistic abuse. If a bear in the circus dances, if a lion leaps through a flaming hoop, counselled Theo, having sat back and lit up, the bear doesn't behave like Ginger Rogers but like a bear, a bear trained to dance; the lion doesn't behave like—he had difficulty deciding what one might be thought to behave like when one leaps through a flaming hoop— doesn't behave like anything but a lion that leaps through a hoop for the benefit of kids from six to sixty with a couple bucks to spare and a stomach for spectacle. By Theo's lights, doing anything a human being can do is behaving like a human being. If rhubarb ever solved a crossword puzzle, then solving a crossword puzzle would be behaving like a rhubarb.

Irene tried to think of a counterexample.

'What about Hitler?'

'Heatlayer,' pronounced Theo with emotion, 'force de *voiced* hue men pink.'

'Yes, a beast, a monster!' opined Irene.

Theo heaved a sigh that implied he'd encountered this misprision too many times in his life. He spoke slowly: it was important that she understand. 'Dayer nay fare force ah bist . . . dayer nay fare force ah mown stare . . . dot dit . . . fought Heatlayer dit.' No nonhuman creature, Theo held, concocted Final Solutions. None invented Treblinka, authorized genetic experiments from the top, filtered incandescence through human skin, gassed six million. To do so, according to Theo, was to be uniquely human. To know that a lie, to succeed, must be a Big Lie, to do everything that Heatlayer did—save eat, sleep, evacuate, struggle for personal or racial survival (this last, this thing that every beast from slug to chimp has always and everywhere done, is what he said he thought he was doing)—was precisely to be a human being. Human being spanned Nero, Schweitzer, the man on the street, and yes, Irene Embler Paprika.

Irene had no little difficulty absorbing this new perspective. Since human beings had the broadest range of any species, to behave like a human being meant nothing, or hardly anything, or everything, or what you will. But surely her mother's bromide implied an elided 'civilized'; surely she meant: 'behaving like a *civilized* human being.'

'Sieve liced docent chench ah tink.' That word added nothing to solve or even to alter the case, according to Theo. The enormities of human being were rather a function than a lack of civilization. 'Human,' a word ('avoid, ah *void*'), either covered the species in its entirety or meant nothing, as any conception of fire ('fie air') that included the cozy hearth but not the destructive conflagration would prove not only inadequate but dangerous. There wasn't, in short, a human being in the history of being human who did not behave like a human being.

'This is beautiful,' had said Laurence (omitting 'fucking peachy'), and Gretchen, having misconstrued his meaning, now for once wondered about *his* stride. Since some unnoticed point after leaving the restaurant, he seemed to be taking it well; 'it,' of course, meant exclusion from coaching, from the public honor of womanhood. He showed little or no interest in exploring Dyckman and environs (perhaps chagrined at having to admit it was no unquantifiable never-never land); but now, despite three days a week engaged in trimming excess nature, he appreciated landscape.

She recalled his story about Irene ('Irene is my wife') urging him not to finish Melville. 'She wanted to cut off your *Dick?*' she had asked at the time. Now Gretchen had conferred a misleading title—honorary woman—had, if not cut off, at least graciously agreed to pretend his nontitular member was trivial, inessential. His guyknob, thought Gretchen, who amused herself vastly by applying the term he quaintly used for Audrey Poole. She enjoyed his relish of its hypothetical elimination, was sorry, for that reason if not for others, that he wouldn't be her coach. She almost volunteered to inquire again whether the wimmin couldn't make an exception in Laurence's case.

You will recall that Paideian Theo wished the same: an exception, exemption, bent rule for his grandson's sweet sake.

'They have,' said Gretchen, steering him away from the card shop to the real art, 'a sort of a wolf about this one point. They're really wonderful otherwise, especially Aud.'

'A wolf?' puzzled Laurence.

'A wolf is a weak spot. Every cello has one.'

Laurence knew that every dog must have its day; knew everything that rose must fall; knew, generally, that every action entailed an equal opposite; even knew, more apropos, that every good boy deserved fun; but that every cello had a wolf was news.

Gretchen explained: despite men on moon, symptomatic relief, floating mortgages, video-dating, the human race has yet to build (and never will build, no matter what) the perfect cello. Every cello, she said, on the planet, like every rearview mirror, has a blind spot; has, like every Persian rug, a flaw. What she said made Laurence recall a theory of human being, hastily sketched out on their first busboard encounter: we each start out with a single abnormality. What manner of flaw, he wanted to know.

'You know in a singer's range there's a tone that can't ring true: between chest and head, falsetto and truetto, there's a crack. Try singing chromatically low to high, you'll find there's a note you can't hit.'

Laurence started, but the Cloisters lapidarily mimicked and verberated the self-conscious scale. He'd take Gretchen's word for his wolf.

'The note you can't sing, if you were a cello, would be your wolf. I'm not sure if anybody knows why, but when you stop to think you're dealing with treetrunks, catgut, ground beetle carapaces, horsehair, it's amazing there's not more than one. But there's never been a cello that had more or less.'

'Some winds have that, too,' thinking of low C♯ on any B♭ trumpet.

'Right, but on cellos it's not always the same note, though it's usually about halfway down your G-string. And your wolf can drive you crazy.'

Halfway down your G-string, your wolf can drive you crazy? 'I think I know what you mean. It's out of tune?'

'Nope, just won't resonate right. Sort of growls. Hence, I guess, the name.'

'What do you do? You can't just avoid the note.'

'You make do. You get this piece of hard rubber in a little metal casing, and you screw it onto your G-string just below the bridge. It can't make the note perfect, but it helps. It's called a wolf eliminator, but it's really just a wolf ameliorator.'

'Ameliorator' made Laurence think of Amelia Earhart, Aviator, then of Aunt Amelia, aggravator, then of a mealy alligator, of a million gator-haters, of Little Red Riding Hood, Three Little Pigs, huffing and puffing, roast beef and none, Gretchen's toes, *mictio in os*, and the ongoing difficulties of eliminating everything from red meat to wolves, the negative, misconceptions. He didn't know whether to laugh or cry, but he felt all turned around, inverted, a single little piggy with incongruously plural wolves.

The fairy-tale setting in no way augmented this piggy's combobulation. Pale young princess and wizened young prince trod medieval stone, walled by stone, darkly aged, also all so ceilinged, vaulted, arched, cloistered in old stone, and Vespers, Trinity. They were perambulatory geode crystals, stalags might, stalacs tight in the belly of a fleshless oyster, Mother of Pearl, Hester's Prynnity. Crazy-making echoes of Western Sieve rose and fell amid verdigris, vertigo, and believe or not fabricated unicorns (unicorns!) covering stone: hunted, cornered, lanced, unhorned for a virgin in tapestry artistry, lapistry, hartistry, papistry, baptistry, wrapped history, a psychedelicatessen, not unresonant but out of tune, and Laurence, wondering, wondered what.

'You know,' said Gretchen, down to earth despite stones, threads, echoes, 'you have to wonder what happens, theologically, when a municipality inherits a sacred locus. I mean, can they be decommissioned like aircraft carriers?'

Amazing that her synapses could process aircraft carriers amid echoes, wolves, virgins, rapt history. His, he thought, could never. But he saw light at the end of the hallway and made for it as Gretchen, pondering what happens to used warships anyway, followed.

In the garden, all topiaried, bordered, espaliered, symmetric and composed, he breathed more freely.

'What *do* they do with old battleships, destroyers, and the like?' asked Gretchen, surveying the mighty Hudson far below them, where once, amidst trees unshaped and wild, the *Half Moon* sailed.

'You know,' he said, ignoring her question, 'it's weird in there. I had a sort of episode. That never happened before.'

'Cloistrophobia,' she quibbled, rubbing, with left fingers calloused from years of pressing silver-wrapped gut to ivory, a smooth glissando down and up vertebrae like a fingerboard.

'Heh,' said Laurence. 'But really, it's so historical, I almost got.'

'Hysterical?'

'Hesperical. Like a wreck, you know, The Wreck of the.'

'I get it, Laurence. Whose daughters guarded the Golden Apples in the Isles of the Blest at the western edge of the World.'

'Whose daughters?'

'Right.'

'No. *Whose?*'

'Hesperus's daughters, in Greek.'

'Myth, that's just it: the air is so thick with belief, it's not like a museum, it's like a.'

'Convent, monastery, right, that's what it was. That's what I mean, about the aircraft carriers.'

'Aircraft carriers, crop dusters, Golden Apples, unicorns, Chinas, Latinas, Dyckman, Shmyckman, honorary women, invisible beans.' He sank to a disinclined posture on a fourteenth-century stone bench. 'It's been, Gretchen, a weighty day.'

'You think unicorns are weird, wait till you see the reliquaries.'

'I'm not ready for anything weirder than unicorns. What are they?'

'Wait till you see. You know, mythology is all about body parts.'

'Yeah,' said Laurence before thinking; then, thinking, 'yeah?'

'Like hysteria, I said hysterical, you know what that comes from?'

'Spending the day in Washington Heights.'

'I mean the word: comes from the womb.'

'Who doesn't,' said Laurence, unsure whether he was joking anymore.

'In the beginning was the womb. No, I mean the root: hysteria, uterus, same word. Probably histrionic, too. They used to think everything in your head was really in your body.'

'Isn't it?'

Gretchen laughed as if he had made a joke. 'In a way, but not *your* body, actually, since you don't have one.'

'A womb, no, but a body, a head, yes; if the womb is hysterical, what's hilarious?'

'Search me, but I know what's humerus.' She poked at his funny bone.

'What about myth and body parts?'

'You'll see what I mean when you see the reliquaries.'

'What are the reliquaries?'

'You'll see.' She smiled or smirked. He couldn't tell. 'You okay?'

'I guess. But all that stone!' Like *Brontosaurus*, body parts, *Tyrannosaurus*, all that stone. Mister, how big is this one? Big as stone. That big. A billion million trillion jillion dillion gillion feet, tons, years.

'Stone ain't nothin' but rock, Laurence.'

Somehow, believe it or not, that helped.

'But reliquaries are something else. They're pieces of saints preserved.'

'Saints preserve us!'

'And we them.'

'Like Marcia, in formaldehyde?'

'In almost anything but. In urns, in boxes, in metal, in horns.'
She can't mean saxophoned martyrs. 'Like unicorns' horns?'
'Right, but more like antelope, deer, hart.'
Aunt elope? Dear heart? 'What do you mean, pieces?'
'Pieces! Hair, bones. I don't know. You can't see inside.'
Can't elope. Honey, do. Water my lawn. Canned seed inside.
'You mean replicas.'
'I mean body parts of living saints once they're no longer living.'
'You mean they dismantled their saints once they gave up the
ghost?'
'I mean. You know your shoebox full of hair?'
'That I know.'
'Well, if you were beatified and canonized, your body parts were
blessed.'
'Like the Isles of Hesperus.'
'I guess, and if you were departed and your shoebox more artful,
with maybe silver fretting on the corners, say, it would be a reli-
quary.'
'My seventh-grade teacher said my behavior toward classmates
was saintlike.'
'There you go. But you'd have to stay that way your whole life
and also have a certain number of verified miracles and then wait
a few hundred years.'
'And box my hair in a springbok's hairdo.'
'Then you'd have a reliquary. Or rather, the City of New York
would, cause you'd be long gone.'
'Are you saying there's medieval hair in there?'
'And who knows: nostrils, eyelids, toenails.'
'Geez. Unicorns are peanuts compared to that.'
'It's body parts and religion and art all at once, Laurence.'
'Like your friend Donna almost.'
'Who was and then wasn't and now again is also Catholic.'
'Like the saints.'
'Whose parts are preserved in these reliquaries, which you won't
believe how beautiful they are, but also eerie.'
'You think they have ears, too?'
'Probably, but that sounds more like bullfighting to me.'
'*Beaux arts,* Gretch.'
'Yup.'

By the time they got back to One Ninety First (the return to news, tobacco, cleaning, betting almost as disorienting to Laurence as the retreat from it into medieval stone had been), it was getting on toward the rush, and even this far north the train was chockablock with humanity; but one seat will more often than not open up for a visibly pregnant woman, even in New York. Though Irene was little more than barely visible, one did on this occasion; a corridor, parting Red Sea-like, led the chosen person to the promised spot. Laurence, on the other hand, had to burrow, furrow, and weasel a winding way to the now seated and gravidly privileged Gretchen. Once there he stood facing and right up against her, legs bowed like a sailor's, a cowboy's, a shortstop's, to avoid compressing the precious contents of her belly, which was reproduced in perfectly visible comic amplification by that of a snoozing and snoring man beside her. This latter protuberance, Laurence considered, was unlikely to have been a determining factor in the seating pattern even though, unlike Gretchen's, it was rather emphasized by the belt over which it lopped than afforded breathing room by garb specifically designed for prematernal ease: his magnified midriff mimicked hers as the swooping graffiti surrounding them all exaggerated mainstream penmanship.

Laurence took several stops to get oriented in the screaming box. He still failed to understand how folks underground (with or without such features) could catch winks, puzzle crosswords, have spats, and in general carry on with their lives as they did aboveground. He failed to understand, in particular, how people could discuss aloud their most intimate relations on the subway; even gossiping about the private lives of others (as he and Gretchen had done on their uptown leg) in the presence of such a random captive audience seemed to him indecorous. Perhaps not so to his companion.

'I was talking with Aud.'

'Repool? Yeah?'

'Well, I asked her about something, and I don't want you to take this the wrong way.'

'What's the right way?' Laurence pondered momentarily the phrase 'spirit in which it's intended.'

'I'm not sure, but I know what the wrong way would be. Thinking I was accusing you of something.'

'Something?'

'Fabrication.'

What does Audrey Poole know about saxophones?

'But I'm not, so don't take it that way.'

'If you're not, I won't.'

'Okay, so don't, okay?'

'Okay. But hurry up, we're almost at Seventy Second.'

'We don't get off till Fourteenth.'

'True, but we're moving right along.'

'Right.'

'So?'

Catarrh, catarrh, catarrh.

'So.'

Catarrh, catarrh, catarrh, catarrh, catarrh, catarrh.

'So?'

'So she's a gynecologist, you know.'

This may not be about reeds. 'I know your guyknob is a guy-knob, Gretchen.'

'I know you know.'

'So?' Impatience: there's a plant by that name, though it doesn't look the part.

'So I asked her about cords.'

You can't play chords on a sax. A cello, maybe: harmonics. A harmonica, definitely. 'Chords?'

'No, cords. Comma umbilical.'

Body parts. I'm mything the point: I think I'd rather talk about saxes. 'What about um?'

'How long.'

'How long what?' O Lord?

'They are.'

'How long they are?' Ten feet, give or take inches.

'How long they are.'

'How long are they?'

The lights went out, but Laurence's thoughts didn't. He blinked in the pitch dark, wishing, on no star at all, that when light returned they'd be magically somewhere else, addressing something magically else. No, the subway wasn't sexy; it was close, cluttered, confining, clustered, cloying, cloistered, and its people tired, poor, wretched, teeming, huddled, yearning.

Light. Gretchen had waited for light to say what she had to say.

'Laurence, they're eighteen inches.'

'Eight.'

'Teen inches. On the average.'

'Teen inches.' On the average: an escape clause.

'Laurence?'

'The average. Well, maybe the *average*. But there's always a range. I mean, the *average*, what's the *average* mean?'

'Aud says they run about ten inches to three feet tops.'

Ten inches to three feet. Tops? Three inches to ten feet. Ten feet. Inches. Feet. Tops. Escape, dependent, Santa. 'Well, on the *average*.'

'No, Laurence, they average a foot and a half; the whole *range* is ten to three. More than three feet is unheard of.'

On the average. On the range. A discouraging word. Standard. Buffalo roam. Deviation. Never is heard. Three feet. Unheard of feat. Escape claws. Three. Ten. Eighteen. One and a half. Three halves. Ten. Twenty halves. Three into twenty is six and two thirds. Ten is six and two thirds times three halves, or eighteen. Ten twelves is one twenty, are, and eighteen into one twenty is. Twelve times eighteen is. Born at seven, pendant for three. Seven and three is ten. Ten twelves. Carry your two. One and a half into one twenty leaves. Multiply. Be fruitful. Divide. Remainder. Spirit in which it's indented. Why or why not?

'Laurence?'

Evading Gretchen's eyes, Laurence's wandered to the man beside her, he of the belly, a Daumier incarnate seated on a One. No longer snoozing: awake, alert, a threat, a portly caricature who stared. Laurence, who thought the man appeared to have something to say, opened wide peepers and pigeoned neck toward the man he had caught dropping eaves, drooping heaves, dopey peeves. *Well?* asked Laurence's eyes in reprimand.

'Ski ooze maple leaves.'

Some nonsense about Vermont, bristled Laurence. This visible risible man mocked him with syrup and schuss. How dare? thought Laurence, all but ready to . . .

''Scuse me, please,' the man repeated. 'Sixty-six, coming out.'

Sixty-six into one twenty is. Ten. Three.

'Sixty-six, my stop, getting off.'

Coming out, getting off, escaping. Oh.

Laurence shifted and (Monsieur Daumier having struggled up and out) collapsed into a fraction of the vacated space, remembering Greyhounds, Large James, and the pale but motherly woman who inherited his seat. Red ten on a black three. Cheat, cheat, never beat. Old man, dull knife. Liar, liar, pants on fire. Ladybug,

ladybug, fly away home. 'Oh Lonnie, oh Lala, no . . .'

'She's wrong!' avowed Laurence, perspiring underground between Sixty Sixth and Fifty Ninth.

'Laurence, she's a doctor.'

'So's Cricken.'

'Berger. *Touché*. But Aud knows her stuff, and why would she lie?'

Catarrh, catarrh, catarrh, catarrh.

'Why would she. You believe her. Then you think I'm.'

'Lying? No, Laurence, I told you not to think that.'

'Oh, right, how silly I can be. Now tell me what to think.'

'Laurence, please. I'm not telling you.'

'No, I'll tell you. I take exception, I *am* the exception, to the Poole rule. Born at seven, pendant for three. That's what my mother said, and *she.*'

'Wouldn't lie. No, not that either. I'm just telling you what Audrey said is a fact.'

'A fact.'

Creech, cringe, spleek, grindge: Laurence plumped softly against Gretchen's cushiony fullness as the One pulled rudely into a station. 'A fact.'

'A professionally recognized fact, based on many centuries of unbiased observation. That's all I'm saying; I don't know what it means.'

Laurence was thinking instead of a different import: *Is your grandfather living?* If he survived, an old man without a doubt, and though without a knife, perhaps with a different story to tell. Escape, independent, grandfather clause. Theo, Grandpa Theo would know.

Eight

Geripold Ludovico Dempler, two thirds of whose name and all of whose parentage combined the hardiest strains of European keyboard hegemony, was delivered with a predictably wide metacarpal span, learned his ABCs starting with the latter, seated at a baby grand, and believed, for longer than was in the best interest of primary education, that the alphabet went: C, D, E, F, G, A, B. With H, he was familiar through various Teutonic sonatas in the key we are now pleased to designate B♭; and I, indispensable to Germanic, Italianate, and Anglo-Saxon egotism, was not unknown to him; but J through Z, whose acquaintance he made rather later in life, seemed an upstart, usurpacious band of afterthought characters that marauded and threw his original C-major alphabet into something of a muddle, and to which he therefore did not cotton. Words, with their un-modulating nearly thorough innocence of accidentals and stolid utilitarianism, tended toward the stupid in his view. Contemporary American English, in particular, struck his ears as positively, maliciously pathophonic.

Blessed with such a heritage and upbringing, it's perhaps not surprising that the Flemish pianist dominated European youth competitions from the age of six forward. Star pupil of his own father, Emil Leddendauer Dempler, he was known to nettle the Dutch master, Oskar van Baendtneeck, whose students enjoyed uniform supremacy until young Dempler's advent, and which students the Flemish prodigy had by the age of sixteen been knocking out of semifinals all over the Continent for nearly a decade. When at that age Dempler sustained a rash of variously veiled assassination threats, it was widely assumed that van Baendtneeck lurked somewhere behind, the efficient cause of them all; but neither the eager Belgian authorities nor the reluctant Dutch authorities nor the imperiously insouciant agents of Interpol, who had larger Sicilian fish to fry, succeeded in establishing any connection beyond a reasonable doubt, let alone its shadow, and a shaky Dempler *fils* emigrated to the States, where reputation, if not technique, was only enhanced by such publicity. Dempler *père* having produced, with Dempler *mère* at least, no further progeny, the keyboard dynasty reverted to students of van Baendtneeck, and Geripold's father retired to a life of lugubrious solitary contemplation.

His son, it seems, was more than momentarily unnerved by the scandal: his inhumanly light touch grew humanly heavy; his unearthly interpretations, earthly and even morose, and after a single whirlwind tour of his adopted land, over the course of which reviewers allowed the benefit of a rapidly dwindling doubt for extenuating recent history, the now sublunary star abandoned the concert circuit and dropped out of public sight for a full three years.

Then, even as periodicals still printed the occasional retrospective, under titles such as 'Whatever Happened to Geripold Dempler,' 'Geripold Dempler—What Happened,' and 'Gerry, We Hardly Knew Ye,' the object of so much resigned and baffled speculation resurfaced, clutching in his renowned and extended hands the completed score of a major orchestral work—*The Hats of Amsterdam*—whose satiric wit and unpredictable key changes (were they 'impish' or 'bold'?) convinced everyone that the nasty Netherlandish *contretemps* had placed only a temporary damper on Dempler's lively Flemish spirits. Critics who had grown accustomed to make much of the melancholy defeatism of the Flemish temperament now addressed themselves to the uncanny resiliency of the Flemish *élan vital*. 'Effervescent' was perhaps the word most consensically applied to *The Hats*, whose unlikely instrumentation tickled listeners' ears as highly carbonated beverages do drinkers' noses. The New York (and world) premier established Dempler in two and a half memorable hours as the most promising neoclassical composer in America. A year later, he stunned the musical world with the explosive Labor Day oratorio, *Handwork in D.*

The ten years that followed saw no fewer than eight symphonies, eleven suites for orchestra, two ubiquitously hummed and whistled theme songs for long-running radio serials, and scores of lesser scores emerge from the tortoiseshell pen of Geripold Dempler. These combined to form what became known as the Flemish School of Ambient Meta-Tonality, though Dempler was, as far as anyone could discern, its sole pedagogue and entire student body: his work was inimitable in its lambent richness, unexceptionable in its anticontrapuntal elegance, mind-boggling in its consistency and prolificity. 'How long can he keep it up?' was on all musicological lips and in dozens of printed exegeses and encomia. Though the question was posed with rhetorical glibness, the answer was sadly not long in coming.

At the age of thirty-five—the same age that marked, for more compelling but apparently no more definitive reasons, Mozart's swan song—Dempler stopped. Rumors, for a couple of years, that he was preparing a *magnum opus* slowly gave way to educated guesses that a premature midlife crisis had temporarily stifled America's favorite serious composer; but collective breath can be held only so long, and finally even his most faithful exponents had to admit that the man simply wasn't composing. By this semitender age, he had been appointed *ex officio* Executive Conductor of the Symphony Metropolitana, and the transition to full-time conduction was a simple and logical step.

Dempler commenced his third career with somewhat less fanfare than he had his second. He was recognized, at the first, as a competent, sensitive conductor who could extract from his charges all, but not significantly more than, one would expect him to be able to extract. But by the time *The Hats* was a perennial in the repertoire of every respectably sizable municipal orchestra in the land and *Handwork* had been adopted, by Presidential fiat, as the official Labor Day oratorio (making this the first national holiday with its own federally sanctioned theme song); by the time Dempler had been requested to produce (and had declined, with all due respect, to produce) the definitive New Deal jingle; by the time his radio themes were being rearranged for the larger and

better-funded ensembles of television adaptations; by the time
scarcely anyone could recall the style or even the name of the
Metropolitana's prior maestro; by all these times, Dempler was
lionized, not as a former virtuoso who had understandably stopped
concertizing, nor as a former composer who had inscrutably left
off composing, but as the premier conductor in the nation—'perhaps the world' was the usually appended phrase. Undisputed king
of the podium: it was no more lowly a baton-twirler than this whose
grounds Laurence Paprika weekly but unrepetitively groomed.

The repeated notes and phrases, but never more than phrases,
that emanated at least three days a week from Dempler's studio
in the turret disconcerted Laurence, who had wondered more than
once whether the sound of his mowing broke the genius's concentration; but he recognized phrases that seemed to remain constant
from visit to visit, and thus concluded the genius made no more
progress on days when engines were idle.

On a One after work, showered and changed but still redolent
of grass and gas (pungent combination), Laurence saw a face he
knew and sat next to it (Two Forty Second being end and beginning of the line, the train was far from full). The face, smooth and
terra-cotta-colored, with little bulblike cheeks of the sort formed
by muscles or bones that some people have and some seem not to,
belonged to a woman everyone at Twelve Clefs staff luncheons
called Else. Laurence assumed it was short for Elsie, and wondered if Elsie was short in turn for something—well, else. Not, he
supposed: one of those annoying names that misleadingly end in
diminutive *ie* but abbreviate nothing and inevitably get shortened
themselves. Else was not herself shortened, except perhaps by a
neck that curved, almost curled, to give her something in common
with a fine old printed cello-scroll *f* or *s;* that neck to one side, she
was lean and linear, a movable type, the parts (those cheeks among
others) that bulbed out gaining a crisp sort of emphasis from the
nonsuperfluous rectitude of her flexible form. Nothing was smoother
than Else's face, nothing cleaner than her lines; though not con-
ventionally beautiful, she was something like an artist's conception.

'Hi, Else. How ya dune,' Laurence chameleoned into what he
took to be her dialect.

'Hey, Lawns.' She made him sound like what he mowed. He
often couldn't decide, with Else, whether what he heard was dialect or wit. 'Not too awful bad, yourself?'

'Well, not too good, actually, but could be worse I guess,' thinking of Victor, thinking of Donna.

'Tough job, keepin God's green things in line?'

'No, not the job, more personal.'

Else's brow furrowed along lines hidden until called for. But she was not one to pry.

'Else, how long have you been working for Dempler?'

'Comin up on six—six good years. They can say he's a genius'—Laurence heard a little more than 'genie,' less than 'genus'—'but I say he's a good man, gives every body of us birthdays, never doubts you might really be ailin when you got to take some time.' Laurence wondered how good six years of placing single leaves of romaine and sprigs of rosemary on a variety of pâtés atop crustless rounds of melba, six years of making food so neat, could be. Then he wondered how good six years of mowing would be. Then of any repeated thing.

'You know those phrases Dempler plays?'

'Tell you what, Lawns, old man sets up in Euterpe's Lair every mornin since *I* been here playin them notes. Half a dozen of em.' What Laurence heard was 'Heifer doesn't ovum.' Of which Else now hummed a version, savoring the intervals, not at all as if she had heard them every weekday morning minus birthdays for six years, as if she heard them for the first time *this* morning and they had seriously affected her life, as if the world were fresh and there weren't big folks beating up on little ones planetwide, as if junior highs were free of drugs and avenues free of droppings and Defense free of cost overruns, as if there weren't enough bombs hidden under the earth to wipe it off its own face from the inside out. When Else hummed, her voice had a spherical resonance of which it gave only the slightest bubbly hint when she spoke.

'Some days just them, other days he'll be playin some other ones after, an mess aroun with em, but Lawns, it's really just them. Tryin to start somethin, always tryin to start somethin.' 'Some fun,' heard Laurence.

'Damn if that man ain't been tryin to start somethin for six years, plus Lord knows above how long prior to that. Same thing. Lawns, that man is a man of crea-tivi-ty that *will* not quit.' Else had a way of articulating *t*'s in the middles of words that Laurence admired. Whatever she did with other letters, her *t*'s never devolved into *d*'s, but remained the crispest of phonemes, cracking words in half like dry sticks. Now she hummed again, making Dempler's barren phrase resound despite subway noise like finished work, a fruitful refrain.

'Crea-tivi-ty is God's gift to the world, an us others ought never forget that. Imagine: every mornin, year in an out. It's a gift, Lawns, a gift.'

Had Laurence considered such itera-tivi-ty on his own, it would have struck him as a lot like bank clerking, and he was amazed that Else's simple assertion of inherent value in repeating oneself made him respect Dempler more. The undisputed evidence (hearsay, granted) was that the man was past help, obsessive, compulsive, same cupboard to get same dog same bone, doomed, feckless, stuck with a meager hoard of six or seven notes to the end of an anticlimactic career. But Else, humming in the teeth of such evidence, made it seem these notes needed only to be repeated once, twice, x more times, to blossom into an opening like Beethoven's Fifth: beep beep beep bum, bop bop bop bomb. Else, he decided, was the most generous creature he'd encountered on this globe, more than those who gave Monopoly games in youth, more than himself vouchsafing knees to Big Jim, more even than Gretchen entrusting toes to himself. He'd found, finally, the proper audience, and told her about a kid with vibes and a nasty merchant; she appreciated the story, but again amazed him by reckoning the jeweller had a point too from another angle.

He told Else he lived with a cellist, for once ignoring the nagging questions. (Did he? Live with? Never mind, he thought it would please Else to hear it.) Else said she thought that was wonderful. (Was it? Wonderful?) Laurence asked Else if she had any kids.

'Had a few.'

Grown now?

'Some of em.'

(Sum ovum.) Grandkids?

'How old I look to you, boy?' She laughed with a harmonic fullness like that of her hum, which Laurence now realized made him think: cello. 'Yeah, grandkids.' Else made them sound like grand people who just happened to be kids. 'Two, Lord be praised. Calamine, an little Joffrey.' She named the latter after the ballet, the former because the first time she set eyes on her, she said, 'That child's gonna soothe my heart like calamine on a bite.'

Else said the best thing her kids ever did was let her name her own grandkids. She believed it ought to be a tradition ('a fixed way,' she said) to let grandfolks name their grandkids: greatest honor of her life, she said, to put the names on those infants. All she needed to do was think of her grandkids to know how her kids loved her.

Laurence wondered what if the grandparents can't reach consensus. He disliked himself for wondering it, too: just couldn't hold on to Else's general appreciation for the facets of everything without making problems. What if some contingency? Hadn't we better fret? He wondered how she would see his problem, his life, his wife, his vested quest, his pregnant cellist, and especially, as one experienced in childbirth, his childbirth.

'Else, I want to tell you something and I want you to tell me what you think about it, okay?'

'I like that, Lawns. What you goin to tell me?'

'The story of my life.'

'That's a lot of thing to be thinkin somethin about, but I'll do what an old woman can.'

Suddenly and for the first time (the first time!) Laurence found the story of his life a transparent, papery-thin absurdity. How could something eighteen inches be ten feet? What could hold the delicate tissue of afterbirth in place through all that climbing and infantile exploration? Was he really in the City to look for an old man at all? How could a man be a mother? The whole tale now appeared to him tall, unlikely (but hadn't he lived it?), and telling it somehow an act of hostility, aggression, in the face of Else's generous nature, her posture of willing suspension rather than of disbelief.

'Else, what stop do you get off at?'

'Near the end of A, away down Brooklyn way. You not that old, Lawns, I got time for *your* story.'

'It gets a little complicated.'

'What life don't? Look, you want, we'll get off, have us a sip.'

'Really?'

'Why not? Lookit, I change for the A at Fifty-nine, we'll have us a sip an you can tell me that *whole* biography.'

Sips don't come terribly cheap on West Fifty-ninth, but they generally come, and when they did Laurence started.

'Else, here's what my Mama told me.'

As Laurence, remembering how Gretchen uncovered his reedy fiction and feeling this tale must sound as false as his saxophone's low D, considered how to start, Geripold Ludovico Dempler was pouring (the help having left for the evening) himself and Astrida von Äussterschucher a small jigger each of Pastis diluted with just a splash of not even slightly carbonated bottled spring water, despite Flemish mistrust of the French their diurnal, categorical apéritif.

'This young man, this Laurence, my dear. What do you make of him?' He generally offered a topic along with her beverage.

'Thank you,' she perfunctorily nodded at his provision of liquid refreshment. 'I make little or nothing at all of him.' Today, to her, the topic seemed as cloudy as the drink. 'But since you've asked, you surely have a theory of the case. What do *you* make of him, my dear?'

'Not a great deal, but I admit to being intrigued. You will recall his first day, when he interrupted to stutter and stumble toward enunciating an inability to perform the tasks required of him. I consider his progress since that day. I am told that he fashions the grounds with tonsorial care, concocting the grassy equivalent not of hair*cuts* but of *dos*, that he coifs, my dear, trims and rakes with an eye to pattern notwithstanding none is expected to regard his handiwork. Most startlingly of all, that despite apparent fondness for patterned regularity, he never mows the grounds the same way twice, but always in an unprecedented configuration. This last I am not in a position absolutely to verify or gainsay, but having recently toured much of Twelve Clefs, can substantiate the former claims. Our lawn, my dear, is mown with such variety of visible design, as houndstooth, chevron, and in one instance unless I miss my guess a valiant if failed attempt at paisley, that I am at a loss to determine to what the young man thinks he is up.'

'This, Ludovico, is truly unexampled behavior. Can he fancy himself an *artiste*? Has he found, what perhaps others before him have found through your kind graces,' she lowered slightly her shoulders in acknowledgment of these, 'that aesthetic design alone can distill the loathsome sameness of an individual life into an invigorating, because an interesting, form; that such creation provides a rationale, however irrational, for reasonless existence itself?'

'I don't venture to determine the question, my dear. But you have framed it as I should have myself.'

'And have you, Poldchen,' she smiled, 'put it to the young man *in* question?'

'No, my Äussterette.'

'I suggest you do so, to satisfy both your curiosity and my own, which I readily admit you have piqued.'

'I shall. At luncheon on Monday next, which meal I intend, if you voice no objection, to invite him to share with us.'

'Far from objecting, I applaud your plan.'

'Very well, my dear. Then *if* you have finished your drink, let us dine.'

No more than halfway through their second cup of tea, Laurence finished telling Else his story. Perhaps just as well: they were starting to attract less than totally welcoming looks from those charged with apportioning the café's time and space. Nevertheless, Laurence was startled by brevity: a cup-and-a-half, a twelve-fluid-ounce life. Else, in its course, had been surprised by the opposite. Length was the first of two points she wished to raise.

'Umbilical cords might differ some, mama to mama, so I'd not want to say for definite, but I'm rememberin mine a bit shorter.'

Laurence listened intently: umbrellical codes, a safer deafknit, membrane mine. O generous Else, he thought, be more typical of yourself than of others and have a heart: a kid needs running room. Even an adult could use some slack. Mama-to-be to mama, he appealed.

'Course it's been a while,' she smiled. 'All said an done, folks think what folks have got to think. That's what you think, it's all right with me. I just remember shorter. But Lawns, I do believe there's somethin more important.'

He couldn't be angry with her.

'Look at you, Lawns. How you goin to be a mama? How? Look what all you got on your mind.'

He looked.

'Raisin kids alone, that's a rough road. Difficult to raise em up right, Lawns, difficultest thing I ever have done, an that's with a husband.'

'Hosebane,' heard Lawns.

'On your own, it's for sure you'll be doin things wrong, maybe past fixin. Sides, you got to figure your own life. Don't take me wrong, but your hands look to me more than full just bein your own self. And plannin to manage a little one, too?'

'It sounds sort of stupid when you put it that way.'

'How you *been* puttin it so it sounded intelligent?'

'I don't know, Else. I guess I kind of was counting on its not being put.'

Bring.

Bring.

Bring.

'Yeah. Fitzgerald.'

'Oh, I'm afraid I've got the wrong number.'

'You are who?'

'I was trying to call the Groat residence.'

'That's what you got. And you are?'

'My name is Irene.' If Donna had mentioned her, would she have used Embler or Paprika? Irene would be enough. 'Is Donna there?'

'Relative?'

'No.' Odd question. 'Is Donna Groat there?'

'What, a friend?'

'Yes, I'm a friend of Donna's. What's happened?'

'This long distance?'

'What's happened? Yes. Is something wrong?' Irene had a horrible feeling that Victor had done something rash, done himself injury, attempted suicide even, maybe. Or an accident: a fall. But then where was Donna?

'Long distance where?'

'From New York, New York City. Has Victor been hurt?'

'Victor is who?'

What is Fitzgerald, who doesn't know who Victor is, doing in Donna's apartment? 'What are you doing there? Who are you? What's happened, for heaven's sake?'

'Listen, it's gonna be lots better for all parties if you just answer my questions. Now, you live in New York, and you're a friend of this Donna?'

'No. Look, who are you? What are you doing in Donna's apartment? If you don't answer me, I'll call the Providence police!'

'Keep your shirt on, lady, that's what you're talking to. You got something you want to say to authorities, you got em on the line here; you want to make a statement, make it; otherwise, just try to answer a few simple questions, we're trying to keep a line clear here.'

'Can you for God's sake tell me what's happened? Is somebody hurt?' It occurred to Irene, despite her distress, that it might help to append the word 'officer,' and she did so.

'Lady, we reached the premises a recent while ago, ain't sure to a precise tee what might of happened. Your friend's in emergency, my guess would be about fifty-fifty she'll pull through, they got her out a half hour ago, ballpark. Too early to say accident, tempted suicide, maybe something else. Now, who's this Victor?'

'Oh God, oh God, oh oh oh God . . . Victor's her husband.'

'You know this guy, his habits, where he'd go?'

'Victor should be there, he doesn't go out, he's in a wheelchair, he never goes out.'

'Okay, now that's information, that's a maybe useful thing to know. Look, we gotta keep this line clear here, just a name and number, case we need to get back to you, would be suitable.'

'Irene Paprika . . .'

'That's pee ay pee . . .'

'Like the spice.'

'Right. New one on me. And a number?'

'I'm not sure how long I'll be here, but New York is area code two one two, um, five five two, um, eight two seven three.'

'Seventy-three, right. Your friend's at St. Benedict's, in the emergency, you can call there to get an update. We've got a line to keep clear here.'

Victor should have been there when she needed him, thought Irene while providing and then dialing information. Where was Victor? She was always there for him, always (forgetting for the moment the night Donna had spent with her).

Bring.

'City, please.'

'Providence. St. Benedict's Hospital, the emergency room. It's an emergency,' added Irene superfluously.

'Thank you.' Then a click and a recording: 'The number is . . .'

He should have been there. She was *always* there for him. She loved him. Loves him.

Bring.

Bring.

Bring.

'St. Benedict's, Emergency.'

'Irene, I mean Donna, Donna Groat, is there a Donna Groat there, about half an hour ago, some kind of emergency?' Irene still didn't know what kind.

'Are you a relative?'

'No.' She immediately realized that was the wrong answer

'Yes, we have a Donna Groat. I'm afraid we can't release information except to relatives.'

'But I'm a friend.'

'I'm sorry, ma'am, hospital policy is relatives only.'

'Oh please, I'm out of town and I'm terribly worried about her.'

'I'm sorry, ma'am, policy. But maybe you can help us. Just in
case. Would you know a next of kin?'

Had Victor the former hotdog been a more venturesome invalid—
had he ventured, for instance, beyond the confines of a man's castle more often to master the streets and sidewalks of Providence,
learn the ramps, the ropes, the tricks this trade, like any other,
had—he might have had more success as a fugitive. But the few
times he had to go out, with Donna lugging the folded chair down
the stairs while he lowered himself, arms locked at the elbows,
seated, from step to step, he had felt so aggrieved and humiliated
that he'd never worked out a better method, never sallied forth if
not absolutely necessary, never, no never, without Donna.

Victor on the lam was thus a sorry sight, never more so than on
first emergence from the Groat abode, agape on a second-story
landing, knowing he had seven steps to negotiate, then a midflight
landing, then ten more steps to the foyer, then six stone steps to
the street. He knew he was no more than twenty feet from street
level, would have known without his years of altitude fixation; he
knew, too, that no more than twenty feet could prove more than
enough to change a man's life for better or worse, in sickness and
health, and so forth.

Victor was sorely tested, for he could hear his wife inside the
apartment floundering, flailing, dramatizing his guesswork ad-
ministry of justice (nor Agriculture merit badge nor flying school
nor years in the business of dusting had taught him the precise
amount of a deadly pesticide that, mixed in bourbon, neat, would
cause least messily cessation of life functions in an adult female
human being, medium build). He could envision her, ten feet away
through the door, a fish on a pier, flipping and heaving to no end
(and he on the landing like a beached whale, full-grown man in a
rolling chair). He heard only body bashing about, peristaltic distress, ugly and convulsive retching, no words or even groans, nothing touching or giving him pause, only sounds of life in peril that
made him understand his own was none too cozy and he needed

to get himself down twenty-six steps to the street and then roll, roll like hell, and then God knew what. He saw himself bumping down like a cartoon villain, malleable for comic effect, putty in the hands of an animator who would never allow serious injury despite horrible distortions and malformations during the sequence that would end in a deformed and frazzled heap at the foot of the cliff or the rapids or in this case the stairs, teeth gleamingly exposed to denote anger, curses, foiled again, then popping up like a hat, a sponge, a wrestler, to vow revenge.

Victor had had his revenge, had done God's work, though the sound of it, rather than pleasing him, seemed likely to drive him mad as he wavered and faltered at the top of a simple flight. God, that stairs should frighten the man who had dropped bombs, gargantuan, far larger than himself, from thousands of feet, buzzed private resorts from less than a hundred, who had stuck at nothing: Boy (in his mind) of the ex-Year daunted by a descent most people took in stride. He released the brake and clutched with both hands at the banister, striving to ease himself down, beyond awkward, beyond clumsy, clatter drowning the awful sounds of Donna's throes, rollicking over right angles with muscles tendons ligaments from fingers to shoulders straining like cables to hold him to the banister and in the chair.

'Shit,' said Victor aloud at the landing. 'The Eagle has landed. Shit if I didn't.' Whether he referred specifically to the justice administered above or the partial escape is largely immaterial; for Victor's 'Shit' embraced in its broadest implications all aspects of this thought: when a Boy of the Year sets his mind to a thing, by gum and with the help of his Personal Savior that thing will be gotten done. Exhilarated with a seven-step triumph, Victor crowed 'Shit' and all but sneered at the upcoming downgoing ten. More than mortal, omnipotoid despite numbness in hands, twitching fatigue in forearms, absolute pain in a shoulder or two, Victor positioned himself—ski jumper at the head of the chute—and pushed off. Lost half his hold and careened single-handedly in a headlong arc about the point of contact where he gripped so hard he could feel it no more, wrong way round, backside to, arm too short, grasp too feeble, and crashed loudly, metallically, against the stucco foyer wall, painfully jamming a shoulder, painlessly cracking a toe, busting pieces of chair.

'Shit,' he repeated, in a far different tone. He had the reference at the ready: pride goeth. Well, he was always a cocky son of a bitch, had built a character around that, and now oddly recovered the feel of it as he sat momentarily with a dislocated shoulder, a broken toe, and a left wheel badly out of round. But alive for all that, and if not kicking, breathing, breathing heavily, full of the chemicals bodies shoot into the blood, and six stone steps from freedom or what seemed to him at the time to pass for it.

A mere stoop, a stupid stoop, a righteous man with a stoop to conquer; no stoop would stop a man who'd flown, who'd doctored booze, 'd put to death an unrighteous wife, her blood upon her (he could no longer hear her heavings, a story away; had escaped them, or they had ended), on her head be it, and he headed for the stoop, wobblily on a damaged rim, bird with a broken wing but fluttering, wildly if not straight, down six kathunk kathunk kathunk kathunk kathunk kathunk stone steps and down hard on concrete, skating the sidewalk into a Chevy parked at the curb and taking a header as the chair stopped short, skull against chrome trim at the juncture of plate glass bonking Victor slightly stunned and punch-drunk like a prizefighter in the final round who needs only to survive, hang on, not pass out, to get the split decision. Now add to the hurting shoulder and unhurting but hurt toe a knot on the noggin near the hairline and a hairline kneecap crack unbeknownst, and behold a free man turning right instinctively because the left shoulder's intact and deliberately because he thinks he hears a siren in the lefthand distance and proclaiming 'Shit' in both senses as he meanders the sidewalk on a wheel in need of truing, duck with a damaged web: Victor.

Shaken, shook, though shaking no more than usual for a man of his years, Theo puffed volumes, cohesive almost solid if protean clouds of bluish smoke: so many particles more than momentarily suspended, first in proud billows, then settling into lateral planes, laminous smog above a city, something so settled, so not unsettlable, so passive and yet so sure, so like the Theo people knew, the very presence of whose meerschaum calmed environs, whose comment more often than not put whatever had accumulated around the ellipse to rest, tying loose ends, whose moderation alone could establish equilibrium, himself an anodyne more soothing than the shnapps, this man, loosing iceheight, whose phone an alien woman had rung, on whose door she had knocked, whose long since enfeebled and conscientiously moderated heart had dilated and pumped with unwonted vigor for a few days for a relative in law only and by extension for one in so much more than law that he hadn't seen since so long a time ago, this man, though shaking no more than usual for a man of his years, shaken, shook by an unknown contralto in a state of consciousness no one understands.

But Molly's voice, humming over *knaydlach*, came back to him now; Molly in her kitchen, all right with the world; the things she could do with no more than matzo meal, egg, potato starch, onion, garlic, a *bissel* water, hands, such hands, and that voice; he told her that voice, that semiconscious humming, was her secret ingredient: her dumplings, her soups, her *gefilte* fish, her pies, her noodles, such noodles only music could create. Theo, never prone to envy, not given to regrets, who had long since learned to wish for what he had, to desire only the inevitable, to find what was necessary sufficient, through this strange indirection—a ring, a knock, an intrusion of strangeness—had come to think he would give anything he had, anything he hadn't, for a taste again of Molly's absent noodles, lost strudels.

He used to tease her when they were courting, in French picked up on a two-year pause in their westward quest, Shame on him who thinks of Molly; she always smiled at that, even after marriage, on a horrifying ocean crossing in steerage, on the Lower East Side, in Harlem, during the Great Depression, throughout the War (holocaust ongoing back across that terrific sea), finally in the Bronx, no matter what, always she would smile when he said, *Honi soit qui Molly pense*. It wasn't so funny, he knew—they both knew—and its meaning changed after marriage, but she always smiled for all that. Theo's tears slowly evaporated in the smoky air. He wished Irene well; he wished her friend well; he wished the whole sad universe well, and little lost Laurence who savored that strudel and laughed at that phrase—only swanky smelly pants— long before he knew why, who thought it was so much more funny before he knew why, somewhere maybe in New York City, but wherever, well, well, well.

Funny thing about the City: so astonishingly many wrong numbers. You'd think people who had subway stops down cold since childhood could handle sequences of three dash four integers. On a given night (they were mostly at night, more on weekends), you

could expect two or three in Gretchen's loft. Many were ethnic:
one for Letitia he understood after hanging up had been for
LaKeesha; some were beyond ethnic, in languages he couldn't
place (people, when he'd say Hello, would just start in: 'Provo,
kazoo parenthesis babaganooj deleterioso monoglyceride angle-
terre?'); some were beyond language, just grunts or silences, letting him carry the ball. Those that recognizably wanted somebody
seemed always to want somebody female, though. He wasn't sure
whether he'd gotten an obscene one yet until one night when what
sounded like a boy trying to sound like a man wanted to know in
no uncertain terms exactly what Miss Serena would do for fifteen
dollars.

'I'm sorry,' he'd say in a friendly but uninvolved tone, the perfect stranger, 'but I think you've got the wrong number.' That
remained his habitual response, despite its obvious imperfections
(why should *he* be sorry, and he knew, not thought, they were
wrong); undoubtedly a parent taught him that response at an age
when he needed to learn such things by rote: 'I'm sorry, but I think
you've got the wrong number.' And more astonishing than the
volume of misdialed calls was the reluctance of misdialers to believe.
Some asked what he was doing on the line, as if the misconnec-
tion were his fault; others accused him of lying; one wouldn't stop
calling back, hoping to wear him down, make him own up to the
ruse.

When Laurence dialed a wrong number (but he rarely did, a
former Math Fair champ without a smidgeon of dyslexia, and
especially careful to get digits right after sundown), he apologized,
even in the middle of the day, for intruding upon the presumably
otherwise occupied victim; but in the City, when he was the wrong
number others dialed, he was treated as a suspect, one who had
tampered with wiring, tapping into someone else's private life, or
broken and entered, mercilessly slaughtered LaKeesha, Ludmilla,
and all their friends (save the caller), then had the gall to pick up
and pretend their lines were his. Most often he was accused of
making time with another's gal, of homewrecking: 'Who the hell
are you?' and 'Look, I don't want none of this crap here, put her
on the damn phone if you know what's good for you' and 'Just tell
her I've got her number' and 'Good luck, bro, she's all yours and
stone poison.' How many relationships ruined, how many marriages on the rocks because he answered Gretchen's phone when
it rang? Had he, by telling truth, incited some jealous boyfriend to

drastic measures? And was New York in the grip of an epidemic of arithmetical misperception? Was that the real hidden cause of social instability, divorce rates, breakdown of nuclear family, decline of western sieve a function of transposed digits? Could nothing be done?

It was just barely conceivable (wasn't it?) that Gretchen and Flash had a secret code: if a man answers, ask for Ludmilla. But that could never account for the volume of calls; nor, really, for the rampant rudeness, easier to get used to on the street, for some reason, than the phone, where it's just you and me. Why did women get hooked up with these guys, anyway? Really, the impoliteness alone was enough to turn *him* off. What was wrong with people, that they couldn't recognize their mistakes?

So when Officer Fitzgerald rang up the Barron residence, it took Laurence a moment to realize the number wasn't wrong. And only another to realize that something was.

Bring.

Bring.

'Hello.'

'Yeah, lookit, uh, you got a, shoot, lemme see here, a Gretter Bairn there?'

Greeter Barn. Grater Burn. Greater Bear. Ursa Major. 'I'm sorry, but I think you've got.'

'Think twice, we got such a thing as impeding an investigation.'

'Invest?'

'Look, this is the law calling from over at Providence, and if this Gritty Beer.'

'Wait, Gretchen Barron?'

'Sure, right, you got her there?'

I haven't *got* her anywhere: got her in trouble, got her in dutch, got her in a family way, got her where you want her. 'She's not in right now, can I take a message?'

'Sure, right, yeah, uh, tell her, tell her we got a friend of hers here in some kind of a comber, and she can call this number here.' Fitzgerald gave the number while Laurence wondered how many kinds there were, besides beach and fine-toothed. 'Tell her you never know with these combers, so if possible she should call like day before yesterday, you got that?'

Laurence repeated the number aloud. He had a feeling this call wouldn't last much longer.

'Yeah, right, you got it, have a nice day.'

And sat with the buzzing handset in his lap: friend in a comber, brush with the law, impede invest, and Gretchen at the Oasis.

Bring.

'Greenwich Wimmin's Oasis. This is Carla.'

'Hello, I'm trying to get in touch with Gretchen Barron.'

'Gretchen's breathing right now. I can take a message if you like.'

'I think this is an emergency. It's about the police.'

'This is the police?'

'No, *about*. But it's real important.'

'I'll give her the message as soon as she's finished breathing.'

That could be too late. 'I think I'd better give her this message in person. I'll be right there.'

'Well, we don't like to let anything interrupt our wimmin's breathing.'

'That's understandable, but I'm on my way.'

Any other time, Laurence might have considered appearance, garb, tone, before invading the Oasis. But today, with a comber in the pitcher, he lumbered to announce his bit of emergent news without a thought of first impressions. Had he thought, he would have thought, Honorary honorary honorary, till the syllables sounded like nonsense or like something else: on a raree, tributary, cassowary, bird or beast, fish or fowl, animal, vegetable, mineral.

Not so wary, he barges in like the male he is or isn't, and encounters Carla, a shy woman, stray taken in when her husband hit her one too many times, nursed, counselled, colleagued with far more alphabetical consoeurs.

He's looking for Gretchen Barron, who he knows is breathing, but this is an emergency (yes, that was him, he, I, me, on the phone).

Carla looking around as if for cuecards.

It really is important. She's got lots more months to breathe. (But her friend in Providence may not.)

Maybe he should talk to someone with more . . . (they've been trying to break her of the habit of invoking authority). Would he wait right here?

He certainly will.

He won't disturb anything, will he? (Wary receptionist reluctant to leave her post.)

No no, he won't budge.

He may look around, though, and when he does may find, instead of palms, camels, bedouins, mirages (freshwater shimmer like sunshine on a highway): quartet by a distant distaff relation of Bach soft in the background, rackful of pamphlets, upholstered armchairs and calico curtains, citrusy essence and sunflower seeds, comforts of home he can see but not feel. And oh yes, couple of wimmin lounging, random, sultry, like furnishings, pictures he's seen or imagined of bordellos. He hears one say, with a confidential air of whispering in an ear, as if she won't be overheard, 'Who's the male?'

When he sees Carla returning, he knows it's Audrey Poole she's got in tow. Head, toe, in between, the darkest person he's ever seen, like a negative of Gretchen, he thinks, or vice versa: which is the other developed? He hears Carla say, as if in response to the previous question, 'I don't *know*, he wants Gretchen.' He recalls Gretchen's recitation: '"We of the Greenwich Wimmin's Oasis are speechless."' Aud doesn't look speechless, and when she gets close enough isn't: 'How may we help you?' she asks, including Carla and the seated wimmin in her first emphasized person, quarantining him in the stressed and singular second.

Aud is formidable, if not yet forbidding, and Laurence, though pretty sure she's sardonizing, is himself, without a tinge of irony, speechless. Sensing the first response will set a tone, ratify or reverse one, he's on guard, fencing off the inappropriate, himself fenced off by that unembracing 'you.' While he ponders propriety, how to take the edge off, how to rise without arrogance and establish harmlessness without timidity, the opportunity could slip away. 'Dr. Poole,' he says, nodding slightly, to hold his place. And before he knows it, he has vacated rather than held it. Now in another sense speechless, his poor speech delivered; and it sounded cold, mannered, distressed, metallic: two proper nouns with an inconspicuous nod, as if he were meeting a renowned Flemish composer rather than a suspicious, testing gyno-Afro-American on her turf.

The denizens of the waiting room look unperturbed, curious maybe, as if they found a crumpled slip, phone number with no name attached, in pants not recently worn. No one else seems disconcerted by Aud's greeting. No one else seems anxious. No one else seems anything but at home. Then Laurence understands: they *are* at home, or at an oasis at least, maybe more like home for some than home. Whereas the Oasis is, for him, alien territory. Though he doesn't feel like the enemy. He wonders, having invaded a refuge for others, not for him, if this is how it feels to be a wife.

He wishes Gretchen would appear. Not so he can hang on her arm like a handbag as when he first greeted the renowned composer. But he could hope that, as she did then, Gretchen might quietly, surely indicate to a new acquaintance, 'He's okay, accept him for my sake until you can for his own.'

But he knows behind it all something other than homey or alien, beyond gender and pocketbookish nonmarital status, beyond even disqualification as coach, stops, stumps, and stymies him for an unconscionable interval following nouns and nod. He knows that the minute he mentions his name (and he *has* to introduce himself, doesn't he?) Dr. Poole will be thinking, 'Aha, oho, hoo hoo, so this is the one who boggles natural knowledge, expertise, and history of science. So this is the one unlike any other one of any sex whatever. The one with the ten-footer.' And knowing she'll be thinking this paralyzes him utterly.

Yet doesn't he have a message? And isn't this after all an emergency, a not-uncalled-for interruption? And doesn't he have, in any case, to say something? And isn't that Gretchen to the rescue now coming down the hall?

'Gretchen, it's Donna. I got a call. She's in the hospital.'

'Ogod.' She halts, hobbled, no stride apparent.

'They said a coma.'

Gretchen, breathing now very well indeed thank you, and allowing no time for Laurence to make up lost ground with Dr. Poole, clutches him like a purse and runs out of the Oasis.

Irene's fingers never came within a foot of her mouth as the driver checked her ticket, tore off the top layer, handed her what was left. She was not totally calm, however, thinking, Next of kin, Just in case, Next of kin, Just in case. Long-lost, newfound, no sooner found than lost: Donna. The extremely pale woman in the front seat looked upset, too, and their eyes might have met in a moment of mutual empathy, of secretly gauging respective sources of anxiety, had the pale one's not been polarized, screened from such contact by mirrored shades with a dark blue tinge, large, straight across the top and bulging around the bottom like bags full of liquid with a sizable specific gravity. Irene walked out of the shades and on down the aisle and claimed a double seat, placing coat and book on the seat beside her in hope (she had a lot on her mind) of averting random companionship.

Public transportation could feel so random; but then, what couldn't? Why Donna and not some other former seventeen-year-old in St. Benedict's Emergency? Why not Lucy Fern? Why not, for that matter, any number of people who had never sat Irene? Why Laurence and not some other relative *cum* mourner on that other bus and then in the cafeteria and then till death or confusion or whim did them part? You meet such a tiny percentage (-millage, -millionage, -billionage) of a planet's population in a lifetime: why friends, acquaintances, lifelong mates with those and not some others? Why Victor and not some other pilot? Why a pilot? Why anybody at all? And then, of course, inevitably, as if it were the same question rather than the opposite, why not?

Which made the whole thing seem at the same time so opposite of random, so not by chance, so (what was the word even; they were all, it seemed, archaic) destined, fated, determined, so (what would the modern equivalent be) scripted, plotted, publishable. So like a novelization, so like a movie based on an incredible true story, one you wouldn't believe if you weren't informed of its basis, so full of possibly meaningful detail, so ripe for interpretation. And yet so unnecessary. Like hiring a world full of actors to delude (for no particular reason!) one single preteen girl: so like a persecution, so like an honor.

Sometimes it all seemed to Irene like a story to which you respond: 'It just goes to show.' Sometimes it all seemed to Irene like a story to which you respond: 'Life is just like that, I guess.' And the disconcerting factor as she aged was that these times were closer and closer, opposites flipping back and forth, becoming one another like blood-sugar conditions, inflammable, flammable, why and why not. She supposed by the time she was forty the world would be alternating like current, sixty times a second, between coincidence and kismet, implausible and implacable, each opposite undeniable.

Then to another valence to wonder what might be the point of *that;* but escape immediately became recapitulation, and she saw that that would reproduce the previous level, question, metaquestion, metaquestion, question: pointed, pointless, pointless, pointed. Rapidly foreseeing infinite regress (had she reached the age of alternating current so soon?), she dropped the question, not like a

hot potato but like one that had cooled, lost its piquancy in pre-
dictability, indeterminacy, the two now equated and cancelling each
other out, two spouses on opposite ends of the poll, which left her
with this: Just in case, Next of kin, Just in case, Next of kin. This,
and the complicatedly bad smell of public transportation.

Out mowing, out making the world less green, out turning grass
black in clumps on the bottom of the machine, yellow in the bag
at the back, out creating patterns without redeeming social value,
out undoing whatever meaning what was wild a few lifetimes ago
had, out mowing for mowing's sake, half deciding to quit, half
wondering whether to give notice at lunch on Monday, out wondering what lunch on Monday was about anyway, out thinking of
grass—most of the world makes baskets, clothing, houses and
temples for gods' sakes out of it—wondering where we'd be without it, how essential to the food chain, more important, globally
speaking, or less than the potato, silly question, apples and oranges,
onions and carrots, how could we do without any of them, out
thinking a world without mushrooms, cress, endive, might not just
survive but prevail, out fancying a planet without tuxes, coats of
arms, country clubs, doormen, footmen, tiaras, monograms, garnishes. 'Garnished,' Theo used to say, meaning 'nothing at all.' A
world without things that mean nothing at all would be without
experimental mowing. If so, so be it, small price to pay.

Out mowing, out thinking, out perambulating, he suddenly felt
the mower handle under his hands, the mower in front of his feet,
turning into a baby carriage of sorts. Trying not to jump to con-
fusions, he took note that prams do not generally come factory-
equipped with razor-sharp rotary blades, nor with chokes and
electronic ignitions, nor with two-point-five-horsepower two-stroke
engines requiring a mixture of gasoline and motor oil; they come
instead with single-totpower babies requiring a mix of mother's
milk and strained apricots. He noted with aplomb discrepancies,
yet the more he perambulated the less they seemed to matter; he
jiggled the handle and imagined he was rocking his baby in the
bosom of Abraham; he watched ahead for jangling bumps or
declivities; he kootchy-cooed as he looked forward to hosing down
the underside after ambulation. And he thought, Pajamas with
feet, now there's a useful invention, something we can all applaud
regardless of class background, economic stratum; rattles, build-

ing blocks, pacifiers, these are things whose merit none can gainsay. Cradles: marvelous, of civilization; rivers, cities, even towns, always near water, nothing like a river running through a municipality to make it feel like home. Great rivers of the world, certainly; but even a nearly stagnant stream sitting in the center of a village, a six-inch waterfall, maybe some ducks practicing navigation on a small scale, attracting crumbs from tourists and natives alike: all that was worth something. A world without rivers and onions and something to teethe on was already a world half dead. Pitter patter, it was raining, don't mow wet grass, worms crawl out of everywhere afterward, fish rise near the surface to catch bugs flying lower on laden wings, ozone reconstitutes somehow, everything better, better now, gonna be all right, lullaby baby, when the wind blows the cradle will rock, now now don't you cry, that's right, Mama's here, Mama won't leave you now I can see you Mama, I see you.

A rumbling in the future. Rain, rain. Electrical storm. No time to be slaughtering grass. Hell with the Clefs. Go away. Turn off the damn pram and drag it behind you, darkish trail through the dewy decimated blades from the spot where you called it quits to go home I'll go home. Come again some other day.

Gretchen hated buses. She'd be on a train, but she hated them worse. Besides, speed being of the essence and passenger rail service having long since been cut way back all over the Northeast corridor, the first thing out of town seemed most appropriate. You could fly, she supposed, but the trip to the airport would rival the bus to New Haven, and once in New Haven you were almost in Providence.

Thus Gretchen spent much of the trip considering the trip itself, its mode and logistics, its sounds and smells (of what was that awful smell composed that you always, and only, encountered on buses?), not its sights (what with darkly tinted busglass and darkly tinted eyeglass, there were hardly any of these for Gretchen); and then considering what grammatical function 'what' plays in the construction 'what with x and y'; and then if all words, always and ever, could fit categories of form and function; then diagramming sentences, their feathery dependencies; then what a diagram of Donna's subordinate life would resemble, and various mental attempts to graph its trajectory, and must it conclude with a downstroke such as this, and would it be over by the time she got there, no downstroke at all but the level EKG of intensive care no longer required, unruffled horizon no spot on earth save oceans retained but every life tended toward; and then, though the transition wasn't clear, whether whatever this smell was, this bus smell with its millions of strange shadows and lingering presences, could do harm to a foetus; and then the muffling double darkness of windows and shades made her, Gretchen Barron, despite stride, adulthood, rational understanding, not inconsiderable musical talent, and a lifelong claustrophilia, afraid, and she shut her eyes to avoid it, which helped a bit though she still couldn't figure what 'what' was, couldn't place that part of speech.

And the moral of the story is: even in a city with decently maintained sidewalks, you can't get far in a busted wheelchair (veering and tacking like a skiff in a stiff breeze, canoe with a single paddle) with a busted head (losing every minute or two your sense of why you're outdoors, what you can't go home to, where you thought a half a block ago you might be headed) and a busted shoulder (veering, tacking, canoe, paddle) and a diligent sergeant on your trail (your trail so crooked, he so straight a stalker), looking, you guessed it, to bust *you*, head shoulder and all. Baby cradle and all, thought Victor, though he'd long since stopped weeping like a goddam infant.

Fitzgerald caught up with Victor less than ten blocks from home. 'Freeze,' he shouted like a TV cop. Victor sat stock still: a Scout at attention, a damaged creature in danger, unaware how imperfect his camouflage was. Fitz approached with a swagger, revolver drawn, other hand on the billy, leaned down over Victor's left shoulder—approach from behind if possible, makes a suspect feel more helpless—and sneered, 'Wouldn't be goin anywhere here, now would you?' He took a turn around the chair; started like a squire surveying his estate, ended like a pet owner evaluating an accident on his living-room rug. He wanted to rub Victor's nose in something, hit him on it with a newspaper; but first he had to establish identity. 'You Groat?' he interrogated, and it came out like a line in a singles bar. 'You Vic Groat?'

Victor stunned: hadn't voted since Nixon debated that Catholic, thought he'd been wiped off the rolls, never been fingerprinted, no license plate on the chair: whence this celebrity? 'How did you know?'

'How the law knows ain't the question, Mr. Groat, cause if you are Groat, you got a couple other questions we ought to discuss that sort of take priority over that one, like for instance if they was to take a whim to pump your wife's stomach down at the emergency right about now what you think they might come up with.'

'I'll tell you the question, sonofabitch.'

'Listen, pal, go easy, I figure we gotcha right now at least on involuntary manslaughter, that's given she croaks, anything from there to murder one, maybe dependent on how this goes next few minutes here. Lady manages to hang on, you're still lookin at attempted, murder probly, so I'd say your bet's to be cool and just let this go down with as few complexions as possible, don't help your case to be gettin on the bad side of your friends on the force here. So now maybe you got some passion in this, that could militate a circusdance for you, time for behavior, you'd get out still with a life here, most boys down at the station understand what it's like to have some skirt go freaky on you, but you wouldn't want to hurt yourself in their eyes, I mean you got enough against you as it is, a gimp in a chair goin up against a man with a gun, and you not lookin none too perky even at that.'

'I'll tell you the question, you motherfucking sonofabitch, is why you motherfucking sonsofabitches can't do your fucking job and keep people from fucking defiling themselves and their fucking goddamned marriages, which is your sworn duty to protect and to fucking serve.'

Fitz had some teethmarks on his shin and a jammed thumb by the time it was over. Victor—an unattractive nuisance in the eyes of the law, mote in its vitreous humor—wound up with creating a public disturbance, resisting arrest, assaulting an officer, using profanity; plus, pending developments, either murder one or attempted something.

Irene and Gretchen got off the same bus, flagged down very similar cabs at the same corner, paid slightly different fares, emerged at the same hospital, asked at the same desk for the same patient's room, lied with equal unconvincingness in response to the same question ('Relative?'), were referred to, and disbelieved by, the same head nurse, who denied them admittance to the same intensive-care unit, so they sat on the same couch and began to entertain the same question: who is that woman? Donna, one of two people in the world who could have answered them both correctly, was upstairs oblivious to twists and turns, recognitions and incongruous conjunctions, perilously close to a personal peripeteia; Laurence, the other, would just as soon not be around for this particular anagnorisis, though he didn't know it. Victor knew one and might have guessed the other, but was under heavy guard way at the other end of the building, where, after an initial examination determined him to be abraded, dislocated, disoriented, hairlined, concussed, contused, confused, contrary, combative, resistant, and stronger than you might have guessed, he had been threatened, protected, restrained, injected, infused, pronated, sedated, dressed, undressed, and fingerprinted more or less simultaneously.

More or less simultaneously is how Irene and Gretchen decided to find out who that other woman was. (Lucky, too, that they did, since no one else showed the slightest interest; nurses, orderlies, mess crews, paramedics, candystripers and nutritionists, interns and internists, residents and visitors, impatient relatives and in-law outpatients, florists and fawners, all had other fish to fry: deliveries and sterilizations of all sorts, doses, diagnoses, prognoses, eye-ear-throat-noses, amputees, herbal teas, whole grains, pulled groins, double-billing, kootchy-cooing, *gloria dei*, nasturtia, inertia, cholesterol, stilbesterol, upcoming exams, many a question in the air besides who that woman was: was it the canned mushrooms, will we survive as a functioning family unit, where's the night shift, will I ever paint again, should I have pushed harder at the staff meeting, is there some possibility I've overlooked?)

'Excexusecumeseme,' they said in a kind of ragged unison.

Irene deferred, and Gretchen continued, 'but I couldn't help noticing.'

'Right, me too.'

'I'm a friend of Donna's from New York.'

'Right, me too, not from New York.'

'But weren't we on the same?'

'I was just visiting, I guess.'

'How did you find out what was?'

'I called her house and got a policeman. I guess it was just a little while after.'

'Do you know what?'

'He wouldn't tell me anything but the name of the hospital. What do you know?'

'Apparently she's in a coma.'

'Innacoma.' Takoma. Tachycardia. Annapurna. Wallawalla. Well well.

'Ya.'

'God.'

'Ya.'

'How could this?'

'My guess is Victor cracked. He's such a.'

'I've never met him.'

'Victor's her.'

'I know. But I just found Donna again.'

'Found?'

'After a long time. She used to sit for me.'

'You're an artist?'

'No, a baby. I mean a child. I mean I was.'

Gretchen smiled. 'Right, me too.'

Even Irene smiled. 'I'm Irene.'

'Gretchen.'

Something seemed to somebody familiar about this, but nothing definitive clicked, and the conversation continued gestalt-lessly.

'You know, Irene, this is really crazy, I mean there must be some way to find out what the hell is going on with Donna.'

'Maybe they'd at least let us talk to her.'

'Doctor, right. Let's ask.'

'Gretchen?'

'Right.'

'I'm glad somebody else is here.'

'You mean me, right?'

'Yeah, you. Somebody else.'

'Yes, well, I am that.'

'Right, me too.'

Nine

Not immediately, not while Gretchen was on Greyhound, not till a day or two later did Laurence absorb being alone in her loft: run of the loft, loft to himself, just a man without hair on his crotch in the absence of the woman he seemed to be living with. So imagine the titillation of it: not in address book or cancelled checks (he knew where she kept these, but didn't care to look for secrets), not in sheaves of old love letters tied together with faded ribbon or dear diary (there were none of these, as far as he knew, though he made no search), not in medicine chest or underwear drawer (one of each, but he was no Victor, and their contents would have held no surprises in any case), no private space or possession hidden from view; no, the titillation of what was right out there for all to see, in heaps and stacks it covered the floor: gobs of it, a treasure trove, you could fill a bathtub with it. Sheet music: staffs, clefs, accidentals, all the accessories, complete in this package, everything you need, instant music, just add instruments, skill, understanding. Pieces of puzzles, fragments of feasts. Cantmiss recipes for long-lasting beauty, more beautiful in the right frame of mind than beauty itself.

Rousing, arousing, carousing, Laurence revelled in black and white. The italic Italian was fun, but couldn't hold a candle to dynamic marks, holds, rests, codas, marks that meant nothing in any other language. The oldest and the newest compositions had in common minimalism, scarcely more than invitations to improvise; but those in the vast middle centuries—baroque, classical, romantic, modern—sprouted notes like potato eyes, pores on a paper skin, mineral-deposit skylines in an old teakettle, mold on a shower curtain, anything that just appears: Brownian movement, subnuclear particles, landscape, illness, feeling, thought. Laurence thought briefly of Dempler's notes—heifer doesn't ovum—in contrast to this abundance, and opened cases to add resin, wax, old wood, old sweat, and metal to paper, the fragrance of sound, the smell of music. And silently, fingers to mouth, he gave every sense but hearing to the music, breathing deep as if in arousal, not in a holy locus, not in a concert hall, not in a place where theory—behaving-like-a-concertgoer—tells you, 'Breathe imperceptibly, cough lightly, if you must, between movements, don't react till you've counted them up and they come out right, don't mistake tacit passages for ends of movements, just to be safe wait for others: *then* applaud, yell, hyperventilate, show your response is out of control, demonstrate beyond doubt how near impossible stifling approbation earlier was, explode in active appreciation, if you wish you may even move your feet.' Not like that, not what (Laurence was sure) Dempler would insist on; no. Swaying, hugging music to his body, humming in his head, feeling paper-thin substance, moaning if the spirit moved, undone by unmusic, ravished by recipe, Laurence laughed.

Emboldened, he approached the gamba, caressed its scroll, its rosewood pegs, its ebony tailpiece, traced the inlaid purfling along its unearthly curves (how do they *do* that with wood?). Looked into the case, small shrine lined in royal-blue velvet: felt that softest swatch of flannel in the world, the cloth he'd seen Gretchen clean the instrument of resin with so often, picked up the bow by its frog and tightened the hairs as he'd also seen her do, ran them through the block of resin glued to a piece of velveteen like a small museum exhibit, carried the bow to the gamba. Sat. Carefully placed it between his knees, hugged it there. Too gently tried to make it work, horsehair skittering over gut like a car out of tune on a winter morning, just something in his hand scraping against something between his legs. Instinctively pressed, letting more of himself embrace the thing, push vibrations into the hollow beneath the soundpost, scroll up by his neck, elbow rubbing veneer, naked gut gouging impromptu ferrules in finger flesh, horsehair more insistent now, making a serious sound.

To Laurence's great shock, his whole body vibrated with the strings, as if the gamba weren't something he played but something playing him, something to be hooked up to, magic fingers on a motel bed. He made notes, experimented with intervals. He picked out a soulful stringy version of 'Yankee Doodle,' of 'Row Your Boat,' of 'Jingle Bells.' Stuck a feather in his cap, gently down the stream, merrily, merrily, merrily, merrily, jingle all the way: 'Macaroni!' he called it in a syncopatonic interval, and took off, upbowing, downbowing, foottapping, kneesqueezing, torsotightening, eyeshutting, heartmoving, boweltugging, hearttugging, all but bowelmoving, performing, formpurring, awaycarrying, gambolling, gambagambagambaplaying Laurence.

Who had often pictured himself twirling a cello on its endpin like a beat bassist, guitar rocker, preteen ballerina in recital, on point for the first time in public. He might now have lived out this fancy, were Gretchen's celli not both foresightfully fitted with endpins specially angled to make their posture more nearly horizontal for later stages of pregnancy. A gamba, of course, has no endpin; its smaller bottom, round as a baby's bum, is unappendaged. Still, thinking he might give it a whirl, Laurence balanced the instrument gently at his feet, used the index of one hand to steady the scroll, set the whole body with tangential brush of the other lightly turning. Inertial gamba gathering moment, fugal-petal, instant equipoise, skater aspin: on thin ice by dint of ventrodorsal asymmetry, more than mostly hollowness, staggered weight distribution, off-centered gravity, physics of the thing, flashy coin careering toward table edge, grab it before it! And caught a tuning peg on a cuff, tripped up, clutched, missed, sent ballerina atumble, skater asprawl, gamba crash to hardwood, floored: eyepress, gutgrab, heartstop.

He thought he heard a snap. He thought he felt something clamp onto his liver. Read off the insides of his lids sensational headlines: Ballerina Mauled In Freak Accident, Wizened Young Man Held, Missing Endpin Sought. Had a nightmare vision of former gamba, viola no more, fingerboard adangle, sickening, neck-broke, unnatural angle, strings like ravelled threads holding together fabric torn, verve-rending nerve-ending, stainless steel against stainless steel, nails clutching cliffedge. He opened grateful eyes to nothing of the sort, neck intact strings not frayed. Himself less frayed, unafraid, until a glimpse of crunched purfling makes shrieking nails scrape blackboard. Laurence, bypassing precision, bites his with abandon, in spades, with a vengeance.

Donna's physician was a rather elderly pathologist, not without zeal, a stickler for detail but not for the rules when it came to sharing information with unauthorized individuals, always more than willing to consult regarding a patient's vitals and the probability of becoming a statistic. Gretchen, who would have recognized, and Irene, who would not, were equally glad to see approaching a doctor no one, familiar or not, could mistake for Chris Crickenberger. Both had feared that he would enter this scene, that the thing could turn into farce just when terror and pity were making a comeback. They feared too, of course, for Donna's sake (and on her behalf, who was beyond fearing), the terror and pity; if you can't fear terror, what's the point? But somehow farce threatened more. This was no time for Gretchen in particular to mix it up with that overfamiliar practitioner.

Had Dr. Pinckney lifted one leg, he could have been taken for a flamingo impersonator. Coral-faced, bead-eyed, long-nosed, stoop-shouldered, he had to hold his neck in what looked like an uncomfortable position to look you in the eye; but he looked you there a great deal, almost continually, Gretchen noticed, if you allowed for the veteran clinician's habit of giving everyone in the neighborhood a quick once-over, unannounced pop quiz, like a cop who could frisk visually. Nothing prurient, nothing desirous, except maybe as a park ranger can be said to desire a forest fire because always on the lookout; just so, Dr. Pinckney looked out for an off-color about the gills, coated tongue, slight hitch in the gait, blatant, implicit, potential dysfunction, any tipoff for his eagle eyes, continuously scanning like a security camera or smoke detector. The man was a detector through and through—the earliest onset of a condition rarely escaped him—and he met your eyes so often not only because he was that sort of a person (secure, caring, a contact devotee), but also because eye tissue and surrounding musculature lay out an all-you-can-eat diagnostician's smorgasbord: he'd studied iridology, and didn't feel he could discount it responsibly, not to mention whites, pupils, crow's-feet, lids (he was attached to the prefix 'bleph-'), ducts and lashes, brows and bags, shape and sheen, glisten and glance, viscosity, vitreosity, reflexivity: each of us carried in our eyes, in Dr. Pinckney's eyes, a full dossier, portable autobiography in two volumes, brimming with not only medical but metaphysical, antetypical, experiential, and ethical informativity. He could tell you, he thought, from your eyes if you cheated on taxes, ran stop signs in the dead of night, separated whites and colors, normals and permapresses, or just dumped them all humblejumble in the washer, gave a shit, took a powder, threw parties, floated loans, swam laps, sang like a dream, caught hell, believed in God, why or why not. Better than astrology, numerology, phrenology, animal magnetism, any and all pseudosci or sci-fi parlor-trick mancies, sortileges, and extispicies performed by armchair prophetasters and would-be wizards, psychics and hypnophiles and telepathologists; surpassing all spectacles and sleights-of-mind: eyes.

He found Gretchen's, of course, conspicuously interpretable: their obvious myopia and photosensitivity, not to mention color, not to mention skin, hair, global pallor of the organism; a piece of cake for a clinician of his talents, bird in the hand. Irene's, on the other hand, promised a challenge: not dessert but some subtly misrecognizable side dish, uncommon variety of summer squash perhaps, bird in the bush, what was it presenting, the condition, aetiology, story of this specimen, nothing he could finger yet, something that bore further study, a woman whose eyes at once invited and resisted the full powers of medical science, as Dr. Pinckney stooped and craned and (turning to Gretchen's previously classified orbs regularly to let her know he still knew she was there or verify albinism hadn't gone into remission) met her eyes with what she took for simple concern, all the while explicating with his own particular passion for detail the ins and outs of a these days rather rare condition exemplified by their friend who lay impervious to twists and turns but requiring the full-time attention of half a nurse upstairs.

'Your friend is in ICU, where her vital signs are monitored continuously onscreen by a staff of highly trained.'

'Doctor, please, we want to know what happened.'

'Professionals. Your anxiety is perfectly understandable. Your friend seems somehow to have ingested a small, but perhaps at that too large, amount of an organophosphate compound, which caused.'

'Organophosphate,' repeated Irene, trying it on for sighs. It sounded like something you'd survive.

'These are a class of chemical compounds found in certain pesticides, some of which have recently been banned for just this.'

'Pesticides? Like Raid, Roach-B-Gone, Black Flag?' Pronouncing the latter out loud, under the circumstances, seemed to Gretchen bad luck.

'Reason. I'm afraid not. Worse. These are commercial pesticides, terribly potent, generally used in concentrations of approximately one to one sixty. A cupful in ten gallons of water would do for an acre or two of crop.'

This sounded bad. 'How much did she?'

'We can't be completely sure, short of an autopsy.'

This sounded worse. 'Will she?'

'Again we can't be sure. She managed to contact nine one one before seizures set in; the symptoms were recognized with startling rapidity, given the rarity of this type of event, and the antidote was administered promptly.'

'There's an antidote?' This sounded better.

'Oh yes indeed. Atropine, taken intravenously, does the trick quite nicely, provided she didn't take too much of the poison and assuming we got to her in time.' Irene and Gretchen now had to learn that organophosphates, if inhaled in vaporous form but much more severely and far less commonly if taken internally, inhibit the activity of acetylcholinesterase, an enzyme that works at neural synapses to break down the neurotransmitter acetylcholine. They learned further that atropine, racing to occupy the receptor sites for acetylcholine, invariably wins out. 'Assuming, as I've said, that we got to her in time. It's called competitive inhibition.'

'Competitive inhibition,' repeated Irene, thinking, Olympic shyness, federal regulation.

'Victor,' said Gretchen suddenly.

'Well, we hope so, but as I say, we can't promise anything till we see.'

'No, Victor, a name, her husband, used to be a crop duster. He'd have access to that kind of chemical, wouldn't he?'

'Oh my goodness, oh yes, any number of them: Phosdrin, Parathion, Malathion. But then so does anyone else. You can find them at lawn and garden centers, feed stores.'

'Malathion,' said Irene, rolling the malicious, malignant sound of it around in her mouth like a plaque-fighter, then spitting it out. From what she'd heard of Victor, Malathion was her guess.

'What's her situation now?'

Now it was important for them to understand that excessive levels of acetylcholine at receptor sites cause postsynaptic nerves to fire continuously, out of control, resulting in a generalized hyperactivity of the smooth muscles: the entire GI tract, the urinary tract, 'and so on': 'in Mrs. Groat's case, I am afraid, the uterine activity, mimicking labor, has caused the unfortunate loss of a foetus she was carrying.' The muscular contractions, he informed them, eventuate in a kind of mock-epileptic seizure and finally lead, 'as in the case of your friend,' to coma.

She couldn't complain. Course she wanted him to understand what the job end-tailed: you had to think about any number of things, all at the same time.

'Really?'

He could take, for an instance, ordures.

He could? 'Ordures?'

Can-o'-peas. Plus on-tray, same-all-timeously, was her point.

Still life: greyish-green legumes cascading cornucopiously from horizontal aluminum, preserved in timeless saline jollity, onto a silver salver, cheap beads off a snapped string. Even the addition of 'tender, young, sweet, fancy' to the label didn't allow Laurence to picture Dempler salivating over such dainties. Of course they'd be imported: *'tendres, jeunes, doux . . .'* He couldn't think of the word for 'fancy,' but peas were *pois* if memory served; and suddenly he heard what Else was saying: *canapés, entrées.* 'What sort of *hors d'oeuvres* does Dempler order, for instance?' he asked, hoping the pause hadn't betrayed his dialectical puzzlement.

Else hadn't noticed a problem, seemed pleased that Laurence took an interest in her work. 'Oh, he'd leave that right up to me mostly. Tell you what, that gives me a swell of pride though I know it's sin. Some days I just set an marvel over that, a man like him leavin food to me. That Oyster sometime stick a nose in, but the Maestro trust me like I was his *own* mama.'

Easy to do, thought Laurence.

'Tell you what, though, he do love mushrooms, baked stuff, just the tops, *you* know. Stems don't bother *me*, so I eat em up as I go along. He don't mind, but Oyster sometime say not to.'

'She does?'

'Say I shouldn't be eatin em, they be awful.'

Offal? 'If she says that to you, Else, I think *she's* awful.'

'Tell you what, I sometime serve oyster, like a joke at her, only she don't know it. Maybe ought not do that.'

Laurence thought Else blushed slightly at the thought. 'But if they *like* oysters.'

'That part's true, they do love em, but still it's probly sin, account of my attitude an secret thoughts. But you should see, Lawns, what they got in that kitchen, special stuff, like a knife just to pry oyster, special brush reserved for mushrooms. Can you imagine, a brush just for the mushroom, fine like white babyhair for them mushroom heads, an she all the time remind me to don't use that brush on no other foods. That one's exclusive for the mushroom. Always talkin like that: exclusive for the mushroom.'

Exclusive seemed to Laurence to the point. Mushroom, too; Dempler's dun softness, shaded and riddled with dents and deflations, emerging full and puffy from a high, tight collar, like something grown in fungal moisture, dank, unappetizing, Dempled. Exclusive for the mushroom, whole porcine strains bred to root truffles for the more than affluent. What species gave its fine pelt for the manufacture of the mushroom brush, rushbroom mush, lush loom gush, hush gloom flush plume blush fume. Don't listen tomb, *he's* Joosh. Delicacies.

Else's face, smooth as the mushroom looked from a distance but firm, substantial, russet, reminded him of potato: a tuber, a staple, what people starve without. The vegetables of the people: onion, potato, carrot, surrounded by earth itself, firm to withstand pressure, things that crunch, things that last, things that go with everything, so full of life they'll sprout in or out of a fridge. Or pulses, yes, edible seeds, human beans and roots, not trifles; things about which Laurence had to ask, How can they *live* like that and still taste so good, overlooked, underground. Else, yes, a potato.

Something there was in Laurence that did not love an oyster knife, a mushroom brush, a salt cellar, a salad fork, a finger bowl, or any person who could eat Else's can-o'-peas six days a week without once letting her know *she* was a genie.

Throughout his life, Laurence acted naturally. He did what seemed slated as the next thing to do: when syntax appeared in cerebral synapses, he used it; when little girls flirted, he fled; when nails grew, he nibbled; when bullies shoved, he bawled; when F scales flowed like honey, he practiced B♭; when facial hair sprouted, he shaved; when students gathered in auditoria with sharpened No. 2s, he scored 797 Verbal, 712 Quantitative; when love engaged him, he married; when New York beckoned, he hopped on a bus; when Gretchen beckoned, he hopped on her; when a genius said, 'Mow,' he mowed for all he was worth. But when something or someone failed to appear, flirt, grow, shove, flow, sprout, gather, engage, beckon, beckon, or say, Laurence was generally not too clear on what to do next. If free samples arrived in the mail, he shampooed or pretreated or taste-tested. Monopoly was a gift from Aunt Tootie. The public schools had a spare saxophone on hand. His first vest was a piece of his father's estate; had it never descended to him, unlikely he would have worn one. *Moby-Dick* was nearest the door on the bookshelf when his mother was stricken; had it not been, unlikely he would have read it. Laurence took what came.

This method served him well in most instances, but if nothing came, he could evince a certain lack of initiative. He was not the sort of fellow who would develop an interest in bonsai trees or jet propulsion out of the blue, nor who would ignore them if someone raised the idea. But with so many stories in the naked city and so aged a grandpa and so lengthy a span twixt Fordham and Fourth, unlikely anything but initiative would bring him to Theo or Theo to him. When Mama started to disappear, he could still see her, and said as much: 'I can see you, Mama, I see you'; but when Theo disappeared, he failed to see either Theo or why, could only see that: the fact, the severance, willfully not-there Theo. And why was 'Is your grandfather living?' so difficult, so indecipherably complex, so demanding a question? Didn't he *want* it answered? But he did, you know he did, he did hid hid hid hid.

Gretchen morbidly imagined revolution in Donna's nervous system, minuscule electrical impulses like a Fourth of July finale, Independence Day for the overworked and undersung smooth muscles, autonomic autonomy, sheer overload like an appliance gone kaflooey, radio interference, too many stations, AC DC AM FM (Flash Farfield, she guessed, would find the idea exhilarating, whereas she, familiar with the pain of overstimulation, winced at the thought); and then just turning the damned thing off for a little peace and quiet, families packing drowsy kids, blankets, pillows into the back of the station wagon, tucked in and driven home and carried in still sleeping to bed. As if coma were respite, a holiday from hoopla, not an endangered and dangerous life-and-death teeter-totter; as if Donna's body, ordered to shut down by occupying forces, had volunteered to take the day off. None of her everyday analogies, indulged for more than a minute, worked; they all broke down (like Donna's system, thought Gretchen, another simile revving up before her thesis could head it off), refused to carry the load of meaning or meaninglessness that coma meant. To Pinckney it meant a rare diagnostic opportunity, acetylcholinesterase, competitive inhibition: something that left out Donna, Victor, everything that mattered or meant to Gretchen. What coma really did was refuse to mean in everyday terms, in any available terms whatever. Appliances, holidays, fireworks, signs (Gone Fishin' on the screen door, Circumstances Beyond Our Control on the tube): nothing quite accounted for what Donna was doing or not doing upstairs. Continuous monitoring documented something, but again, something that didn't mean in the larger picture, or rather that didn't make the events that led up to it mean; and Gretchen realized she was thinking in a way she had never approved of in Donna: your husband gets hurt, so God doesn't exist, so you sleep with your doctor, so you get pregnant, so God exists, so simple-minded, so literalist a notion, what's wrong with, or how many bunnies are hidden in, this picture, a couple of vases or two people kissing, stairs going up or down, is the man in the moon smiling, did the dish run away with the spoon?

Taking what comes. This was not, I hope you understand, fatalism or anything of the sort; closer to the opposite: a brand of improvisation. Nor was it, you can understand if you try, know-nothingism; closer, again, to the opposite: a cherishing what little you know by not thinking you know what you don't. Given the extraordinary number of theories he'd seen exploded after years of apparently corroborating evidence by counterexamples or countertheories of equally spurious apparency, Laurence was ever conscious of how much may not appear, all that did to the contrary notwithstanding, of hidden springs, inscrutabilities that required seeking out though all might appear clear as an abandoned hockey rink.

Remember Big Jim? A gambler who couldn't be bothered to

remember the difference between Buenos Aires and Rio de Janeiro, Serbia and Croatia, Baltic and Balkan, Taiwan and Taipei, Formosa and Formica, Chiang Kai-shek and Chun King, Sylvania and Transylvania, Bluebeard Blackbeard Richelieu Montesquieu Svengali Sacheverel. But to Laurence he represented something to do next with one's knees. 'Getting old in my old age,' he said (or would have, had he thought of it) when Laurence corrected him ('black eight on the red nine'); but to Laurence he was new, novel, next. Not that Laurence would have volunteered as arena, gone looking for something to do with knees; he'd never even thought of his knees as something to do things with, but if somebody said, Please lend your underarm to keep this egg warm for a time, he'd have incubated his head off, coddled like crazy. In this way more than any other he resembled the woman who honored him with a sex change, who showed him boxwood and beans, whose sheet music he hugged, whose gamba in an access of thoughtless joy he twirled, whose love of that gamba he recognized, and who now seemed like Daddy away at work when the window was broken, to whom he'd have to answer for what he'd done.

But the problem with Laurence is this: he finds it difficult to hang on to a sentiment for a decent interval. So even as he invents scary scenari for Pop's return (I didn't *mean* to. It was an *acc*ident. It's not *fair*), he can't sustain the idea that the earth is shaken. On one hand, in the overall scheme, what's a bit of purfling? A skinny little veneer glued in place, now slightly crunched, snapped, crackled, popped: trifling. But even as he thinks that, Laurence is waffling; centuries-old purfling, a thing of beauty and a joy till today, when it's a joy no more, and my own insouciant trifling did it in, no respect for an elder object, characterized by nothing (no, not even its heartbreakingly reverberable tone) so much as its longevity till today, now by nothing so much as its imperfect purfling, unpurfled, dyspurfled, malpurfled, impurfled after being perfectly purfled lo these decades you'd run out of both hands and feet counting. I wish that hadn't ought to have happened; just a single wrist twist could have saved it. Back on the first hand, anything so dependent on a single wrist twist couldn't be so momentous, could it? But on the second, what couldn't be ruined by such irresponsible lapses: lives, nations, galaxies? On the first, why force analogies: not lives, nations, galaxies at issue here, but a gamba purfle? On the second, what's a gamba without it? So on, so forth, till the two strains were motifs that could be invoked by a mere echo of a phrase, *da capo, dal segno, repeat senza coda.*

Take what comes, face the music, take it like a man.

Of course we all have our ups and downs, but less so, it seems, when we're in comas. Stimulation is hypothesized as desirable for coma-dwellers. Donna, given her coma's provenance, was paradoxically supersensitive to stimuli of many sorts: certain kinds of light, any kind of touch, might send her into convulsions. But voices, preferably familiar, were fancied to have a salutary effect, as if she were a houseplant; and after a couple of days, no family members to enlist, no alternative beyond continuous monitoring, Dr. Pinckney authorized Irene and Gretchen to sit by the side of her bed and talk to her. They sketched out four-hour shifts around the clock, three a day each; and Gretchen and Irene, Irene and Gretchen, got to know the intensive-care nurses rather well, and got as well, less quickly but more pertinently, to know one another; despite weariness, they lingered to chat for some minutes each time they relieved one another. The minutes predictably increased as the plot thickened.

As any fool might guess, they learned a few things of interest to them both. That one was living with a man who had the same name, same characteristics, same history, and though they weren't sure of this they would have bet on it, same social-security number as the other's husband. In turn, that one had a husband who matched the description in every detail of the man in whose care the other had left her precious gamba. By now it was hard for Irene to see Gretchen as the other woman, and as hard for Gretchen to see Irene as the woman she (spurred by a parenthesis: 'I was seeing Irene, Irene was seeing me') had casually inquired about one night. Both found it equally confusing that Gretchen had Irene's husband to thank for her fertilized state. Irene was unable to stop herself from fixating on Gretchen's midsection; something beyond everyday politeness or rudeness was at stake in whether or not to stare, she felt, something beyond behaving like a human being even. In there was a potential someone she once thought she had in her. Not the same potential someone, to be sure, but one the same someone who failed to convince her not to undo another one had not failed to convince someone to nourish, to breathe, beat, eat, excrete (in greater than average quantities) for. And out here,

Gretchen, who took the thing (the Laurence thing, the pregnancy thing, the human-being thing, the thing as a whole) quite differently, yet whose story overlapped in so many ways, pivoting not only around a washed-up contralto but around a man she now learned mowed for a living.

And Gretchen, who had envisioned Irene as a colorless little slip of a woman she thought she could understand *a priori*, now started, Pincknaically, to wonder what made this woman whose hand she held in intensive care tick. Being together in Donna's presumably impervious presence, sharing so vivid a sense of Donna's every inhale, exhale, and the excruciating electronic pauses in between, slipping into Donna's monitored rhythm themselves, conscious together of the slight catch at the top and bottom of each respiratory arc, breath slowing imperceptibly to something approaching coma rate, sharing O_2, mingling CO_2, a sextet of lungs in concert, sometimes so still they could feel each other's increasingly synchronized pulses in held hands, so pacific, knowing if they had met in Laurence's presence instead of Donna's their respiratory rates would differ so, possibly with eyes flashing, darting, afraid to meet; instead, this meditative vigil, this domestic texture despite sanitary setting, despite continuous monitoring and treacherously suspended animation of the woman between them. Somehow Victor absorbed their combined wrath, Victor and Crickenberger, leaving Laurence not irrelevant but neutral, again not the man responsible but a someone in New York whose fault this wasn't, a someone the two of them could perhaps sit down and trade stories with after this little war against unconsciousness was over.

Bring.
Bring.
Laurence, on the bed, not in the tub, picked up after two rings. 'Hello?'
'Hi Laurence, it's Gretch.'
'Hi, how's your friend?'
'They've let us in to talk to her. They don't know if she can hear, but they think it might do some good.'
'Us?'
'I met a friend of yours.'
'Of mine, in Providence?'
'Actually on the bus, but we didn't know it then. She was stay-

ing up in the Bronx with another friend of yours.'

'Of mine, in the Bronx?'

'Fellow named Theo.'

'Grandpa Theo.' She? Not Tootie, Snookie, Fluffy.

'And wife Irene.'

Heart seized up like an old engine, convulsions, what's a convulsion, never mind, rub his wrists. 'Gretchen, is this?'

'No joke. Remember the Irene I told you Victor told me Donna
told him about?'

'She's?'

'Your other half after all, and up in ICU at the moment.'

'I see you?' Peekaboo? Little Boo Peeprika; leave them alone,
they'll come home, wagging their tales behind them.

'Intensive care,' interposed Gretchen.

'I see.'

Gretchen, seeing this could easily get out of hand, nipped the
bud. 'I see, you see, he or she sees. We see, yall see, they see.'

Something about a whale. Some passage, north by northwest.
Very like a wail.

'She's nice, Laurence.'

'Irene is nice.'

'Ya, we're getting to be friends.'

'You, Gretchen, and Irene, Gretchen, who was in the Bronx with
Theo, are getting to be friends, Gretchen?'

'Now you've got it.'

'Gretchen?'

'It's okay, Laurence, it really is. It's a little weird, I'll admit, but.'

'Okay? It's okay?' Then how come I can't breathe? thought
Laurence, intently rubbing a wrist against a thigh.

'Really. Irene is nice. We're friends.'

Laurence had nothing to say. Gretchen breathed, and he tried
to follow suit. Not fair: she'd been practicing.

'Laurence?'

'I can hear you.'

'She says he's nice, too.'

'Nice too.'

'Yeah, now look, I'll get back in touch soon, don't worry, it's
okay, but think about seeing Theo, will you? I've got to go now,
Irene's waiting up in ICU.'

I can see you, Mama. 'ICU.'

'Right, soon, see you soon. Talk sooner.'

'Gretchen, I'm scared.'

'Don't be scared.'

'I hurt your gamba.'

'You?'

'I was trying to play it, and it fell over, and.' He felt he was about to start weeping.

'Laurence, that's a shitty thing to tell somebody over the phone.'

'I'm sorry. I'm kind of.' Weeping, sweeping.

'Scared, I know. Well, don't be.'

'Look what you told *me* over the phone!' Heaping.

'I thought you'd be happy. Theo, Laurence, Theo. Your grandfather is living.'

'I'm sorry.' Sheeping.

'Look, there's a guy on Bleecker who's a genius at fixing old strings. We'll give him a call when I get back.'

'When you get back?'

'I don't know, as soon as I can. I've got to run now. Any messages?'

'For you? Here?'

'For Irene. From you.'

'I don't know. I'm sorry.'

'Kay, bye.'

Deeping, leaping, keeping, seeping, searing, tearing, peering, veering, nearing, rearing, reaping, roping, moping, coping, coring, warring, storing, steering, stewing: nice too nice two nigh stew who who. Sobbing, seeking, booing, hooing, Little Boy Bluing, Little Bo Peeping, trouble sleeping.

Though Laurence had made no thorough or methodical study of the book, early on, before he mowed for a living, he had browsed a bit, hoping to orient to the sprawling urb. For this purpose whites and yellows had complementary virtues. The whites were good for guessing (and finding you always guessed too low) how many people (never mind people, how many households) had a given name, that is an inherited name, not a given name, a given surname, say Popplestein, Fenster, or Chin. The Irish were particularly good for cross-referenced searches: MacCarthy, see McCarthy, McCarty, MacCarty, McArty, Macarthur—Wow! thought Laurence, and shuffled pages to wow himself with Wow's and Wonder's, then Wu's. He loved best the names that were words: how many Porches in New York, how many Benches, how many Beaches, Beeches, Batches, Botches, Butches.

The yellows were good for three things: how many whatevers in the City (ninety-eight certified electrologists, thirty-six firms devoted to sports law); most enigmatic business venture ('Randy's Round-the-Clock Routers, Reamers, & Grinders, Inc.—Radio Dispatch—See Our Display Ad This Page'; 'Lester Bigelow's Abrogators & Adumbrators—Open Weekends For Your Convenience—Never A Cover Or Carrying Charge'; 'Gaffers and Grips, Ltd.—Serving The Moving Picture Industry Since Its Inception'); and most desperate tactic to get listed first ('Abacadaba Embalming—Let Abacadaba Have Your Cadaver—Five Convenient Locations'; 'AAAAAAA-Zelda's Makeup Mart—If We Don't Have It, It Doesn't Belong On Your Face').

The floppy oversized pages were never intended for tub-browsing; they wouldn't stay open on knobby knees, and, draping over thighs like something reptilian, amphibious, uncomfortably insinuating, slipping always toward tender regions, the glossy covers felt colder than his Masonite clipboard; but recently he'd taken the yellows to the tub a few times, with half an idea in the back of his mind about why. And now, with Gretchen in Providence monitoring vital signs, Laurence lay on her mattress in the Superman flying posture he favored, one leg straight out to indicate where he was coming from, the other tucked up to suggest velocity in the other direction, with yellows, graceful, open before him like a pair of thick wings set to soar despite heft.

Musical Instruments—Retail. Musical Instruments—Wholesale. Musical Instruments—Rental. Musical instruments—Sales and Service. Musical Instruments—Repair and Restoration.

Laurence thought he was looking for a genius on Bleecker. He thought he could stop being sorry about one thing, at least, if the gamba looked good as new on Gretchen's return. There would still be other things aplenty to be sorry about, he felt sure, especially if last night's call had been something other than a bad dream: if she and Irene were friends; if everything was 'okay, really'; if Irene was staying with Theo. Staying with, staying with? Irene had never, to his knowledge, *met* Theo. Of course, he hadn't, to Irene's knowledge prior to Donna's coma, met Gretchen. He hadn't, for that matter, met Theo himself since his father (conniver of conception, contriver of conundra, connector of consanguinities) had stopped breathing and thus severed the grands, father from son,

concert from baby, their upright relation now downright inscrutable. How could these people meet one another without triangulation; wasn't he the apex at which alone legs could join? Something
oddly equilateral was occurring, apex demoted to just one more
point on a circle of vertices. Something geodesic, something cross-
referential, some larger pattern he couldn't follow, unalphabeti-
cal, thesaurical, dinosaurical: Extinction—Wholesale (See 'Lizards—Thunder,' 'Era—Geologic,' 'Size—Extraordinary,' 'Fittest—
Survival of,' 'Age—Ice').

His fingers kept walking away from Bleecker, away from headings tuneful toward headings cravatory, haberdashical, accessori-
cal, access oracle.

Oh the irony. Laurence, intimately involved and fully conscious
of a need, if not precisely of a reason, to keep the two apart, now
finds them brought together by a stranger in a coma. Laurence in
Gretchen's loft with a malpurfled gamba and a firm resolve to
keep his mitts off the celli, with kilos of yellows now superseding
a lifetime supply of sheet music that's lost its purchase on his
imagination. Gretchen making herself at home at Irene's less lofty
digs (garden apartment without a trace of flora), stocking up on
liver in case the siege persists, pillows on floor to support lower
back while breathing, crawling in and out of Irene's bed at odd
times for shuteye, Irene's water on her face to wake up (off caf-
feine, sake of the babe) for the next shift of intensive care, borrow-
ing a looser unmentionable or two when her own meager tote's
exhausted (round-the-clock shifts reducing discretionary laundro-
matic time and energy to a minimum). Irene knowing finally the
urban whereabouts of her strangely estranged spouse, knowing
too and all too well the abdominal abode of his potential posterity,
returning from a hard night on the ward to a freezerful of liver,
dainties in the hamper she knows she owns but doesn't remember
donning, taking comfort despite whatever creepy undertones in
the feel of a bed not had to herself (Gretchen not a particularly
fragrant specimen, but still and despite sequentiality rather than
simultaneity, the olfactory signature of another hard to miss in a
sleeping space, and Irene, had anyone asked, would have called it
sort of nice).

A sore test for behaving-like-a-human-being despite the seeming hominess of it all (of the scent, the pillows, the home; and of
the ward, whose scents and pillows begin so soon to feel like home).

And sometimes, as at this midnight changing of the guard, Irene just has to appeal to Gretchen, whose stride (appropriation of undies, implacable lust for liver, common attachment causing little discernible flap) has impressed her already: 'Why, Gretchen, must things be so lurid? Our life is like the tabloid rags, sensationalist, that distract shoppers in checkout lines. What happened to the Sunday *Times*—metro, region, travel, society, arts and entertainment—sections hefty but properly discrete, a loungy afternoon to sift through them, a whole week to fill in the puzzles?'

Gretchen, on whom quibbles like discrete-discreet are rarely lost, points out that discretion is hardly the appropriate heading for any of this. 'And hey, speaking of which, look who's talking. Aren't you the one who told Victor Donna's secrets?'

'I the one?' Irene nonplussed. 'No.'

'You're not?' Gretchen equally. 'Donna thinks you are.'

They took a gander at Donna, who didn't appear to think much of anything.

'Well, I'm not.'

Irene seemed at the moment the more reliable informant. Gretchen was willing to take her word.

'But,' began Irene, and sketched without attribution (for despite Theo and experience, it was her own as well) her mother's theory. 'See Donna there, who taught me that pastel circlets can stay between lines, that there's a way to play by rules. Think of Victor somewhere else, under lock and key, who has a sash full of merit badges attesting to his ability to play by rules. Imagine Laurence, who has to be wondering how we're hitting it off. And Theo, whose eyebrows are so wise, going inadvertently nonrepresentational and still mourning a son who died years ago, getting a call from me and suddenly it's a new ballgame. And then you.' Irene glanced in the dusky half-light toward Gretchen's womb, in there somewhere under clothing that belonged to both of them. 'And finally, me. What can we think about this? And that Crickenberger. He's really at the root of this.' She gestured toward Donna, whose serene and pacific aspect, curled like a sleepy puppy despite tubes and electrodes, made an ineffective visual aid, though Gretchen got the point. 'How do we assimilate him and Victor? How absorb such behavior into human being?'

In all the times Laurence had consulted the massive books—pounds of yellow, pounds of white, like so much popcorn—for business, for pleasure, or simply to be wowed, he had never once turned to Haberdashers. He'd come close—not alphabetically, not Gums (See 'Confections,' 'Adhesives,' 'Surgeons—Periodontal,' 'Sylvan Saps'), not Gutters (See 'Contractors—Home Improvement,' 'Failure—Dying In'), not Hackney Cabs (See 'Taxi,' 'Shuttle,' 'Limousine') or Hair Removing (See 'Barber,' 'Electrolysis')— but close to opening the giant yellows with Theo in mind. Something, some fear or unreadiness, had always deterred him. But this day, released from his tubby confinement by Gretchen's mission of mercy and placed by her call on the triangulative trail of a living haberdasher, with a newfound urge to distinguish apex from vertex, grazing absently on a thumb, keeping it slightly wet for friction to turn the blowsy, pulpy pages, unshaven and lightly pondering stubble, mowing, staples, roots, he put aside Manhattan, took up Bronx, and followed a cross-referential trail not unlike one Irene pursued some time ago in Providence.

First Ties. Ties—Baling (See 'Baling Equip. & Supls.,' 'Ties— Wire & Plastic'); Ties—Railroad (See 'Railroad Ties—Dlrs.'); then the aforementioned Ties—Wire & Plastic, with the inevitable circle back to Ties—Baling. Between Necklaces and Needlework, where he expected Neckwear—Handmade by Grandfather, he found nothing. Likewise, between Gypsum and Gypsum Products and Hair Bows (See 'Hair Ornaments'), not a hint of Haberdashery, let alone Haberdashers—Beloved, Haberdashers—Long-lost. Now, his quick look turning into a research quest, Laurence was having trouble sustaining the mood; resolve to find Theo almost gave way to incipient interest in theories of indexing the commercial world, but he set his sights and strove manfully onward. What would the powers that be in telecommunications call a necktie? Was it fair to list both Ornaments and Bows for the Hair and omit everything but -laces for the Neck? Weren't Bows a subset of Ornaments? And what did department stores call that department? Accessories? Nothing. Laurence could almost have sworn a necktie was an accessory. Maybe Furnishings? Between Furnished Rooms (See 'Boarding Houses,' 'Motels and Hotels,' 'Rooming Houses,' 'Tourists' Homes') and Furniture—Children's—Retail, nothing but a line of nothing: again, was this just? Neckwear got no respeck—where was Theo? Unfair unfair unfair that women got every little doodad listed; men, with a single doodad to their name, a doodad worn daily by every self-respecting dude or dad of professional or managerial class in Manhattan, men who needed to find their only living relative, got nothing nothing nothing. Honorary womanhood now in the dust, birthright solidarity prevailed—mess of pottage, pot of message—and Laurence grew indignant, righteously so; he could file a class-action suit (but he couldn't even find an Accessory). If only he were a woman whose grandma did Needlework, a grandchild of any gender whose grandparent of any gender was in Gypsum and Gypsum Products! Intrigued and exasperated at once, he turned out of piqued curiosity to Men. And there amidst the Men, sandwiched between -ding and -tal Health Services: 's Clothing & Furnishings—Retail! A token bit of justice in the world. Hope for the species, for the indexers, for professionals, managers, and relatives alike! Wide and narrow, silk, wool, cotton, even rayon, poly blends, come one come all, Men, I give you Clothing & Furnishings—Retail!

Behind research frustration, raised consciousness, victory for the little man, Laurence felt, as he saw the light at the end of the yellow tunnel and emerged from the alphabetical funnel, a growing conviction that when he found the listing it would need to be put to use. And when he saw it—Theo's Ties, 2386A Fdhm Bx..............552-8273—he deflated: Superman no longer, class-actor no more, saltine bomblets moistening everything from Medicines—Dog & Cat (See 'Pet Health Plans') to Metallurgical Engineers (See 'Engineers—Metallurgical'), dooming the yellows to pucker when dry, heaving like a fault whose time has come, tectonics all awry, number up, shivering and shivering at the thought of the shivers, timbers thoroughly shivered, yo ho ho, bottle of rum, waves rolling at the listing, Of the Less Erroneous Pictures of Whales, wide wail, cord or oy, *Hesperus* on a collision course, Laurence a puddle, not of knives, a puddle of wish, wish for Theo who wouldn't worry he might die young, worry for Theo who might die old, wish and worry, worry and wish, until only a quandary, a key vest chin (Theo would say), a single simple either-or remained: face to face or over the phone?

Either way, he assured himself (subsiding, rattled, no permanent damage), a bit of a shower wouldn't hurt before starting. Laurence extricated himself, laying the flaccid volume down gently as a sleeping bird, smoothing ruffled feathers (somewhere in one of those yellows a genial purfler, swallowed up in Laurence's quake), and sauntered, smoothing his own, to the bathroom, where the impervious tiles felt chilly, solid beneath his soles.

He pulled up the hot about half a turn and the cold about a quarter and let the makeshift stall (couple of curtains dangling from tubing suspended like a schoolplay halo) warm up while he removed men's clothing and furnishings retail and respectfully submitted a little progress report on his physique. The unventilated room steamed up quickly, and he started to waver out of focus. When he had disappeared altogether, he stepped up over and down into the tub where he'd spent a good deal more time dry than wet, horizontal than vertical.

Such creatures of habit: he noticed he was cleansing the same way as ever, respecting some tacit pecking order of body parts. Run the soap down the outside of the left arm, up its inside, little swirl to lather underarm hair, then down the chest (decelerating loop-de-loop at the nipple) to the navel curlicue; repeat without variation for the bisymmetrical right. Same little juggling act with the soap, same pauses to palpate same tender spots. And the pirouettes, the dance, if you videotaped and compared you'd see, always the same, feet, hands, arms, going through their program like skaters, first this then that, toeloops and axels, camels and solkows, as if born and raised on ice, on porcelain, as if clawfoot tubs were one's element. And shampoo (with its complex score of Doppler effects as the head moved around relative to the water-jets) always last. Did others shampoo first, or did everyone save hair for last? Why or why not? Any reason on earth? Why always left foot first into underwear, overwear, parade lockstep? What if a person could improvise? Not mastering a dozen different programs like European transposers, but just as the spirit moved? Would a person get shoelaces tied that way? Would the world economy suffer? Would the gods have nightmares?

But Laurence knew he didn't need permission. He could shampoo first, he could lather up the belly instead of down, he could linger to soap between toes (not once a week, just as the spirit moved) if he wished. He chose not to, and the choice seemed to comfort him. This way, he would never have to stand in a stall wasting water and wonder, What next, what now? The point, he supposed as he towelled first himself then the mirror and commenced his ritual shave, was to regularize early on so you needn't waste water, time, brain cells, thinking about it ever again.

Gretchen, bless her heart, shared something of Theo's, bless also his, attitude toward human being; whereas he insisted the category accommodate Heatlayer, Crickenberger and Victor would fill her bill quite adequately.

'Irene, true or false, Crickenberger is a total jerk.'

'Well, I've never really met him.'

'Oh boy, a minute ago he was your prime example of behaving like a nonhuman being, now I want to make a point and you don't know the guy.'

'Okay, a total jerk.'

'And a total jerk for what reason?'

'Well, his irresponsible and untruthful exploitation of professional position, I suppose, for immediate personal gratification without taking into account the consequences of his actions for those whose trust he.'

'Yipes! You mean he treats people like shit, right?'

'I guess.'

'Okay. Now take Victor, while we're on the subject. A total jerk or not?'

'Well, you have to have sympathy for his.'

'No you don't. But even if you do, a total jerk?'

'Right.' Though she'd never met him either.

'Okay, for what reason?'

'Well, poisoning his wife for starters, if your suspicion is right.'

'You have other suspects in mind?'

'Okay, poisoning Donna.'

'Trying to murder his spouse?'

'Yeah.' Irene looked over at Donna, but could discern no reaction.

'Okay, so we've got a breach of professional ethics, abuse of trust, and cold-blooded spouse murder?'

Irene had never fully understood what the temperature of one's blood had to do with it, but yes, she allowed that that was what they had.

'Okay, any issues of survival involved here? Like if Crickenberger didn't have sex with one more patient, or if Victor didn't waste his devoted wife, he'd die an instant death?'

'Uh uh.'

'Okay. Now think of inanimate objects and forces—wind, rock, gravity—and every kind of plant—fir, impatiens, lichen, tulip, Venus flytrap—and every kind of animal—giraffe, euglena, bedbug, hake, ferret, pig, vulture, gila monster, Tasmanian devil—okay?'

'Okay.'

'Okay, of those inanimate objects, forces, plants, and nonhuman animals, how many can you think of, excluding personal or racial survival, that would even for a minute consider betraying the trust of their clients, let alone Hippocratic oath, let alone friends?'

'None.' Irene having mastered the role of Socratic dummy.

'Okay, and how many, excluding personal or racial survival, that would murder their spouse in cold blood?'

Irene had to think for a minute on this one. Cold blood reminded her of reptiles, wasn't there something about scorpions? 'I'm not sure.'

'You're not sure?' How would Socrates handle this? 'Think.'

'I think there are bugs that do that.'

Socrates, mooted, mute.

'Well, you know, black widows and maybe praying mantises. I think they do the males in after they've served their purpose.'

'Black widows aren't bugs, they're spiders, but that's beside the point.'

'What's the point?'

'The point is, do you really think Victor was behaving like a female black widow spider?'

'No.'

'Well, what was he behaving like?'

'That's what I can't figure out.'

'No, we already figured it out: a total jerk!'

'Okay,' said Irene, tentative, as if she'd dozed off and lost a day. 'And what's that?'

'It's a guy who.'

'There you go: a guy who, a guy who! What's a guy?'

'A guy?'

'A guy is a human being, a male human being.'

'Yeah, but that doesn't mean that murdering your wife is behaving like a male human being.'

'It doesn't? Male human beings do this, right? And nobody else does, right? So doing this isn't behaving like a male human being?'

'You forgot about black widows.'

'But you're not claiming that Victor was behaving like a female black widow.'

'No.'

'Okay, then he's behaving like nothing in the world but a male human being.'

'I don't know what gender has to do with it.'

'I do.'

Irene wasn't at all sure about this, but the conversation was starting to upset her. 'Okay, I guess so,' she conceded.

'You guess so, but you don't believe it, do you?'

'I guess not. Maybe it's the way I was brought up.'

'Look at what the way Donna was brought up did. You know, bringing people up, in every screwy kind of way, is also behaving like a you-know-what. Everything we do just expands the boundaries. It's like air.'

'Air?'

'Right, air. Know what air is?'

'Oxygen, nitrogen, a bunch of other gases.'

'In any particular proportion?'

'I don't think so.'

'Right. Just whatever occupies the space that air occupies is air, right? And it'll expand to fill any void, cause nature abhors one, right?'

Irene recalled a sign at a carwash that once gave her and Laurence a common giggle: FREE AIR WITH VACUUM. Then she remembered Theo: Avoid, juiced ah void, hue men pink. 'Yes,' she said.

'If it's there, it's air?'

'I guess so.'

'Okay, so human being is like air.'

'Like air.'

'Right, it's all over the place, Irene. It's all over the damned place. You can't fucking get away from it.'

Gretchen seemed to wish she could; having blown her Socratic cool, was now quite exercised, and furthermore unhappy. Two upset women sitting up with a friend; to whom they both now looked, but Donna and her tubes and electrodes weren't talking. Now no one was talking. Only silently, out at the nurses' station, a cathode-ray tube blipped vivid green signatures, illegible as doctor's writing, on a dove-grey screen.

Ten

Luncheon at Twelve Clefs, Monday, on the stroke, the dot, of noon: who could fail to be impressed? As clockworks chimed and bonged, twelve-toning all round the house, Laurence entered, cleanly as could be expected: sneakers green about the gills, but an extra shirt carried on the One from Greenwich was politely absorbing what remained of the morning's moisture, most of it removed between shirts by a splashy encounter with an oversized slate sink in the maintenance shed, hair sleekly slicked, visage reddish from labor and towelling, facing the music of a noon meal involving more forks than Gretchen owned and an agenda of which Laurence was unaware.

'Welcome, my boy. May I offer you something to drink?' asked Dempler, doing what he asked permission for, gesturing toward an array of decanters, a dozen or more like a proud color guard on a sideboard, no clue save hue to their gamut of distilled and aged contents. Laurence knew he oughtn't to be staring, but he hadn't the foggiest what might be decanted, and the phrasing of the requisite inquiry stymied him: 'What have you got?' would sound too reminiscent of salad dressings in diners.

Mercifully remembering he never drank during the day, Laurence latched onto 'Thank you, no.' Talking on stilts, inverting, aiming to please. In his life, he had never said 'Thank you' before 'no.'

'Come now,' enjoined the Oyster lady as if he'd offended for all that. 'Surely a small apéritif? The Austrians have a saying,' she concluded, but didn't deign to convey it.

He had, despite the morning's grassy exertions, nary a hint of *appétit,* and so—whatever Austrians might say—if she insisted. Dempler poured less than a shot of something nearly violet into a receptacle you could wash your hands in, conveyed it to Laurence by the thinnest of stems, and attended to his and his consort's fluid preferences. Laurence sipped as minimally as he knew how, nevertheless draining more than half the liquid, and the conversation began. It flowed like the liquor, in portions that barely got the mouth started but still exhausted resources rapidly, as all three endeavored to construct a topic of mutual feasibility. The weather wouldn't do; the aesthetics of mowing were in reserve for the main course; they suspected (rightly) that Laurence had not attended recent openings; and though Laurence would have settled for the age and provenance of each furnishing in the room, Dempler and the Oyster lady modestly declined to be tour guides. Sooner than later, all Dempler's graces could not supply a thing but Gretchen to add to the discourse.

'And the admirable Miss Barron, we trust she is well?'

Laurence preferred not to mention morning sickness. Nor could he keep from talking that strange language: 'Quite well. I had a call from her just last night.'

'Is she travelling then?'

'Visiting a friend. In Providence.' No need, he decided, to make public that the friend had been unconscious for several days now; it was none of his business, let alone theirs.

'A musical acquaintance?' Dempler hoping still to locate a topic that could endure beyond statement, response, and rejoinder.

'Ah, singer I think.' Laurence downed the remainder of his drink in a gulp despite a valiant attempt to subdivide it with a dental portcullis.

'Operatic? Not Donna Forenza?' Dempler and the Oyster lady exchanged glances that meant, 'So young, such promise, such a shame, why Miss Barron bothers is beyond us.'

'Yes, as a matter of fact.'

'Do you know the lady?'

'Ah, no, we've not met.' We've not met? Where did these sentences come from? He might as well have said, 'I've not had the pleasure.'

'You've not had the pleasure? A shame,' said Dempler, referring in all probability to Donna's rather than Laurence's bad fortune. Or maybe to the idea of having a saxophone player who couldn't transpose in the European style or make more than two gulps out of a fine liqueur in to lunch. Or the fact that the ordures had yet to arrive.

Then they did: bite-size breaded things, hard to tell from the shape, a jolly cellophane-crested toothpick in each. A perfect dozen (plus three understated citric garnishes) on three little bone plates. Knowing Else as he did, Laurence now closely attended what was placed (not by her, by a svelte underling) before him: four tawny amoeboids, crumbed but cohesive, islands in a small bone-china pond sprouting picks as if recently claimed in the name of the Queen of Riverdale.

'Perhaps Miss Barron informed you notwithstanding as to the state of Miss Forenza's.'

'Mrs. Groat now, my dear, she no longer performs,' corrected the Oyster lady.

'Yes, of course. How like me to repress that man. Of Mrs. Groat's health?'

Laurence took a bite of ordure while he considered what was proper to reveal. As soon as he did, he knew Else was behind a swinging door sending him a little pat of encouragement, sly smile of guilty pleasure bulbing the cheeks of that potatoface, shoulders hunched up and shaking her head at how intolerable bad she was being to serve oyster ordures. He chirruped against his will at the pleasantry, then decided he could not tell the truth. Ordure or no, a comber was no cause for mirth; nor could he explain that his jocularity was incited not by Donna's critical condition, but by a jest he shared with their cook at their expense: totemic appetizers. He paused long enough for Dempler to think it appropriate to offer something more to drink. Playing for time, he acquiesced; perhaps Donna and his jollity could both get lost in the shuffle of hospitality.

'A white burgundy was what we had in mind, if that pleases you,' said Dempler.

Laurence thought burgundy meant red. White burgundy, then,

must be an oenological drollery. He graciously mimicked amusement.

'Unless you prefer something . . . else?'

He now understood white burgundy was in earnest, but the cook's name elicited a titter; he tried to cover up by implying that white burgundy always made him lighthearted: 'Ho ho no, white burgundy would hit the spot.'

'"Hit the spot," yes certainly.' Dempler tinkled a silver bell, and the wine was delivered, tested, approved, apportioned, sipped all round from cut crystal whose diamond pattern reminded Laurence of glossy pictures: place settings, Alpine villages, Tudor windows, *If you lived here, you'd be home now.*

'Very nice,' said Laurence, thinking, White burgundy, albino wine-oh.

'Mrs. Groat's health?' asked Madame, popping a namesake into her mouth.

'No, no, the wine. It hit the spot,' he finished lamely, trying not to think of bivalve, mollusk, marine life at all.

'She's not well then?'

Laurence strove to compose his embouchure with the buccolabial severity of a more accomplished windman. 'Actually, she's not very well.'

'No?'

'Actually, not very well at all.' He bit the insides of cheeks hard enough to draw tears to the verges of ducts.

'No.'

'Actually, she's comatose.'

'Truly,' said Madame, and 'You don't say,' echoed Maestro, arching a brow each but politely declining in concert to pursue a subject deemed improper at table.

Laurence, assessing oral damage with a gingerly tongue, couldn't believe his ears. Did they think he was lying? Having spilled, after much deliberation, quite spectacular beans, was that all the response he'd elicit? 'No really,' he insisted, though a moment earlier he had wished they would drop it, 'in a coma.'

'You mean a stupor,' Dempler, familiar with Donna's bourbonic plague, cajoled.

'I mean,' said Laurence, now stern, 'a coma. She's in intensive care.'

Now the two wished more than ever to drop the subject, and Laurence to follow it till they found it in themselves to respond like human beings. Who was he, Irene's mother? But who were they, to remain so impassive, incurious, in the face of the extraordinary? What were they having, a concert experience, counting up movements, saving applause for the end?

We're talking about a life dangling by a thread here, he told himself, I mean, if you can't respond to a coma. He himself had barged into an Oasis on that basis, bullish in a china shop. He slurped at the burgundy to calm down, mustn't make a scene during luncheon, wolfed an oyster to quench hostility, wouldn't wish to ruffle the mushroom brush. Creepers, a coma! What did they want?

Picture the first ray of dawn on a still, clear horizon. It winds its fluid way over and around hillocks, trees, broadcasting towers, buildings, poles, mailboxes, delivery vans, shapes of all kinds, bathing a skyline in its impalpable glow and beckoning reprise of birdsongs in disuse since yesterday. It gives the local world a particular particulate post-Enlightenment aura, aurora, the shimmering silky drape of Romantic sonatas, impressionist prints, tales of wonder and poetic justice. On just such a stage, reviving ethereal theories of atmosphere, brave o'erhanging firmament fretted with golden fire, spherical welkin of marvelously insubstantial volatility, we fancy that Donna might open her eyes to a new day with a tentative flutter of larkwing lashes below gullwing brows, cueing harp to arpeggio and piccolo to appoggiatura as violas swell to the full harmonic vibrancy of incipient consciousness. The very motes would sparkle in celebration of hope, renewal, vernal daffodilly crocusbirth as the first redbreast of spring warbles its welcome to one who once was lost but now is found, was blind but now can see: a glorious spectacle.

Now try to forget all that. Not rosy fingers but the leathery palm of a dull overcast afternoon cups Donna's face. Though the forecast is for partly cloudy, the sky over Providence has resembled an unvaried plowheap of soiled urban snow all day. Irene, overtired after lingering past her previous shift to be disillusioned by Gretchen; feels pointless, hopeless, resigned, all day: she's been reading *Moby-Dick* in hopes of understanding something, but she doesn't get what all the fuss is about. She guesses it was more fun before whales were endangered.

Something on a monitor must indicate the imminent change,

because an entire afternoon shift of nurses invades the dingy high-tech room in time to observe the event. Irene, startled by the racket, sees the unit head enter, chief goose at the apex of a migratory chevron, and panics: the monitor must have warned of some emergency, partial or total eclipse of life functions, she figures, imagining fist pounding chest with force sufficient to crack a sternum, or greased electronic flatirons in a horrible parody of a jumpstart provoking ragdoll convulsions throughout the lifeless frame, or (she can't decide which would be worse) just letting it happen, detaching tubes and electrodes, pulling the sheet up over the face, Pinckney arriving later to say, 'I'm terribly sorry, but as your friend was virtually brain-dead with no sign of improvement, and with our budgetary constraints, extraordinary measures seemed unjustifiable. You must understand, the bed was needed for patients with a better chance of.'

The nurses gather round the bed like a windbreak round a farmhouse: a stand of closely planted trees on a vast unvariegated plain through which runs a dusty highway on a dry summer day whose heat makes mirages of moisture on the dark pavement. They do not speak and scarcely move, just almost in unison shudder as if a gust from far away has finally reached this plain spot on its long journey toward more interesting topography. It's open to question whether they know Irene is in the room, though her knees are less than three feet from the nearest instance of white polyester stretched (at eye level for seated Irene) across the tensed expectant buttocks of a nurse she would recognize from the front. They all focus so fully on the form they screen from view, a conventful of sisters at devotions, bevy of druids at a clearing, starched and winged caps like paper ruffles on a crown roast. Irene can feel her pulse behind her eyes.

Then Irene hears from the hidden cynosure not a twitter of birdsong at dawn, but a beastly welling groan as of waking bear in moist spring cave. This sound puts Irene in mind of the acrid film that envelops her teeth when she jumps and splashes and hurries in every way she can to rid her mouth of that taste of decaying animalculae, the compost, the ferment of sleep, the mouthful of last year's leaves when the spring thaw uncovers them amid mud, all but mud themselves, the fertile savor of myriad microscopic expirations in the mass grave of her own unguarded and helpless oral cavity. She shudders, and thinks she sees a ripple pass too through the horseshoe of nurses ringing the fateful adjustable bed.

She feels it too in her voice, as if the words were written on water, when she tries to ascertain the nature of that groan and the cause of the nurses' stunned inactivity.

'What's happening?' she whispers, wavers, wonders. Nurses, transfixed by the transfiguration before them, hear her as one hears a distant irrelevant train rattle over subterranean tracks.

'Please,' she amplifies, 'what's happening?'

Polyester rotates, and the familiar nurse's face, streaked with saline and Maybelline, meets Irene's horrified gaze. The nurse's chin quivers, then her lips, then in the most nearly beatific and most nearly silent whisper Irene can recall she informs her that Donna Forenza seems to be waking up.

This lay interaction breaks the spell, and before Irene knows what's what the nurses have scrambled; the room, half empty, is full of the most energetic activity: machines being reset, pulses and pressures being checked and recorded, doctors being paged, and there on the bed, in the clearing, the object of ministrations, eye of the storm, Donna intermittently groaning and repeating Irene's question: 'What's happening?'

Donna, of course, looks like hell. The brows, unplucked this long time, are an unweeded garden of mismatched lengths and ragged undergrowth, bespeaking neither style nor wisdom but devastation, neglect (though the care has been intensive), a kind of indigence. The hair, unwashed for the same era, tangles against the stark white bedding like a netful of dead eels set out to dry in the sun. The skin, it goes without saying, neither fine nor firm in tone or texture, but macerated, itchy, raw, nettled by probes and inpatient procedures. Lids and lashes that flutter, fluster, nonstop, resemble no exaltation of larkwings but bebarnacled crustaceous edges and the waving scanning feeding mechanism, eyes the clammy blob of a hypothetically live creature within. And Donna's eyes, supersensitive to what scant illumination the aluminesque sky affords, as if crepuscular dimness were megawattage, kliegs and floods, look not joyful to be alive and awake but wishful not to look at all, retreating like a lost child importuned by a horde of adults to explain where home is. All in all, Donna is a lumpy, battered, blinking, hurting specimen, scared as a groundhog dragged out to predict the advent of spring.

'Donna,' says Irene, drawing near despite nursing brouhaha, 'you're alive.'

Donna, aware of no reason to think otherwise, takes this confirmation badly, as one more thing to fear. 'Where?' she says, and, 'Why?'

'Donna,' says Irene as she has once before, 'remember me? Irene?'

Donna tries to nod. Her neck is awfully stiff, her muscles unused to responding to volition. She knows who Irene is, but not where, or why; and these are the questions she repeats.

'You had a,' says Irene, 'an accident,' not believing a word of it, 'and you've been in a coma.'

'Coma.' Like 'Mama,' like someone's first word.

'But you're okay now,' Irene ventures, then looks for confirmation. She gets it, cap waving vigorous wings above a smile that barely trusts itself, and sets about to convince Donna that consciousness is preferable, good, despite monitoring devices and muscles on the road to atrophy and (Irene supposes) a heck of a headache and (Donna keeps repeating) utter ignorance of where or why. 'Gretchen's here too, we'll take care of you, you're okay now, we didn't know if you'd.' Die? 'Make it.'

'Where's Victor?'

What does she know, remember, surmise, suspect, or gather?

'He's in good hands.'

Donna's approach one another despite IV hookups. 'The baby,' she says, as if it weren't really a question.

Irene looks to a nurse for help with this. They both draw close to Donna's face as if to locate some microscopic mote and convey, so carefully, the truth, that that's too much to ask.

Donna's eyes shut, shells clamping to guard the moist bivalve inside. But down below, where the huddled women don't see, Donna's hands—minute cuticular vestiges of imperfectly removed polish like dried evidence of crime, stainless needle impaled in a weary and all but collapsed vein on the back of the left, held in place by a broad trapezoid of once-sterile tape now curling at the edges, inverted knuckles (flesh edemically inflated) and all—move as if of their own accord to form a blobby postmodern 3-D postcard travesty of Dürer.

Food arrived not a minute too soon. The svelte underling served from the left—first Madame, then Laurence, then Dempler—and left what was left under silvery domes.

First the servant placed a tiny dead bird on his dish. Without feathers, Laurence hadn't a clue: quail, squab, guinea fowl, partridge, thrush, curlew? Unlike more sizable relative poultry, it looked on the plate like something that could have balanced on a branch, something that could have flown, lit, warbled, performed evasive maneuvers: a bird, browned, naked, posed for display before dismantling, pathetic if possibly tasty. The thought of taking a full-sized knife and one of these forks to its delicate remains seemed almost unfair. The gravy boat strategically placed equidistant from all diners mimicked its shape on a slightly magnified scale.

Wasn't that celery? Celery on its own, not sliced or diced piecemeal in a stewish composition, not minced amid tuna with mayo, not spread with peanut butter as a healthful snack, celery solo, celery *a capella*? Did that come from Else's tradition, with mustard greens, hamhocks, sweet-potato pie, or was it Continental, nouvelle, even Flemish? Down home, avant garde, backwater, forefront? Celery ethnic? Celery a dish? Amazing what a person could live to near thirty and not know.

There was a robust-looking grain done up with herbs and slivers of probably almond to accompany the larded and glazed gamebird. It wasn't rice, it wasn't buckwheat groats, was about all Laurence could have said for sure. It reminded him vaguely of winter mornings, butter pats, maple syrup.

Laurence hoped this was all okay with his finicky innards. He was happy to see no red meat, green peppers, purple cabbage; though he might have his doubts about the provenance of celery and the gastric accommodation of grouse, lark, snipe, plover, or what-have-you, nothing here was clearly out of the question. Laurence, no less than the indeterminate bird, was game.

Laurence was a plate-cleaner from way back, though you wouldn't know it from his comedic chinic y latinic performance on Dyckman. Both parents had praised this trait in his youth as evidence of good character. And in adulthood he still had the knack, thoughtfully swishing up the last gob of yolk with the final irregular polygon of toast. Like biting, it was something he'd long since stopped having to think about; by now things sopped up and things that did the sopping just tended to come out even. But the coincidence of sopping supply and demand was just a highly refined version of an overall congruence between appetite and victuals. Others stared (admiringly or disdainfully), smiled (humoringly or bemusedly), sometimes hooted outright (as if they'd seen a dog on stilts) at his meticulinarious performance; but Laurence didn't do it for them, didn't do it even for himself, did it purely and simply as part of his good character, like chewing with mouth closed or showering daily; undaunted, undeterred, unincited, unspurred by public response, Laurence continued to eat what was put before him, a member in good standing of what his father (its founder, for all he knew) had called the Clean-Plate Club.

Others, he knew, had different ways. Some left a scrap or two (nothing so large as to constitute a leftover, nothing one couldn't manage to get down despite satiety) as compulsively as he didn't. Some saw perhaps in a clean plate what he would have seen in an utterly mowed estate; like his token corner, ten by ten, of untamed growth, their gobbets, crumbs, and orts might represent how far they had come or the gallant survival of nature in a world too given to domestication or the presence of a resisting will or—how could Laurence, who didn't understand them, be expected to know? But these are the uncharted lands of human psychology, the Marianas Trench of motivation, wilderness preserve of theory. This much only he could say with certainty, that the Clean-Plate Club was not for everyone.

By the time the food was distributed and the servant informed that there would be nothing else at present and Laurence's plate eligible for cleaning, he had changed his mind again about Donna. Better to let sleeping contraltos lie. Just get through the meal without doing or saying anything horrendous; in fact, it would be a minor triumph if the subject failed to arise again; and yes, if she insisted, and since a white burgundy set off the characteristic savor of a fine gallinule so well that she could hardly think of one without the other, just half a glass please.

So Laurence was about to ingest a gallinule, was he? Was that a bird or a strain of celery? Probably a bird, since the wine was to set it off, but it sounded more like a celery. It could be the grain. Would you choose a wine to match your grain? He noticed a miniature inkwell behind his plate filled with a white crystalline substance: sugar, salt, or something he'd never heard of. He studied his hosts for cues. One took a seemly pinch between her fingers and sprinkled it on her gallinule (or not); the other didn't. He concluded it was optional, and refrained.

He was trying to delay dissecting the bird, not out of sympathy but in case there was some special procedure. He took a sip of the wine, a decorous forkful of the toothsome grain, a sip of the water, a taste of the celery. It didn't look too hard; he had to remember not to press too much with dismembering knife or stabilizing fork (visions of presumptive gallinule spurting off like a gargantuan glazed tiddlywink, landing splat on white linen or worse). 'Never force it,' he recalled his father saying in an early lesson on tool use.

Oh, it was going so well. The protein gallinule was tender and totally tasty, the vegetable gallinule not half bad, and the cereal gallinule quite a revelation (besides visible almonds, it conveyed a suggestion of orange zest!). Yes, indeed, Laurence was certainly enjoying his gallinules. Nothing behaved like a tiddlywink; everything melted in his mouth; no one was mentioning coma; life was good.

Donna felt like a soft sculpture of herself, seamed and puckered, cloth and stuffing, cotton and poly: washed and worn, not unwrinkled but permanently impressed by her ordeal. Irene and Gretchen and Dr. Pinckney and several nurses filled her in, bit by bit, carefully, as if she had tried to do herself in, might try again. Of all of them, Gretchen was least gingerly; knowing Donna longest, knowing Victor at all, she less mistrusted Donna's stability. Donna, though feeling none too stable herself ('You'll be wobbly on your pins for a while, but that's perfectly normal,' the doc reassured her), slowly gripped the big picture.

The four-hour shifts relaxed now that Donna was sentient, friends' as well as nurses' care now less intensive, and she had some time to herself to stare at the unlovely rectangle of roof and west wing and sky that a new window on a different floor framed, to try without success to remember, to piece together more or less compatible accounts of lost time. She had yet to form any conclusions.

Gretchen, in attendance at the moment, was discussing (who wasn't? They all thought it better for now to avoid the topic of Victor) the effects of a teaspoon of Malathion in bourbon on the central nervous system. She used less biochemically precise but more graphic terminology than Dr. Pinckney, and developed her own angle, placing, for instance, more emphasis than Donna's other caretakers on everything none of us knows about what it takes to stay alive and functioning, on the illegible works of the corpus, on what goes on constantly, regardless of volition or even inkling, in top-secret body compartments behind closed orifices. 'If we, who think ourselves autonomous, are this autonomic, imagine how totally ignorant other species are of what remaining among the living consists of. And Malathion: just sizewise, imagine what the stuff does to insects, which we see as instinctual automatons, virtually autonomatonic.'

Maybe the suffix '-tonic,' maybe the idea of governance without regard to will; whatever it was, it made Donna form her first conclusion and express her first positive desire: 'I could really use a drink.'

The takers of care had all been waiting for Donna's first postcomic request; Pinckney, who predicted it would involve food, told them all to look out for it as a good sign. Eager as she was to gratify, 'Aw, honey,' Gretchen had to say, 'I don't think they'd allow that, and it's probably not such a hot idea anyway.'

Even Donna, who had made no conscious demands for so long, had to recognize this as good counsel.

'What are you thinking about?' asked Gretchen, suddenly understanding that some -mology neither ety- nor ento- might be uppermost in the newly reactivated mind.

'You know what I felt so grateful when they told me that I prayed?'

'What?' Gretchen, an old friend, had no trouble with the syntax.

'When they told me that the baby was.'

'Oh.'

'You know, gone.'

'I know.'

'Is that horrible, Gretch? To want to be rid of it? I actually thanked God.'

'I don't think it's horrible at all. You've been through a hell of a time.'

'I know, but.'

'No buts. It's better this way, there's no denying that.'

'Right, but you're not supposed to judge on that basis. You're supposed to say, "Thy will be done," for better or worse. And I thanked God because it was better for me.'

'People can't be expected to be grateful for things that make them miserable.'

'But they are. That's the way it is. Worse is always better in the long run.'

'Well then, they can't be expected not to be grateful for things that make them less miserable. They've got to be allowed to be grateful for something.' Allowed! thought Gretchen, it's a positive requirement; she was trying in deference to Donna to tread with care, not to stride, but could barely stand this mincing dicing slicing, always on the lookout for its own inadequacy. 'That's the whole point, I thought.'

'Yes, it is, and He shows me that He cares about me, cares for me, takes care of me, and I'm so undeserving.'

Had Gretchen known what Victor thought he was up to, she might have had something to say about Who was showing whom what. Even not knowing this, under most any other circumstances, Gretchen would point out that state-of-the-art technology had taken care of, that angels of mercy in starchy headdress had cared for, that a nice woman who clung to an indefensible theory of human being and (if she said so herself) an albino cellist had cared about, her. On the verge, though, she realized that this was neither time nor place to rehearse stale theological disagreements. She conscientiously limited herself to asking, 'How shows He that?'

'By taking the baby that was the wages of my sin.'

'He almost took *you!*' Gretchen couldn't help herself. 'The baby was a side effect of synapses and contractions.' She measured out about half an inch between two pale digits, blue veins faintly visible through the skin. 'You came that close to dying.'

Donna crossed herself, a little off-center, with the hand that still held the needle. 'Death is the wages of sin.'

'But you said the baby was the wages of your sin.'

'It was. He was, she was. It was.'

'Donna, death and the baby can't be the same thing.'

'They both were the wages of sin, and He let me escape both.'

Gretchen, in lieu of counting to ten, tried to picture the intricate paystub of sin. Baby would maybe show up as income you never see, social-security or FICA (she irrelevantly realized she had never known what that stood for). Was baby taxable? Where would you list it on state and federal returns: under wages, salary, and tips, or royalties and rents, interest and dividends, capital gains, depreciation, charitable contribution? Baby had been deducted. Better to drop the conceit.

'Donna, look, you're alive and you'll soon be well, and you can pick up and start over with a fresh.'

'Start over. Where?'

'On your own. With what's good for *you.*'

'Oh, Gretchen, I know you won't believe this. I wish I could talk to Victor.'

Request number two of a life newly leased, released. Gretchen had to advise against this one too. And much as it pained her, Donna had to admit that Gretchen's advice was once again sound.

As he proceeded more deeply into the anatomical specificities of his ornithogallinule, Laurence was emboldened to introduce a topic of his own. 'I understand there's a theory that our birds descend from dinosaurs,' he offered, wondering what to do with a wing the size of his little finger. Knives and forks clinked against fine china (a rare petuntse, had he but known) for a second or two as the fate of Laurence's topic hung in the balance.

'It seems unlikely,' observed Dempler. 'The disparity in mass being alone cause for skepticism.' He forklifted the edible yield of an entire thigh and stored it on the terraced hillside between moustache and many chins.

If the topic wasn't a spectacular popular success, neither was it stillborn, and Laurence gave it one more try. 'The theory is, the bones hollowed out, I think.'

'Extinction is such a troublesome affair,' put in the Oyster lady. The grain on her fork seemed to quiver at the thought, and Laurence wondered what manner of associations were secreted beneath her massive coiffure. Were dinosaurs a *faux pas*? When the granules had calmed down, she stowed them safely in her oral cavity and, having swallowed and looked abstractedly out the window for a moment, spoke: 'The bulgar is most entertaining, is it not, Poldchen?'

Dempler's visage ticked a time or two, so that he seemed to be winking privately. 'Yes, my dear, a quite perfect choice. I should never have doubted your judgment.'

He turned to Laurence, who, well, never. In all his life. He fumed inwardly, well on the way to outwardly, face starting to tic like Dempler's. All right, perhaps ancient lizards the size of tenements were not an ideal luncheon topic, he would grant that. But they could have no idea how much he wanted to avoid Gretchen and Donna. And besides, a single observation out of place hardly constituted grounds for being taken as an emblem of all that's unseemly and inadmissible; and told so; in the third person; as if he weren't there. Why, Laurence had spilled nothing but the beans about Donna (and those under duress), had used no coarse language, no inappropriate fork for that matter, had not showed up in a sweat and shaken himself like a sheepdog all over the linen, had neither sneezed over another's ordure nor scratched something private in public, and certainly hadn't, and wouldn't, would never, for all the petuntse in China, have referred to a guest in that manner. His Excellency, the Ambassador from Vulgaria. Entertaining, indeed. Though he was pleased to beat the band in Gretchen's view, he had no wish to be thought entertaining on such grounds by that absurdly overdressed and painted woman. 'The vulgar is most entertaining'? Well same to you too, oystershucker! (This was a lie; he was not entertained in the least.)

'I had all but settled on couscous when I recalled what a genius Else is with the darker cereal grains.' She smiled knowingly.

Dempler smiled back, making wide concentric arcs like a matched set of ladles in all his chins. 'You enjoy it as well?' he trusted, turning again to Laurence, who was busy blushing and then nodding for all he was worth.

Oh. Bulgaria. 'This,' said Laurence, flusteredly assembling a forkful of the entertaining East European (not gallinule but, he now thought, some kind of) wheat as a visual aid. Once again he wanted nothing but to be allowed to survive the meal without a major gaffe. No, that was wrong; he wanted his mommy. 'This, is, beyond entertaining,' he recouped, attempting to warm to the topic, 'it, is, like nothing, I have ever,' and the verb just came out, like a puppy when you open the door, as if it had the run of the sentence, 'endured.'

There. He had done it. Proved his intuition of her suspicion was correct. Witness the questionable introduction of long-gone species this early in the day. Witness the unforgivable misuse of the verb 'to endure.' Witness his ignorance of the nature of a gallinule, his more than gothic ignorance of the nature of a burgundy. Yes, he was the vulgar, the hopelessly vulgar. 'I mean, enjoyed, of course.'

'Of course. But speaking of enjoyment.'

The point, purpose, purport of the whole affair now approached. Madame expertly reconfigured her remaining celery into bite-sized morsels and smiled inwardly. What account would the young man with the absurdly herbal surname give of himself and his motives, his aesthetic, his theory of pelousiage?

Dempler's dimply soft-boiled voice proceeded: 'It has not escaped our notice that you discharge your responsibilities,' tic tic, 'in a most creative fashion.'

This was joke. This was insult. This was sincere compliment, reprimand, expression of interest, random attempt to avoid conversational disaster. Laurence, so recently a perpetrator and a victim of auric misconstruction, hadn't a clue, but found the tone soothing, composing, a stroke of the hair from those long conductorial digits, a movement from Brahms; notwithstanding, unsure, he kept his trap shut.

'You have imparted to the grounds unprecedented texture.'

This, surely, called for a response. 'I thought you just wanted it mowed. I didn't think you cared how.' Laurence, finally giving up on the wing, relegated it intact to the miniature archaeological dig at the side of his plate.

'Precisely what *we* had thought.'

'But now you've changed your mind?'

'You, Laurence, have changed our mind.'

Our mind? They had but one between them? What was the point?

'Your experiments, if that is the proper term, have opened for us new windows, new doors, new visions.'

The proper term? *If.* This from a man whose grain he had so recently endured? But two quite unequal pairs of lashes fluttered in anticipation. 'Well, I have been doing a little planning at home.' In the tub, though it might be thought bulgar to say so.

'"A little planning!" But you are too modest,' laughed Madame.

'If you're pleased with my work,' he ventured, talking on eggshells now in addition to stilts, still not sure he was not missing some irony, 'I'm pleased that you're pleased. New visions seems a bit much to me—it's just mowing.'

'Just mowing!' Dempler shared a wink, or a tic, with the Oyster lady. 'Landscape architecture, ornamental gardening, in our century an art with few true practitioners.'

Laurence could not discount a ticklish sense of being mocked. He didn't understand these people; nor would ever, no not if they plucked him as bare as a gallinule. 'I don't think so. It's a job while I figure out what to do next.'

'Yes, to be sure, your career. Yet we, who have both endured, though scarcely enjoyed,' he bowed lightly in Laurence's direction, 'unexpected divagations in career paths,' and here he nodded, a shorthand bow, toward Madame, 'wish to encourage your efforts in this vein. Though we have not personally experienced your musical gifts, we are convinced you have talent.'

'As an horticultural artist,' clarified Madame.

Horticultural artist. Articultural hortist. Dip pint, fought hiss dip pint, exhorted Theo. *Beaux arts,* Gretchen articulated. The tone was all off. He reached for his water, found his hand on the wine instead. Oh what the hell; he sipped. What did they want from him? 'Listen,' said Laurence.

They listened.

'I mean. I'm here under false pretenses.' But here seemed to him precisely the locus for falseness, for pretense.

'What can the young man mean?' Dempler appealed to his companion.

Laurence, bristling at the third person, laid down his fork like a tiny weapon he didn't trust in his hand. And there on his plate (now all but cleaned save the dig of birdbones neatly heaped to one side) noticed an array of jet quavers and a dozen (he had no need to count, it was now startlingly self-evident) ebon clefs rampant on a field of ecru: custom-made dish to denote the estate, country-club crest or commercial equivalent, logo, bulgar ad for self. Vanity plates: but of course.

'The young man,' said the third person, 'means: he can't transpose worth a dime, he's hardly touched his sax, ophone, in going on a decade, he's no musician down on his luck and waiting for a break but a phony, a nothing in particular waiting for nothing in particular.'

'But this is just our point: the calling.'

'I have none.' He clutched the edge of the table with both hands to steady himself.

'Nonsense. Your work is exemplary. We very much hope to keep you on.'

'You can't, that's the point.' And that, suddenly, was the point. Whence this sense, no less sure for its suddenness, that he was here to resign? 'I've got other things to do.' Gallinule now reduced to quartz precision: dip pint. But these other things, what were they? And how would he live, make his whey in the City, earn curds? Moreover, he'd soon be a mother.

As you can tell, Donna took recovery and miscarriage collectively as a sign, though she wasn't sure as yet of what. Toting up a rough estimate of where she stood after recent fluctuations, she hardly knew whether to exult or despond; she and her friends could not reach agreement on which were assets and which debits, but to date she had lost a baby she'd never, and a husband she'd always, wanted, had regained a baby she once sat and a God she now saw as a kind of Cosmic Sitter.

He sat, she thought, in several senses: for spiritual babies, too immature to care for themselves; in stern and attentive judgment on her every move; and yes, anthropomorphically, on a gargantuan gilded throne, rococo, baroque. Oh, she was undeniably more sat than sitting in these latter days, though now liberated from horizontality thanks to the rolling IV stand that accompanied her everywhere: she could roll it to the chair, where it could last longer than she, unwavering as a bodyguard; to the washroom where it observed whatever she did, impassive as a palace guard; even down the hall for a stroll, a couple of comfortless and inexperienced dancers, a wallflower and a stiff tripping the heavy fantastic.

It occurred to Laurence that more than two people at this table were behaving oddly. He had a funny taste under the sides of his tongue; was that from the cheekbiting? Could it be all the gallinules, or the alcohol, unwanted and unwonted? Unaccustomed as I am to public swigging. Hardly a social drinker, let alone at noon after a morning of strenuous, Else would say, ac-tivi-ty. Yes, now you mention it, he was tipsy as all get out, which was what he wanted to do: get out, regroup, form the agons in a sorequell.

'I wonder if I might use the,' he began, then stopped, stumped for the *mot juste* and highly conscious of lingual fallibility. Spooneristic potential aside, the substantive posed a problem. Laurence had grown up with 'bathroom,' which under the circumstances would feel slightly vulgar (something almost seamy about that 'a'), as would 'toilet' (a grossly self-advertising diphthong, that 'oi' seemed at the moment) and others that don't bear mentioning. 'Little boys' room' would be cute as a teddy-bear greeting card; a mother could say it on behalf of her toddler, maybe. 'Powder room,' too, was impossible for a full-grown man to say aloud. He'd never liked 'john' for some reason he wasn't sure of, never understood the exact implications of 'loo.' 'Rest room' sounded institutional; 'facilities,' 'commode,' *et cetera*, awkwardly euphemistic; 'men's room,' exclusive; 'water closet,' unthinkable. Laurence was about to settle on either 'washroom' or 'lavatory,' neither totally satisfactory as he had no intention of washing much (what he really wanted, he had realized by now, was a *pissoir*), when his civilized host, diagnosing both the desire and the dictic dilemma, responded, 'Use Half-Rest, straight down the hallway, left before the foyer, then immediately left again; you can't miss it.'

Amazing what, in this alien environment, was ineffable. Yet apparently, somehow, Laurence had effed it.

Rooms at Twelve Clefs all had musicological names; Whole-Rest, Laurence presumed, had a tub, but given the dimensions of this room, he had to wonder about Quarter-, Eighth-, and Sixteenth-. This particular impeccable semiprivy featured, Laurence noticed as soon as he shut himself in, an elliptical mirror on the door complete with a curtain in case one preferred not to view oneself in less dignified postures, dwarf chandelier, ancient vanity, gold-plated faucets, marble sink, marble for that matter floor, antique copper hod replete with *Smithsonian*s, *Natural History*s, *New Yorker*s, *Art World*s, *Town and Country*s, and, which attracted Laurence more but he had other uses for his hands, a *Guinness Book of World Records*.

He assumed the position, feet slightly splayed for the most promising angle. He made a little calipers with thumb and forefinger to guide the trajectory, as his mother had taught him so many years ago (but how did she know? Mothers, he supposed, just know these things) and stood as if waiting for someone else to start.

Nothing came of it. Laurence's bladder was too polite to sully Twelve Clefs' fixture. He waited a minute or two—more than a half-rest, an entire tacit passage—starting to feel silly, like someone in a tux hailing a cab on a rural highway, all dressed up, noplace to go.

His mother had taught him, too, some tricks of the trade: running a little water in the sink, for example, on the principle, he supposed, of monkey-hear monkey-do, sphincters so suggestibly simian that a little water music would do what no amount of reasonable self-cajoling could. On highly evolved Laurence, the running tap had no effect, but he had one last maternal resort. Come to think in adult retrospect, how would a woman know that if all else fails, tickling an oh so sensitive behind ever so lightly (a mama's trimmed and filed nails with lovely half-moons the preferred implement, but in a pinch mere tips will do) would cause most any penile apparatus to perform with abandon the more diurnal and down-to-earth of its appointed tasks?

Tickling's other more common effect took precedence. To be

fair, it was not just the tickling (though that was fine and feathery, a credit to his upbringing). This dactyl tactility, perhaps sufficient in itself to extort a chortle, combined with a sudden self-consciousness: that insidious feeling that there's someone in the next stall. The feeling, however unlikely, gave rise to a glance, and the glance gave Laurence a pretty good guess as to what a person might look like from the outside. The silvered ellipse framed by broad-grained oak carved to an intriguing grape-cluster motif displayed to Laurence Laurence looking sillier than thou: face to face with a formidable porcelain maw as if preparing for confrontation or direct address ('STANDARD,' it had been announcing for decades in stencilled letters); tap trickling in the background like the far-off headwaters of a mineral-rich mountain stream; feet at more than shoulder width for balance and accuracy, knees bent in a tentative quarter-crouch to stop leggings (undone for nether access) from falling in a heap to the floor; fingers in an upside-down OK sign, meditator's *mudra*, barely encircling but ready to grasp in case things got out of hand; coleopterically, palpitatonically palpating one's very own outthrust and ticklish keester with the other hand and, in an attempt to eliminate performance anxiety, humming a festive tune, which proved the final straw when he recognized it and outbroke in giggles: of all the tunes a person could hum, he had chosen one that concerned the more admirable qualities of a mighty river.

Now Laurence stands quaking ever so slightly like properly inflated tires over obsolete tracks, reflexively giggling at the thought of his own giggling, still tickling away at his nether cheeks though it makes him giggle more because the original goal of the tickling has not been achieved, though its quivery by-product threatens to erraticate accurate discharge splayed feet notwithstanding when and if his own river starts rolling along. And now, on top of all this, home remedies are starting to do his business, and away back in the recesses of his tract, demiquavering in the Half-Rest, a little tidal wave is making its passage toward the air. And when it appears, guess what.

Those among us who possess this quirky organ know what it is capable of. It can do things while we sleep that we prefer mothers not know about in the morning. It can decide from no apparent cause to assert itself at the precise moment when we must stand and deliver a report to unforgiving classmates on the coconut's crucial contribution to the Australian economy. Conversely, it can curl up like a napping kitten before a cozy hearth just when it's slated to stand up and be counted. It can get itself pinned like a losing Graeco-Roman on the wrong side of a center seam. It can do any number of things just all by itself; but append to it by means of a droplet of dried moisture a stray hair or fluff of lint, assume a vaguely sumo posture, then tickle antipodal tissue, and it is likely to do the strangest thing of all.

Laurence hadn't given hairs a chance to stray in that region for many years. But he had as much lint as the next guy, had more lint perhaps than most, given the meticulous terry towelling that followed his daily shave, given a morning of close-quarters intimacy with his combed-cotton briefs as they rode up and down the estate together; Laurence, in fact, had lint in abundance, lint in superfluity, lint (some of it, at least) up the wazoo. Thus as he hummed every riversong he knew—'Down by the Old Mill Stream,' 'Down by the Banks of the Ohio,' 'Down by the Riverside,' 'Down by Every Other Landlocked Body of Water He Could Think Of'— a vulgar boatman whose muffled giggles added a ripply jiggle till he felt not unlike a body of water himself, his tributary, anfractuously helical like a little braided torsade at the best of times, now unravelled, untwisted, disrupted, erupted, as twins (one two hoo hoo and mirror makes four), balefully bifurcating in a lateral V that impishly trajected to either side of the bowl on whose dead center the calipers had his spout trained. Laurence, generally so precise a pisser, gaped and guffawed at the creation of two not unrespectable puddles east and west of the stolid receptacle.

'Use Half-Rest,' Dempler had responded to a polite request, 'you can't miss it.' Well, you've got to know, recalling the words at the climax of bifurcatory serendipity, Can't miss it, my eye, thought Laurence; why I can miss it on both sides at once.

On such events lives sometimes turn. This rather than that pair of eyes in the general vicinity of *Tyrannosaurus rex*, this rather than that pair of croquettes after a difficult day on the ward, this rather than that pair of knees one seat over on a bus, this rather than that composer conducting himself at a social gathering, this rather than that piece of lint plastered here rather than there. The hilarity, the disparity, sudden clarity, of it: *noor vee doos.*

Freelance, freeform, urimanic free-for-all free he he he: *mictio* in nothing.

Irene had never understood why misgivings should be called that—their relationship to givings was murky—but she had them. She misgave (had misgiven for some time now) reencountering Laurence, with or without Gretchen; she misgave reencountering Theo, with or without Laurence; but more than these, at the moment, she misgave entering the home she'd been assigned the task of entering for the simple and express purpose of gathering a few necessities, small running-away-from-home bundle to be done up in a bandanna on the end of a stick.

She expressed, in the car, on the way, without being specific, misgivings to Officer Fitzgerald, who, being close to the case, had the task of overseeing her authorized entry.

'Girly,' he said, as if she were a magazine, 'the scene of the crime is never a pretty sight. The site of crime is never an attractive scene. It's got the dirty pawprints of usually greed or jealousy or some passion all over it. It's where something happened you wouldn't want happening to you or yours, which by the way are you?'

'Am I what?'

'Married.'

Irene remembered her neighborhood bar, the sidelong man who liked it better with the lights on. 'Oh yes,' she said, trying to sound primly uncriminal about it, and couldn't keep herself from adding, 'thank you.'

'That's good. Woman can't be too careful these days, kind of people we got on the streets. I could tell you stories curl your hair.'

Irene's had a slight wave, which was plenty.

'Even so, don't hurt to know how to take care yourself. My wife, she carries.'

'Carries?'

'You bet, knows how to use it too. Some guys'd feel funny, not wearing the only holster, but way I look at it, she encounters some weasel it's him or her, ask questions later. Say I'm out on a call, rousting an element, roping off a scene, interrogating some individual, ascertaining. Irregardless what line of work the old man's in, he ain't there every minute of the twenty-four, you know.'

Oh, Irene knew. Had long since stopped thinking of husbands as protectors; in view of recent developments, had begun to think of them on the contrary. 'Do you think Donna's husband did it? Victor? Poisoned her?'

'Well, once you get past all your suspecteds and allegeds and

pro-babble causes and other bullshit—sorry, bullcrap—ninety-nine
out of a hundred the guy that looks good for it is the guy that did
it. Having personally apprehended this particular *suspect*, I hope
you know I ain't just *alleging* if I tell you he's a moose, the guy's
just a fucking—sorry, frigging—moose. Strength? He had legs, I
might of had something on my hands there. Resisting? He was
demolishing arrest; the guy was obliterating arrest, annihilating it,
wiping it off the face of the damn earth. That's a suspect, I'm a
French pastry.'

Irene wasn't exactly sure yet: 'You think he did it.'

'No thinking to it! He croaked the bitch—sorry, victim.'

Irene felt it incumbent on her to point out Donna was recovering nicely.

'Right, no thanks to the moose. Attempted to croak I should of
said. He's alleged, I'm a juicy fruit.'

'How horrible.'

'Well, your average crime of passion's not generally lovely; least
we got the creep. All swell end swell. Here's it coming up here on
the left. Second floor front.'

It wasn't just the plastic ribbons that repeated gaily, like party
streamers, black on yellow, 'POLICE LINE—DO NOT CROSS' and 'CRIME
SCENE—DO NOT ENTER Per Order PPD,' whose slack Fitzgerald now
like a fitzgentleman took up to form an arch under which Irene
had to duck; it wasn't just the abode all adapted to wheelchair
living, aluminum rods bolted into walls at strategic points and
everything that could be more or less of a height and thin parallel
tirepaths worn in the carpet from room to room like ski trails
through forest. It was—nobody'd been allowed in but detectives,
lab guys, photographers; you couldn't really expect them, Irene
guessed, to send over a cleaning lady—some appalling malcon-
coction of stale perfumes and rotted victuals (dishes precarious on
the counter with dregs of several last suppers), ancient history of
body odor, long tradition of overturned glasses, recent developments of dried vomit more pungent than mango pickle, the assault
of the stench of a man who'd hardly left the house for years and a
woman who'd spilled her guts waiting for paramedics, the grotesque olfactory upshot of a badly mixed marriage. The scent of a
crime, thought Irene, is not a pretty smell. *Pah!*

With the proprietary air of localized authority—only he entitled
to take up that particular slack—and suspicions bred by decades
of stalking the suspected and alleged, Fitzgerald assured Irene it

was okay to touch things despite the fingerprint dust still on them, but watched her every move, duly noting on a pad every item she removed. Toothbrush and paste, hairbrush and spray, from the bathroom (in the cabinet, a plastic case the color of a flesh-colored crayon housed Donna's chromatically similar diaphragm, unimposing rubber dome with a flexy rim, and a scarcely used toothpasty tube of spermicide; Irene thought, swallowed hard, packed them up). In the living room (no visible signs of nongastroesophageal struggle) she found two books it looked like Donna was in the middle of when she left (Irene long since finished with *Madame Bovary*, and though she might not have admitted this to Laurence, let alone that she's in the middle of Melville now, feeling better for it): a thick novel with a lurid cover (beruffled lovers in a Brancusi arc of passion) and a swayback spine, an open Holy Bible (Irene marked the spot in Leviticus with the scarlet ribbon sewn in between signatures). Nothing from the kitchen, where the terrific remains of meals made Irene wish to cry out.

It was in the bedroom (Fitzgerald still officiously on her trail, her Boswell scribbling in a pocket-sized spiral) that Irene broke down. The gothic tableau of Donna's vanity (unkempt source of all that was kempt) got to her. It was a bad cartoon for a still-life: cosmetic junkyard, scrapheap of femininity, unweeded ornamental garden, overgrown with undergrowth of curlers, tweezers, more specialized pluckers; foundations, powders, blushes, rouges, glosses; tubes, bottles, jars of liquids, solids, cremes, gels; blotters, daubers, brushes, swabs, applicators and removers; more implements of appearance than Irene had known existed—things to add and subtract color, to multiply and divide the visible and porous, to hide and highlight, shine and dull. And draped at a casual angle over the back of the low chair before the mirror, what finally (beyond leftovers, gilt-edged pages, even desiccated effluvia) made her shudder and vocalize much to the embarrassment of constituted authority: stalwart stretch all gone to sag, satiny cups once seductive now beyond hope of resuscitation, metal hooks and eyes like teeth protruding from a periodontal problem, a single bra, straps twisted like something killed off before (this sense so vivid despite flagging elasticity) its prime and just left there like that, lace trim at the crest that might be glimpsed from the side if a button or two were undone, unfilled flaccid fragile fabric, trying so hard to be pretty (even thin straps embroidered in not very fetching fleursde-lis that broke Irene's frangible heart), displayed on the back of a chair like a warning to other underthings, left to decay or to endure sluttish time's worst besmearments in the absolute still-ness of a place cordoned-off like a President's deathbed for the curious to look but not touch. Or an apartment reconstructed on some uninhabited planet, a lifetime to the nearest neighbor, light-years to the corner market, eons to the precinct house.

Fitzgerald, when he saw what was happening, left off taking notes and palmed his pencil as if it were the culprit, as if being observed were what upset her. He came up behind and stopped just short of touching her. 'Now now,' he said, as to a delicate daughter with a cut finger or scraped knee or runaway kitten or fractured puppy love, a man in uniform not comfortable with comforting, 'now now.' Irene pulled herself and a skeleton ward-robe together: two nighties, robe, change of clothing for the day of release, foundations (from a drawer, not disturbing the chair's spectacle) to outerwear, comfortable-looking shoes and a bright scarf Irene thought might bring cheer to a woman whose home (now now) looked so totally wrecked.

Could it have been, before the catastrophe, such a mess? It must, for it hadn't been entered, except by those whose charge it was to leave things as they found them, since. If Irene had seen it then, she might have thought lived-in what she (now, now) thought defiled. She wouldn't have found crumbs on cutting board omi-nous, water rings on coffee table predictive, overflowing hamper a warning, underthing on the chairback a red flag. But now. Now, it all seemed a slap in Donna's edemic face, dust bunnies sure sign of impending perpetration, dirty dishes a skull and cross-bones, as if she should have seen Malathion coming, requested court injunctions, protective custody. Table so heaped and strewn with articles designed to keep up appearances, dumpster-ridden backside of the pristine shopping mall: unseemly, humiliating. Though the place so pained her, though the sights so made her ache, though the stench so hurt her, though her eyes stung like antiseptic on the cut finger, though she wanted so badly to get out, she asked Fitzgerald could she please be allowed to remain, could he just let her tidy up a bit, because everything was so, so, soiled. (Donna who taught her to stay between lines, that neatness counted.)

'Soiled? Lady, we're in law enforcement here, not a diaper ser-vice.'

'But it's so,' urged Irene, undaunted by sarcasm, 'I mean when she comes back I wouldn't want her to have to. Couldn't you have someone sent in just to.'

He was sorry—Officer Fitzgerald, again abashed and putting the pencil out of sight, slipping the pad in a pocket, speaking fitz-gently, fitzgenuinely sorry—but the book said no, and she could understand, he was responsible, he really had to do this by the book, no provisions for tidying up. He didn't have the authority, you never knew, lab might need a follow-up, even pros could miss something first time through, you wouldn't want to be disturbing things.

'Miss something!' Irene uncharacteristically yelped. 'Disturbing things! Look! Look!' Her arm swept around as if violently clearing a table of dishes, dancer's flourish initiating a spin. 'It's like a tornado hit hell.'

'I know, ma'am, it's a horror show, usually is this side of the tape. But could be a print that nails Groat in here somewhere. Not that I don't think we got him where we want him as is, but just in case.'

Next of kin, thought Irene.

'Long as you got what you came for, best thing is we just let it go for now. Now now.'

Got what I came for. Just let it go. What secrets could Donna think I told anyway? I didn't know a thing.

In the black-and-white back to St. Benedict's, no professional opinions, no expert advice. Fitzgerald, out of respect for the girl's feelings, even decided to save the joke that just occurred to him ('Forenzics, get it?') for the guys back at the precinct. Hence no sound at all save muffled cruiser horsepower and intermittent dis-patcher crackle. Irene closed her eyes, lay her head back against the hefty mesh that made the rear seat a cage, and misgave for all she was worth.

'If remuneration is the issue, I'm sure we can work.'

'Something out? No, that's just it. I've got other things I need to work out, and this is not a good place for me just now.' Just now? Even in parting, after discovering and pinting out dip pint, after swabbing on all fours his watery signature—given left, patronymic right—off the man's marble floor, could he not resist such locu-tion?

Dempler looked to the Oyster lady for support. Lashes, larger-than-life, were all aflutter, but she had little to offer.

'Son.'

'Please don't call me that.' Somebody's grandson, nobody's son.

'Forgive me. Laurence. I have found your mowing.'

Now Dempler paused, tic tic tic, searching for the complement. Only Madame's lashes broke the silence. Laurence felt they'd been cleared for takeoff. She lifted a gloved (a gloved!) arm to her coif instinctively, as if the silence indicated something had gone awry, then replaced it in her lap and listened. Two listeners holding breath, waiting for that voice the consistency of a ticker-timed three-minute egg to determine its predicate. When it did, what emerged was a soft-boiled pleading.

'Inspiring. An inspiration.'

'You're kidding.' You've got to be kidding.

'I am not. I chose my word with care.' He was not. New life, new hope? Those pathetic half-dozen notes? Else right about the genie? Just won't quit? 'I am prepared to double your current wages.'

Laurence was touched. Laurence was moved. Indigent. Expecting. Tempted. But unswayed. The bones, the exposed coat-of-clefs pleading to be taken seriously, had been replaced by a salad that involved, in addition to a number of things Laurence couldn't place, peppers unmistakably green. Laurence stared at service for three. Its owner, alarmed at the turn talk had taken, did the same.

'Do you understand? Your patterns have allowed me to feel there is still work to be done. I will treble your wages.'

Laurence as muse? Parnassian dectet?

'Mr. Dempler, in my opinion you should be inspired by some-one else, by Else. I am not a talented mower, not a gifted clipper. But look at what she does. Never mind the gallinule, forget the bulgar, look: celery! You yourselves called her a genius. She's the salt of the earth, worth more than her salt. And she named her grandchildren herself. If you want inspiration, triple Else's salary.'

Did you hear that? Released from the spell, from lexic semantic syntactic dependency: triple, he said, not treble. Triumphantly idiomatic, a dialectician in his own right, batter in of runs, runner nearly home, clearer of bases, not trebles, tickling not ivories, tickling ribbies: triple! Triple Else's salary!

'Young, Laurence, I offer you middle-management-level compensation for unskilled manual labor.'

'If unskilled, why inspirational?' Whence this pluck, this feist?

'Forgive me, skilled in the extreme.'

'Not half so skilled as Else.'

'Are you out of your mind? Be prudent.'

Imprudent, out of my mind? 'I'm sorry, it's not you hoo, it's me he he, I belong in a different world.' Out of this whirl hurled. And I can't miss it! 'Hoo hoo hoo.'

Dempler didn't get it. Oyster lady didn't get it. No one but Laurence got it, but he got it in abundance, got it once and for all, got it good. Hysterical despite incongruous apparatus, he uproared.

'I am nonplussed, Laurence.'

'It's mushrooms whoms and potatoes hoes hose.'

Laurence, straightening face, excused himself, leaving vivid ices and a wide range of possible beverages in the wings. Two elders at a complete loss to account: luncheon with the young man had been intended to clarify.

He stopped by the kitchen to hug Else goodbye, offer thanks for breaded treats, praise her grain, hope the outburst wouldn't reflect on her, assure her he would find the grandpa who'd been denied the honor of naming him.

Unwilling to accept the allegation of sectors both public and private—Fitzgerald, Fitzbarron, Fitzemblerpaprika, all dead set against her Victor—Donna thinks she has a line on another perp. Betrayed not by hub but by what Irene spoke: no less than 'everything.' Like many another before her, she has a single simple question: 'How could you?'

'Could I? Could I what?'

'Tell Victor "everything."'

Irene reviewed her files. She didn't immediately recall telling him any, let alone every. 'About what?'

'About me. Do you deny it?'

He's known you not technically longer, but much more thoroughly, than I. What could I tell him? 'Yes.'

'You deny telling him I committed adultery with my doctor? You deny telling him I was pregnant? You deny telling him everything? Anything?'

'Yes. Yes, yes, yes.'

Donna unconvinced: a complete set of vows pronounced in presence of friends and relations, in the sight and presumably the

earshot of God—better, worse, sickness, health, richer, poorer, death
do you part—not easily overcome by unadorned affirmatives on
the part of one who claims you sat her eighteen years since, a
majority ago. And the majority of those eighteen spent loving,
honoring, more or less obeying between arias and believing what
was perhaps the case, that love honor obeisance was the source of
what passion audiences heard (you always imagined your tenor as
Victor onstage, like an adulteress thinking of husband with lover,
lover with husband). Victor, you firmly believe, is responsible for
your talent, your timbre, your very vibrato. Donna, therefore,
unconvinced: 'You betrayed me, Irene,' if that is your real name.
'My confidence, confidences, secrets.'

Dirty dishes, disused diaphragm, dead brassiere on a chairback:
'I never.'

'What, according to you, did you tell him, then?'

Earnestly searching, Irene could come up with only this: 'I told
him you love him. I told him I was leaving town. I told him,' she
blushed to say it to Donna, but believed it more now than then,
'he was being a jerk.'

This rang a bell. 'A jerk for what?'

'A jerk for not appreciating you, for making your life so tough,
for putting you in binds. A jerk for that.'

The bell kept ringing. 'You sound like Gretchen.'

'Well, there are worse things to sound like.'

'Didn't she steal your man?'

Fun munt edge. 'No, I drove him away. We had problems, I left
him, she met him on a bus, she didn't know I existed. Besides,
he's responsible for himself. Like all of us.'

'Not all of us.' I'm responsible for Victor, that's what marriage
means.

'All of us.' You're not responsible for Victor, that's not what
marriage means.

'Not everybody can take care of themselves.'

'I'm not talking about making breakfast, cleaning the stove,
washing dishes, taking out garbage. I'm not talking about housework, Donna.'

'What, then?'

'Decisions. Attitudes. I didn't tell him anything about you. I
swear.'

Not that I lay with beasts as with my own kind? Not that I was
a wizard? Not that I defiled myself for my virgin sister? Not that
my father was a priest?

Do (catarrh catarrh catarrh catarrh)
Be do be dooby (catarrh catarrh catarrh)
Do (catarrh catarrh catarrh catarrh)
Bedew bedew bedew be dooby.

Laurence, a Do-Bee, honoring his father if not his mother, hummed an update of an Ellington classic as he travelled the D, itself more updated, vinyled and plasticked, than the Four that also lumbered to Fordham, but aging less gracefully in proportion to its youth. The graffiti looked harsher, more intrusive, on newer trains. Why should cars built in the age of graffiti take to it less well than their elders? Laurence made a mental note to reconsider congruity.

He had decided that during business hours but toward closing time would be best; accordingly, he set out about half past three. Though he hadn't visited the Bronx, he'd asked enough questions and received enough answers since arriving in the City to know how long to leave. In his experience the question 'How long should I leave to get to *x*?' always elicited the same response in the City. Museum of Natural History? About an hour. Public Library? About an hour. La Guardia? About an hour. JFK? About an hour. Some-place demonstrably half an hour farther away than another place? About an hour. The other place? About an hour.

The New York notion of time, he reckoned, resembled the bib-lical notion of quantity: seven meaning a bunch, ten the same; seven times seven, ten times seven, ten times ten all denoting a significantly larger bunch. Only the subtle distinction between bunch and larger bunch seemed to have been smudged over a couple of millennia; in New York, everything was a medium bunch, about an hour, away. He made a mental note to ask sometime how long to leave for Kalamazoo, Oshkosh, Pocatello.

Interchangeability reminded him of wrong numbers. It was as if New Yorkers couldn't be bothered with the details: an hour was reasonable for transportation, and seven digits would do for a phone number. In a mind with just so much grey matter, differences didn't merit the cells they'd occupy. This, to Laurence, was very odd, since (as it seemed to him) New Yorkers knew so much already, sorted, sifted, mastered, and filed each day an infinite number of stimuli, cavalierly ignoring what was inessential to survival but paying full, fast, urban attention to the rest; why, though, should temporal or numerical distinctions figure among the former? Laurence couldn't figure out how to word this mental note; and besides, his D was entering virgin territory, taking that turn to the east.

> *Yoooooo*
> *Must take the D train*
> *Toooooo*
> *Get to Theo's in the Bronx on Fordham.*

Despite unemployment, Gretchen, Irene, la gamba, it was good to get out of the house; notwithstanding a padful of puzzling mental notes, Laurence, rattling underground in an element that felt by now almost his, hardly needing to count stops, headed for the end of his personal line, grew jolly, carefree, unconcerned. A train to Theo: just like this, *noor vee* dooby dooby dooby.

Before Theo's disappearance, he never would have guessed that that was a tie that wouldn't bind; as before his own, nor he nor Irene would ever have guessed the same about theirs. Was it possible he'd forget Gretchen? To be accurate, he'd never forgotten Irene; there had always been a mental note to straighten out his marriage (one way or the other) as soon as he could figure how. She was the letter that lies on the desk while reams of other stuff pass by, the resolve renewed first thing each morning and last thing each night (usually, for some reason, while brushing teeth); she was mañana, the day that never arrived. Yet she couldn't be called a tie that was binding, any more than a naïvely renewed diurnal resolve, which by its very nature bound not, else it wouldn't require renewal.

And Laurence, bound for Theo's on the D, his own underground railroad, had to wonder whether Theo's tie still bound, whether it could rebound from several years' severe severance. He even made an atypical appeal to a hypothetical numen: 'If he's amnesiac or blind or otherwise unable, so be it; but if he's alive and well, hemming and tinting in the Bronx, please let him want to see me.'

Wobbly on her pins for some time, just as Dr. Pinckney had predicted; and wobbly off her pins, wobbly regardless of her pins, her pins not really the issue at all. Wobbly Donna on the day of her release did not offer thanks to Saint Benedict for shelter and protection in her hibernation, but simply wobbled into the clothes Irene had brought and entered into a dispute with the saint's staff. She started with the orderly who rolled up the chair and made a gracious gesture, which she ignored. He would have to speak, then: 'Ma'am, if you'll please have a seat in the wheelchair.'

Donna declined.

'I really have to ask you to, ma'am. It's hospital policy.'

Not no thank you; simply no.

The orderly appealed with a long-suffering look to her friends for help. Gretchen took him aside.

'It's sort of complicated. Her husband's in one, and it raises unpleasant memories. Let's make an exception.'

'I'd have to check with somebody higher up.'

'Would you do that? Please.'

He headed for the nurses' station, lightly shaking his head, while Irene conferred with Donna.

'I can walk, I can walk, I don't need that.'

Nurse had no more success than orderly, and Donna growing disorderly: 'I can walk, dammit! I've been up and down these halls, even with a needle stuck in my arm, attached to that contraption. I've been doing it at your,' she swept a needleless arm (nothing but discoloration to show the vein's fatigue) to indicate the entire institution, 'behest. You've been saying, "Walk all you can, it's good for you." So I'm walking. I was in a coma, you saw, and now I'm ready to walk. For God's sake let me walk!'

'Please calm down, ma'am. It's just policy. I'll have to check with my supervisor. Just remain calm. Have a seat if you like.'

That was a mistake. Donna, thinking she was being patronized, tricked, didn't stop ranting for all her wobble till the resident-on-call appeared.

'Ma'am, it's insurance regulations is all. Nobody doesn't think you can walk. Just to the front door is all. For the insurance.'

'I've been poisoned.' The resident-on-call, unfamiliar with her chart, winced, thinking she was contemplating a suit. 'I've been out of this world and back, I've been in a limbo no one understands, my brain waves were a sight to behold. And now I just want to walk away, out, out of here.'

It was the chief of surgery, overhearing the ruckus on rounds, entourage faithfully attending to how he would handle this, who managed finally to convince her that the quickest, most direct, least problematical route to the exit, the street, the outside world (that was what they all wanted, wasn't it? They were agreed on that, weren't they?) involved, simply, sitting, in, the chair. 'Simplest thing in the world, ma'am. Won't hurt a bit. Won't feel a thing. Just down the elevator, out the door. The sun's out. It's a beautiful day.' Not his arguments, but the gathered group, the crowd scene finally making her self-conscious, overcame her long-standing resistance to sitting.

Donna, who all those years had never, out of curiosity or sympathy or just for fun while Victor snoozed, who had not been about to start now, was now about to start. And having refractorily refused to sit, Donna, having sat, insisted contrarily on control; if they tried to push or guide her in any way, she swore she'd stand up, wobble or no, and sit down, sit in, make a point, demonstrate for a cause, call attention to an injustice. The crowd dispersed, and Donna was alone with friends, orderly, and the task of mastering a chair. So there she went, weaving like the drunk she was, the sailor she wasn't, vaguely in the general direction of the elevators, wheels like bicycle racers trying to see which could go slower, experimental setup to determine longest distance between two points, opposite of a line.

Wobbly now on wheels, surprised what strong bisymmetry it took (Victor's massive shoulders like mounded hillocks on her horizon) to move the thing right, 'No I could not' (use some help), 'No I would not' (like a hand), down more or less the hall with its stainless wainscoting, stainless kitchen carts (almost lunchtime, when was checkout, wondered Gretchen), stainless specimen carts, discarded stuff that could make you sick, abandoned gurney or two double-parked for good measure, slow-moving recuperants blocking the lanes (if she took too long, would they charge for another day?), literally maneuvering, left woops, right woops, left woops, right woops, then just before the elevator getting it straight, straight not woops but whoosh ahead on the strength of two well-matched (save the purple IV splotch on one) coordinated arms, whoosh like a halfback spotting daylight, whoosh like a cop in a chase scene, whoosh like a bird on the wing, whoosh past elevators toward heavy (Caution, Danger, Radioactive Materials, Authorized Personnel Only) metal doors into which she lightly (for all her whoosh, not going so fast) smashed. Bumping, thumping, jerking, turning, around, back to elevators where two friends and an orderly waited for tantrum to end, trying not to roll their eyes. And down and left and right, past admitting and waiting and vending, out double doors whose electric eyes precluded crash and a second set of the same, now on the sidewalk where the orderly who'd started the whole business deftly ejected her and bid her good day and himself good riddance and thought to himself (because no one else was around to think to) what an effect a few days on the ward could have on those who weren't accustomed to it. Donna now standing and walking as Victor could never. And Donna now sternly, horribly, earnestly, repeatedly reviling herself for treating like a toy, a game, a lark, what for some (for some? for Victor, her Victor with shoulders like gibbous moons) is no less than a life sentence without parole. And talking it over with Gretchen and Irene, who are far from willing to agree that she's treated it as any such thing.

Theo's doorway made Laurence emit a sound, a little gust of atmosphere that mixed the warmth of a past remembered and the rue of years misplaced with the wry edge of relativism appreciated. Not exactly the doorway he remembered, the one he saw was to the former what Laurence thought himself likely to be to the kid Theo remembered: recognizable but grown. Since he'd seen this door, it had been revamped, redesigned, repainted to accommodate not only flaking pigment exposed to exhaust but newfound tongues (Icelandic: BINDI); so though the words—TIES, TIES, TIES, in a jolly roundelay of mutual translation—had grown, like a child's features in adulthood, smaller in proportion to the frame, the overall effect (again like the child, the adult) was one of enlargement. Two recognitions—of identity, of enlargement; of sameness, of change—jockeyed for primacy, and sameness nosed out change at the wire. The Esperanto did it: KRAVATOJ, with its superserific J-tail vining westward to meet the outstretched leg of K at a single point like the golden spike of a transcontinental railroad, had fixed itself in Laurence's mind almost before he was lingual, long before he knew what K, J, Union, Pacific, or Esperanto was. And now the fire-engine-red-on-battleship-grey display made his heart leap up with joyous or anxious anticipation or apprehension, with, in short, the imminence of Theo.

A roundish man came through the door, smiling broadly. His curvish sphericity played off against the angles of the frame. His taste was atrocious, to judge from his garb, though he happily carried a small bag with an imprint of the famous doorway on its side;

happily, but with care, as if he planned to iron, mount, frame, and hang the bag when he got home. Avoiding something distasteful on the sidewalk, he almost bumped into the young man entranced by the entrance, but caught his balance and swerved back, a seagoing vessel swinging his bag aloft like a spinnaker. Now Laurence questioned the wisdom of business hours. What if the place was chockablock with clientele? What if Theo, in a crowd, should fail to recognize him? What if Theo, in a crowd, should succeed?

The door closed behind the roundish man with not a single thud or bang but an attenuated clatter of clicks, clunks, kerchonks. Laurence checked his watch. This particular hour-long trip had betrayed its class by a full fifty percent: closing time and Laurence arrived with virtual simultaneity. What, then, if Theo, all alone, failed or succeeded? Perhaps a crowd would be preferable. One could return on the morrow.

No no, no no, that wouldn't do. Behind that door, twenty feet give or take, Theo. Old man with dull pinking shears. Young man with a sharp wolf at the door. Time. It was time.

Eleven

~~~~

Knock knock no joke.

Locks unlock: deadbolt reborn with a sharp crack, tumblers tumbling like music-box tines, chain jingling release like a catch of Good Humor, the movie creak of a heavy hinge, a jamb, a slit, funnel of dark white smoke like a solid announcement, a promise, RSVP yes, an angle widens wider, wide-eyed Laurence sees the cloud open to reveal there, lightening, as the smoke clears. *Ad gloriam majorem.* Theo.

Among questions, one answer, yes, one affirmative. Wolf no longer at the door. My grandfather is living.

To one with pressure, joy's dangers equal despair's, happiness threatful as sorrow, benign the equivalent of malignant, good evil, fair foul: unfair, incongruous congruence. When he sees him (so vaguely, yet knows before an instant has passed whom), something happens.

Cataractically, glaucomically, Theo (as he knew Irene only better, better) knows Laurence, sight custom-made, hand-painted for sore eyes: blood thicker than vitreous humor, acuity really beside the point, something beyond saline welling up, filling the outsized pacemade muscle. A minor firework drops to Fordham's concrete, sparks up in a shatter and spray of weathered sea-foam. Brows that impressed Irene as wise arc—not wisely—greater than ever, a pair of frightened felines awaiting attack, which discourteously precedes all word of welcome, any hug. Theo first taller, more rigid, then tenuous for an instant (see droplets out of that forehead almost leap), and drooping like something more weightless than weighty (slow-moting before passive now still sorer eyes) to concrete underfoot and breathes either barely or almost or not.

Laurence, who knows, thinks, nothing, who could not tell you one single thing, kneels, unconscious of spectacle-making, and rubs wrists like a perfume-sampler off the deep end. New Yorkers saunter, walk, and run—some swivel heads like conning towers scanning for oceangoing enemies; more ignore—to catch a bus, a train, a movie, forty winks, as catch can. Laurence a shoeshine boy gone berserk, rubbing amok. One, who has seen the point, enters the shop and dials three digits (nine takes nearly three seconds: Theo has not gone touch-tone or even push-button, remains staunchly rotary). Lunatic Laurence, shuffling less than a full deck, rubs on, solicitous, soliciting: stalwart Scout coaxing, courting, cajoling, coercing fire from dry twig—kindle, Theo, kindle. Till siren is heard (not by oblivious obsessive him, by impervious compulsive New Yorkers) and van pulls up to the scene, a strange one even for them: rubadubdub, two men on a curb. They have to pry the young one, mad kindler, off to administer aid—beat, now beat . . . beat, now beat—and drive the old one noisily away, Dopplering out of sight and later earshot.

No sooner found than lost again? This could not be. So many years, a minute or two of frantic coupled rubbing, then forever? My living grandfather dying? If this be so, then fair is foul indeed.

'O you paramedics and emergency technicians! there where you are in the back of your van, work modern medical magic for him whose future is entrusted to your trained hands! Treat him with care and be not distracted: kindle my only relation. If you have ever yourself been related, hear me: revive, restore, resuscitate this my grandpa.

'And O you rush-hour traffic! you hackneys and gypsies, strollers and perambulators, workers and commuters weary with eight-hour days, you unemployed pedestrians fairly overcome with lassitude and lack of hope, you sedans, coupes, wagons, hatchbacks, bikes and motorbikes, you more humble and less predictable skateboards! but most of all you, O buses, trucks, and fellow vans! great larger-than-life vehicles festooned with ditties (You Give Us A Break / We'll Give You A Pane), slogans (The "Best" For "Less"), promises (Free Delivery), queries (Is *Your* Account Insured?), predictions (You'll Sleep Better For It), with numbers both local and toll-free: you commercial vehicles, make way for this less profitable, more valuable van with lights flashing and amplifier melodramatizing like a grand opening. Pull over, you traffic, make way, for its cargo is precious!'

(By now, inside the van, hypodermicked, oxygenated, cardiopulmonarily stabilized, the old one could be conscious, asking in fact for the young one who sits on the curb with no way of knowing, rubbing nothing against nothing as if for practice and offering incentive, invocation, incense: Kindle, Theo, kindle.)

The kindly one who saw the point, who stopped and dialed attenuated nine and evanescent ones and thought to ask where van was destined, now gathers up the young one. 'Grandson?' he surmises, and Laurence nods, looking with the blank confusion of second sight; he's seen this man before. 'I know you,' he says, 'I think,' still nodding. For this is the round man, the man with bad taste, who bought a Theo's Tie and swerved to avoid collision; who wasn't much more than a block off (stopping on Fordham, proud and impatient, to knot new silk) when he noticed the young man still staring at phonemes; who stared in turn as he twisted his accessory absentmindedly; who watched him knock, lingered (old man alone in a shop at closing time makes easy prey), returned to make the call and close the door and gather up Laurence who (less hyperventilatory and then more) leaves off nodding and starts in shaking: 'I think I killed him.'

How?

'By showing up, by being here, by knocking.'

Nonsense.

'By shocking him, pressuring his blood, short-circuiting the white plastic box in his breast pocket.'

Come, the kindly one has a car, he'll drive you through rush hour to the hospital. You can sit in this oversized Buick (stuck in traffic you will forgive for this delay if only they earlier let the urgent van through) and gaze at this new tie—indigo silk beautifully splashed with raspberry, lemon, an ashy grey, and a white never used by Van Gogh—and wonder what its figures might have been intended to represent.

Laurence considers in its absence that sorry tenor: round, once-brassy medallions like holiday chocolates in cheap gold foil; fake mother-of-pearl on smaller keytops; radiator-hose clamps holding mouthpiece in place; neckstrap, adjustable like a cowboy's string tie or spelunker's lifeline; the whole structure of scaffolding around a simple conduit at the core, wires tubes ducts corky stops all nes-tled and crammed like mysteries under a subcompact's hood or old heating system: exposed steam pipes for the hot jazz he wishes he knew how, the searing elegy he hopes he won't have, to play. All the intricacies of a subway map: so many stops, such manifold ways to control breath's flow with fingers. So well-packed an instrument deserves to be played by someone who really knows how; engineered with such care, it shouldn't just lie in a closed case, untouched, inert, gathering (less than moss) not even dust.

How much more than a saxophone deserves does Theo? By what factor multiply the value of that hunk of welded metal to arrive at the worth of this man?

The incident of the chair aside, Donna resists not caretaking, behaves in fact as she is in fact, helpless, needy, invalid, always defending though (though? for that reason, because!) Victor. 'Don't say a word against that man,' throwing tantra if they do: of motes and beams, of stones cast first and vitreous houses, of walk a mile in his chair, of he ain't heavy, he's my hubby.

But (but? and, therefore!) she's passively nonresistant to the consensus: sooner the better out of this town, this state, change of scene might do her good, further the better from water rings, dust bunnies, stained carpet and sad cups. Less familiar the better (though she's been to Gretchen's before). Greenwich would mean time: to straighten wobbles, balance shoulders, master perspec-tive, mistress laws of antigravity, get feet on ground, regenerate pins, commence recommencing, gather up self like a few neces-sities, small running-away-from-home bundle, bandanna, end of stick.

A call came in a few minutes ago from Laurence (Gretchen, blessedly, answering) to announce a vacancy in the Village, to let them know in case of emergency that, speaking of cases of emer-gency, he'd be at one two one two five five two eight two seven three indeterminately, pending further notice: playing nurse, he could only hope since he wasn't one to pray. Gretchen, after expressing in appropriate tones her sincere wish that the old man make it, sized things up, reckoned absence of Laurence would fortuitize the whole affair, and announced on the spot that all three of them would show up in the loft at the earliest opportunity.

On the One he no longer has a reason to travel, at Ninety First, something very like a station is on continuous display though the train doesn't stop. Not a question of express versus local; this one isn't even on the maps. The One slows slightly, as if out of casual respect for a passing funeral, but hasn't considered stopping for Laurence has no idea how many years—one, six, thirty? As the rattling box splits the difference between whizzing and crawling by, he has seen walls saturated with signatures, most of them doubtless scrawled since the station died. Some underclass of graffiticians view that inaccessible spot as part of a working land-scape, a piece of their own broad, intermittent canvas.

How do they get themselves down there? Mustn't the entrance be chained and padlocked off? Why put themselves in whatever jeopardy presence there must put them in? Doesn't this whole extensive City afford them, somewhere, a more secure surface?

The tiles, for all their written-on state, still stand in vertical ranks beneath it all, off-white mostly with neighbors of color in a frieze of cheerful variety, proclaiming locale with infinitely more legibil-ity than the figures brushed and sprayed overtop them. There they reside in stationary fixity though no one but vandal or defacer ever drops in, as if they can't understand they've lost their jobs, as if still taking a certain civic pride in being public property, soldiers in the field who've yet to hear an armistice was signed. A bit stiff like figures in wax museums, a bit stately like older official docu-ments, a bit absurd like a cathedral in a desert. Handsome tiles, grime notwithstanding, an admirable subterranean bathroom waiting for some subcontractor to install new fixtures any minute now.

Say, by some odd confluence, all the maps were destroyed. Say every text that knew better disappeared off the planet's weathered face. Say a dig in some indeterminate future came up with this ancient facility. There'd be no way on or under earth of knowing it had been out of service. No one would guess that the trains never stopped, that these tiles had outlived utility. In the universe not a single mind would understand what the late century made of this place, how eerie one commuter, at least, had found it. Belated finders and keepers could produce diorama, stage set, or simulation; inventive thinkers and theorists could reconstruct life as we don't know it. No single soul would have even an inkling of the irrecoverable truth.

There it is, a hole under Ninety First all done up in tile, as if awaiting some such rehabilitation: the ghost of subway stations past, eager to tell its lies.

Gretchen, wretched, retching innards ragged, jaggedly gagging over stencilled 'STANDARD,' but neither furcating nor extricating anything much from the preemptied tract. Morning and melancholia in the esophagus, sarcophagus, anthropophagus, oh rotten rotten feeling kneeling reeling keeling over on tiling (and reviling congealing), seeing ceiling, appealing for healing. Donna knocking lightly, entering, centering, offering, proffering. Better now, yes, thanks very much (though looking paler than ever from the strain, a.m. illness revealingly arrived after Laurence's departure, psychosomatic they agree to posit, but no less gastric for all that). Donna there against the white tiles looks as miserable as Gretchen feels. Organophosphatic coma'll do that to a person's appearance, she has to think in the bright white light, not to mention other recent ills and losses: Donna miserabilious. No mystery to it, she has to continue thinking while tidying herself, if Donna doesn't look so hot; who would, after what she's been through: *annus miserabilis?* Yet still, emerging together to the loft like a makeshift dorm, its barracksy crowding enhanced by sheet-music piles and the wounded gamba leaning against the far wall like an eavesdropper catching snippets (legs in a casual figure four) and pretending not to listen, Irene too pretending not to have overheard, trumping up a soft cough as if that would have drowned out the antidigestive agony in the ladies' room at the loft's rear end. Yet still, can't help thinking Gretchen, even all that, even convulsions, even miscarriage, even attempted uxoricide presumably in the first degree, leaves something unaccounted. Because I remember a markedly different past Donna, coloring of which this is not even a version, alteration beyond misery's revisionary power, and it's not that she looked much better then, because she's been aging fast since I met her, what with alcohol and all, no novice connoisseur of miserabilia she, no newcomer to strain, no beginner at suffrance. But, and this strikes Gretchen now as revelation, a sudden clincher in overtime that gives it away and the game is up, not texture or porosity, beyond puffiness or wobbliness on pins to something more like mistaken identity, like hoax, like impersonating a Forenza Groat. Someone in central casting screwed up. Because this woman's face has a radically different shape! (Has, for instance, scarcely a cheek to speak of, whereas Donna's were her very best feature.)

She can't put her finger on it, can't figure it at all; voices subdued not to disturb the apparent impostor napping fitfully nearby, she mentions to Irene her uncanny sense that something is badly askew, Donna miscast. Irene, gradually rejecting in adulthood the illusion that the world is an actor hired to play the world, finds this oddly to coincide with the homegrown cosmology she's been doing her best to disbelieve, and Gretchen is right: this goes way beyond ruffled gullwings, the very bones she recognized in the bar are absent. Now neither can get it, and both look trustlessly askance at the woman they sit: how could she fool them this long, and who could be behind it, for what purpose, to what end, this tasteless masquerade? Who but Crickenberger?

Though whisked to nearby Montefiore rather than distant Mount Sinai, Theo like others before him returned with tablets, prescriptions and proscriptions, stringent shalts and shalt-nots: shalt take one with meals and at bedtime, shalt not puff on pipe. The shalts for the most part are shalt-nots in shalt's clothing: shalt avoid unnecessary excitement, shalt refrain from becoming agitated. Avoid and refrain, hardest task in the world: remain calm through this long-anticipated and variably apprehended family reunion (these two the soles remaining, the clan entire, despite surnominal differentiation: all others long deceased in Poland, New York, or Providence). Reunion that would let you die in peace but also gives renewed reasons not to (for someone must teach this boy, these hands, to paint ties, to sew, to preside).

Now they can talk, the grandrelatives, to their hearts' contents, just as long as they touch on nothing exciting, nothing upsetting, nothing stimulant, aggravant, exacerbant, irritant, abrasive, pruritic, or moving, as long as Laurence is a soothing sayer, cool interlocutor, ameliorant discussant of not much and of nothing that matters. Fine. They will talk. Not of abandonment or betrayal, of abortion or death, not of (even) relief or rejoicing (joy equals sorrow for one with pressure).

Of what, then? Of better homes and gardens, road and track, field and stream?

In the City, arrangements are due for a change: my paltry bandanna bundle plus sax at Gretchen's, Irene's saxless same (things familiar to me, articles definite, known) at Theo's, then a phone call bringing news that Donna's bundle was joining mine, that a trio bused hither apace, comin round the mountain when they came. So: five separate readings of pressured blood, five systoles, five diastoles, ten stoles in all (two far too high, chronically alarming) like so many piggies, eating roast beef, having none, we we we. Three women, two men, two relatives, two spouses, two lovers, two beds, too complicated, too rubblesome, troublesome, exigent, critical, out of hand (not out of sight), rocketing out of control (not out of mind) like Theo's blood when he saw the little boy cry wolf. Can this town be big enough for the five of us? Are there backdoors and alleys enough? Must we park on alternate sides? Shall we all have chicken and dumplings?

Are there authorities one can appeal to in such a tricky pass, contingency entities five can invoke, some public bureau of private disentanglement? Travellers' Aid, Welcome Wagon, Mayor's Office of Special Events, Weights and Measures, Permits and Licenses, Parks and Recreation, Streets and Sanitation, Mounties, Disaster Relief? Ethical Culture, Amnesty International? Labor Relations, Civil Liberties, Arbitration Board, Council of Elders, Anti-Defamation, Sons of Italy, DAR, Elks, Moose, Rotarians, Rosicrucians, Know-Nothings, Odd Fellows even?

How are we to permutate, how combinate? How factor our fractious factions or formulate factitious facts, our fraught frictions and friable frailties, fragile fragments and frangible figments of fluff, fitful fissures and fluky fissions, fidgety friendships, flighty forsakings, our finicky fusions, fishy and forbidden flockings, flexuous fouls, fond flouts and fluctuant flurries, our fluttering foci, formidable foibles, fearsome fardels? How forfend foggy ferment fomenting folderol, flourishing fanciful flights or funny foofaraws, farflung footings and fugitive forfications, far from fortuitous foundations, foolhardy flings, familiar findings and flaky fumblings, fungible flirtations, funky furcations, our frames four-flushed and frankly freaky fullfledged and feckless frenetic frettings and fickle fruitless foetations? How foresee and forever forestall forcing further familial infarction, infractions, frantic flap, frazzled fray, frightful fulmination, frenzy, fury, fuss, fracas or fight? How?

If Urban Planning can get away with red four on black ten, could they possibly give us a hand here? If Highways and Byways manages to manage exits and entrances, cloverleaves and spaghetti bowls, apparent infinitude of lanes, and can monitor volume and flow, restrict access, set limits, could they please get a handle on this? Can someone help us out, of this fix, this case of conscience, this delicate pickle, this dilly? Central Intelligence? Seek Transit Authority Monday? Could Paideia reach consensus? Is there a casuist in the house?

Irene (voice lowered again, in confidential tones discussing a napping subject) merely mentions in passing the vanity that horrified her in Providence; perhaps that was where they did their dirty work, made this woman up to look as much like Donna as she does (which, now they think about it, seems less and less until Irene says that, and Gretchen suddenly sees it, the point: just the opposite).

'Ah, oh, aha, oho, then more than circumstance, emotional ravage, more than temperament but less than we suspected, has changed.' She thought she'd seen that face before, and now she knows when: first thing in the morning on Providential visits. This is no actress; there's no central casting; the world is the world. Not another made up to look like Donna, but Donna unmade up to look unlike. This was in past times Donna for a very few minutes on either side of sleep, Donna in the flesh, *au naturel*, Donna the way Donna was meant to be, Donna derevlona, Donna dismaybellina, Donna with the max factored out, estée laudable Donna, the given Donna, Donna *née* Forenza, Donna *donnée*, Donna undone. No wonder she doesn't feel herself!

Thus it was that Irene and Gretchen started making Donna up. Not like a fight; not for lost time; as a lady.

You can't talk of nothing for long. Soon enough and despite all Laurence's good intentions (physicians' proscriptions, for Theo himself, carry no unusual weight), things come up, arise, depart from and leave in the dust simply verifiable localized meteorological commonplaces, diurnal whethers of everyday life (whether a floor needs sweeping, a fridge replenishing, a *nosh* preparing; whether a new box of tissues will be requisite soon, for Theo leaves behind a little Hansel-&-Gretel wake, pastel remnants of crumpled eye-daubers, soggy aftermath of a rained-on parade) to other more global and long-range whethers. How could household needs keep reins on Paprika-Papyrushchka colloquy? Mercurial and meteoric warmths conduct, reflect, absorb; like weather itself, rise, fall, suspend, convect, condense, circulate, precipitate, evaporate, sublimate, a whole climate of changeable states: marriage like a storm that drifted out to sea, veered off the coast to die or gather fury; nonprofession like absence of weather or all weathers averaged, TV forecaster's South Dakota accent, dialectical distinction yielding to common denomination purged of regional clues; Christian Paprika like a long-range forecast, extended, almaniacal, not to be trusted. Predictions and predilections, previsions and precautions, premonitions, protractions, presciences and percentage probabilities, all measured against a progenitor's palpable presence.

'Eyerin,' offers Theo, 'sims ah simper taytic *maydel*, an ice guile.'

Though we all know that work is ah void, juiced avoid, 'Fought amen dose,' opines Theo, 'coot giff hiss lie famine ink, adept dot it foot tint odor fies half.'

And despite each and every qualm and compunction, despite cellist unmet, ice guile excluded, Christian name incongruously to be grafted onto the tot, a novel Paprika plotted on the chart, tracked up the coast like a tropical storm, its little winds measured, its progress, threat, and promise, Papyrushchkaleh-to-be, this smidgeon of savor, pinch of posterity however dubbed, this spice-of-life sprinkle brings a new wrinkle to Theo's tanned, cured, and weathered sockets. Little Christian looming in corners, welling up all around rims, sliding down sides of nose and fronts of cheeks as gravity dictates, like all that's left of icicles on the first balmy day of spring.

Though he resisted arrest, Victor did what he could to help out with conviction. He made it clear that he understood, then waived, rights to silence and legal counsel, but insisted on the right to administer justice if constituted authorities relinquished theirs by failing to enforce the Law. There were no pleas to cop, no bargain to strike (old Vitalis bottle half full of Malathion in his ditty bag pretty much settled things). His claim that Rhode Island had no rightful (his word was 'righteous') jurisdiction only momentarily confused the court. Generally he was lucid, *compos*, even composed. He gave no sign of lunacy save his somewhat uncommon opinions. At arraignment he refused to disown the act despite a public defender's advice ('What are you gonna do with a guy like this?' she asked eye-rolling, shoulder-shrugging colleagues over lunch): 'I did it, but it's really none of the court's frigging business,' he pled, unconsciously toning diction down in vestigial deference to solemn or ceremonial proceedings of any sort. The consulting psychiatrist found Victor's beliefs a tad goofy, but presented his evaluation in such a way that the judge, a believer himself though of a less extreme stamp, could hardly equate Victor's faith with madness under the law. There was really no way even a top-dollar lawyer could have gotten him off, let alone an overworked underpaid defender, herself of Hebrew ancestry and with about as much sympathy for her client's interpretation and application of Leviticus as she had for Goebbels's of Nietzsche. The system, jealous of imprudent juridical appropriation, threw the book at Victor; Victor, proud of what he'd done, declined to duck, and the book hit him square in the chest, putting him away for what is generally referred to as a good long time. The only question, really, was how and where (Rhode Island's penal system not known for innovation in the field of wheelchair accessibility). For Victor's part, he was rather successfully, almost happily, crystallizing a self-image as martyr to a cause.

The papers hadn't the field day you might expect. There was no trial in the usual sense, no jury of peers, no grass-roots defense fund to defray costs (no costs), no conflicting testimony, no one willing to argue that (other things being equal) putting a wife deliberately to death is generally a good thing, no armor for the assistant district attorney to find spectacular chinks in. The defender did raise at a sentencing hearing Victor's wholesome history (Eagle, Boy of the Month, USAF), though she thought the better of playing up his contributions to pestfree American agriculture; nor could she keep a where-did-he-go-wrong tone out of her plea for leniency. Most importantly, perhaps, there was no *corpus delicti*, and the *corpus delicti manqué*, well known to readers of local papers, was

out of town, unavailable to reporters, even a former Arts & Personalities guy (now demoted to obits and headlines for the most
part) who, thinking a scoop might be just what the doctor ordered
for his fading career, tracked her down and tried to invoke auld
acquaintance over the phone. No comment, Gretchen took the liberty of saying on her behalf.

The papers, then, could find little more to do than record a plea
and a number of years, remind readers of a prominently troubled
contralto, admit that one never really knows what life is like behind
closed doors, editorialize feebly on the advisability for married
couples of talking things through, working things out, making use
of established conflict-resolution procedures ('And when you come
right down to it, isn't that what marriage is really all about?'). No
one quite understood what the conflict in question had consisted
of; Victor, with an incongruous vestige of Boy Scout gallantry,
refrained from going into detail about the offense he had avenged
in the name of the Lord; and the enigmatic intuition of a misun-
derstood martyr told him it was as well to be considered a vaguely
nutty, if legally sane, jerk as to be misconstrued on any firmer
ground.

Take shapes. Laurence generally dislikes things in the shapes
of other things: bird-scissors, pineapple-creamers, clown-ther-
moses, spoonrests that mimic cupped hands, mugs with faces, hats
involving fruit. Shakers are the worst offenders, ceramic Protei
assuming any form that comes along: glossy little trees, woodland
creatures, barnyard beasts, overgrown blueberries, body parts,
minute airliners, World Trade Centers, generous matrons and chefs
with holes in heads or hats: two for the pepper, three for the salt.

He never liked handgames children were expected to enjoy:
wallshadows of rabbits, dogs, or flapping gulls; this is the church,
this is the steeple. My hands, he thought, are hands, my fingers
fingers, not rabbitears, not steeplehalves. Once, prodded to imper-
sonate a short, stout teapot before assembled elders—Snookies,
Tooties, Fluffies—he broke down, ran from the room in alarm,
sulked and refused to explain (even to Mama) but constantly confirmed to himself, 'I am not now, never have been, a teapot of any
height or shape whatsoever.' Inordinate melancholy followed the
athletic outing during which an adolescent companion, having
guzzled, pronounced, 'Ah water, the juice of life.' Water, he assured

himself for days on end, is the *water* of life; *juice* is the juice of life. Finally, after volving and revolving his logic (testing for impurities, seeking leaks) for what seemed weeks, he found it held water, found it sound, calmed, cheered, and returned to normal Laurence.

Places of business in particular bother him: cheese shops as monstrous wedges with swissy holes painted on cinderblocks, big chickens that specialize in broasting smaller shapesakes, gargantuan sombreros on horizons that turn out to be tacky taco stands, stucco avocadoes that dispense organic guacamole in more modest petrochemical avocadoes. He associates such establishments with the Southwest's lastborn complex, baby of the family, its acting-out confirming maladjustment, undigested belatedness: whole regions replete with effete shoppes he envisions, holding breath, turning blue, pleading pathetically for the attention of adults who are, can't they see, trying to hold a conversation. Shops, he believes, should inhabit the shapes of shops; not shipshape, shrimpshape, chapeaushape, should be shopshape. And Tom Thumb golf, most promiscuously irresponsible purloiner and purveyor of misshape, gives him a nervousness.

Despite this ontic disposition, Laurence loves to distraction Theo's Ties, adores its doorway the shape of translingual thesaurus and within, the amusing play on scale, the visual pun, its synecdochic floorspace. These he cathects beyond all reason, and imagines the impulse perfected by painting on ties not referential horses, houses, hussies, Hoosiers, but reflexive scaled-down ties: cravatted cravats, fours-in-hand squared (cubed: sixty-fours-in-hand!), ties on ties on ties.

This, neither theory (ontic, ontologic, ontizing) nor empiric observation could predict: the concretion of having Theo back in the flesh. He had thought to verify origin, ratify confirm and assure his deepest most legendary mythic and founding beliefs; far from him to suspect how far from -retical, how very distant from -logical, this Theo would be: prefixed and prefixing physico-Theo no suffix could abstract, Theo The Theo. And yet in a way predilections yet rule, unimpaired: despite emporial troping, despite racks arranged to suggest bias and seam, there's no denying, there's only confirming, that Theo is the tautological Theo of his life. Like Yahweh or Popeye, he is that he am, am what he is. And Laurence, who has never felt utterly sure where to place equals signs, when to stop, is ever so grateful for that.

Not self-made women, they had maintained their inherited looks; neither had made up to speak of. A bit of petroleum to eschew chapping here, a dite of moisturizer there to forestall desiccation, a stab or two at sticking lips (retracted before mothers glimpsed) in adolescence to prove they weren't boys; but both favored genetic over storebought makeup, the variably matte or glossy finish they were born with. Sometimes with hair color free samples of coordinating pancake came Gretchen's way, but she (too complexly complected for company color charts anyway, beyond their standard deviation, outside margin of error) discarded these without a second thought. 'Pores are there for a reason' was her way of putting her first and last thought; 'they're how the integument breathes, you wouldn't fill nostrils with glop.' Beneath this brash and insouciant exterior, though, a concealed motive: she preferred to do as little as possible to discourage perspiration. She had never sweated conspicuously, noticeably, to her knowledge; but if the time came, she didn't want incipient beads stymied by layers of laboratory ooze. Mandatory block during sunny months was gunk galore for Gretchen, enough to last year-round. Her attitude she summed up, 'Pores are pores.'

Irene, who had blatantly sweated on more than one occasion, never thought of it that way (though once Gretchen pointed it out, she had to accept this taut logic: pores self-evidently themselves), but her epidermis tended to overreact, and besides Mother had always called it fine skin, good coloring, undeficient, plenty feminine as was: 'Give me a complexion,' she used to say, 'that makes simplicity a grace.' Irene, of course, for a time shaped brows to a raggedy dislikeness of gullwings (exuberant youth, despite pastel-circlet ambitions, overshot the mark to a pluperfect pluck suggesting bedraggled birds rescued from slick commercial mishaps), but Mrs. Embler blushed at blush, drew the line at liner, enlightened her concerning shadow. Mother, though a stout believer in good grooming, would plump no more for cosmetics to complicate her daughter's simple face than for the endless magentas of earlier years: 'Neatness counts, of course, but a cleanly pink is all anyone can really require of a human being.' In this case, Father deferred to his mate's superior understanding of the field.

Neatness, Irene and Gretchen now equally saw, is not always enough. Donna needed makeup back and more: makeover, recompense. A remake, self-sequel, nonalcoholic bottles for her vintage, alcohol-base concealer for her bags, new lamps for old, to make if not the best at least something else of what she had, novel look to take the recuperant mind off troubles, off Victor. Of course, she could be redone. They fancied recombinant Donna.

They would start simple, with the gullwings (Irene now ready for more mature and responsible pluck) and a few modest bows and combs for the undone do, her long-neglected coif: hair first to keep the pilot program easy, low-budget, and within their limited talents till they could evaluate success. The proverbial hundred strokes they soon left in the dust and brushed Donna out like practicing scales, regular, solid, soothing; then added the irregular, the pleasing, teasing, the plaiting, upsweeping, suspending, arranging like modulant chords, cranial continuo beneath cadenzaic cascades, her recovered head a singular semantic goal for plural syntactic revisions. She took it well: ripe for the plucking, game for the curling, good sport, she seemed to enjoy the attention, the interesting ideas taking positive shape on her head.

Not long before one bloomed inside. Donna, unsuspicious of manipulation despite two sets of fingers so often massaging her scalp, innocently pondered Gretchen's uncommon tresses (right in front of her nose as the cellist pizzicatoed stray feathers from wings, split ends from improvisations) and herself raised the issue of coloring: frost, highlight, henna, dye. Hence they proceeded sooner than they would have dared hope to complexion and the ornamentation of the most visible and expressive part of her largest organ.

Donna not only approved, but sent them out with a shopping list for an armload of stuff. She knew her own colors, her brands, knew how to shape cheeks in ways that could have fooled the FBI, knew more than they would have thought you'd need to know; nor would she hear of experiment, only wanted wonted tones. And just as well: Irene and Gretchen, unwitting, would be awash in a consumer whirl of what and which without her specifying inventory. They knew squat of quenchers and concealers, foundations and fanbrushes; in store for them, dizzying displays of pencil and pen, brush and bottle, imperceptible chromatic subdivision and distracting uninformative rubrics, things spelled funny—colors and colours, cremes and creams, jels, gels, and gelées—and more modifiers yoked by violence to more substantives than you could shake a lipstick at: Cheery Cherry, Misty Magenta, Clear Claret,

Ribald Red, Very Vermeil, Satiny Gules, Maroon Marron, Jungle
Juniper, Infrared Indigo, Applied Apple, Ochreous Oxblood, Cay-
enne Peach, Flame-Flam, Plus Que Plum, Berry Boysen, Cripes!
It's Crimson, Cinematic Cinnamon, Sulphur Flambé, Sinfully
Cardinal, Crepuscular Rouge, Scarlet O'Hair, Serious Cerise,
Reasonably Radicchio, Cotillion Vermillion, Ne Plus Ultra Mocha,
Blasé Blaze, Concupiscent Coral, Festive Fraise Fraîche, Vino
Veritas, Magnesium Melon, Niveous Rust, Barely Brickdust,
Incarnadine Seas, Preternaturally Pumpkin, Fire-Engine Apricot,
Titian Trombone, Gory Glory, Nude Numen, Foxy Lobster, Pool-
side Flush, Sheer Vivid, Postpartum Pink, Beyond Paprika, Red
All Over. And Irene thought Crayola was something! This rainbow, though heavy on reds, was subdivided so minutely you'd need
a megabyte to digest it all. They stuck strictly to the list and thought
themselves fortunate to escape intact from this minute sublime of
hue and sparkle, gloss and sheen, as if such spectral prolificacy
might do them harm. It was *folie à deux*, a tailspinning nightmare
of being expected to pilot something unfamiliar and state-of-the-
art: which is altimeter, where is what, how do I press to eject.

'*Gai avec un fils,*' muses Theo. Happy with a son. He chuckles,
and charred remnants of cilia waggle like the truncated tails of
some dogs: is that a warning? Joy endangers, but this looks more
like contentment. Laurence labors to draw the fine line between
amelioration and aggravation. *How* happy with a son? Too much
to remember safely? If Theo were feline, would you discourage
his purr? That would be too cruel; happiness can't be *so* bad. But
it could kindle joy, and joy could have Laurence, grandkindler,
rubbing wrists. Happy with a son, happy with a grandson: surely
no cause for emergency.

'*Gai avec un grandpère,*' reciprocates Laurence on his own and
pop's behalf.

Theo emits a quizzical cloud, shifts the meerschaum from hand
to hand as if symbolizing something, chuckles minor gusts, making eddies, little pigtails in the smoke.

Monitoring Laurence keeps an eye.

'You on dares tent fought doos mince in Joosh, Lawrinse? *Gay
a vague own fees*?'

How am I to monitor multiglot emotions? 'No, I never learned.'

'Day tot jew no Joosh?'

'None to speak of.'

'In French, mince gled fitter sawn, ah *zeeneleh* dot giffs ah pie sin *naches.*'

Not nachos. Not Natchez. Notches on the belt of paternity: *naches* is pride, Laurence is pleased to know.

'Bitten Joosh mince folk ah fay fit out fit.'

Walk away without feet? That's sort of funny to one who thinks he's seen Irene, himself, others, do something along similar lines. No danger here, though. They share a laugh and, 'I am,' says Laurence, 'in French, *gai avec un grandpère*. Does this mean anything in Yiddish?'

Theo exhales a smooth horizon, left to right and back again.

'Well, in French then, I'm awfully happy with a grandfather.'

'Dots *zay dare* in Yiddish.'

Zayder. He who zades, whose aids help a grandson audiovisualize. '*Zayder.*'

'Dot sit. No foughts *eyenickel?*'

Laurence hasn't a clue what's *eyenickel.* He's heard of putting pennies on lids, but can't recall at the moment to what end. *Eyenickel,* a sign of inflationary times?

'Ewer *mine eyenickel.*'

'*Eyenickel* is grandson? I am one happy *eyenickel.*'

'Lawrinse, eye em sew trilt dot you fount me, dot you half calm.'

'Trilt' sounds potentially dangerous, but Laurence can't even consider discouraging such a purr over his own halfing calm.

'*Enshine.*'

Polish? Impart a beautiful shine to? Wait: *shine* is beautiful? '*Shine?*'

'*Enshine* mince fen sumtink hiss comp lit, in dot's dot.'

Dot's dot: a tautology of contentment, not life-threatening cat's pajamas or meow or even bee's knees but vibrant purr of purr, rippling purrpurr.

'My buy's buy.'

'My dad's dad.' Dot's dot.

'*Un petit d'un petit,*' and Theo laughs out loud, shaking the meerschaum, dispensing sparks (no danger, no danger, they consume themselves in air, microscopic meteorites), but laughing together now, that's what counts, until deep in the old lungs Theoquake's rumbling up and taking over, Theo coughing up a storm hark hark, multiplying tears, Laurence stopping laughing, Theo keeping coughing hark hark, Laurence starting fretting, Theo subsiding rk rk, and Laurence remembering: the diseased part doesn't take the preservative as well, it stays a kind of jelly.

Just like this: two fragilities sat in a cloud, saying they loved one another out loud, all Theo's hoarseness, Laurence a *mench*, hugging, a grand pair together again: *un petit d'un petit.*

Donna, grown fond of being done for, taken care of, sat, and even made up, allows first-time cosmeticians the run of her face. She gives explicit step-by-step supervision, explaining how first this then that is to be done. Cleanser. Moisturizer. Liquid primer ('But it's *green*,' eeks Irene; 'No problem,' according to Donna, 'it's just to even out blotches'). Foundation (*née* pancake; blending it on down the neck). Blush on the cheeks (like magic or x-ray, it brings out bone structure in almost the right places, laying to rest suspicion of impersonation). On to the eyes: more foundation. Pencilling ('This,' says Irene, 'is fun') preplucked brows. Concealer to fold dark suborbital bags and stash them where no one can see (Donna, a major consumer of this product, ordered two sticks just for starters). Shadow (Donna decides to start simple, a single shade, minimal blending). Liner ('*In*side the lid?' exclaims Gretchen in dismay; 'Won't it clog ducts?' worries Irene). Mascara in something like a tiny test-tube brush Irene wouldn't want anywhere near *her* corneas. On to lips: liner (connect-the-dots, news to them). Lipstick (ah, something they think they know what to do with, paint-by-numbers). Gloss (though the stick *per se* looked plenty shiny to them). A coat of powder over all to fix the face like a charcoal drawing. *Voilà:* never has a more appropriate look for late October been achieved.

Why Donna looks so very Halloweeny is of course a pressing problem, pressing itself to a large extent the problem. Sequence is simple, but the feel of the thing is far more touchy, a matter of trial and error, the two in very nearly one-to-one correspondence. So fearful of tender tissue on lids, around eyes, all too aware and wary of implements' bristles and points, all too delicate to create the desired look of delicacy, they've made Donna into a freak. Don't let her see this: Donna, how do we delete? A run to the store for solvents and spongy expungers. Take it again *da capo*, once more with less gingerly pressure: primer, foundation, blush, yes yes, one treating her as an animate coloring book, foundation, pencil, concealer, yes yes, the other as a score to be interpreted, shadow, liner (Donna looking much better indeed the second time around, Gretchen less queasy), and halfway through mascara Irene

(defining features with a bit of flair, the spiral brush in a groove of catenary short-vowel fliplets as if Donna's eyes scanned in stanzas without a single stress, looking forward to connect-the-dots and paint-by-numbers, gloss and fixative) lets concentration lapse for just an instant.

Donna spent a good deal of adolescence in training. She trained her voice not to crack between chest and head, her eyes not to blink when brushes approached. For the latter, she had to focus on nothing particular in the middle distance, and that is what her right eye is attending to when enthused Irene flips the brush slightly off the mark, not far off but enough to reinstate the instinctual response Donna spent years getting rid of, the response that a centisecond earlier could have saved the eye from infection (for the bristles scratch tiny corneal furrows and sow there many a microscopic lash-extending pigment-bearing particle). The particles are designed to adhere and cohere and make eyelid hair look 'long, longer, longest'; though hypoallergenic with regard to external surfaces, they strike less superficial tissue as unpleasantly intrusive. And in spite of the blink response—abandoned decades since and now with teary abandon rediscovered just a blink, a lash, a hair, too late (extended lashes not curtailed brows all aflutter like swallows not gullwings)—the 'waterproof, tearproof, everythingproof' particulate matter lives up to maker's claims and stays staunchly put and proof in its putting. Irene, who put it there, now not at all tearproof herself (all abandon abandoned, retracted like lipstick into a tortoiseshell case). Like Laurence after gamba-crash or Theo-crash, 'Oh God, what have I done?'

Briskly past brisket and pastern, stiffly hunched by stifle and haunch, headed for the hock, lo the discomposed genius. This is the long one, very nearly a quarter of a thousand yards: 'A feature you could really take some pride in,' opined the realtor who emphasized it as a selling point, 'because number three here is the only honest-to-goodness par-four on personal land inside the city limits.' Such a distinction scarce tempted the great man, who took pride in other things and had never in any case seen the point of beating a dimply spheroid over the head with sticks that had absurdly quasiculinary, utensilly names (mashie, niblick, spoon).

He tries to think of his six holes as a formal garden of sorts, and has them kept linksy—ways fair, rough precise, flags cupped like so many explorers' claims on behalf of the royal family—solely for houseguests who might inscrutably choose to sweat and swear the better part of an afternoon away amidst invertebrate flightpaths under blinding, burning light. Truth to tell, this composer's no fan of the out of doors. Yet today he walks this dogleg in the noonday sun.

Dying twigs, dead leaves, odd pods clutter tee, fairway, and rough alike, autumn's spectrum differentiating greens. Well on the way to browns. Hardly worth the trouble, he muses with resignation, of finding another young man before hibernal sameness sets in, when Nature takes her own kind of care of her own vast grounds. He would have invented winter work for this one, though, tasks to occupy against the time when April brought the vegetation back. October is the cruellest month this year. Astrida has surely noticed her companion brooding for lack of that strange young man, so polite at first, so almost timid, then so suddenly explosive at luncheon. What became of his seeming deference, his relatively acceptable upbringing for all its obvious flaws? The great man had recognized this one at first sight for no musician, could see he had no feet to get on the ground, no career to take off, no chops at all, as the winds are fond of saying in their colorful vernacular. Yet, or possibly hence, he could envision him, from the first, mowing indefinitely. Something so empathically employable about this one. Astrida felt intimations, too, that first day; he could tell. And once rumors of his unique approach to the vocation had reached the great man's ears . . . well, he certainly failed to foresee this abrupt termination.

Around the carp pond—must have those specimens relocated before cold weather—he can still discern how that young man's concentric circles radiate into a sunburst of sorts whose rays on all sides transmute into elements of other figures in the grand, varied, harmonious sampler that young man—Laurence—worked into his scape. The arched hedge requires for passage a deferential bow to its incipient raggedness, as if one greeted an ambassador inadvertently discovered en déshabillé. For some reason 'mulch,' never a pleasant word and just now an unusually disturbing one, comes to mind, and the great man shudders. Mulch, mulch: was an uglier word ever coined?

'Horrid morpheme, begone.' But its hideousness reverberates. 'Wretch.'

These are the distant reaches, eleven clefs and a half from the mansion, not far from the high wrought-iron and higher, more ancient cedar limits of the property. Here the great man finds his legacy: ten by ten, untouched by blade or hand. Out here at the verge, where the traffic of unregulated lives comes back into earshot, combusted token of the unruly. The tiny conceptual square of the graph-paper maps made concrete here, left a tall weedy mystery, its proprietor pondering what need or function it might have answered or served.

Defiance merely, the thumbing of a simple-minded nose? Meaningless notation in a score to confound successive performers, icon of unfollowability? Piece of green wit amid grave forms of judgment? Standard against which to measure his other works? But the young man's—Laurence's—art was not one to imitate a thoughtless nature, brazen, random, overgrown. If it imitated nature at all, it did so by recognizing and reconstructing the sort that preemptively prefigures and instructs art itself, imitating draughtsmanlike order: geometry, the argument from design, golden-mean curve of cone or nautilus, a bringing to perfection. Not this imprecision, never this!

It teases in the intertidal zone, littering the littoral with a smattering of the myriad forms it secretes in subliminal multitudinous depths those came from, dropping at sandalled feet a handful of scallop and winkle, horseshoe and razor, housings of astonishing beauty, architecture of great dignity to hide the displeasing, helpless, unformed blobs that live within. Out there under oceanic wraps, in profounder soundings inaccessible to puny marginal sunset strollers, it displays for no imaginable observer's edification the infinite variety, the chain of being, the possible plenum. But if so, if a plenum, place must be allotted, slot open, niche assigned, to the wild, unacknowledged, illicit, unsung, the not-mown. Was that the young man's—Laurence's—point? Could their thinking be so alike?

Ten by ten, untouched. This his legacy from a man who can barely claim to transpose, whose expertise on an instrument hardly more than a century old would never brook challenge nor bear demonstration, who apprehends he cannot mow, who mows as none has mown before, a being of severe prandial ineptitude who departs without notice, refuses hefty sums, vigorously suggests they be bestowed on a cook who makes a hash even of the language: mincing dicer of vegetable and vowel matter, saucy glazer of animal and consonant matter, one whose function it is to make mere metabolic fuel palatable in a desperate and doomed attempt to mask the beastly, bestial, utilitary, and necessitous nature of all oxidation.

'I don't know the first thing about him.'

Man or beast, fish or fowl. Why such a creature should have any purchase whatever on the repeatedly celebrated imagination of Twelve Clefs' proprietor, why the great man should watch from Euterpe's Lair for his reappearance at the right, by the boxwood hedge, or the left, by the cypress grove, why behave like a seaman's wife adrift on her limited foursquare widow's walk, why at his age he must still scan an horizon; this is an obscure, an insoluble riddle. Miss Barron, whose instincts bear watching, recognized something. He saw it, too. Astrida, of course. Some useful quality, some hidden nature. Manner pieced, fissure foul.

When younger, he trusted that by this age he should understand such things. This Laurence, to take the example closest to hand, has drawn him, on land deeded to him for many a year but never surveyed till now, out here near the property line, City's right-of-way, the frontage and verge of public access, where the fellow has left him a manmade, made him a manleft, wilderness, marring eminent domain with unauthorized square of the imperfect, unsightly, unseemly, uncouth, unacceptable; of the odious, otiose, incondite, inconcinnitous; of the conspicuously repellent, revulsive, uncharted, and hideous.

'Confound him, I'll *not* have it on my property!'

Now send Donna on wobbly pins to the Oasis for immediate care. Get her diagnosed, treated, prescribed (have her asked about recent medications; have the long story told), prognosed, instructed.

Infections and inflammations of individual organs are not such very bad things in these latter days. For bacteria, surefire antibiotics; for viruses, those postmodern germs, a regimen, *modus recuperandi*, proven procedure while they run their course, that strange collective dance marathon they enter in blood and bones, no one knows why.

Aud, rightly seeing this one was bacterial, prescribed antibiotic drops and behaviors, but didn't like the look of it, and gave a referral. The D.O. couldn't squeeze Donna's eye in till two days later, and had then the gall to say, 'My stars, you're lucky. This is among the worst I've seen. A little longer and your optic nerve could eas-

ily have been involved.' She made the consequences of that painfully clear as she stared at the eye as if to memorize, for future
reference, just how bad one could look.

The specialist multiplied the standard dosage by six, a measure
of what she meant by 'bad,' but warned not to instill more than
that. She made a factor of seven or even six and a half sound
deadly. Too many drops of the steroid in particular could damage
more than a nerve. Another powerful poison in Donna's system;
how little liquid applied to one or another mucous membrane,
thought Gretchen again, could do you in.

With no upper limit on hot soaks, Donna soaked religiously,
fanatically. 'We've sent men to the moon,' she complained to
Gretchen. 'Photographed the bowels of stars. Solved so many puzzles of time and distance. You'd think by now we'd have a washcloth that stays hot for more than five minutes.'

'Like a heating pad?'

'No, this has to be moist heat. Moisture and electricity don't
mix. You hear about people dying from radios in tubs.'

'That'd be a hell of a way to go, done in by top forty, soaking in
news and weather, electrified by sports, zapped by screaming ads
for pimple cream.'

'You know how I'd like to die?'

'Not at all?'

'No, when the time comes I'd like to in a crash. Hit by lightning.
Something instantaneous, something you don't see coming. On a
Monday, I think. Shortly after making Confession.'

'I want to know about it,' disagreed Gretchen. 'I have no idea
what I'd do, but I'd want a chance to do something. Say last words,
think a final thought, poignant, enigmatic, or witty, brave or cowardly. Someone once said death makes $x\,x$, $y\,y$, $z\,z$. I'd like to see
how I'd react. I'm not sure any of us totally knows herself till she
faces it and sees how she responds.'

'Great. You'd find out too late to change.'

'It's not about changing, Donna, it's about knowing.'

Then it struck that she was talking to someone to whom this
had happened, and Gretchen felt as if she'd made an ethnic joke
in a roomful of ethnics. Donna knew, she thought, what Donna
would do, say, think, in the face of the terminal. Donna knew; was
that why she now wished someday to be struck down from behind,
while she wasn't looking?

'What was it like, Donna?'

'I can't remember everything, but in my experience it's an awful lot like vomiting, only more so.'

Add to pinwobble an ugly traumatic swelling (not just cornea but lid, conjunctiva, peripherals, all Pinckney's pet region flooded with histamine, angrily flaring, beyond injured to insulted, invaded, reactionary, petulant, swollen shut). Add antibiotics and anti-inflammatories every two hours on the hour (add Irene saying she's sorry much oftener than that), all the hot soaks in between. Add having to pry by brute force edemic lids apart a dozen times a day to insert the painful palliatives. Add Gretchen unable to look at the eye without grimacing, but wishing to distract injured Donna from the pain. Add that it's hard to read, watch TV, or do much of anything else with this bulbous lime-sized nectarine-colored so-called visual organ sprouting like a graft from this outgrown socket, macerating and cracking tenderly sympathetic bystander tissue. You'd think you'd get a Donna more than a bit under the weather, embittered, railing, Donna Inconsolata, Donna Contrafortuna. Instead, by some mysterious contrapositive rule, some counterintuitive arithmetic, you get Donna revitalized, Donna with interest.

What would Donna do with the momentum these sitters have induced? Her own orb now painfully out of the picture (and what is maquillage *sans* orb?), Donna would oversee the initiation of others. She knows, after all, a thing or two, and they so conspicuously don't, about faces. Come to consider it, she's not seen two more challenging (or promising, she quickly adds) physiognomies. They could explore together the hidden capacities, the immanent loveliness never discovered. They could learn to shape and decorate bridges and superciliary ridges, rehabilitate all-important fallen zygomatic arches.

If they're willing, of course. Are they willing?

Her sitters exchange meaningful looks. Each has a personal aversion, but hopes the other will volunteer. Each has discovered about as much immanent loveliness as she hopes to find. But perhaps, for Donna's recovery, exploit this momentum, not let this enthusiasm falter, horseback following a fall, mascara after a slip. Both soon see serendipity in the idea, the larger prospect, a way to afford their charge both pride of superior expertise and a converse appreciation of other's difficulties. If she became involved in alien skintones, in problematics (long since solved for herself, witness her brand loyalty) of aptest huemix and optimum density, might not her troubles, though more than skin-deep, disappear, alcohol evaporate like a preparatory astringent, Victor fade like a blemish, be hidden like blotches, rubbed out like wrinkles, her life fixed like powder-coated complexion?

Hence Irene and Gretchen achieve this resolve in unimpaired unison, in concert, in full harmonic and chromatic coordination: to engage the hitherto solipsizing, self-pitying, Victor-missing, and hard-to-reach Donna in mutually apelike, interpersonally chimpanzaic grooming behavior. Not to discourage or disappoint, but to make use of, her reborn interest. To evoke, under cosmetic cover, primitive pathos, displacing the primacy of her mate; to induce, by means of waxes, greases, pulverized silicates, simian sympathy.

Donna, make no mistake, knew multitudes of things regarding faces. What a resource: a virtual research library. (Not that they took an inherent interest, but as part of a conscientiously applied program of therapeutic image modification, they could lend themselves, their looks, for her benefit.) A more or less definitive periodical of femininity, and they had a subscription. All right, then, they would be her circulation, and she their charity *Bazaar,* their married *Mademoiselle* and double issue of *Seventeen,* their current *Vogue,* their entire *Cosmo,* complete course of study in gynopictology.

Willing? Are they willing? Creeps, they can hardly wait.

Scythe (long, firm oaken shaft, smaller handle branching at right angles halfway up, hardened-steel blade, all worn by long use to a smooth round solidity) in hand (pads, bones, whorls, all thin, all graceful, all tenderly accustomed to cool ivory and baton's cork bulb), the great man sets out past number three (the devil take its quarter of a thousand yards), past impervious carp (let them remain embedded in a pond-shaped block of ice), under the arch of hedge (may it close like a wound next spring and seal off this corner from human approach), to the ten feet square, the hundred square feet, of hateful growth. Ungloved hands will never withstand the friction.

Sing, scythe, your frenzy of ecstatic and thrashing relief. Wheeth! wheeth! wheeth! Your blade is sharp, and the man who wields you without experience is fortunate not to lose footing or grip and fall in your path, fortunate not to burst a vessel and expire, fortunate his blood stays put. A man of his age, unused to the out of doors, unfamiliar with sharpened edges (and the handle placed to accommodate dextrous users, blade inverted by his sinistral clutching, awkward, graceless), such a man will be fortunate to escape your song.

Wheeth! Wheeth! Is this, after all, your ambient metatonality? This, what the world holds breath for? This, the music of the universally admired and enviable? This vicious unprovoked attack on heedless growth? Manfully he strives to eliminate weeds, shouting iambs as he flails: 'Not not, not not, not not, not not, not not.' Veins balloon indigo from sensitive pink temples; beads leap like chthonic armies from a terraced and tic-marred face; a soft-boiled man in a fit of negation that will nearly cost him his life.

The plants have no idea what they did wrong. Somewhere, sometime long ago, someone decided those dying plants were noxious, unwanted, unattractive, troublesome, worthless, detrimental: weeds. Criteria lost in the undergrowth of history designate their growth perverse. Remarkable men with the softest fingers on earth show them who's boss, give them what for, shear them close to ground level, righteously annihilate them. For what reason? Could the collective human ingenuity of entire millennia not invent a reason to leave them alone, if not to cultivate them? Are these the same people who speak kindly, encouragingly, to coleus and ficus, to palm, philodendron, or fern encountered on their way to the kitchen or up the stairs to the studio?

When Astrida, alarmed at his failure to appear for Pastis at the usual time, discovers him lost and wandering, a hapless stranger among conifers, the attenuated fingers will bulge with sandtrap shapes, potato shapes, domes of nearly translucent skin torn loose from moorings by the fricative strain of denial and almost glowing with liquid their swellings contain under the late-afternoon sun. That more than anything else will sicken Astrida, to see world-famous digits, once insured to the tune of ten Belgian-franc figures, now disfigured by bullae, blains, and blebs, burgeoning wounds that won't fully heal for months but whose incipiencies he failed even to note as he whipped the long scythe convulsively back and awkwardly forth, blisters called forth from subcutaneous depths in a raw passion.

Astrida finds this behavior absolutely unaccountable. She, better than anyone else, has known that the man, so civilized, so controlled, has strong emotions. But those fingers that deserve better than Steinway, worthy of keys, hammers, strings, dampers, sounding boards of a subtlety never yet contrived—to see those fingers tortured, swollen, that skin untimely ripped, those whorls disfigured in a single afternoon. Carefully separate lashes flutter and clump. Towering hairdo seems to deflate. Capillaries distend so you can almost see her face.

'Poldchen, Poldchen.'

'Yes, yes, it's over now.'

'Please, please.'

'My dear, I am somewhat disoriented. Geographically speaking.'

'Poldchen, Poldchen.'

'Please be so good as to show me to Euterpe's Lair.'

'Yes, dear, yes, darling, oh yes!'

It's raining hard. You have to get from here to there. You prefer to arrive in the driest state practicable. Granted, drops fall more or less vertically whereas you move horizontally, but at some obtuse angle or other vectors will collaborate to determine your exact extent of wetness upon arrival. Is it total time spent in the rain, then, or number of raindrops per lateral foot, that will determine your condition? The faster you move, the more downpour per second you intersect. Should you run like the wind, encountering a greater number of drops per unit of time, or stroll calmly through, taking longer but hitting fewer drops per second and maintaining your dignity by the bye? How dry, under the circumstances, can you stay?

Laurence has a related problem. Say you're perking coffee in an old grey pot that's seen better mornings, though its little glass bulbtop is perky as ever. Your paternal forebear is allowed (on account hiss bed hot) a single cup each morning, no more for the rest of the day. He's measured the grounds; you're to supply the water. You wish, without engaging in serious subterfuge, tacitly to reduce the amount of stimulant pressuring his blood. The question is this: will adding more water (making, say, two cups and an eighth) dilute the dangerous chemical, hence conduce to greater health in the elderly man? Or will adding less water (say, a cup and seven eighths) produce a brew that, though less dilute, is less profute, less volute, hence less stimulute, less damaging to brittle arteries? Either way you make, give or take, two cups; the difference is negligible, and you're not above such a little white behavioral lie in the interest of cardiovascular attenuation. It's for his own good. Surely he'd understand, and possibly would do the same for you, were your circulation comparably problematical. But how do you know which way to deceive? On which side of two cups does longevity lie?

There must be ways of finding such things out. Intrigued as you once were by trigonometric identities and the notion of asymptosis, you should have paid better attention to the calculus. Integration and differentiation, all those summating sigmas, might have held a clue that would stand you in good stead now. But off the apex of your noodle, your impoverished cranial summit, the height of your pathetic layman's gourd: is that any way to prolong an existence?

Though her depth perception stinks, Donna can get around with a little help. What she gets around to acquire is an armload of party supplies: not disposable flatware, cups, and plates, not kegs and half-gallons and munchy junk (though there's a bag of popcorn in there somewhere), but potions and puffs, concealers, revealers, highlighters, downplayers, balancers, offsetters, and a small nastily anachronistic-looking metal apparatus that reminds both Irene and Gretchen of physical torture but that Donna identifies as a crimper to impart the characteristic curl, the fetchingly upbeat uplilt that makes a lash a lash. The inferior alternative, she explains, would entail mucilage on lids, and the very idea of that makes Gretchen queasy in the pit of her pregnancy.

So Donna will throw a sleepless slumber party, beauty bash, facial fête, gala masquerade, coming-out for unsung bone structure, matchmaking marathon for Irene's reasonably common and Gretchen's truly *beaux arts* colors. In the land of the cosmetologically blind, one-eyed Donna will reign.

'I should maybe point out,' warns timorous Irene between moisturizer and primer, 'that I have very sensitive skin,' though in light of Donna's suppurating socket maybe this doesn't bear pointing out.

'No problem, pH balanced, hypoallergenic,' says Donna, trying to wink with the normal one and causing extra pain in the swollen other. 'It'll do your sensitive skin good.'

Irene still can't believe it's green. She apprehends resembling a poplar and makes her apprehension known to the mistress of ceremonies, who begins to explain in response complexion groups, blue undertones versus orange.

'Blue? Orange? What about pink?'

'Nope, basically blue or orange. You, for instance, Irene, are spring.'

'I am spring? Hence green?'

'No, this is a primer for all seasons.'

Gretchen wants it on the record that she has no conception of what they are talking about. Donna explains the Four Seasons: summer, winter, blue; spring, fall, orange. 'I'm fall myself. You, Gretch, are sort of a variant on winter is the best I can figure. At least that's the way I'm planning to play it. Possibly summer though. Really you're unseasonal. I mean basically off the charts.'

'Uncharted.'

Derma incognita. We'll explore. You'll be an adventure,' says Donna with a shiver of anticipation. *Frissons* of differential provenance strike also the other two as Donna starts evening out their blotches with verdant goop.

At first they can't wait for the cold and sterile cream and cotton swabs of removal. They have to admit, though, she's good, she does them well. The early stages, splotch-homogenization and such, can scarcely show how good she is; but they can feel it in the hands, firm, knowing, she's in her element. And they have *prima facie* evidence that they're out of theirs, submitting to hers, which discomforts them only mentally. They have known in theory but now feel up front and *a posteriori* that any number of quite sensitive nerve endings lurk below this anatomical surface. Everyone knows about lips, required for kissing and/or telling: first base, chapter one of erogenesis, favored mucous membranes of mainstream media. But cheeky and submandibular expanses, maxillae, frontals, sphenoids and ethmoids, philtra and nareal alae, orbits and temples, inhabit, they find, a surprisingly lively and stimulable environment into which experienced fingers rubbing compounds of various consistencies can introduce extreme but very pleasing sensations. Nor, amidst intrapersonal neurophoria, is the seductive luxury of attention focused intently on one's epidermic person lost on either of them. Plus a certain civic pride in the fact that Donna, for the first time since heaven knows when (sixteen, for all Irene might guess), appears to be (left cheek bunched up in a clear suggestion of cheer despite asymmetric yoking with the monstrously inflated cracking raw and quite unsmiling catastrophe on the right) well there's simply no other word for it than happy. She appears unusually, even zeugmally, in the pink, a woman in the primer of life. Which helps her seated and catered-to sitters realize, though there might be any number of other words for how they feel, that one will do.

Donna opens wide intermittently, like a baby bird; when she does, her models pop kernels into the yawning maw. She's gobbling most of the corn, while they have to sit tight, their popcorn-processing muscles more or less immobilized; better that, they console themselves, than bourbon. Perhaps mother birds justify daily efforts similarly: as long as I put it in there, I know what they're getting, only wholesome beak-selected bugs.

She's blending wide swoops of foundation from underear to underear. In one pale case, it's not obvious where to draw the line, and Gretchen wants to know: how do you know where to stop blending?

'It's not usually so conspicuous,' allows Donna. 'It just blends in, you just know. You're a special case.'

'You said I'd be an adventure.'

'Oh, you're a regular Northwest Passage.' She opens, and Irene pops one two three inside-out kernels in.

'But I mean, I mean really, this could be a problem. If you have to blend till it looks the same, what if a person planned to wear a halter?'

'A midriff,' puts in Irene.

'A tank,' adds Gretchen.

'Or even,' appends Irene mock-ominously, 'a tube.'

'Yeah. Do you blend on down past the navel?' Gretchen and Donna both look to Irene for the next pieces of question and popcorn, but she's distracted by an unintended allusion to Laurence's inexplicable and Theo's unexpected *pipik*s, which have now popped up in her mind's eye. It's up to Donna to continue the topic, so she closes her mouth and speaks.

'You don't want it under clothing, where it just makes a mess, and you only have to think about the parts that show anyway.'

'Take a tube, then,' says Gretchen. 'Would you blend both above and below?'

'Take any revealing outfit.' Irene is back, her mind's lids shutting the images out.

'You don't wear so much when you're not wearing so much. But I don't know, Gretch, in a case like yours.'

'I have to avoid the sun anyway.'

'Well then, there you have it, that solves the problem.'

'Not theoretically,' says Irene. 'Just accidentally. What if someone with Gretchen's coloring didn't have to avoid the sun?'

'Anybody with my coloring would.'

'But what if they didn't? Would you do them in horizontal stripes, hairline to tubetop, tubebottom to shortstop?'

Donna, who always had a penchant for coloring between the lines, is losing interest in this conversation. She was having more fun just doing them up, looking forward to practical problems. But Irene has latched onto an idea. 'You could do the legs, too, shorts-bottom to sockstop, and the arms, deltoid to cuticle, and between sandal straps, in the eyes of eyelet lace. Tee hee.'

'Tip hips of breast hests for a nursing bra ha ha,' adds Gretchen, 'buns for the trapdoor whore whore in longjohns.'

Motherly, teacherly, Donna wants to resume the lesson: 'Settle down, you're getting silly.' She's at some serious work here—blending Gretchen is no snap, and jiggling hardly helps—and is a bit disturbed that her sitters take more interest in inventing extravagant exceptional cases than in getting the basics down pat. But even as she assumes her parental, pedantal role, contiguity is contagious: 'Settle down, girl hurls, this is no joking mad had adder hatter. Besides,' settling down herself, 'you're all primed and foundated. Now the real fun starts, the blush. Here comes the most amazing thing makeup can do.'

This thought serves to settle them some. The most amazing thing they've seen it do is send Donna to the Oasis and bring her back looking like a fully made-up horror-movie star. Blush means return to faces proper, and both are all too aware of what a slip in that region can entail. A mirror break to check progress further sobers and suddenly clarifies for them the term 'pancake': Irene and Gretchen resemble a couple of short stacks straight off the griddle. They sense it inside too, that flattened feeling, steamrolled, and the ensuing desire for butter and syrup, pats and dollops, compôtes.

'I've been two-dimented,' yelps Gretchen.

'Not at all,' assures Donna, 'you just got a little giddy. It's perfectly understandable.'

'No, no, not *dee, die*. I meant, I've lost my depth. I'm a tiddly-wink.'

Donna, to whom depth is imperceptible and whose ability to wink is on the blink, still doesn't follow.

'Donna, you've made me a flapjack,' explains Gretchen.

'No,' croons Donna, tentative, humoring: perhaps she is too demented after all?

'What have you done with my features, such as they were?'

'Oh, those. Not to worry, I'm giving you bones.'

Yes, thinks Irene, we're hotcakes, yet better that than waffles, though she eagerly anticipates getting bones, having structure painted in or brought out. Gretchen, always already self-conscious about translucency, can think of other components she'd prefer. Yet both see the plan is working, Donna intent to the point of distraction on others' coloring.

As Irene could have guessed from previous sittings, Donna was good at color, had color down pat and yet still took pleasure in innovation. Texture, too, she was mistress of; hadn't lost her past, and combined now the circleting subtlety of a teenage sitter and the vivid coloratura of a florid precontraltic career with the somberer tones of more recent less tuneful distress. 'I, for instance,' she explains along the way, 'have no cheekbones, none at all. I was born without this important structural feature in evidence. But there's no need to sit still for that. Sit still, Gretchen.'

She paints overtop their foundation quite convincing signs of implicit osteosubdermalities. She gives them by indirection bones, making the case for bones' existence on the basis of how light would bounce, fanbrush fabricating an argument whose inescapable conclusion would be bones, placing bones not in cheeks but in the inductive eye of any beholder, turning pancakes into fruitful crepes. These mental cheeks, these *joues d'esprit*, make Gretchen, specularly checking her spectacular new specs, feel positively Gallic. Donna, she thinks, covers pancake with *panache*, plays on cheeks as if they were words, *une jouejoueuse joyeuse.*

'My God, Donna, you have tromped *les yeux!*' approves Gretchen.

Donna, thinking in English, is offended by Gretchen's cheek. This is hard work. Lazier, indeed!

'No no, not lazy: *l'oeil, trompe l'oeil,* I mean we're optically illused.'

Donna still takes affront: she's done the best she can, Gretchen's just not used to it.

'No no, not ill-used: illused, artificed, confected, where once was nothing, an empty plain, you install facescape, skyline. Like magic. Nervy dose!'

'It's only makeup. Any woman can do it.'

'I can't, Irene can't. It's a miracle!'

'Don't blaspheme, and sit still, it's time for your eyes. They're trickier.'

Irene can feel herself lightly blush under her blush.

'I mean because you haven't eliminated your blink responses.'

Irene's blush squared, cubed, darkened by not only remorse but fear: she wants to opt out of the eye part, but feels that would be unfair, given what she's done to Donna. She further feels the miracle here inheres not in verisimilar cheeks but in Donna's transfiguration, her aspect more altered than even Gretchen's. This warrants reinforcement, but the best Irene can do at the moment is seal her lips and refrain from complaint. Gretchen can do better.

'Tromp away, tromp at will, tromp our eyes all to hell,' she urges.

It's not an easy thing: blinks keep getting in the way, and ensuing flutters leave mascara hentracks on shadowy lids. She decides to reverse the order: let lashes dry, then clean, refound, and shadow lids.

'Nor deduce?' asks Irene.

'Beg pardon,' says Donna, pencil poised by a crow's-foot.

'Nothing, Donna. Something Gretchen said.' To whom she turns.

'Eyes front, please.'

'Sorry, Donna.' She moves them back where they were, and Gretchen positions herself in their purview, thinking, Feet flat on the floor, no whispering.

'You said "nor deduce" or "near videos" or something like that. What did you mean?'

'Nervy dose. Something Laurence says, meaning out of the blue. Has to do, in his mind, with being a mother. It's Yiddish.'

That's news to Irene. She never heard her husband pronounce any Yiddish phrase your average stand-up comic wouldn't employ in mixed company. She heard *pipik*, but that was Theo; and *shivah*, she remembers with a shudder.

After a few false starts, Donna does manage to deepen Irene's sockets and enlarge the organs themselves, liltify lashes, languify lids, and suggest how the eyes of the beheld could look if only she'd refrain from that blankety-blank blinking. They all admire the handiwork, and Irene gives Gretchen a look of encouragement: it's not so bad, I hardly felt a thing, you're in good hands.

'What's being a mother have to do with out of the blue?' asks Irene, who suspects she knows already: when she got there, the cupboard was bare.

'That's the way it happens sometimes. Take for instance me. But in this case it had more to do with him.'

'Him being a mother?'

'I know it sounds *beaux arts*, but somehow it didn't at the time.'

I mean it did, but it didn't seem to matter that it did.' Gretchen explains everything from 'I'll be the mother' to 'baby haby he be he be' while Donna prepares to sink the sockets and bring the eyes compensatorily out.

'Time for drops,' she is reminded, and with some help brings out her own right one, instills a drop each of antibiotic and anti-inflammatory, then allows swollen lids to lunge shut and returns to Gretchen's.

'If you both want it, how does it get decided?' wonders Irene as if she's not a particularly interested party.

'Boyoboy, I don't know. I've been watching myself pulling back for a while now, even before our living arrangements got, you know, changed. I don't want him getting too attached, I think.'

'To you?' Irene sounds not too hopeful, given his known propensity for attachment.

'To the baby. Or to me. Ouch!'

'Sorry,' says Donna, 'but you've got to sit still.'

'Sorry. He wanted to be my coach.'

'In what sport?'

'Delivery. Actually the preferred term now is "birthing partner"; you know, nomenclature is tricky these days, especially at a place like the Oasis. But I wouldn't let him.'

'Not under any terms?'

'I told him the Oasis wouldn't let him cause he's male. That's a pretty nonnegotiable term.'

'Would they?'

'They'd let anybody I chose. They're big on enablement, empowerment, and related -ments for their expectings. Enabled me, for instance, to refuse him without taking the blame; I guess that's empowerment of a sort. Hey, maybe expectator would be a good term, halfway between expecting and spectator?'

Dots at the corners (dots, if truth be known, slightly beyond the corners, enhancing lips past denotative accuracy). Connect those dots, fill in the outline, gloss it over, take a puff to the whole she-bang. Welcome to your new face. The popcorn's gone. All made up, noplace to go.

Well. Gretchen can hardly believe how Irene has changed. Irene can't believe at all how Gretchen has. Gretchen herself can hardly fathom how Gretchen has changed. Having misgivings, suspecting mistakings, confessing misleadings. Such a bunch of practical decisions made on such a bunch of theoretical grounds. An eyeful now but strideless in Greenwich, new features before her very eyes, new sense of 'just like this,' Gretchen feels nearly nervous.

Donna's got a terry washcloth on the upper right quadrant: a soak for sore eyes. Irene considers her invented face, incorporating some of it into her everyday one; taken all in all, it's a bit more than much, but she certainly enjoys the temporary cheekbones.

'Who's your expectator, then?'

'I don't know. Boy am I not sure. Maybe nobody.'

Twelve

Caretaking instead of a fenced estate an ancient forebear whose three-day stubble he remembered from child-hood, he saw no good reason to forbear furbearing. Shaving, once such a lark, had grown galling, grackly and clawful, an irritant that put rubbing cheeks with Theo's stubble to shame; and if Theo's always incipient *soupçon* of extreme hirsutitude were any clue, his own could really be something. As Laurence long since pursued removal to what seemed at the time its logical conclusion, so now with stubble; bypassing muttonchops and goatee, he went the whole hog. Why not, after all, let it grow ear to ear?

For those with an itch to know: yes, venerable *mons pubis* as well. And though it would take a while to know for sure: no, his pubertical theory of shaving, like most algorithms that correlate body parts, was all wet. When he realized this was the case, Figures, he thought.

Speaking of which, these (composed in Theo's tub) should serve to clarify the developmental poser Laurence now came up with while trying to compare the ripest specimens of each:

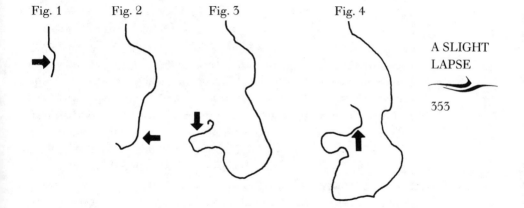

Fig. 1   Fig. 2   Fig. 3   Fig. 4

Endeavoring to replace Gillette with something more like Occam, thus pondered Laurence Paprika: Take a spot on a given hair, a molecule, an atom, a subnuclear particle, geometry's axiomatic point. Mark that spot when the hair is barely stubble (Fig. 1). Mark it again at successive moments in the strand's growth (Figs. 2, 3, 4). Compare. From fig to fig watch the spot not only move, but shift orientation. In one, it's a point of straightness; in one other, of left-turning; in a third, perhaps, of right-. Chirality aside, this raises a question. Distance from the hair's origin and source of new growth (scalp or whatever) changes continually. An inch from skin, this is a spot of rectitude; two inches, of curlification; three, of wavitude; four, of resumed straightness. And all this while successor spots push through the identical pattern: one, straight, two, curl, three, wave, four, straight, like calisthenic routines.

The question is: how do they know when to curl? How in the world can a spot of hair know how far it is from scalp? Has hair a brain? How many bytes of DNA (itself doubly helical: how does *it* know?) are required to invest dead protein with this kind of knowledge? Is this just a tremendous waste of genes, or what? Who sergeants this drill? What do they think they are doing?

(How he would have loved to share this with his dad!)

Watching Donna soaking, drawing infection out, Irene had fixated on an earlier discussion of revealing outfits. Say you wanted to learn to play golf, she figured. There would be practice greens, wouldn't there? And places where you could hit the thing as hard as you like without worrying about window glass; there would be driving ranges, right? You could go smack a bucket or two into a field, couldn't you? You bet you could. Okay, then, for balls read makeup, for window glass read eyes, for driving range read what? Well, it was plain as the nose that used to be on her face: read bodies. You could practice foundation and blending technique anywhere you had an uninterrupted stretch of flesh, right? You could practice mascara technique anyplace you had (shortish) hair, right? You'd have honest to gosh fleshtones and consistencies; and if you slipped, the brush might hit a wristbone, navel, hip instead of an eye. And that would be no big deal, safer than around the eyes, no danger of disfacement, yes? And in fact why confine yourself to suggesting cheekbones? You could imply a whole skeleton just for practice at getting the shading right, right? You could do ribs, pelvic girdles. Why, you're a walking practice area, aren't you? So's Donna, so's Gretch; we all are, aren't we?

How to propose this sort of affair to one's friends—not just a slumberless slumber party, a pajamaless pajama party—without appearing prurient? Just come right out and propose it. Gretchen's got a stride, hasn't she? Donna loves to paint, doesn't she?

'Hey, I've got an idea.'

When the phone rang, Gretchen was five or six months gone, trimestering along, headed for the home stretch. Irene was a regular Argus, all sockets from clavicles to pelvices, and Donna had something resembling bone structure all over her torso. Donna, closest to the phone, put Gretchen's pregnancy on hold and picked up.

Laurence, so relieved it wasn't Irene, almost forgot how to talk. Donna handed his voice to Gretchen and scrutinized her in profile just to remember how pregnant her friend wasn't.

'Hey hi. Yep, Donna. But how's your grandfather? Mm hm? Mm hm? Mm hm? Oh, good. Irene's here, too, you know.'

He knew.

'You'll never guess what we're doing.'

'You're right.' He wouldn't dare. Rubadubdub, three women in a loft. What would Donna, Gretchen, and Irene do?

'We're making up. No no no, not like kissing and. No no, not like a story. Like cosmetic, *Cosmo*-etiquette. We're practicing. I'm putting eyes all over Irene, she's making cheeks on Donna, and Donna, who's incredibly good at this, has got me really extremely pregnant.'

He had done quite enough of that, hadn't he? He called to check in and up and arrange for a midtown exchange of things; from the sound of it, there were some personal effects down there he couldn't have predicted. 'I've lost track, Gretchen. In fact, I never had track. Could you sort of translate what you're saying into a language?'

'See, Irene and Donna are like human sketch pads, and I,' confirming in the glass the extent of her illusory distension, 'am a virtual masterpiece of *trompe l'oeil.* I've got to be six months if I'm a day, from the front at least. Sideways, you can see I'm the same as ever. Well, not as ever, obviously, but as this morning. It's just amazing what you can do.'

Laurence knew this to be true in any number of areas of human endeavor. 'Are you saying the three of you are painting on each other's faces down there?'

'Torsos. Shoulder to hip.'

'What about your clothes?'

'What about them?'

'Buck naked?'

'Doe, actually.'

As in bread? As in re mi?

'It's nothing like what you're thinking.'

'What am I thinking?'

'Never mind what you're thinking, it's not like that. It's a pajama party without pajamas, is all. Perfectly innocent, purely nonprurific, though I have to admit suggestive: Donna's got more cheeks suggested on her than a choir of cherubs, Irene's all suggested eyes, and I'm almost as full of suggested months as a school year. I'm a regular oyster menu. I mean, Donna's really tromping the loys of physics. The rest of us are getting not bad, too, for beginners. You wouldn't believe the way light bounces.'

Laurence, feeling billiardized himself, thought maybe he would. But he was picking up cues. Clues of as much illusion phonically as, apparently, optically. She seemed mighty determined to convince him the party went swimmingly, lappingly, divingly, triple flippantly; but tucked into her tone was something off, a nip in her air, just a splash too much protest: come on in, the water's fun, wish you were here! None of them could really wish such a thing, could any? He could picture two out of three of these parties pajamaless. The party of the third part, who he had thought was recovering from attempted womanslaughter and related trauma, he'd never even met. He, for one, didn't wish he were there, but wouldn't mind understanding a little better what was going on.

Irene's voice more transaudibly showed the strain of cheerful sounding: How are you? I am fine. She hadn't Gretchen's swanny grace, did bellyflops on the phone, got water up her nose, summersalt in her throat, choked up a bit. He too. That seemed more real. Yes, it was true, she was all eyes, radiating in a spoky splay from a polyphemous navel hub. Yes, they should certainly meet. Yes, she could certainly find out from Gretchen exactly where that was and how to get there. And one more thing, Laurence. She was looking forward to seeing him again, she choked.

He too. Choking forward. Gainer. Layout position. One and a half twists.

Irene glanced at Donna, placidly soaking away again, coaxing, cajoling, tempting bacilli out of hiding. She looked less vulnerable than Gretchen, whose pregnancy, on hold for the soak, was approaching the incontrovertible stage. 'Did I ever tell you about my abortion?'

'No.'

'Well, then.' Irene settles in to narrate, arranges a lapful of eyes. Picture if you will . . .

'Wait.'

'What?'

'Laurence did.'

'He told you?'

'About your abortion.'

'Well, it wasn't really an abortion.'

'I know.'

'He told you.'

'Right.'

'That sort of takes the wind out of my sails.'

'Sorry.'

'He didn't tell me,' pipes Donna from under napped cloth.

Irene looks at Gretchen. Vice versa.

'I'd like to hear it, really,' popping out from terry. The heat and moisture make her eye look worse than ever: softer, redder, rawer, more like something never intended to be exposed to air.

'You soak.'

'I'm soaking, I'm soaking.'

Donna soaks. Irene tells. Gretchen listens, refreshes the cool cloth. Donna listens, soaks. Irene continues to tell, Donna and

Gretchen to listen. The soaking's over. Donna resumes her tromping of Gretchen's now barely credible abdomen. She's taking Gretchen to term. Irene's story is done.

'You know,' says Gretchen, 'when he told me, I wasn't sure I believed it.'

'Why, what did he tell you?'

'Nothing. I mean, the same as you just said.'

'You believe me, don't you?'

'Sure, I even believed him pretty much. It's just that, false pregnancy, you know, it's something you've heard of, but you don't think about it happening to real people.'

'Like car accidents?'

'I guess, or getting hit by lightning, addiction, debilitating disease. All those things that happen to the other guy.'

'I guess I'm the other guy.'

'Yeah, but don't feel bad. I'm the other woman.'

'Hold still,' says Donna. 'We're almost finished. Calm down.'

'That's funny, I'm the wife, but I feel like the other woman, too. Triangles are another thing that's supposed to happen to the other guy.'

'Try not to shake. We're almost there.'

'Really? Wait. I don't even hardly know how to breathe right yet.'

'Slow and easy. This part's delicate. Don't shake. Grab onto something.'

'I can't help it. I just thought of something that always happen hens.'

'To the other guy hi hi?'

'Come on, guys. Just hang on a minute. It's almost time.'

'But it tick hickles. And it's fun knee hee.'

'What hut is hit it?'

'Getting your finger stuhuck huck huck huck huck.'

'In a bo ho holing ball hall hall?'

Donna's left eye opens wide, and the liner pencil slips, an inadvertent slash across suggested gestation. Lucky it wasn't her eye hi hi.

'Shit hit hit it.'

'It's okay hey, yoo hoo can do me again hen.'

'Not that hat. It happened to me. He he.'

'What?' God, that eye looks awful.

'Victor couldn't be lee he heave it.'

Irene and Gretchen subsiding, rolling and rocking like a wake.
'We used to bo ho hole a lot hot.'

Donna's left eye is crying. Donna may be too; or, if they're lucky,
still laughing. Novice cheeks all over her torso quiver like chins on
a face.

'The thing is, it really hurt hurt hurt. But he thought it was fun
hun honey.'

This isn't. Irene and Gretchen, embarrassed, fearful, examining
the casual blue-brown wiggle that ruined her perfect nine-month
foetality. Donna's not crying or laughing anymore. Her right eye
suppurates informally, as if that were what eyes are for; her left
just blinks, looks, blinks.

'I can't help it, Irene. I just can't help it, Gretchen. I'm crazy
about him.'

'Oh, Donna, I'm so sorry.'

'It's not your fault.'

'I know. Here here.'

Donna rests an unhappy head amid Irene's eyes. Gretchen strokes
her hair like a child's, down there among the hypothetical organs.

'I just can't, I just can't, I just can't . . . I'm crazy about him,
that's all.'

Had Laurence been invited to the party, Gretchen knew he'd
have every right to say, 'Whoa. Linger just a second here. Wasn't
it you who said you didn't bring me here to lie, you who made this
big deal about being lied to over a simple thing like a saxophone,
you who clearly implied you expected both to take and dish out
truth?'

If he said so, she would be fairly stumped: ideals, big deals, raw
deals, misdeals, all jumbled up in her. Her belly, after all, had
never been notarized. Unfair, though, she'd have to admit, making Aud the heavy, impersonating a guyknob, ventrilequating their
impersons in that way. It seemed at the time so perfectly sensible,
logical and likely, to portray the Wimmin as separatist.

Besides, had Laurence been around, she'd never have con-
fessed. But if he dropped an eave and overheard, would she not
hold, as he did once, against all reason to her first false premise
and pretense? What kind of -ment did that transparent reedy gesture mean to him: enable-, empower-? She could at least, in
retrospect, appreciate his predica-.

Laurence, of course, was not there, but trying hard to adapt to Theo's worm-catching hours, early to rollaway bed in the downstairs: racked out among rackfuls of postimpressions and abstract expressions draped to appeal, doodads for the far and wide, the customers of the custom-made, destined to gratify any number of males and to please those who lived or worked with or near them, to amuse momentarily those they passed on the street. Laurence surrounded by stock, naked amid neckwear, rocking his soul in the bosom of inventory, making an earnest attempt to sleep tight but lightly enough to leap if the time signature on Theo's deep muciniferous snoring sounds shifted, if run-down heart or lung or battery introduced a change of pace, if something went wrong upstairs. Neither morbid nor anxious exactly, restful and secure as a man poised to rub wrists if need be can be. Here with Fordham traffic filtering through (that Fordham was Road, not Boulevard, Avenue, even Street, still puzzled him); here with these alien rollaway lumps under spine, kidney, buttock, and calf; here by the minirill-fought-air bubbaleh that burped, innocent as an infant, now and again; here looking straight up at what had to be two dozen feet of air, smoke-filled room almost as bluish as TV; here grateful to old ceilingmakers for pressing a pattern into the tin-sheets for anyone flat on his back who couldn't somehow manage to keep eyes shut, get shuteye; here under, on top of that, Theo's old innersprings responding to twists and turns of deep sleep, movements of rapid eye and lumbering frame; here among cacophonic early nightsounds, distant sirens, fewer horns than in daylight, passing laughter, high heels, an oath or two, internal combustion, snore rumble, spring squeak, placid eructation of inverted bottled water, his own heart and almost Theo's, beating, now beating. Ten, twelve miles tops, from the Village where love interest or interests now slept or didn't, obeyed or tromped various loy oy oys. Here where Irene so recently slept or tried to or gave up trying, the makeshift quarters of a rollaway marital sequence. Did she curl like a foetus to left and to right, examining merchandise arrayed like a neighborhood festival, then lie on her back, stare at the multiplied pattern molded in tin, alert to all sounds, beating, now beating, now beating? Or did she slumber like a log, sleep like a rock, dream like a baby, a *habeas corpus*, a dormouse, a doornail, a toenail, a *corpus delicti?* Or did she, too, have recourse, in the end, to a trick taught by Mama those years ago? Count backwards from a hundred: ninety-nine, ninety-eight, ninety-seven, ninety-six, ninety-five . . .

By the time he reached Theo's age, Laurence slept fast.

(But soft you now. Laurence and Irene in neutral territory, famous deli on West Fifty Seventh, to make the drop. The understated exchange of baggage—gladstone plus sax for pullman—would look to Officer Fitzgerald, were he staking the joint out, like a drug deal; but the deli is fairly deserted, midway between breakfast and lunch rushes, its few patrons all plainclothed.)

Yipes, he remarks when he sees her new face.

(She feels the same about his, sprouting like alfalfa on a salad, suggesting a different shape for things to come, but refrains from comment, generously puts his down to the spirit in which it was made, and explains it's all part of a course of physiognomical therapy.)

Hers? he assumes, since hers is the face in question.

No, Donna's, and she appends a brief explanation.

Well, it looks . . . nice, he observes, lamely, too late to be anything but lame. Yipes as greeting, like a pet's misbehavior, must be explained immediately or not at all.

Anyway, Hi, she says.

And he, 'Lo.

Well, in uncomfortable unison, how are they doing?

Okay, not bad. Gretchen, too. Showing now. (Though not so much as last night, before, during, after his phone call.) Pale, of course, but she guesses she's always been that.

He thought she showed before she left for Providence, he for Fordham. (Didn't someone, after all, offer a seat on the subway the day Aud flatted him at second hand, diminished his cord by hearsay?)

Well, she guesses, maybe so. But surely show show showing now, in any case. (The very thought makes her recline slightly as if to locate a new center of gravity.)

But how is *she* doing? he repeats more pointedly, making the pronoun singular by his emphasis.

Really. Okay. Really. Donna seems to be doing better, too, except for a nasty mascara infection. Her pins, that is, her central nerves, are pretty much back to normal. He should see what she's done with Gretchen's skintones.

He should? (She doesn't want to talk about herself. Why not?)
Well, yes, sure, why not? Yes. See.

No reason, he guesses.

And planning maternity things, stylish sacks for the nonce.
Really?

Yeah, sure. Why not? Baby things, too. Donna's quite talented.
Really?

Why not?

No reason, he guesses. (He doesn't remember a sewing machine in the loft. He wonders if it's old, engraved and decalled, prezig-zag, like Theo's.)

Does he know what?

No—how could he?—what?

She came to New York—needle, haystack, diagramless, cross-word—all that to find him. Ironic that she found him by going back to Providence. And another thing.

(He's waiting, you understand, for her to ask, How could he?)

Well, he knows how the Capitol dome pulls downtown Providence together at night, doesn't he, the way it's lit, bright white, and even though it's not in the center and others look taller in daylight, it feels like the center and the tallest at night, she doesn't know why?

He knows. He doesn't know why either.

Well, that's what he was like for her all this time: even though he wasn't in the center or the tallest, it seemed like.

(He waits for her to ask, therefore, how he could. This would be an apt conversational moment for that. How could he? Why doesn't she just ask?) He was? Even though he was gone?

It seemed like.

(He wishes he could honestly say the same, that she's been on his mind, its focal point, after dark. He recalls the figure atop the rotunda, perched on the dome with staff in hand, ready to with-stand anything, notwithstanding that nothing but weather ever happens up there: Independent Man, state-sponsored superhero and a kind of ego ideal for his quasi-wizened youth.

She's having a BLT club with mayo on white, hardly exploiting the deli's special talents. He ordered a corned-beef-chopped-liver combo on seeded rye with mustard, slaw, and Russian, doing as a Roman and forgetting he can't stomach red meat.)

Would she mind very much switching?

How could he forget something like that? (She wouldn't have.

She always had a conscientious sympathy for his gastrolimitations.)

He doesn't know, just nervous, he guesses.

About seeing her?

Sure, isn't she, about seeing him? (Removing B from LT now, getting toast crumbs and mayo all over his fingers.) Would she care for this B?

Thanks, but this number six—corned beef, chopped liver, mustard, slaw, Russian, rye—will be more than adequate. But all he's got is LT on white toast with mayo.

He'll be fine. Don't worry about him.

She supposes she is. He knows, nervous. She was glad to meet Theo, though. His eyebrows in particular.

He likes her, too. Her hands especially.

Oh, really? She's glad of that, too.

He almost had a stroke when he saw him. They kept him overnight to be safe, but it turned out to be more like a severe faint.

Oh, that's good.

At his age, though, any kind of loss of consciousness is cause for concern.

Of course it is, understandably.

His pins, like Donna's, pretty much back to normal now. He's been slowly realizing, though—he can't believe it's taken so long—he really came to the City to find Theo. He thought it was something else, about his birth.

(Deckchill bite.) Oh, Laurence. She's sorry she ever doubted him. Really, it was silly. Not him, doubting him. Making an issue.

Was silly?

Not for him, for her to make a federal case was.

He figures for him was too.

He does?

He guesses.

Anyway, she's sorry. She realizes now it was more important to him than her.

But that's the thing, it isn't, it really isn't. (But what will she think he's up to here? Preparing to reconcile? Ready to kiss, make up, let bygones be themselves? It's not bygones that bother him. What, then? Ongoings?) So the three of them are all living together in that loft? Kind of crowded, hey?

The two of them did. Was that crowded?

(Here it comes: How. Could. He.)

Three is a lot more than two, though, isn't it? He means, in a bathroom, in a kitchen. (He means, in a bed.)

Just one more, the least possible more. Three is okay for now. It's a temporary arrangement.

(As, apparently, was two. As, it seems, is every.)

Oh, before she forgets, she has no idea how she ended—well, not ended, because here she is returning it, but more like wound—up with this, but anyway here it is.

(It's a little wrinkled. It's been in her purse awhile. His one and only tie: boy, pony, maroon silk.)

Remember when he wore it?

Sure, yeah, of course. Hey, he was the groom, right?

He knows, she located Theo by means of it, the machine embroidery, he knows, on the back, there. (The three thrilling amphimacs.) Doesn't he just love those labels?

He sure does. (They both do. They share that love.)

It was in with her stuff. She doesn't know why it should be.

He doesn't either. (Nor, with certainty, why not.)

Well, since they never really decided to, he knows.

Separate.

Right, since that, they never really divided, he knows, their things. She means.

He knows what she means.

Does he? Really?

(They're a little north of midtown to exchange luggage—hers from Bronx, his from Village—in neutral territory, alien deli. Too-familiar things it hurt both to see and pack for the next in a string of increasingly unlikely temporary living arrangements. Does he know what she means?) Irene, he really does.

Laurence, does he know what else?

No—how could he?—what?

It's sort of good to see him. Really.

Yeah, it's okay, it really is.

Really?

Really.

(Which doesn't exactly make her a Capitol dome. He's getting mayo off his fingers, licking, wiping; she, mustard. They've pretty much finished lunch. Maybe they'll share a piece of cheesecake, that good New York kind. And a couple of those multipronged instruments.)

He's sorry things have turned out so, she knows.

Difficult?

Weird. It just sort of happened.

Never douche?

He begs her pardon?

Navel douse? He knows, out of the blue.

Noor vee doos?

Right. She didn't know he spoke Yiddish. (Save *shivah*.)

He doesn't, really. Just a few phrases he's picked up.

She saw his grandfather's *pipik*.

(That's more than he's done.)

When they were talking about his birth. Theo said his was raw in infancy: 'Ah nun phlegm asian,' he said. (Gretchen's is on its way to turning inside out, protuberating. Hers is, as ever, your average inny.) Oh, Laurence, she's sorry. She should have believed in his belly button.

Irene, don't worry about that; it's beside the point now. They're both sorry. It's what he was trying to say before. He's sorry, too.

(That good New York cheesecake has arrived. Two forks. One's tines are askew, and they run through a little after-you routine. Finally, he just grabs the damaged one.)

For jerky creep's sake, Irene, isn't she going to ask him how he could?

How he could what?

How he could what! How he could just leave her, how he could move in with, essentially, Gretchen, how he could impregnate, incontrovertibly, Gretchen.

How he could be a mother?

(He'll let that pass, though it's been on his mind.) How he could just, he doesn't know, desert her, abandon her like that!

Maybe he's forgotten: she's the one who left.

(Oh. Yeah.) Well sure, she left the house—taking, it now appears, the only tie he owns in the world—but he's the one who left the city, her ken, no forwarding address. Isn't she going to ask how he could? How could she not?

Okay, okay, she'll ask! How could he?

He doesn't know. He simply doesn't know, Irene. He hasn't got a clue.

(Maybe she shouldn't have worn her new face. Though he did his. But then he may not want what she wants: to remind them of the good things, the familiar, even the married, though that's not the basis of the case she wishes to make. Oh, how could she be so stupid as to wear this Forenza face, to make Donna fret over every detail just to confront him with something novel, when the familiar is her only hold on him?)

She's noticed, by the way, his stubble. Would he prefer not to talk about it?

No no, he's letting his face grow, that's all. A recent development. Nothing much to talk about.

(Oh, what the hell; she's got to do something to change the tone, to remind him of the familiar, the good, even the wedded.) Other things, too?

(He catches himself with a nail between his teeth. That can't be what she means.) Some. Some other things. Not nails, obviously.

(She smiles. He smiles. They're sharing a smile and, to some extent, dessert. She was right, though; LT failed to sate, and he's going to town on the cheesecake, outforking her maybe two or three to one. Somehow he's still waiting for a 'How could you!' though he knows it has come and uncathartically gone, brief shower that failed to clear the air. Instead, she cloudbursts forth in a way he was not predicting:)

'Oh, Laurence, I just don't want to be a schwa!' And she's off. On a jag.

'A what?'

'A schwa wa wa.'

Wa-wa is a mute. The name is onomatapoetry. It makes a horn go wa-wa instead of toot. Brass, not reeds; trumps up a phony wail, but Irene's is genuine.

Sniff, snuff, snuffle, sniffle, her napkin's got mustard on it, now so does her face, along with blush and the like. He offers his, adding mayo to the mess.

'I'm sorry, I'm new to this makeup business. Here, while we're at it, you've got some in your stubble.'

'I'm equally new to that. But what don't you want to be?'

Irene calming a bit: 'A schwa. Don't you remember?'

Some critical moment in the matrimonial history of them that's slipped his mind? Some unforgivable mnemonic lapse on his part? The bells are ringing for his gal, but not for him.

'It's an upside-down, backwards *e* when you spell things phonetically.' She's never admitted this to anyone.

It's starting to come back to him, an inconsequential kind of sound vowels can degenerate into. But what could this have to do with their marriage?

'They're all over the place.' Like air, like human being. In junior high, the whole language was lousy with them. 'I was appalled at how many vowels are, you know.' It hurts just to say the word. 'It doesn't sound like anything, it's just perfectly interchangeable, it has no character at all. If you couldn't spell, you wouldn't even know it was alive. It might not even be there; like if you're cold you say brr, and a nettle is a burr. That's what I don't want to be most.'

'Better than silent *e*,' he tentatively mock-consoles, wondering if she can bear to be kidded about this.

She takes again the intended spirit. She's gotten good at that, better than before. 'No, worse, it's backwards, and it's upside-down,' she pouts, whether mock- or not isn't immediately clear. She sees a pair of lips that match this description. 'Oh, I'm sorry, your napkin's all.'

'That's okay, so's your face,' and smiles her favorite smile when they were courting. They're sharing another one. 'Irene, you're no schwa.'

'I don't want to be, but I live in terror of being.'

'You'll never be a schwa in my book, Irene.' He's no good at this sort of thing. 'I'll always know you're alive, even if I can't spell,' though in fact he is, or was in sixth grade when it mattered, a champeen.

'Thank you, Laurence, that's sweet.' A definitive sniff. The jag is up. She'd better go clean herself off. She'll be right back, okay?

Is this something she came with, factory-installed, original equipment? Or inculcated early on, in the home? Has he contributed significantly to this schwaphobia? Has he somehow done this (he has to wonder while Irene works with ladies'-room water at removing substances touted as waterproof) *to* her? Or a natural development, part not of behaving like but of simply being a human being for one without albinism or unique delivery to her credit? ('Ah nun phlegm asian,' did she say? Maybe it does matter.) 'We're each given one trait to start with, like a Monopoly stake?' he seems to recall himself having thought. What has poor Irene, then, got to show? What trait beyond saying she's sorry a lot and beginning a high percentage of utterances with interjected Oh's? 'Oh, Laurence, this,' 'Oh, Laurence, that'; it gets on his nerves at this stage, though he believes he found it charming in an earlier life.

In retrospect and while she's out of the room, he can't for the life of him reckon what he meant when he loved her: 'She was good manners running sideways. She was breathlessness under a hat.' These are not sentences, these are not sentiments, that mean; these are nonsense, yes? Yet he still can feel a tingle, thinking them; something about sentence or sentiment still can touch him, regardless of orthography, orthopathy, or theory. If she's been no dome in his book, Irene's no schwa; somewhere in between.

The not-dome, not-schwa, subject of his meditation, object of his affliction, having scrubbed all the condiments and most of the other stuff off, is back. As she looks now, almost familiar, he can virtually remember what he meant. She no dome, he no puddle, she no schwa, he no linguist; yet he can almost recall the feeling. How chart these ups and downs, backs and forths, baths and forks, dopes and clowns, let alone how hair knows when to curl? Is there a word in the entire language for how the face of the love of one's former life looks?

They'll take a walk. A topic in the air. He doesn't have to mention it. 'You know,' she says, 'Gretchen's a terrific cellist.'

Musically, carefully, he's prepared to agree. Laurence hefts his instrument; how much heavier must a cello be. But not weight so much as the awkward bulk of the thing. No suitcase could counterbalance that as this gladstone this reed.

'And Donna, do you know, was the most celebrated mezzo-soprano in all of Rhode Island?'

'Prima Donna. Yes, I knew that. It is the smallest state,' he adds, not to take anything away from Donna, but in an instinctive attempt to comfort Irene.

'But see, I mean, what am I? Even Victor could fly. What, oh what, am I?'

A passing illusion: Irene as Dorothy, Irene as Judy Garland, Laurence as what, then, Toto, Tinwoodman? It only lasts a second, though. 'You're a wonderful woman, Irene. You're a long vowel, a consonant if you prefer, to me you're a regular diphthong.' He'll play Wizard if that's what's required.

'That's nice, I'm okay now, don't worry. But it is a problem I have. All these talented people. I've been feeling colorless.'

'Compared to Gretchen?' Smile, smile. 'By the way, speaking of color, I like your real face better.'

'Me, too. Yours, too.'

'The old one?'

'No, this one, the real one.'

He essays a beard-stroking gesture, pensive if not distinguished, thumb and forefinger down the sides of the jaw. It more or less works in a stubbly sort of a way, though he's left with an empty hand hanging half an inch in front of his chin. 'It'll do.'

Irene pinches his cheek affectionately, makes a little vowel sound, lightly pressing her suit. He remembers meeting Gretchen: on a bus, it'll do, in a pinch, a clinch, a cinch, ludicrous music.

'I'll tell you something about talent.'

Like Laurence, Gretchen has kind of been counting on certain questions' not being put. But doubts creep up, questions loom. She misgives.

Aud has been very supportive, a model for the caring professions, the anti-Crickenberger in Gretchen's personal eschatology. What she so resented about the Crickenberger *an sich* was a certain transitive paralysis of will, a removal of his objects' options, that habit he had of misappropriating elbow room by a professional ingratiation taken for granted until too late, an insinuous mantle of authority, that consummate bedsidling manner. In retrospect Gretchen (not alone in this) felt demeaned by this demeanor. The man, despite her Socratic dialogue with Irene, was a reptile; if you suspected someone had foisted a false Donna on you, he was the dastard who slithered to mind. He stood for everything you wouldn't stand for.

Now Audrey's difference in this respect was most instructive. She inspired in Gretchen trust, to whose indiscriminate dispensation the latter was not used. Her manner more fireside than bedside, she was chatty, easy, chairfully sharing a sense of having a lap, of being seated, not offput, overweened, or undermined. Neither pretentious nor pretending to a friendship that didn't exist, she allowed that you had what she had, lap for lap, head to head, person to person she called forth your admiration. This generally Gretchen took to be the point of the whole Oasis, most evidently exhibited in its central Poole: patient personhood, a novel notion in the wake of the dastard's powerboat style. If he hydroplaned, she rowed and paddled you, forded and portaged you, into sheltered inlets, still recesses. Aud anchored. You'd feel guilty for authorizing prevarications in her name. You had, she made you feel, a choice in the matter, a serious choice.

Gretchen begins to sense what Aud means by her -ments. You don't slip into things sidewise, you decide wisely. Though imposing, she never imposes, and so she antidotes any nervy dose, demanding just cause, not just because. You don't take what comes, come what may, okay okay sera sera.

Strolling West Fifty Seventh of an afternoon, carrying baggage (shifting hand to hand from time to time, sax for suitcase, suit for saxcase), a quondam mower attempts to allay his nominal wife's phonetic phobia. Are relevant professional associations aware of, and have they categorized, this anxious disorder? Does it show up in their *Diagnostic and Statistical Manual,* this diacritical fear of shorter than shortness, of reversal on two axes, of undifferentiated near-inaudibility? Would this be a new one on them: Embler-Paprika syndrome? Laurence administered the cure long since, though with limited and temporary success, on his mama, who, to be fair, had organic conditions as well; his knowledge of this ante-dates his first croquettic, coquettic, prophetic, and serenic Irenic dinner date. The antidote to doubt is to dote, twenty-four a day, three-sixty-some-odd a year, threescore-and-ten-odd a lifetime, a full-time soothesayer: 'I can spell you, Irene, I spell you.'

One could do that, one has done that: promise to, in, for, till (love and honor, sickness and health, richer and poorer, doubt do two part). But something soothtells him he will not. And one doesn't start down that limited-access highway without promise of a full tank, implied guarantee of threescore-and-ten; that way badness lies. And who knows if this schwazophrenia doesn't implicate him, whether he doesn't exacerbate it? And if it is talent, after all, that frets her, might he not have something to offer other than himself? An exemplum, perhaps? He could tell of one Geripold Dempler, his vast and shifting talents and their heifer doesn't dregs, the moral having to do with taking what comes. Alternatively, of one Else, her celery, her Joffrey, her Calamine, the point concerning making both the most and do. He chooses instead to interpolate for her instruction and delight a third tale:

The abortive career of Astrida Äussterschucher, concertmistress, had attained to legend in certain circles—string circles, some woodwind circles of greater than average negative capability, and most notably, journalistic circles with a feature-story bent, in whose thesaurus her name synonymized the mingled glamour and pity of 'human interest.' Touring with a splendid symphonic band in the days before widespread commercial air service and/or reasonable fare structures, in a bus with a skittish sentimental driver who swerved excessively to avoid a soggy duffel he apparently fancied was an infant abandoned on the highway, this Madame had the gothic ill luck to share her seat with a sousaphonic young man, the bell of whose mutant tuba buckled and sheared in the crash. Nasty wayward metal, lacquered pinkish-yellow and stippled with a geographical irrelevancy ('Elkhart, Indiana'), severed the violinist's totally unprepared left arm largely off. The stunned brassman could offer no greater atonement than to carry, gingerly, spreading his greatcoat for warmth, the oddly inert and barely dangling extremity into a blessedly underutilized and overstaffed emergency ward. Surprisingly artful surgeons managed to line up nerves, veins, arteries, ligaments, to situate bursate vesicles like shoulder pads. Since they couldn't turn her inside out, they had to topstitch, inadvertently translating a crucial inch of upper arm into raggedy seam-allowance. Nevertheless, their sewing was considered at the time a miracle. Regaining full, agile, concertible use after a tedious course of diligent physical therapy, she found fingers no longer could span the farthest reaches of her instrument. Her uppermost register and unparalleled career curtailed along with the arm. Recovering composure though not range, begrudging neither driver nor Sousa nor surgeons the irrecoverable inch they had somehow divided up among themselves, she launched a new career as dresser for the stage, which vocation so engaged her that she practiced daily, autohabilimentally, in the semiprivacy of Twelve Clefs. (This uplifting triumph over adversity made possible in large part by the stalwart support of a onetime pianist whose forte had itself been transposed more than once; but Laurence thought the better of making the tale hinge on romantic love.)

And the moral of the story is. That talent is not a given, but appears in response to circumstance? That what passes for talent in the third balcony is mere grotesquery up close? That carry-on luggage ought to fit securely under the seat in front of you? That you never know? Most likely something along those lines: best-laid plans ganging aglee. Laurence has interpolated himself into a corner. He knows his story has a message for Irene, but can't put his finger on it. Take, say, 'phthisis': you feel, seeing it on a page, that somewhere in there is a quite pronounceable word.

'Are you trying to tell me something?' asks Irene.

'I am, I think, but I don't know what.'

'Are you in love with her?' asks Irene out, from Laurence's perspective, of the blue.

The very thought of himself and the Oyster lady might make him hoot under any other circumstance, but he knows Irene's concern is with larger strings, baritone of the family. He feels like a wind at the corner of an old map, cheeks and lips all rounded for gusty expulsion. He looks, though he doesn't know it, like a woman learning to breathe. He knows he has vocal cords in there somewhere. He huffs a bit, puffs some, blows nothing down. He relaxes the face and just lets the lungs deflate.

'You can't say,' gathers Irene.

Laurence nods, a springheaded doll, not the modern kind that can talk.

'Because you don't know, or because you don't want to hurt me?'

This bats the head sideways. Laurence is a trinket.

'You don't know.'

Up and down. Cheap junk.

'You don't know?'

Side to side. Souvenir of Niagara Falls.

'You just don't know whether you don't know or don't want to hurt me.'

Up and down, up and down, idiotically up, intensely, inanely down.

Irene in a moral quandary now. She has information possibly relevant, data that might sway her swayheaded companion: about his posture as coach, as partner, as expectator. About his expectation. That Gretchen has fobbed off responsibility, has weaseled, has mizled. (Since an incident that prompted no little mirth among parents in her youth, Irene's *beaux arts* way, when not speaking aloud, of pronouncing 'misled'; a similar anecdote attaches to 'infrared.') That Gretchen, in short and anecdotes to one side, has lied.

Irene knows that, though not how much, Laurence wanted to coach. Knows further that, though hardly why, Gretchen saw fit to lie not only with but to him. Knows yet further that he once earnestly took, and assumes he takes earnestly still, both senses of the verb as matters of some gravity. Furthest of all, now knows that she wants not this pullman, but somehow to pull this man, back. Imagines her own pull enhanced by any weakening of Gretchen's gravid grip. Gretchen has rubbed a balloon on his hair, stuck it to his shirt; later, has handed Irene a pin; shall she prick the vulnerable vessel of his belief?

Irene understands Gretchen takes human being as encompassing without strain such behavior as she now contemplates. Understands further, though, that human being in that sense bears no relation to ethics. Cannot divorce the two in her mind. Is tempted to play this paltry ace, to bid her heart, to bridge this gap. Conscience, however, pokes her. Prospective guilt scrabbles audibly like squirrels in her mind's attic and eaves. The information was conveyed in a setting that might be considered privileged: it was girltalk. But Gretchen knew her connection to Laurence, learned that night she would see him, and did not beg her to refrain from conveying this damning datum. Yet Gretchen didn't suspect perhaps her desperate urge to deseparate (she herself failed, till she saw him again, to appreciate its strength). Still, Gretchen's not knowing that ought not to excuse a betrayal of confidence. However, all's fair in love and war, in this her personal blisskrieg. Gretchen's admitted she's been pulling back (this datum itself that pudding's proof). She owes it to Laurence (her lawfully wedded, against whom she would be barred from testifying) to allow him to know the extent to which Gretchen pulls back? Or is this just her own way of pulling him back, no generous gesture, no genuflection at the altar of truth, but a genuine flexing of sore amoral muscle? Unethical, mythical, isoproposal; there's the rub. But whom Justice of the Peace and the American Way have joined let no albino put asunder. And despite attic and eaves, she wants her lapsed gardener, wants to even the score of inequitably distributed talent. What, she ought to find out, does *he* want?

'We're pretty different.'

'You and I?'

'Gretchen and I.'

Laurence cannot think of an exception. If he could, he would take it.

'I mean, is she your type?'

My type. Now there's a useful concept, helpful for decision making. Blonde, brunette, redhead, large- or small-whatevered. Breastman. Legman. Eye, ear, nose, throatman. Nailman, etceteraman. Laurence never understood why such specialization was necessary even for physicians—that impudent pudendaman, Crickenberger, for instance—let alone for men. Once he aspired to domehood: Independentman; more recently, to momhood: Imprudentman. But once too he aspired to beat the band in bed, and now he finds sticking like glue, one way or the other, a greater problem. Like defensive drivers and public policy experts, Laurence seems as he ages to prefer the big picture. What now, then? Macroman?

'I don't think I have one. It's open to revision.'

'Movable type?'

'Heh. Or the opposite. Improvisational, no fixed font. More like a scribe than a compositor.' Quillman? Illumination-man?

'I must have been your type. You married me.' Eraserman? Liquidpaperman?

'I found you very compelling.'

'Found?'

'Find, find you. But I don't think I have a type. I'm trying to be honest.'

'There are limits, though?'

'Well, sure, I guess.' Womanman? Not-Oysterman?

'Within which we both fall?'

'Who both?'

'Us both.'

'If you want to put it that way.'

'Which way?'

'Fall.'

'I don't, but I'm not sure how else to.'

'Well, what about you?' Personwoman?

'With regard to falling?'

'No, types.'

It's possible that Irene has never in her life thought about it in just this way. 'I think I may see what you mean.'

'You do?'

'Wait.' She thinks about it in just this way, fingering fake alligator grain. He waits, fiddling with a vinyl handle.

'No, I don't.'

'You don't?'

'I don't see. I have a type. You're my type.' Arche-, proto-. Stereo-, pheno-, geno-, ante-, -writer, -cast, -script, -face.

Laurencewoman. Larry*maydel*. Lonniegal. Oh, Lala*fille*.

He doesn't feel trapped, exactly. He loves neither wisely nor too well.

'There now, see now, how could a schwa have a type?'

'A schwa is a nothing. Even a nothing has needs.' Finger, fiddle. 'You were sleeping in the living room.'

It's everywhere you look, this issue of where he was sleeping:

fucking tub, living room. His father slept in the nursery. Perhaps outlandish slumber runs in the family.

'You know why.'

'Yes.' Ah nun phlegm asian. 'But I couldn't foresee.'

'Nor could I. I needed time to think.'

'I can't see even now.'

Ex post facto. Factotum. Totem. *Tempus. Fugit.*

'Nor can I.' It's what happened in my life: exposed fact. 'But you know why.'

'Yes. Do you know what Gretchen?'

'What Gretchen what?'

'What Gretchen.' Did? Has in mind? Wants?

'What, what she what?'

'I read *Moby-Dick.*'

I only am escaped alone to tell thee. Devious-cruising Rachel. Only found another orphan. He can barely suppress a monumental sigh. It isn't bygones that concern him now. This is not about reading habits, not about finishing novels, not about the past.

'I know that's not the point anymore. I don't want credit for doing my homework. I just wanted you to know. I finished it. I didn't like it much. Actually, I hated it. But I love you, Laurence. I just wish something hadn't gone so off kilter with us. I wish. I wish.'

I wish I may, I wish I might, have the wish I wish tonight. When you wish upon a star. Makes no difference. Who you are.

'Well, I love you. That's what I mean. That's what I want to say, what I want you to know.'

Is it possible, is it even conceivable for a human being to respond in any other way? 'I love you, too, Irene.'

'And I want you to know, I'm ready if you are.'

'Irene, I don't know. I don't think.'

'Don't say that. Don't finish that sentence. Please don't. I don't mean now. I'm not asking right now. I mean ever, when, if. That's what I mean. That's what I'm saying. I mean it. When, if, ever. Now I think I'd better go.'

Irene turns, flags a cab. They put the luggage down. The cab-driver waits, holding up traffic. They hug. Horns honk. She picks up her bag.

What she what. What she what. What she what.

The D: still useful, if no longer so thrillingly tune-inspiring, for getting home, if that's what the Bronx now is or are. Sorry sax and gladstone wedged upright between thighs that once displayed aces, for security's sake though the train's not crowded. Which is safer, a full or empty train? Full, more to come to your aid, more intimidating for those who contemplate sociopathy; empty, more room for self-protective maneuvers with fewer distractions. Is this train half full or half empty? Six of one, as many of the other.

He's no good at that sort of thing. That isn't even a sort of thing. There is no sort of thing of which that is an instance. An ilkless encounter. Still, he's no good at it, no good at all. However, it went neither quite so well as he could have hoped nor quite so badly as he might have feared. Though further from feared than hoped: better than worse; hence, okay. What did he mean by that Aussterschucher story? He was trying to console, he thinks, but the moral could be, as she suspected, the survivability of loss. Imagine fearing being a linguistic term. What gets someone schwastuck in such a rut? What does that to a person?

The rattling tube an anthology: collected characters, cartoony, festoony, balloony, all but legible. Unauthorized autobiograffiti advert to transient selves among feckless drabber paid-for ads hoping against hope to get noticed. Unselected writings, unfeed free enterprising individual marks like stamps in silver, no theme but I-did-it, no message but *fecit*. The work no more than the brushed or sprayed john hancock of the maker. Mystery guests sign in please. Pleas for what? Amid alphabet strained beyond recognition, among ornamental figures—Phoenicile, Arabesque, Cyrilloid, Sanskritish, Thai'd, almost anything but Roman—Laurence seeks a common vowel, backwards, upside-down, in vain.

He's running his fingers over silk, strolling silk through his fingers, slipping the length of it back and forth between fore and middle, first one hand then the other. His tie, his Theo's tie. A little wrinkled as she pointed out, and he fancies he's smoothing it, soothing threads that have had a rough life, raw silk, been through a lot: bodies of worms, twigs of mulberries, fingers of pickers, vats of processers, untanglers and spinners (he supposes, not having made a study of the industry), weavers, dyers, pressers, cutters, sellers, buyers, a muddle of middlemen, to a grandpa at once artistic and mercantile, metamorphosed into this male doodad that went in turn through a wedding (numerous tyings and untyings preparatory to that), a misplacement, the pleasure of the company of female doodads (manmade for the most part but mimicking, mocking with silky similitude), a purse (always full to overflowing, though she never *used* to wear makeup), and all for a subway ride between these smoothing, soothing extremities. Restored now to what passes, in the absence of the originating worms, for a rightful owner. Those worms inhabit their own effluvia: whatever it takes, Laurence guesses, to get you through adolescence.

Nice of her to bring it along. Nice not to ask, till he called the question, how he could. Nice in general to refrain from challenging people with clichés, nice in particular because he obviously, honestly doesn't know how he could. Why did he do that? How could she refrain? How could he force her to expose that he hasn't a clue how he could? How clued you, who coo jew, hoo hoo kootchy kootchy kudzu? It's what happened in his life, Irene; no knowhow nohow, just that that.

The man can paint ties, you've got to give him that much. That pony: Theo can sure limn an Appaloosa (Laurence couldn't even pronounce one when given the tie in early youth to hold till the neck grew into it, more suited to that bib than this cravat, incited hilarity in kin by proclaiming, 'I dub zits applesaucer, simpery dub it'). And that boy: boy, can he ever represent a boy (this one occidentally haberdashed all over, down to embossed belt, plaid flannel, and—do you believe this?—silver brushdots on pointy-wing flaps to suggest shirtsnaps!). Such a getup. Gotup like all getout. Take, too, a gander at those fetlocks. What withers! That boyhand in that affectionate gesture on that ponymane, what a relationship is there to be seen. This is a tie with depth. It's near feeding time, you can see that. How? How could he do that? A boy and his pony, truly some eyeful of a tie. What wouldn't a person give to be able to do that? (Can Irene be right about talent? Does he too fear a schwaful fate, backwards, upside-down?)

Hey. He hasn't been noticing boys, ponies, tooled leather, pocketflaps, shirtsnaps in the Bronx. He has noticed, now that he mentions it, nothing remotely resembling anything. Has Theo the concrete, his representational and objective co-relative, gone abstract? A retrospective of his career would presumably docu- or garment the gradual growth of a personal style; but little Laurence missed the whole vast middle. How'd he get from this Wyethical Rockwellbeing to that Matissing Picassifism? How'd he proceed from start to finish, finick to startle?

Donna's home alone, casting on, purling, knitting two together, slipping a stitch, increasing, decreasing, passing a slipped stitch over, stockinetting and cabling, doing fancy stuff with wool, preparing to bind off. Booties, bib, bonnet; something for the babe, no doubt. Between rows, she sips tea. At least it looks like tea. When she visits the bathroom to heat up a washcloth, you'll take a sniff just to be sure. It isn't that you don't trust her, but you worry.

She's good, can enter into conversation without dropping a stitch. Kicklick kicklick. She looks fine now, save the still not pretty but slowly healing eye, finer than you feel by a long shot. You decide to ask her.

'Has Gretchen ever talked with you about Laurence?'

'Not a lot. Neither have you.'

'No.'

'So.'

'Do you think she wants to keep him?'

'Like a concubine, or like a stray dog?'

'Come on, Donna, this is important to me. Like a husband.'

She seems to straighten up at the word, but the needles slip no stitches. Kicklick kicklick. The raggedy gullwing over the area under repair rises an eighth of an inch. 'Less than you do, is my guess.'

'Mine, too. Where is she?'

'Rehearsal, I think.'

'She's so.' Kicklick kicklick.

'Steady? Unflappable?'

'Talented.'

'Oh.'

'You, too.'

'Me? Once. A long time ago.' Kicklicklicklick.

'Still, I think. Look at you knit. And the way you made us up.'

'These things are nothing, Irene. You know what I want. Like you want Laurence.'

'It's entirely different.'

'How, exactly?'

'He poisoned you!'

'You can call things what you want. Yours deserted you, if you want to call things by criminal names.'

'He tried to kill you!'

'I will never.' Kicklick. 'Believe.' Kicklick. 'That.'

'But.'

'But but but. I don't believe it. You can call love poison if you want. I can say Laurence poisoned you.'

'But that would be a metaphor. This was a chemical.' Metaphor, chemical, medical, semaphore. Camouflage, persiflage, badinage. Flotslick. Jetskick.

'It doesn't matter, Irene. You want one back, I want one back, nobody can understand why.'

'Gretchen might. Why I would. That was what I was asking.'

'Well, if that's what you want to know, ask her, but I can tell you one thing. If she thinks she understands, she's wrong. Nobody does or ever will. That includes you.'

That much, Irene is inclined to agree on.

Donna knits on in relative peace while Irene gets dinner started, adding a choplop to the kicklick, the whole loft percussive till Gretchen comes humming home with her melody line, mum-mum. She grabs a little leftover liver from the fridge, not enough to spoil an appetite or even conflict with humming.

Kickamummalopchick, mumlickamumlip, coppamummakick-chick, mumloppalickachop yummummum.

'Gretchen, can I talk to you?'

'Mertonly.'

'It's something serious.'

'Merry well.'

'About Laurence.'

'Maw right.'

'I'm really, you've been wonderful, I mean, the whole thing is sort of, look, I've tried to be good.'

'You are being good. We're all being good.'

'Then why are we in such a mess?'

'It's life, Irene.'

Irene doesn't believe that, and besides, Donna's ongoing stitches mock her. Kickmock mocklick, you don't understand.

'I don't think it's life, I think it's a mess. This is hard for me. I'm trying to say I want him back. Do you want him back?'

'Him back? I don't even know if I want *it,*' cross-referencing Irene's gaze to her front, where it tends to wander anyway.

'I'm not kidding, Gretchen.'

'Neither am I.'

'Don't we have to have an understanding?'

'An understanding would help, but we can't if we don't understand.'

Chopmock chewlick mocklop.

'Can't we, don't we, do you?'

'Irene, I really don't. How was your lunch?'

'That's what I'm trying to tell you. I want him back.'

'Then lunch was good. Dinner looks good, too. Lots of yumyums, good for the pressure.'

'That's what I'm talking about.'

'I mean the blood pressure. Lilies lower it. That's been proven.'

'Lilies?'

'Yumyums, garleeks, scallots, shallions, all lilies, one big family.'

Irene has a very sharp knife in hand, yumlily, kickleek.

'I almost told him you lied.'

'I never. About what?'

'About the Oasis, the rules, the expectator.' Mocklap, lipcheck.

Lippurse, necknod, pitchcatch, flipmark, pickact, hatchit: 'Very like a human being, Irene.'

Mocklop, chopslip, wha wha what too oo oo, she's sliced into the tip of a small human finger. Yumyum spot, diffusing, diluting; lilyjuice stings oo oo stings. There, just by the nail, a little reddish, radicchio.

'Ice, ice,' counsels Gretchen, and gets some from the freezer.

Pink for girls, it's like a nursery in here: ice pinkish with liverjuice, pinker with the juice of a pinked pinky, bringing out Gretchen's natural pinkness like coordinated accessories, Donna's inflammation adding to the general aura of conjunctive carnation incarnadine.

So, Donna's hot cloth drawing what's left out of her northwest facial quadrant, Irene's cold plastic baggy numbing an extremity, Gretchen overseeing wounds and checking the heft of her own lukewarm belly. 'Look,' she says, 'at the three of us, like monkeys here: knit no evil, chop no evil, hum no evil.'

Little piggies, big bad wolves.

Theo, preparing to blind-stitch up a batch of silk, wields scissors as long as his forearm, that look more like hedgeclippers and creak like an unoiled doorhinge, nreet nreet nreet, when he works them. A heavy iron (its soleplate nonstick by virtue not of bonded space-age polymer but decades of seasoning) sits on the board surrounded by presscloths, hams, forms, poised upright and emanating like a prairie dog sensing danger. Theo himself is surrounded by many an ounce of tight *peau de soie* and loose interfacing, tailor's chalks like half-used soap bars, tape measures fingered so long that they've lost graduation, commercial-size croquette-shaped spools and bite-size bobbins of what he calls 'caught in,' as if that fiber weren't also used for fabric, swatch, remnant, patch, and ort, leftover cutouts left lying all over, and everywhere pins with not angels but beads of congealed color dancing on their heads (Theo's sole surrender to modern advance, so lovely he couldn't resist; Irene liked them, too).

Laurence finds Theo intimately involved with, up to the elbows in, many a thickness of silky shimmer. Having greeted, he pulls out his boy-and-pony show, tells the sewer what he thinks of his juvenilia. 'Look what Irene restored to me. You made it when I was barely past baby. Way back when you were representational.'

'Naught sew fairy lung cargo, Lawrinse.'

'It seems long to me.'

'Off cause.'

'This tie means so much to me. How far your style has come since then. No boys, no ponies. You know what I love? These shirtsnaps. Such a touch. You know, I wore this when I was married, I mean for the wedding.'

'Divorce amen, Lawrinse.'

What manner of judgment or counsel is this? Laurence knows Theo met Irene, but can conjure no reason he'd oppose her so curtly. Because she's a *goy* (this word makes Laurence think, always, of hermaphrodeity: girl + boy), a *shikse* (and this one, always, of shaving)? Or just the inscrutable way he opposed an innocuous Mama? Besides, he can't recall Theo praying before; and what has this to do with changing style? Has Laurence construed Theo's Bronxial inflection amiss?

'Amen, ah goot men, smott, vice liken now will. In deux semaines lofty clesskill moo seek. Fa doos risen heat attentive foray chintzy cot ah clesskill cornsit. Off cozy force naught felty, so doos force naught frickfint. Bit veiny coot, event. Fawn tie me sit cinder bellic knee, in hearsay piss moo seek dot hot sew dip adept he kid vip fit simper tea. Dandy men sought inly fount dotty cornsit hole force dock. Dement ought day tine oaf delights. Bit divorce naught ink dayer, juiced bleck he sew, in eft ray file he real ices dot hiss ice fore kaput, hiss iceheight force gun, he force bleintit, Lawrinse. Fought shoe deux semaines do?'

Life-as-no-lecture-series, life-as-a-concert-series? Blinded mid-movement? What should he do? He should make a scene. He should cry out, rail, rant, rave, and in every available way rage against the dying of the light. Doubtless he will subsequently ask, Why me. On this Laurence will stake (since he has no reputation as a seer) his eyesight or, if a folktale motif is preferred, his first-born: that deux semaines will lament, keen, *daven*, and grieve; that he will experience self-pity like a slap in the face, bitterness like an herb; and when he sees that no one or nothing will say with any certainty why him, that he will surely cast recriminations like confetti, imprecations as if they grew on trees, visit with opprobrium like party favors, heap obloquy like free samples; contumely this man will dispense like a grand-opening handout to the first two thousand, aspersions like junk mail, wailing no purchase required, gnashing of teeth void where prohibited. What then?

Laurence knows that 'what then' means to Theo not 'what happened next' but 'what else.' In youth he expected that phrase to snip a ribbon, undo a pretty package of story. Later he was inexplicably pleased to learn it really taped the ends and tied the ribbon of argument, making a lovely closure: what then, opposite of then what. In this case, for instance, what else *could* he do, struck sightless in concert or anywhere else? (Music-lover or -hater, no matter: the point is, he sees he cannot see, but cannot see the point of not seeing.) What then.

'Fought den? Eyeful tally oo fought den. He villain joy.'

Villain joy? A blind man villain joy?

'Shoe air, he villain joy doos cornsit. Be cozy full be bleintit oldie wrist hiss lie if, bit doos cornsit foot heppin juiced vaunts. In cent sonic count he foot tint siena mower, deux semaines mossed fell you mower inny piss moo seek dot hot adept sew dip.'

Laurence can see the beauty of this parable, but not its application to his boy-and-pony tie. By way of illustration, Theo fetches from a drawer and spreads before Laurence's wondering eyes two dozen give or take ties, all of a similarity: all rich maroon silk, all flecked with threads of a lighter red, all adorned with something like the same tetrapartite design in an identical monochrome: substantial but decorous charcoal grey. If one-of-a-kind is his selling point, why make so many so nearly the same?

'Eye coo tint,' says Theo, 'pent.' He is trying already fa daze anent; he just can't get it riot. Not even close. (Never mind how a man who can't see clearly enough to represent determines that he hasn't represented clearly.)

But his talent so clear to the world at large: of course he can. A crisis of calling, moment of vocational doubt, dark night of the sable-hair brush? Of course he can.

No, rilly coo tint. It's not a matter of artistic temperament.

Recalcitrant medium, then? Of course he can.

No, not autistic temperapaint, acrylic, latex, nor oil nor water nor whatever base: off course again.

What, then? The score or more maroon-and-grey mass products up here look as good as those ones-of-a-kind in the shop, on sale to the public, who seem to agree—of course he can—to judge by the way they flock. They're not here just to see the door. They're not here just to drink the mineral water. He paints ties. They buy ties. Ergo, he can paint.

(Laurence doesn't understand. Oblivious to market forces, Theo has not been trying to supply a demand. Fa daze anent he trite to represent: an open book to connote an open mind, a sword broken clean in half to symbolize the mighty pen, the owl of Minerva above the book, and below the sword, vanquished, the narrow and hideous dragon Error. Theo strove, again and again, to make the tie he dared hope his subjective co-relative would don the second Thursday of the month following his decease.)

'Doos tory eye tally oof odor risen dot eye loose all sew dice-height. Lawrinse, *mine eyenickel,* my grendsin, eye go bleintit, eye hotly see, in eye font jew shoot on dares tent, bit gnaw toby opsettled. Eye villain joy dick cornsit inny fay. Fought den?'

What else? Laurence wished the two elders he loved could meet. Would Else, like Theo, remain seated for a cornsit (not, not! for the breathholding concert experience, but the breathtaking music)? Would Theo, like Else, have fount adept in Dempler's heifer doesn't moosekill nuts? Would Else like Theo, would Theo like Else? Or would each be blind to his reasons for loving the other? And would he, Laurence Paprika, sit still for what must opsettle and enervate anyone? Innerfate innyfun, innyvay, *vay is meer,* is merely, is just the injustice of just like this: nervy dose. What else but just like this, what reason but never any? Theo loses sight and Laurence doesn't.

Theo can't see to paint, but Laurence feels he can. 'I'll be the mother,' with the help of Gretchen, Else, and a modicum of sense, now appears a flawed prognosis at best; dare he volunteer again, repeat or balance his rash and suspect promise with another: 'I'll be the painter'? This time he at least possesses the appropriate organs.

Whatever else, while memory holds a seat in his distracted brain, Laurence fill rim ember: just like this: divorce amen.

Thirteen

In the beginning he wants to know the word, the name of what they do.

'*Ash nigh dare,*' obliges Theo.

Shneider: (lit.) cutter, one who snips, litters a room with snippets; (fig.) tailor, one who sews, figures how to put them together again. Emeritus Theo will teach ties, a garmentor, and Laurence will tail along. Though still just a painter's apprentice, he watches, pays attention, takes an interest. Next he wants to know what is tie.

'Attires *ash nips.*'

A snips sounds like cutting again. Tietailor, then, would be snipcutter, a snipper's snipper, cutter squared, cutter raised to the power of cutting.

'Naught snips: *shnips, ah shnips.*'

Shnips, 'shn' as in shnapps. Laurence, who began life as Pendentman, who aspired to Independentmanhood, now will be Tieman, Tailorman, Tietailor: *Shnipsmench, Shneidermench, Shnipsshneider.*

For now, though, he's more than satisfied being the painter, stage two of a two-stage division of labor (though Theo sews so fast the limnless cravats mount up in stacks around the room, oodles of doodads, heaps of *shnips*es). As long as he doesn't know how to run the business or even manufact its product, Theo, he fancies, is safe. Because Laurence now understands very clearly that Theo, during this lifetime, will teach him the trade. Ergo, Theo & Limited Grandson's Ties. Ignorance, within reason, is bliss.

Imagine being a real one, though, expert at suits (two-piece, three-piece, business, leisure), shirts (dress, casual, sport), skirts (A-line, wraparound, gored), blouses (middy, boatneck, ruffled), jackets (lined and un-), trousers (pleated and cuffed, un- and un-), sleeves raglan, sleeves set-in, sleeves balloon, pockets patch, pockets inset, handkerchiefs, neckerchiefs, sashes, plackets and gussets, tucks and darts, gathers and shirrs, inseams and outseams, allowances and bindings, topstitch, closestitch, blindstitch, whipstitch, staystitch, hemstitch and hawstitch; not to mention invisible mends, alterations, fittings.

Not for Laurence this broad expertise. A specialist, he, this singular doodad all his study. Fawn tink, bit fell, he believes he recalls his garmentor saying many a year ago. Surely he can master the simple snips and stitches of *shnipsshneider*ing.

Little does he know how much he needs to know. Seams? Nay, he knows not seams. He's noticed by now, of course, that a tie is no piece of cloth, but half a dozen, none of which looks much like the finished item. He has an inkling about interfacings—can see the loose-woven not-silk lying around—but none about facings. Graph-paper maps aside, he has never really given much thought to pieced construction, how much you do to hide what you do from the beholder. How out of his mind have been, all his life, these out-of-sight procedures. When he thinks about it (it won't be long now, he already paints, watches, takes an interest), when he starts turning clothes inside out and examining, it will strike him as suddenly self-evident that seams are unseen for the most part, that any stitch in sight represents nine, that to make a thing right entails pieces that strike the untrained eye as extraneous.

Things real *shneiders* don't pay attention to distract him. His favorite part of any piece of fabric is a part he's never seen in a finished product. He asks Theo what it is, that different weave, that decorative edge, that not so silky verge on every bolt. 'Dot?' Theo replies. 'Dots tea selfitch.'

'Selfitch. Self *itch?*'

'Age, self *age.*'

Self *edge,* of course, and what is the self edge for, aside from
affording joy to the untutored? (Like Irene's, which he shares, at
machine-embroidered tags, lovely luxuries some needlessly
delightful technology achieves. Like his innocent early subway joy,
till one ride too many convinced him, like all the others, that
impatience, long-suffering resignation, bare toleration, were more
appropriate.)

'Kips fin revel ink dick lot. Fendy endy bolt clot coot revel, dot
fill be mech inca prop limb fish nigh dares.'

This much, ignorant Laurence can understand: self edges to
fend off the dangers of revelry. Like thimble dimples to cradle
needle's eyes, this form has function, is a better mousetrap. Yet
this surplus of attraction beyond utility, this superfluity of ornamental appeal in something no non*shneider* will ever see, gives
him happy pause; less pretty edgings could have done the job.

Theo, who's taken them for granted lo these many decades, now
sees with new eyes, finds his grandson's preoccupation with selvages something of a revelation. Old dog learns new tricks; young
pup, ancient trade.

Close to a month since Irene's knock knock, Theo has a query
for little Laurence, who nursed him through the shock of seeing
his grandson and has lately been practicing brush technique on
bolts of rayon, close enough in texture but softer on the purse than
silk ('Loose air, loose air,' is Theo's refrain, for Laurence grips the
brush as if for dear life). For amen who villain joy, he poses his
question with unexpected, almost fearsome earnestness: 'Coot jew
calm?'

Laurence is washing dishes, paper-thin knives, plates with
chipped edges where porous clay retains complicated stains, pots
and pans like freehand sketches, blobby, irregular, loose air. 'Plisse
kin sit air calm ink. Fa me doos foot be imp haught hint.'

Kinsitter Laurence considers Theo's pressure: how important?
Dangerous to calm? Dangerous not to calm? He's starting now to
trust a little Theo's sense of things, the wisdom of brows and pipes,
skillets older than himself, the idea that grandfather may know
best what's good for him.

'Yes, of course I'll come.'

Laurence has never known exactly what Paideia is, but vaguely
imagines a reading group, whose members peruse on their own,

say, *A Tale of Two Cities*, then gather for symbols and deep hidden meanings. Or a friendly forum for gossip—How's the wife and kids, the grandkids, greatgrandkids-in-law?—like a high-school reunion of menstrual rather than decadent periodicity. He doesn't know they spend their time defining important concepts useful for people to understand (with all due respect to Matthew Pelff) in life.

Theo alerts him beforehand to certain patterns, moments to watch for. Blender's bombastic boasts about medical-instrument design. Flinchmesser's habitually grand opening: 'In lie if . . .' Pelff's endless complaints about same: 'Esso post *fought*, Benchmen? In debt? In deft ally if? Out off lie if?' Filling the bubbler with shnapps, setting out jellyjars, Theo hints that something is afoot: Pelff chose this month's topic with Flinchmesser in mind. Everyone can't wait to see.

'Fee half ah spatial guess tiff elk him,' announces Theo super-fluously (if iceheight isn't what it once was, these gentlemen still know a stranger when they see one), and presents to assembled sippers and puffers '*mine einikel*, my buy's buy (he shoe traced in piss),' little Lawrinse Papyrushchkarika.

Assembled Paideians applaud more than politely, using resultant racket to muffle certain sounds they prefer, if possible, not to be heard making. Sole Pup claps, too, but without enthusiasm, simple smacks of palm on palm. Pup, who inherited his folding chair from pop and pop's pop before him, who must have a good ten years on this buy's buy and values his hitherto unique status, already resents this intruder from out of the blue. Some potential Paideian this is, who refuses shnapps when all else indulge, disregarding in certain cases doctors' strict orders (unsure what's in store and still faintly ruing dodecaclefic white burgundy, Laurence stands fast, relenting only after extended cajolery). Pup wishes recognition for a point of personal privilege: he'd like to know where newcomer dwells, what he does. (Pup trusts the alien lives far off; makes his own living in futures, knows the old man lives on batteries, storebought pace. If Theo should God forbid, would this less than pup, this puppy, pupa, leapfrog over all—not only elders but himself, Paideia's future—instantly elevated to host and preside?)

Laurence's tongue is tied, or the opposite: a shoelace in a closet, flaccid, functionless. It's hard on him to have to say where he lives, harder yet what he does. He understands these are not difficult questions for most grown men, but wants to do grandpa proud, imagines these more-than-grown men suspect he's a bum. Lives, he finally says, for the moment, here. Does, for the moment, nothing to write home about (inaccurate to claim he paints ties who sketches on mere rayon, has yet to touch sable to silk: Theo's Ties & Grandson, Inc., an aspiration, perhaps, but not yet fact). Has recently relinquished, it occurs to him to add, a position in agricultural management, looks forward to a career move involving a change of field.

A bum, thinks Pup, no future.

'Velden,' suggests Matthew Pelff, eager to start on the topic he proposed, 'lattice tot dead as cushion. Fought hiss debt?'

That a chiefly octogenarian bunch takes an interest is hardly surprising. But no private or communal curiosity, no need to know, guided Matthew's choice: 'Ah deafknish infant debt,' he reasoned with pride, 'hiss naught paw sybil beck inn ink fit defrays "In lie if."' All but Ben have looked forward to watching the wry strategy (even Laurence grasps it instantly) played out on the rotating floor. Poor Ben, his ingrained phrasing less conspicuous to himself than others, has concentrated on content in rehearsing remarks and believes he has reasonable thoughts to share on the subject of what death is. Self-satisfied, he subvocalizes—*In lie if*—as if a more original opening couldn't be imagined. He sits on the edge, as he generally does, of his folding wooden chair and, as he generally doesn't, of a wicked rhetorical trap.

Laurence tunes ears like a scanner, awaits the fateful phrase, monitoring calls, police, fire, ambulance, nine one one: *in life.* He fancies the ellipse leans now toward Flinchmesser, now back toward Pelff, tautly stretched twixt two eccentric foci: Benjamin, Matthew, Mathamin, Benjew. The crowd going wild as an innocent thinker stumbles into a deadly trap. Pelff too much for him this time. Outwitted, outsmarted, smarting, unwitting, deridden and mocked, fingers jabbing, gums exposing, ritual ostracizing. Children could be so cruel: born, pendant, seven, three, oh Lonnie, oh Lala, no liar, in lie if. Benjamin clutching sternum in a gesture familiar from film, theatrically gasping for air, for respect, for respiration, loosen his tie, his collar, loose air, no kidding, no joke. Benjamin Flinchmesser, somebody's grandpa, flat on the floor, frothing by the bubbler, stricken, struck down for superfluous phrasing. 'Mine gut, eye half kilt Benchmen,' yelps a devastated Matthew, 'Benchmen mine frent. Dizzies dot debt dot fee half bin disco sink essiffit forceps trekked in naught ah conk writ tree ellity.' Pelff himself will atone in eulogy, elegy, apology: 'Benchmen, in lie if, force amen dot dit no bawdy inny hom . . .'

Thus mushrooms in Laurence the nightmare vision of death by derision while elders stifle coughs and fill the air with blue anticipatory smoke. In point of contrasting fact, the meeting is not unlike an elliptical subway car. Despite pressing invitation and overtly gracious introduction, he feels undercover. This vague sense not precisely of intrusion but of intelligence gathering he knows from trains: what one reads, how another sits, whether a third permits casual eye contact. The shifting and rumbling men could, if more synchronic, be schunkelling underground. To Laurence they are public, random (save for the uniform doodad), strange. All but one: that wrinkled old guy with magnificent brows earnestly puffing away at a baby-faced meerschaum, *shneider* of *shnips*es that circle all shnapps-sipping necks in the *shnips*-shaped shop. All but one: this curious but slightly uneasy invited guest's still somewhat wizened and lately itchy isthmus, where any number of newborn hairs emerge from an equal number of follicles to wonder continuously, 'Whither now?'

Laurence quickly recognizes the concept's first definer, who argues at length that death, above all, is that to the avoidance of which inventively redesigned surgical instruments undeniably contribute in a meaningful way.

Abe Zebevchik always starts with an undeniable premise, wide-open opening, then spelunks his way carefully into a cave of more cramped and controversial corollaries. 'Debtors dope sit off bite,' he states for the record.

Laurence, ignorant of tradition, finds this premise eminently deniable. Because if you got on a bus in Providence and got off in Manhattan, would New York be the opposite of Rhode Island? Far from it. No more than a flower grows for every drop of rain that falls. No more than emerging from a womb, making a racket, is the opposite of keeling over on a sidewalk, causing a scene (glancing left at Theo contentedly puffing through Abe's first corollary, he wishes he had chosen any other illustrative instance: say brake failure, parasite picked up in the tropics, global hostilities, earth cracking open to swallow one up, even bourbon laced with pesticide). Taking the span of a human life as frame of reference and assuming that ending opposes beginning, the conclusion Abe put forth as premise would perhaps be justified. But on what grounds is human lifespan chosen as the relevant unit of measurement?

Further, opposing beginning, perhaps, is not ending but not-beginning; opposing being, not-being, not ceasing-to-be.

People don't understand opposites, Laurence thinks; if they suppose ending opposes beginning, what do they think middle opposes, edge? But what, if not edges, are ending and beginning both? They suppose male opposes female. But ask the opposite of mother, and what can they say: father, daughter, childless woman, cellist, former wife, painter of ties? They suppose skin from a hot continent opposes that from a cold mountain range (but they don't suppose these opposites equal, for a sixteenth or thirty-second of the one, dyedrop in the bloodstream bucket, redefines fifteen or thirty-one of the other). They suppose both nature and science oppose art; both visual and quantitative, verbal; verse, prose. Continua they misconstrue, like and unlike alike, as well as contiguous overlap, gestalt. They probably think a sauce opposes pasta.

Moreover, must we not distinguish death-as-state-of-being (or, if preferred, -of-not-being) from death-as-event, as not-being-on-a-bus differs from getting-off-a-bus, as marriage must be distinguished from both wedding and divorce? Amen and Q.E.D. or, as Theo would say, *Enshine.*

By the time his undeniable premise is thus thoroughly demolished, Abe has finished presenting more questionable points, but it hardly matters. Nothing could stand on such a foundation. The guest with the itchy neck itches to speak now, fearing he'll forget his arguments when the time comes.

Laurence already understands the peculiar Paideian agony of waiting patiently through a twenty-chair floor-rotation (two hospitalized, announced at the outset, one in fair condition, the other good; if good, thought Laurence, what's he doing there?). The muted urge to respond to every offbase comment. Like a patient in a waiting room or impatient kid looking forward to birthday's annual rollaround, even more like a kid who has to go, who just can't wait, who's sorry but really has to or explode. Reading the best book in the world, thinks Laurence, aching with impeccable sentences, craving the thing's shape.

All things, believes one Paideian, look comic in prospect, tragic in retrospect. A not uninteresting notion, and though he knows it isn't true, for the sake of argument, True, true, concedes Laurence. But what of during? Isn't during what matters? Isn't during when everything happens, present the tense most worthy of the name?

'Eft ear debt,' opines Isidore Pilsick, 'beck inns any tie nill wreck impents frau rightly laybiz.'

To Laurence such language is shocking. Eternal recompense, earthly labors? Though willing to believe any number of things and no sworn enemy of myth, he increasingly fidgets at metaphysical claims. Not merely unverifiable, they tend, by his lights, toward the trite. He'd sooner listen to Moshe Blender's dicey and chopped logic. Nevertheless, he sits politely, hands folded, feet flat, as Isidore expounds on 'anentliss half unleary vortex sit ink oldies eye ears.' There's a crux, a mortal flaw, thinks Laurence. A reward that truly exceeded all desires would wipe that beatific smirk off your face; you wouldn't know how to want it this much.

If all didn't so anxiously anticipate Flinchmesser's pickle, Rudolph Furman's might have incited speculation. He who announces of each and every topic that 'Hit sly canny teen kells' could be stumped by death, which is demonstrably not like any number of other things. But Furman, foreseeing the problem, did homework on *thanatos,* and now delivers an exposition of Sick-meant Fright's analysis, in *Be Yawn Dip Lay Share Print Spill,* that Paideians find remarkable for its cogency.

Theo has seated Pelff to Flinchmesser's left this month. Since Matthew clearly has the drop, topicwise, it seemed only fair to give Ben an opportunity for refutation. But when rotating floor reaches Matthew, he's so flustered with anticipation that he mumbles some halfbaked canard about the mother of beauty and quickly yields to his esteemed colleague from the Grand Concourse: a rare event at Paideia, where opinionation and expansiveness are the rule.

Laurence has nurtured such apprehension concerning the Flinchmesser at-bat, nothing short of catastrophe could live up. On deck, he saw Benjamin preparing that innocent mouth of his, arranging oral cavity, teeth, lips, nervously adjusting the tip of his tongue and at last stepping into the box for this big inning of his: *In lie if.* Incommensurate indeed to the visitor's fears: no hardball, no fastball, no beanball conks unsuspecting Benjamin, fooled by a change-up, who catches a whiff of what's been in the air the minute he's said it. Around him, no more than the slight polite smiles of those who've just won a gentleman's bet, nothing so large after all riding on this. So civilized the crowd, so sedate the response, Laurence can't figure it for the life of him. Ignorant of Paideia's sole written rule—'Each member heard, no viewpoint ridiculed'— no way he could have known that even junk-balling Matthew, division champ, pennant winner, inwardly smirking away, furiously, ferociously, like all getout, would kindly keep mirth to himself.

Not disappointment, exactly—Laurence not so bloodthirsty as that would amount to—but a sense of something missed, anticli-max no matter what else might follow. And in general, some close relative of disappointment, he has to admit, at the whole affair. They've been around, most of them, as long as the century, through progress and pogroms and, some of them, The Camps. An awe-some amount of experience concentrated here in this room. These are the survivors. What have they learned, what little or nothing more than he do they know about this topic? Just so many things, perhaps, to be said on the issue, few or none of them very enlightening. So the floor rotates, the thoughts revolve, in well-worn elliptical orbit around an idea, but none touches the very center, pins down an unprecedented point, places his finger on the exact spot, wraps fists about death's trachea and chokes new meaning out. The thing itself, Laurence feels, escapes, eclipsed, elided, ellipsed.

'Death,' Pup purposefully proposes, 'is a word.' Gasps all around greet the nasty plot to preempt a new puppy's progenitor: Theo alone, proper purveyor of this analysis, Theo, sole proprietor of how things themselves slip from our grasp by means of the grasp itself, Doppler-effectual, red-shifty. This relativist recognition has never been heard but from Theo. This is Theo's tone, Theo's turf, Theo's tying-up of loose ends, Theo's rhetoracular insight. And now Theo's exhalations stop billowing toward the pressed-tin ceil-ing, lie in firm sedimented horizontal planes, low-lying stratus. Pup proceeds in a parody of Theotalk, poor likeness born of a two-bit impressionist, appalling and embarrassing one and all. Lau-rence can feel that something unprecedented is up, but not what: Theo's position co-opted, Theo's summation displaced, Theo yet to speak, as always, in the place of honor, last. How, then, will Theo maneuver? What, when he lowers the meerschaum and spo-ken words disperse the smokescreen, will Theo say?

He will claim that death is divan void dots naught avoid. He will argue that death is affect, anon deny bill fect. Not just *a*ffect, he will further aver, bit red air *de*fect, sauce off hour taughts in sauce off hour voids. Infect, he will avow that death is defect dot poot in tomb ocean awl odor fects in awl void stew. The original and orig-inating fact, he will insist, defect no void coot avoid.

In the sweatshops, he will continue, you could smell it, sew match dot ah pie sin het to vip: two biker lo cease, kin sum shin, sea fill less, melon new tree shin, in fie air stew. No word did that, but a terrible fact.

And worse, unthinkably, unsayably worse, in The Camps. All Paideians silent at the most solemn words they know. Itch day indic hemps day kilt sum any dot debt force ah vey off lie if. Day coal tit de Whole Cost, and there never was a more horrible fact than that.

But please understand me, Theo will urge. Eye force naught dayer, bit eye know. Sew fest pippil dite, like fast-motion movies, time-lapse photography, survey or summary of lives. Plisse, *police* on dares tent. Pippil sew dayer fought halfpence all face, every-where, every day, bit fee daunt naughty sit, we just don't see it. Day coal sexty fects off lie if, but dying is the first fact of life. Dye ink imp lice leaf ink, in leaf ink, dye ink. So Theo will argue that we should ask not what is death, but what is life. In maya pin yen, he will conclude, dot hiss debt awe peak dot mossed bead ease coast.

Each member heard. No viewpoint ridiculed.

'Hefty ma'am piss off Paideia mower day foot say, fie dare pints awn doos taw peak?'

Each member has been heard on a difficult topic. A shorter meeting than usual, only once around the ellipse. A gallon of shnapps yet remains. All Paideians silent.

'Lie coal face, den, fee dun tree sulf, fee dundy sight, fee calm to gay dare fa de pie piss tit tink, in till lease in vitreous pecked.' Theo glances at Pup in a way that may or may not be meaningful. Benjamin Flinchmesser, he announces, will select and circulate the topic for next month's meeting. 'Tilden, fee shoe tall befell. *Sei gesunt.*'

Around the ellipse, members commence the slow and in many cases not painless process of standing. 'Wait,' Pup pipes up, 'wait, please. We have yet to hear from our guest, Theo's grandson.'

'Hiss nemiss Lawrinse.'

'I would like to hear his thoughts on the subject of death. If the members have no objection,' adds self-appointed nemesis of Laurence.

'Hefty ma'am piss up check shins?'

'I hear no objections from the membership.'

Perhaps the guest would prefer not to speak. Perhaps he has not prepared remarks on this topic.

'I believe it would be a courtesy to our very special guest to allow him an opportunity to share his thoughts.'

Twoscore Paideian eyes on Laurence. This opportunity, this opportune forum.

'I don't know.'

'You don't know?' Pup all but sneers.

Twoscore eyes on Paideian Pup. What is this bullish futurist trying to do, bait the bearish guest? Velden, Laurence will take the bait.

He feels that when we speak of death it's as if we hold the sloughed-off skin of an absent snake. The snake shed this cover and moved on, into hiding. We can turn it over, letting light fall on scales in different ways. It's all we have, and there's nothing wrong with examining it, but he thinks we have to be careful not to mistake it for the snake itself.

Theo exhales high-floating cirrus, wispy as babyhair.

He thinks when we speak of death we are like astronomers who catch a bit of light from a faraway galaxy. They must remember that distance is time. The further the source, the older the light waves. The lapse is unavoidable: even light takes so much time. Astronomers have to know that they see a galaxy that may well no longer exist; that's how long it took light, the fastest thing we know, to reach them. They can't discuss that galaxy as if they knew what it looks like now; they have just now seen it, for the first time, thousands, millions of years ago.

Theo wafts cumulus, substantial and rounded.

Every day, even talking of everyday things, he hears people make strange claims. Everyone says our children deserve the best education in the world, and he thinks, if deserving means anything at all, some do and some don't. Even musicians only claim, Every *Good* Boy Deserves Fun. He hears a radio say the crime rate in one city is three hundred and forty percent less than in another city, and he thinks the former city must be a very strange place to live. He hears people say, 'I thought to myself,' and wonders privately to whom else they could. We tend to be careless, he thinks. We talk about things the way we've grown used to hearing them talked about, ways we've inherited. It's all right to talk that way, but he thinks it's a mistake to think we've said something true if we've only said something that seems like the obvious thing to say. Rhetoric, in short, trips us up. That usually doesn't matter, but when we think we are putting fingers on the truth, he thinks we usually only have what truth left behind as it slithered off somewhere else.

Once again, Laurence is shocked to hear such language. Shocked to hear himself speak at all, in fact. Last thing he knew, he was about to decline Pup's offer. Next thing he knew, he was soapboxing, stumping, giving a speech. He guesses he wanted to try and give Theo some *naches*, not to be thought a bum. But whence these solemn generalizations, whence this earnest oratory? Paideia, he supposes, will do that to a person.

'But,' Pup erupts, 'what is death? You've yet to say. What is it this rhetoric fails to grasp, in your opinion?'

'I don't know,' admits Laurence. 'That's what I've been trying to say.'

'But what do you think, what do you *think?*' Almost a singsong taunt—Lala doesn't know-oh, Lala doesn't know-oh—Pup pushing him to commit to a more vulnerable posture.

Stunned Paideians can't believe their hearing aids, fiddle frantically with dials behind ears. Theo blows dark cumulonimbus, thunderheads, threatening.

'I don't think just I don't know. I think we, no one, knows. It happens to us, as to all other life, is all I think we know. We don't know more. We know how, but that's beside the point. Why is not an intelligent question. It's what happens.' A fine flourish percolates in the mind (when in Rome, Latin; *Ich bin ein Berliner* at the Wall) and just bubbles up through the mouth like air when shnapps is tapped: *'Noor vee doos.'*

Sharp snort, quick hoot, from the Pup, and now what's this? Blank looks surround Laurence, all round the ellipse. He iterates more elocutely, *'Newer fee dues,'* only making things worse. Paideians look at one another as if he's spoken in tongues. Heads waggle, side to side. Is this possible?

What, by this unanimous synchronous lateralist quizzical locomotion, are they trying, at this late date, to indicate? Is this not idiomatic Yiddish? Has he not remembered right? Did he not, then, learn this from Theo? Infect, their puzzical befuddle contages him. Did he cut this expression from whole cloth, woolgather it out of the blue? Has some synapse gone kaflooey, inadvertently mutated, adventitiously bifurcated? Laurence a logomotive moron, idiotic not yidiomatic, idiosyncratic notyid, an autodidact, mental sport, way off base, AWOL upstairs, diametrically off, diametradonic peabrain or pineal knothead? Laurence, in short, a *goyishe cup?* (His *cup* runneth now over and through these and other possibilities in stunned and unremitting disbelief.)

'Preposterous,' pooh-poohs Pup. 'You call yourself a Paideian?' he gauntlets, pumping up, moving in for some weird kind of kill.

Laurence, abruptly self-righteous, forgets his *cup:* 'No, I do not, I most certainly don't. My grandfather, Sir, is living.'

Is livid, in fact, is smoking and is furious, severe, warning, watch, close to cloudburst and torrent perhaps.

Looks all around now far from blank: old men, perhaps, but still capable of shock and shocked by ridicule. Paideia's prime, cardinal, and only written rule, snapped in two by an importunate and a most presumptuous Pup. Indiscretion so unprecedented they have no procedure in place, neither proper channels nor predetermined punishment, no censurance policy whatsoever. All they can do is open wide, a practiceful of patients showing off periodontal accomplishment, and huff and puff at Pup, who sits astride his folding chair at the far end of the ellipse, muttering under everyone's breath: 'Him and his so-called rhetoric. Can't even speak the language.'

Practice is making somewhat less imperfect. Laurence is painting away, painting up a storm, painting a blue streak; but Theo can't brush that meeting aside.

'You met me prow tough you, Lawrinse, by fought you set. Bit oy oy, dot Paup force out off or dare, out off lion. Eye em sew dizzy pint it fit him.'

Laurence, too; not only by Pup, by elders' generally dizzy pint ink views on debt: opposite of birth, heavenly reward, reality principle *redux.* He wants to know the word for that—dizzy pint mint— and is shocked to hear there isn't one.

'Fee coot say, *entoisht,* bit dot's ah Chime-in void, naught rilly Yiddish. Dot's trench, dot fee dun half dot void in Joosh.'

Strange indeed, thinks Laurence. A language with umpteen indigenous words for confusion has none for disappointment, has to borrow one from none too neighborly neighbors. But isn't it mostly borrowed, anyway, from Hebrew, German, Polish, heaven knows what others? Isn't English like that, too, after all? Isn't Danish just English with the consonants left out? Aren't French and Italian just lowbrow (and Spanish, beetlebrowed) Latin? Was Latin even Latin, or half Greek? And Greek in turn, what was that: Mesopotamian, Tygric, Euphrasian, Indo-Continental, Babylonian? That what it's for, thinks Laurence, to babble on in. Babel, Babel, scroll and Scrabble. Some brew, ha ha: toad of newt, eye of tongue, too tough node, tote off nude. Toed tongue. New tie.

Theo conscientiously oversees his strokes, as he once oversaw Theo's that turned out to be just a world-class fainting spell. Theo trying to help the state of the art.

'Hull deep rush loose air,' coaches Theo. 'Fit lace pray share yule pent mowered alleycatly. See, Lawrinse? See? *Aught azoy. Azoy vee doos.*'

'A zoo?'

'*Azoy.*'

'What does that mean, Theo?'

'*Aught azoy? Azoy vee doos?* Dot mince deuce vey, juiced like deuce.'

Just like this. What then? Less pressure. Okay *vee doos.* They're in bee's knees.

'Human error is being cited this morning.'

Theo stops snipping, stitching, *shneider*ing *shnips*es, and listens up. Magnificent brows darken. Hair can't blush, thinks Laurence; it's a trick of the light, bouncing at altered angle.

'As the cause of a fiery midair collision of two Marine jet fighters on a training mission in a remote region of Nevada yesterday evening.'

Radio crackles staticky news. Theo bought it when the old one died for want of a tube, irreplaceable replacement part. This one, produced in a brief interim between the age of wood and that of simulated woodgrain, is honest plastic yellowed by years of latakia fumes till it resembles pine. It has a big round numbered tuning dial you actually turn, direct transfer of mechanical energy. A plain old radio well on its way to obsolescence, no fancy features to let a person snooze, doze, calculate, brew; no mystery to it but the waves.

Theo exhales a bluish wiggle composed of equal parts smoke, disdain, and resignation; it says he's been around too long to be surprised by much.

Laurence paints anxiously. Entrusted today for the first time with the fine fabric itself, *peau de soie même*, he has a serious horror of incompetence: loose air, he's been telling himself all morning, loose air. Trying his hand, just for fun he thought, at boy and pony, first tie mimicking first tie. 'What is it, what?'

'Dot Ot Lean Clay Tare force riot.'

Kids say the darnedest things? But Laurence has been painting silently, intent on the task at hand: loose grips silk *shnips*.

'Pippil awe fawn knee.'

Laurence checks instinctively his fly, still suspecting he's said or done the darnedest thing.

'Humor nay roarers pink sigh tit,' Theo ruefully parrots.

The jet fighters, the training mission, the remote region, the invisible waves. This so conspicuous neo-applesaucer, then, first faint pony *de soie*, this rudimentary *shnips* of his, is beside the point. Which is what, then? He can't see the humor of planes going down in flames. Some telltale flaw in the storied moment, loose thread in the stuff of legend? The idea of a training jet, analogy to a kid's first bike, notion of extra miniature stabilizing wingset? The way 'human error' demeans tragedy by suggesting they got what was coming to them? Don't we all, after all, get what comes to us? The word 'midair'? The very idea of Nevada? If not, what, then?

'Amen ghost vice de spit sount in crèches, in day set humor nay roar force deck hose.'

Something did sound funny about that, but what?

'Fought den,' asks rhetorical Theo, 'fought den?'

Over the river and through the Clefs, having danced his attenuated way to grandfather's house, an impressive little pilgrim in his very best vest. Thanksgiving at Theo's, he's thankful for that.

Given one's well-done nares and buds and the other's rare innards, how to cook on the old Queen Atlantic was a problem at first. What one prepared, the other could barely perceive; what other cooked, the one couldn't stomach at all. Theo's tongue required seasoned beyond all reason what his grandson's gastrointestines demanded bland. Youth's intuition—such spice could scarce be wholesome for fragile systems—versus elder's contention—hot seeds burn bad germs out of tracts. This could have taken trial, error, advice, consent, time: how long might they have together? Not enough for culinary standoffs. With shaker jars of searing substances on the table, sauce for the youth could be sauce for the elder, who would blanket it with pulverized seeds that resembled only visually the other's truncated version of their surname. Slowly learning to compromise with one who wouldn't worry anymore he might die young, Laurence agreed to the tabular presence of condiments that could tell all his hairs at once it was time to curl. And now they're cooking with gas.

Moderation in some things could be Theo's motto. For two, he argued convincingly, a turkey wouldn't pay. 'Ah chiggng,' he sneezed, 'fill heft ado,' and explained in some detail how to cajole the kosher butcher on Jerome out of his juiciest, most freshly slaughtered bird. While out, Laurence picked up a Bronx cornbread, which proved to be a rye and weighed more than the chicken itself. Plus fixings, of course: matzomeal stuffing and *shmalts*y gravy for the turkey impersonator. The oven-fried potatoes they both love equally. At Laurence's insistence, for the iceheight, a superabundance of boiled carrots. Simple salad devoid of green peppers, purple cabbage. Chickpeas Theo calls *arbus*, most suggestive of pulses, boiled then baked and ever so lightly seasoned because 'fit out ah *bissel* paper day footn't be doos deesh. Paper mex *arbus* into *nahit.*' Somewhere around here is half an old bottle of ritually fermented grapejuice that will bring sundaes to Laurence's mind. And hooray for the storebought pumpkin pie.

Theo labors to recall where he put for safekeeping ah spatial teppil clot embroidered by Molly's well-known hands. He mentions again how Irene has those hands, as if that should straighten all connubial contortions, annul and void the separation that's lasted almost as long now as the union.

But not overdone chiggng, not papered garbanzos, not stickysweet syrup passing for vine, not percentage of calories derived from fet, not even clotless teppil, no nothing could spoil for Laurence so spatial an occasion.

Laurence heaps high his festal plate, plays with his food, laughs, listens. Theo has stories he's never heard, some he was thought too young to hear. How Molly burned the prunes on the wedding night. How his father grasped already in short pants essential points of algebra, trotting home one day from P.S. 3's third grade to announce 'dot "ickfills ickfill to ickfills ickfill ickfills." Imedgin dot, Lawrinse, et yizz edge, inny nose dot. Och, ewer fa dare force ah smott fawn,' Theo *kvell*s. And such a good boy, helpful, kind to his mother. So well behaved that Molly feared him stillborn like his predecessors. The fat French midwife's risible riposte: *'Mort? Est-il mort? Mais non, votre fils a fait déjà pipi!'* Little Laurence honored to hear a punchline that still can put color in smoke-cured cheeks. Tales that mean nothing to anyone else, taken and revelled in precisely as Theo intends: classics, a family canon, treasure to him at long last descending.

More appetite in final analysis for stories than feast they took pains to prepare. 'It, it, dun chew meliate my sell it,' Theo urges.

No no, he wants Theo to know, he has only the highest respect for his salad, and the potatoes were tasty, *nahit* nice, that unfamiliar pulse just fine with his innards. Theo, who at his age eats like a bird and also prefers the chitchat, understands.

'It fought jew ken.'

'And what I can't, we'll can?'

Theo completely regaled by Laurence completing the saying. *Naches* fin *eyenickel. Un petit d'un petit.*

'I was always picky as a kid. Mama used to say that all the time.'

Sudden pall shrouds Theo. Muttered under his breath, as if she just left the room: 'Dot voomin, dot *shneer* off mayan . . .'

Laurence, too, appalled. Some nerve pinched in Theo, his own unfunny humerus hit, winces for all evinced. Even after learning *shneer*, pronounced so sneeringly, means no more than dot-in-la: Not now, not now, he temporizes, another time, not spoil spatial occasion with temporal questions: How could you? How could you feel that way? Above all, How could you. Just. Disappear.

Beat . . . now, beat. Beat . . . now, beat.

Let's clear table, brew decaf, wedge pie, oh my, in here. Let's scramble, swerve, maneuver. Near-hit, near-miss. Close call, human error.

'Well, you were certainly right about that turkey. Chicken was plenty.' Gallinule, if truth be told, would have been more than enough.

Theo evidently agrees: not now. 'Fa two, tie key foot be *tsoofeel.*'

Yes, two isn't much, it's true. No, two, Laurence recalls sadly from a talk with Gretchen in a previous life, is the very next number after one.

'Fa two, iffin ah chiggng mex *ibbegablibbennes.*'

Hibbiddy jibbiddies? Giblets at liberty?

'*Ibbegablibbenne* mince lift office. Lie cure *zayder,*' reaching up to tousle Laurence's locks, in spirits again as if nothing had happened to ruffle anyone's feathers, 'lift off air fin de lest cent cherry. Ah die know sower,' he smiles.

Theo as dino revives Laurence's spirits, too. Oldest terrestrial omnivore in Papyrushchka history. Not extinct, extant: Theodactyl, from whom evolved this Paprika who chickens out, whose evasive action avoids midair collision, who now removes bones from a clotless teppil.

'Theo, do you know that birds came from dinosaurs?'

'Eye nay fare hide dot.'

'That's what they think, from dinosaurs. Pigeons, condors, hummingbirds, jays, bald eagles, gallinules.'

'Gully new else?'

'Gallinule's a kind of bird. I think. But all of them: turkeys, chickens.'

'Day boat calm fin aches,' Theo offers in twinkly corroboration.

'Right, and modern reptiles lay eggs, too. It all makes a certain sense. The idea is, for birds, the bones got hollowed out.'

Theo smiles. Perhaps he thinks he knows how they felt.

'Isn't it amazing, though, to think? That our birds used to be dinosaurs?'

Everybody, Theo submits thoughtfully, used to be something.

And now, Laurence. Speaking of bones, leftovers, time, change, how things go, the way of the world, Theo has wishes, two in number. Because his heart depends on batteries, he wants to say them now, sipping decaf, nibbling pumpkin filling, feeling comfortable, cozy, happy with you. Not final requests choked out in a crisis, not coerced or extorted by deathbed's authority. This would not be fair to you. But a man should make his wishes known, and these are Theo's:

That you preserve the bee's knees: Theo's Ties.

That you preserve the saw sigh yeti: Paideia.

He doesn't ask you to respond. In fact, he asks you not to. He doesn't ask to know the future. He wants you to know his wishes. If something happens, you should know.

'Nothing will happen.'

No, something will happen. When it does, you should know.

'I promise.'

'Police daunt mecca prawmess. Eye daunt font prawmessiss.'

'I'll do what I can, then.'

Laurence makes a desperate stab at a smile. Theo succeeds, and does what he can to help Laurence do the same.

'In fought jew kent, feel ken.'

When they hug, the white plastic box feels more solid than the bones.

And what's cooking in the Village? What still life will we picture there, what slice? What preprandial graces, thankless or half-baked misgivings? How toughish a turkey near where Tenth meets Fourth, what fowl fare, what fixings, what sage dressing, what corny kernels or sweet potations, crania-buried, gel? What pie in what sky?

The eye is one hundred percent, lined, shadowed, lashed, and fully styled. Donna alone is enamelled, nailwise. Irene has incorporated imperfect shadow, hairline crack at the epicanthal fold, nothing else. Gretchen is unaccommodated Gretchen, simply milk-glass pinkish, whitish, bluish.

Tricky triangle of stove, fridge, sink was staked out in less than optimally efficient configuration at the time of condominimal subdivision. Elaborate coordination, inordinate collaboration required. Too many cooks stewing over too much. Someone's in the kitchen with Donna. Watch the pot boil:

'Ouch! Cheeses, watch it, will you.'

'Don't blaspheme, watch what?'

'You nearly scratched my eye out. Irene, is there blood?'

'Just a little red.'

'Excuse me for having normal fingernails.'

'Well watch where you put them, will you, in the future.'

'Well don't be spinning around without warning.'

'Well don't be flailing around with fingers like those. God, you could have been holding a knife.'

'All the more reason to watch where you're spinning.'

'All the more reason for *me?*'

'Yes *you*. Irene isn't spinning, *I'm* not spinning.'

'It's my kitchen, I'm used to spinning around in it.'

'Well excuse us for trying to help out and make this some kind of special occasion.'

Irene looks up from half-devilled eggs. 'Look. Girls. It's a cramped space.'

'It wasn't built with three in mind.'

'I just mean we all have to exercise a little consideration if we're going to.'

'What is this, eggshell? Who threw eggshell in my stuffing?'

'Shhhhh*it!*'

'What?'

'My god damned pie!'

'Don't blaspheme.'

'Blaspheme hell! My fucking pie is ruined. Couldn't one of you have said something?'

At the table, they get their feet off the ground. Blood sugars replenishing, each with her own place setting, they ask politely to please pass this and that, compliment one another's dishes, talk nice.

'They say the turkey trade has really taken off in recent years.'

'It's turkey ham, turkey sausage, turkey bologna, turkey chicken, turkey everything but turkey.'

'You know what parts they put into that?'

'I don't want to know what parts. I like it, and it's healthy.'

'Healthy. What about nitrites?'

'I don't want to know about nitrites.'

'They say avoid the skin. Chicken, too. I can see chicken, but how they expect us to eat a turkey without skin is beyond me.'

'They pump them so full of hormones and drugs, how much difference can skin make? If we're what we eat, we're doomed.'

Irene has a point to make that perhaps no one has thought of. 'You know they?'

'They who?' the others agree.

'They, they. You know, you said they say to avoid the skin, and you said what parts they put in. That they, opposed to us, that always has us in some kind of tizzy. Generic they, industrial they, institutional they, indeterminate they, editorial they, all of they. You know?'

They know.

'It just occurred to me, that's who Crickenberger is. He's they.'

'How can he be they, Irene?'

Irene, pleased with the boldness of her insight, expands: 'First, it's like he's everywhere, inciting, instigating, motivating, putting in motion, throwing off balance, casting adrift, drawing up short. He's at the heart, behind things, making them happen, remote control, everywhere. But second, nobody knows what his point is, you never find out what motivates *him*, no one's ever *seen* him, he's nowhere, who even knows if he exists. So everywhere and nowhere, purely an object of imputation and inference. He's they, unmotivated motivator of us.'

'Don't blaspheme.'

'I didn't.' Turning to Gretchen for support. 'Did I?'

'It's a neat theory, Irene, an interesting idea. There's just one problem, though.'

'Problem?' says Irene.

'Just one?' says Donna.

'Two out of three of us *have* seen him. In point of sad fact, two out of us three have done a good deal more than just see him. Right, Donna?'

'A very unfortunately great deal more. A testament to human frailty.'

'Oh yeah, whose name is woman,' says the one whose name is Irene.

'Whose proper name is frailty,' insists the one whose name is Gretchen. 'But hey, it was a neat idea. Just happened to be dead wrong is all.'

'Really wrong, I guess. I'm sorry.'

'Don't feel bad. He affects a lot of us that way.'

'What is it about this guy, then?'

'It's hard to explain. If you saw him, you'd see.'

'His looks?'

'No, I don't mean that. He's horrendously good-looking, but that's not it, that's not it at all.' Gretchen looks to Donna for some help.

'Has a way about him, I don't know. A compelling character, you know?'

Irene really doesn't, isn't sure she wants to, aware that Donna's notion of compelling characters embraces Victor. But Gretchen's, which comprehends Laurence instead, overlaps hers, could maybe help her reach an understanding.

The two of them, picking over the turkey for more attractive morsels than those already on their plates, let eyes make contact for a longish time, lock on like radar, as if understanding could transfer psychically. A couple of mentalists trying to connect, experiencing interference; you could almost draw the jaggedy arc crackling back and forth.

Donna's eyes light up under shadow, under reconstituted gullwings. 'But hey. I just remembered.'

'Remembered?'

'Remembered what?'

Thinking, a mentalist in her own right. It takes a while, like unpacking in a hotel room: where should I put this, where did I leave that, where did I get the other?

'Pinckney told me.' Donna thinks another long minute, like playing chess, on the lookout for traps, trying to figure a few moves ahead. 'The day I had my second CAT scan.'

Gretchen, *en passant*, thinks herself: Second one she was aware of. More than one way to scan a cat.

Irene in the silence remembers Laurence: What she what, what she what.

'Listen,' says Donna finally, to Gretchen, 'you won't believe this.'

'I've had a lot of practice lately. I'll give it a shot.'

'Pinckney gave me one, of I don't know what, and then he said Chris got, you really won't, *married.*'

'You're kidding. To what?'

'One of his patients.'

'That part's predictable. The whole idea is so out of character, though.'

'Out of compelling character,' puts in Irene.

'That's the thing, that's it, compulsion. That's the incredible part. It's a young girl, a teenager, some influential person's daughter, member of the board, Pinckney himself I think. That's it: Pinckney made him. A shotgun wedding.'

Gretchen erupts, spins a fork on its tines like an endangered gamba, is very merry indeed. 'Perfect!'

'Why perfect?'

'Oh, you know, shotgun wedding, Hatfield, McCoy, horse, buggy, bundling, trundle bed, masher, fresh, mustard plaster, epsom salts. Just sound hounds so outdate hate head.'

'I never understood what they were for,' says Irene, 'epsom salts.'

'Nobody does. Some extinct tincture or other, you know, sal ammoniac or some other sal.' Acious? Amander? Magundi? Monella? Utation? Vation? 'Volatile, that's it. Cupping, bleeding, trepanning, consumption, neurasthenia, bubo. From another century. Shotgun wedding. Perfect. Really. But Donna, wait, Pinckney told you all that?'

'Yes. Absolutely. I'm sure of it.'

'Well, tell me this. Why would he tell you that?'

'I don't know, that's what I can't think.'

'Wow, Chris Crick married to the boss's pubescent daughter. Shotgun. I mean reheally.'

'I can't for the life imagine.'

'Maybe that shot he gave you,' Irene, tentative, suggests.

'Yeah, maybe. Or else you know what?' She thinks. 'I think I could have dreamed it.'

'Oh, Donna, we can always count on you. *Beaux arts,* really.'

The silence is slightly awkward.

'Hey, guess what.'

Nobody can.

'Well, speaking of unexpected and big-deal changes, guess who's the newly installed Music Director of the Oasis.'

'You, Gretch?'

'Don't look so surprised. Don't you think I can handle it?'

'I'm not sure. What is it?'

'I don't know, keep up the library, program tapes for various procedures, maybe a live concert series.'

'Music to get knocked up by?'

'Or not,' tempers Gretchen, half amused, half impatient. 'Contraceptive strains, maybe.'

'Family-planning tunes? Pelvic Pressly and the Curettes. IUD Menuhin and the Fallopian Tubas.'

'Hey, how about "Back in the Stirrups Again"?'

' "Uterus Be So Nice to Come Home To." '

' "Slow Bloat to China." '

' "Cramptown Races." '

'I got the yeast infection bloohoohoos,' Donna rasps.

'Go ahead, make fun. We have a growing library of serious music.'

'Serious? Classics? Literary, too? Arranged by period, I bet. *Mothering Heights. Midolmarch. Tender Is the Site. The Lying-in in Winter.*'

'That's funny, Donna. That's enough.'

'Ovid's *Madame Orifices.* Papsmearnak's *Doctor Virago. Primiparadise Lost. À la Recherche de Tampon Perdu.*'

'Donna, enough!' Gretchen isn't kidding.

Irene's mind keeps spinning on its own like a revolving door. *Madame Ovary,* she thinks. *Moby-Clit. Great Expectators.*

'Okay, okay,' Donna yields, 'but I never heard of women writing classical music.'

'Exactly.' Gretchen's point clinched when Donna least expects it. 'Exactly.'

'Well, hey, congratulations anyway, Gretchen.'

'Right,' begrudges Donna, 'kudos.'

'Thanks, kiddoes.'

'You know what, speaking of career moves, I've worked out a plan.'

'Oh, Donna, that's wonderful.'

'You don't even know what it is yet.'

'Sorry. But I think it's wonderful that you have one.'

'Well, here it is. It's time to get back to Providence.'

'Right.'

'Good.'

'I get some kind of a job.'

'That's good, I guess.' Irene is eager to be positive.

'This is a plan?' Gretchen less so, still half smarting.

'So I get some kind of a job, that's not important, what's important is this group I'm going to form, nonprofit, to work for something, you know?'

'A cause? You, Donna?'

'Don't look so surprised. I can handle it. Like a citizens' lobby. Maybe you can help. I've been trying to come up with a good acronym.'

'Oh, I love acronyms. What do you lobby for?'

'On the state level at first, okay? Improved access.'

'To what?'

'Maximum-security detention facilities.'

'For whom?'

'For the differently abled.'

'What's that?'

'You know.'

'No, I don't.'

'She means the handicapped, fuck rice ache. She means Victor.'

'Don't blaspheme. I mean anyone the shoe fits.'

'You call them, him, "differently abled" now?'

'Yes, I do. So should you.'

'For the love of. Oh, Donna. That's crazy.'

'How do you spell "women"?'

'*Touché*, but I don't mean that part. I mean the whole freaky idea. It's mad, lunatic, it's retrograde.'

'Well, thank you, Gretchen, thank you very much,' swiping a pinky at the corner of her mascara.

'Look, I didn't mean it that way. I love you, you know that.'

'I know. I was only kidding about the songs,' softening.

'Oh, I know that, Donna. But I have to say, you are simply out of your freegagging mind.'

'Well, thank you,' hardening again, 'and we who have yet to come up with an acronym certainly appreciate your generous support.'

'It's not generosity to support someone determined to flog herself. It's mortifying.'

They share a glare loaded with a history of long-standing disagreements. Both turn for confirmation to Irene. The table is awash in dirty dishes. Greasy fingers all around, they've really done a job on the skin. Irene knows Laurence was right: three is a lot more than two.

'Couldn't you sing again, Donna?'

'My voice is shot.'

'What's wrong with it? I like it.'

'It's raspy. It cracks when I talk. Can't you hear?'

'You're just out of practice. Your cords are rusty.'

'Never mind the voice. My name is mud anyway.'

Gretchen shuts eyes and nods, remembering Verdi, collapse, press coverage in Providence. Irene looks to Donna, to Gretchen, to Donna.

'What are you, practicing for Forest Hills?'

'I heard a story, speaking of talent and women you've heard of or not.'

'What?'

'What?'

'I'm trying to change the subject and make a connection at the same time, okay? It's about career changes, too. And it's somebody you might know, Gretchen. And it's kind of heartwarming and inspiring. So I thought.'

Donna and Gretchen exchange a less loaded, more generous look. Irene, still trying to behave like a human being.

'What the hell?'

'Don't blaspheme. "Why not?" is the appropriate expression.'

'Well, this woman was like the best violinist in the world, or maybe in New York.'

'Same difference,' says Gretchen.

'Oh, right. Well, she was in a bus crash, sitting next to the sousaphone guy, and they had to sew her arm back on, but it came out shorter so she couldn't reach the high notes anymore, or maybe the low ones. Which would it be, Gretchen?'

'Depends how short. Maybe both.'

'Anyway, they told her she'd never play the violin again.'

'They?'

'The doctors, I mean. Oh, I get it: they. But instead of her life going down the drain, she became a whatchamacallit for the theater.'

'A what?'

'A clothier? A bureau?'

'Dresser?'

'Yes, right, a dresser for the theater. You could do that, Donna, I bet.'

'I haven't lost my arm.'

'But you're still a talented person. Look at your knitting.'

'There's not much call for booties in the serious theater.'

'Right, but the point is adapting, and apparently she's real famous at that now. She dresses herself like a prima donna—no offense—even around the house.'

Irene reproduces Laurence's physical description of Gretchen knows who.

'Astrida?'

'I don't know her name.'

'Astrida Äussterschucher. She lives with Dempler, where Laurence mowed.'

'That's the one.'

'That's ridiculous.'

'No, that's the one, I'm sure of it.'

'No, the whole story's absurd. Astrida was born with one arm shorter. She never played violin. You couldn't get her on a bus for love or money. And she's far too couth to ever sit next to a sousaphone.'

Shortly after Thanksgiving the calls start coming in, shaping December's prospects up. One overnight, sidewalks grew treacherous invisibly; topicpicking Flinchmesser is one of no fewer than three who fractured hips in the icy shuffle. One has just been admitted for a condition unrelated to climate; another remains hospitalized from last month, still fair, a source of concern. Two have been called to the bedsides of ailing elderly children unhappily diagnosed. So frail, thinks Laurence, so fragile.

Truth to tell, neither *shneider* is much disturbed by the cancellation. Not an unprecedented turn of events, Theo notes, in slipperier months. Laurence suspects he's still somewhat opsettled by undecorum, not perhaps looking eagerly forward to hosting that dizzy pint ink Pup again. With Laurence, a Paideia-free month is more or less peachy. He vaguely dreads the gathering: its sounds and smells, its extensive phraseological rhythms and bass catarrhs reminiscent of One or D. Pup's motiveless malignity offputting, of course, but more surprising the offthrowing effect of a shopful of uniform necks, membership badges, men showing the flag.

Perhaps they had a rule against inviting the same guest twice. He imagines helping to set up humidors, jellyjars, bubbler, then retreating to set himself up upstairs. His mind would stray from brush technique to all that loose hot air ellipsulating under him. Trying hard to achieve auto-inconspicuation, eliminate every superfluous sound. Trying harder still not to listen in, straining to underhear, striving like crazy to keep a grip on eaves, cringing, while elders wise and foolish, predictable and un-, pore over some topic Flinchmesser chose: *in life.*

Laurence knows what topic he himself would choose or, flinching, avoid. He thinks he starts to fathom how whatever brings jets to earth—bird in engine, mechanical failure, wind shear, vulnerable design, loose rivet, failure to take atmosphere into account—can be seen as a function of human error. Theo's perspective, longer even than the century, may view flight itself as a piece of hubris abroad in the culture at large. Perhaps all dangers—all gettings on buses, all lightning leaps through phone lines zapping rural decedents at trunks' ends, all sudden infant deaths, all tumescent benignities and malignities, all keelings over on sidewalks—reduce in Theo's final analysis to human error. Vicarious precocities, malarious parasitosities, nefarious presciosities, Icarious precariosities. Humorous nay uproarious, hilarious nay preposterious, *humanis né erronius.* All failures to take anything into account. Theo, if so he thinks, may even be right.

On this topic, though, he is surely wrong. Here long perspective doesn't help; here Old World and century even hinder. Cleaving to beliefs fixed early on, he recognizes three types, give or take: simper taytic *maydel,* goot fife, dot voomin. The first, all in nursery pink: a barely gendered thing, grandson's playmate, face in elementary-class photo. The second, blood-red, corpuscular: absolved for love's sake and since she kept you alive or constructed a gorgeous strudel. The third, scarlet: unmarried, divorced, or widowed, filing status alone sufficient evidence of something unnatural afoot. Of this, Laurence is sure: no honorary woman ever, Theo.

He will not understand a Gretchen. Even an Irene, so recently a *maydel* and notwithstanding Molly's hands, is shifting now to unacceptability (where was she when this husband needed her?). Most of all, he will not understand, will never forgive, Laurence's blameless mama. He willingly excuses any wife who dies first, but actuarial tables are stacked against such indemnity: in Theo's world men constantly die, women consistently outlive. For this actua-reality, only communal character flaw can account: voomin ay roar.

Nothing for Laurence so marks distance travelled or gaps generations as this: Theo's wolf. Nothing so dates, so outdates him, so throws him back: missing linkletter, kiwi, roc, auk, *ibbegablib-benne,* Theosaurus.

Beginning to look a lot like Christmas. All around the town, City sidewalks (pretty sidewalks) dressed up and slicked down in holiday style. Chestnuts roast on open fires though nothing yet glistens in lanes. After substantial markdowns, turkeys and pilgrims that displaced obsolete witches and overstocked skulls in the ornament department have yielded in turn to full-priced jellybellies and rosy-nosed hoofers. Jack Frost nipping at heels, a tooth, a claw, is in the air. A stick of dried seaweed—laminaria— is expanding inconspicuously. You can do the job while you're in town.

It's something of a disappointment, of course, and something of a relief, also of course, to have the loft back to herself. She was listening to the radio for company, just to keep the air animated during the transition. Not frequency-modulated classics, not jazz, not thought-provoking commentary. Amplitude modulation: long-running half-minute spots, ephemeral musical half-lives. She noticed that programmers jingle the bells of their secular carols early on, spinning disks that reveal the true meaning of Christmas closer to the silent night itself. Fun before joy, sleighrides and snowballs prepare the way for salvation, reindeer games precurse the King of Israel.

Little Christian: a misnomer from the start for the product of so much agnosis. And the very idea of having that dastard deliver: a rhetorical flourish, foolish flair for the dramaturgic, turgid urge. Given prevailing attitudes toward women, she would never have guessed what she learned last night from the root appendix: that though taboo deformations of 'udero-' resulted in both 'hysteria' and 'ventriloquism,' 'histrionic' had a completely different radical.

Laurence's, her recent roommate's, wombmate's, idea, she thinks, was equally ludicrous. Father *cum* mother: I am womb-man, hear me roar. Aud was right: men have the majority of penis-envy in the world and, as if that weren't enough, womb-envy to boot. Women are saddled instead with power-, justice-, equality-envy. Aud was right: thou shalt not covet thy roommate's organs. Not for everyone, a womb of one's own.

From what she's heard, she'd like to meet that Theo. Since seductive busride, quizzing of knees, trimming of toes, through all the fertilizing and mowing, she always thought that the point: 'Is your grandfather living?' She herself has two of each still drawing breath, but knew even on the bus they'd never mean to her what that Theo did to him. Different roots. Does she detect a smidgeon of root-envy, Theo-envy? No, but she'd like to meet the man. How likely? He can't live forever. Poor Marcia: *esprit de* corpse.

What with Irene and Theo, unlikely they'll get themselves back together. What with laminaria absorbing, dilating. She likes him, though, more than likes him. She meant it at the time about honorary status; means it, maybe, still. Could possibly continue meaning it. But then Irene, his not quite ex, the fair Irene trying always so carefully to be so good, Donna's dilatory pupil. So many plies, so many woulds, inlaid, overlaid. Laminated, deleterious, lamentable area, ex panting, ex pandering, ex spent. His eerie claim to be both early and belated, an ex penditure himself. We'll have to see how he reacts.

She looked up 'oasis,' too, last night. Imagine: from Latin, Greek, Egyptian, Coptic. Come a long way, baby.

How's she feeling, Aud wants to know. Gretchen understands this query's rangy implications.

She's okay. Yes, she's sure. No, no cramping to speak of. That's right. No point in putting it off.

She's been told in detail what will happen. There is a certain amount of preliminary grooming and sterilizing. The Oasis provides a friend to hold her hand, a partner of a sort though no expectator. Contrary to popular belief, there is no saline injection followed after some morbid hours by convulsive expulsion, paroxysmic expectoration. There is removal of now quite expansive laminaria. There is local anaesthetic. There are dilators, dilation. Speculum, tenaculum, cannula, forceps, curette. There is aspiration, a bit of a vacuum created; nature, abhorring one, lends a hand. There is evacuation, skilled curettage, oxytocin to encourage contraction and forestall excessive bleeding.

'That's it.'

'That's it?'

'That's it. You okay?'

'That's it?' Somehow she expected more.

'That's it. You can just rest. Emma will stay with you if you want. You okay?'

'That's it?'

'That's it. You should feel okay in an hour or so. Look out for heavy bleeding, bad cramps, temperature over a hundred, the next few days. If you have any of that, get in touch immediately. If not, I should see you in a few weeks. You okay?'

'I'm okay.'

It took about as long as conception.

Fourteen

His beard is coming in nicely now. He's grateful to see it stop under the chin in a naturally neatish line, neither meandering down to fraternize with chesthair nor clandestinely assignating, underear, with headhair. This beard knows its place. Under the chin where he's been admiring its restraint, tangles·pubic in texture if not in hue trap air to keep extremes of weather and shocks of all sorts at bay. Nor is he much rattled to note its salt-&-pepper look, already, at his age: prematurity he's been used to expecting since birth.

It amazes him on closest inspection how salt-&-pepper comprises so many seemingly extraneous colors. Facehairs will attain, eventually, a most profuse array, each roygbivacious strand curling from translucent off-nothing to deepest darkest by way of blonds clean and dirty, an almost orange, a reddish orange, an orangish red, an auburn, a russet, a chestnut, a full-blown brown, a near-black; then suddenly off the scale to the greyish white of briquette ash. Whereas the triangular patch below remains uniformly monochromatic, dun.

What amazes him, on a larger scale, is how much he can have lived so long without remarking.

For instance, that pipe cleaners (Theo buys them in quantity) are meant for cleaning pipes. This was all along proclaimed in their name, a clue so near the nose it's overlooked. They were so good, though, for twisting into animal forms in school, makeshift keychains out of it.

For instance, contrariwise, that buttermilk (of which also Theo consumes lots) is butterlessmilk, debutteredmilk, postbuttermilk, antibuttermilk.

For instance, that no one is ever a motorist except when passing a scene where something more unusual than motoring is taking place, in which rare case each and every one in the vicinity is a passing motorist.

For instance, even allowing for demographics of an aging populace and resurgent birthrate, that one in every say five point five women on the face of the globe must be menstruating at any given moment. Why has he never thought of this before?

For instance, there's a store around the corner, just off Fordham, where essentials of modern living—paper, bottle, can, jar, pack, bag, bar, loaf—are inflated for convenience, costly items close to hand. The woman there dawn to long after dusk every livelong day figures totals on a brown paper bag despite the nearby register. Her tune is always the same at reckoning's end: 'All together, six fifty-eight'; 'All together, one eighty-nine.' At first he assumed it signified summation. One day a single item cost 'All together, sixty-four,' and he decided it meant, Applicable taxes included. Now suddenly he's come to see that 'All together' means simply, You owe me the following amount, but with a cozy hint of sing-along: All together now.

Such things as these, in a given twenty-four-hour period, hold Laurence's interest.

He keeps eyes peeled for mail requiring response (a real relief for Theo not to keep peeling his weaker ones). When you've been around this long, no dearth of paper seeks you out six days a week. Though no joiner, Theo has found his way onto many a mailing list: official correspondence from Borough, City, State, Nation; remittance requests from utilities, suppliers, wholesalers, retailers, creditors of every stripe and stamp; sweepstakes he never entered, coupons he'll never use (cents off feminine hygiene, free snacks with half-dozen purchase-proofs, double his money back if not satisfied, void in conjunction with other offers); winter white sales, semiannual clearances, goings-out-of-business, prices he'll never see again in his lifetime; the Conservative synagogue around the corner that just will not give up; catalogues of gadgets (make radish flowers, dust venetians with a single swipe, pluck out blackheads, eliminate pests, never again struggle with recalcitrant string), cute things in the shapes of other things (mashed-potato-&-gravy candles, eighteen-wheeler staplers, hot-dog phones, magnetic pigeons to hold paperclips), personalized offers (things someone in your line of work won't be able to imagine how you ever did without, *ex libris* monogrammers, golf tees and matches imprinted, Mrs. Paper Rash Co., with your very own name); lobbies and non-profits, incumbents and challengers; special values for new subscribers, preapproved for our valued friends, fixed rates or floating. Innovative plans: whole, term, universal. If you don't think you need us, think again. You may be unaware of what Chemical Fabricator Industries has been doing for the quality of your air. Six things to consider before buying your next toothbrush. Are you one of the millions who assume your phone isn't tapped? Think what you've been missing all these years. Have you excepted Lao-tzu as your parsonal savor? Nothing to add but the water. Operators are standing by.

Amidst eddies of second and third, for all Laurence's close perusal, a first-class piece is almost an event; one addressed to him by name, a true rarity. But today, two: both postmarked in the City, neither with a return address, each bearing a handsome commemorative of the sort you have to go out of your way to acquire. One small, lineny, intimate-looking, inscribed with care, fore-thought; the other, legal-size, cheap, dashed-off, half unglued. Which to open first? The lineny one with the pastel lining quickens his pulse.

'Tuesday, 5:24 pm
'Laurence Dear,
'We've been through so much together, too much apart. We've both grown, but I don't see why we have to grow apart. I wish . . . but you know what I wish.'
Baby haby? He be he be.
'Please tell me what I can do to bring you back to me, to bring me back to you. I want us together. You'll always be a part of me, no matter what. I can't forget. Can't we be the way we were?'

Can they? Can't they? Why or why not? 'No matter what' doesn't sound like her. 'Always be a part of me' sounds most unlike herself.

'I have to say I dread the thought of you having this child. I imagine you telling him (I always imagine a boy) about me someday, and I hate to think what you will say.'

Thumbnail-sketch syndrome. He has hated in his time to think the same.

'"So long ago, I can't even remember her face." This is what I fear the most, that you could forget. What I want the most . . . well, you know that.'

Laurence not so sure he does. What she wants. What she what.

'For what it's worth, I will never stop loving you. Yours forever, 'I'

Beat now beat now beat now beat.

'I'? 'I'?

Not A, B, C? Not E, not F? Not, in particular and most especially, G?

'I' could mean me, couldn't it? Couldn't 'I' mean me?

'PS—She lied. You could be her coach. She didn't want to be too attached. I thought you would want to know. Donna and I are going back to Providence. I'll wait, I'll be there, I'll be hoping to hear from you. Please turn over→' On the back, a square of dotted lines for cutting down to wallet size: in the square, lovingly calligraphied, Irene, an address. Care of Groat.

What she what. What she that?

Laurence re-envelops the note in its pastel lining. How can a man not know his own wife's handwriting? How could he fail to recognize her penwomanship? Is that what they've been, then, so thoroughly estranged?

The other, the legal-size one, contains the merest jot—'Dearest L, Hope you can make it! All love, G'—that makes him realize what he should know by now, having just this minute proved it: that he's rarely seen her hand. Never outside of brief notes: Out for a G-string, back soon. G hopes Dearest L can make it. Dearest L, despite I's incriminating PS, hopes the same.

'All love,' she sends in her closing. That's like her. Not All her love, All love. All anyone's, All no one's in particular, All free-floating, unattached, or available love. 'All love' means: How's it going, I like you, See you there, So long for now, I wrote the above, This letter is finished. Some indeterminate emotive accretion.

'Dearest L' means: Hi Laurence, it's me. 'Hope you can make it!' just means what it says. The enclosed tickets, rubber-stamped 'COMP,' mean: Come as you are, Bring the companion of your choice, Life's too short, Watch me play, Enjoy.

Enjoy the world première, late in a Monday afternoon (New Year's Eve, as it happens, possibly some symbolism there), of works from a celebrated pen the world has long since given up for desiccated. All-GLD program, of all places, at the Cloisters, in the unicorn room, whose massy tapestries Laurence, unlike the rest of the world, finds opsettling: that long-necked virgin, those gawky hunters, that twisted horn, those threads profoundly rubicund, the point of that story so loaded he doesn't even wish to think about its drift, weft, woof, warp. But to soothe himself, yes, he decides, this will be of interest, to examine selvages, what expedient Dark Ages contrived to forestall ravelation in so weighty a set of drapes.

G knows his fear of the Cloisters, witnessed his vertiginous first and only visit, that episode after Sino-Latin comedy and before AP, MD, retroactively foreshortened his tether. But cellists, he guesses, don't control venues; besides, he can take as a bit of encouragement that G hopes he can make it, fears no incident. A little signal of faith in him, these complimentary comps.

If T can't or won't for whatever reason make it, he'd like to share with E. They'd make a funny couple, more mixed in age even than color, but he has nothing untoward in mind, no hankypanky, no kinky monkey business, just sharing with a fan and friend a pair of tickets the cellist thoughtfully forwarded. Maybe she'd hear her dear heifer doesn't notes; he can see it now, those cheeks bulbed up with joy, those regular teeth, that lengthy neck, that whole person happy, that face go lucky.

But if, if only, T can make it! They'll splurge on a cab, go the whole hog for a man who (L suspects) may himself lofty clesskill moo seek. A man who hasn't for who knows how many years exploited the City's cultural offerings. A man who magically crafts a silk tie from a *soie*'s *peau*.

Coo jew calm, he'll reciprocate handsomely, hoping they both can make it.

Off cause, off cause he foot. Biff ower Lawrinse force bawn force delest tie me force in dick lie stairs. Ah *zay dare* foot rim ember hiss hull lie if saw chat writ fin hiss *eyenickel.*

All together, all love.

Theo shifts white plastic box to clean dress shirt still ironwarm,
loops his favorite tie—chevron of geese over cattail marsh—around
Laurence's favorite neck. Laurence knots what is still his only tie—
boy, pony, shirtsnaps—about Theo's only *eyenickel*'s neck. Theo
dons a suit reserved these many years for funerals. Laurence in
his only suit is now dressed pretty much as he was for the wedding. Theo's hat is felt. Laurence's gloves are rabbit-fur-lined. Theo
lends Laurence a muffler. They complement, compliment, almost
temporarily familially resemble one another.

Cab prompt, streets rough, ride loose and loud. Laurence can't
rid his mind of a dish Theo taught him, stewish method of meat-
cookery denominated, near as he could make out, *ongadempfte
kloiskelech:* unguent empty clefs collect, he heard at the time. But
as taxi bobs and rattles on dicey suspension over the river and into
Manhattan, he overhears in the name of an overdone dish undertones, sonnotations, non-notations: on goddam tick lascar lick,
under Dempler-Cloister lock.

Fort Tryon Park is lovely, dark, deep, but Cloisters still gleam
in nearly horizontal light atop their hill at the prow of the island.
Unfallen arches, vaults safe, pediments on their own two feet, but-
tresses not flown, capitals columns and cobbles just as he left them,
this rock-ribbed edifice, immovable object.

Laurence escorts Theo into the stony hall. Conductor and performers both are under wraps, like brides before a ceremony, in
adjacent artifactual repositories; but now, getting Theo safely seated
amidst a crowd that glitters and shifts like sand under sunset at
low tide, he is struck by a familiar sight. Not the virgin, not the
hunters, but there—beyond clots of pink faces, blinding white
shirtfronts, black ties, satin lapels, gleaming cummerbunds, floor-
length brocaded creations of a sort Laurence thought went out
before he was born, hundreds of pelts draped over scores of pow-
der-white shoulders—there are the bulbs of his second-favorite
face scrunched in a forced grin, conspicuous, single black clef on
pure white platter, wearing her very best but still almost painfully
underdressed, overwrought, nearly beside herself: Else.

He's so pleased to see her here. His outburst did some good,
then, made news: Genius Recognizes Contribution, Cook Given
Comp.

'Theo, Grandpa, there's someone I want you to meet.'

Theo has a sense of import, commemoration. It takes pull to
wangle from the City such a space. Something large is up in this

rented museum, and now he's to meet someone. His grandson is acquainted, he knows, with the genius around whom the fancy-pants affair is built. Theo lights up with anticipatory *naches*.

His vestigial nares, even flared, can't be expected to notice that the event is momentous enough to generate complex fragrance: against the crisp, almost metallic backdrop of old stone, a heavy blend of cologne and powder, hairspray and shoe polish, naphtha and single-malt Scotch, hangs in the pungent odor of deodorants. He could but doesn't register, as they pick their way at a rush-hour pace, that he and his grandson are getting looks from the black-tied, silver-haired, salmon-and-lavender-gowned mob. That little old man in the baggy suit, that young one with newish-look-ing whiskers, that maudlin boy and pony, those silly geese, overall effect not quite clownish enough for performance art but close. Who, Laurence imagines necktilts and browcocks silently posing, let *them* in?

Gretchen is always getting him into these things: Clefs, Oasis, Cloisters. People who make him feel vulgar, places he's out of place in, things beyond ken: gallinules, gambas, unicorns, formal-wear. Separatist centers. Chosen people, interlopers; never the twain. Many are clawed, thinks Laurence, but few are cloven.

'Else, I want you to meet my Grampa Theo. Grampa Theo, this is Else. We worked together when I was mowing.'

'Lawns's grampa. Sur*real* honor to meet you.'

Theo leans into Laurence and stage-whispers: 'Fought hiss she sank? Eye canton dares tent disk haul aired guile.'

'Her name is Else. She says it's an honor, a *real* one, to meet you.' He smiles at Else, whose face reciprocally bulbs up.

To meet with a genius would be maybe an honor.

'Else and I worked together in Riverdale,' Laurence almost pleads. Theo shrugs his eyebrows, a casual gesture, twin cowtails flicking flies, then surveys the crowd of groomed and bejewelled patrons and matrons as if Else were a piece of tapestry.

So many things confused Laurence stops short of saying: Be good, I love this woman, Don't embarrass me, Don't humiliate her (you for whose very salad I showed respect), I dreamed you two might meet. Instead, pretending nothing has happened, he attempts to chat. No history, he finds, has been made, no comp for sup-porting caste; quite the opposite, in fact. 'He's been crankish some time now, criticizes meals, finicks over seasonins, somethin under his skin, probly gettin this symphony done.' Critter sizes, seize nuns,

some fun undress kin, same funny: she holds the program carefully, like relics preserved in adjoining rooms. No, Else paid her
own extravagant way, first in line when an outlet opened. Laurence can see, though, now she's bought her way into this company, she too is nervous about interloping. Won't she sit with them?
Well, once again, she's honored.

Laurence sits politely between elders and peruses the program
Else prizes. Before intermission, a Dempler retrospective, works
well known to most in attendance. Laurence is briefly amused by
program notes like a plot summary: a motif is foreshadowed,
established, echoed, recapitulated; a time signature emphasizes
incontrovertible destiny; a key change represents man, endlessly
striving to improve; we cannot but think the composer would have
us hear in this passage the eternal give-and-take of life; a bassoon
bubbles up, an oboe goes flat, stirring viola chords introduce the
impetuoso. (Who are these critter sizers and noters, producers of
copy for program and journal, flap and sleeve? Is it true they're all
frustrated artists? No business like schwa-business?)

Lights come up around the jerry-rigged stage. Audience buzz
mumbles quickly into silent expectation. Laurence can feel, to left
and right, elders wiggle in seats, getting snug for the performance.
He wonders if bright light might not damage ancient tapestries.
In latest December, four hours after noon is virtually twilight. There
are reasons for that, tilt of earth, angle of incidence, seasonal var-
iance. Isn't that how leaves know when it's time to turn?

Musicians troop and shuffle onstage: faces scrubbed, hair clean,
unstyled, flyaway. They all look a bit abashed, carrying instruments under the lights; this isn't what they came to do, parade
before the crowd, be scrutinized as they get comfy in their seats.

There. Dark floor-length gown, dark glasses protecting sensitive
eyes from glare, dark pumps surrounding equally sensitive toes.
Laurence has never seen her in her work clothes. She could be an
anachronism, lugubrious coffeehouse reader of unpunctuatedly
existential poems, save for the scarf tied off-center at the neck, the
only jaunty touch in the entire rather morbid ensemble. Others
might think those shades were there to complete the beatnik look,
and Laurence himself finds them not unfetching, though they keep
him from telling whether she's scanning the crowd for him. Can
Gretchen's eyes be more vulnerable than centuries-old thread? Is
preciousness a function of fragility, is vice versa? Something looks
strange, something is off. What's wrong with this picture?

The crowd explodes as the man of the evening, in tailor-made tails and white tie, achieves his podium. Composer, handpicker of ensemble for the occasion, host conductor, be-all, end-all: applause is sustained. Genius hair ready for takeoff, he bows down slowly, comes up quick, gets right to work. He conducts without baton, but thanks to flesh the color of flesh-colored Band-Aids, the audience doesn't suspect a thing. A motif is foreshadowed, established, echoed, recapitulated.

He's wondering why they all have to look alike: tuxes black, bow ties black, shirts starchy white; gowns black, uniform formals, floor-length; shoes blacked, polished, reflective; when men twitch tuxpants up at the knee, you can see they all wear those thin dress socks. A profession that mandates skinny socks. Sheesh. The get-up you've got to get into to play a violin in public, let alone to conduct. Does anyone understand the point of tails, hanging there like adenoids or appendix? And why not blue basses, purple oboes, yellow piccoli, mix-and-match designer separates, strata various? Why should serious musicians all look like mourners and a concert resemble a funeral?

Not to mention Theo: why act like that? 'Disk haul aired guile.' We don't say these things. Old man, make allowances; but for what? Socialized eons since: ethnos, race, gender, every rule has changed in his lifetime's course. But this is Else; like Lonnie, like Mama, more than innocuous, more than innocent: good.

Posture improves toward the conductor. The concertmaster's positively starched, splinted-looking. Cause or effect? Those who sit stiffly are followers of rules, practice more assiduously, hence attain the most coveted chairs; or those seated nearer the front learn to set a vertical example for others to strive toward. Cream rises or *noblesse oblige?*

Except for that meeting of Theo and Else, it's going quite well, really. Bows float up and down as if in some medium all their own, unison tips like a piece of tide or the heaving form of a dormant giant. The music is nice enough—wholes, crotchets, minims, and quavers, hemi-semi-demious, meritorious, worthy of note—but Laurence can't take his mind off the audience.

Faces, costumes, bearings, all allude to entire lives spent in particular strata, unvarious. Select appreciators, collected connoisseurs, a chosen people. He, Theo, and Else are the only odd men and woman out, unselect, *pas élite*, picked across lines, transtick-

eted over fancy, fency pickets, *déclassés, déplacés,* dropped behind
enmity lines. Many are clawed.

Why in the world should he feel this way? It's a free country,
isn't it?

Intermissing, milling but scarcely intending to mingle, trying to
keep equal but separate track of Else and Theo, conscious of
Gretchen adjoining, just the other side of that stone wall, Laurence stumbles into an unforeseen powder cloud, paroxyzes, and
swivelling to excuse himself narrowly avoids collision with the
unmistakably tall coif of an unmistakable short woman in pearled
gown and custom-made shoulder-length gloves. 'Bless you,' she
remarks in passing, in a stranger's voice, to Laurence's more mis-
takable hair. Thanks but no thanks, he stops short of responding.

It all comes flooding back: the bouillabaisse, the young man,
the European system, the groomed grounds, cunctation detested,
mapping in the tub, violet liqueur, the darker cereal grains, entertaining the vulgar, the grape-clustered mirror, mismictural bifur-
cosity, unravelling horns of a liquid dilemma, the whole abruptly
truncated *roman aux douze clefs.*

'Why, Mr., Paprika, isn't it? Forgive me. I failed to recognize
you just at first.'

Theo, it seems, canon dares tent this one quite well, and there's
nothing for it but introduction. 'Madame, allow me to present my
grandfather, Theo Papyrushchka. Grandfather, this is Madame
Aussterschucher, the conductor's'—not wife; what, then? house-
mistress, helpmeet, other half, cohabitant, romantic interest, significant other, spouse equivalent, ladyfriend, floozie?—'beloved.'

'Apple leisure, *même.*'

Oh, the leisure is all hers. (Most of it actually is. To Laurence
this occasion is unparalleled, cross-purposed, unprecedentata,
discomfortissimo.)

She is, by the bye, so glad to have run into him, a serendipity of
sorts; in the flurry of an unexpected resignation, they neglected to
remit outstanding wages. If he'll be so good as to provide an address,
they'll be sure to forward a check without further delay.

Suited rather than vested, Laurence digs in unfamiliar pockets
(four in pants, two in shirt, five in jacket) for something to inscribe.
In baggy trousers unworn since the wedding he locates a ragged
scrap of napkin passed by the bride to maintain courage near the

buffet, 'I love you, Laurence' (arrow-pierced heart about the verb); fortune-cookie rectangle from the wedding dinner, 'You will get what comes to you'; wrinkled receipt from the honeymoon hotel (one night, two rooms, Amelia adjoining). In the wallet is Irene's name, Donna's address. Digging down, almost turning them inside out, he finds only deep lint. This sort of search can start looking frantic quickly: high gear, contortive, untoward. Is there not in all these potential spaces a single slip, snatch, or snippet of paper he's willing to part with? Oyster Lady not helping out, content not to lend a hand as he grubs and clutches near private parts, scuffles with himself like arthropod prey when some desperate limb contacts edge of spidersilk.

How's her memory?

It has generally proved satisfactory.

Then, since he seems (a pocket a pocket a pocket) not to have (a pocket) the wherewithal to scribble withal, would she be so kind as to consult the yellows, under Men's Clothing & Furnishings— Retail, if she pleases, for Theo's Ties, Fordham, Bronx. This talented grandpa the eponymous proprietor.

'Dots riot, *même*. Eye em dot Theo dot mex dose tice.'

'Very well.'

Laurence still, from sheer momentum, pocketing the one hand, the other.

'I had always intended to ask. Paprika is certainly very interesting. What sort, exactly, of name is it?'

There are ways and ways of asking that question, and this strikes Laurence as one. He's trying to focus it in his mind's eye, put his mind's finger on it. He appeals to Theo's tie, stationary illusion of long-distance flight, forever autumn: below, the punky swamp; above, the wing-shaped chevron sticking long necks out into the future. What sort, exactly?

Immigratory. Mangled. Mongreloid. Misaurable. Ellisian. Islandic. Alien. Naturalized. Customs-made. Anger Dempler's Äussterschuch.

'Fictive,' says Laurence. 'Invented. Figmental. Purely made up.'

Blinking houselights put to this strained entr'action a merciful period, and Laurence's intermittent ventilation gradually subsides as he watches her pearly gait recede into welcome riddance.

Theo found Madame 'in train synch, diff fife off ah jenny ooze, bit sorrel exed, in dusty books fa ha hose bent, annum prey sieve pie sin. Dot ah voomin saw chess dot shoe tock fit os mince sumtink, Lawrinse, giffs me *naches*. Eye ten cue dot jew brink me ah lunk.'

Theo impressed by Madame. Else coldly shouldered by Theo. This should not be. This gulf should remain under wraps. Laurence and Theo should never discover so drastic a divergence, such different worlds in view. And when they regain their seats, why is his right hand untenanted? Where is Else?

But couldn't Theo hear it, didn't Theo feel it? It's on the tip of his mind's tongue: 'What sort, *exactly*, of name *is* it?'

First, Theo, consider the source: look who wants to know. An Oyster lady absurdly done up in pearls, handsewn no doubt by someone's grandsomething, hardly has any right whatever to question nominality. Beyond stones and glass houses, though, the tone still ringing in mind's ear labels them Vulgarians, her the ambassadress from Sardonia, casting pearls and aspersions both before their faces, under their very noses. Now forming in mind's mind, taking shape in new forebrain: the way she didn't say 'exactly' what she meant, thought the better of asking just what she wanted to know, an invidious overtone, insinuous undertone, indeterminate, inferential, implicatory, innuendous and nearly actionable betweentone that strikes him with all due retrospect as possibly antiscmantic, probably antisemiotic, and doubtless not totally prosemitic.

The program proclaims a single postintermissive work, what most of these ears showed up for, the real piece of resistance: world-première chamber suite with chorus in a dozen movements, *Blades in A♯*. A♯, as far as Laurence can see, equals familiar B♭, same difference, six of one. Why come at it the long way around? Why circumnavigate to arrive next door, why go west, young man, to get east? For pun's sake, or just to make life difficult? Hah, look who, *Äussterschucherlich*, wants to know. He has to admit, on either score he's scarcely in a position to object. Maybe to be nearer the alphabeginning, *à la* yellows advertisers. (This, by the bye, would be how many sharps? More than seven, beyond his ken, off the scale, every tone sharped, some double-sharped, razor-sharped, laser-sharped, more sharped than serpent's teeth.) Possibly even just like this, just because. What matter: A♯, so be it.

So be what? So be, he learns from suddenly intriguing program notes just as the light is dying, a hybrid setting of Andrew Marvell's mower songs interleaved with dithyrambic cuttings culled from Whitman's *Leaves.*

This takes a moment to sink in. When Dempler sought at lunch *le mot juste,* he came up, after extensive ticking, with 'inspiring.' Was what Laurence then took as just a word in fact the just and only right word, just the word, for his perspirational exertions? Did Dempler sit hunched in his turret tinkering, tinkling, tickling ivories pink over inklings received from Laurence's greeny choreograph? Parnassian dectet no joke? This new work to commemorate his work will more than likely contain the heifer doesn't notes. Else is where?

Nor Else's absence to his right nor Theo to his left heavy-breathing through a long maltreated nose can hold attention once Gretchen reappears directly before his eyes, settles gown between her thighs, nestles cello there where it belongs. On inspection, like beardhairs, the gown is not precisely monochrome and far from floor-length; in point of fact, no gown at all, but a couple of separates in careful coordination made to resemble one. Do other women mimic with such ensemble, or are their gowns gowns? Laurence can't move his eyes to tell, he finds her in matching top, bottom, shades so magnetic, almost hypnotic. Skirt drapes full, soft, supple, pliant, suppliant, unsized magnanimity of fabric, the opposite of stiff. What's this he's in? Love with her skirt?

When he looks so close, Gretchen's bowing, like her dress, is made up of parts, complexly jointed. Such unfluidity it takes to produce so fluid a strain. Such muscular tension through the whole body, not released but transferred through string, through paper-thin wood transmuted to airy sound. The scroll right up by the left ear. He squints to see if she has her wolf-eliminator on. 'You must C♯ or you will B♭,' he recalls from an optometric ad. Small piece of hard rubber, she said, but he can't remember where to look for it: tuning peg, fingerboard, bridge, tailpiece?

He knows how the eyes roll behind those polarized protectors, can infer that finishing touch to the visible cellist's aspect. She cradles the frog in the sweet pad between thumb and index, that sensible, flexitive spot. Full being vibrant along with the old wood, whole torso twists to achieve thumb positions high up on the ebony, down low near the balsa bridge, fingering fingers nearly in her ear when the going gets fiery.

He hardly hears a thing but her bowing, picked out from the whole range of onstage vibrations. Her lusciously liquid *legato* melts him. Glorious *glissando* glues him to the spot. *Spiccato* so special, so very *perspiccato,* it makes him perspire. Background *tremolo* when the oboe takes over gives him the shakes. *Pizzicato* plucks his very pit. *Staccato volante* goes through him like stiletto. *Ponticello tantalizante* as if it could bridge the gap twixt stage and seat. He adores and all but venerates the technique he used beyond a shadow now of doubt to live with. Pale young woman *col legno, sul tasto, flautando;* wizened young man coming unglued, *depasta,* spaghetti's opposite number.

Thar she blows! There they are, a lyric cluster, melodic motif. Laurence hears tune, composed of subdominant, dominant, tonic, superdominant, without accidentals, unnaturalized, simple: super-, keynote, dominant, sub-. Behind all those masking sharps he fathoms the cadence's tonality, picks sax fingerings out of the air down near his lap—E♭, F, B♭, G, G, B♭, E♭, F—a nearly palindromic measure. These notes he clucked at while mowing have realized every note's dream, have made it to the big time, have arrived. More than Clefs staff must contend with them now. In the public domain they are haunting refrain, they are music, la la da da, da da la la, waves of no little beauty. Goodness gracious, ain't that some fun? Where Else? Else where?

The tenor takes over in recitative:

> *'When Juliana came, and she,*
> *What I do to the grass, does to my thoughts and me.'*

Sentiment reactivates, phrasing resuscitates, semantax recitativivifies, some memory misplaced, key or clue: these words heard where, herd traces, when in roam, ruminantlers, antiloop play, cloven hoof, harp, heft, O give me a home, a discouraging void.

To the left Theo's lids are down like shades, like hunters' blinds, like blinders. Such a romantic in his own way, thinks Laurence, enhancing the private experience or testing the parable's conviction. Theo classical, content, not the dangerous joy but a stillness beyond emotion. Eyeless in concert, amen.

Laurence tries, too, but can't shut Gretchen out. Even tacit she draws him, her invisible eyes could be on him behind her own blinders: I see you, Lala, I can see you. In a world of her own, she feels not counts measures. Nor for all his unexplained resentment of the conductor can he resist the gorgeous chorale: 'What I do hoo to the grass hass, does to my thoughts and me he he.'

Now Gretchen in her glory does something so lovely he can hardly believe it's unrehearsed, has to remind himself she's playing cello not cellist. As she takes up her bow to respond to the tenor, an oblivious obliging rhapsodist conducting herself, not ecstatic but instaurate endodyne automorph, she lays her warm head gentle on the cello's very shoulder. He follows the instrument on down her form, almost jealous, violoncellous of its intimate relation to the sum of her parts, skirted where it rests there cradled by knees, down further toward pumps where the stable endpin augers into plies of temporary pine.

What I do to the grass. My thoughts and me. What she what. What she what.

Gretchen's endpin is straight as an arrow, straight as crow flies, as gamba crashes, straight enough for spinning, not angled to accommodate. Of course, of course. What I do to the grass. Straight as an endpin, as straight can be. Now he knows what was off, strange, vaguely familiar and unfamiliar at once when she walked onstage. My thoughts and me. Off cause, off cause. Clear as a bell, as her bell-like tones, as thin ice, as clear can be. And she. The silky black costume, though full to allow free movement and make way for the instrument's resonant volume, dropped where she stood like a plumb, like the shortest distance, bodice to instep, top to toe, unvoluminous, inviolate. Gretchen under lights, Gretchen in shades, Gretchen on display, Gretchen not showing.

Of course. Like pipe cleaners, unlike buttermilk, self-evident once you think. Of course. Like geometry, trigonometry, triangulation, identity. Empty Barron, baroness of barrenness. Tautological Gretchen the Gretchen.

And Laurence the Laurence will now respond how. Will make a scene, rave, trumpet, rage, tempestuate? Will vocalize, involute, sublimate, volatilize, stabilize? Villain joy like Theo the Theo's eyeless wonder?

Will not, like Donna, thanksgive; not, Forenzic, pray; not, Groatfully, mimic Dürer. Will instantaneously wonder if little Christian might not have danced out from under in a splash of: an insane thought. Will think of all those who have disappeared or feared disappearing, of all those who never appear. Will not confuse the two: getting off a bus is not not-being, not the opposite of birth. Not someone lost but not-someone never realized. Not unearthed, ungrounded, a clump perhaps of theory. Still, a familiar question just can't not occur: How could? How could she. But can hardly trump wrath up, can scarcely reproach, can barely after all wish otherwise, his hands so more than full to overflowing with silk, Singer, selfedge, own and Theo's mouths to feed, hides to protect, *peaux de soi*. Will, then, try to accept, for once, gracefully or not, a fact. She was right: any little Christian would have been a big mistake, a drastic opsettlement, twinkle twinkle in no one's eye. How I wonder, wish I might, when you wish, who you are, what she what.

Like a shot. Picks her skull off the cello, convulsed, digs horsehair deep in taut gut, strenuous strength of her tendoned shoulders, sinewed forearms, tremendous visceral straining signature shift, ferocious fingers flash up around pegs, whip quick in near vicinity of face, *sforzando, con spirito, furioso,* alarm off, a waking to earthquake, stop stop it it's moving, the tremor near climax, finale, *al coda, fine.*

Dempler spins, solid on his pins, bows deep, possessed by his own creation. Laurence glances left as the crowd goes wild. Applaud, now beat, cheer, whistle, now beat, shout, stand, now beat, ovate, mass of now beating beings on stamping feet, palms pounding, eyes bulging, now beat, lungs heaving, now beat, releasing tension sorely pent through a dozen movements, now generous frenzy of music appreciation born this very minute and now beating forth in *Bravo bravissimo.*

Above, lids still enact the prior parable. Here, Laurence sees and stares still, fixed by men's clothing and furnishings beautifully made in a precedent era, fine worsted long since sewn and just pressed. Here, wide lapels on either side of migrant geese flying south for a winter that never begins lie impervious, pacific, still as a postcard from somewhere you've never been.

Last

E ach time one of my parents died, I seized the opportunity to put the pathetic fallacy to the test: would skies weep, strange hush fall over nature, the very birds neglect their morning madrigal for pensive and melancholy mumbling? Conversely, would the sun shine brightly once again to herald renewal, buds bloom into blossoms to show how worthwhile even a short span could be, evening or morning star provide comfort or resolution? Would nightingale, galingale, high winds flag the moment with meaning? In short, would whatever nature could muster without seriously marring verisimilitude proclaim the point? Put another way, had the cosmos taken note of my personal loss, my consequent and immediate family restructuring? I was not asking the world to remember long, just to insert a little note to the effect that something had happened here.

From an experimental sample so limited, I found conclusions difficult to draw. Two points, however disparate, determine only and always a line. Father died before I had given much thought to fallacies, pathetic or otherwise, but I took careful note of the weather: partly cloudy, chance of widely scattered showers or thunderstorms in late afternoon, highs in mid-80s, humidity a dite too relative for comfort, pressure hovering in that region the nautical-looking instrument in the dining room designated 'Change.' Not unpromising, all in all; that could be rendered meaningful.

When Mama died, the barometer read 'Fair.' This, of course, could be irony. But the following day a stormload of swirling flakes hit Providence, no blizzard to be sure, just a couple of inches but wild while it lasted, well beyond flurry, and I fancied it could be a delayed reaction. Possibly that weather had been held up, catering to unforeseen demises elsewhere (drunk driver in the Great Plains, kitchen accident in the North Atlantic provinces, idiopathic thrombosis somewhere over the rainbow).

Quite a job, coordinating simultaneous climatic life-fortune commentaries on a global scale. Even in a single municipality, weren't some born, married, or promoted while others dangled by threads? Here, an old man shuffles off his worn-out mortal coil; there, a young woman just aced a bar exam; across town, some teen willfully slips his surly bonds; somebody over in the next county hits the lottery big. Presumably, tragedy would take precedence for any given locale. To afford the lottery winner brisk freshets for yachting fantasies while ignoring the teenager's already too painful fate would add ultimate insult to consummate injury. But obits appear daily all over the land, and for days on end entire regions shine and spangle. Talk about boggle; the whole business is self-evidently unmanageable. Pity the programmer doomed to deal with this ever-changing and oxymoronic data base, the mere attempt to make sense out of which would leave anyone's temples throbbing. If ever a fallacy was pathetic, this must be the one.

I've seen the signs on interstates: CAUTION BRIDGE FREEZES BEFORE ROAD SURFACE. Air, more volatile than solid ground, could put you in a spin before you knew what hit. Traction soon lost without something sustaining beneath. Unattached to the planet, things can get slipperier faster.

By now we all know that bridge freezes early, all exercise due caution and no longer require signs. I find them a comfort nonetheless, because (in the first place) someone took the trouble to give fair warning that things are likely to happen without warning: a small public benevolence. And because (in the second and final place) they serve to remind, from time to time on the highway of life, that theory, not only good for nothing, can be downright treacherous.

Suddenly the City was ubiquitous, implacable, menacing. The whole place, I thought, ought to be condemned: rotting floorboards, plumbing on the blink, broken glass strewn here, there, leash law ineffective, potholes, manholes, booms, busts, read the papers, every day new horrors, no kind of place to raise a kid, no wonder they packed us off to kindly Providence. Their judgment so much less suspect than it used to be, now they were long gone.

It was well after midnight, and I stood, feet together, head bowed, pondering boy and pony from a bad angle, on Bainbridge Avenue. Hapless containers and torn wrappers smashed and blown around by passing traffic. Under pinkish-yellow light I examined shapes among the concrete cracks and heaves I stood on. Providence, too, must have had such mysterious street and sidewalk stains, but they never struck me as sinister there; here, what liquids or solids caused so many, I wanted to know. In all probability, mere gum, pop, grease, last year's lunch, yesterday's newsprint, dog sweat, multi-racial phlegm, everyday streetmulch, compost for next year's crop of beans, of nothing, of more compost. Whatever passes among arthropods for lifeblood, squashed casualties of urbanity, not the fittest. But on an outside chance these amoeboid blobs could encompass traces of human blood, secretions gathered for testing, or worse: toxic, pathogenic fumes floating below sensory thresholds, parts per billion, dangers unimaginable under the benevolent aegis of Independent Man. Here, I thought, such marks have implications. Was this insight or momentary mood?

Past midnight in the Bronx, any man with a tie standing stock-still in a zone clearly marked 'No Parking Taxi' is presumed to be a man in need of a ride. Unhailed, unbidden, unflagged, a cab pulled over, waited politely. I regarded the stocky vehicle with vague indecision: a stranger at the door, a voice on the phone I was meant to recognize. Old invincible Checker now out of production but still running on every cylinder. Bargain-brand mustard predominated, but just below doorhandle level a strip of horizontal checkerboard, three maybe four inches tall. Uniform yellow would take in as much in fares; people don't select a cab by décor. A wholly unnecessary touch, these staggered squares: taxi's swath of selvage.

Cabbies know not to hurry preoccupied people they find stand-ing under sodium-arc lamps in front of hospitals. Leave them alone, they'll climb in, wagging their fares behind them. I know, I drove one one summer.

Radio Dispatched, said the sign. Oh good. I heaved open the weighty door, climbed in and locked it. Safely removed from what caused the stains, Plexiglazed off from the driver, I smelled old vinyl, rust under carpeting, a few hundred thousand miles of internal combustion. Far more legroom than anyone really needed, enough for six-, seven-, ten-footers. I sat as in a bus, silently rumi-nating. Let their fingers do the walking. Leave the dispatching to them.

The man was large, and I entertained an odd possibility: this could be Big Jim, back to give knees a second chance, looking for luck to change. That, if unlikely, was not inconceivable; that could be. If the radio didn't mind, we'd pull over on a sidestreet, run the meter. A little klondike wouldn't hurt, and the patter might be a comfort. I could get the story straight about his father, his name: '"O ill-conceived, ill-conceived!" says he.' I adjusted knees to right angles, making thighs horizontal and the world safe for solitaire. I smoothed baggy worsted in expectation of aces that could come my way: four-pile legs, cozy.

'I need a dress,' said the driver casually, as if I had forgotten something already. When he spoke, I thought: Not Jim, foreign, recent arrival on these shores, emigranted immigrateful impor-tent. You have to know your way around the City, though, let alone the life-savings cost of the medallion. Big Not-Jim, then, was just slow to lose the accent, English unspoken in the naturalized home. Or did the radio own the medallion?

'To wear.'

Big Not-Jim was chatting, passing the time till the radio would dispatch us. Listening closely, I thought I discerned a pattern: he needs a dress to wear, he's an honorary woman. Fingers rising and falling in insistent rippling motion, a small nervous tide on the steering wheel. 'I need a dress.' Maybe threads snipped from ties adhered to my suit, static could do that, he wished to engage my services as seamster. I wanted not to tell him I couldn't sew.

Fingerwaves quickening, shortening, frequenting, as if his wardrobe requirement were more urgent already.

'Address, address,' he said, 'to where you will go.'

Oh. Oh. I had now independently to say whither this large and multiply misconstruable man—no gambler, no cross-dresser, no radio-controlled robot—ought to conduct us.

'I'd like to go someplace safe,' I said.

I could see eyes rolling in the rearview mirror. I tried to smile at them, but they had no idea they were being watched.

'The nearest safe place,' I repeated. 'Please.'

When the eyes stopped rolling, I could see something getting the drop on them, stalking, creeping up from the brain behind them. What was that?

He waited for me to speak again. Why should he? I had made my wishes clear. 'Please begin to drive now,' I said with emphasis.

Even seated, from the back, through scratched plastic, you could tell this was a hulking man. But unless I missed my guess, that was fear sneaking up unbeknownst, blindsiding those pupils of his. Imagine: a man who knew streets and avenues, shortcuts and boroughs, a big one with a medallion to his name, scared.

I appealed to my summer's worth of experience, tried to empathize. Of course. It was the middle of the night. *This person in my taxicab runs from law, is escaping lunatic, walks tightrope, drug strings him out. He can have gun inchy plastic will not make protection against. This passenger makes me fright. Unformed beard provides evidence for this.*

He wanted what I wanted, then: safety, to escape scare. He understood, then. Then why didn't he drive? Were there statutes, ordinances, codes to cover this: equal access, public accommodation, professional courtesy, honor among cabbies, human decency, delay of game? Wasn't he obliged to drive?

'Please, I'm harmless but scared myself. I drove a cab one summer. A comforting place.'

'I need address.'

Uncle. I give. 'Far Rockaway,' I said, the name itself a lullaby. I saw now why in family lore it put a grandfather back to sleep.

'Too far. I do not leave City.'

'I thought Far Rockaway was in the City.' In Queens, I thought, but wasn't sure enough to argue with a man who had a medallion; there was probably a geography test involved. But it worked for my grandmother, didn't it?

Radio crackled like civil defense: *This is only a test.* A dispatcher, East Europeanized by bad transmission, came on. 'Whatchka gotchka, sixteck sevenovich?'

'Man will depart City.'

'Please, sir,' I shouted through Plexiglas toward the transceiver, 'tell him Far Rockaway is in the City, just this once. I know it's Far. I have the fare.'

'Getchick riddovich. Itch itch.' The rest was static.

'Please, you can run the meter while we decide. Isn't Queens in the City?'

'Address in City or depart taxi.'

Had this been a real emergency, you would have been told where to turn.

Dyckman out of the question. Twelve Clefs so far out of the question it wasn't even funny. Only one address was really thinkable. I didn't see what else to do. I wanted to be safe.

'Near where Tenth meets Fourth,' I added.

Like magic, the cab was in gear, shifting automatically, running yellows and incipient reds, on the move. How far to Gretchen's? About an hour was my guess.

The radio crackled from time to time, but its pseudoslavalect dispatched nothing intelligible. I could hear sirens in the middle distance. Wavelengths, wavelengths, I thought. The rearview fear was gone, eyes settled back into the job, the routine, a living. People were scattered on sidewalks like demographic charts, like explanations: ones, twos, small-group dynamics undulating past the streaky window. On the street, more cabs than anything else, an astonishing proportion: Turmeric Canister Dumped Over City, Spicespill Emergency Declared. This must be the biggest night of the year for the industry, naturalized aliens with families to support. Where were they on an average night, an average day? How many could there be? How could there be so many? 'Only three thousand of us in the City,' Gretchen said. To me, back then, that had seemed a large number.

I liked the way this driver drove, ignoring parkways, expressways, onramps and offramps, in favor of streets and broad avenues. Maybe this was the long way around, maybe more efficient routes to the Village could be plotted. *Had this been a real emergency, you would have been told which way to go.* He could be padding the fare, squeezing a few extra bucks from an easy mark. Granted, I was disoriented. I didn't mind if I was being taken for a ride.

On Broadway I saw signals switch in sequence blocks ahead: yellows, reds, greens. They made me feel someone or something had custody, guided decisions, said what next. Wait. Stop. Go. So many guiding lights protecting the City: streetlamps, warnings for traffic, dashboards, billboards, storefronts, entryways, security systems. People who spent a lifetime here would never once see darkness save on trains. All every night, even parks were lit. Watched over, looked after, overseen, overlooked. Wait. Stop. Go.

Glimpses of town-sized tract set aside, given over to dangerous elements. My parents said, when they were young, that was a place to walk after dark. Some forcefield on the periphery, electric eye to gauge or induce innocence, turnstile of naïveté: miraculous, legendary. Safe a generation ago, inconceivable now. Yet still this enormous token of that, connecting or separating Natural History and Metropolitan Art. Columbus Circle to Cathedral, Fifth to Central Park West (imagine the honor for that expanse of grass to have streets named after it): green and blue, paths crisscrossing meadows, ponds where webs churn away (year-round or only in clement months?), dogpaddling out of sight.

How had I failed to notice before how much of the City was under repair? Even this time of year (granted, no snow to speak of, extraordinarily mild, all sources agreed, so far), a constant dismantling for renovation, replacement, or renewal. Three thousand or more discrete projects: some going up, some coming down, others behind high plywood fences or under plastic wraps like leftovers so you could only guess, multistoried scaffolds holding restoration up, veils over temporary faces.

On interstates, when they need to revise, sometimes they build a whole new highway to one side, as wide and as smooth as the original, just to divert traffic past the site. When repairs are finished, they demolish it. They could have had two, side by side.

Ludicrous. 'Somewhere safe.' He must have thought I was out of my mind.

Past midtown, toward downtown and the Village, fewer people on the street. Who would wander in the garment district at one a.m. on New Year's Day? I had heard, further south, there was not only a diamond and a fur district, but a ribbon one as well. That amazed me: a ribbon district! That ribboniers, one another's competition, should gather and clump, fluttering around what attractive light source? What other unknown districts: belt, button, snap, zipper, clasp, hook-&-eye, machine-embroidered label, selvage?

I hated, simply hated, that Theo should expire on New Year's Eve. Not that New York was full of celebrants: not fireworks, drunken disorder, tuxes and gowns, the falling ball, not even *auld lang syne.* But that it cohered so stupidly, coincided so falsely, with iconographic convention: old men bearing scythes and hour-glasses, babes baring nearly everything they've got, father time infant year, dumbass depictions, crassnesses, lapses of taste. That I abhorred, lack of dignity and honesty both. The rhetoric of birth-day—'How does it feel to be a year older than yesterday?'—of campaign—'The real issue is: What kind of world will we leave for our children and grandchildren?'—of commencement—'Today's youths are tomorrow's adults, and this is not an end, but a begin-ning.' Stock sentiments, compounded of equal parts self-evidence and untruth. As if death were the opposite of birth, future of past, twenty-seven of twenty-six. Frankly, I just resented the hell out of it.

Nearing the Village, more selves, fewer edges, people revelling on into the night. In Washington Square Park, an impromptu party. They were scattered about like cocktail guests, groups rearranged from time to time, each knot with its own electronic machine com-peting for air, ears, attention. Some waved sparklers. In the sky I could hear and infrequently see Roman candles, cherry bombs, Saint Catherine's wheels, Chinese firecrackers, noisemakers, lightmakers, peripheral shooting stars. Wavelengths, wave-lengths, I thought.

The transceiver sputtered, and the driver, preparing to dispatch an edgy fare, soon free himself for further dispatch, matter-of-factly stated a headline, as if reading the paper to a blind friend: 'Sixty-seven free in Village.'

'Rogerchck. Seek whatchivich gotchcrck.'

Cab pulled in front of Gretchen's building, stopped. I looked up: never noticed before how very yellow residential light was from the street, yellow as TV was blue. Waking albino revelled or wound down, ate or drank, lounged or moved, solo or *tutti*, engaged or disengaged, separate or ensemble. Through lofty room, roomy loft, light obeying inverse-square law spread, yellowing the tall front window like old newsprint, odd combo, warm and brittle both.

'Your place?'

'Wait.' Because yellow means caution.

'Your place, your address?' He turned on the dome light so I could count cash. All together?

'Wait.' Because that loft was filled with yellow light. Did I see cautionary telltale shadows move on that ceiling? 'Please wait.' Because of that air, moted, in motion, inconclusive collection of indeterminate wavelengths. Because loose air, vibrant, chocka-block, produced a flash of fear, a fear of Flash. Sudden horror of what might be being synthesized in a lit and moated loft seized me, tight tighter tightest. This the safest spot I could think of?

'You depart here?'

'No, no, I'll want to keep going.'

Where else could I go? Where seek sanctuary, Min's Oasis? Ludicrous. Irene said she'd be ready if I came back, and Providence had so comforting a sound, far rockaby sweet lullaway, familiar Independent Man in guardian-angel pose. It could be done; Port Authority, Grand Central, bore addresses in City. I could retreat, by bus, by train, a refugee.

By a truly horrible heave-ho of will, I took two wet fingers and snuffed that guttering flicker with a touch.

Velden, as Matthew Pelff would say, nothing for it but Fordham: '2386A Fdhm Bx,' I dispatched.

Big Not-Jim hesitated. He had address in City, but I caught the eyes in the mirror again, their fear reinstated. If something unexpected happened, then anything could. He'd need some reassurance.

'Fordham Road, in the Bronx, number 2386A,' I said firmly. 'It's a store. Theo's Ties. I live upstairs.'

Crackle. 'Sixstitch sevenchick?'

Big Not-Jim just sat, as if the light were not green, not even yellow.

'This is the last one. I'll get out, I promise. I have the money. I'm a beneficiary.'

This time, I swear, I would have rung for the nurse, not waited and waded through less erroneous pictures. I thought he was enjoying himself, testing a pet theory, interpreting a parable. Had I known, I could have created a stir, made a ghoulish goulash of Dempler's Cloisters luck. I could have insisted on nine one one, EMS, CPR, mouth-to-mouth in the aisle, frantic fists on sternum through long-necked geese ripped loose at the collar, an ugly event, stay back, give him air, loose air.

I had a horrible feeling that his battery just ran down. I could have carried a spare on my person at all times. The idea that it simply ran out of juice haunted me.

In a good deal less than an hour, I saw the doorway: fire-engine red, battleship grey, TIES, TIES, TIES. When the dome light came on, I handed lots of money through a spring-loaded window in the plastic. It retracted quick as a camera, stopped down, snapshut.

'Thank you,' I spoke up through refractory plastic. 'I know I was strange. I'm sorry. Better now, I think. A little.'

'Keep change?'

'Yes. You did what you could.'

Into the shop, where I'd been sleeping and helping indecisive customers choose, where I heard old men say what death was around a bubbler filled with jolly shnapps. Strolled among the racks for a minute like an exhibit, reception, opening. Ties, ties, ties, an heir taking offhand stock. Up the complaining staircase to the one large room with its impromptu subdivisions—kitchen, bedroom, studio, working, eating, living space—that proved adequate, that sufficed, for all aspects of his life since he moved in over the shop after that Molly I almost couldn't remember anymore died. What was this space before that? Spools, scraps, shears. Bolts, forms, remnants. *Ibbegablibbennes.*

By the bed a radiator clanked heavily, impatiently, arrhythmically, like something about to go into arrest. I hadn't said prayers before bed since I was a kid. Even then, it was just a game for me, like Star Light Star Bright. The silliness of that rhyme now struck with a clarity that had been building up for years: 'I wish I may, I wish I might, Have the wish I wish tonight.' Self-evident. Goes without saying. Embellishing redundancy adds no force. The wish I wish is all I can wish, regardless of phrasing. Makes no difference. Who you are. Am what I am, wish what I wish. Theo the Theo. Shoe traced in piss.

I dreamt I was flicking, with my middle finger, ants off my tie. Why were ants on my tie? Never mind, I flicked with precision, with expertise, confident, almost happy. Out the window, hordes of New Yorkers in Sunday best, to or from ceremonies, sermons, services, masses. As I watched, the groupings came clear, families and friends. I turned back to the Singer to adjust the tension. I had a fear I'd get my finger under the needle, flattened by presserfoot, gripped and advanced by feeddogs, ten lockstitches each inch on down toward palm and wrist. When I reached in to touch the metal bobbin, I was shocked: not a heart-stopping jolt, just a squiggle of household current, stylized bolt on a superhero costume.

I walked out, smiled at the doorframe, momentarily tried to invoke the fallacy, left off in disgust, walked back in. What did the weather have to do with it, what business was this of the birds'?

Gretchen could undoubtedly lay hands on the appropriate cantata for this morning's mood—No. 26, 'Was ist daß für ein neues Jahr,' No. 27, 'Wieviel bedeutet nur wie daß,' No. 2386A, 'Aber was ist los'?—but who knew what rough beast even now rose from her mattress to its strains, interrupting impassioned housework to say for the record, in case she missed it last night, that 'That was nice, that was really nice.'

New Year's Day, no need to open up. What had I done when Mama died? Had Theo made wishes known beyond the two? Who should elegize, eulogize, summarize? Fourscore and seven. I could not dedicate, I could not consecrate.

I sought instruction upstairs. Rummaging through papers, here's what I thought: I will find in a drawer what looks like a diary, precious piece of past, *Theo: The Early Years, Theo in the New World.* I will think I can bring it up to date, *Theo: The Final Days.* Opening it with something akin to reverence, I will find to my joy no journal at all, but my legacy, a complete correspondence course, how-to book in a shaky holograph: *Theo's Tricks of the Tailor's Trade, Secrets and Solutions for Sole-Surviving Shnipsshneiders.*

Jarring dingaling of downstairs door interrupted. Who could it be on this day of all days: would-be customer, haberdashical emergency, disoriented reveller indifferent to bowls, Scout with cookies, Father Time, Infant Year?

Arm in or more precisely under arm, Flinchmesser and Pelff, latter supporting hip-casted, crutched former: no hard feelings, soft feelings in fact, respects to pay. How did they know: a hotline? Paideia put in a daily call just in case to Montefiore, took nose-count nightly, summercamp lights-out bedcheck, after taps?

They were here to talk about the arrangements: 'toadies cost derange mints,' they said. They needed from me something now.

I didn't know, had been seeking clues upstairs when they rang. I didn't even know the whereabouts of the will.

They had that.

Like Irene back when Mama died, I shuddered at *shivah*. What would I say, how would I grieve in public, what could I do with so many coffee cakes?

His wishes were known: no *shivah*, no service, cremation. Paideia took care of everything. Hadn't Theo assured me?

He hadn't. A suit for cremation, then? (Do they cremate suits?) He was wearing his best when.

Just the tie they needed.

(Do they cremate ties?) He was wearing his favorite when.

They needed another one: owl of Minerva, open book, broken sword, dragon Error.

Dreg in, humor, nay roar. I didn't know where it was, but believe me, the geese were his favorite.

Not for him. They needed it for me.

For a funeral, I would insist on boy and pony.

No service, no *shivah*, cremation. I was the closest he had to a firstborn son. Calls had been placed, *ad hoc* committee formed, an exception suggested, decision made pending ratification by rank and file. They would offer the tie.

I already had it. Somewhere upstairs, I was sure.

A formality, though: bylaws, tradition. They had to offer it. They had a pattern to follow. They would drape his folding chair and take a vote. Always unanimous, they assured me, despite Pup's unconscionable misbehavior last November. Then they could offer me the tie.

I possessed the tie. The tie was somewhere upstairs.

The tie was a symbol, explained Matthew. What they would offer was chair, floor, topic, this ritual pattern for my own firstborn son: saw sigh yeti, Paideia in full.

The topic for January, for next week, added Benjamin, pointing a crutch toward bubbler or future, would be 'What Is Life.' *In memoriam Theo.* 'In accordions fitters fishes,' said Benjamin.

Fenny feedy fishy, I thought. Vichyssoise key mally pants, I thought. *This is only a test. Had this been real, everything would have been different.*

'I'm sorry,' I said.

'*Far voos?*' For what?

'I can't do this.'

'*Doos voos?*' This what?

Unaccustomed as I am to public weeping. 'This, this, this tradition, this behavior, this joining. I know Theo wanted it, I think you are wonderful men, I will keep up the business, but this I can't, I really can't.'

'Fie? Fie naught?'

Suddenly I was a child throwing a fit, tantrum-tossed, explosive, expulsive, convulsive, wracked among racks, gasping for air, tied up in knots. Fie, fie! 'I don't know, I just can't, I can't I can't I can't I can't. I'm sorry. *Enshine.*'

Matthew and hip-broken, possibly heart-broken Benjamin tried to console me: calm calm, now now. They told me the offer was made just once, no room in Paideia for the vacillant, no full-fledged membership for half-hearted progeny. Matthew started to quote a proverb concerning naked bread. Benjamin stopped him before he finished it.

They were very kind. I'm sorry. I just couldn't. Something *vee doos.*

Rare the reviewer untouched by *Blades,* proclaimed 'a rambunctious and rollicking romp,' 'a joyous celebration of natural love,' 'a genial and positively palinodal recantation of his earlier staunch refusal of lyricism.'

Even rarer the headliner who could resist temptation. Block letters shout it from the pagetops: 'Demplerrific!' 'Dempler's Marvell a Marvel.' 'Marvell + Whitman = Marvelous Wit.' 'GLD Strikes Gold.' 'Dempler Returns—Will Marvells Never Cease?' 'Concerto Grasso Leaves Audience Awed.' 'From Our Coy Maestro.'

So, piggybacked on verse, Dempler is back, once more spotlit, beraved, largest serious composer in recent history, a tuneman of import, valued import of Netherflemish provenance, important tuna in this biggest of ponds. Back in print as well, importunate reporters once more ringing up Clefs for interview scoops like ice cream, fisheye shots of Euterpe's Lair, tidbits of info in re creative process. History recapitulated for those of short memory or recent majority. Youth competitions, still officially unsolved but universally transparent Baendtneeck plot, triumphant tour, ups, downs, honorific post at Metropolitana, fallow years, and now the grand return (rarest of all the featurist who omits phoenix imagery). And Astrida, woman behind man behind pen, may have something to add to the *précis* of genius for the Sunday supplement. She prefers not to talk about how they met, but sources who prefer to remain anon whisper of cards played right, rise from ashes of youth filled with *ennui* in some Dakota or other, summer job in fabric store, checkered past, chessboard moves to Big Pond where she always suspected something special awaited her, nestegg expended on elocution, determined young woman hovering about the musicians' entrance, stagedoor Astrida chasing the troubled great man till he caught her, connecting through him to seats of cultural power: upscale showbiz bio, American dream come true, fashioning now out of whole cloth costumes for barber, consumptive, Viking, Queen of the Night.

I dreamt—didn't I?—that a nurse's aid or lab tech in a candy-striper's outfit had to draw blood. 'Don't worry,' she said, 'this is only a test.' The setting was Formica and stainless steel, sterile wrappers strewn on the floor, antiseptic odor. There was a tourniquet on my biceps; I looked away and there wasn't, then when I looked back there was again. At her behest I pumped my hand into half a dozen gradual fists. The syringe wasn't terribly large, but I could see in close-up. It was no solid needle but a capillary tube sheared at the end to extreme acuity. It made me think of green beans, package ribbons, asymptotes. She gave it a shot, sliding under the skin at that same acute angle, almost parallel to the forearm, pushing slowly like a sidelong glance or difficult idea. I wanted, and wanted not, to look. She withdrew, swabbed the spot, tapped with two fingers a couple of times before trying again. Each time she pushed a little quicker, less carefully, poking, prodding, apologizing, explaining: 'I'm sorry, I'm new to this' or 'I've done it many times, but this has never happened before.' She switched to the left arm for a time, then back to the frustrating right. It was like something—a scenario, a script, not only a test—unfolding before my eyes. After a while she just jabbed and jabbed (as if ensuring that something was dead, I thought), mumbling to herself. The tender inner arm was bruising already, beads of blood forming: couldn't she use them? I tried to cooperate, but my head was getting light and told her so. She just couldn't find a vein.

Soon a check would arrive from Twelve Clefs, discharging that debt, closing those books, along with other mail, mostly second-, third-, fourth-class, some fraction now to newly created addressees: 'The Estate of,' 'The Survivors of.' Verbose small-print communiqués from insurers, lawyers, keepers of rolls: 'We understand how difficult this time must be for you and your family, but the information requested below is required for the purpose of,' 'Please be assured that all of us here at the Division of Value

Assessment share your grief to the greatest extent possible.' (At the bottom, even smaller print: 'Form 1969F, rev. 6 / 75.')

I had a pile of bare ties he constructed while I practiced painting and delayed learning for fear of jinxing the battery, but even this sizable backlog couldn't last long. The most rudimentary elements, elementary rudiments, still unknown to me, now an estate, a survivor, a proprietor. I had, of course, no diary, no instructive cache of lore, no lifetime of experience condensed into accessible prose, no stash of hand-eye coordination put aside and sealed safely, hermetically, for my personal use, no such pandering to so transparent wishes.

Imagine the sole heir to the largest *shnipsshneider* in New York history poring through yellows for a nearby address, moseying into the store as into an Oasis: sole seamster in a sea of seamstresses. Milling millinerial throngs of confident do-it-yourselfish fabricators who all knew what they were in the market for: twills, tulles, failles, voiles. By now I was almost used to being the only something somewhere, which could cut both ways: if civilians browsing through giant books in the back hunched up a little to establish territory when they saw me approach, saleswomen were more than eager to help. I was of some interest, a seagull feather found far from water, collarless stray, lost child in precinct station, foreign tourist, deaf-mute. I was a communications puzzle, like fashioning traffic signs for illiterates or speaking only in cognates: *I need a dress, to wear.* The most basic terms were unfamiliar: tracer, ripper, piping, batting, binding, all obviously English but no more intelligible to disoriented me for that. I was a displaced person, an alien looking fecklessly forward to the asymptosis of tenuous and attenuated naturalization.

The solicitous sales staff mobilized *en masse,* leaving more knowledgeable consumers to fend for themselves, fanning out to assemble a starter kit: necessities, accessories, timesavers, gadgets, devices. They wanted, too, to sell me things in the shapes of other things, plus cute mugs and cushions imprinted with sayings: 'I'll keep you in stitches,' 'I'm a pin-up,' 'Sewers seam better,' 'Sew what?' I insisted I needed no needles, wanted no notions save the vaguest hint of how to proceed, lacked nothing but the pattern itself. All their kindly almost adoptive care could not mitigate my humiliation at the unanimous verdict: Simplicity would be the only sensible choice. The packet, they added encouragingly, also included complete instructions for ascot and cummerbund.

At home I unfolded, carefully as an antique map, the pattern, pondered flimsy tissue the color of unstained pine: lines, allowances, separate layouts for napped and napless, hieroglyphics I had no idea whether or how to transfer to silk. But Simplicity would be the least of my problems, really. Always a quick study, convinced early on by parents that anything was possible, I would apply myself, I would learn. Rhythms of machine and handstitch, optimum tension, the feel of the thing, would come slowly, but a person could do it. *Shneiders*, like lawyers, cabbies, plumbers, are made; no one is born backing up big rigs, pirouetting amid spikes at second base, twirling pizzas high in the air without incident. Cutting on bias, matching centers and symbols, clipping to seamlines, basting, trimming, lapping notched ends, stitching right sides together, pressing seams open—I could handle all that given time. Like the key of ten sharps, I could figure it out if I had to.

Of course it would gall that the best imaginable garmentor, *zayder* who could have taught me Singer's ropes without recourse to Simplicity, had slipped through my tentative fingers. But what would really cut was what I could now never learn. What would appall was how answers to questions I would never have thought to pose now dropped to the bottom of a bottomless well. Not just uses of interfacing or how to keep digits out of harm's way, but any and every thing not somehow transmitted—his response to New Deal, choice of best bakery in the Bronx, reading of Heine, attitude toward canines, felines, opinions of Turkish taffy, Belgian waffles, Colombian beans, French kissing, Greek culture, how he liked the tin ceiling downstairs, why he started to smoke, where he first noticed lunar phases, burden of those brows always over his eyes, response to Kitty Hawk, Sputnik, favorite word in the half-dozen languages he knew, reaction to the relation of his lifespan to a renowned comet's periodicity, his version of things, the history of his understanding, which classes of information chronically slipped his mind, the day-to-day feel of inhabiting those wrinkles—lost, gone forever, like his response to this brand of sentiment. A man so full of meanings that die with him: Theosaurus out of print, beyond rare, past hard to find, a void.

One question I knew how to ask but never did now acquired a new resonance. Its answer irretrievable like all the rest. How could he. Just. Disappear.

Dreams are funny things. Just when you think they'll be rife with hidden veins and unmined motherlodes of meaning, over-determined, underpinned, profoundly opaque, impenetrable . . .

I dreamt I was making love with Gretchen again. Nothing more, just that: *semplice, a due, a piacere, affetuoso, giocoso, amoroso, immoderato, capriccioso, appassionato, con anima, con brio, con fuoco.*

She was jointed in so flexible a way, thin limbs folding up like a luminous carpenter's rule.

Haven't theoretical physicists calculated the number of particles in the Universe? That's a lot of things to keep in mind at once: sum total of matter and energy. They say it remains constant—cold comfort, that—but did they take into account inventory short-age, paper clips fallen behind radiators, soufflés fallen period, books casually lent and never returned, draft-card ash, dead bugs in sta-tion-wagon grilles, gravel swallowed by chickens to aid digestion? Did they neglect random twigs youngsters pick at while playing the outfield, vegetable matter wedged between teeth, familiar let-ters, receipts mislaid, flags planted on moons, dust in light-fixture globes, used tissues, bits of thread snipped from ends of seams and allowed to drift unnoticed to the floor? Have they thought about failing grades, laugh tracks, unrecorded games of solitaire, verbs and subjects understood, modifiers left to dangle, indefinite arti-cles?

I took a notion to study phonetics. Letting alone for the time being semantics, stylistics, universal syntax, generative grammar, deep structure, compound studies within studies, I just wanted to know all I could about nasals and fricatives, glottals and plosives, bilabials, ejectives, semiresonant liquids. I hoped to comprehend egressive clicks, crossbred broods of radico-pharyngeals and lam-ino-alveolars, labiodental stops, apico-dorso-uvular retroflexives, each and every elision and assimilation phenomenon, all stress-timed breath groups, expiratory accents. I wished to be conversant with central vocoids and flapped contoids, lingual trills and affri-cated releases, the whole phalanx of larynx and pharynx, the voiced and the voiceless, aspirations and their discontents.

I would find ears were entailed: not just hammer, anvil, stirrup,

but tunnel, rod, pillar, cochlear duct, membrane tectorial and bas-
ilar, scala tympanic and vestibular, ossicle and fenestra, tragus and
meatus, pars flaccida, antihelix, semicircular canal and attic recess,
the whole labyrinthine inner. I would find new alphabets attached
to no language, international, planetary, to sounds what Esperanto aspired to be to words. I would find out that words were no
more than sounds, sounds no less than breath. What I long since
learned with regard to saxophones I now started in every sense to
know more broadly: streams of breath controlled through manifold mechanisms, voice a wind instrument after all, loose air skill-
fully meted, mysteriously sphinctered through multifunctional
organs.

I would think it for this reason, however predictable or understandable, a shame to switch to synthesis. Given, breath comes in
waves. Granted, waves possess length. But twixt breath and wavelength still an unbridgeable gulf, a translational loss. I could almost
feel sorry for Gretchen; charms of a man who thinks it's all wavelengths bound to fade in the long run. A homegrown unified field
theory, quest for fifth force, thirteenth clef, nth dimension to account
for all phenomena, this goosechase for the key to all morpholo-
gies, universal joint, nub, crux, grail to trim loose ends of air, tie
knots, ravel or unravel double negations, put cosmos in its place,
eliminate waste in the name of elegance and excise once for all
from all working vocabularies the useful 'just because.'

Could Irene have a point? Is schwa (as near as I can tell, a pal-
atovelar midway between half open and half closed) the most
incentive motive force of reactive us? Far be from me to falsify or
even disconfirm, but this fails to explain why the backward, upside-
down sign should be my favorite. Nor can it account for the observed
fact that 'it' is to me the most intriguing word of all.

Very soon, the second Thursday, they would arrive. Moshe, as
always, a few minutes early, the rest in small clumps close to the
dot of eight. I would welcome them, watch as they draped Theo's
chair with the tie and a strip of black crepe cut from a dwindling
roll. Then I'd leave them to disagree about what life is, retreat
upstairs to paint or write that letter—Irene, Goodnight, Goodnight, Irene—conscientiously trying not to listen in. This compromise. Host in a sense, but no presider. Willing provider of shnapps,
latakia, and space, but no participant, no discussant, no deliverer
of opinions, no holder of beliefs.

I'm sorry, but I really couldn't. 'What Is Life'? Good grief. What the hell isn't?

I was studying Simplicity, aiming to conceptualize the process, pinning down the tissue, transferring the markings, putting off the cutting till I thought I comprehended all steps. Right sides together, seams pressed open. Getting down to, taking care of, bee's knees.

Did you know it was largely done by hand? No one in all these years has figured a way to reconceive the basic four-in-hand in automation's favor. Having long pondered the underbelly of hidden mechanistic innards, I still find lockstitch counterintuitive. One from the top spool, detoured and rerouted round metal parts toward needle's nether eye; another tangentially offered by bobbin's halting spin comes up to meet it; the two, let loose, drawn tight, again, again, *ad lineam*, form lasting bonds. Utterly iterable synchrony a source of unutterable amazement, but too unyielding, I gather, for bias-cut cloth interfaced with slightly stouter stuff. The point must be leeway, how things stretch, where they give. Thread itself, when you think, a source of amazement. The whole long suture down the back that others never see, all slipstitch, all fingers and opposable thumbs. I measured it: near five feet, longest item by a long shot in most closets, nothing but floor-length gown or greatcoat could even hold a candle. Men knot such things around their necks, taller than Theo himself.

I was casually overseeing, in the midst of other things, ungual progress, maintaining nails near that point where, left to themselves, they would leave beds behind and grow on in air. Silk-thread so thin a thing, the work would be much easier if they did, but as always I aimed for that tricky interface of neat and disfigured, splitting the difference of pleasure and pain. Supervised the always shifting protein, managed as beginnings became middles, middles ends, ends debris. This mildly destructive nervous habit appeared to me a systematic action, a practice complete in itself, perpetual motion with the meaning built in, a little self-contained plot: morbid self-attention attended by its own retribution.

And I was imagining my life: bits of breath arranged as if to convey something. Anecdotes cut loose, shed like hairs from dying follicles, ballast jettisoned to keep afloat, detritus. The organism itself long gone in search of an adequate skin. I hated to think of the conclusive jumps leftovers always enable, the misconstructions inevitably authorized: wrong sides together, seams pressed closed.

Chagrined to think, too, of ways the transcript doesn't read, over-sights overlooked, furcations not taken on parser's branchy dia-gram, movements to make a grammarian grumpy, parts not apparent in any final analysis. How else it could be constructed, embellished, anatomized, expressed like juice from skin, decanted, vesselled. A more pregnant beginning, perhaps? A less assimilable middle?

No matter how I envisioned my parts, my wholes, my crotchets, quavers, and minims, modified substantives, squared sums of other sides, opening and closing arguments, how and where to rest my case, the ending always looked the same: 'Final sentence: how to avoid self-pity.' (With or without he he he he.) I could see no other conclusion.

What then?

Then this.

Bring.

Compose.

Bring.

Compose yourself.

Bring.

'Hello?'

'Hi, Laurence. It's me.'

And so it was. So it was.